THE CARDBOARD KINGDOM

ROAR OF THE BEAST

ALSO BY CHAD SELL

The Cardboard Kingdom (volume one)

Doodleville

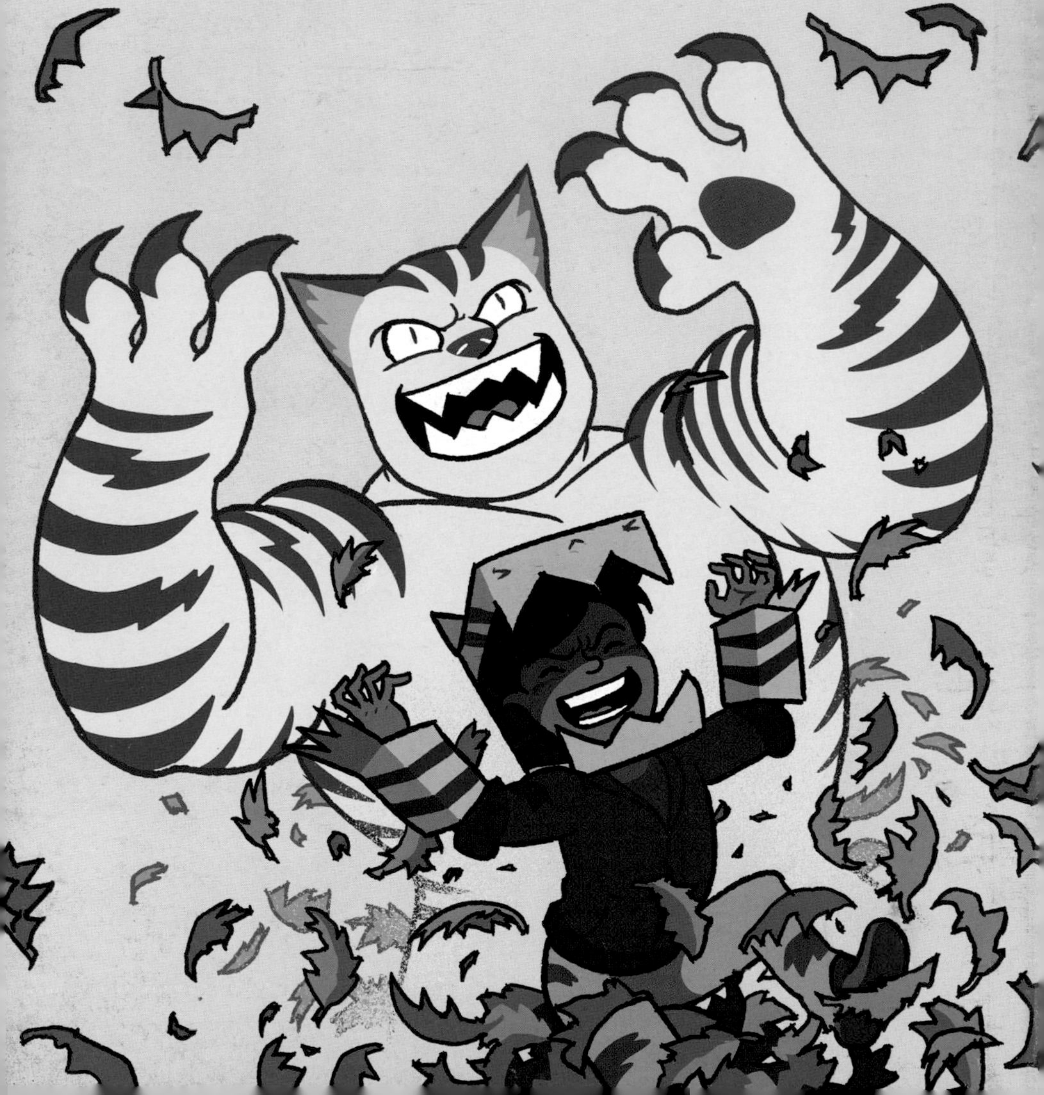

THE CARDBOARD KINGDOM

ROAR OF THE BEAST

ART BY
CHAD SELL

STORY BY

Chad Sell, Vid Alliger, Manuel Betancourt,
Michael Cole, David DeMeo, Jay Fuller, Cloud Jacobs,
Barbara Perez Marquez, Molly Muldoon,
and Katie Schenkel

ALFRED A. KNOPF  NEW YORK

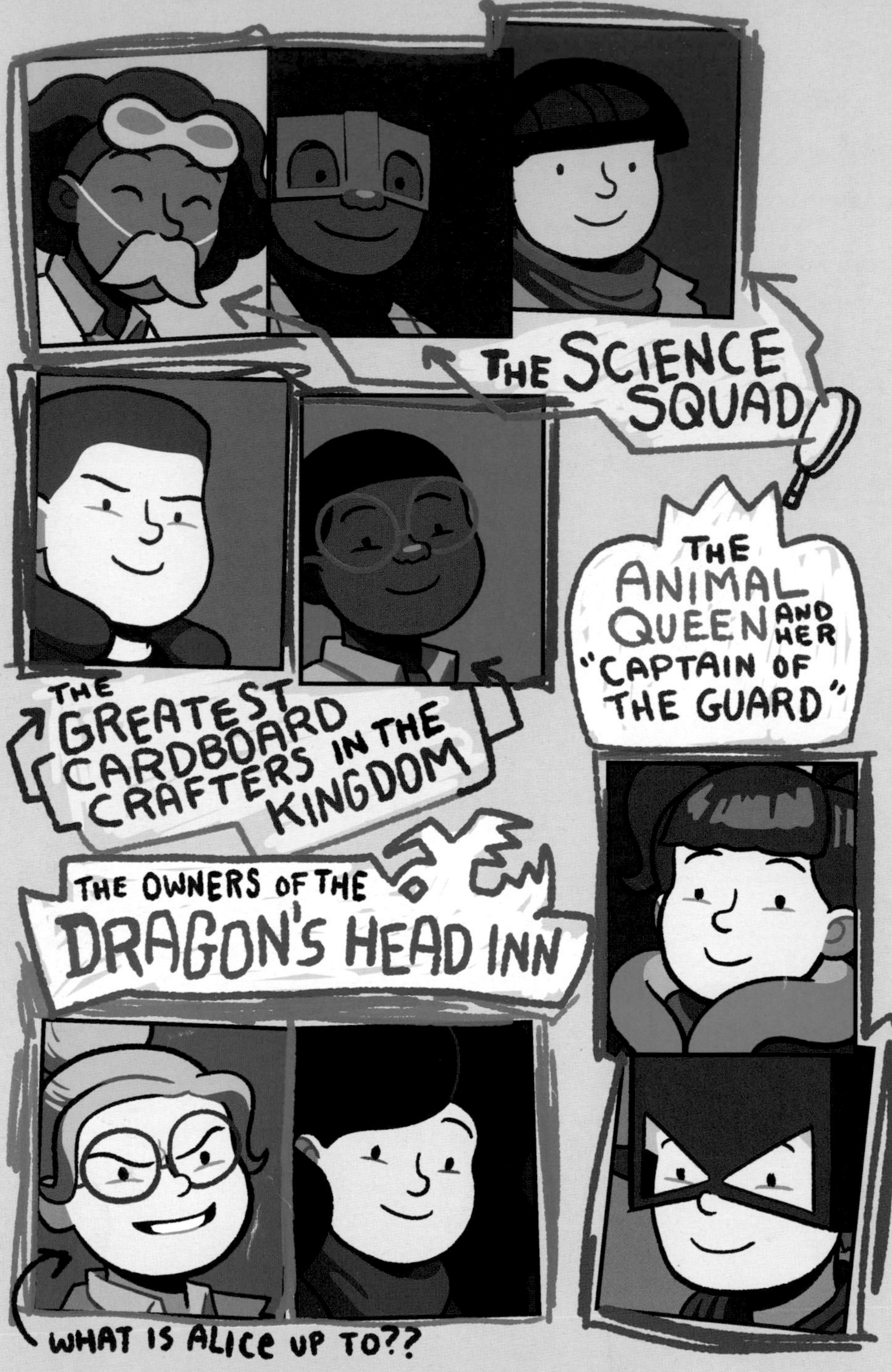
THE SCIENCE SQUAD
THE ANIMAL QUEEN AND HER "CAPTAIN OF THE GUARD"
THE GREATEST CARDBOARD CRAFTERS IN THE KINGDOM
THE OWNERS OF THE DRAGON'S HEAD INN
WHAT IS ALICE UP TO??

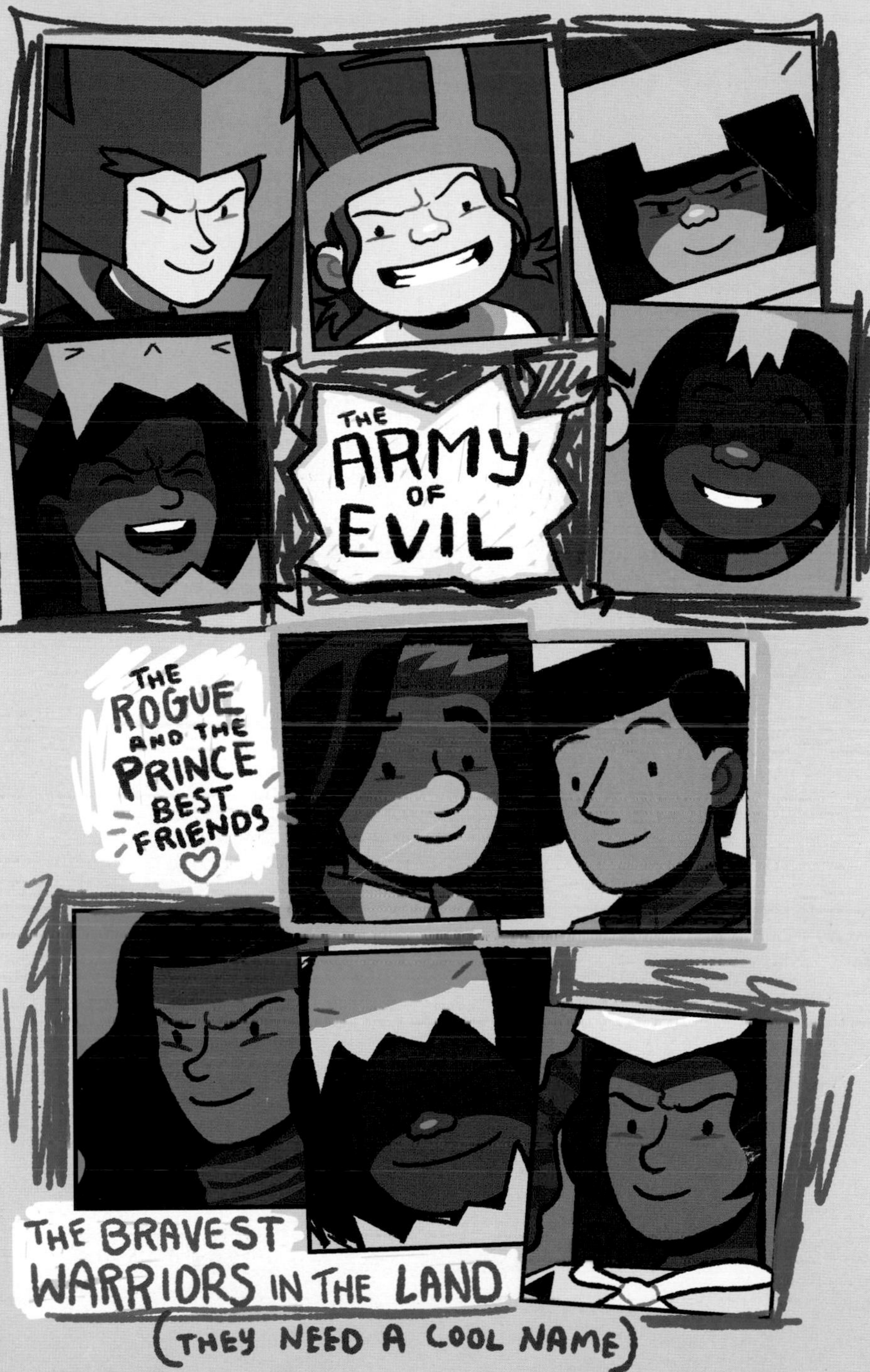

THE ARMY OF EVIL
THE ROGUE AND THE PRINCE BEST FRIENDS
THE BRAVEST WARRIORS IN THE LAND
(THEY NEED A COOL NAME)

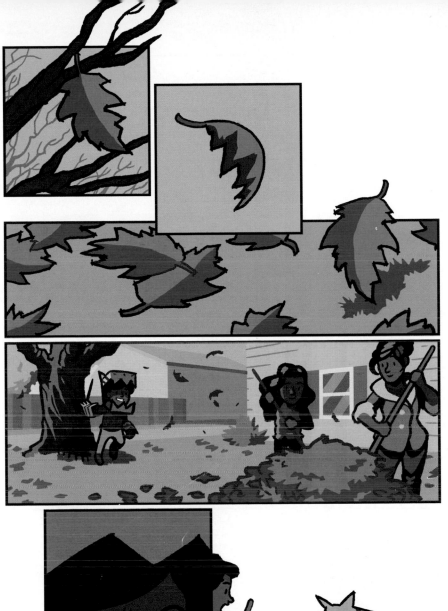

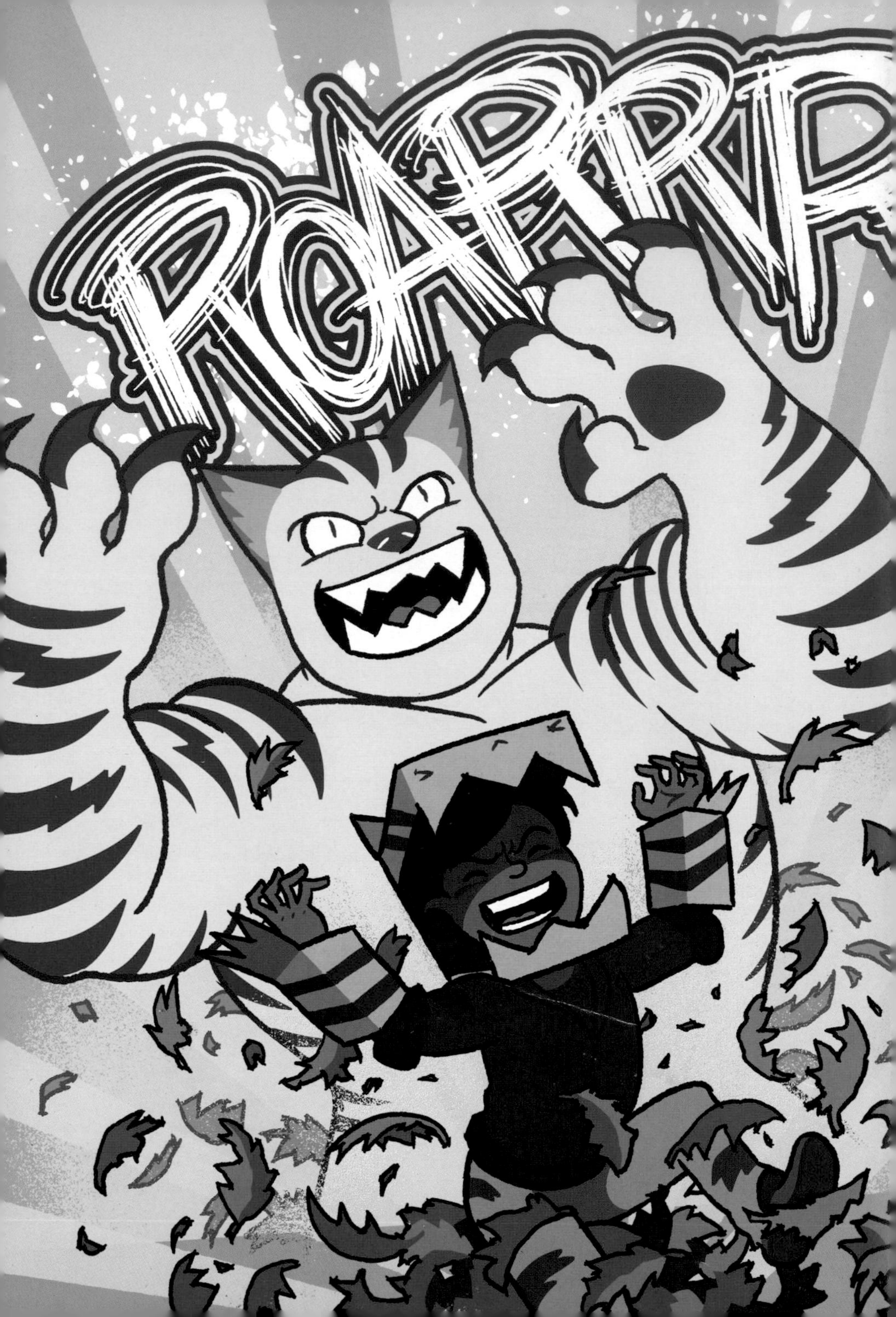
ROARRR

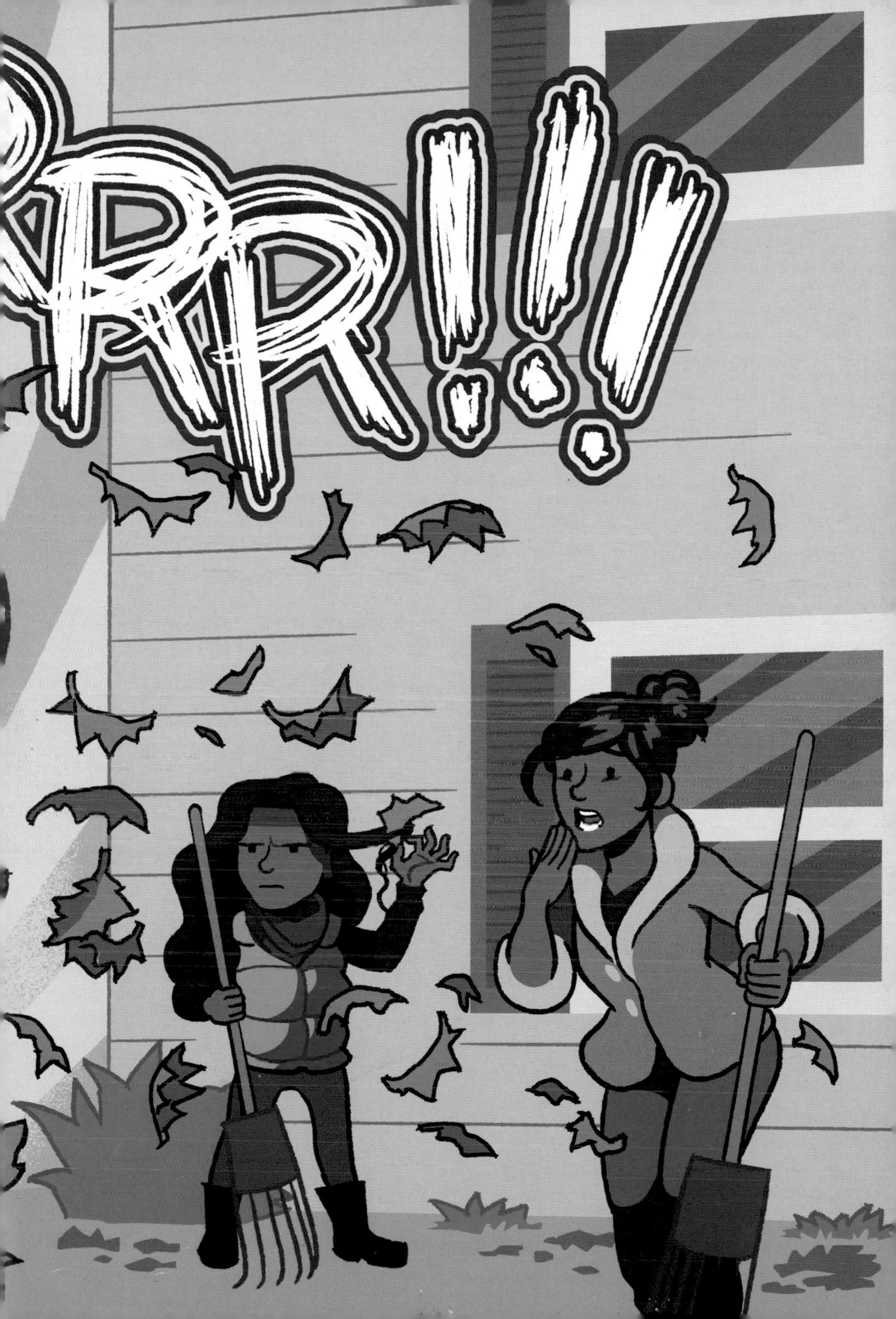
RR!!!

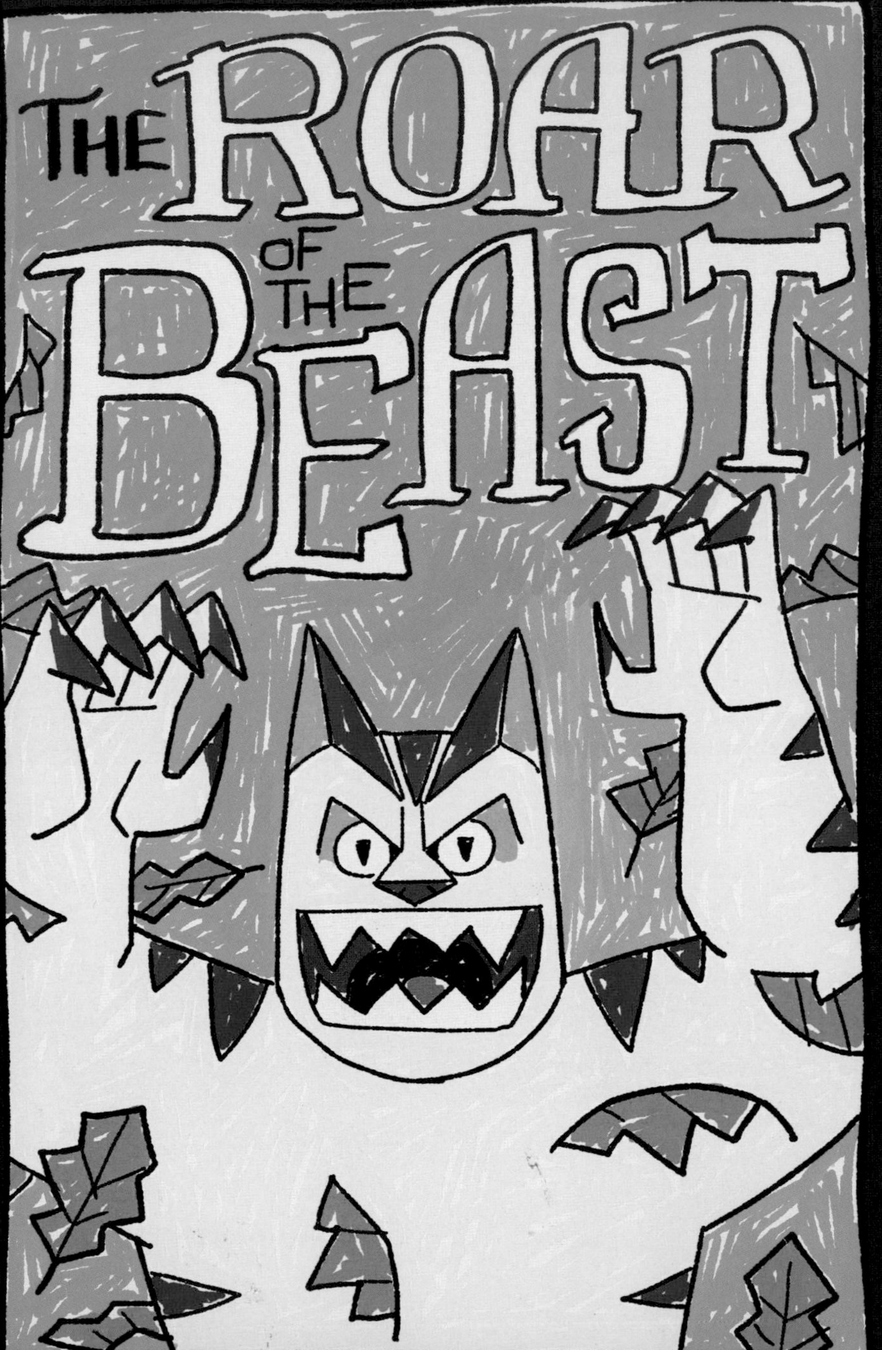
THE ROAR OF THE BEAST

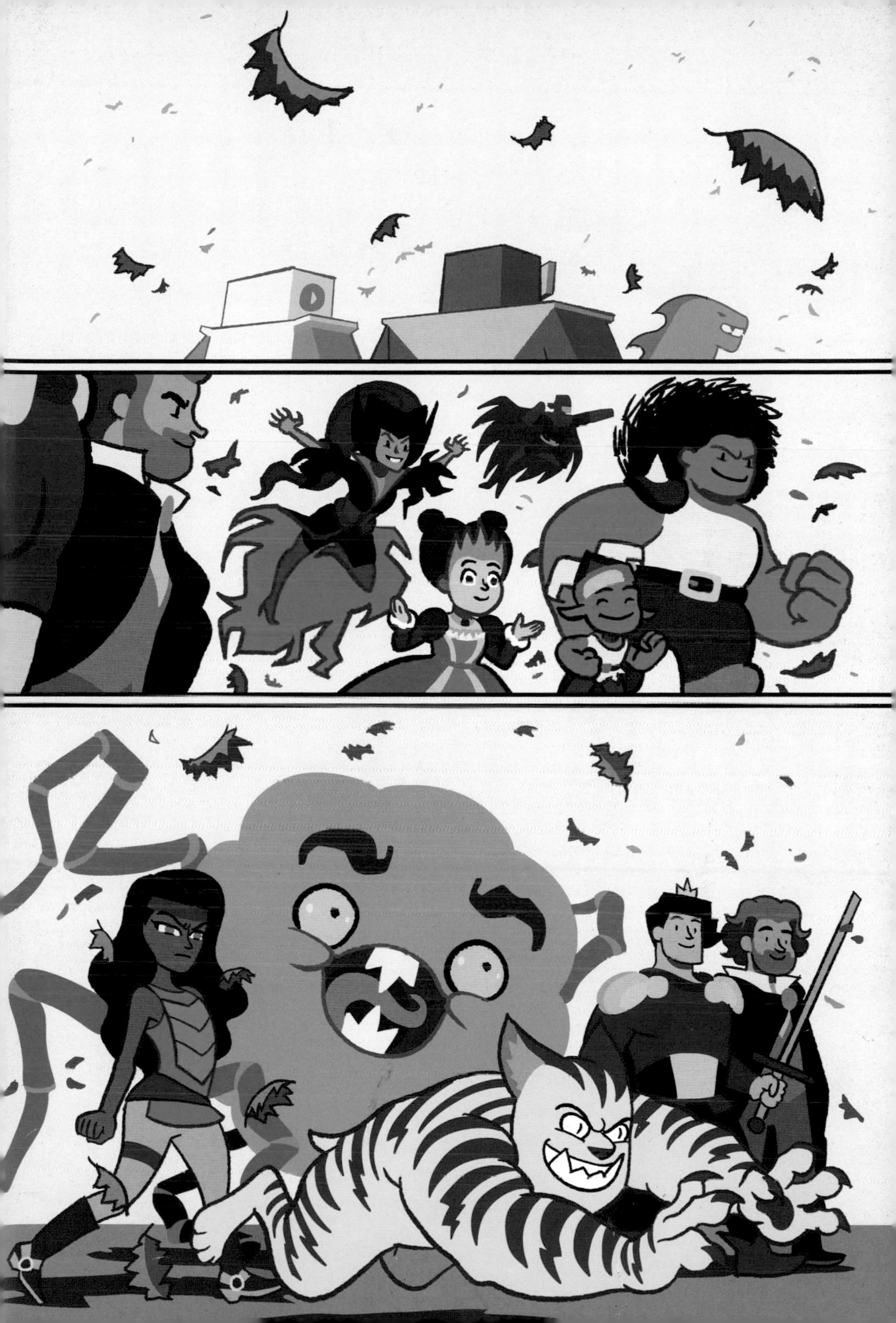

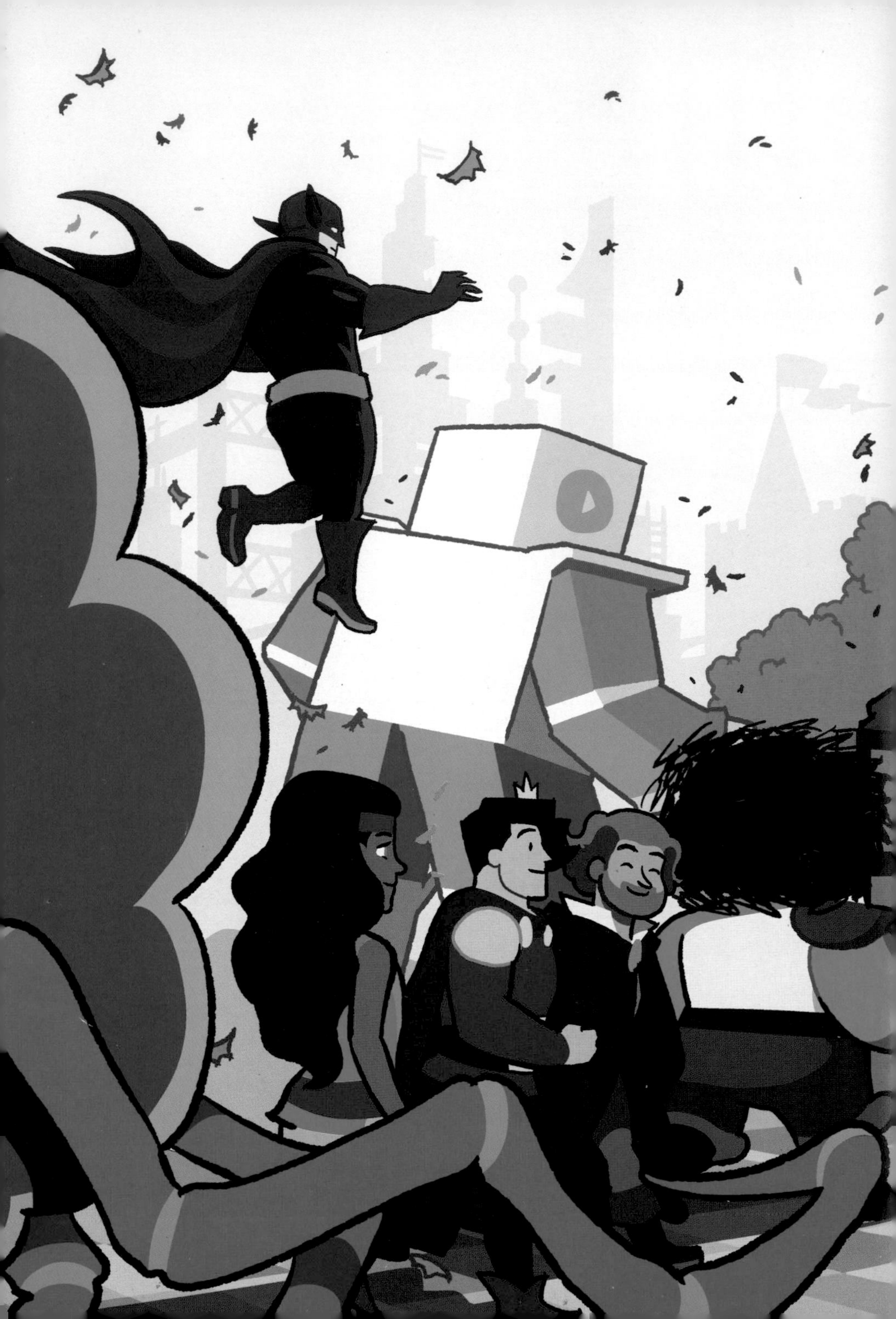

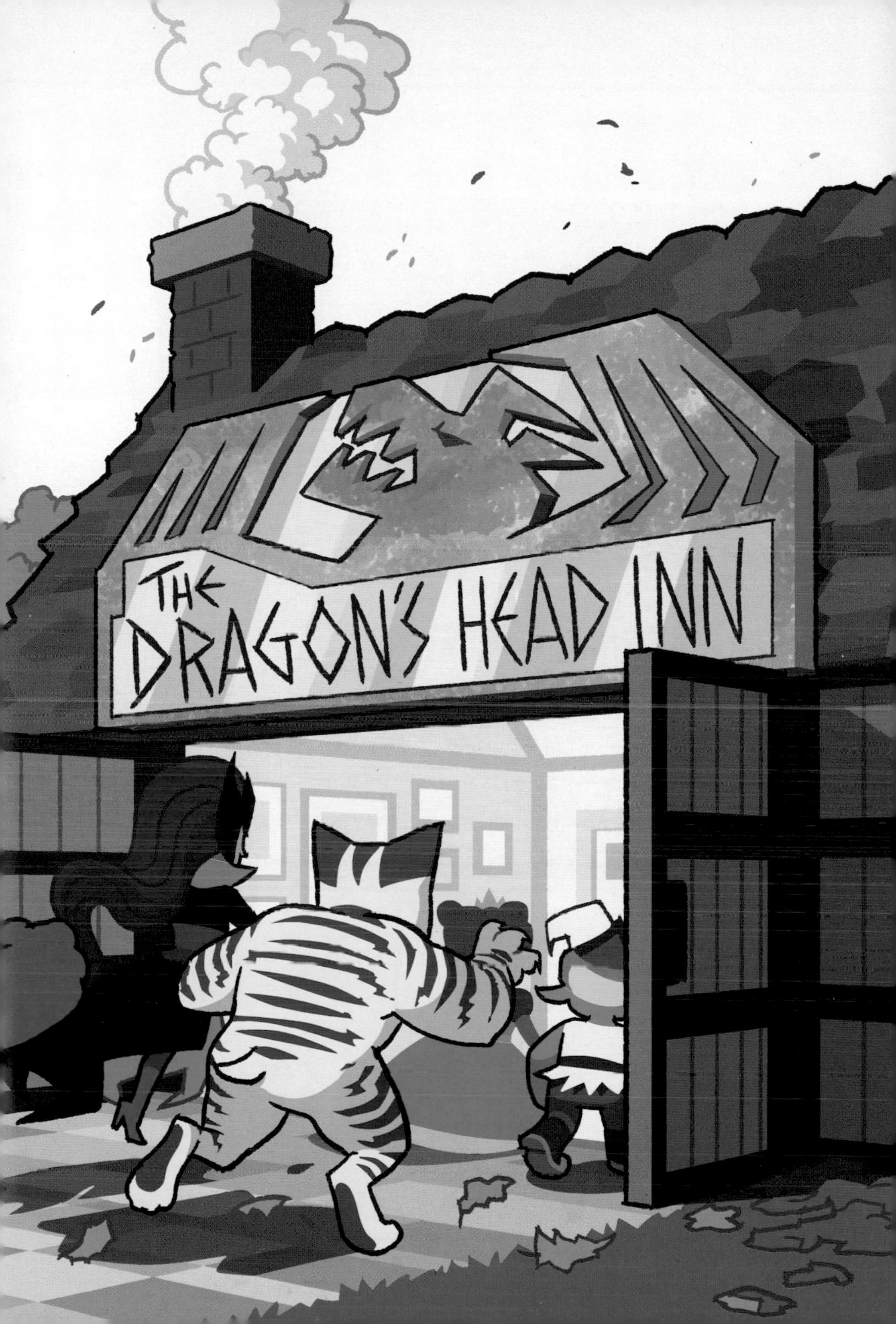
THE DRAGON'S HEAD INN

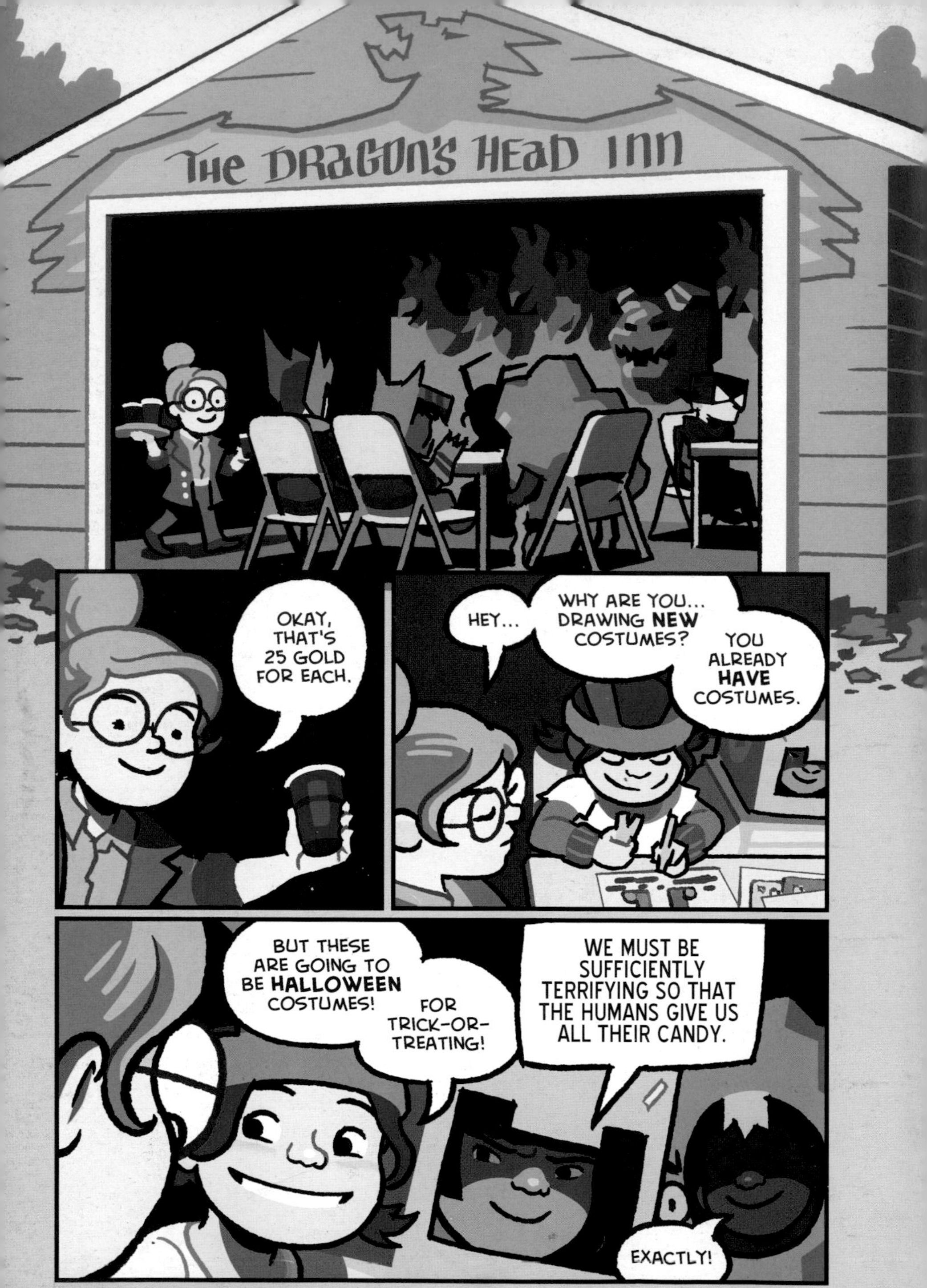
THE DRAGON'S HEAD INN
OKAY, THAT'S 25 GOLD FOR EACH.
HEY...
WHY ARE YOU... DRAWING NEW COSTUMES?
YOU ALREADY HAVE COSTUMES.
BUT THESE ARE GOING TO BE HALLOWEEN COSTUMES!
FOR TRICK-OR-TREATING!
WE MUST BE SUFFICIENTLY TERRIFYING SO THAT THE HUMANS GIVE US ALL THEIR CANDY.
EXACTLY!

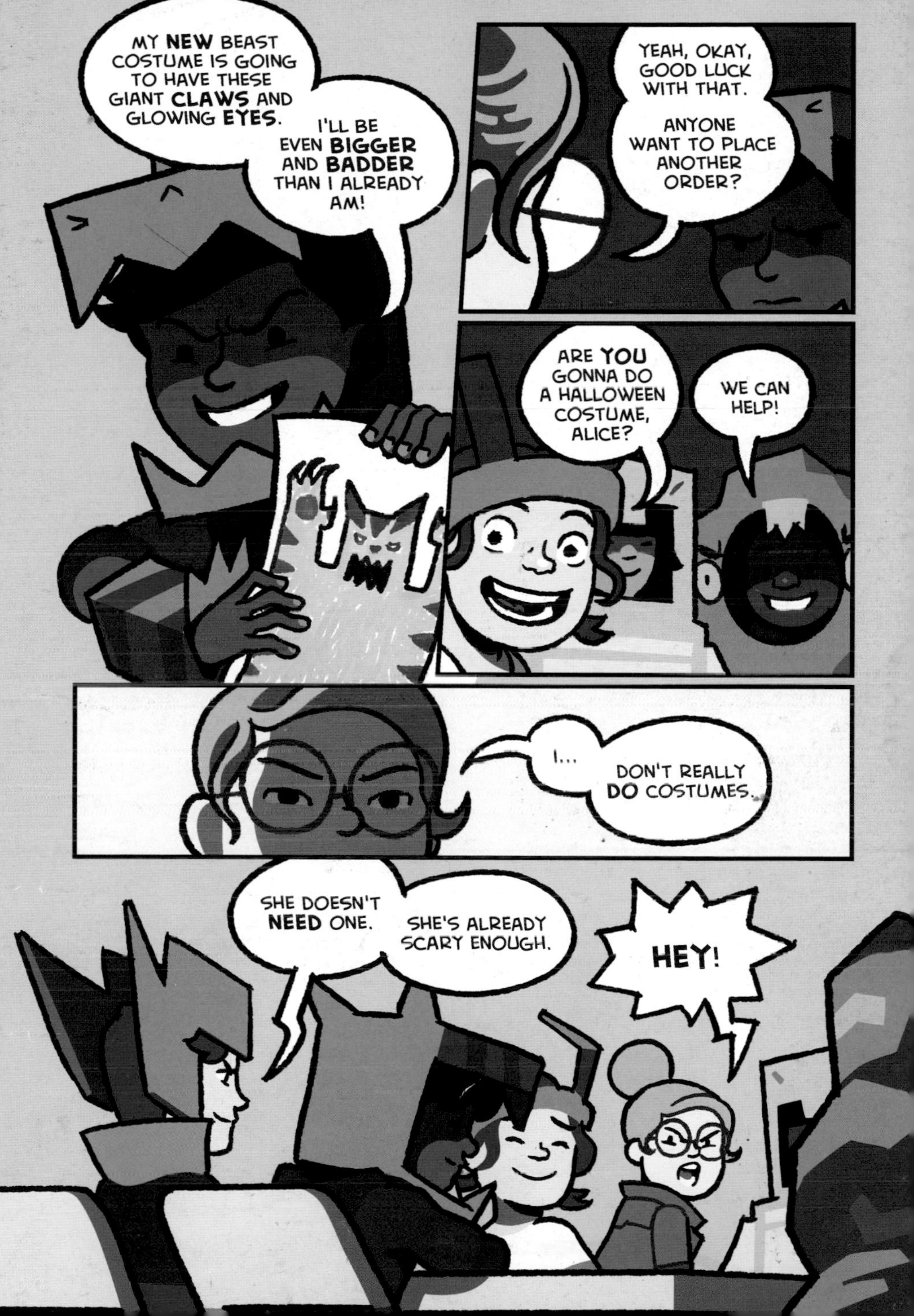
MY NEW BEAST COSTUME IS GOING TO HAVE THESE GIANT CLAWS AND GLOWING EYES.
I'LL BE EVEN BIGGER AND BADDER THAN I ALREADY AM!
YEAH, OKAY, GOOD LUCK WITH THAT.
ANYONE WANT TO PLACE ANOTHER ORDER?
ARE YOU GONNA DO A HALLOWEEN COSTUME, ALICE?
WE CAN HELP!
I...
DON'T REALLY DO COSTUMES.
SHE DOESN'T NEED ONE.
SHE'S ALREADY SCARY ENOUGH.
HEY!

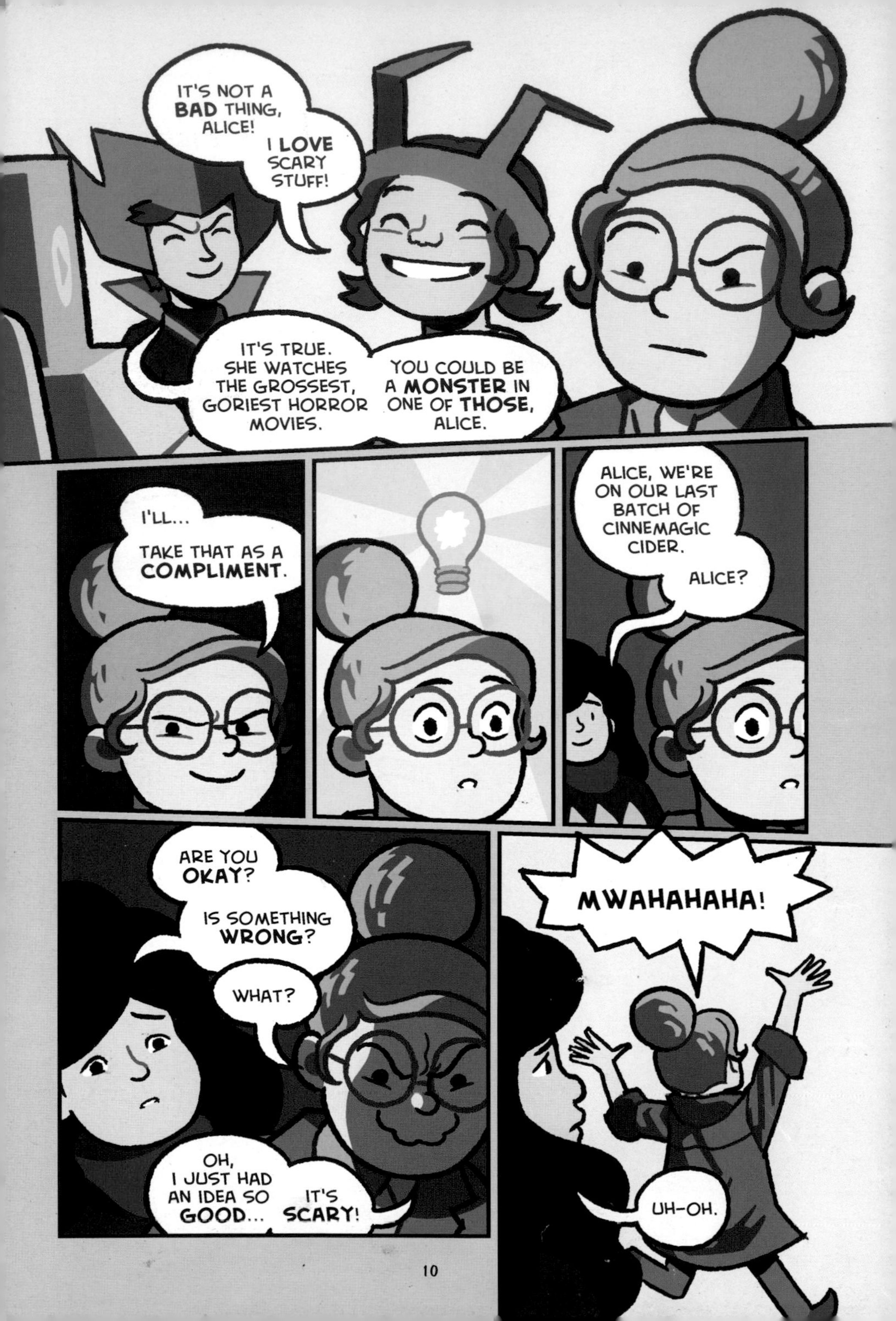
IT'S NOT A BAD THING, ALICE!
I LOVE SCARY STUFF!
IT'S TRUE. SHE WATCHES THE GROSSEST, GORIEST HORROR MOVIES.
YOU COULD BE A MONSTER IN ONE OF THOSE, ALICE.
I'LL...
TAKE THAT AS A COMPLIMENT.
ALICE, WE'RE ON OUR LAST BATCH OF CINNEMAGIC CIDER.
ALICE?
ARE YOU OKAY?
IS SOMETHING WRONG?
WHAT?
OH, I JUST HAD AN IDEA SO GOOD...
IT'S SCARY!
MWAHAHAHA!
UH-OH.

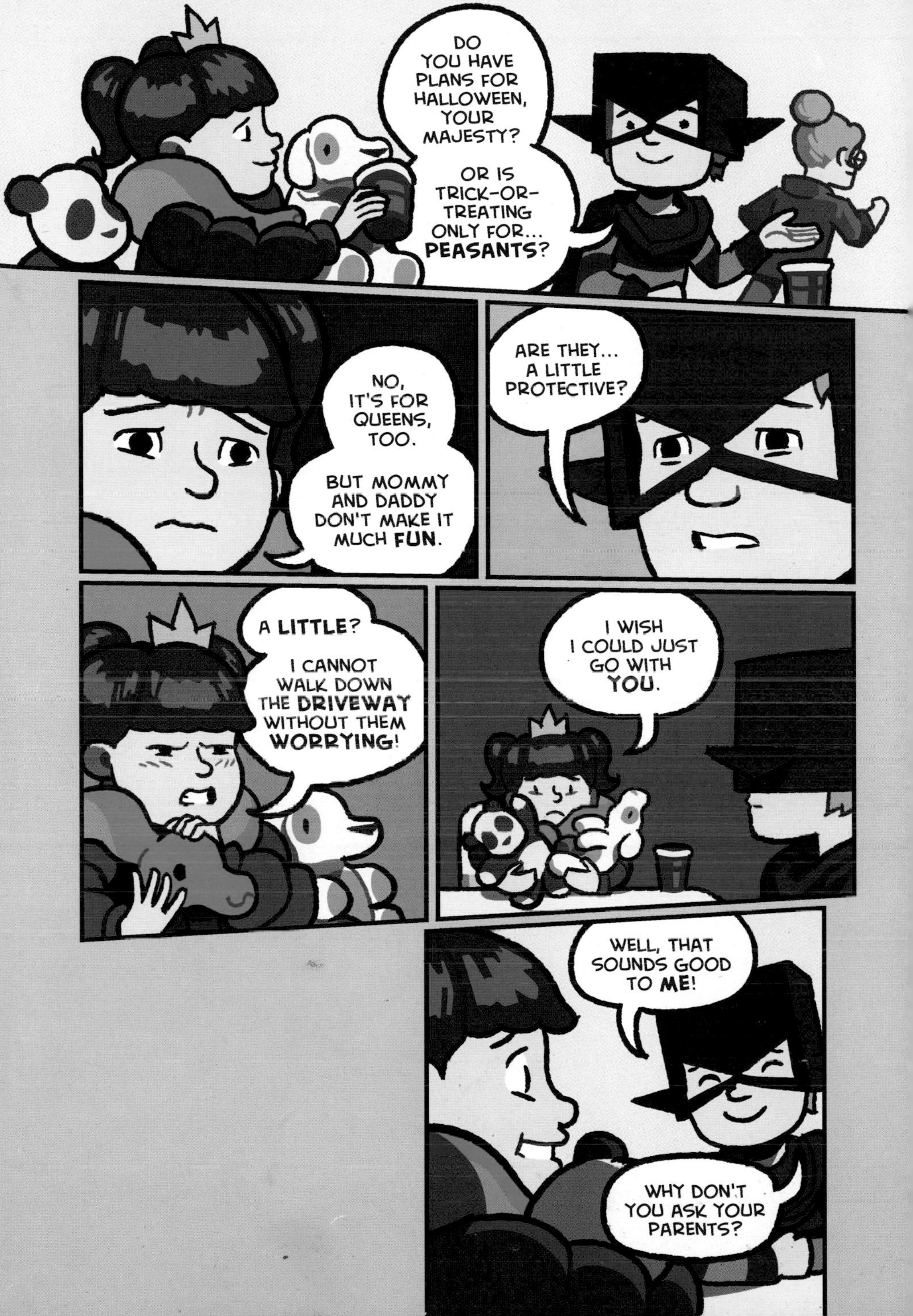
DO YOU HAVE PLANS FOR HALLOWEEN, YOUR MAJESTY?
OR IS TRICK-OR-TREATING ONLY FOR... PEASANTS?
NO, IT'S FOR QUEENS, TOO.
BUT MOMMY AND DADDY DON'T MAKE IT MUCH FUN.
ARE THEY... A LITTLE PROTECTIVE?
A LITTLE?
I CANNOT WALK DOWN THE DRIVEWAY WITHOUT THEM WORRYING!
I WISH I COULD JUST GO WITH YOU.
WELL, THAT SOUNDS GOOD TO ME!
WHY DON'T YOU ASK YOUR PARENTS?

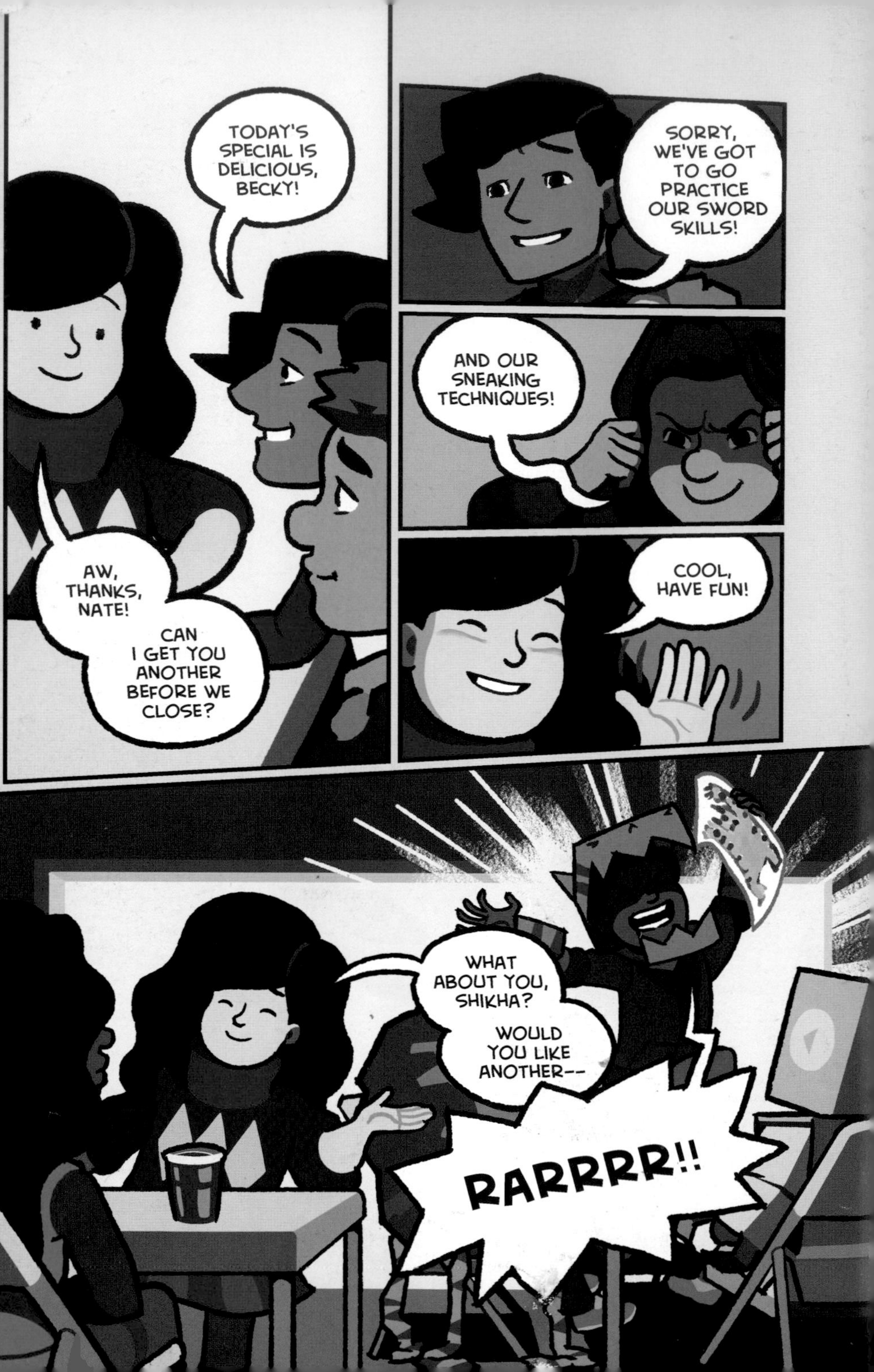
TODAY'S SPECIAL IS DELICIOUS, BECKY!
AW, THANKS, NATE!
CAN I GET YOU ANOTHER BEFORE WE CLOSE?
SORRY, WE'VE GOT TO GO PRACTICE OUR SWORD SKILLS!
AND OUR SNEAKING TECHNIQUES!
COOL, HAVE FUN!
WHAT ABOUT YOU, SHIKHA?
WOULD YOU LIKE ANOTHER--
RARRRR!!

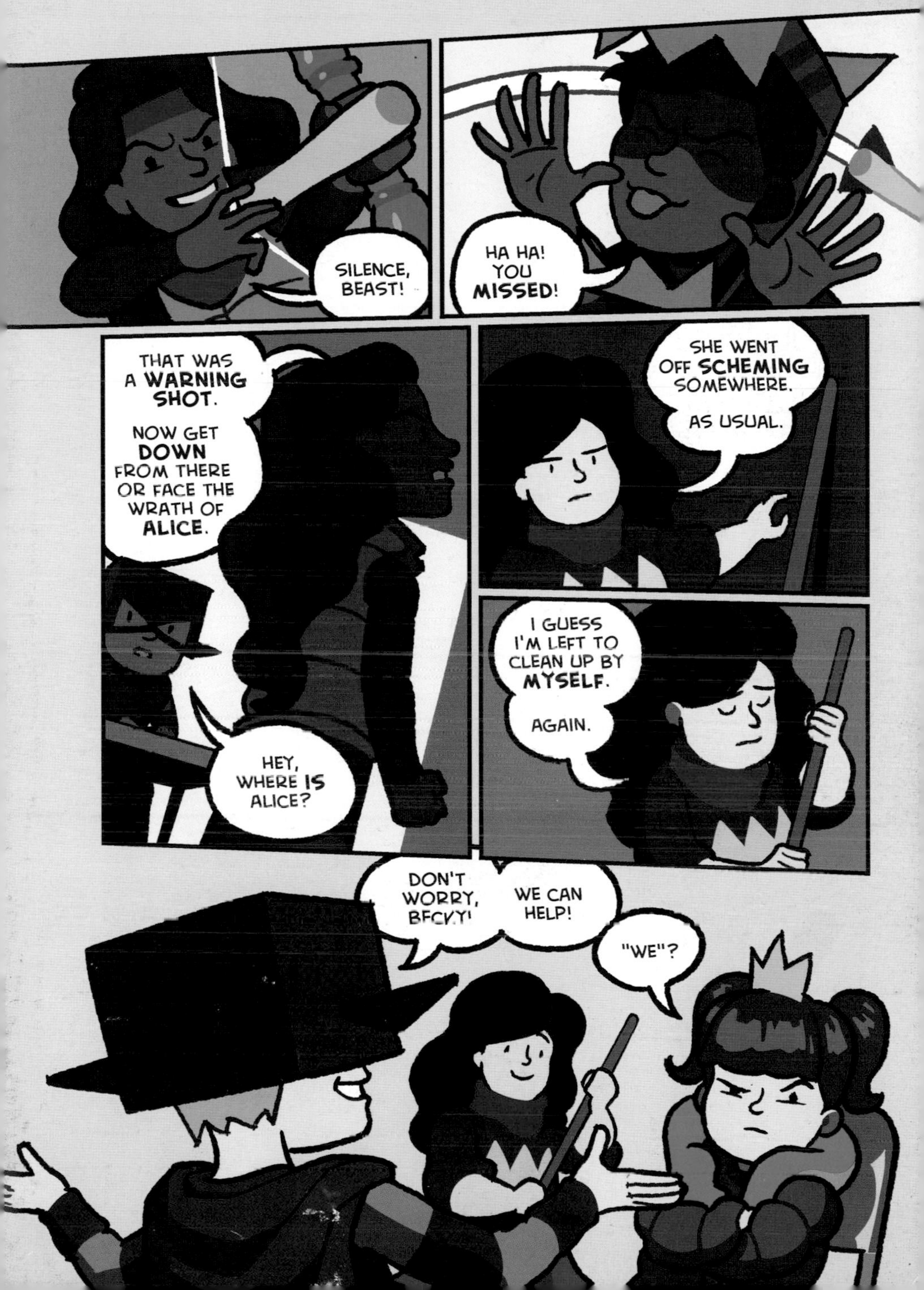
SILENCE, BEAST!
HA HA! YOU MISSED!
THAT WAS A WARNING SHOT.
NOW GET DOWN FROM THERE OR FACE THE WRATH OF ALICE.
HEY, WHERE IS ALICE?
SHE WENT OFF SCHEMING SOMEWHERE.
AS USUAL.
I GUESS I'M LEFT TO CLEAN UP BY MYSELF.
AGAIN.
DON'T WORRY, BECKY!
WE CAN HELP!
"WE"?

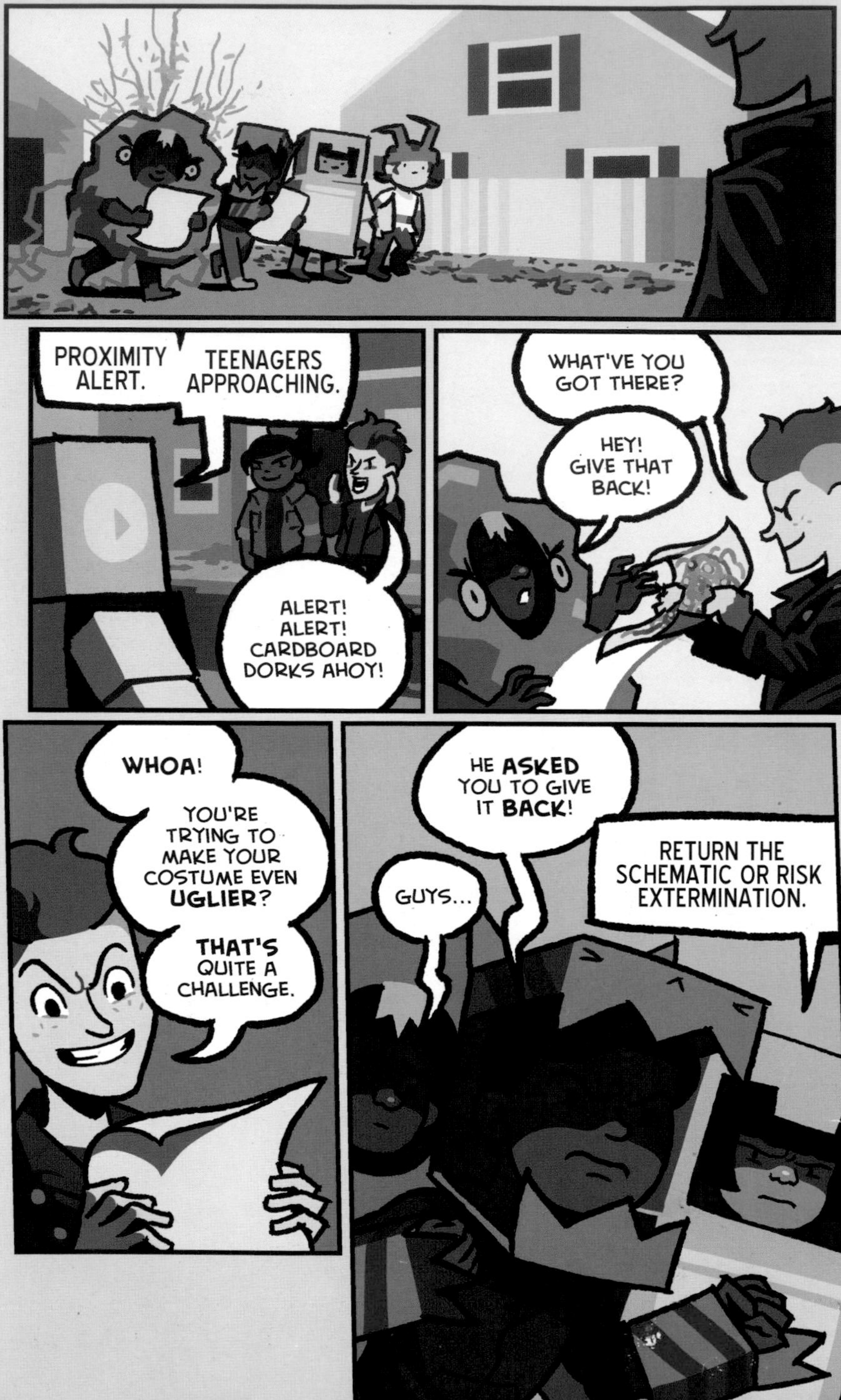

PROXIMITY ALERT.
TEENAGERS APPROACHING.
ALERT! ALERT! CARDBOARD DORKS AHOY!
WHAT'VE YOU GOT THERE?
HEY! GIVE THAT BACK!
WHOA!
YOU'RE TRYING TO MAKE YOUR COSTUME EVEN UGLIER?
THAT'S QUITE A CHALLENGE.
HE ASKED YOU TO GIVE IT BACK!
GUYS...
RETURN THE SCHEMATIC OR RISK EXTERMINATION.

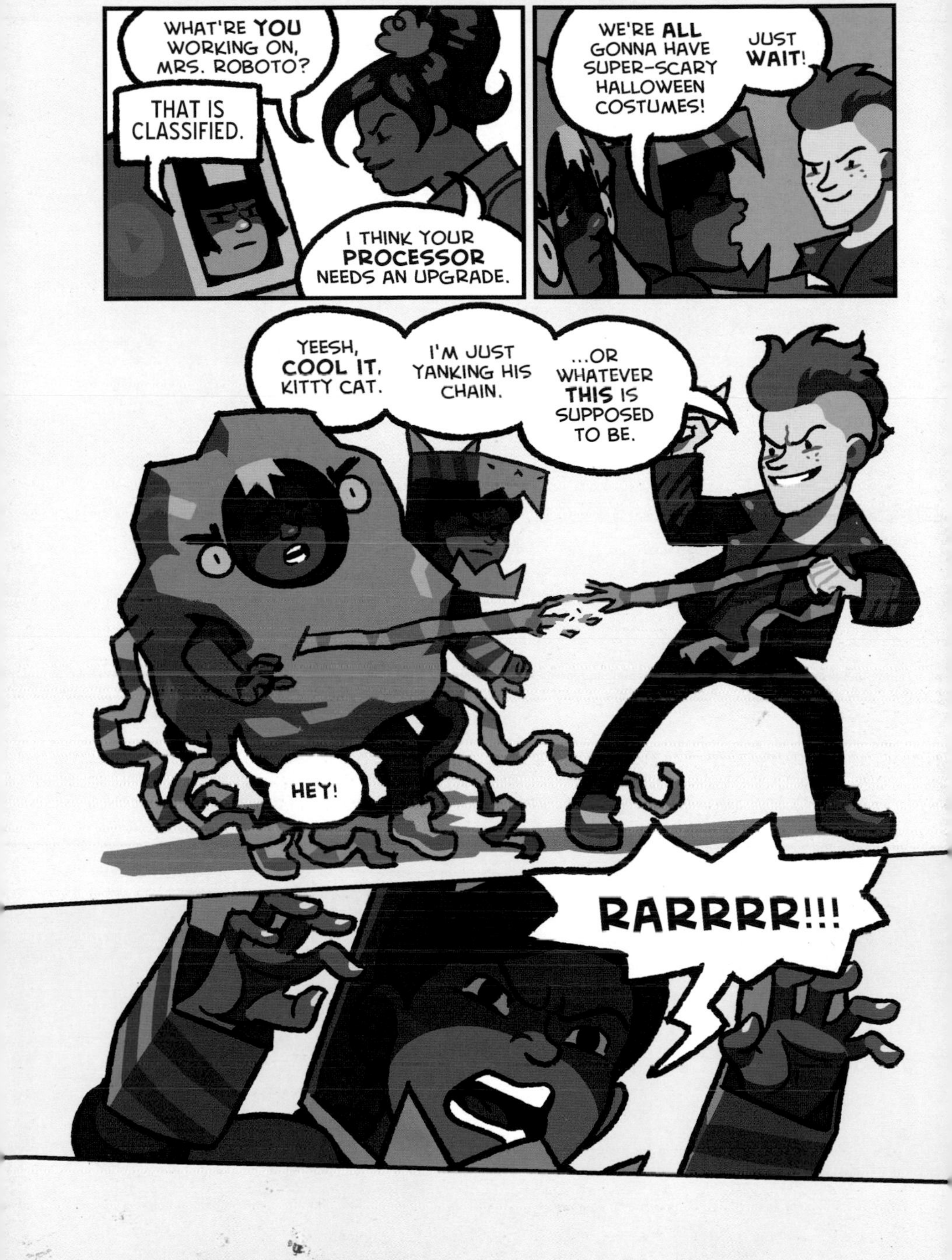

WHAT'RE YOU WORKING ON, MRS. ROBOTO?
THAT IS CLASSIFIED.
I THINK YOUR PROCESSOR NEEDS AN UPGRADE.
WE'RE ALL GONNA HAVE SUPER-SCARY HALLOWEEN COSTUMES!
JUST WAIT!
YEESH, COOL IT, KITTY CAT.
I'M JUST YANKING HIS CHAIN.
...OR WHATEVER THIS IS SUPPOSED TO BE.
HEY!
RARRRR!!!

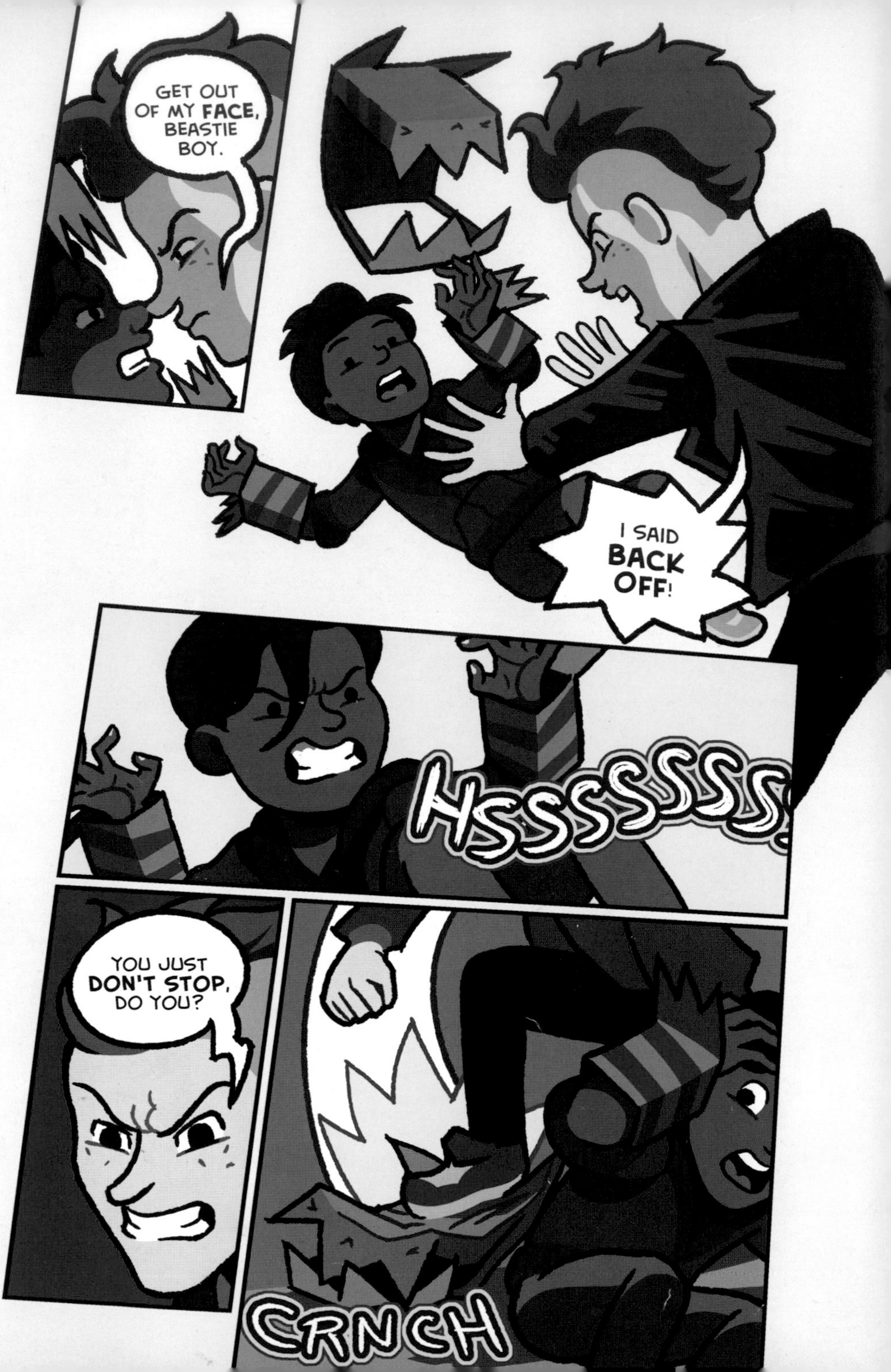
GET OUT OF MY **FACE**, BEASTIE BOY.
I SAID **BACK OFF**!
HSSSSSSS!
YOU JUST **DON'T STOP**, DO YOU?
CRNCH

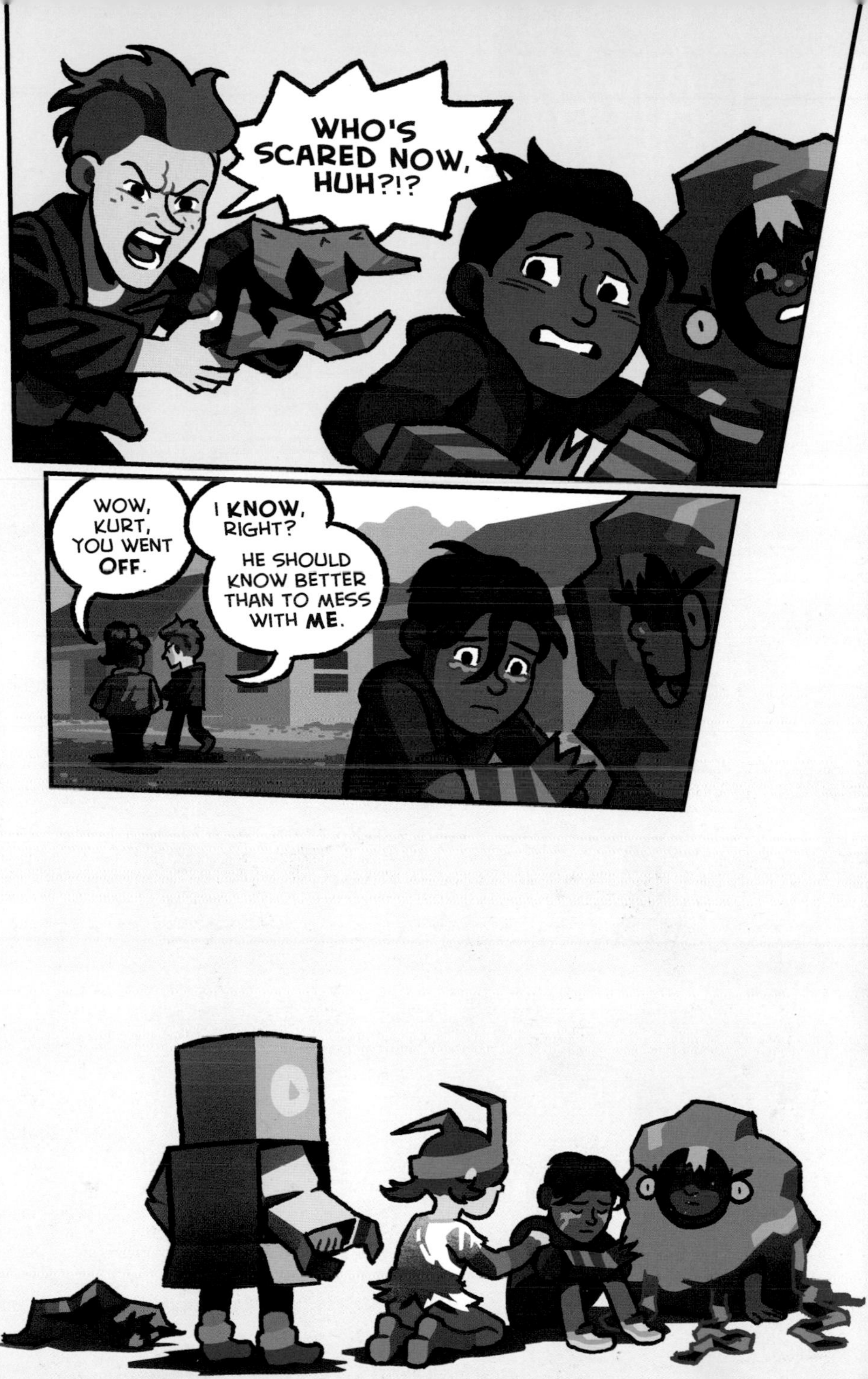
WHO'S SCARED NOW, HUH?!?
WOW, KURT, YOU WENT OFF.
I KNOW, RIGHT?
HE SHOULD KNOW BETTER THAN TO MESS WITH ME.

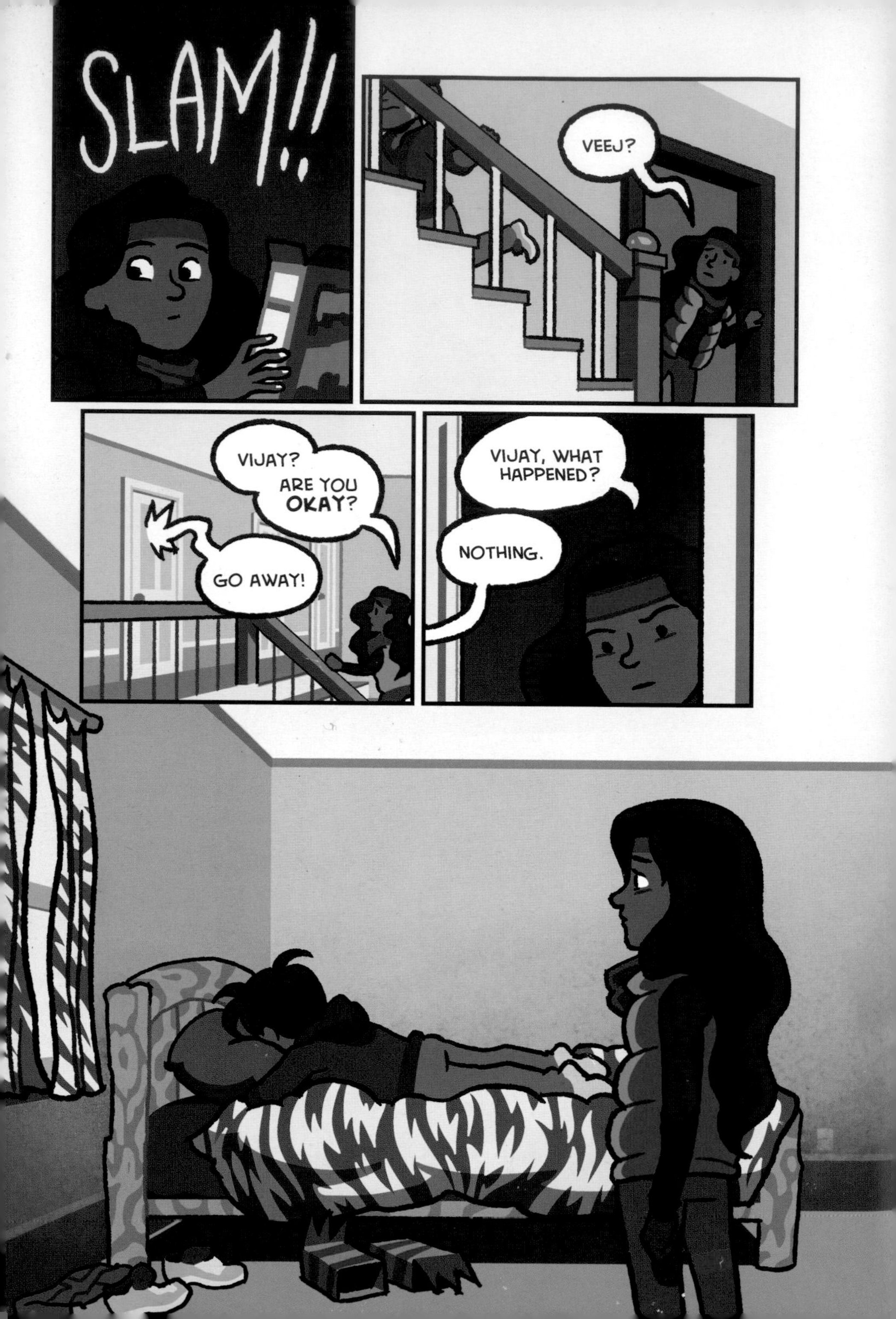
SLAM!!
VEEJ?
VIJAY?
ARE YOU OKAY?
GO AWAY!
VIJAY, WHAT HAPPENED?
NOTHING.

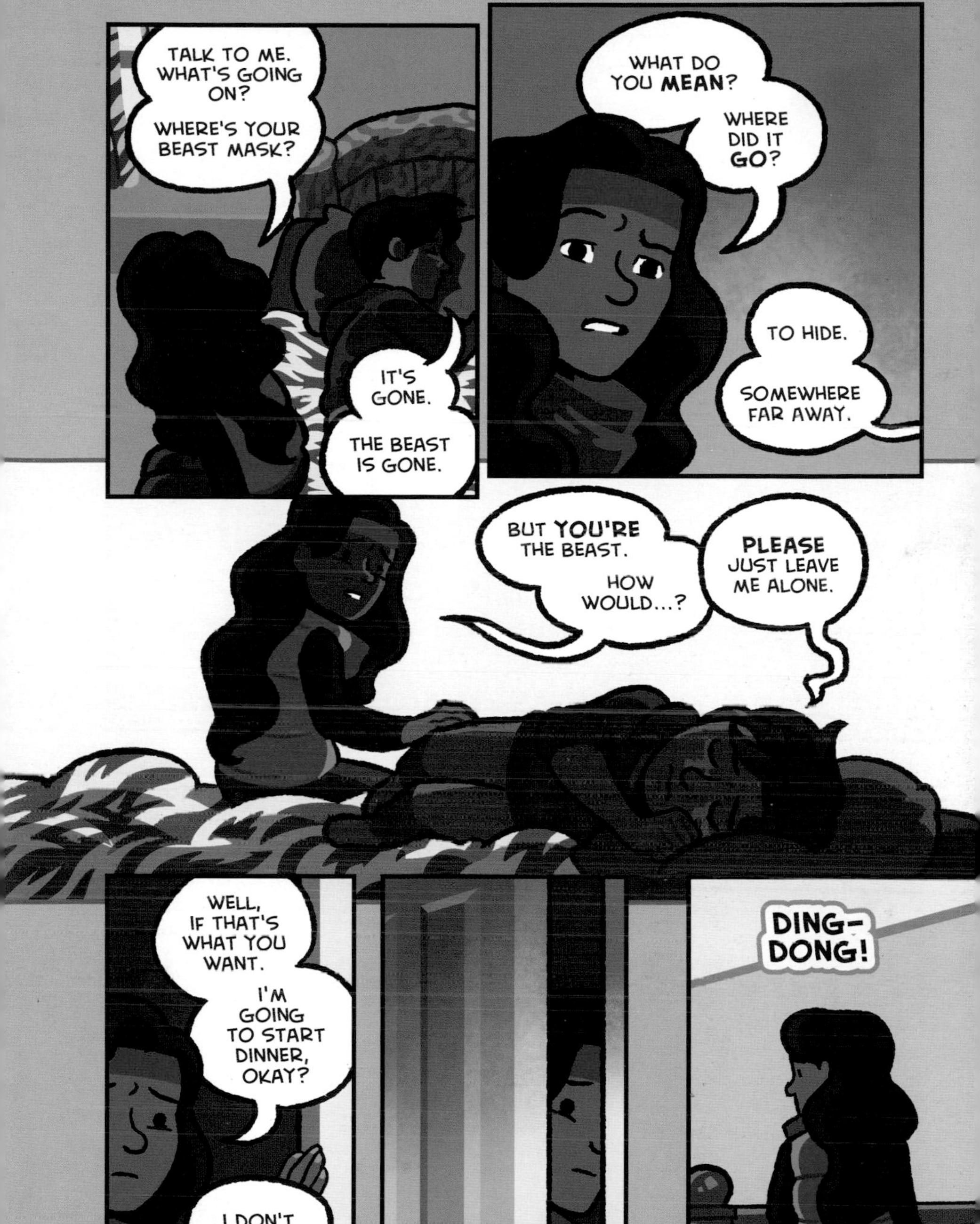
TALK TO ME. WHAT'S GOING ON?
WHERE'S YOUR BEAST MASK?
IT'S GONE.
THE BEAST IS GONE.
WHAT DO YOU **MEAN**?
WHERE DID IT **GO**?
TO HIDE.
SOMEWHERE FAR AWAY.
BUT **YOU'RE** THE BEAST.
HOW WOULD...?
PLEASE JUST LEAVE ME ALONE.
WELL, IF THAT'S WHAT YOU WANT.
I'M GOING TO START DINNER, OKAY?
I DON'T WANT ANY.
DING-DONG!

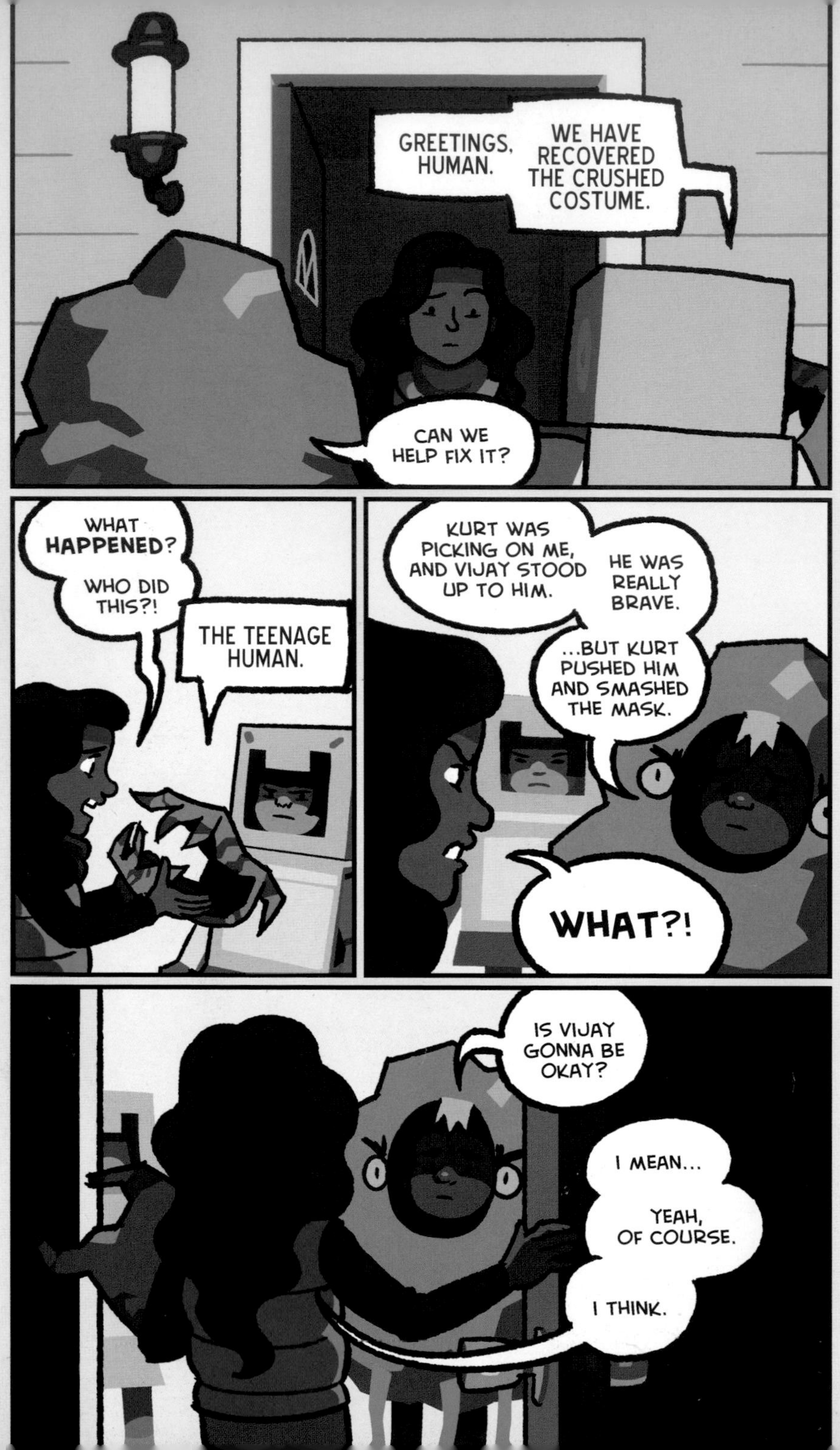
GREETINGS, HUMAN.
WE HAVE RECOVERED THE CRUSHED COSTUME.
CAN WE HELP FIX IT?
WHAT HAPPENED?
WHO DID THIS?!
THE TEENAGE HUMAN.
KURT WAS PICKING ON ME, AND VIJAY STOOD UP TO HIM.
HE WAS REALLY BRAVE.
...BUT KURT PUSHED HIM AND SMASHED THE MASK.
WHAT?!
IS VIJAY GONNA BE OKAY?
I MEAN...
YEAH, OF COURSE.
I THINK.

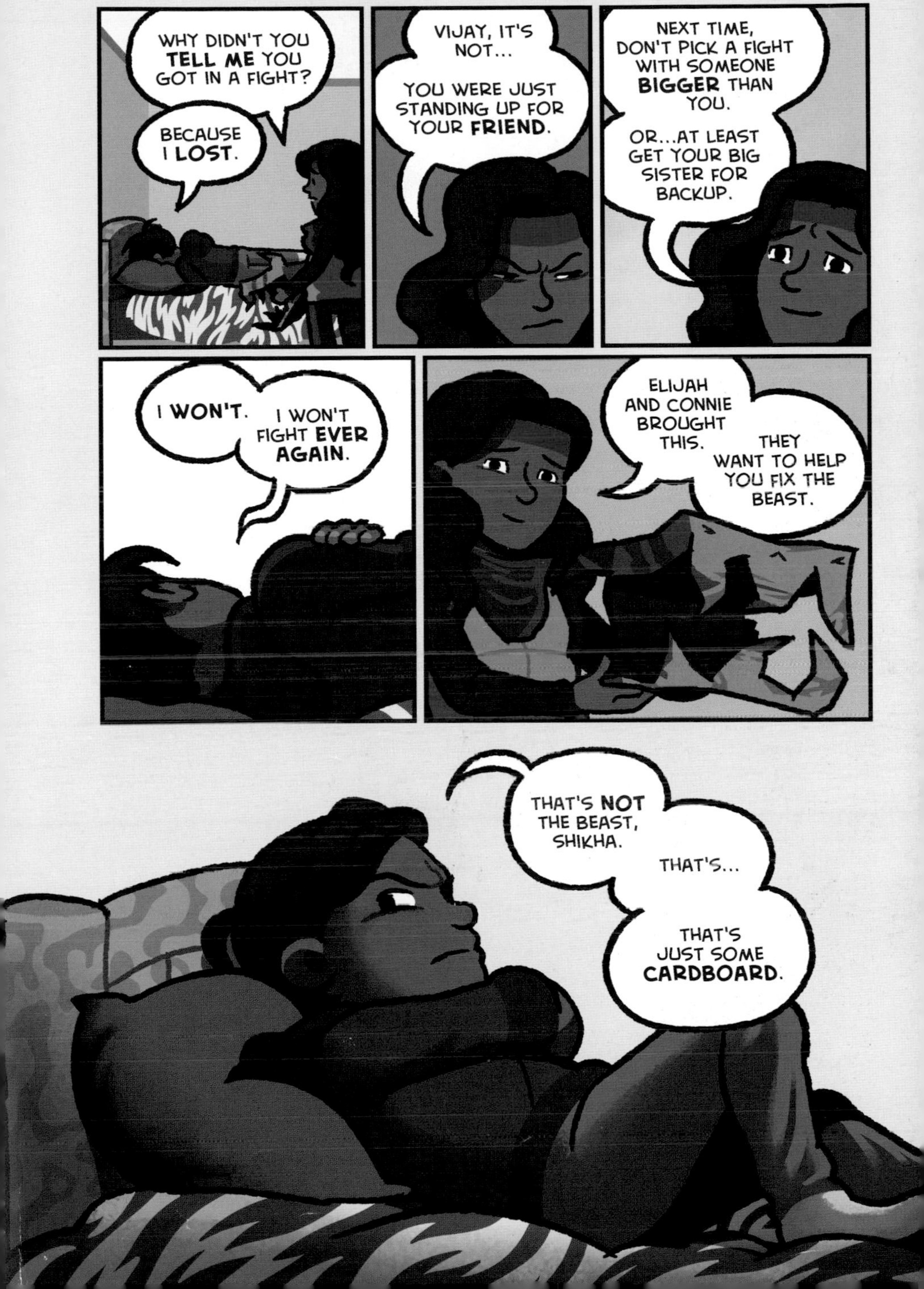
WHY DIDN'T YOU **TELL ME** YOU GOT IN A FIGHT?
BECAUSE I **LOST**.
VIJAY, IT'S NOT...
YOU WERE JUST STANDING UP FOR YOUR **FRIEND**.
NEXT TIME, DON'T PICK A FIGHT WITH SOMEONE **BIGGER** THAN YOU.
OR...AT LEAST GET YOUR BIG SISTER FOR BACKUP.
I **WON'T**.
I WON'T FIGHT **EVER AGAIN**.
ELIJAH AND CONNIE BROUGHT THIS.
THEY WANT TO HELP YOU FIX THE BEAST.
THAT'S **NOT** THE BEAST, SHIKHA.
THAT'S...
THAT'S JUST SOME **CARDBOARD**.

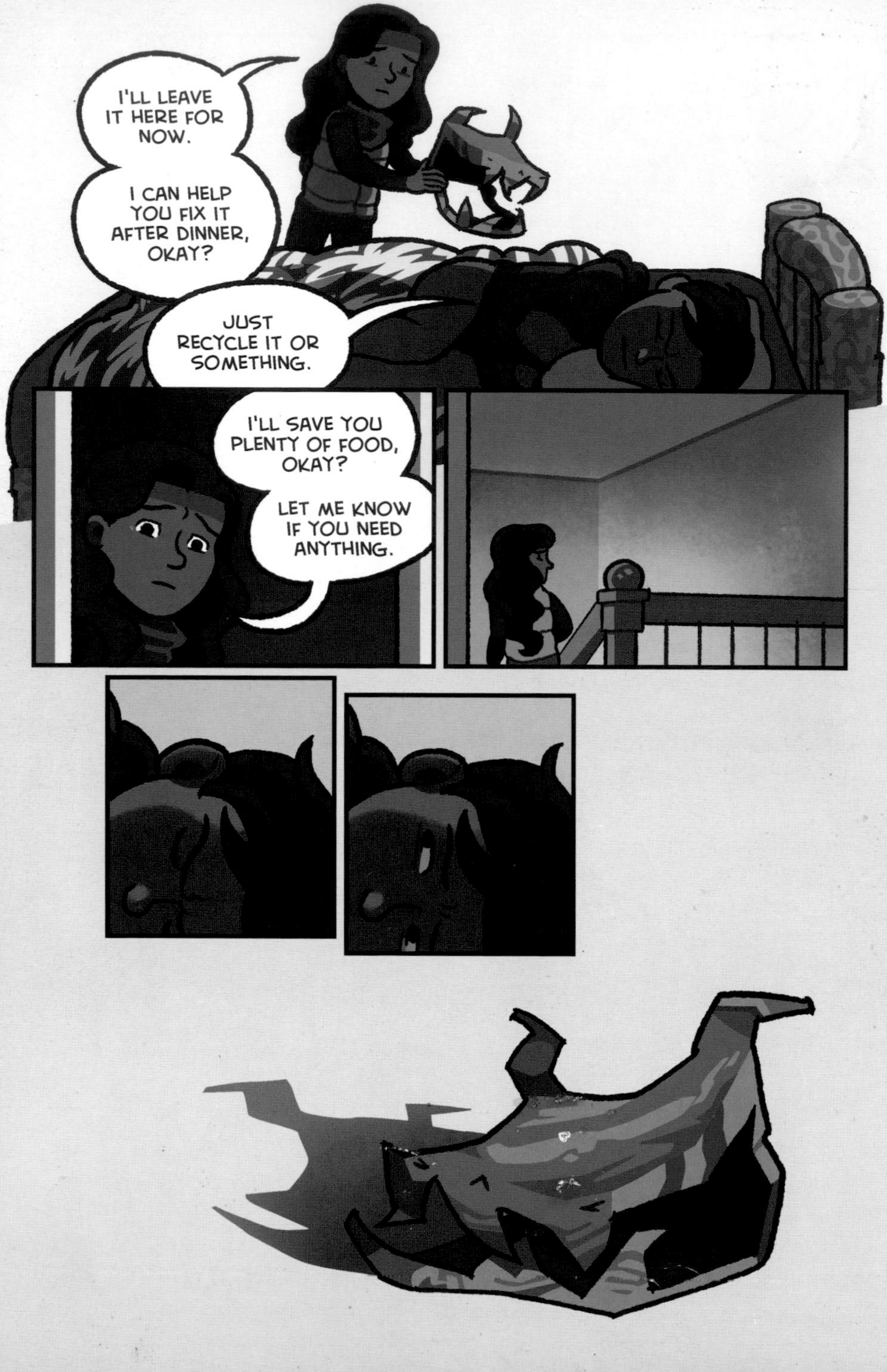
I'LL LEAVE IT HERE FOR NOW.
I CAN HELP YOU FIX IT AFTER DINNER, OKAY?
JUST RECYCLE IT OR SOMETHING.
I'LL SAVE YOU PLENTY OF FOOD, OKAY?
LET ME KNOW IF YOU NEED ANYTHING.

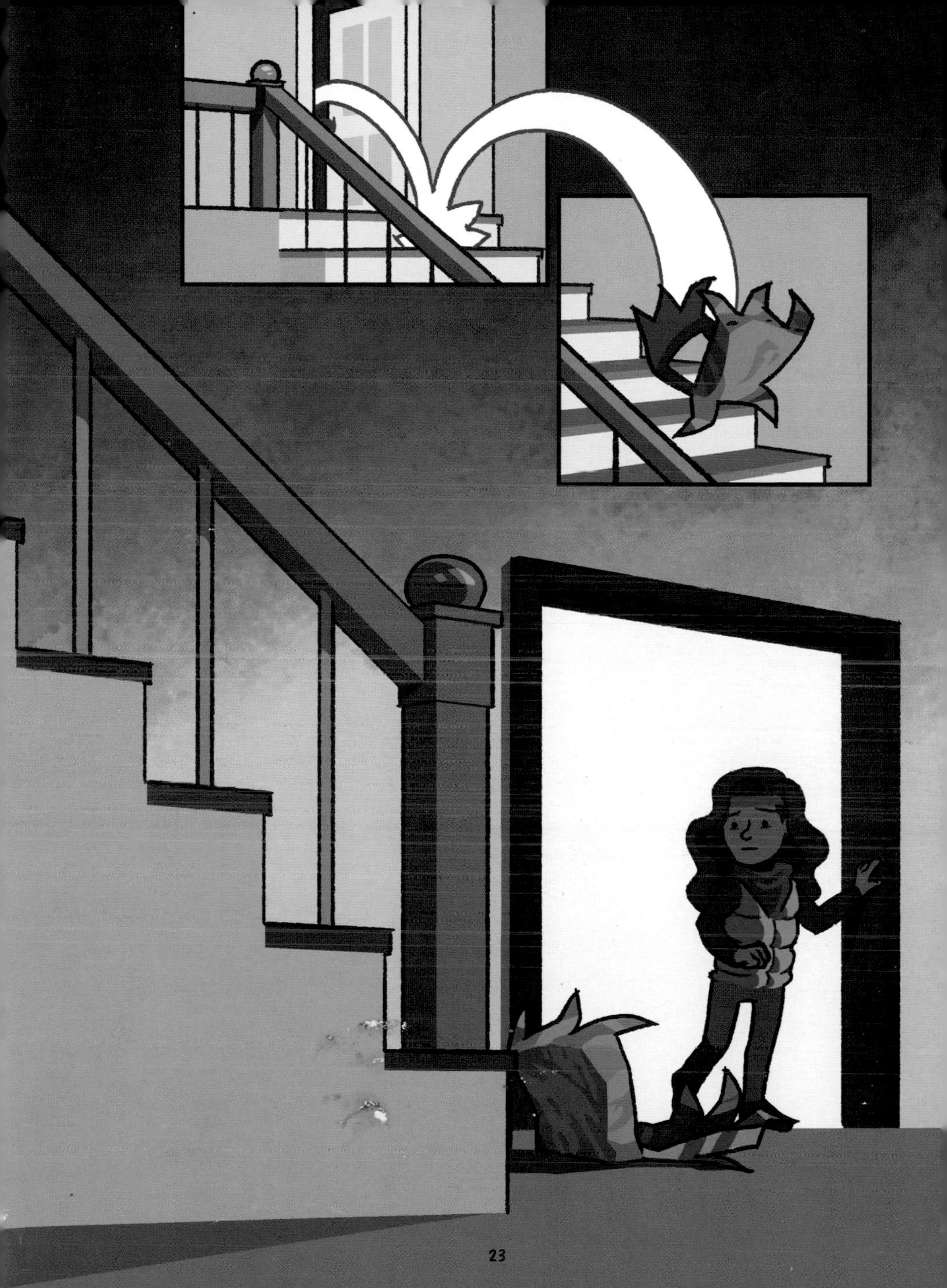

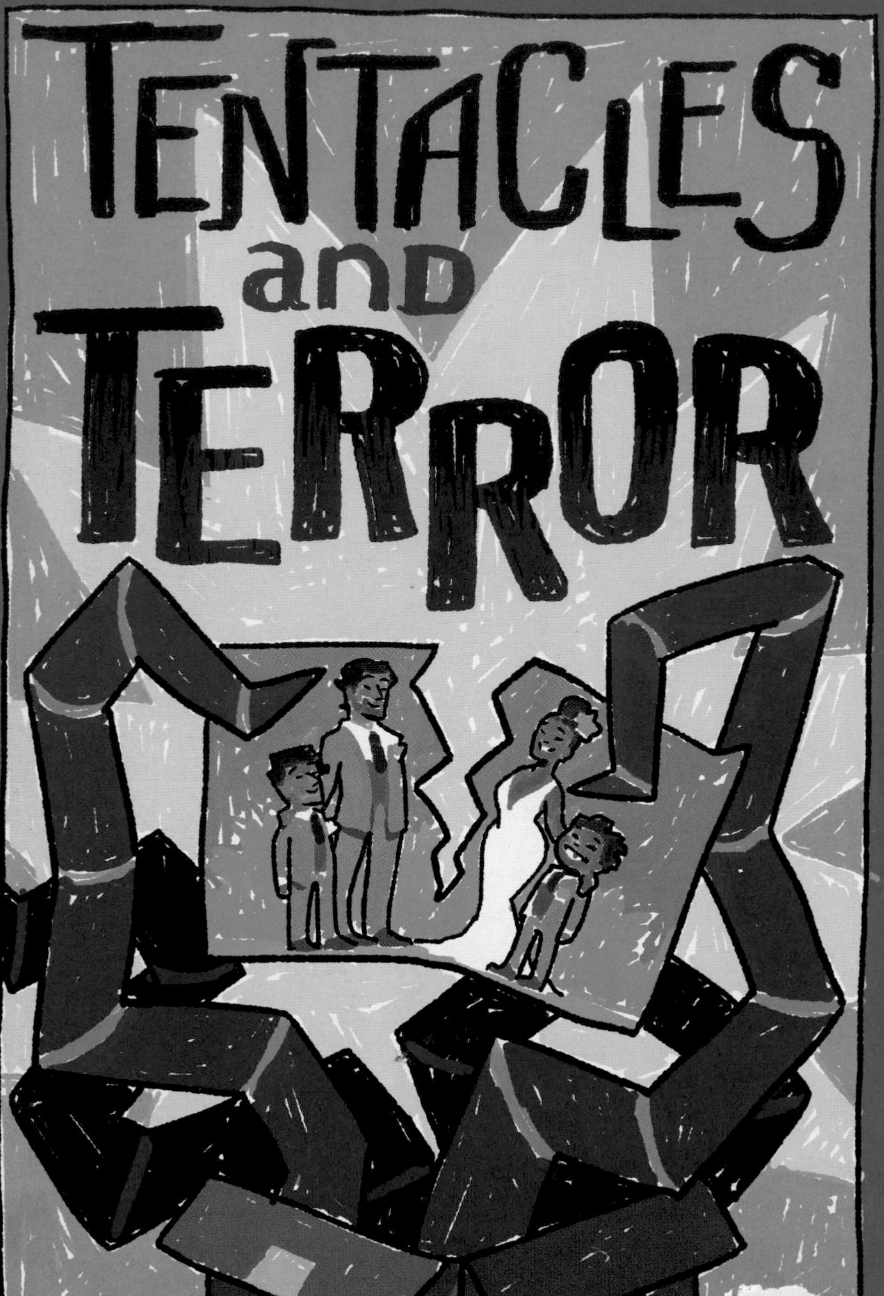
TENTACLES
and
TERROR

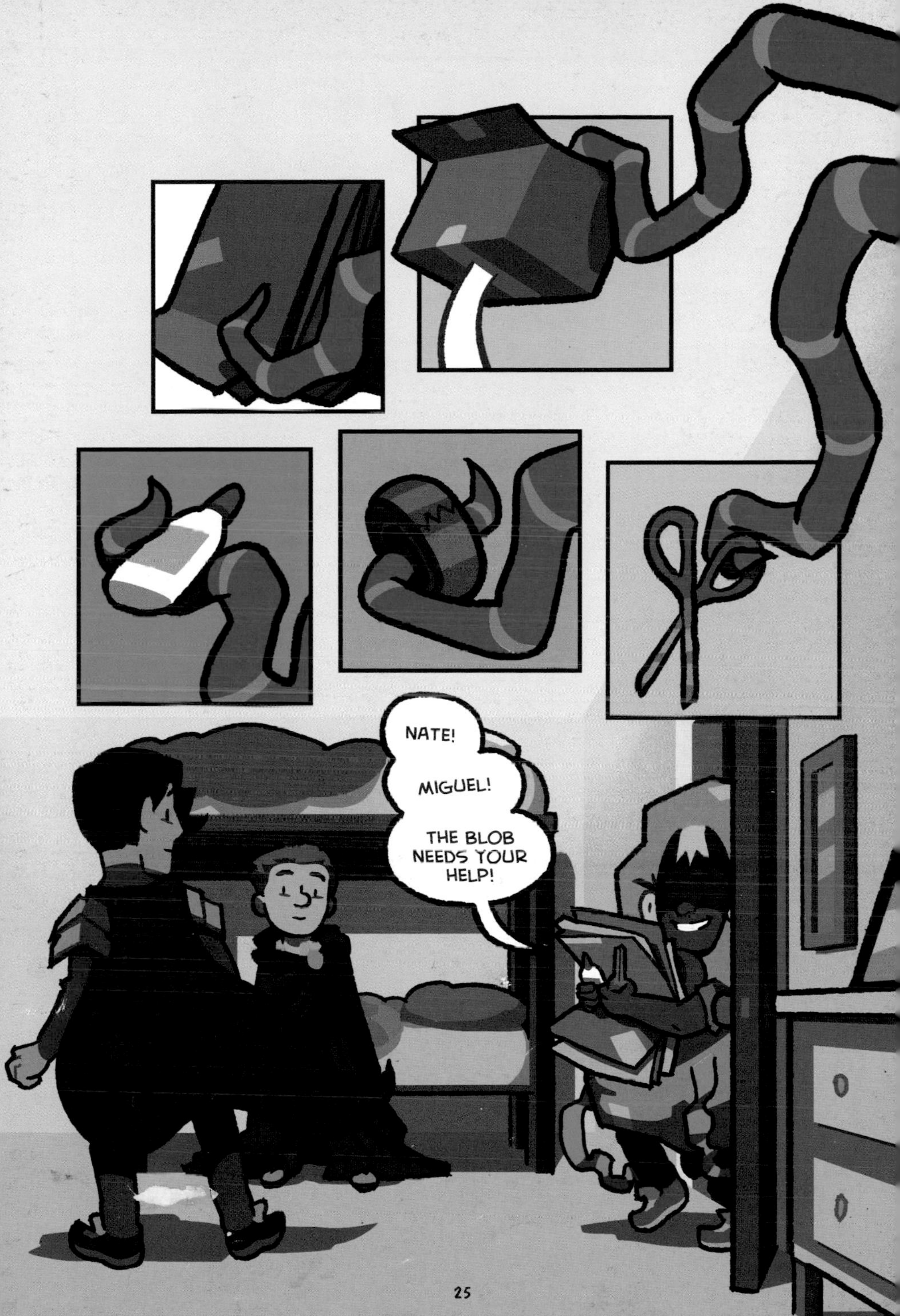
NATE!
MIGUEL!
THE BLOB NEEDS YOUR HELP!

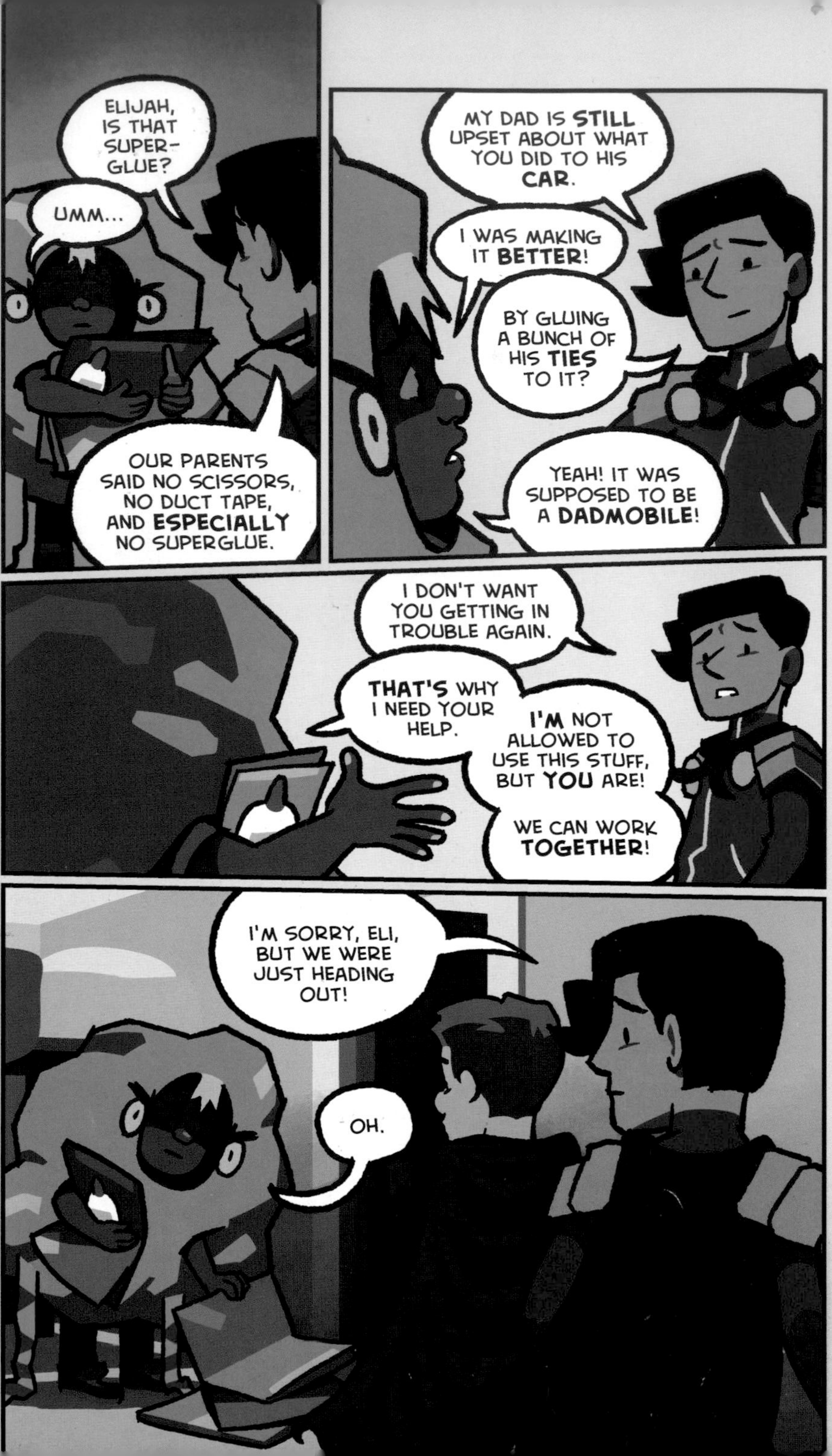
ELIJAH, IS THAT SUPER-GLUE?
UMM...
OUR PARENTS SAID NO SCISSORS, NO DUCT TAPE, AND **ESPECIALLY** NO SUPERGLUE.
MY DAD IS **STILL** UPSET ABOUT WHAT YOU DID TO HIS **CAR**.
I WAS MAKING IT **BETTER**!
BY GLUING A BUNCH OF HIS **TIES** TO IT?
YEAH! IT WAS SUPPOSED TO BE A **DADMOBILE**!
I DON'T WANT YOU GETTING IN TROUBLE AGAIN.
THAT'S WHY I NEED YOUR HELP.
I'M NOT ALLOWED TO USE THIS STUFF, BUT **YOU** ARE!
WE CAN WORK **TOGETHER**!
I'M SORRY, ELI, BUT WE WERE JUST HEADING OUT!
OH.

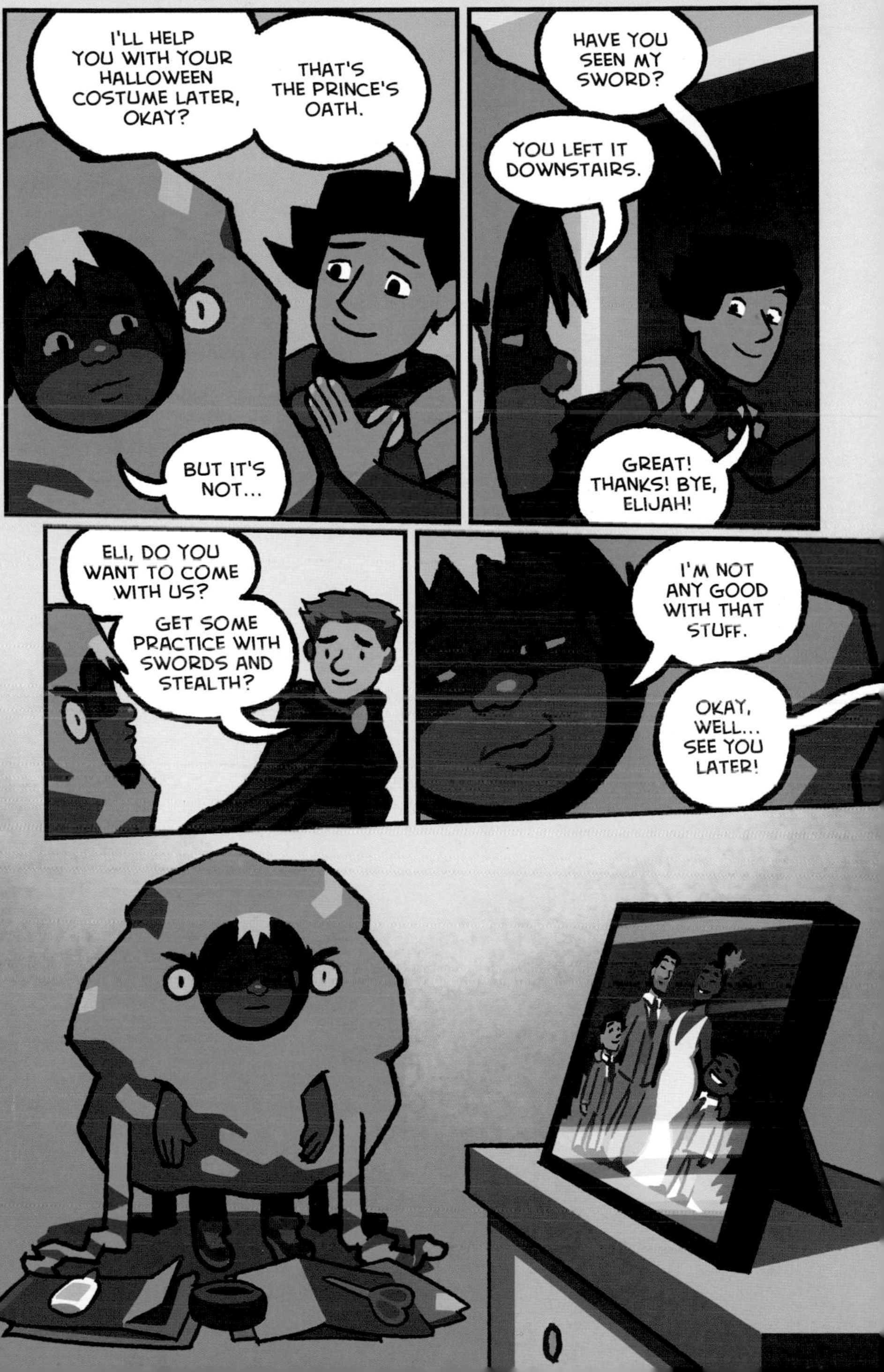
I'LL HELP YOU WITH YOUR HALLOWEEN COSTUME LATER, OKAY?
THAT'S THE PRINCE'S OATH.
BUT IT'S NOT...
HAVE YOU SEEN MY SWORD?
YOU LEFT IT DOWNSTAIRS.
GREAT! THANKS! BYE, ELIJAH!
ELI, DO YOU WANT TO COME WITH US?
GET SOME PRACTICE WITH SWORDS AND STEALTH?
I'M NOT ANY GOOD WITH THAT STUFF.
OKAY, WELL... SEE YOU LATER!

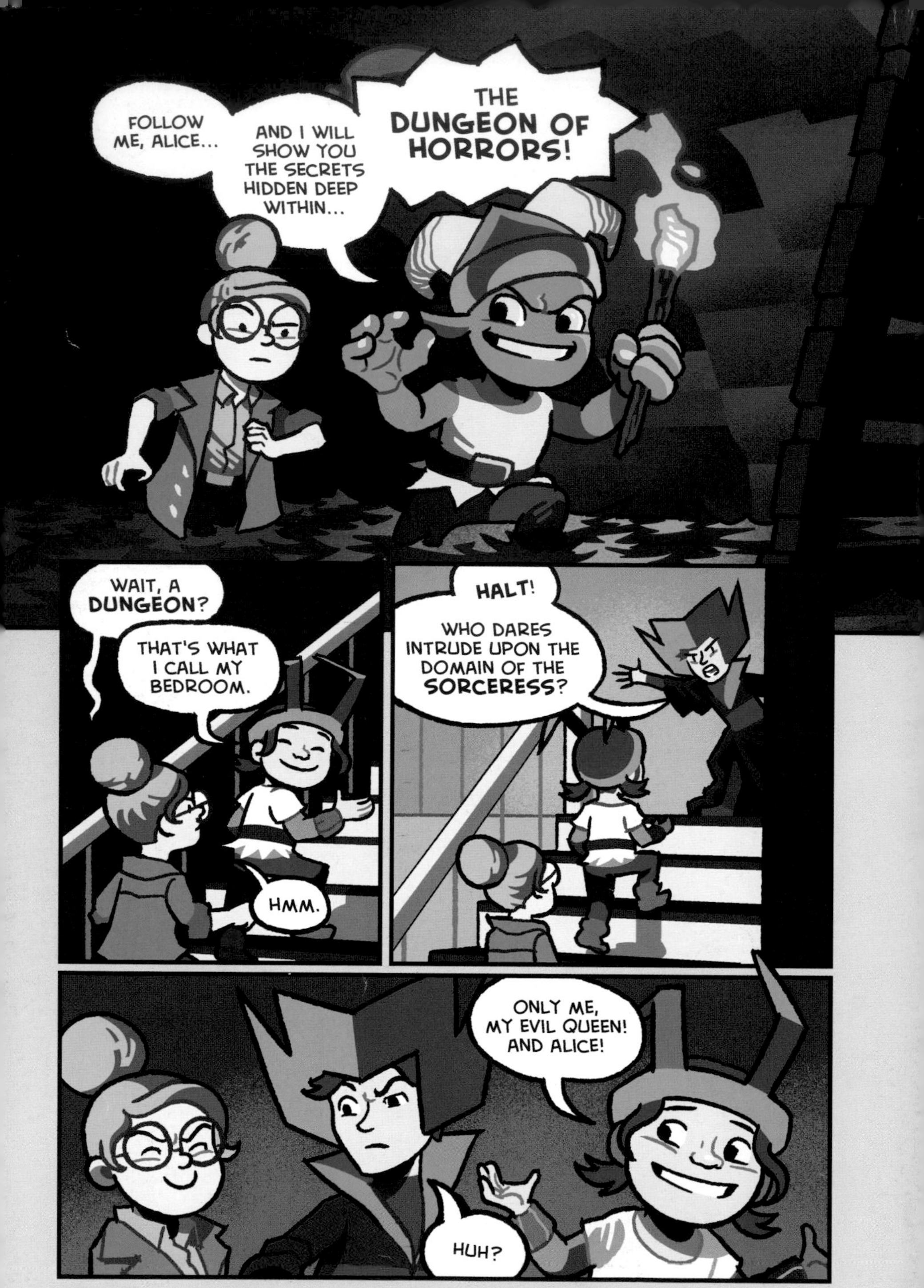
FOLLOW ME, ALICE...
AND I WILL SHOW YOU THE SECRETS HIDDEN DEEP WITHIN...
THE DUNGEON OF HORRORS!
WAIT, A DUNGEON?
THAT'S WHAT I CALL MY BEDROOM.
HMM.
HALT!
WHO DARES INTRUDE UPON THE DOMAIN OF THE SORCERESS?
ONLY ME, MY EVIL QUEEN! AND ALICE!
HUH?

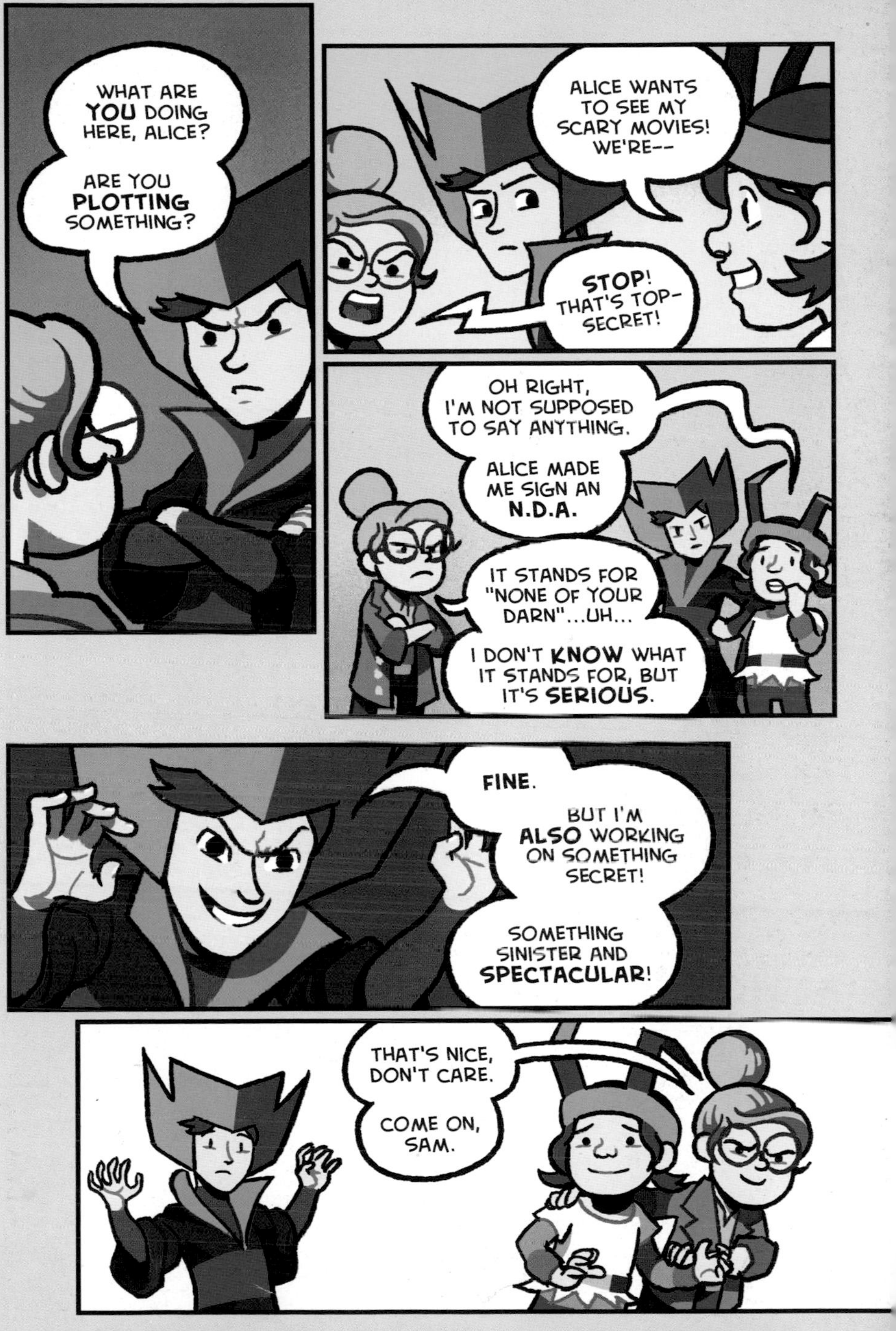
WHAT ARE YOU DOING HERE, ALICE?
ARE YOU PLOTTING SOMETHING?
ALICE WANTS TO SEE MY SCARY MOVIES! WE'RE--
STOP! THAT'S TOP-SECRET!
OH RIGHT, I'M NOT SUPPOSED TO SAY ANYTHING.
ALICE MADE ME SIGN AN N.D.A.
IT STANDS FOR "NONE OF YOUR DARN"...UH...
I DON'T KNOW WHAT IT STANDS FOR, BUT IT'S SERIOUS.
FINE.
BUT I'M ALSO WORKING ON SOMETHING SECRET!
SOMETHING SINISTER AND SPECTACULAR!
THAT'S NICE, DON'T CARE.
COME ON, SAM.

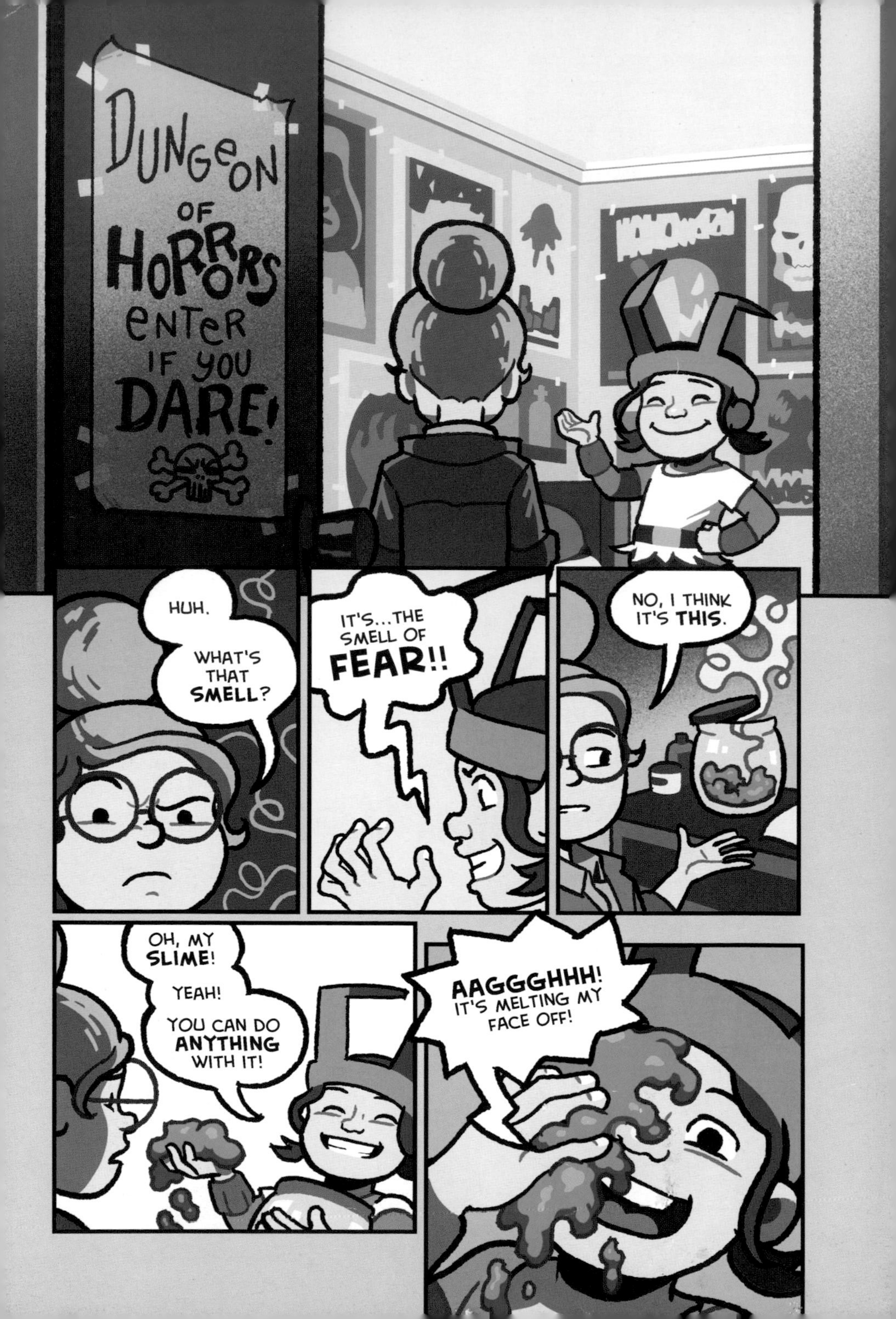
DUNGEON OF HORRORS ENTER IF YOU DARE!
HUH.
WHAT'S THAT SMELL?
IT'S...THE SMELL OF FEAR!!
NO, I THINK IT'S THIS.
OH, MY SLIME!
YEAH!
YOU CAN DO ANYTHING WITH IT!
AAGGGHHH! IT'S MELTING MY FACE OFF!

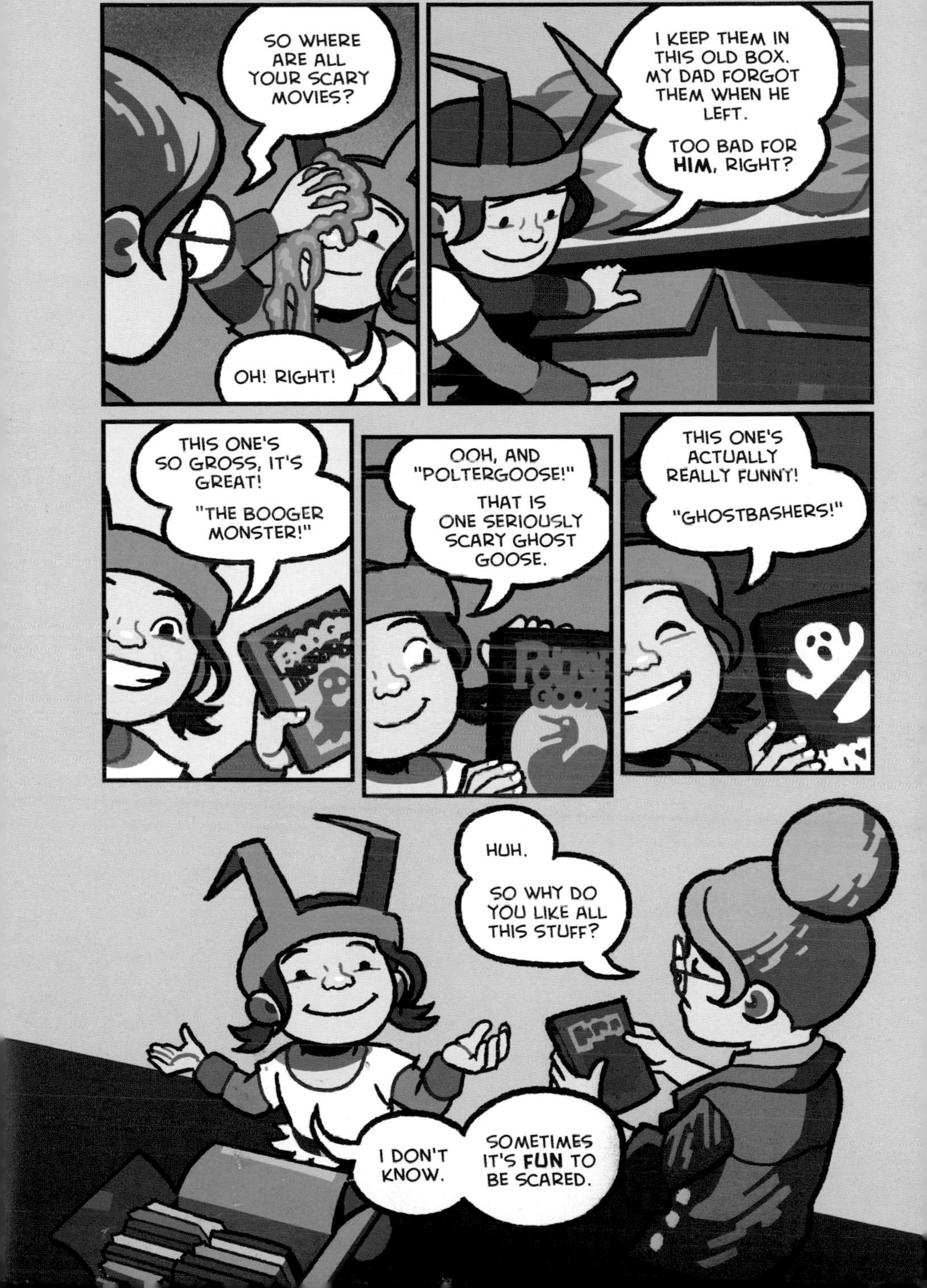
SO WHERE ARE ALL YOUR SCARY MOVIES?
OH! RIGHT!
I KEEP THEM IN THIS OLD BOX. MY DAD FORGOT THEM WHEN HE LEFT.
TOO BAD FOR HIM, RIGHT?
THIS ONE'S SO GROSS, IT'S GREAT!
"THE BOOGER MONSTER!"
OOH, AND "POLTERGOOSE!"
THAT IS ONE SERIOUSLY SCARY GHOST GOOSE.
THIS ONE'S ACTUALLY REALLY FUNNY!
"GHOSTBASHERS!"
HUH.
SO WHY DO YOU LIKE ALL THIS STUFF?
I DON'T KNOW.
SOMETIMES IT'S FUN TO BE SCARED.

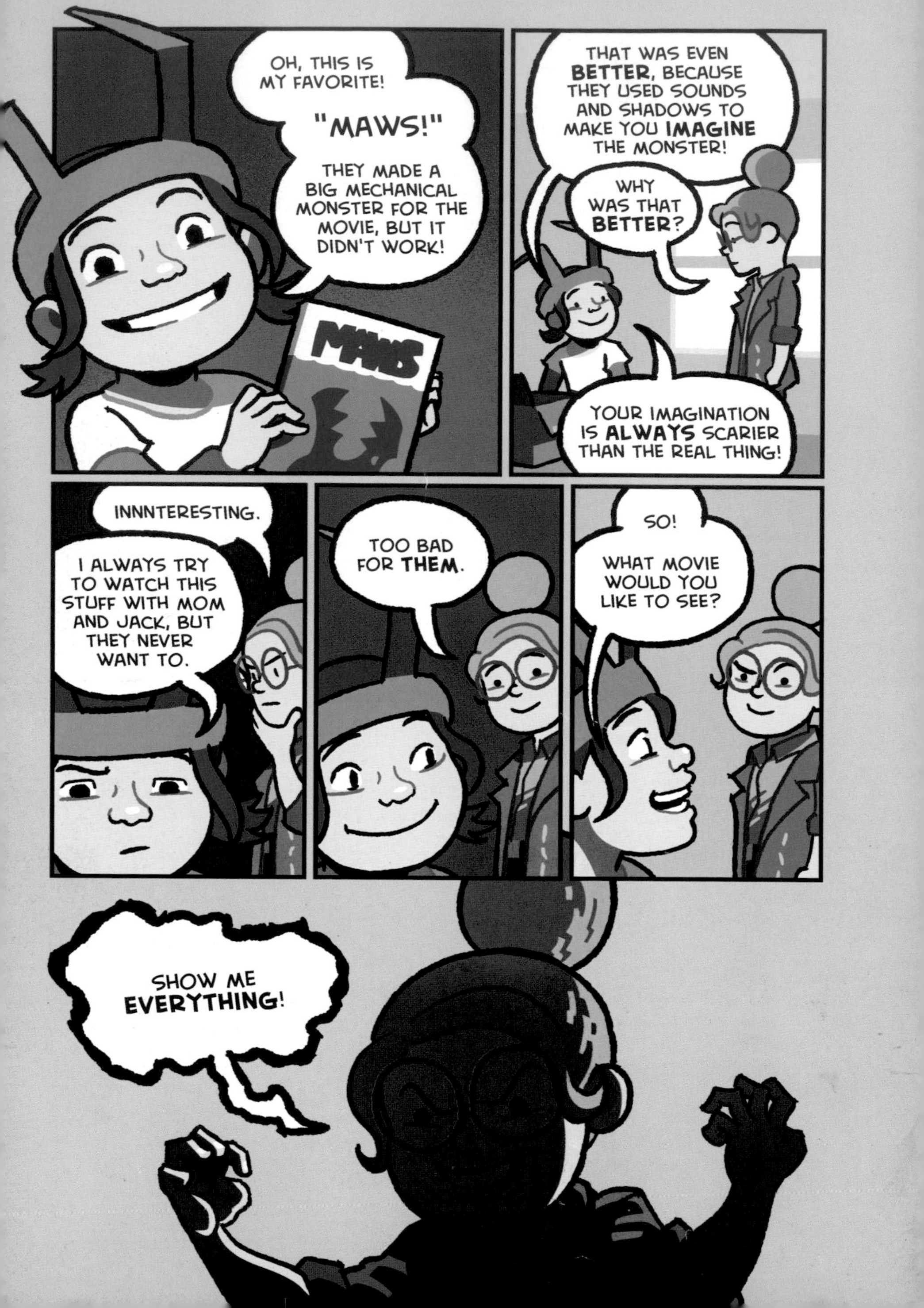
OH, THIS IS MY FAVORITE!
"MAWS!"
THEY MADE A BIG MECHANICAL MONSTER FOR THE MOVIE, BUT IT DIDN'T WORK!
MAWS
THAT WAS EVEN **BETTER**, BECAUSE THEY USED SOUNDS AND SHADOWS TO MAKE YOU **IMAGINE** THE MONSTER!
WHY WAS THAT **BETTER**?
YOUR IMAGINATION IS **ALWAYS** SCARIER THAN THE REAL THING!
INNNTERESTING.
I ALWAYS TRY TO WATCH THIS STUFF WITH MOM AND JACK, BUT THEY NEVER WANT TO.
TOO BAD FOR **THEM**.
SO!
WHAT MOVIE WOULD YOU LIKE TO SEE?
SHOW ME **EVERYTHING**!

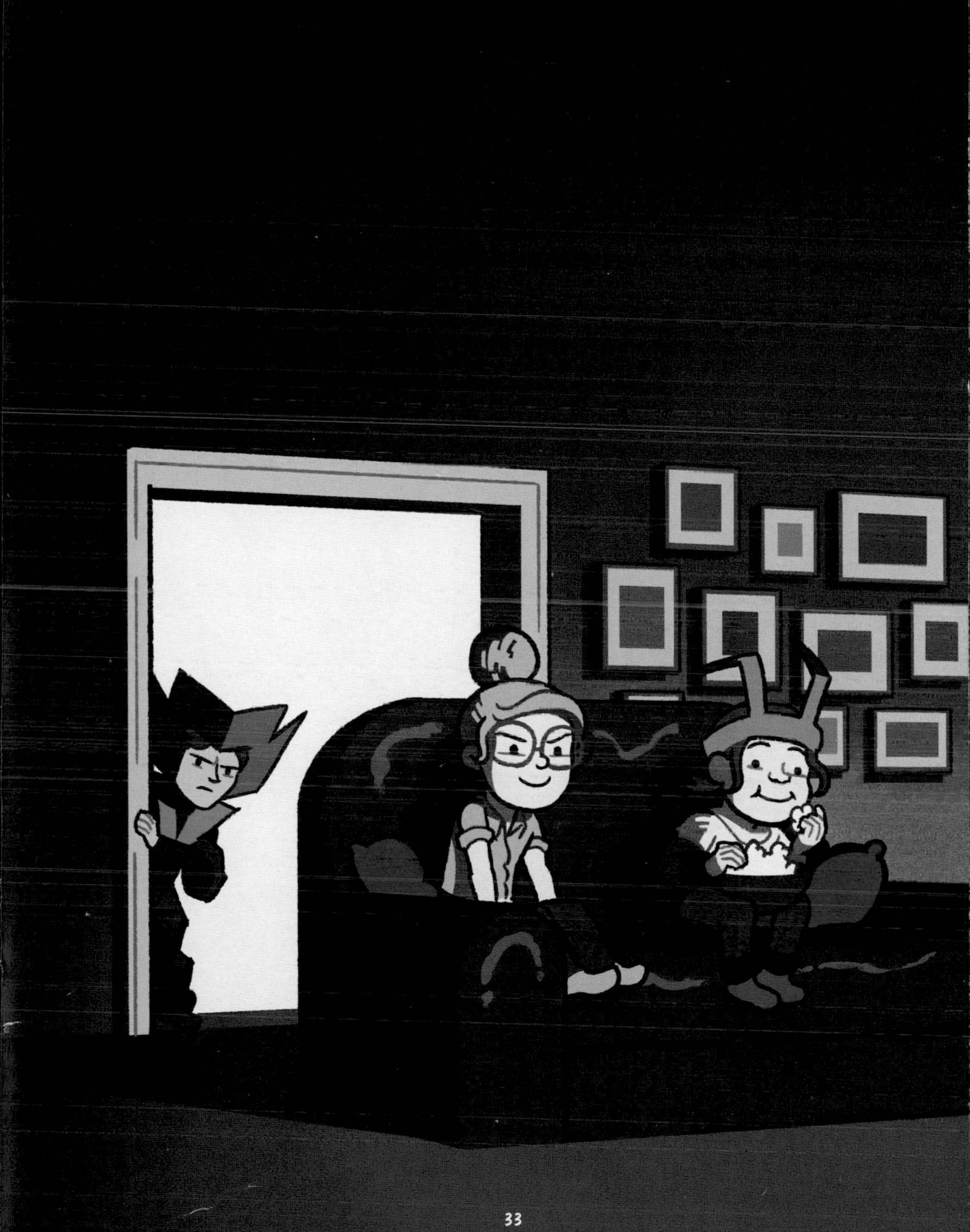

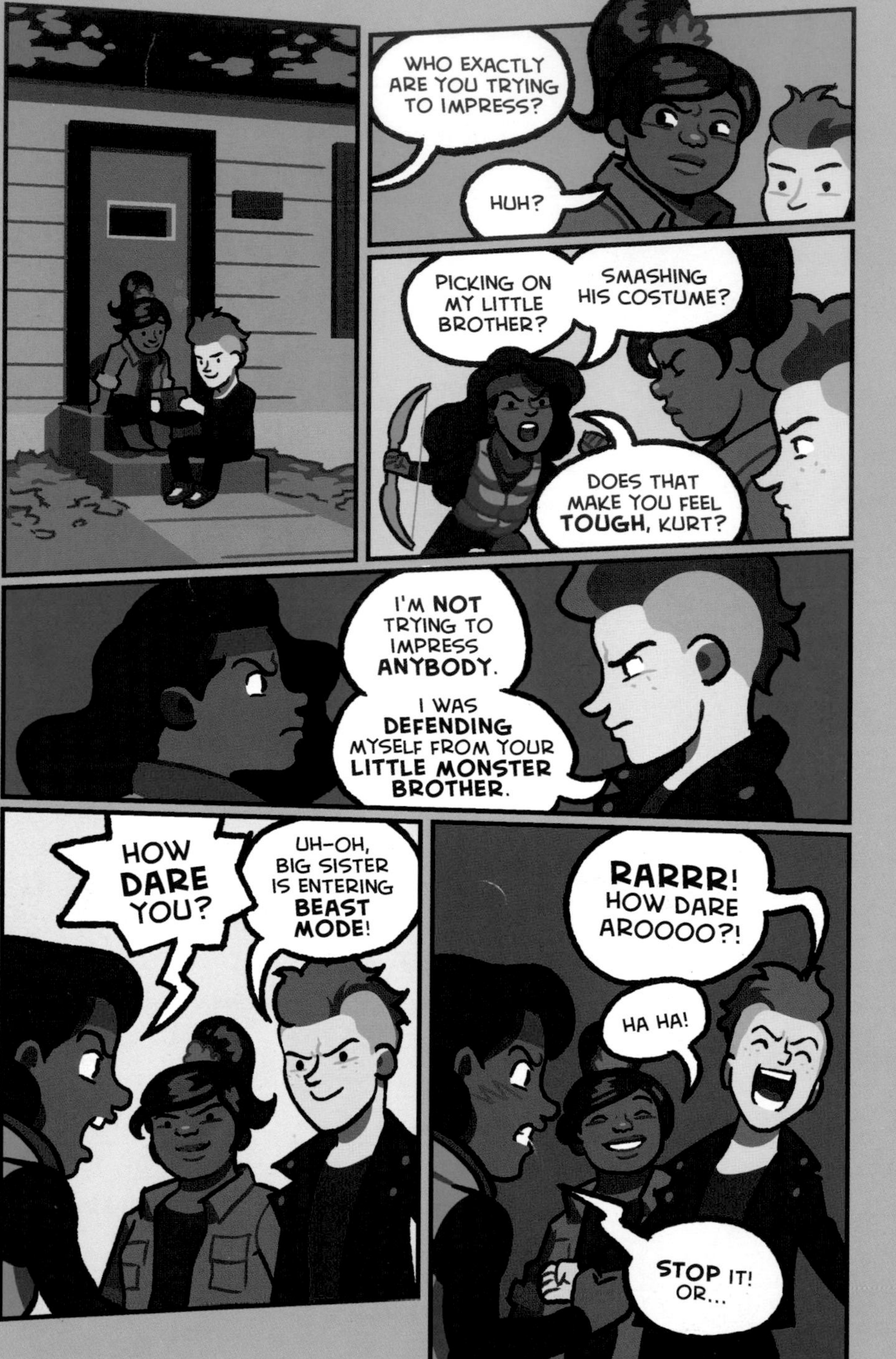
WHO EXACTLY ARE YOU TRYING TO IMPRESS?
HUH?
PICKING ON MY LITTLE BROTHER?
SMASHING HIS COSTUME?
DOES THAT MAKE YOU FEEL **TOUGH**, KURT?
I'M **NOT** TRYING TO IMPRESS **ANYBODY**.
I WAS **DEFENDING** MYSELF FROM YOUR **LITTLE MONSTER BROTHER**.
HOW **DARE** YOU?
UH-OH, BIG SISTER IS ENTERING **BEAST MODE**!
RARRR! HOW DARE AROOOO?!
HA HA!
STOP IT! OR...

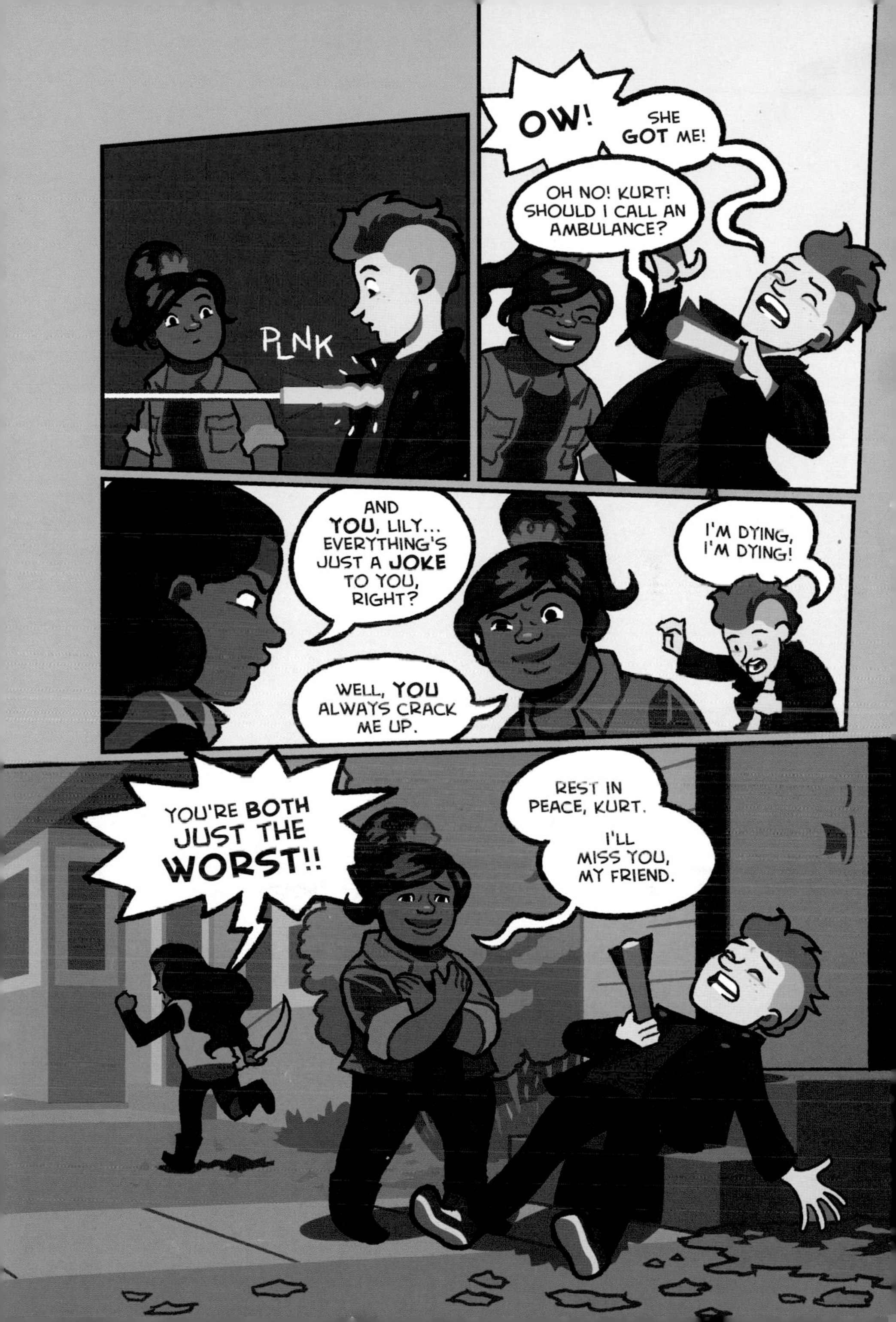
PLNK
OW!
SHE GOT ME!
OH NO! KURT! SHOULD I CALL AN AMBULANCE?
AND YOU, LILY... EVERYTHING'S JUST A JOKE TO YOU, RIGHT?
I'M DYING, I'M DYING!
WELL, YOU ALWAYS CRACK ME UP.
YOU'RE BOTH JUST THE WORST!!
REST IN PEACE, KURT.
I'LL MISS YOU, MY FRIEND.

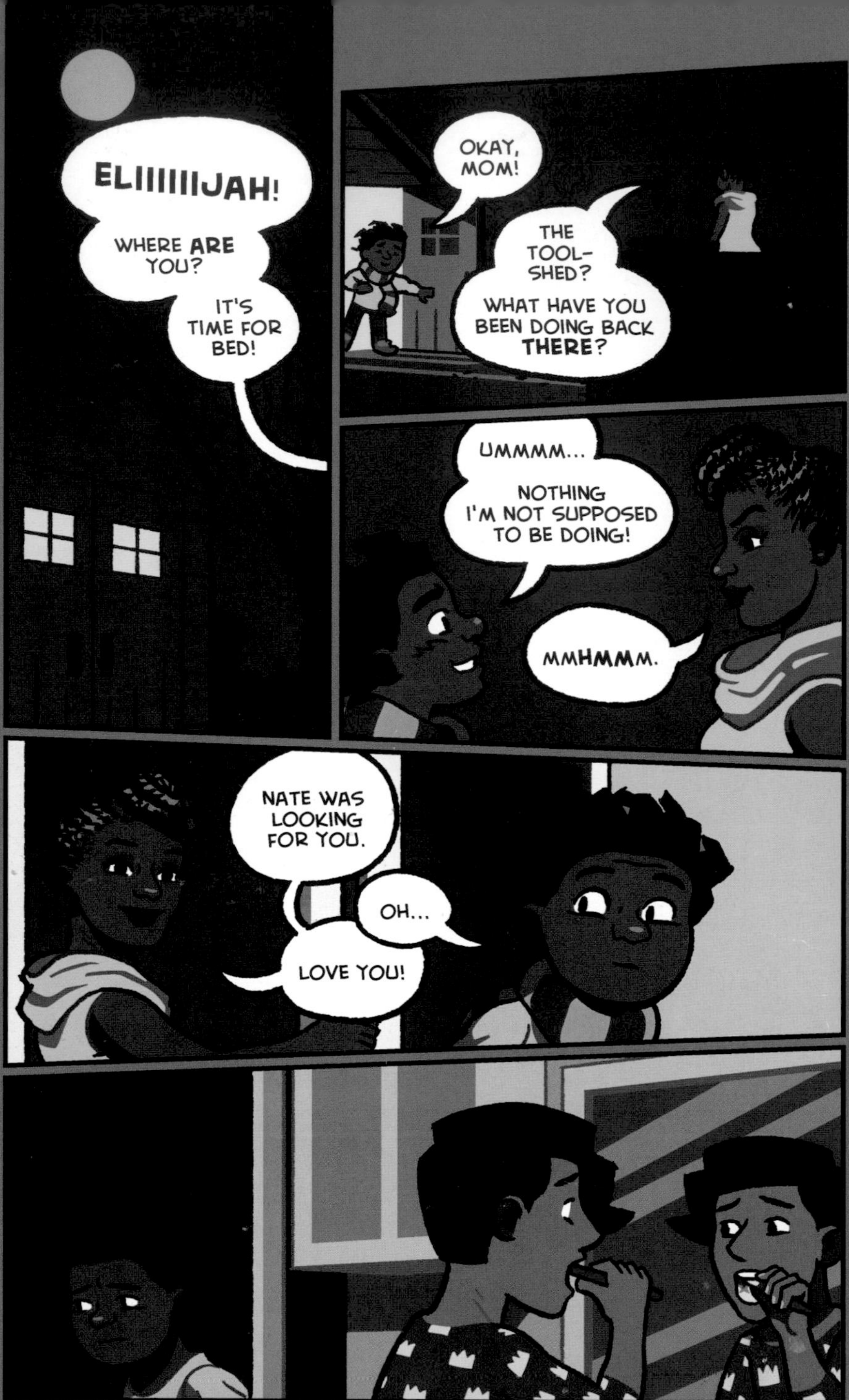
ELIIIIIIJAH!
WHERE ARE YOU?
IT'S TIME FOR BED!
OKAY, MOM!
THE TOOL-SHED?
WHAT HAVE YOU BEEN DOING BACK THERE?
UMMMM...
NOTHING I'M NOT SUPPOSED TO BE DOING!
MMHMMM.
NATE WAS LOOKING FOR YOU.
OH...
LOVE YOU!

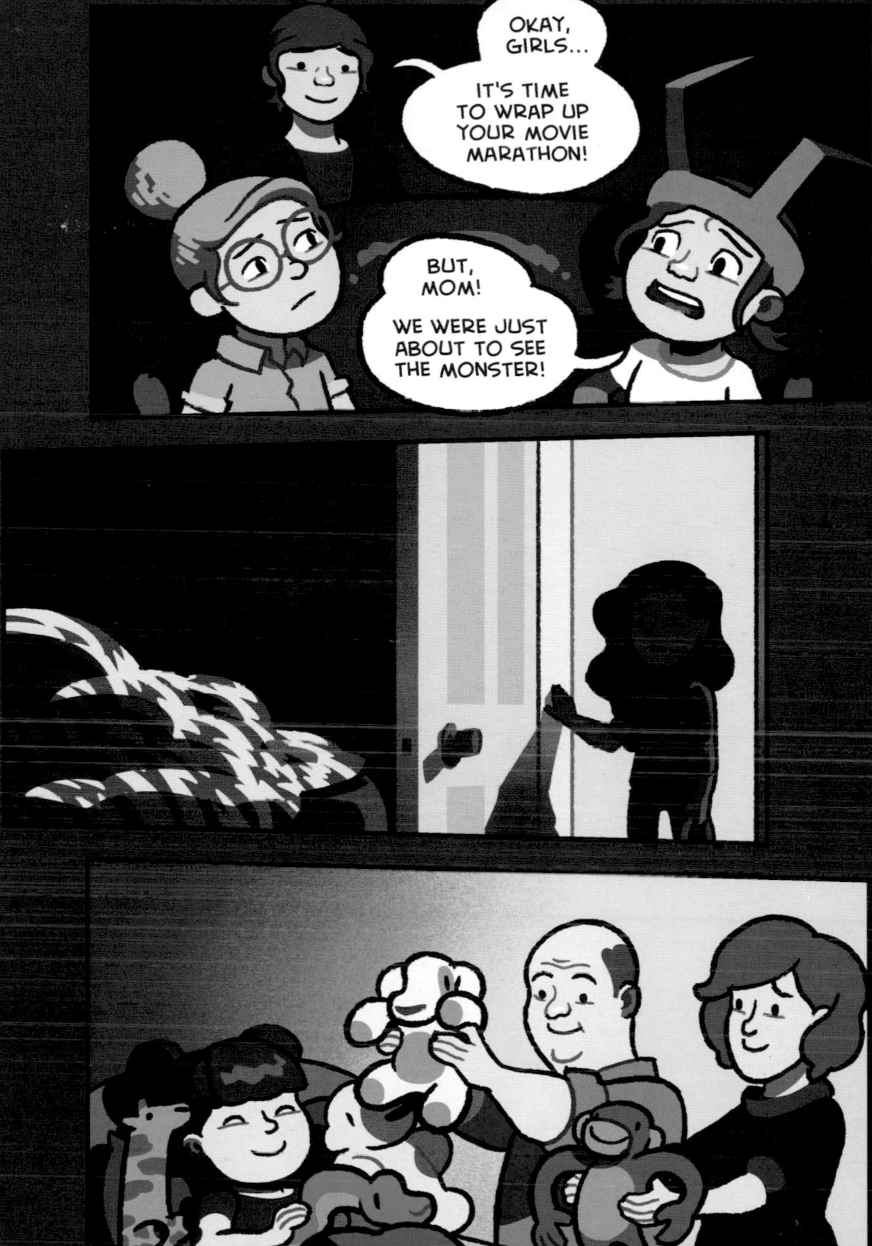
OKAY, GIRLS...
IT'S TIME TO WRAP UP YOUR MOVIE MARATHON!
BUT, MOM!
WE WERE JUST ABOUT TO SEE THE MONSTER!

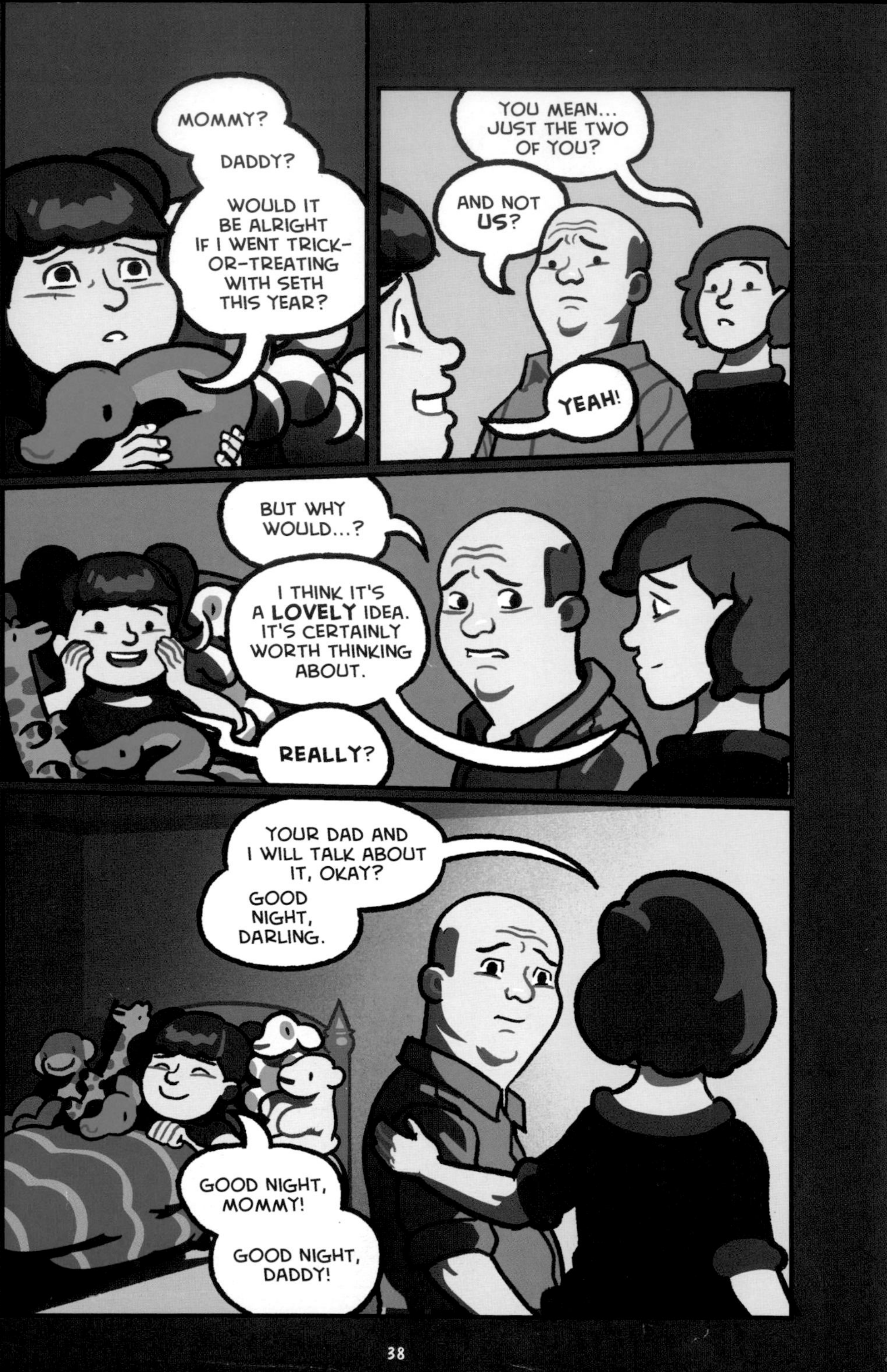
MOMMY?
DADDY?
WOULD IT BE ALRIGHT IF I WENT TRICK-OR-TREATING WITH SETH THIS YEAR?
YOU MEAN... JUST THE TWO OF YOU?
AND NOT US?
YEAH!
BUT WHY WOULD...?
I THINK IT'S A LOVELY IDEA. IT'S CERTAINLY WORTH THINKING ABOUT.
REALLY?
YOUR DAD AND I WILL TALK ABOUT IT, OKAY?
GOOD NIGHT, DARLING.
GOOD NIGHT, MOMMY!
GOOD NIGHT, DADDY!

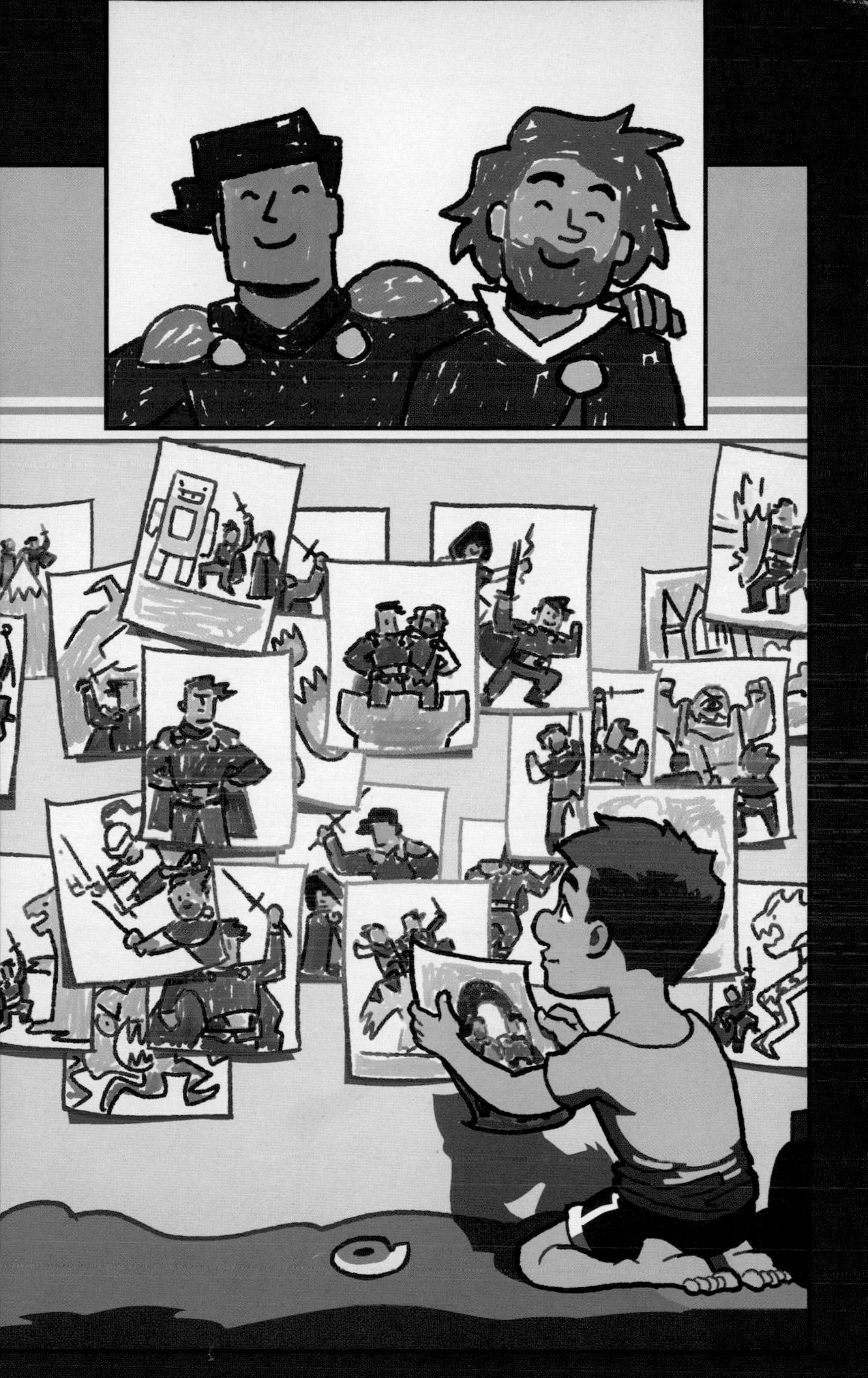

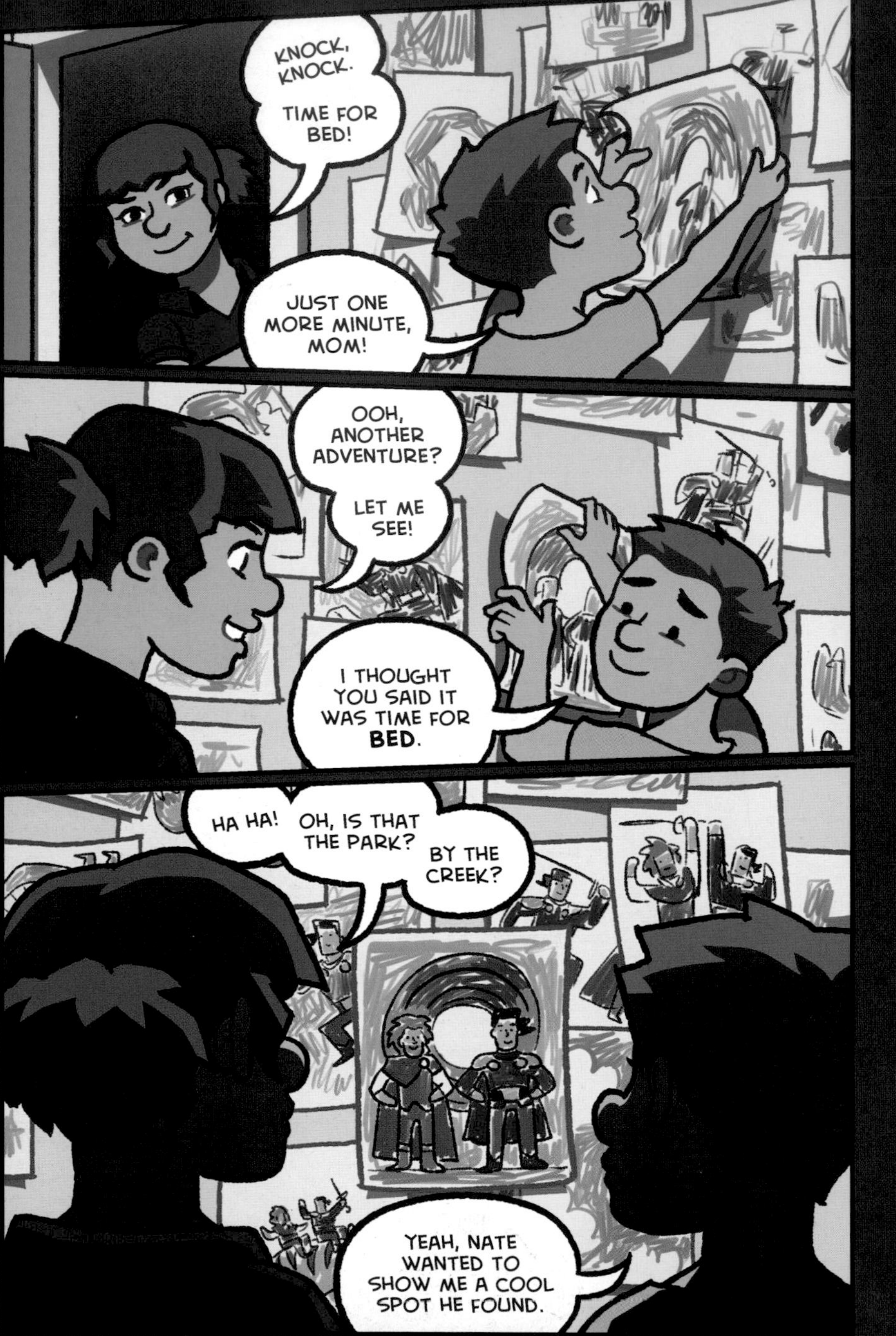
KNOCK, KNOCK.
TIME FOR BED!
JUST ONE MORE MINUTE, MOM!
OOH, ANOTHER ADVENTURE?
LET ME SEE!
I THOUGHT YOU SAID IT WAS TIME FOR **BED**.
HA HA!
OH, IS THAT THE PARK?
BY THE CREEK?
YEAH, NATE WANTED TO SHOW ME A COOL SPOT HE FOUND.

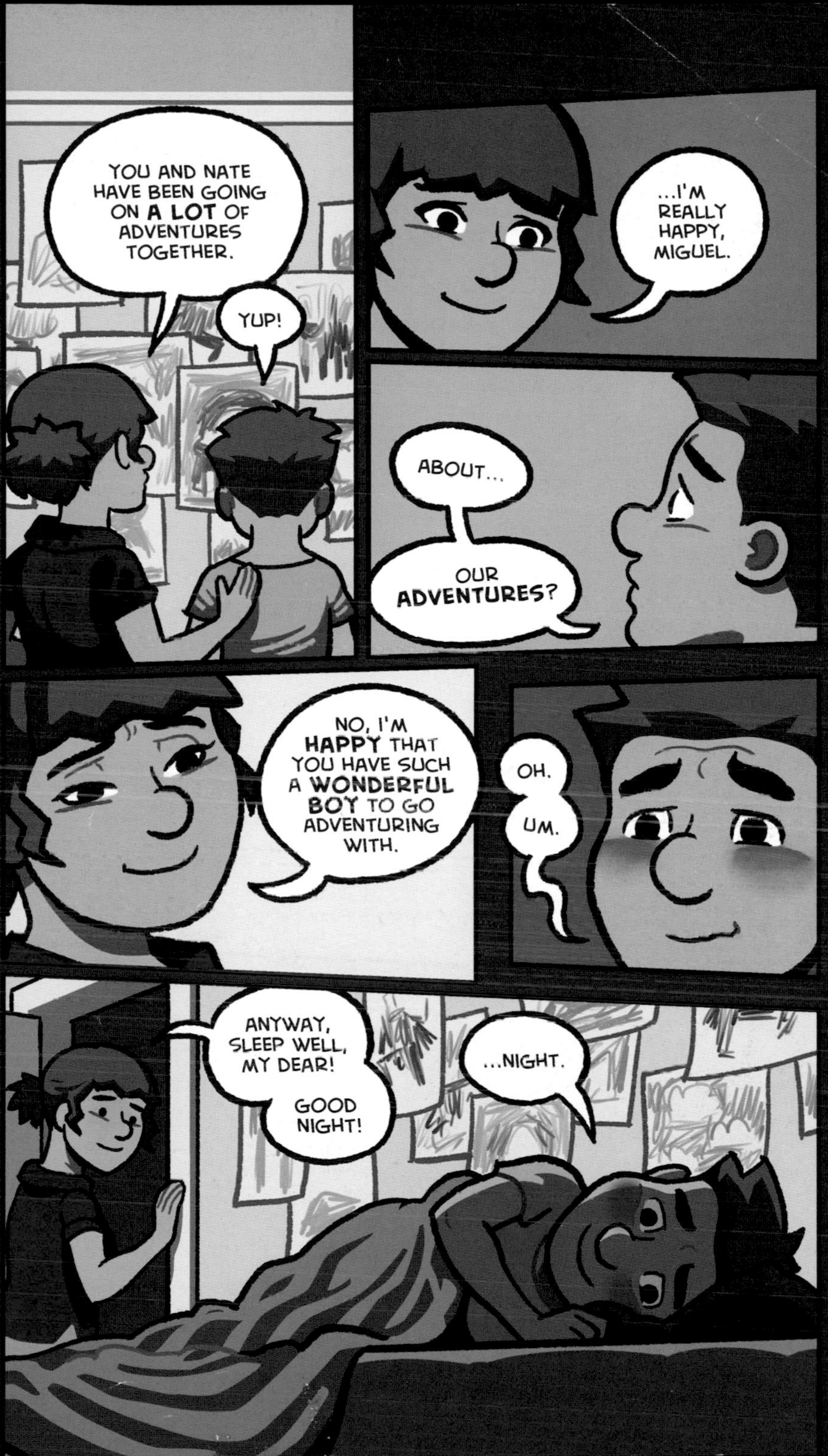
YOU AND NATE HAVE BEEN GOING ON A LOT OF ADVENTURES TOGETHER.
YUP!
...I'M REALLY HAPPY, MIGUEL.
ABOUT...
OUR ADVENTURES?
NO, I'M HAPPY THAT YOU HAVE SUCH A WONDERFUL BOY TO GO ADVENTURING WITH.
OH.
UM.
ANYWAY, SLEEP WELL, MY DEAR!
GOOD NIGHT!
...NIGHT.

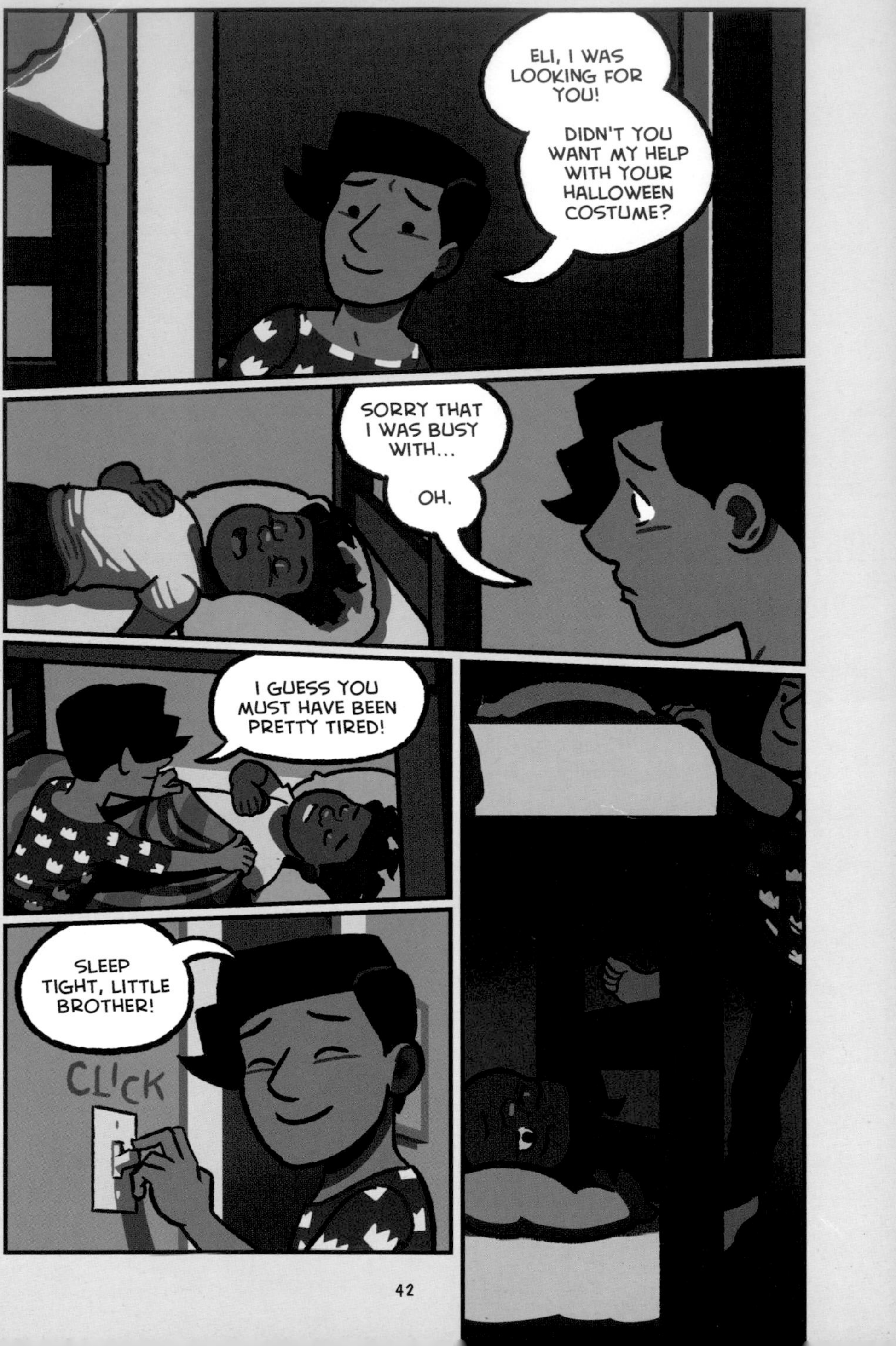
ELI, I WAS LOOKING FOR YOU!
DIDN'T YOU WANT MY HELP WITH YOUR HALLOWEEN COSTUME?
SORRY THAT I WAS BUSY WITH...
OH.
I GUESS YOU MUST HAVE BEEN PRETTY TIRED!
SLEEP TIGHT, LITTLE BROTHER!
CLICK

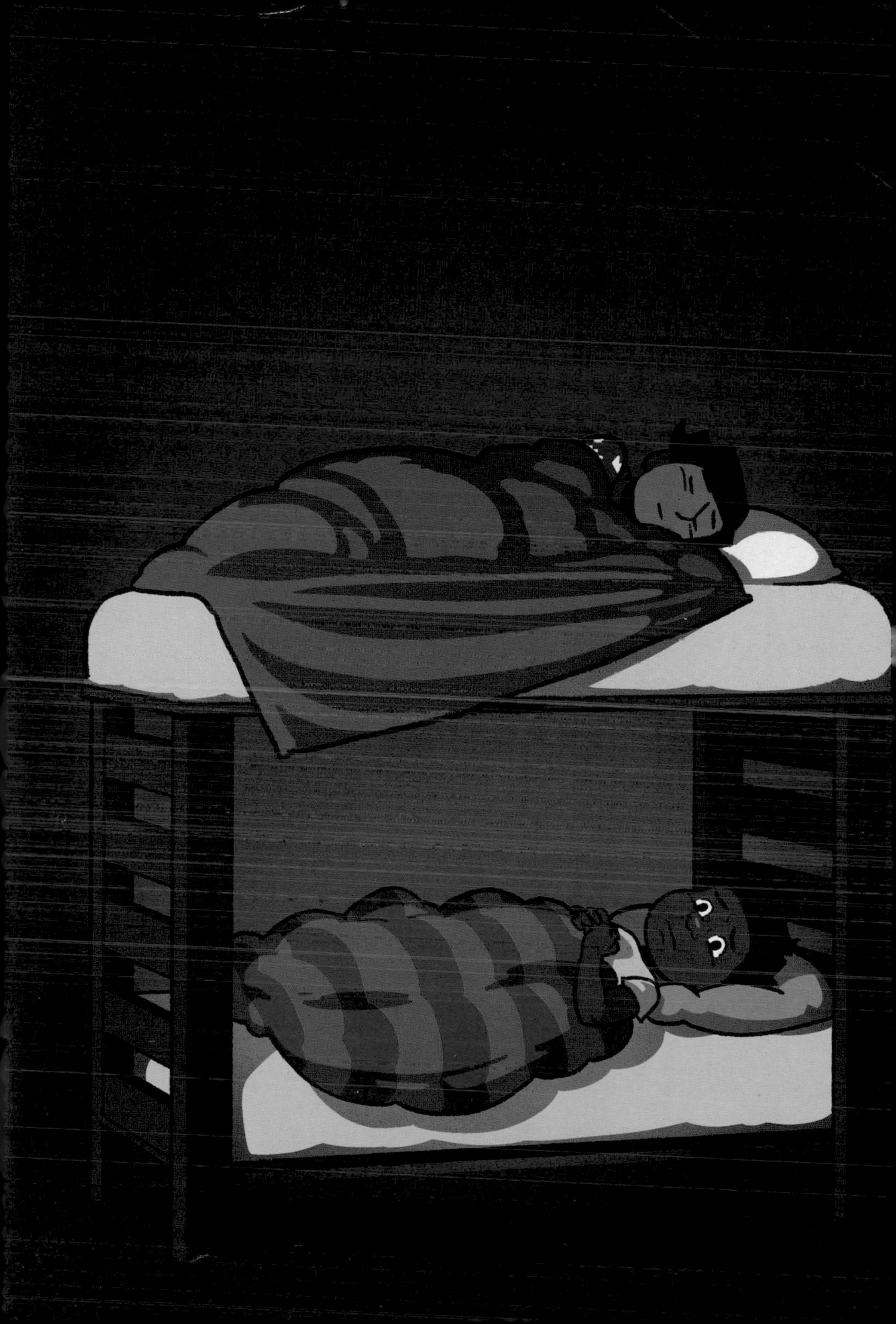

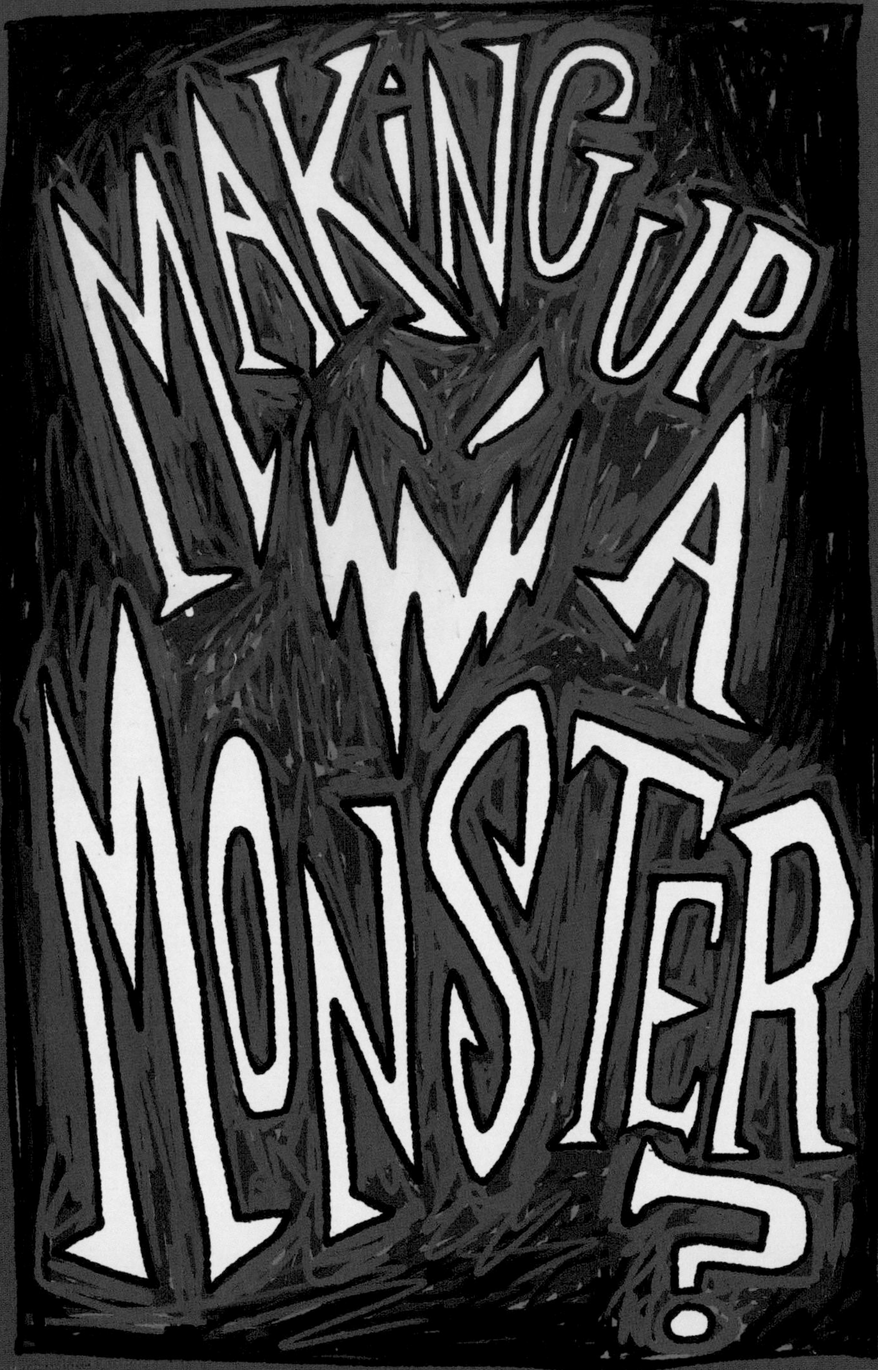
MAKING UP A MONSTER?

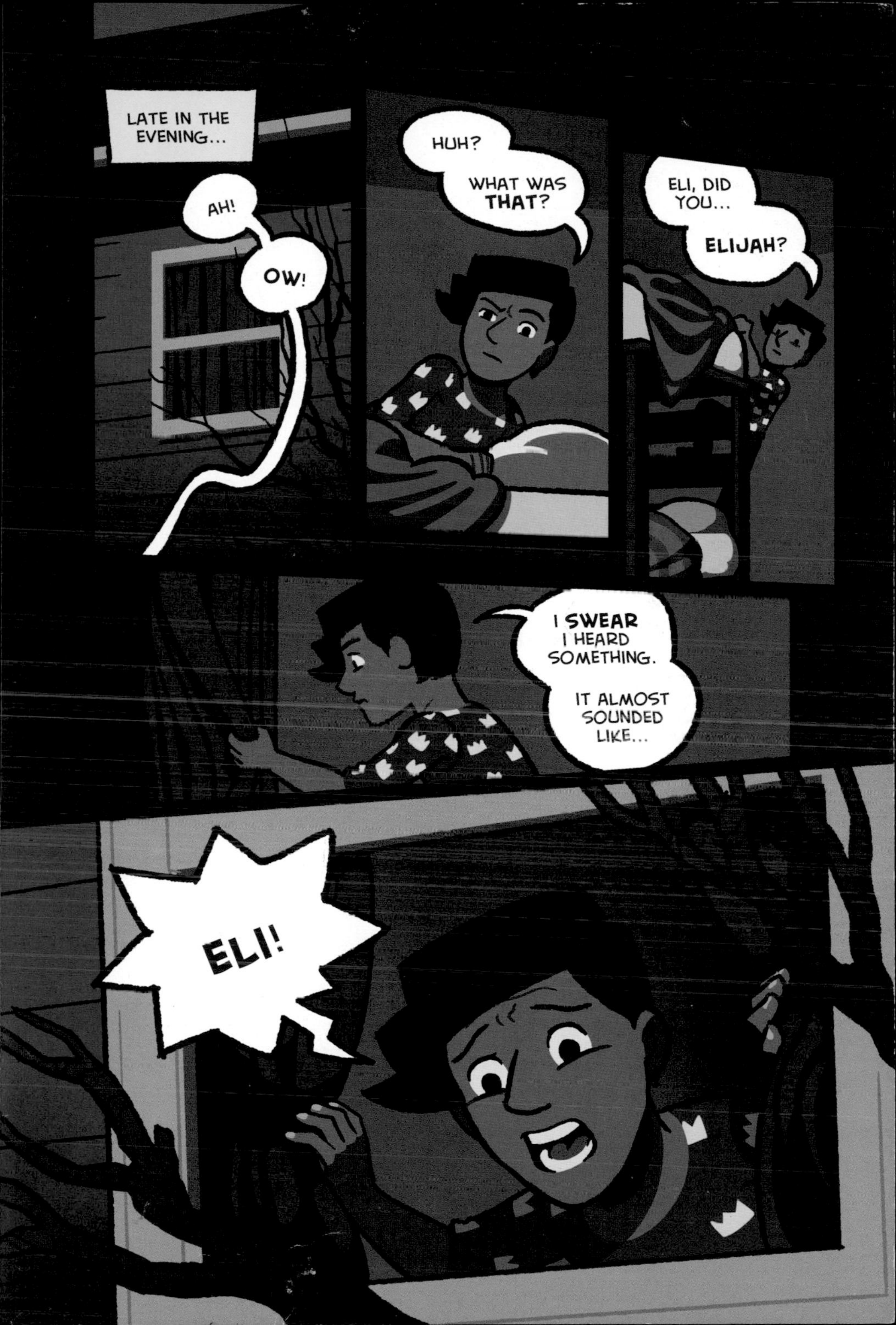
LATE IN THE EVENING...
AH!
OW!
HUH?
WHAT WAS **THAT**?
ELI, DID YOU...
ELIJAH?
I **SWEAR** I HEARD SOMETHING.
IT ALMOST SOUNDED LIKE...
ELI!

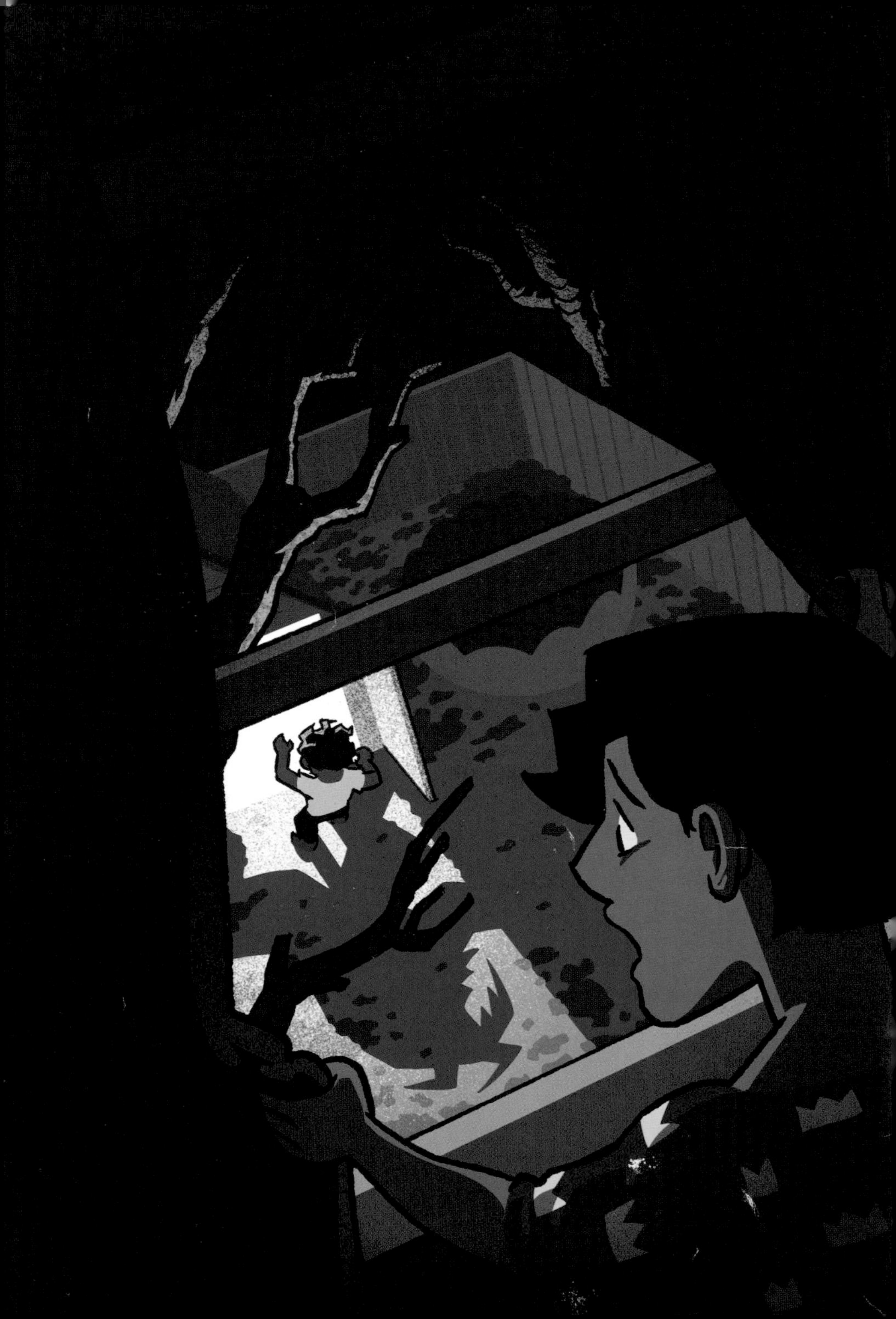

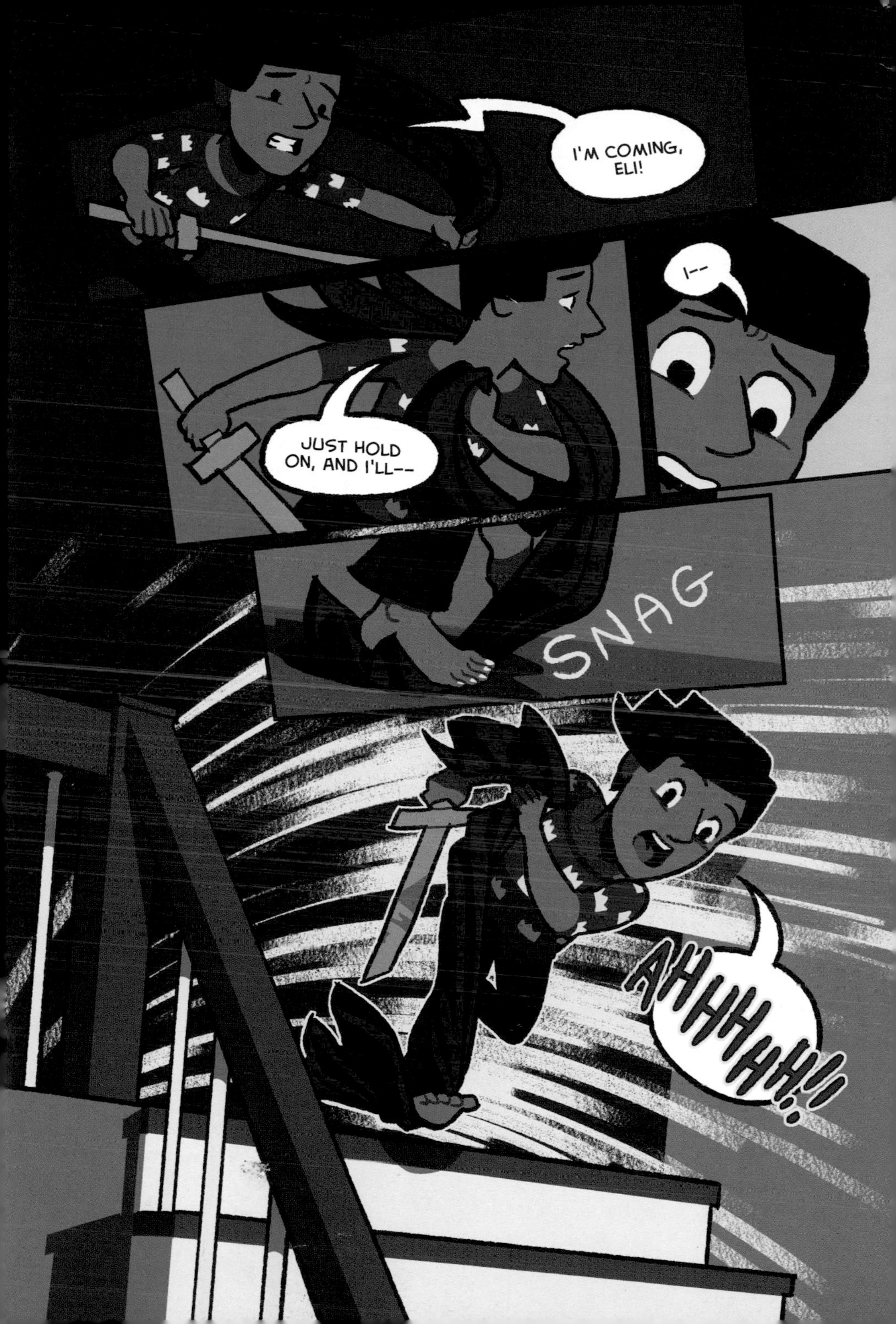
I'M COMING, ELI!
JUST HOLD ON, AND I'LL--
I--
SNAG
AHHHHH!!

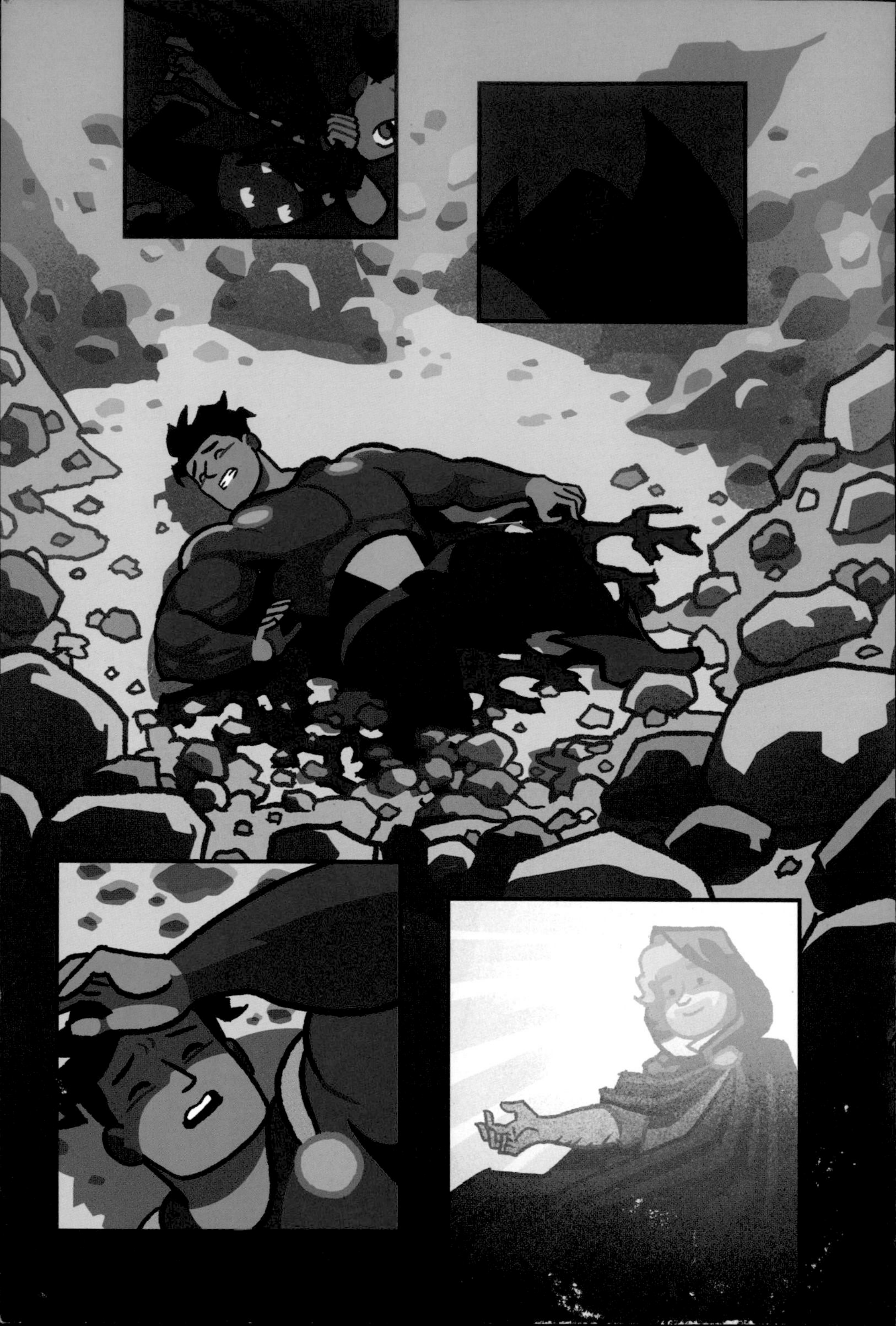

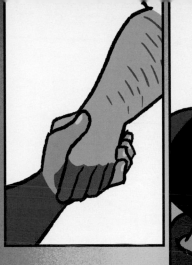

WHAT HAPPENED?

DID...?

WAIT!

ELIJAH!

WHERE IS HE?

WHRSS ELJHH?

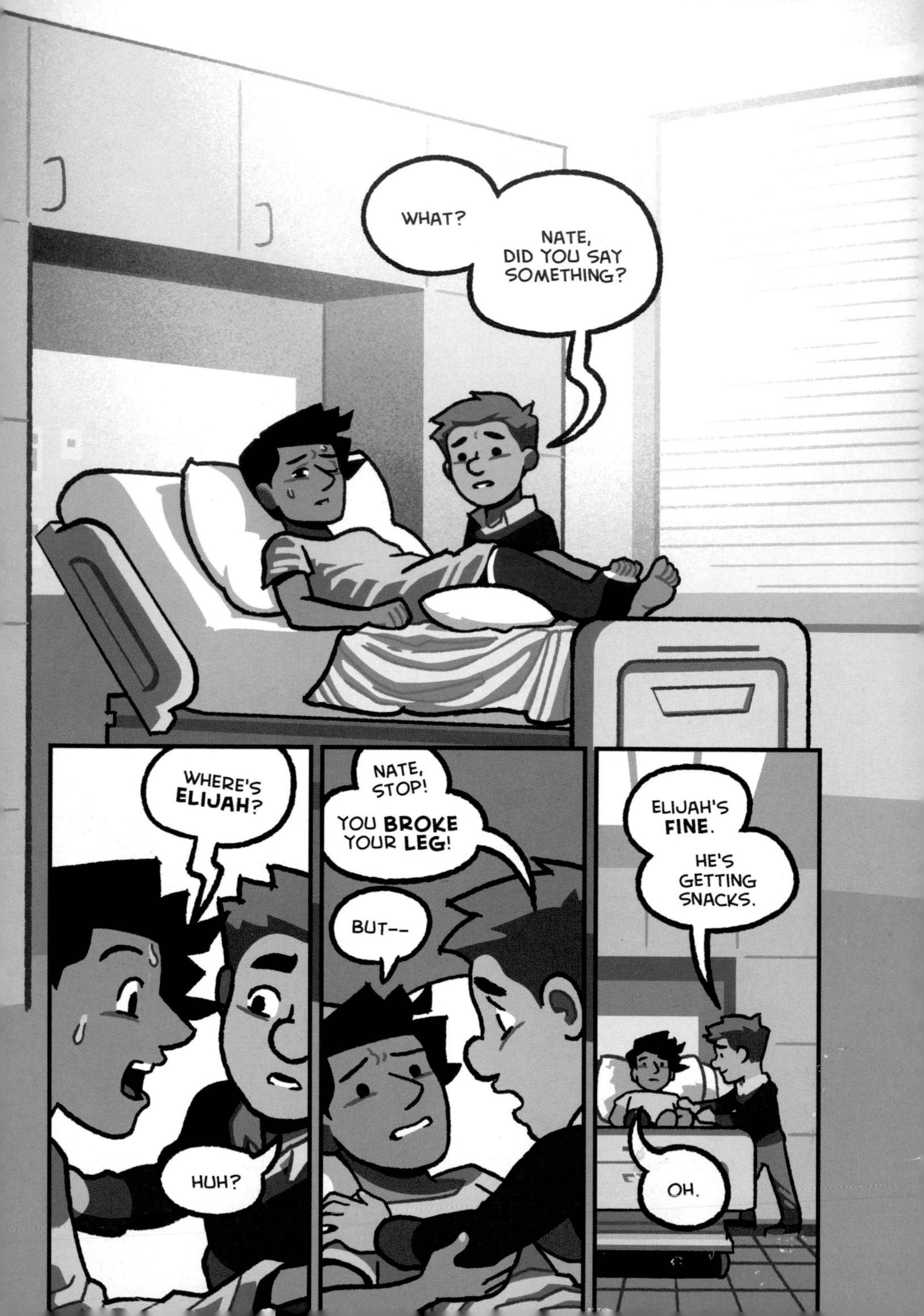
WHAT?
NATE, DID YOU SAY SOMETHING?
WHERE'S **ELIJAH**?
HUH?
NATE, STOP!
YOU **BROKE** YOUR **LEG**!
BUT--
ELIJAH'S **FINE**.
HE'S GETTING SNACKS.
OH.

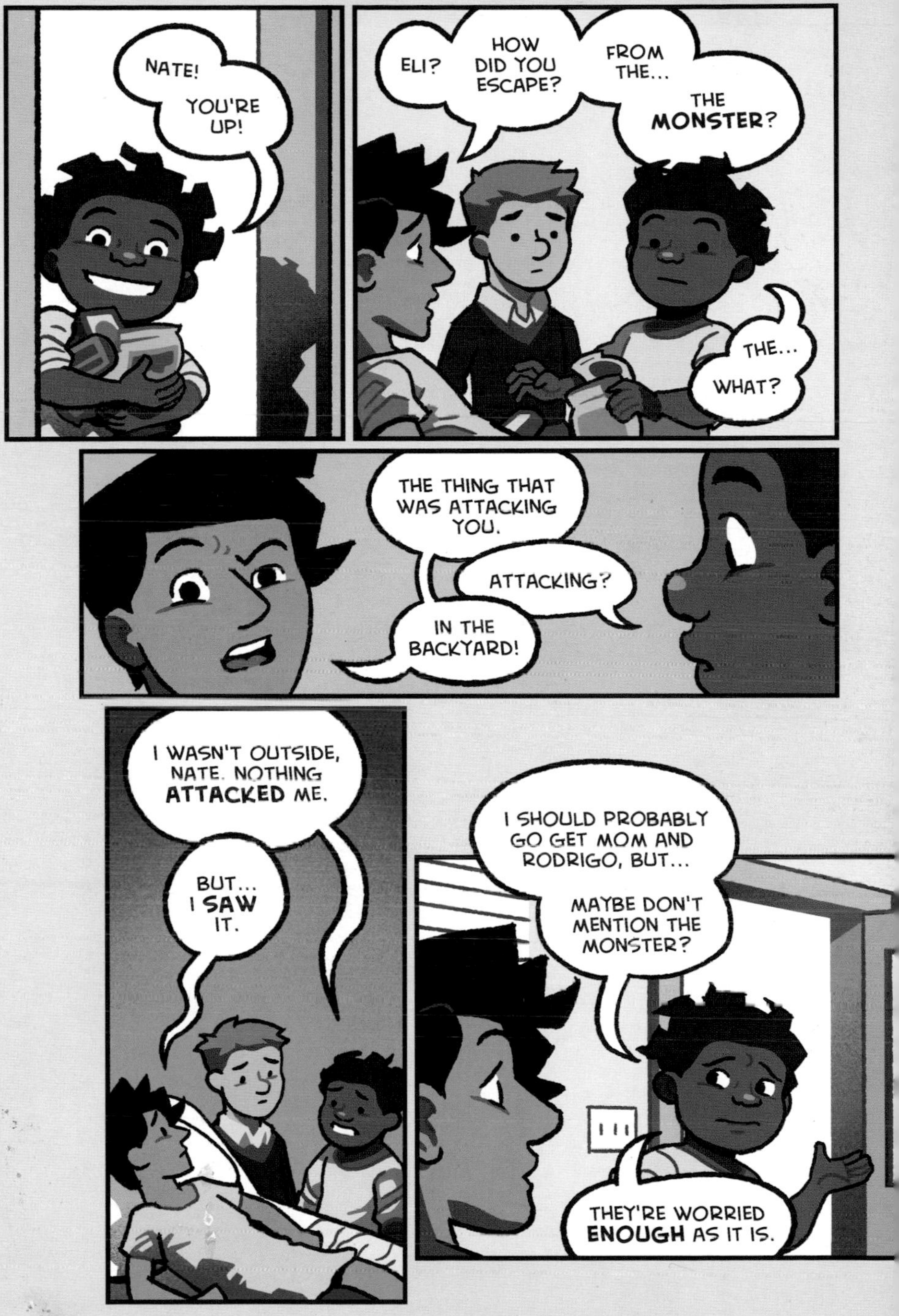
NATE!
YOU'RE UP!
ELI?
HOW DID YOU ESCAPE?
FROM THE...
THE **MONSTER**?
THE...
WHAT?
THE THING THAT WAS ATTACKING YOU.
ATTACKING?
IN THE BACKYARD!
I WASN'T OUTSIDE, NATE. NOTHING **ATTACKED** ME.
BUT... I **SAW** IT.
I SHOULD PROBABLY GO GET MOM AND RODRIGO, BUT...
MAYBE DON'T MENTION THE MONSTER?
THEY'RE WORRIED **ENOUGH** AS IT IS.

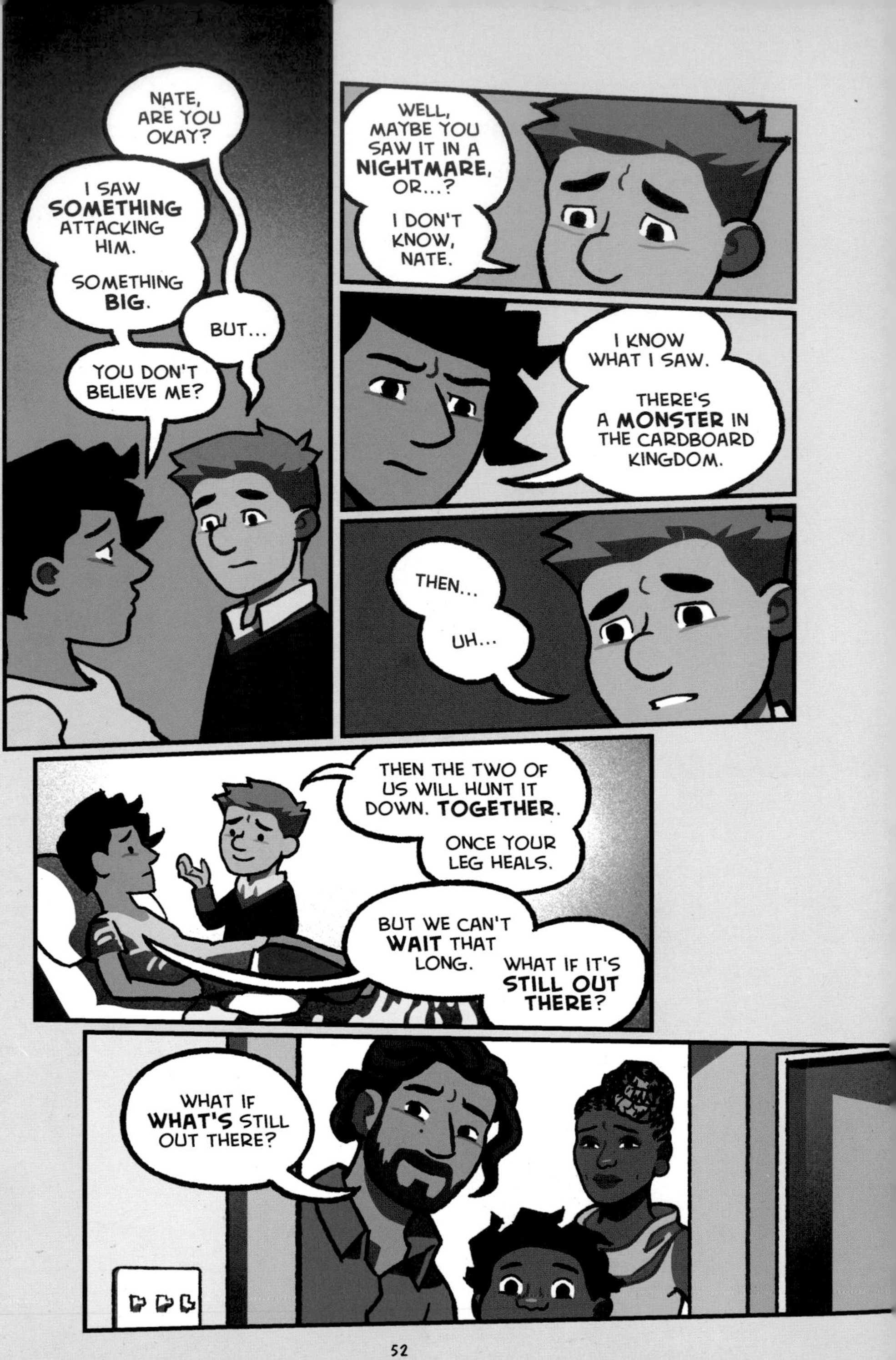
NATE, ARE YOU OKAY?
I SAW **SOMETHING** ATTACKING HIM.
SOMETHING **BIG**.
BUT...
YOU DON'T BELIEVE ME?
WELL, MAYBE YOU SAW IT IN A **NIGHTMARE**, OR...?
I DON'T KNOW, NATE.
I KNOW WHAT I SAW.
THERE'S A **MONSTER** IN THE CARDBOARD KINGDOM.
THEN...
UH...
THEN THE TWO OF US WILL HUNT IT DOWN. **TOGETHER**.
ONCE YOUR LEG HEALS.
BUT WE CAN'T **WAIT** THAT LONG.
WHAT IF IT'S **STILL OUT THERE**?
WHAT IF **WHAT'S** STILL OUT THERE?

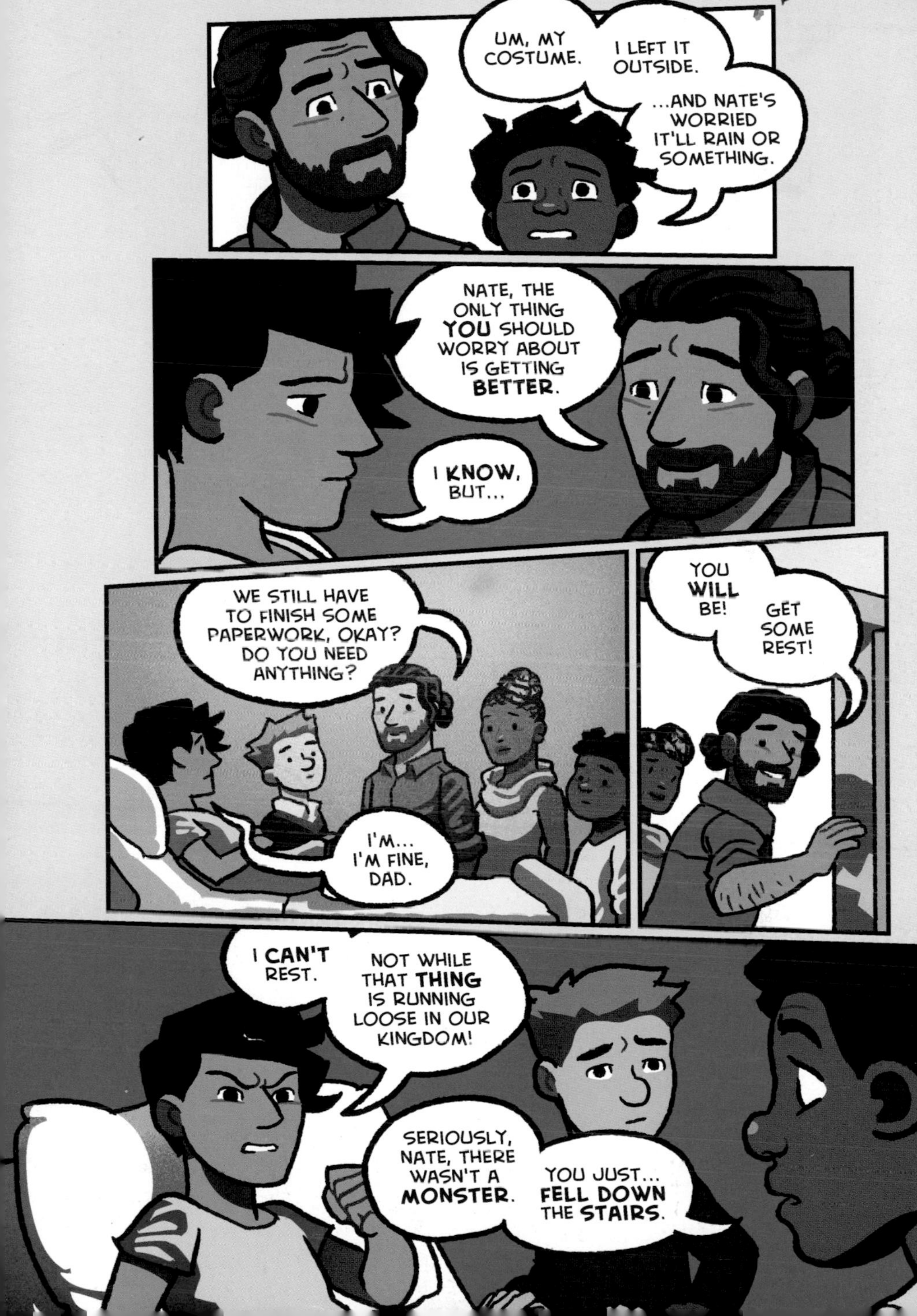
UM, MY COSTUME.
I LEFT IT OUTSIDE.
...AND NATE'S WORRIED IT'LL RAIN OR SOMETHING.
NATE, THE ONLY THING YOU SHOULD WORRY ABOUT IS GETTING BETTER.
I KNOW, BUT...
WE STILL HAVE TO FINISH SOME PAPERWORK, OKAY? DO YOU NEED ANYTHING?
I'M... I'M FINE, DAD.
YOU WILL BE!
GET SOME REST!
I CAN'T REST.
NOT WHILE THAT THING IS RUNNING LOOSE IN OUR KINGDOM!
SERIOUSLY, NATE, THERE WASN'T A MONSTER.
YOU JUST... FELL DOWN THE STAIRS.

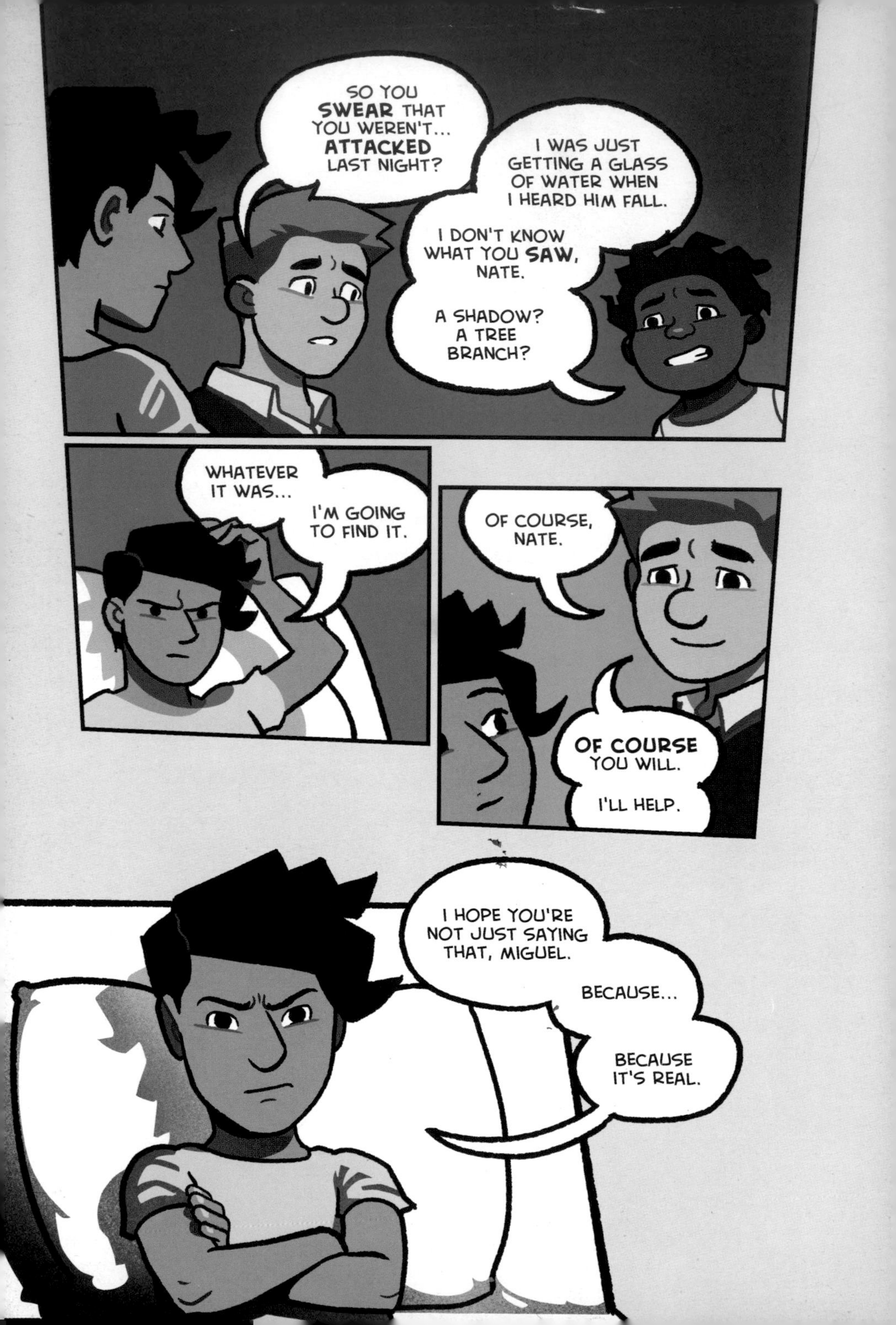

SO YOU **SWEAR** THAT YOU WEREN'T... **ATTACKED** LAST NIGHT?
I WAS JUST GETTING A GLASS OF WATER WHEN I HEARD HIM FALL.
I DON'T KNOW WHAT YOU **SAW**, NATE.
A SHADOW? A TREE BRANCH?
WHATEVER IT WAS...
I'M GOING TO FIND IT.
OF COURSE, NATE.
OF COURSE YOU WILL.
I'LL HELP.
I HOPE YOU'RE NOT JUST SAYING THAT, MIGUEL.
BECAUSE...
BECAUSE IT'S REAL.

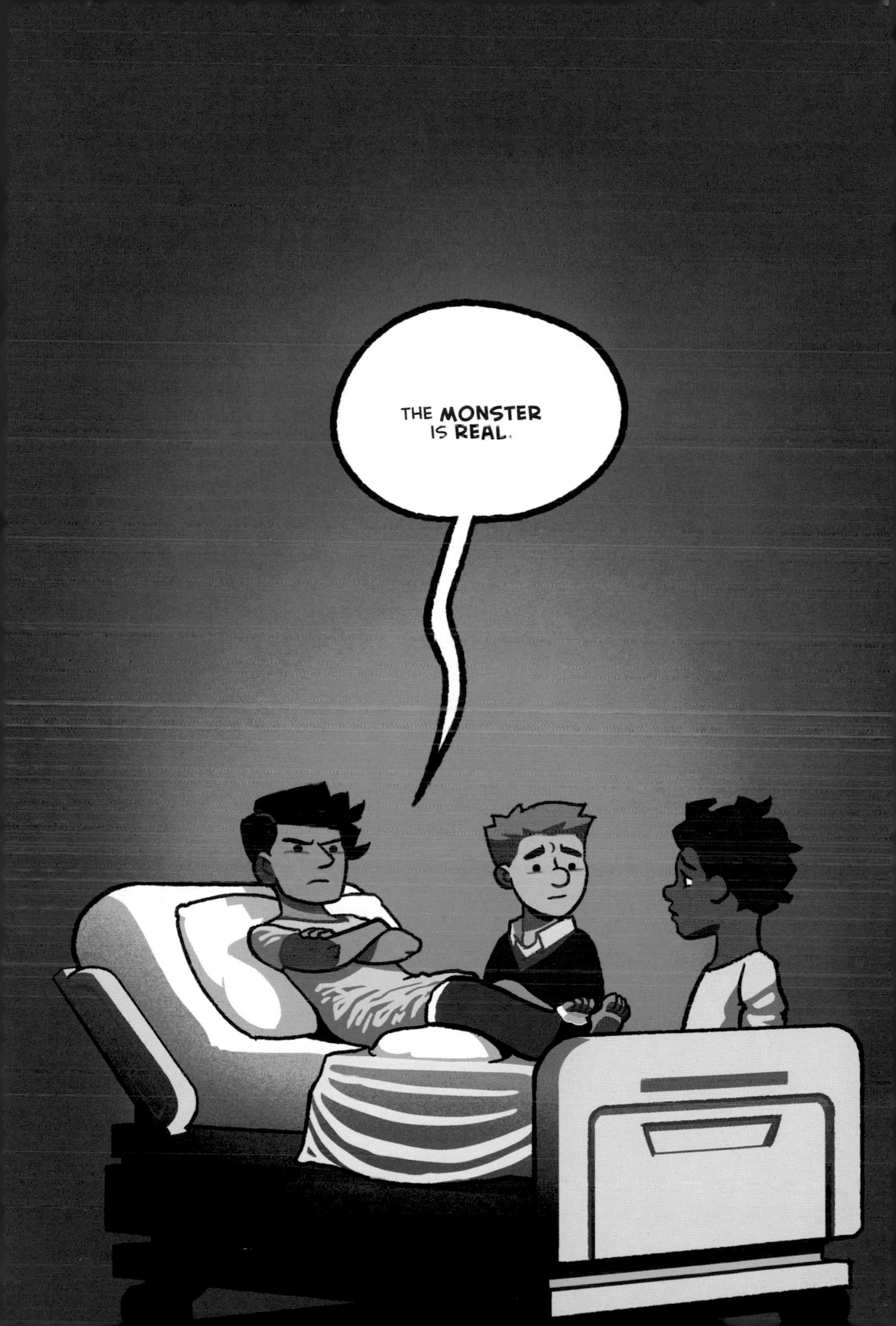
THE **MONSTER** IS **REAL**.

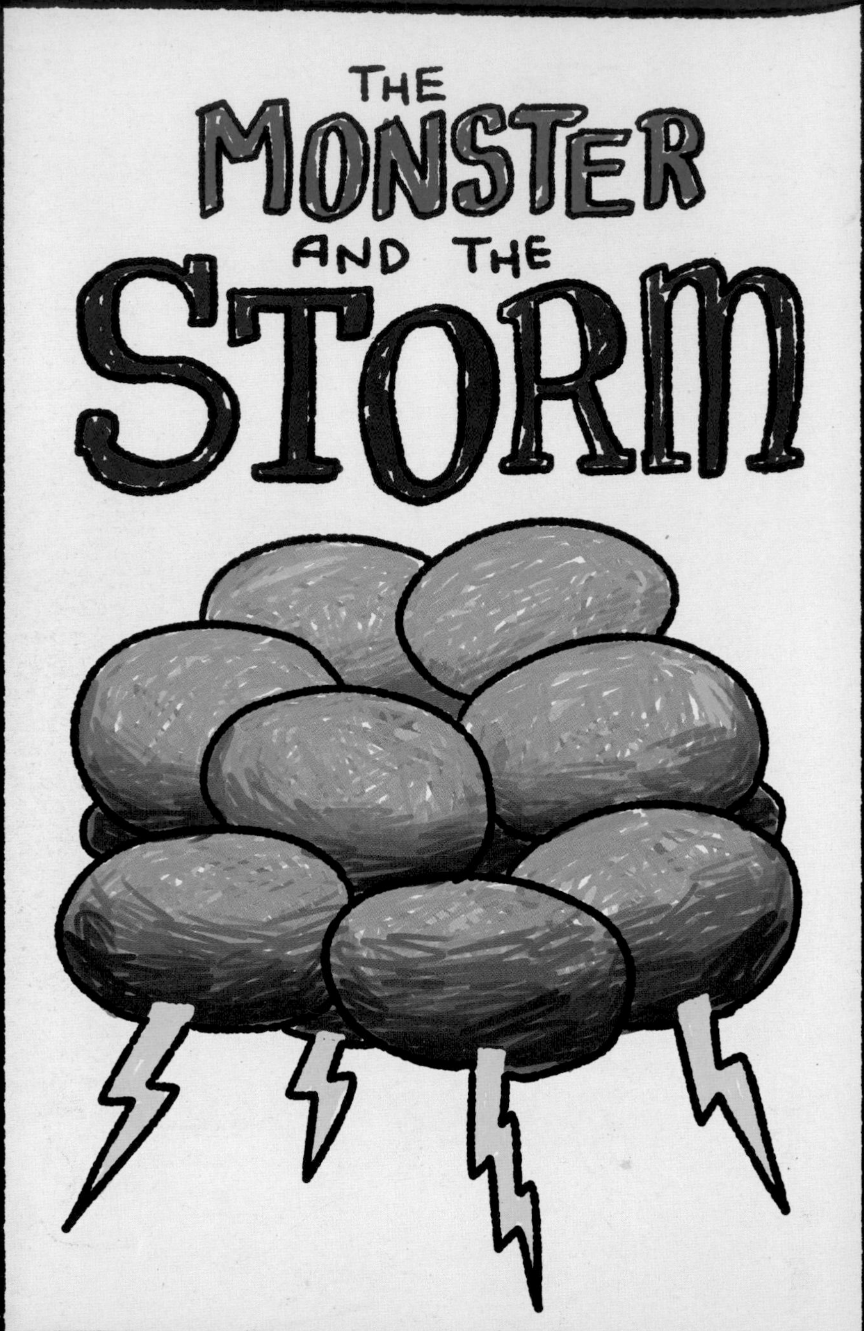
THE
MONSTER
AND THE
STORM

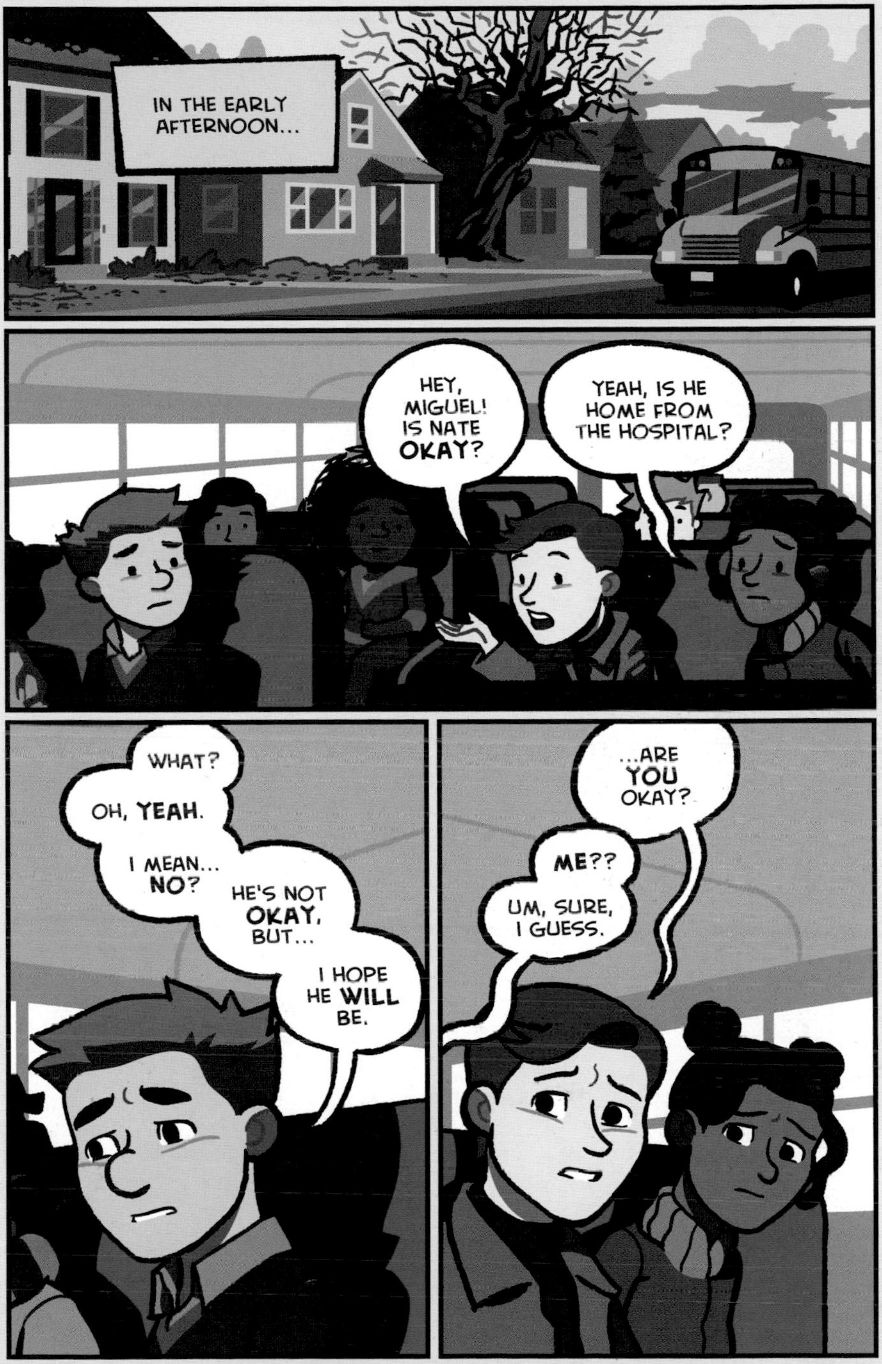
IN THE EARLY AFTERNOON...
HEY, MIGUEL! IS NATE OKAY?
YEAH, IS HE HOME FROM THE HOSPITAL?
WHAT?
OH, YEAH.
I MEAN... NO?
HE'S NOT OKAY, BUT...
I HOPE HE WILL BE.
...ARE YOU OKAY?
ME??
UM, SURE, I GUESS.

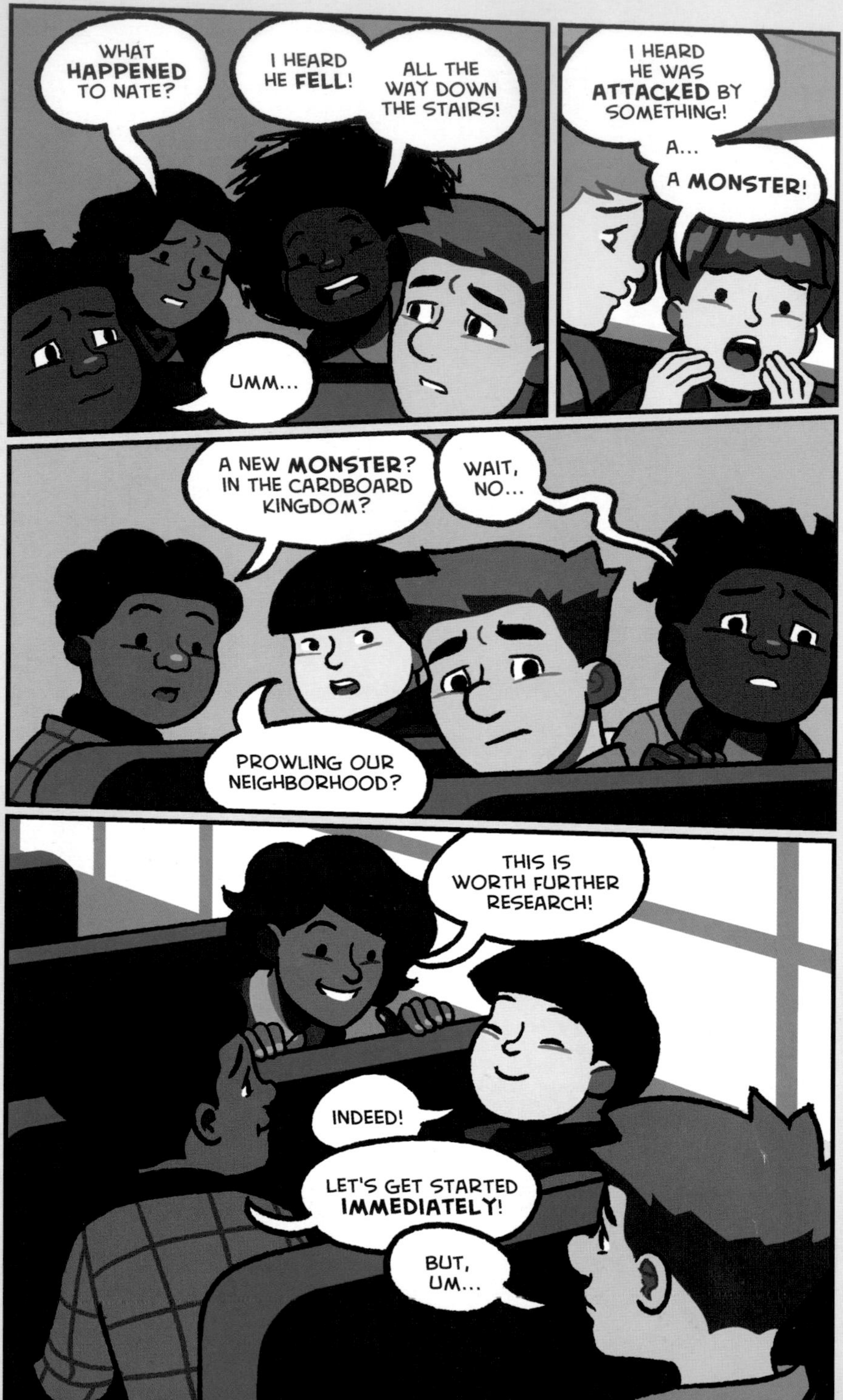
WHAT HAPPENED TO NATE?
I HEARD HE FELL!
ALL THE WAY DOWN THE STAIRS!
UMM...
I HEARD HE WAS ATTACKED BY SOMETHING!
A...
A MONSTER!
A NEW MONSTER? IN THE CARDBOARD KINGDOM?
PROWLING OUR NEIGHBORHOOD?
WAIT, NO...
THIS IS WORTH FURTHER RESEARCH!
INDEED!
LET'S GET STARTED IMMEDIATELY!
BUT, UM...

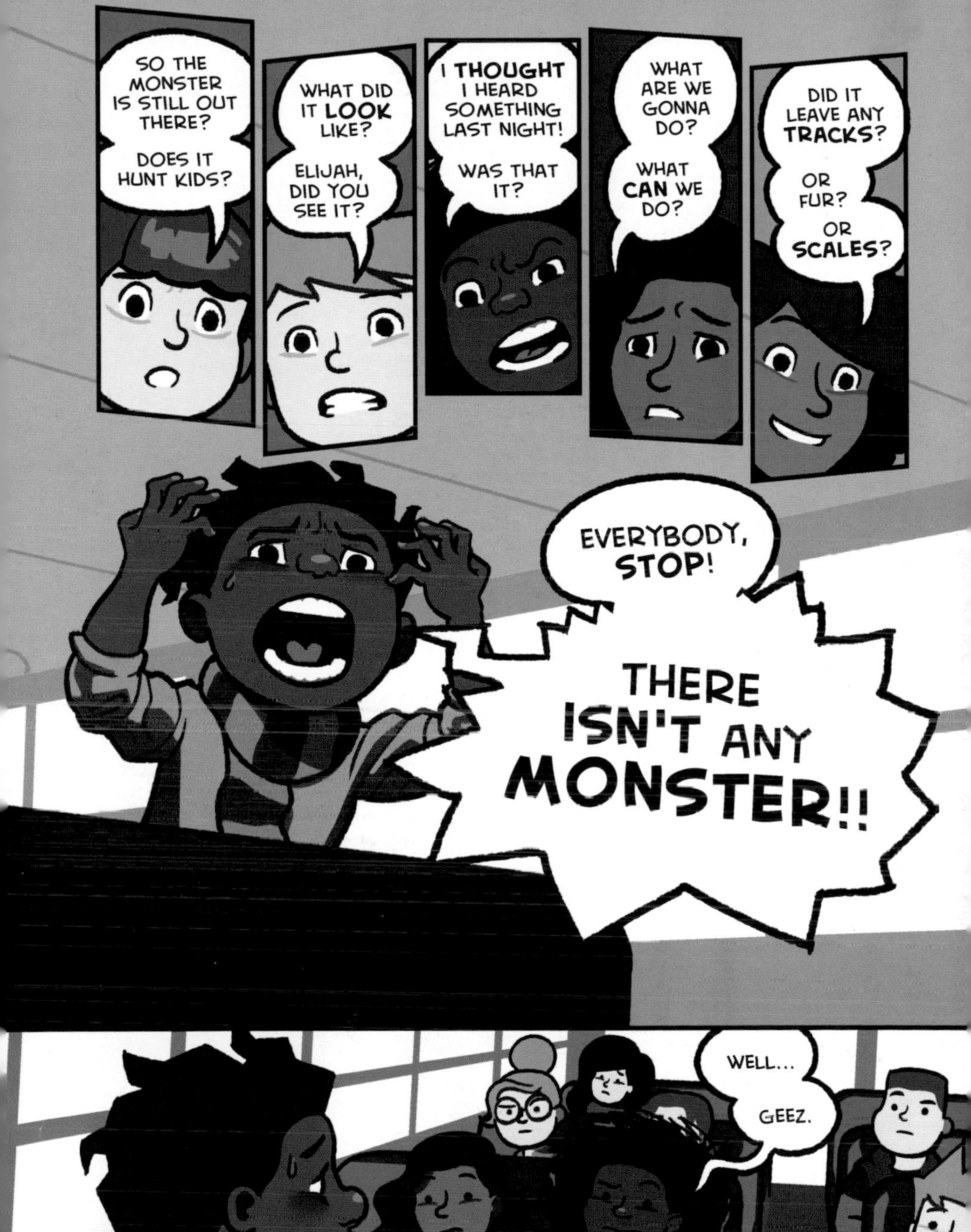
SO THE MONSTER IS STILL OUT THERE?
DOES IT HUNT KIDS?
WHAT DID IT LOOK LIKE?
ELIJAH, DID YOU SEE IT?
I THOUGHT I HEARD SOMETHING LAST NIGHT!
WAS THAT IT?
WHAT ARE WE GONNA DO?
WHAT CAN WE DO?
DID IT LEAVE ANY TRACKS?
OR FUR?
OR SCALES?
EVERYBODY, STOP!
THERE ISN'T ANY MONSTER!!
WELL...
GEEZ.

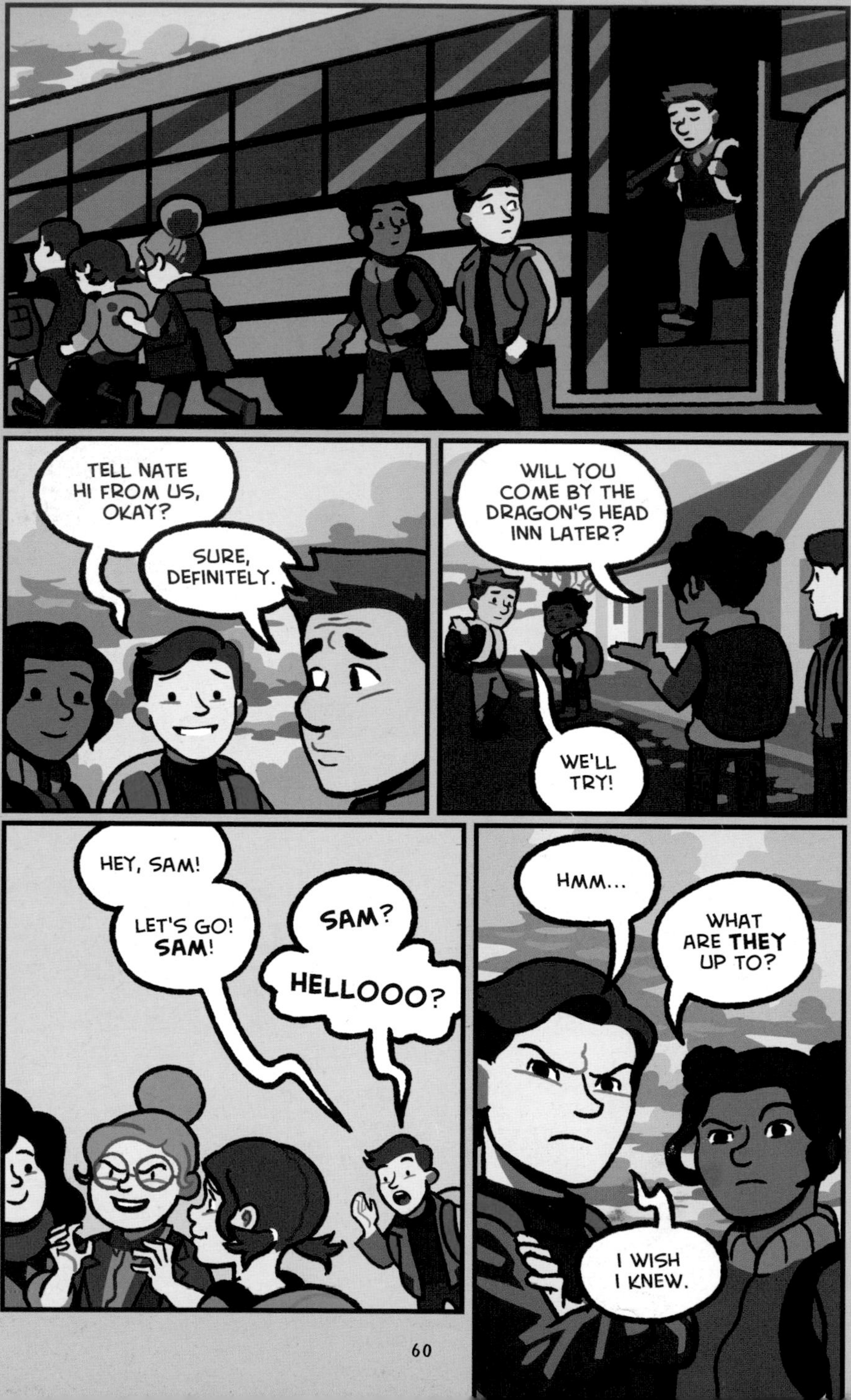
TELL NATE HI FROM US, OKAY?
SURE, DEFINITELY.
WILL YOU COME BY THE DRAGON'S HEAD INN LATER?
WE'LL TRY!
HEY, SAM!
LET'S GO! SAM!
SAM?
HELLOOO?
HMM...
WHAT ARE THEY UP TO?
I WISH I KNEW.

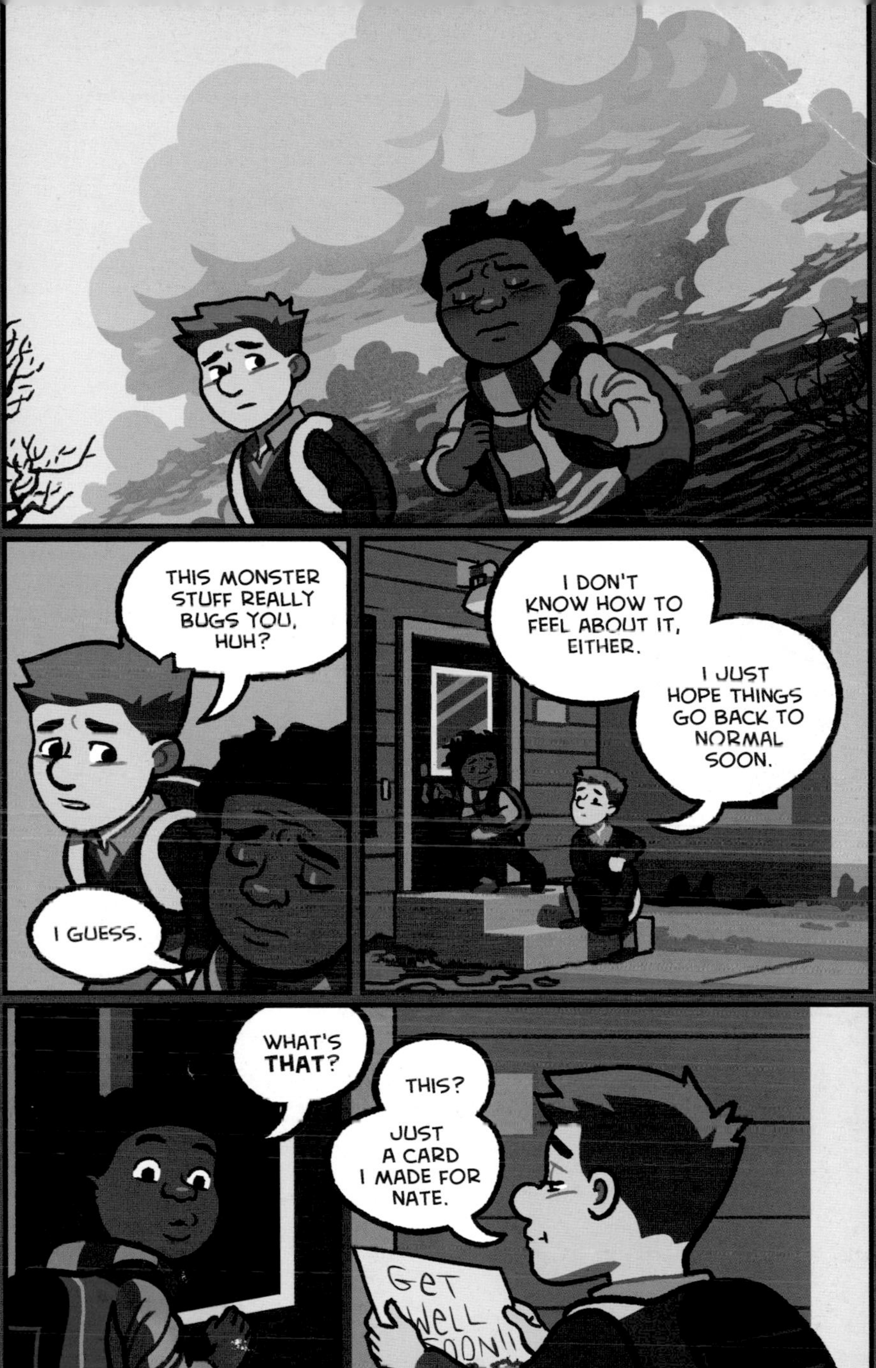
THIS MONSTER STUFF REALLY BUGS YOU, HUH?
I GUESS.
I DON'T KNOW HOW TO FEEL ABOUT IT, EITHER.
I JUST HOPE THINGS GO BACK TO NORMAL SOON.
WHAT'S **THAT**?
THIS?
JUST A CARD I MADE FOR NATE.
GET WELL SOON!!!

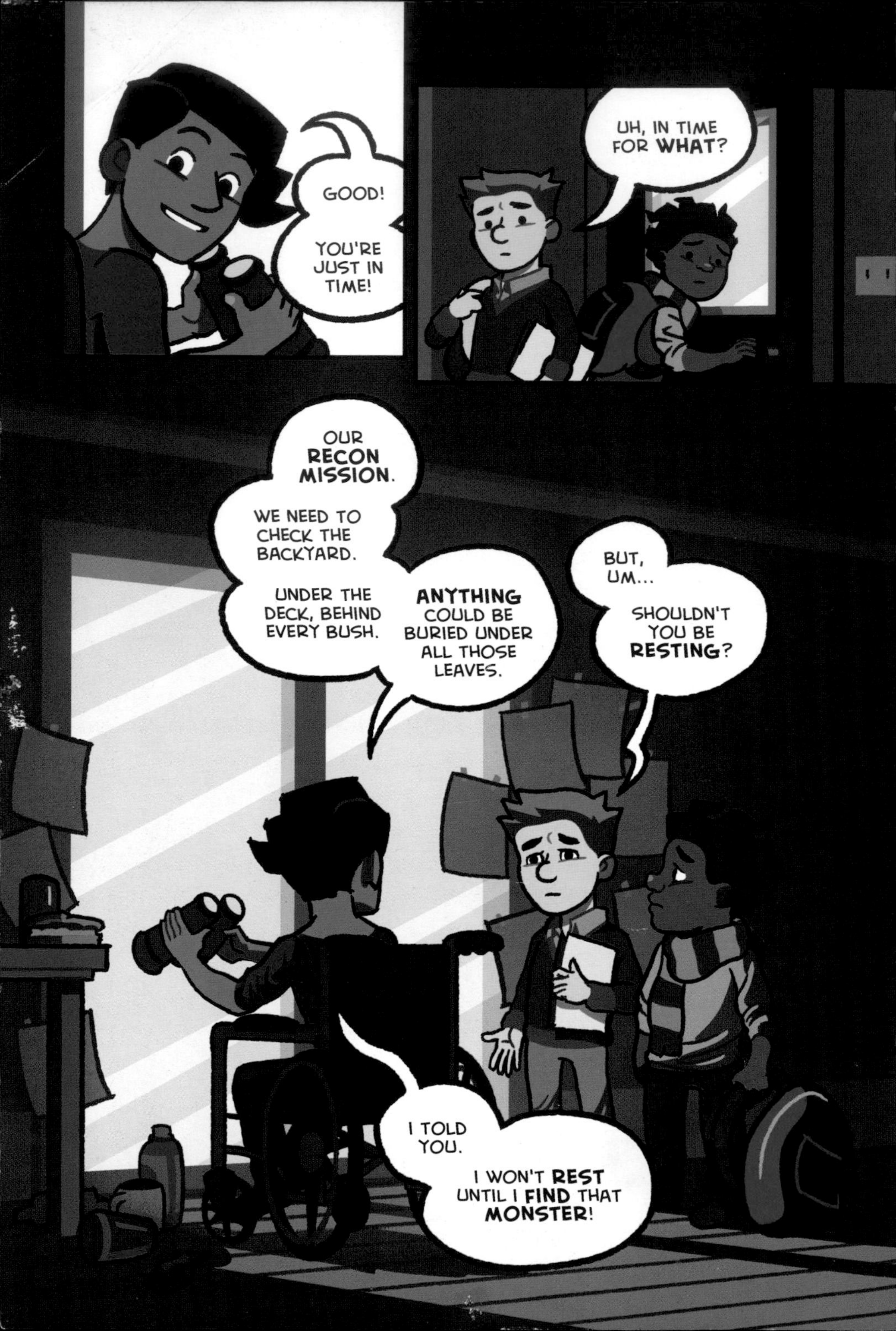
GOOD!
YOU'RE JUST IN TIME!
UH, IN TIME FOR **WHAT**?
OUR **RECON MISSION**.
WE NEED TO CHECK THE BACKYARD.
UNDER THE DECK, BEHIND EVERY BUSH.
ANYTHING COULD BE BURIED UNDER ALL THOSE LEAVES.
BUT, UM...
SHOULDN'T YOU BE **RESTING**?
I TOLD YOU.
I WON'T **REST** UNTIL I **FIND** THAT **MONSTER**!

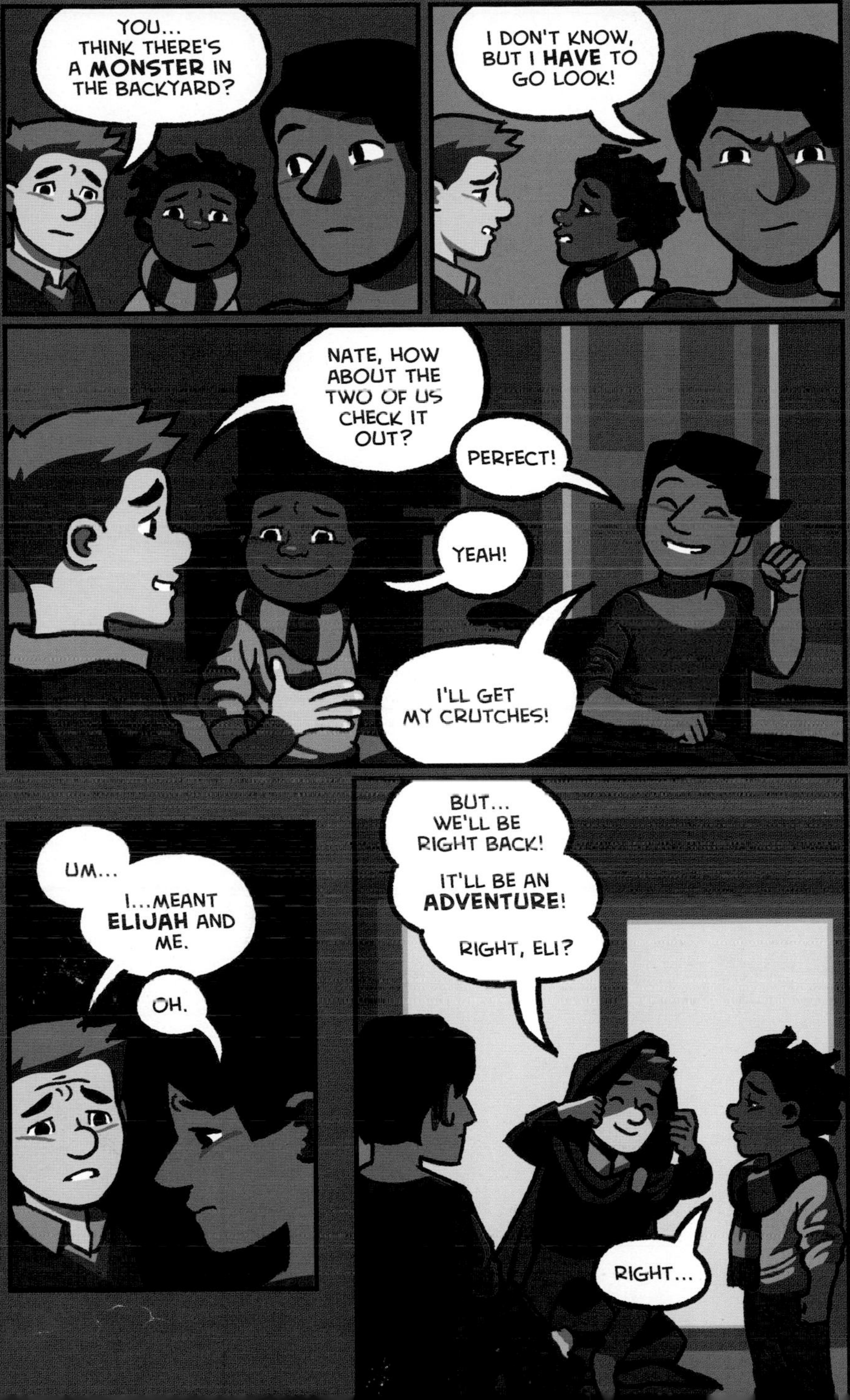
YOU... THINK THERE'S A **MONSTER** IN THE BACKYARD?
I DON'T KNOW, BUT I **HAVE** TO GO LOOK!
NATE, HOW ABOUT THE TWO OF US CHECK IT OUT?
PERFECT!
YEAH!
I'LL GET MY CRUTCHES!
UM...
I...MEANT **ELIJAH** AND ME.
OH.
BUT... WE'LL BE RIGHT BACK!
IT'LL BE AN **ADVENTURE**!
RIGHT, ELI?
RIGHT...

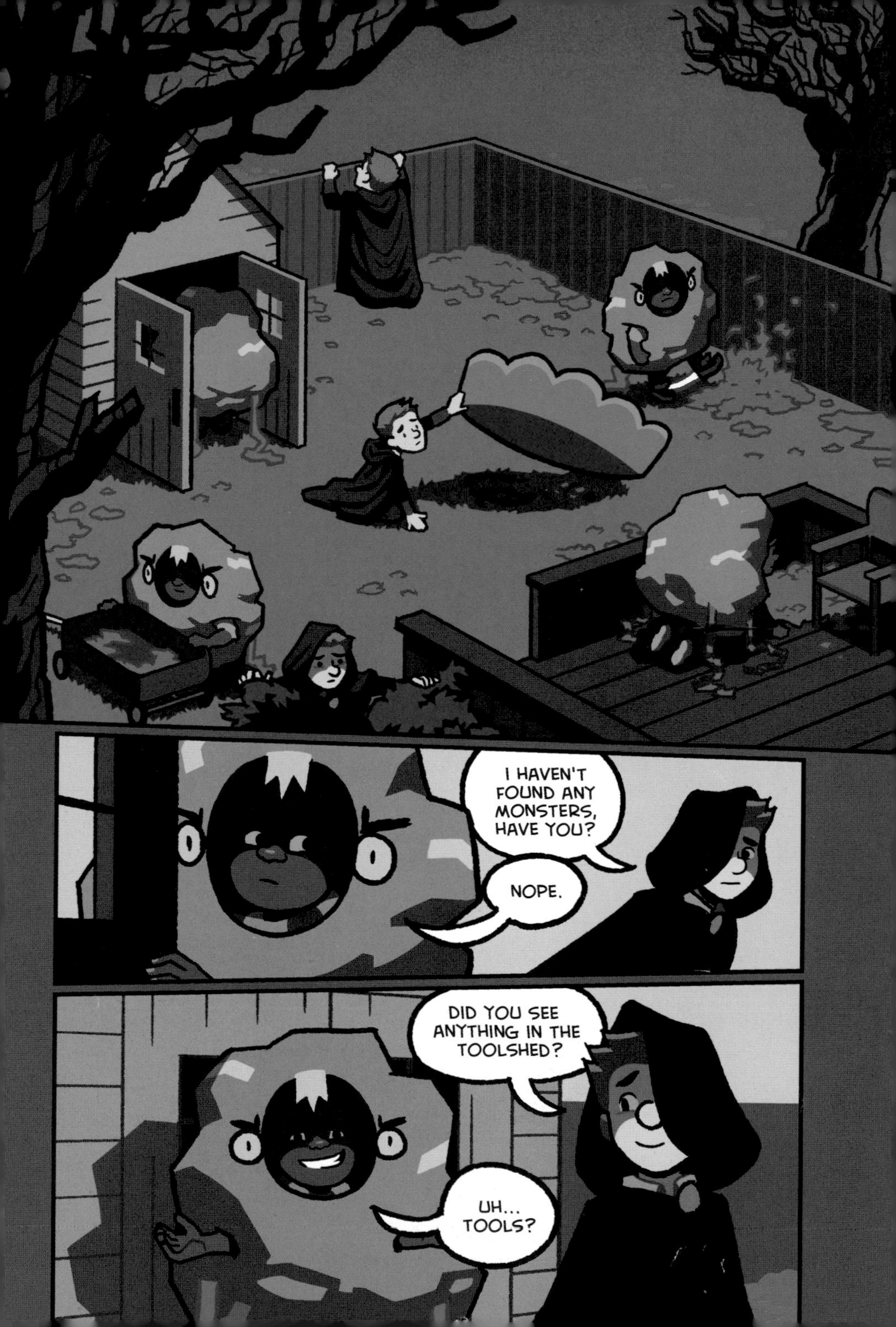
I HAVEN'T FOUND ANY MONSTERS, HAVE YOU?
NOPE.
DID YOU SEE ANYTHING IN THE TOOLSHED?
UH... TOOLS?

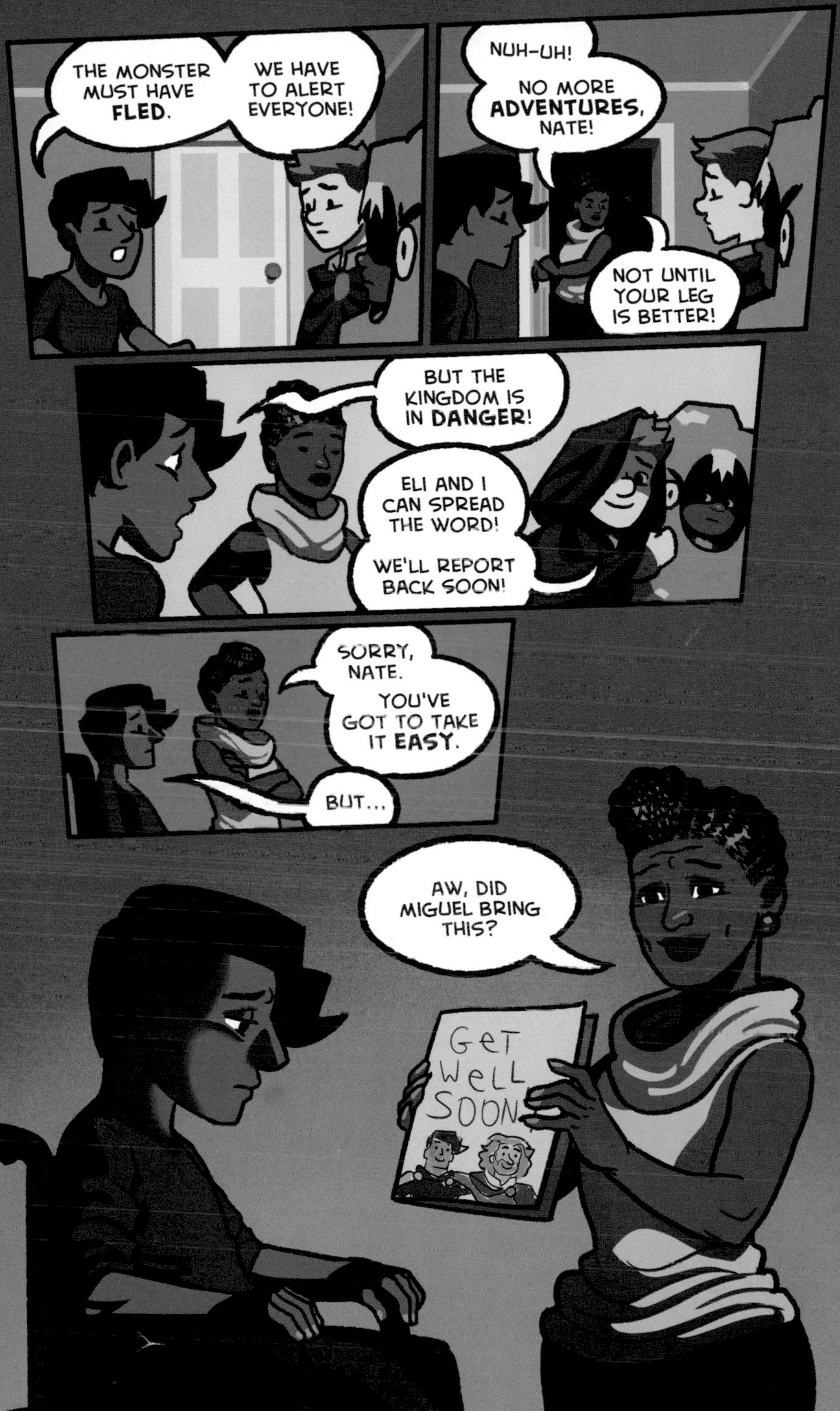
THE MONSTER MUST HAVE FLED.
WE HAVE TO ALERT EVERYONE!
NUH-UH!
NO MORE ADVENTURES, NATE!
NOT UNTIL YOUR LEG IS BETTER!
BUT THE KINGDOM IS IN DANGER!
ELI AND I CAN SPREAD THE WORD!
WE'LL REPORT BACK SOON!
SORRY, NATE.
YOU'VE GOT TO TAKE IT EASY.
BUT...
AW, DID MIGUEL BRING THIS?
Get Well SOON

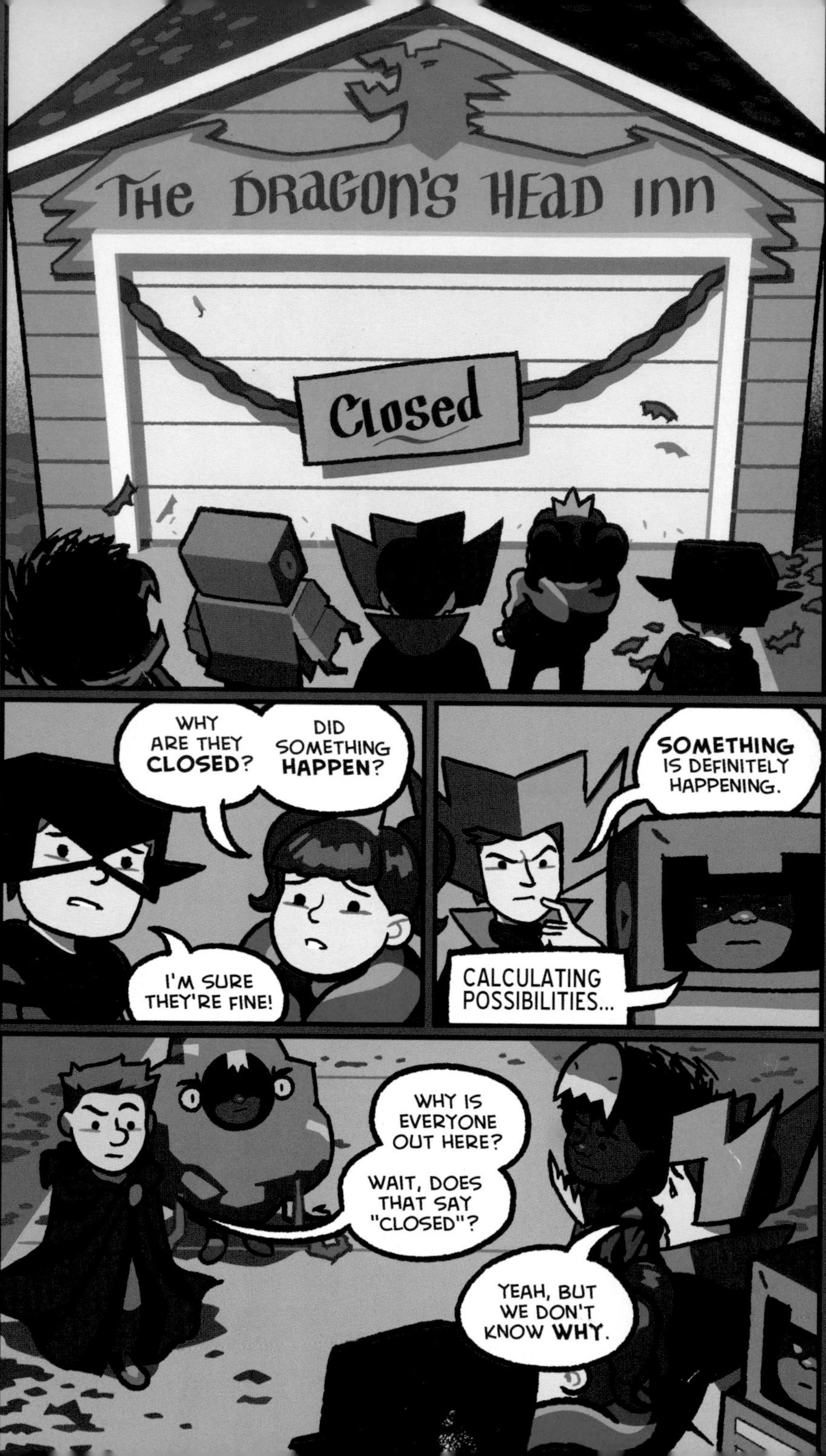
THE DRAGON'S HEAD INN
Closed
WHY ARE THEY **CLOSED**?
DID SOMETHING **HAPPEN**?
I'M SURE THEY'RE FINE!
SOMETHING IS DEFINITELY HAPPENING.
CALCULATING POSSIBILITIES...
WHY IS EVERYONE OUT HERE?
WAIT, DOES THAT SAY "CLOSED"?
YEAH, BUT WE DON'T KNOW **WHY**.

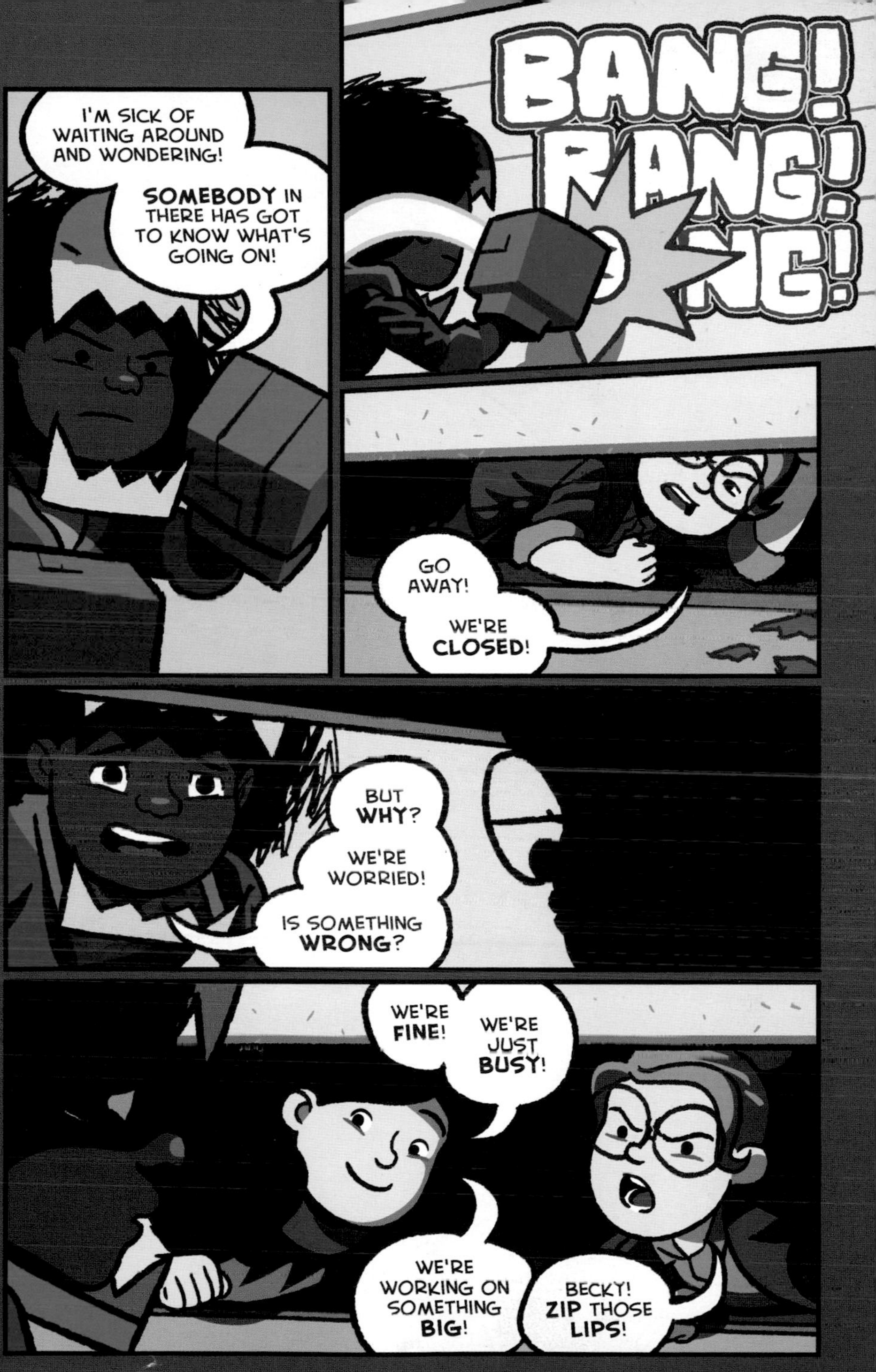
I'M SICK OF WAITING AROUND AND WONDERING!
SOMEBODY IN THERE HAS GOT TO KNOW WHAT'S GOING ON!
BANG! BANG! BANG!
GO AWAY!
WE'RE CLOSED!
BUT WHY?
WE'RE WORRIED!
IS SOMETHING WRONG?
WE'RE FINE!
WE'RE JUST BUSY!
WE'RE WORKING ON SOMETHING BIG!
BECKY! ZIP THOSE LIPS!

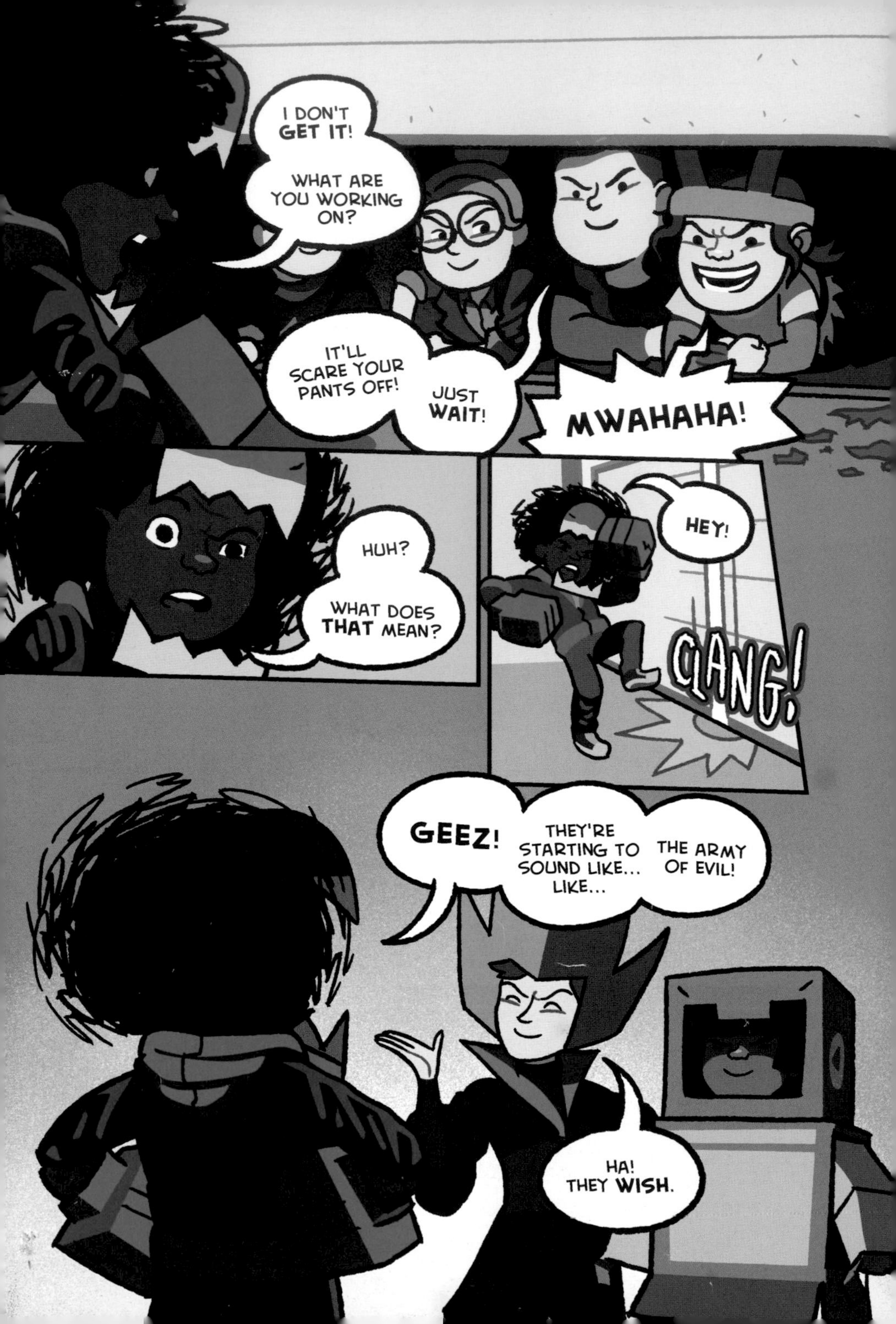
I DON'T GET IT!
WHAT ARE YOU WORKING ON?
IT'LL SCARE YOUR PANTS OFF!
JUST WAIT!
MWAHAHA!
HUH?
WHAT DOES THAT MEAN?
HEY!
CLANG!
GEEZ!
THEY'RE STARTING TO SOUND LIKE... LIKE...
THE ARMY OF EVIL!
HA! THEY WISH.

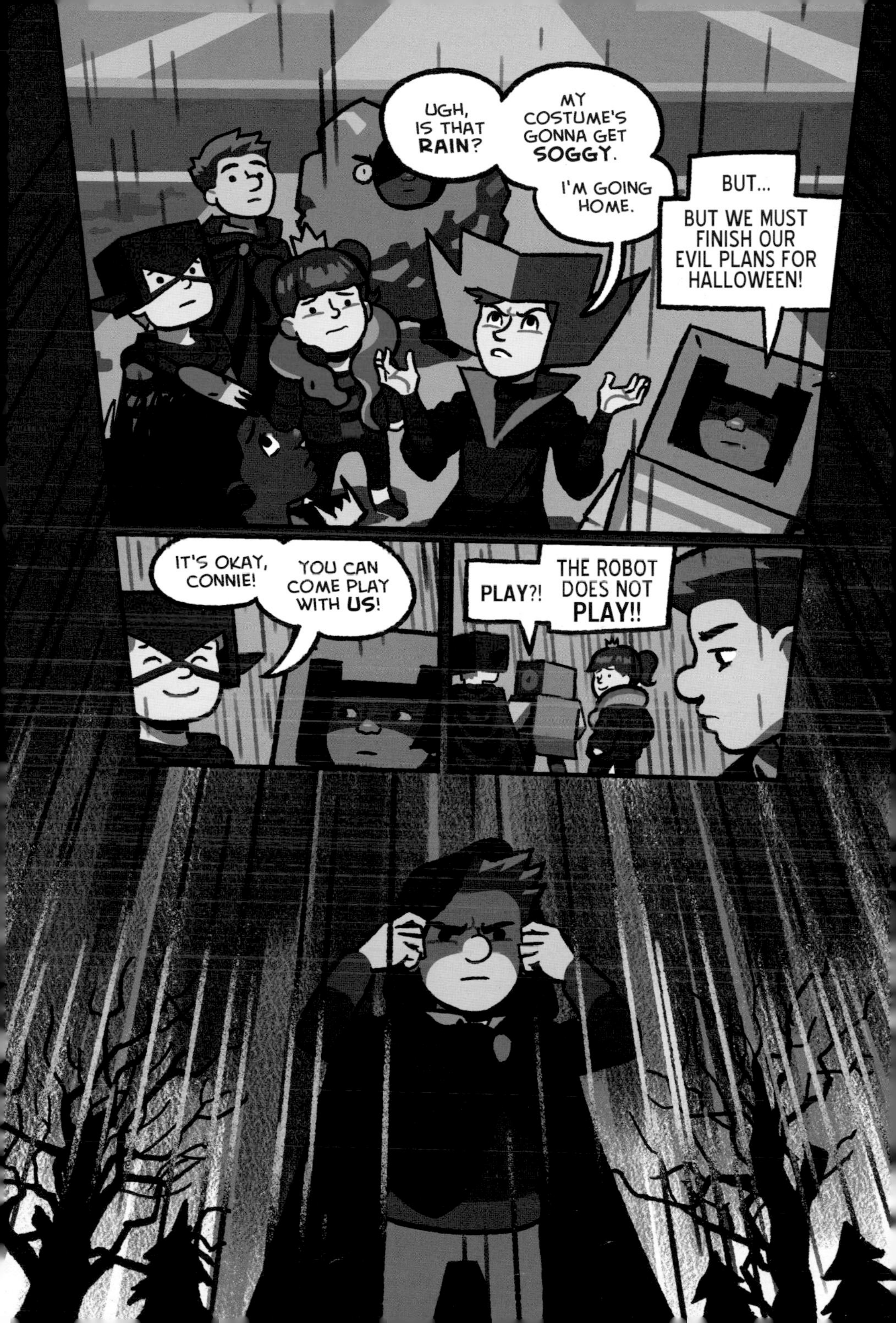
UGH, IS THAT RAIN?
MY COSTUME'S GONNA GET SOGGY.
I'M GOING HOME.
BUT...
BUT WE MUST FINISH OUR EVIL PLANS FOR HALLOWEEN!
IT'S OKAY, CONNIE!
YOU CAN COME PLAY WITH US!
PLAY?!
THE ROBOT DOES NOT PLAY!!

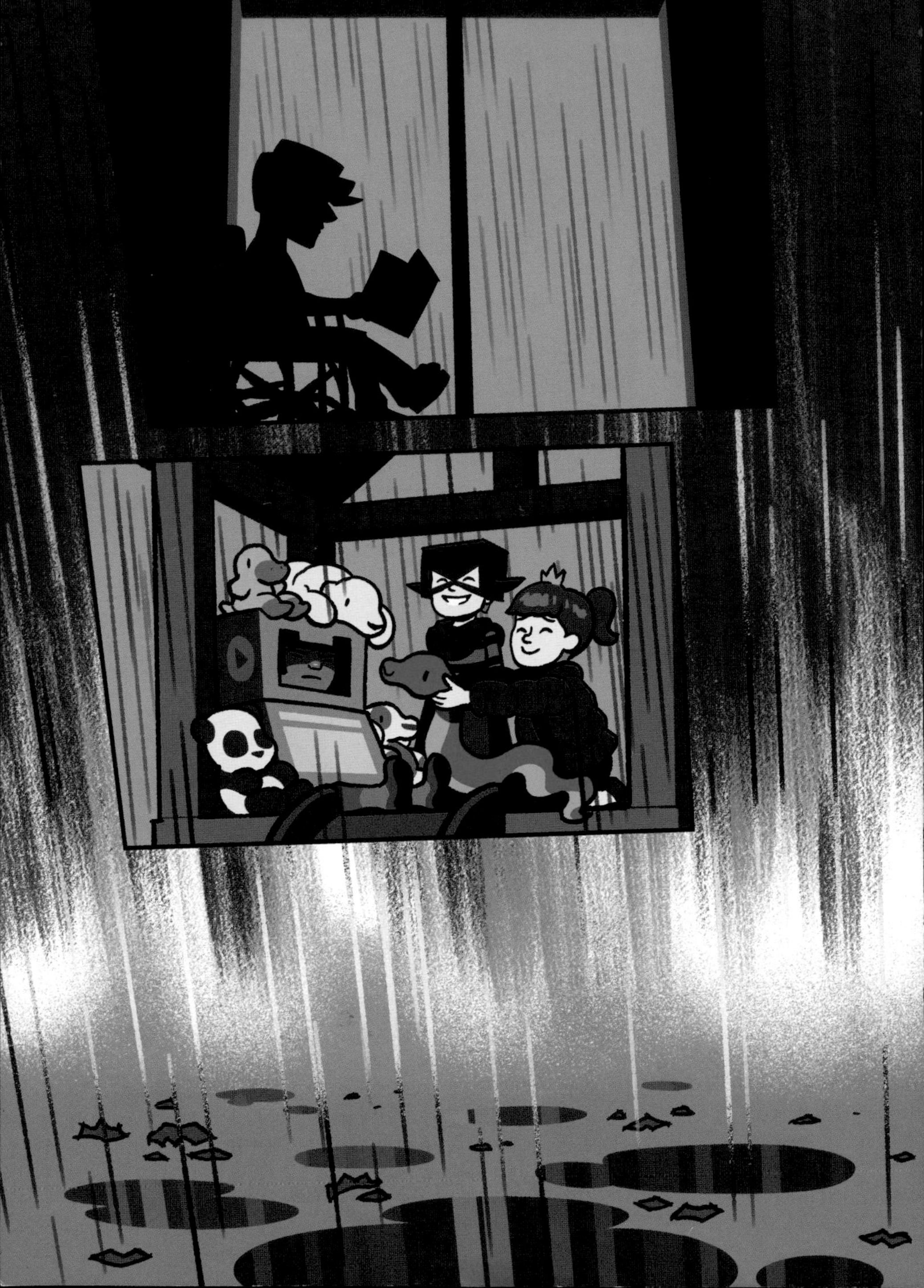

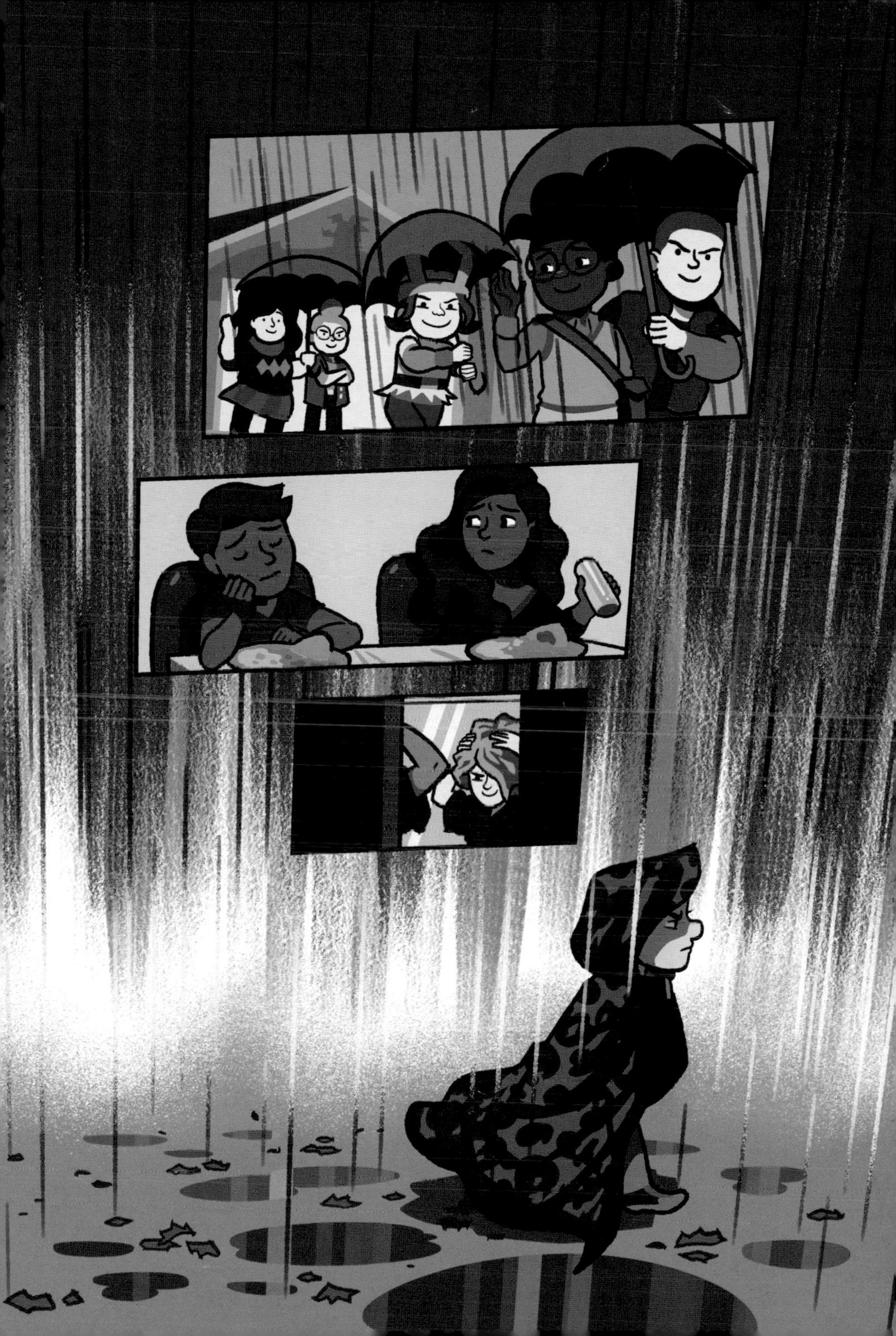

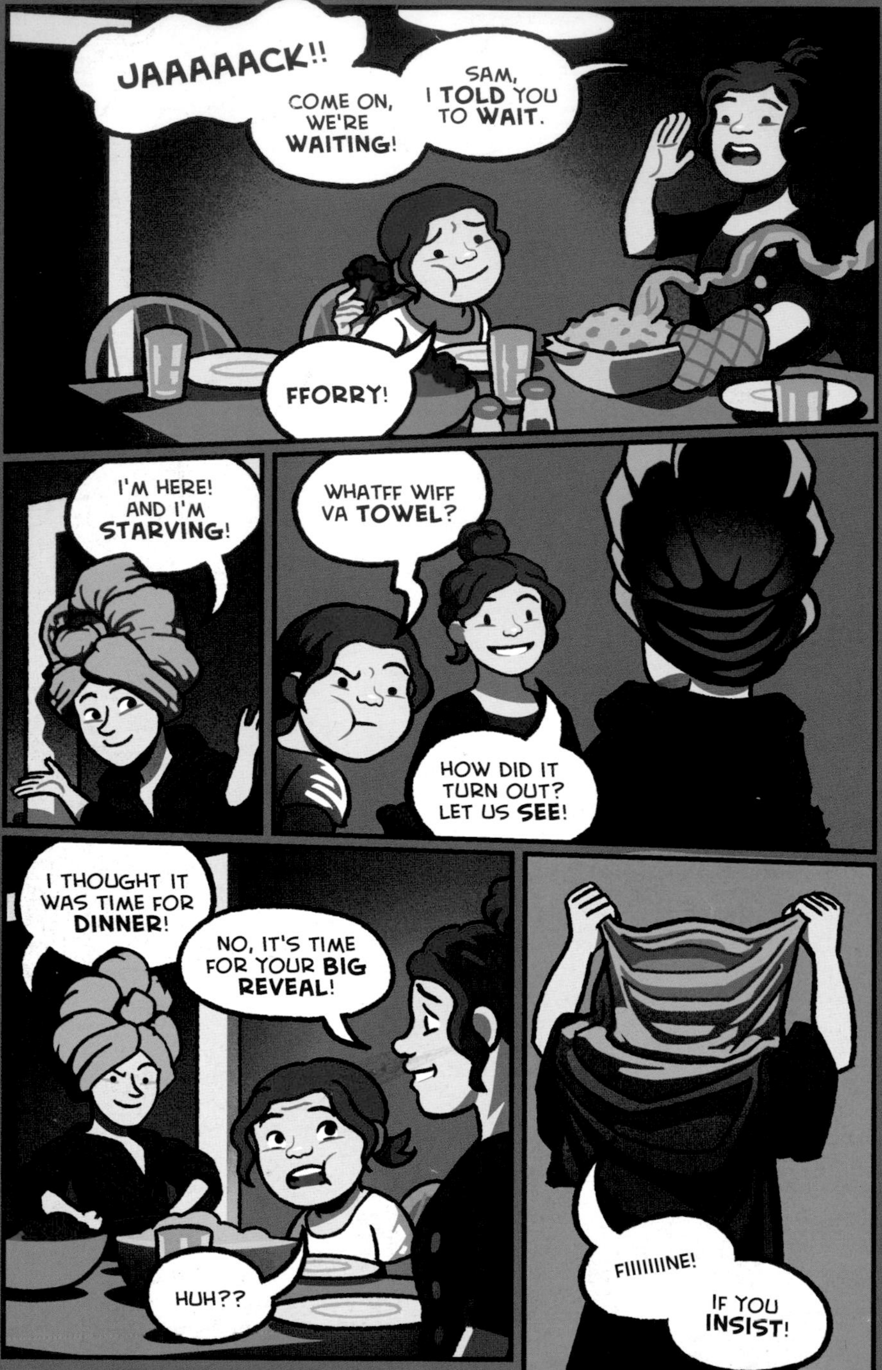
JAAAAACK!!
COME ON, WE'RE WAITING!
SAM, I TOLD YOU TO WAIT.
FFORRY!
I'M HERE! AND I'M STARVING!
WHATFF WIFF VA TOWEL?
HOW DID IT TURN OUT? LET US SEE!
I THOUGHT IT WAS TIME FOR DINNER!
NO, IT'S TIME FOR YOUR BIG REVEAL!
HUH??
FIIIIIINE!
IF YOU INSIST!

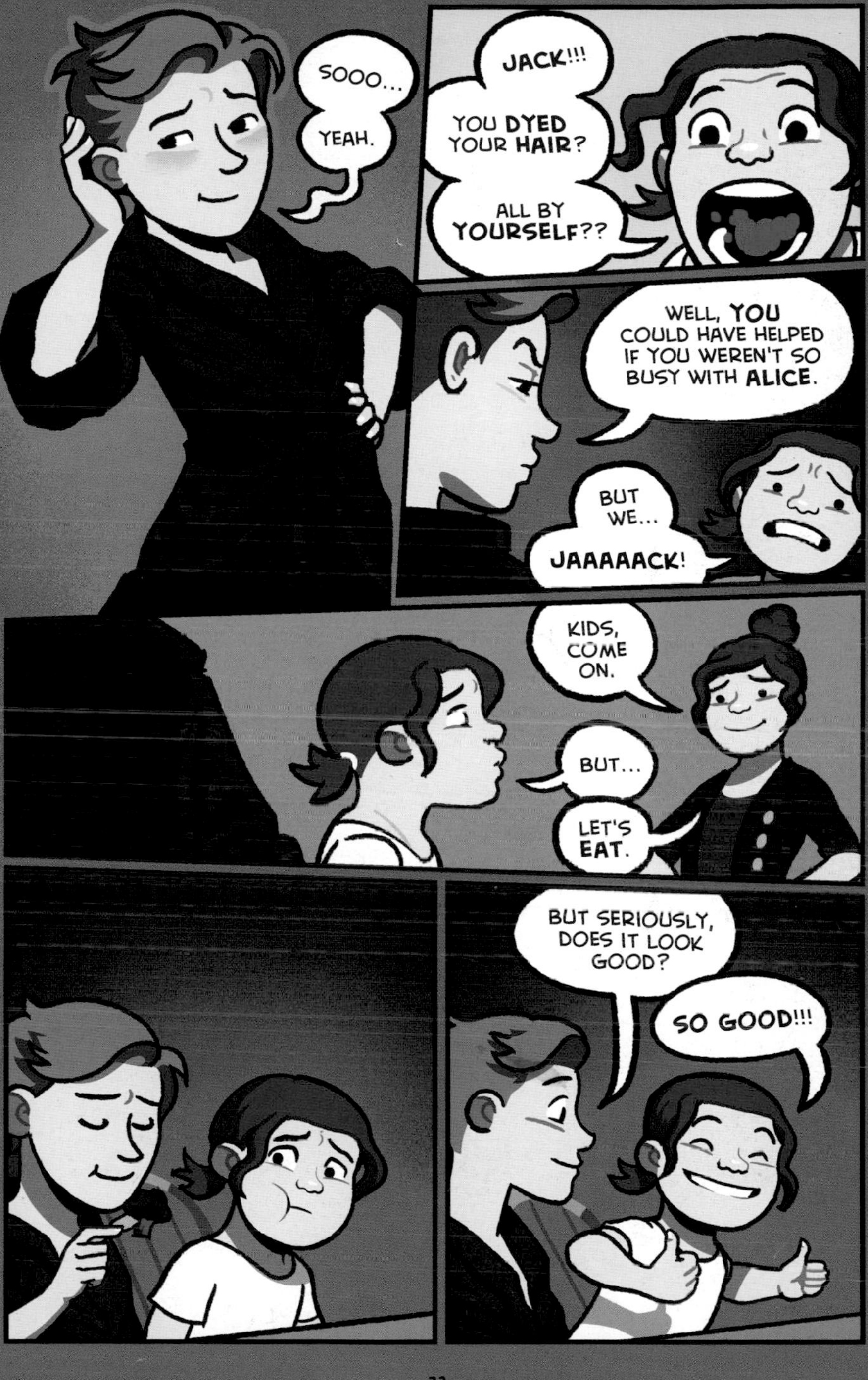

SOOO...
YEAH.
JACK!!!
YOU DYED YOUR HAIR?
ALL BY YOURSELF??
WELL, YOU COULD HAVE HELPED IF YOU WEREN'T SO BUSY WITH ALICE.
BUT WE...
JAAAAACK!
KIDS, COME ON.
BUT...
LET'S EAT.
BUT SERIOUSLY, DOES IT LOOK GOOD?
SO GOOD!!!

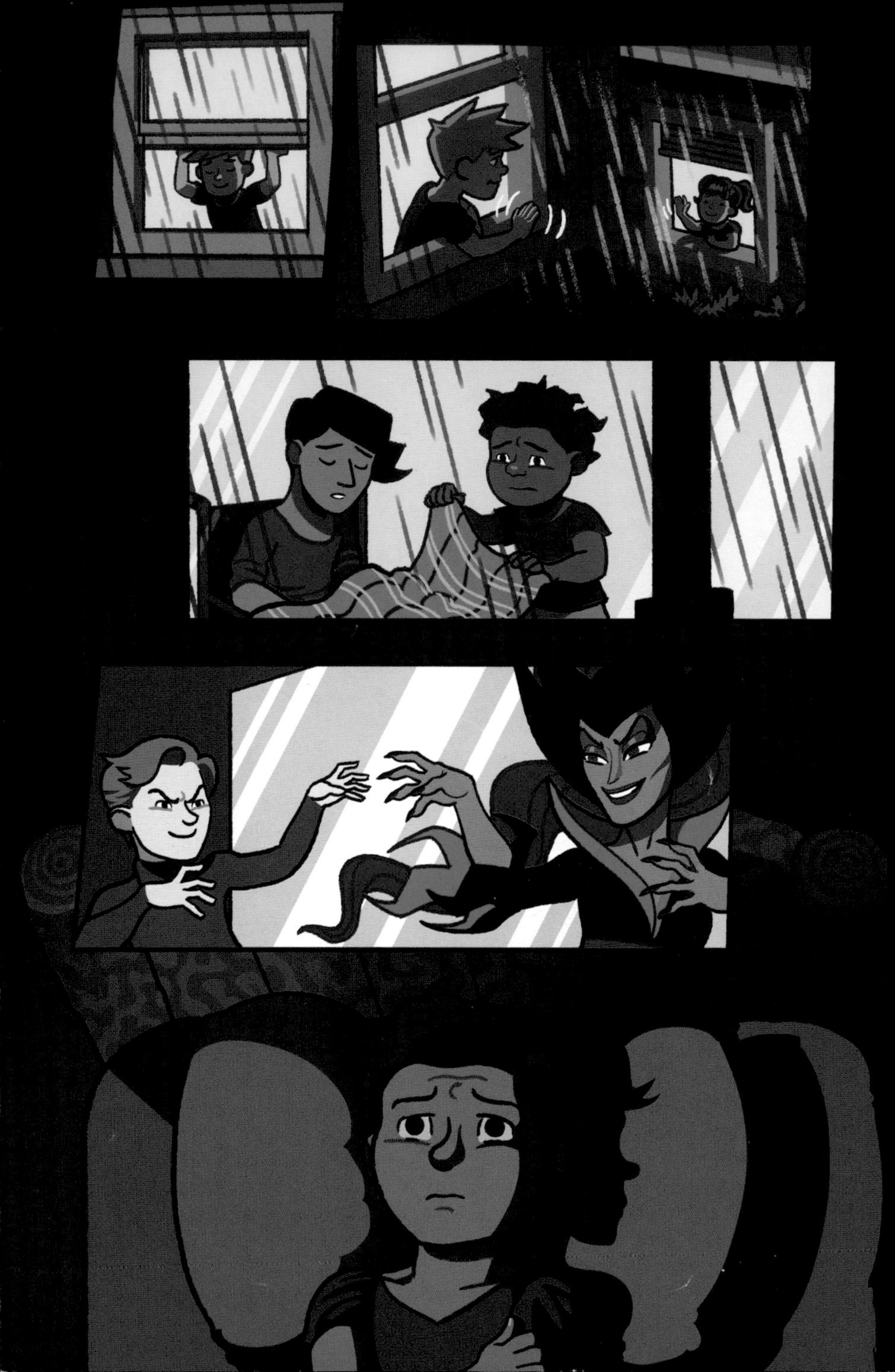

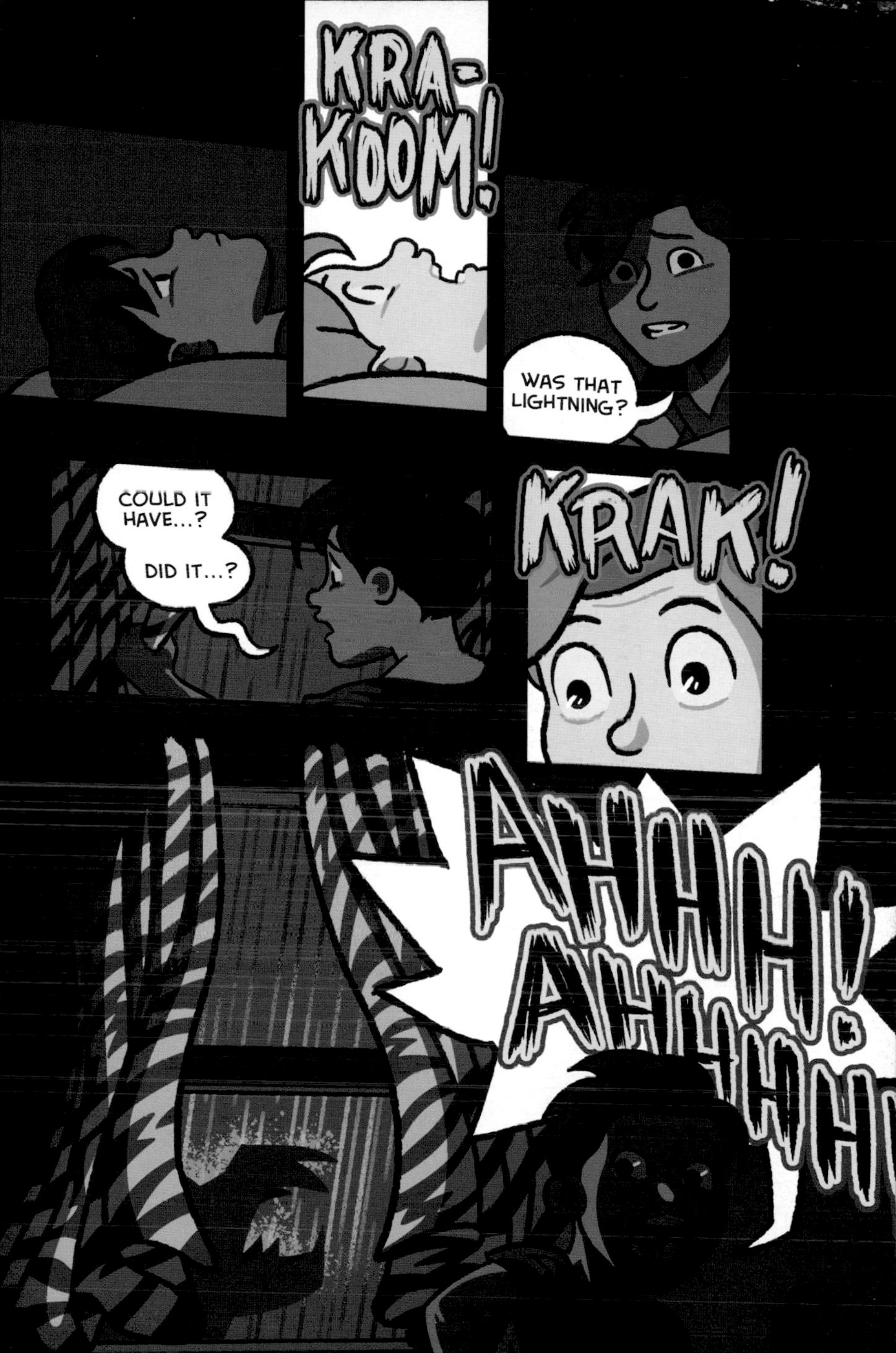
KRA-KOOM!
WAS THAT LIGHTNING?
COULD IT HAVE...?
DID IT...?
KRAK!
AHHHH!

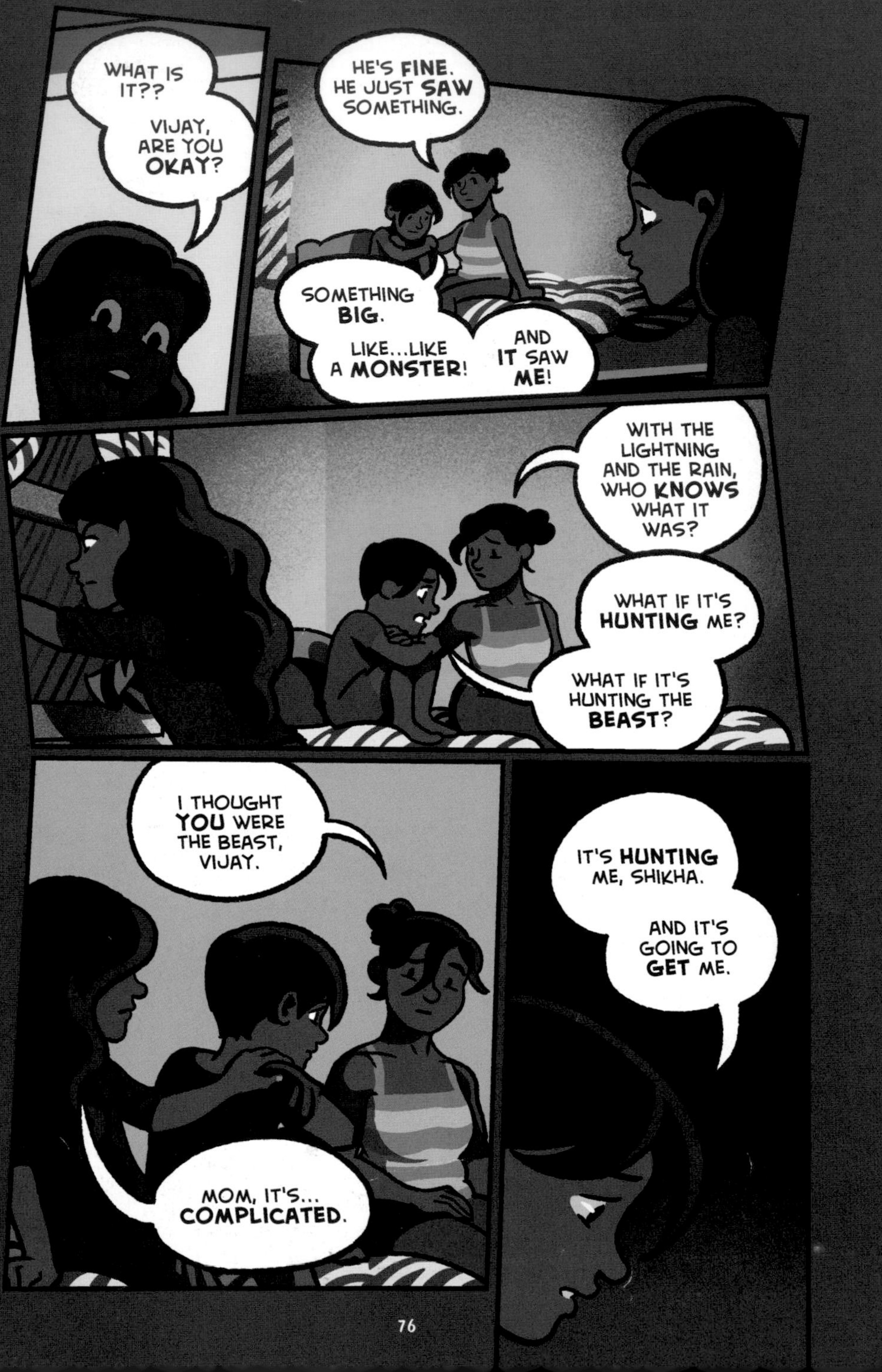
WHAT IS IT??
VIJAY, ARE YOU OKAY?
HE'S FINE. HE JUST SAW SOMETHING.
SOMETHING BIG.
LIKE...LIKE A MONSTER!
AND IT SAW ME!
WITH THE LIGHTNING AND THE RAIN, WHO KNOWS WHAT IT WAS?
WHAT IF IT'S HUNTING ME?
WHAT IF IT'S HUNTING THE BEAST?
I THOUGHT YOU WERE THE BEAST, VIJAY.
MOM, IT'S... COMPLICATED.
IT'S HUNTING ME, SHIKHA.
AND IT'S GOING TO GET ME.

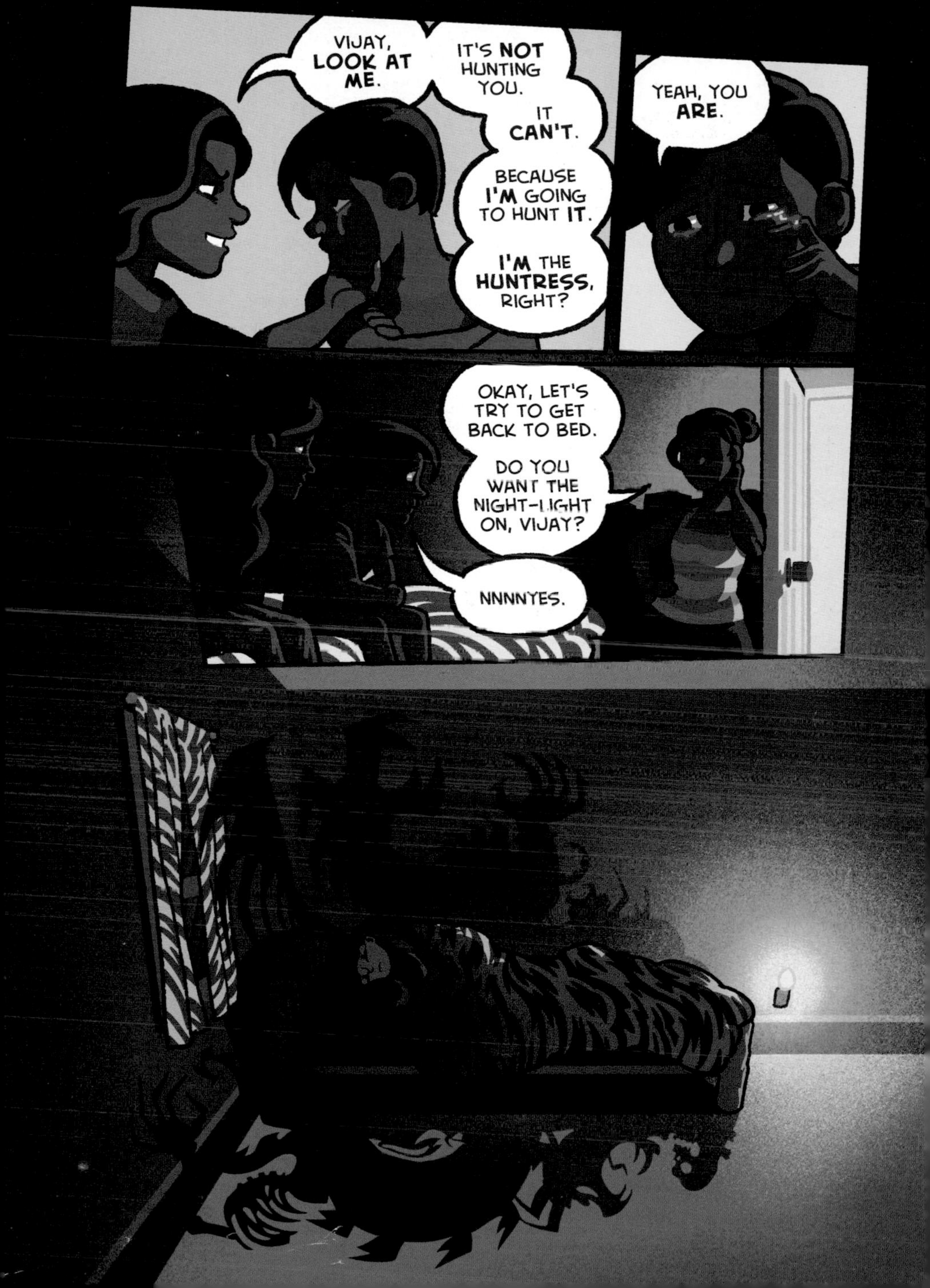
VIJAY, LOOK AT ME.
IT'S NOT HUNTING YOU.
IT CAN'T.
BECAUSE I'M GOING TO HUNT IT.
I'M THE HUNTRESS, RIGHT?
YEAH, YOU ARE.
OKAY, LET'S TRY TO GET BACK TO BED.
DO YOU WANT THE NIGHT-LIGHT ON, VIJAY?
NNNNYES.

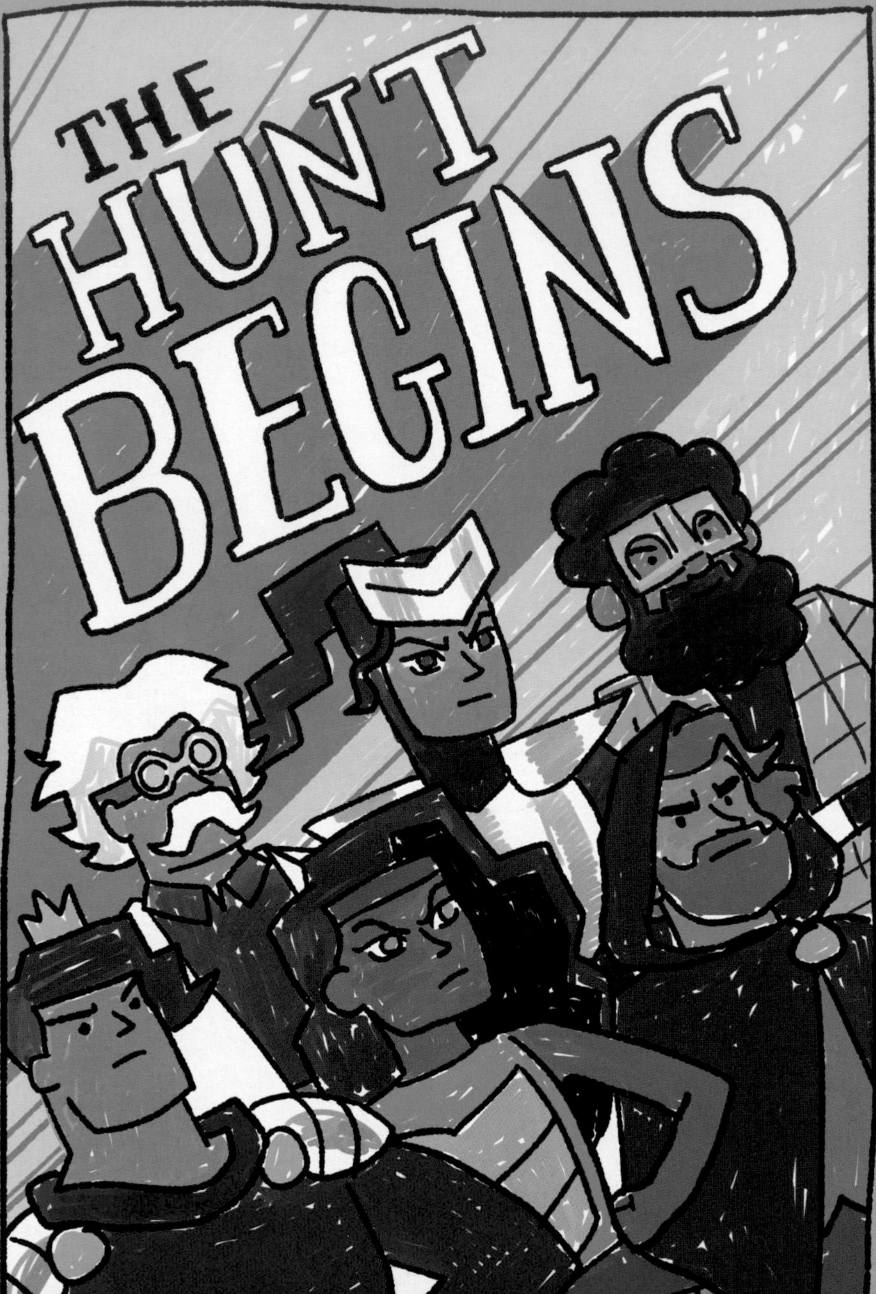
THE
HUNT
BEGINS

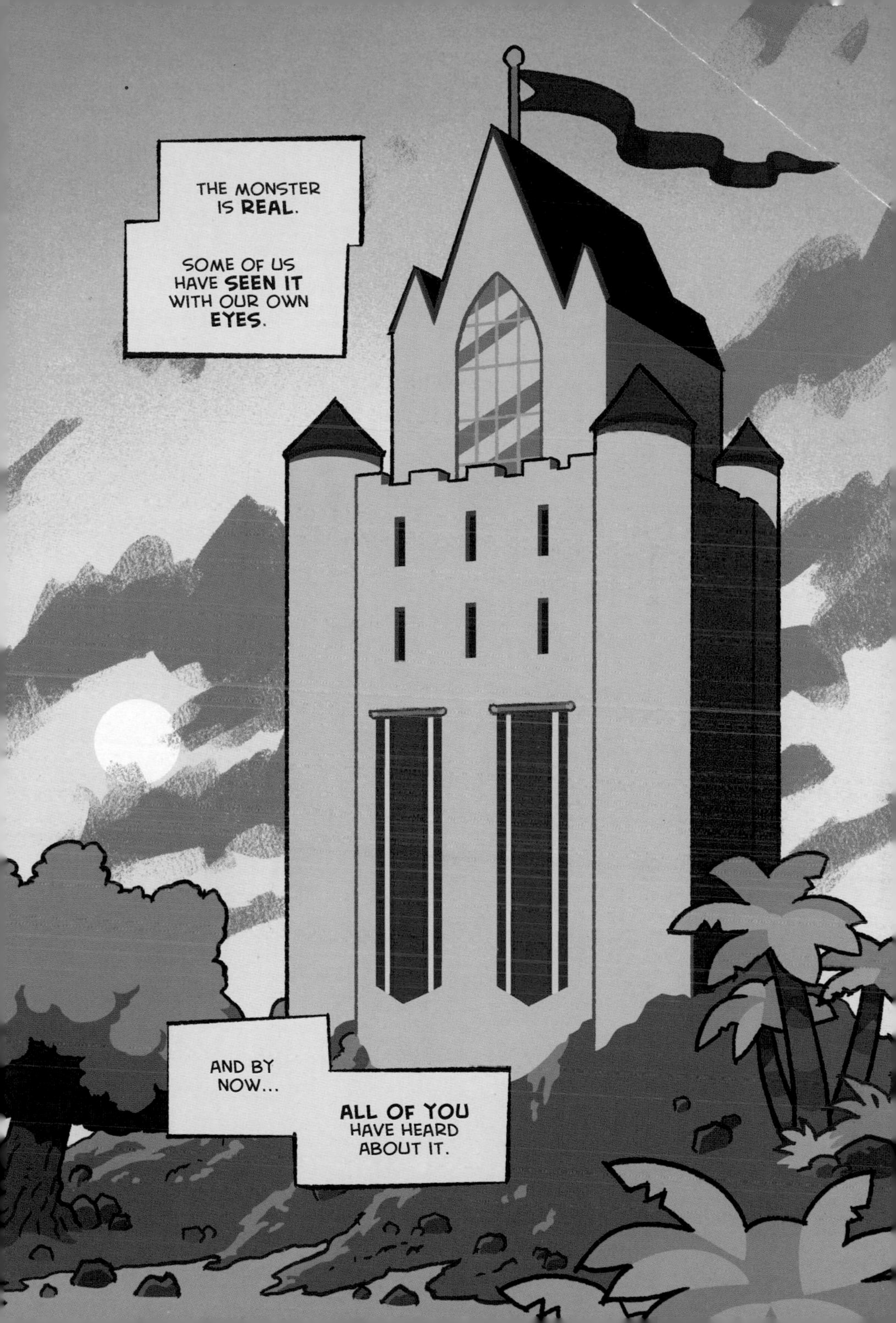
THE MONSTER IS **REAL**.
SOME OF US HAVE **SEEN IT** WITH OUR OWN **EYES**.
AND BY NOW...
ALL OF YOU HAVE HEARD ABOUT IT.

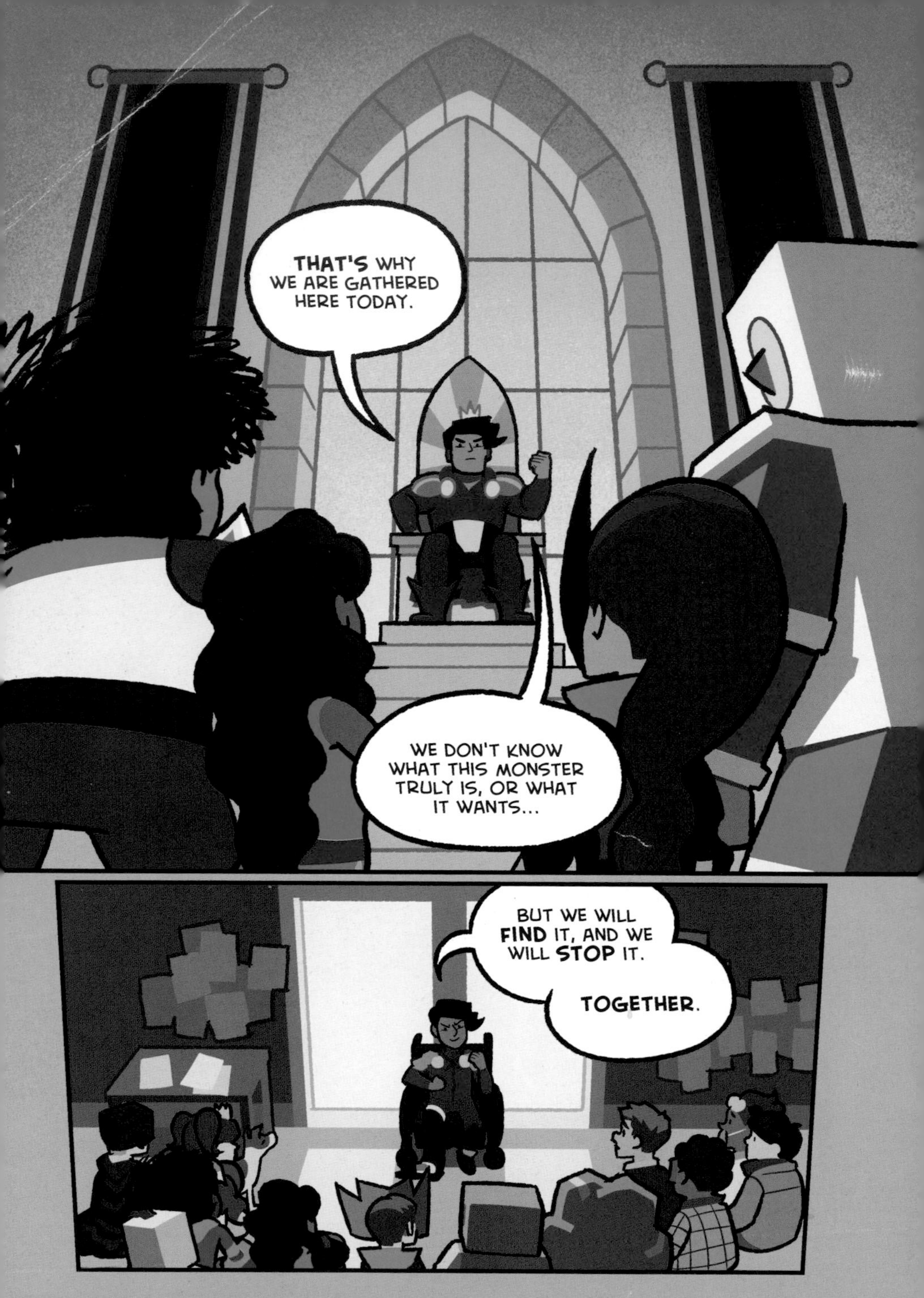

THAT'S WHY WE ARE GATHERED HERE TODAY.
WE DON'T KNOW WHAT THIS MONSTER TRULY IS, OR WHAT IT WANTS...
BUT WE WILL **FIND** IT, AND WE WILL **STOP** IT.
TOGETHER.

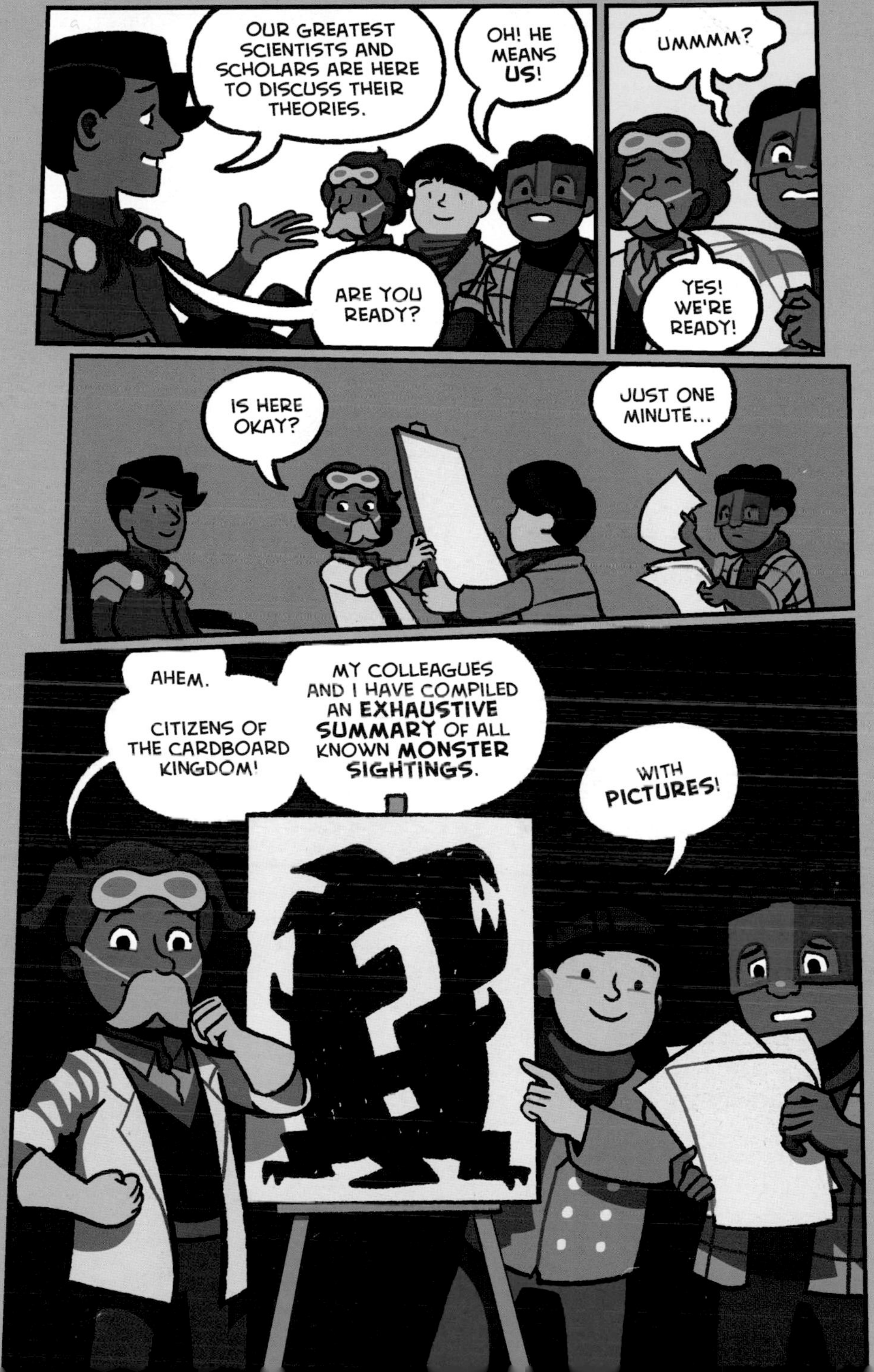
OUR GREATEST SCIENTISTS AND SCHOLARS ARE HERE TO DISCUSS THEIR THEORIES.
OH! HE MEANS **US**!
ARE YOU READY?
UMMMM?
YES! WE'RE READY!
IS HERE OKAY?
JUST ONE MINUTE...
AHEM.
CITIZENS OF THE CARDBOARD KINGDOM!
MY COLLEAGUES AND I HAVE COMPILED AN **EXHAUSTIVE SUMMARY** OF ALL KNOWN **MONSTER SIGHTINGS**.
WITH **PICTURES**!

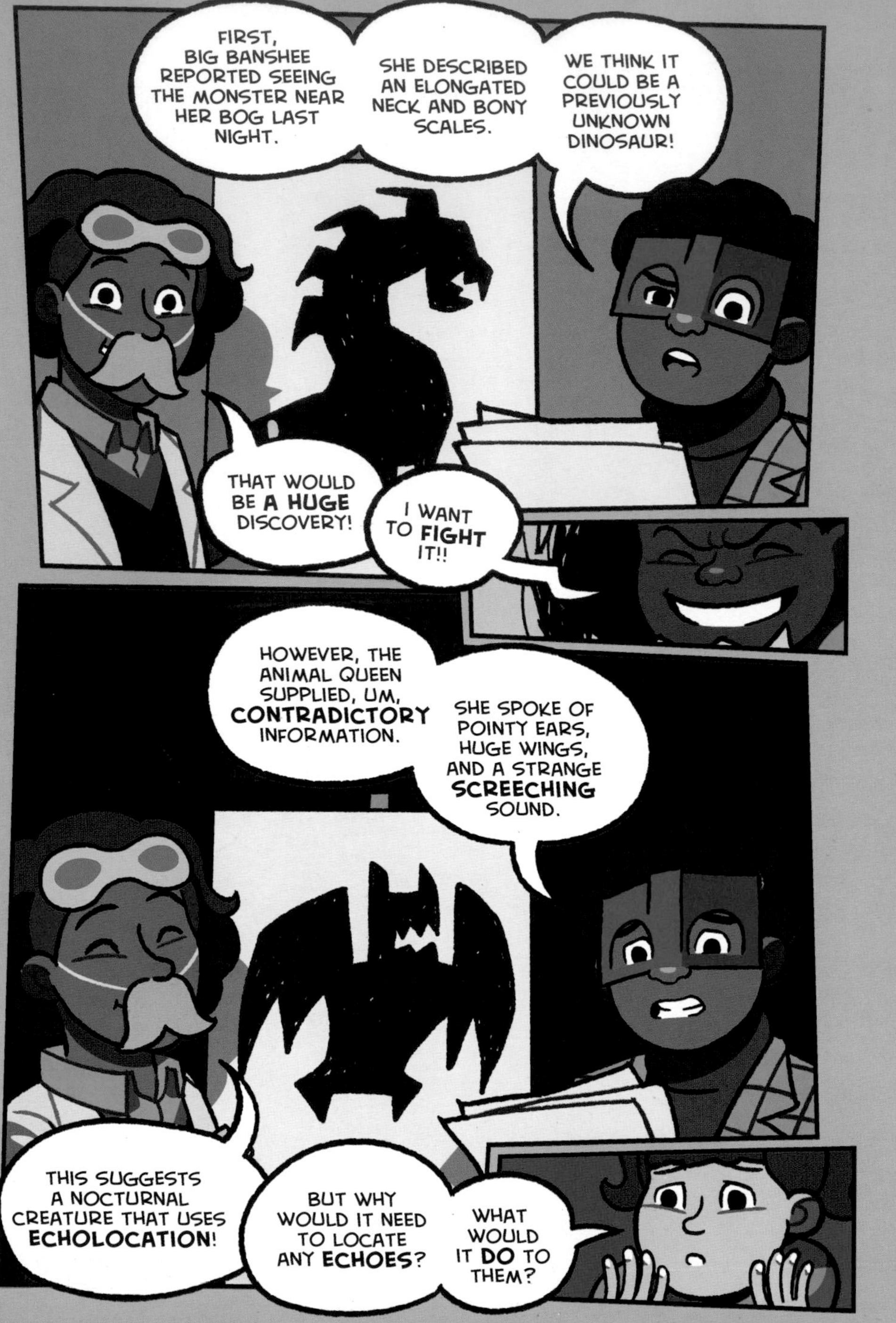

FIRST, BIG BANSHEE REPORTED SEEING THE MONSTER NEAR HER BOG LAST NIGHT.
SHE DESCRIBED AN ELONGATED NECK AND BONY SCALES.
WE THINK IT COULD BE A PREVIOUSLY UNKNOWN DINOSAUR!
THAT WOULD BE **A HUGE** DISCOVERY!
I WANT TO **FIGHT** IT!!
HOWEVER, THE ANIMAL QUEEN SUPPLIED, UM, **CONTRADICTORY** INFORMATION.
SHE SPOKE OF POINTY EARS, HUGE WINGS, AND A STRANGE **SCREECHING** SOUND.
THIS SUGGESTS A NOCTURNAL CREATURE THAT USES **ECHOLOCATION**!
BUT WHY WOULD IT NEED TO LOCATE ANY **ECHOES**?
WHAT WOULD IT **DO** TO THEM?

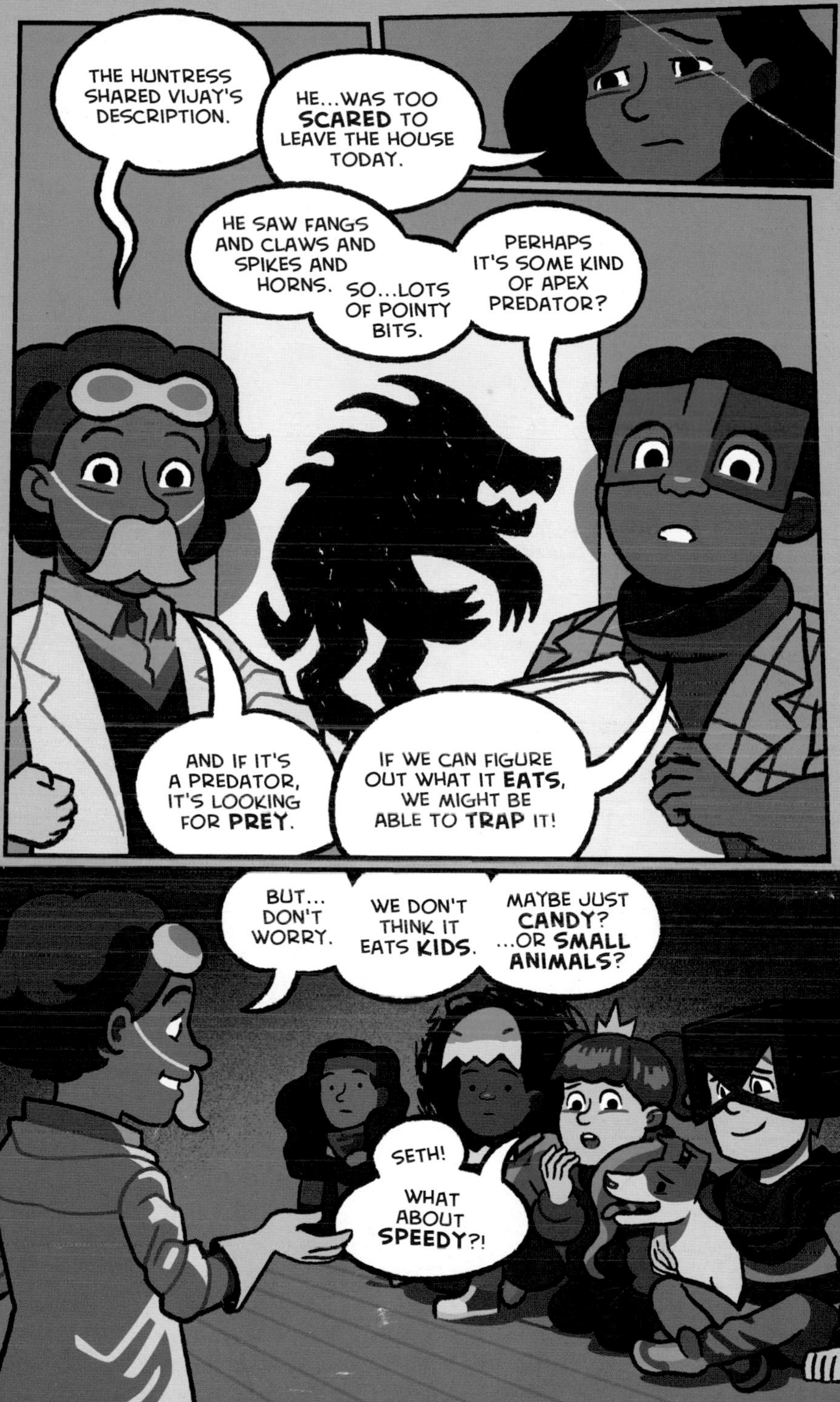
THE HUNTRESS SHARED VIJAY'S DESCRIPTION.
HE...WAS TOO **SCARED** TO LEAVE THE HOUSE TODAY.
HE SAW FANGS AND CLAWS AND SPIKES AND HORNS.
SO...LOTS OF POINTY BITS.
PERHAPS IT'S SOME KIND OF APEX PREDATOR?
AND IF IT'S A PREDATOR, IT'S LOOKING FOR **PREY**.
IF WE CAN FIGURE OUT WHAT IT **EATS**, WE MIGHT BE ABLE TO **TRAP** IT!
BUT... DON'T WORRY.
WE DON'T THINK IT EATS **KIDS**.
MAYBE JUST **CANDY**? ...OR **SMALL ANIMALS**?
SETH!
WHAT ABOUT **SPEEDY**?!

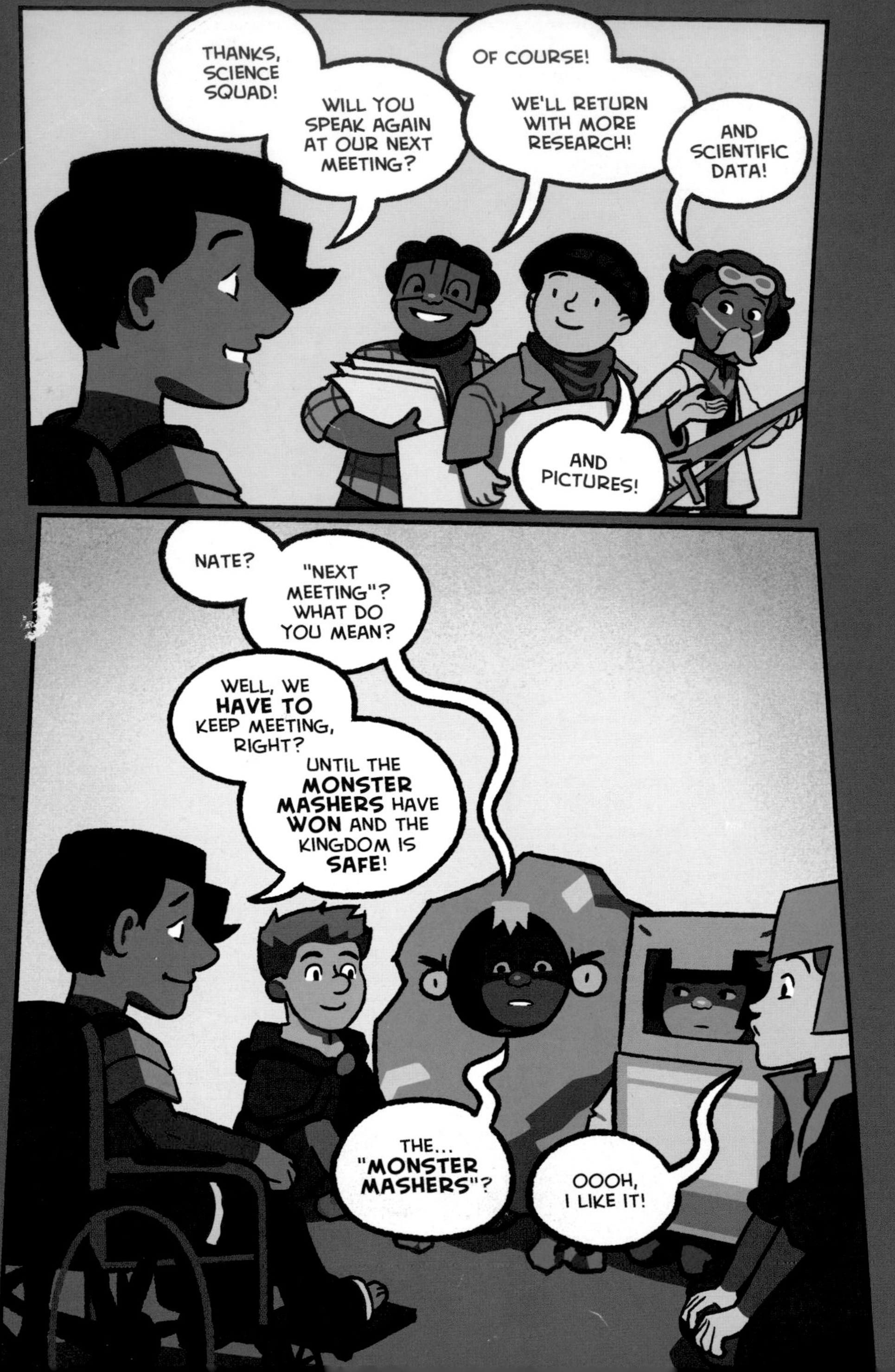
THANKS, SCIENCE SQUAD!
WILL YOU SPEAK AGAIN AT OUR NEXT MEETING?
OF COURSE!
WE'LL RETURN WITH MORE RESEARCH!
AND SCIENTIFIC DATA!
AND PICTURES!
NATE?
"NEXT MEETING"? WHAT DO YOU MEAN?
WELL, WE **HAVE TO** KEEP MEETING, RIGHT?
UNTIL THE **MONSTER MASHERS** HAVE **WON** AND THE KINGDOM IS **SAFE**!
THE... "**MONSTER MASHERS**"?
OOOH, I LIKE IT!

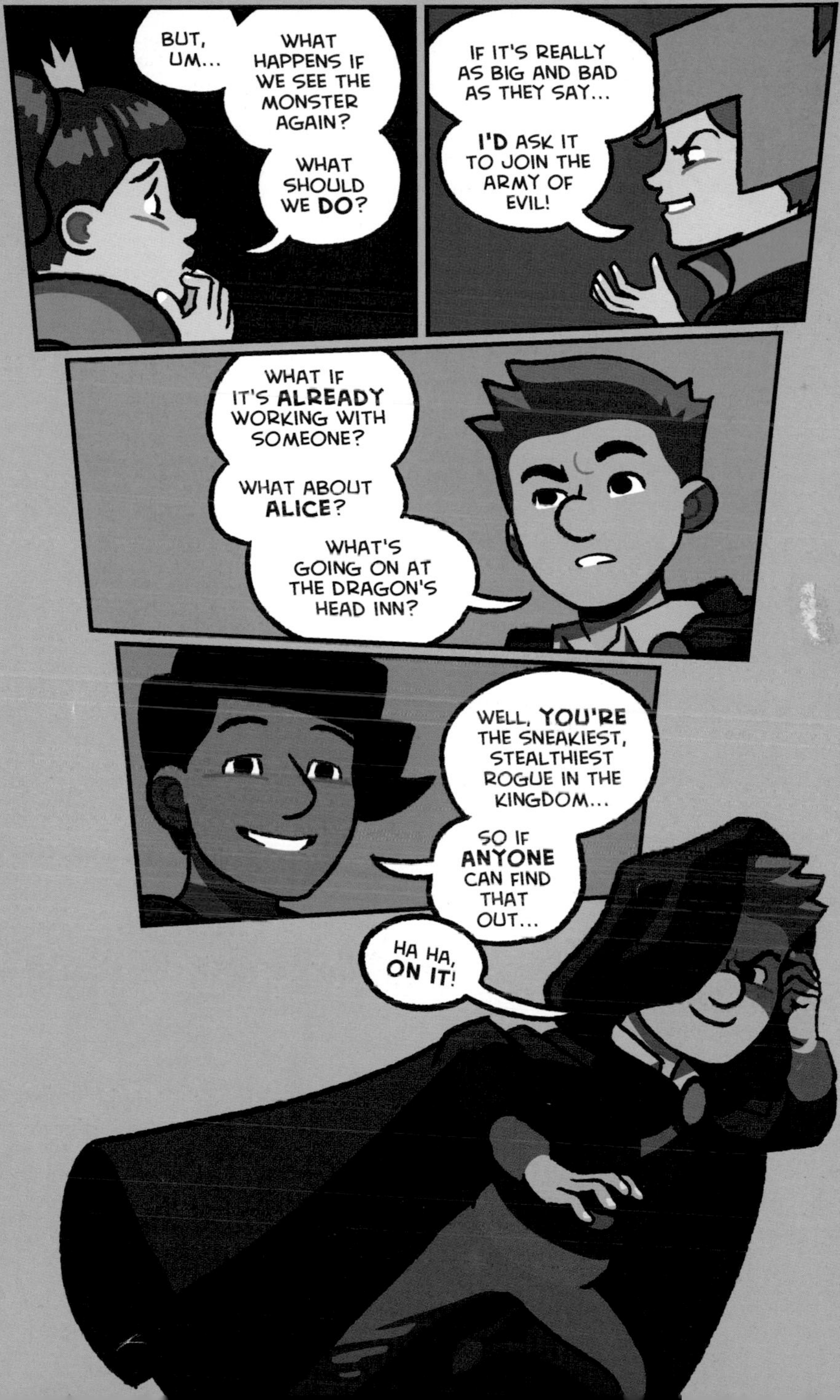
BUT, UM...
WHAT HAPPENS IF WE SEE THE MONSTER AGAIN?
WHAT SHOULD WE **DO**?
IF IT'S REALLY AS BIG AND BAD AS THEY SAY...
I'D ASK IT TO JOIN THE ARMY OF EVIL!
WHAT IF IT'S **ALREADY** WORKING WITH SOMEONE?
WHAT ABOUT **ALICE**?
WHAT'S GOING ON AT THE DRAGON'S HEAD INN?
WELL, **YOU'RE** THE SNEAKIEST, STEALTHIEST ROGUE IN THE KINGDOM...
SO IF **ANYONE** CAN FIND THAT OUT...
HA HA, **ON IT**!

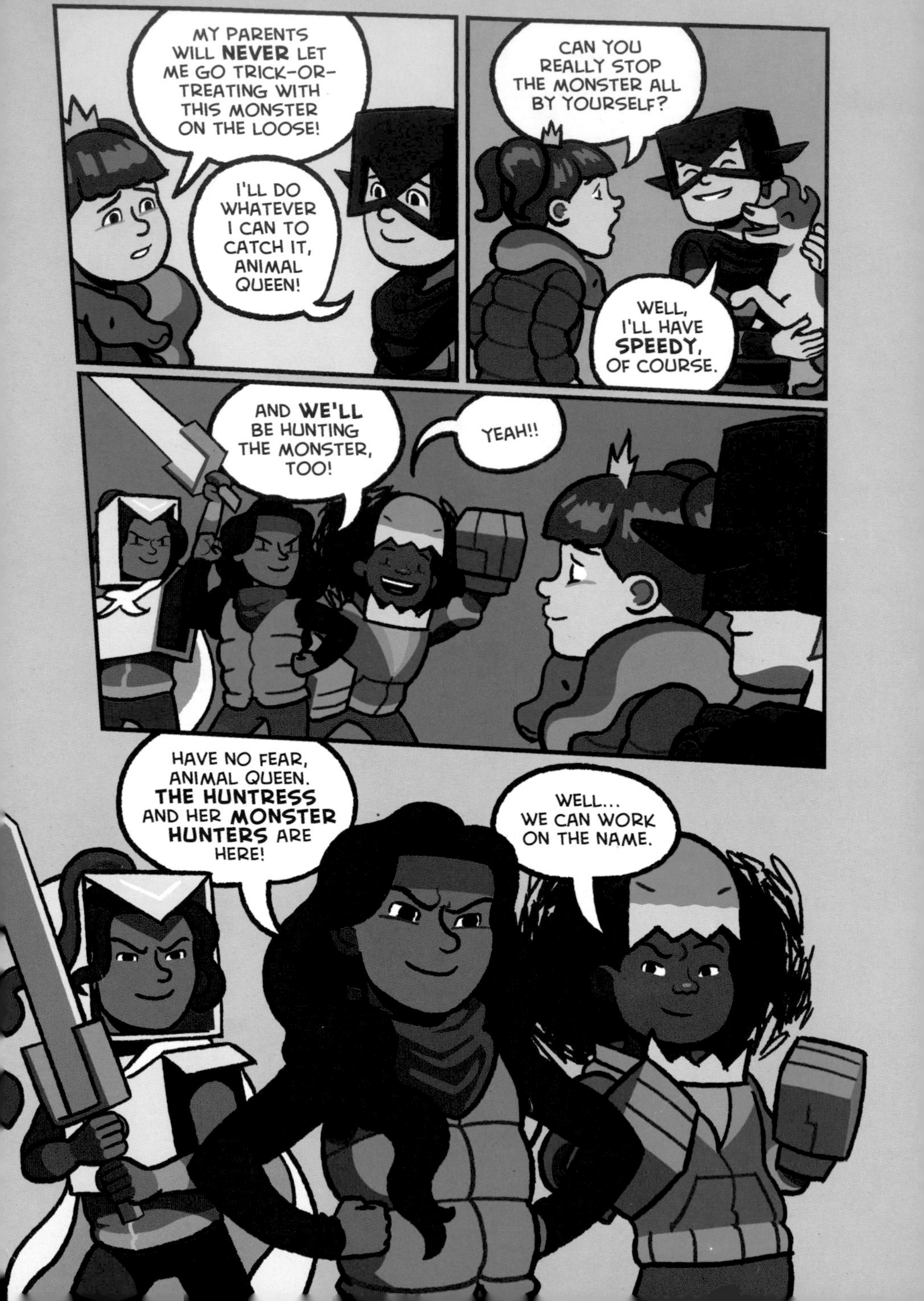
MY PARENTS WILL NEVER LET ME GO TRICK-OR-TREATING WITH THIS MONSTER ON THE LOOSE!
I'LL DO WHATEVER I CAN TO CATCH IT, ANIMAL QUEEN!
CAN YOU REALLY STOP THE MONSTER ALL BY YOURSELF?
WELL, I'LL HAVE SPEEDY, OF COURSE.
AND WE'LL BE HUNTING THE MONSTER, TOO!
YEAH!!
HAVE NO FEAR, ANIMAL QUEEN. THE HUNTRESS AND HER MONSTER HUNTERS ARE HERE!
WELL... WE CAN WORK ON THE NAME.

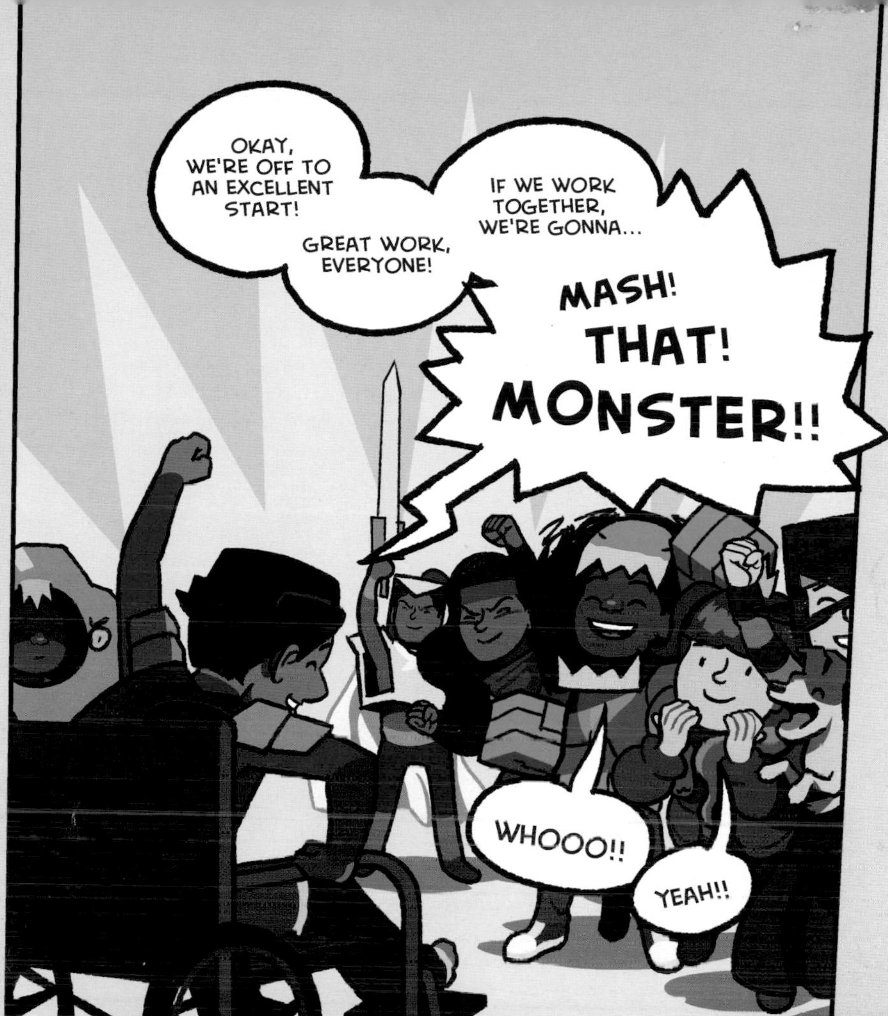
OKAY, WE'RE OFF TO AN EXCELLENT START!
GREAT WORK, EVERYONE!
IF WE WORK TOGETHER, WE'RE GONNA...
MASH! THAT! MONSTER!!
WHOOO!!
YEAH!!

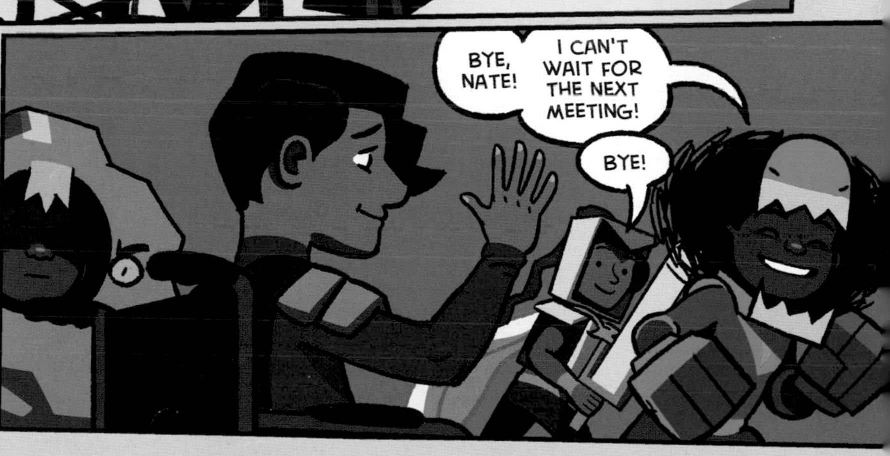
BYE, NATE!
I CAN'T WAIT FOR THE NEXT MEETING!
BYE!

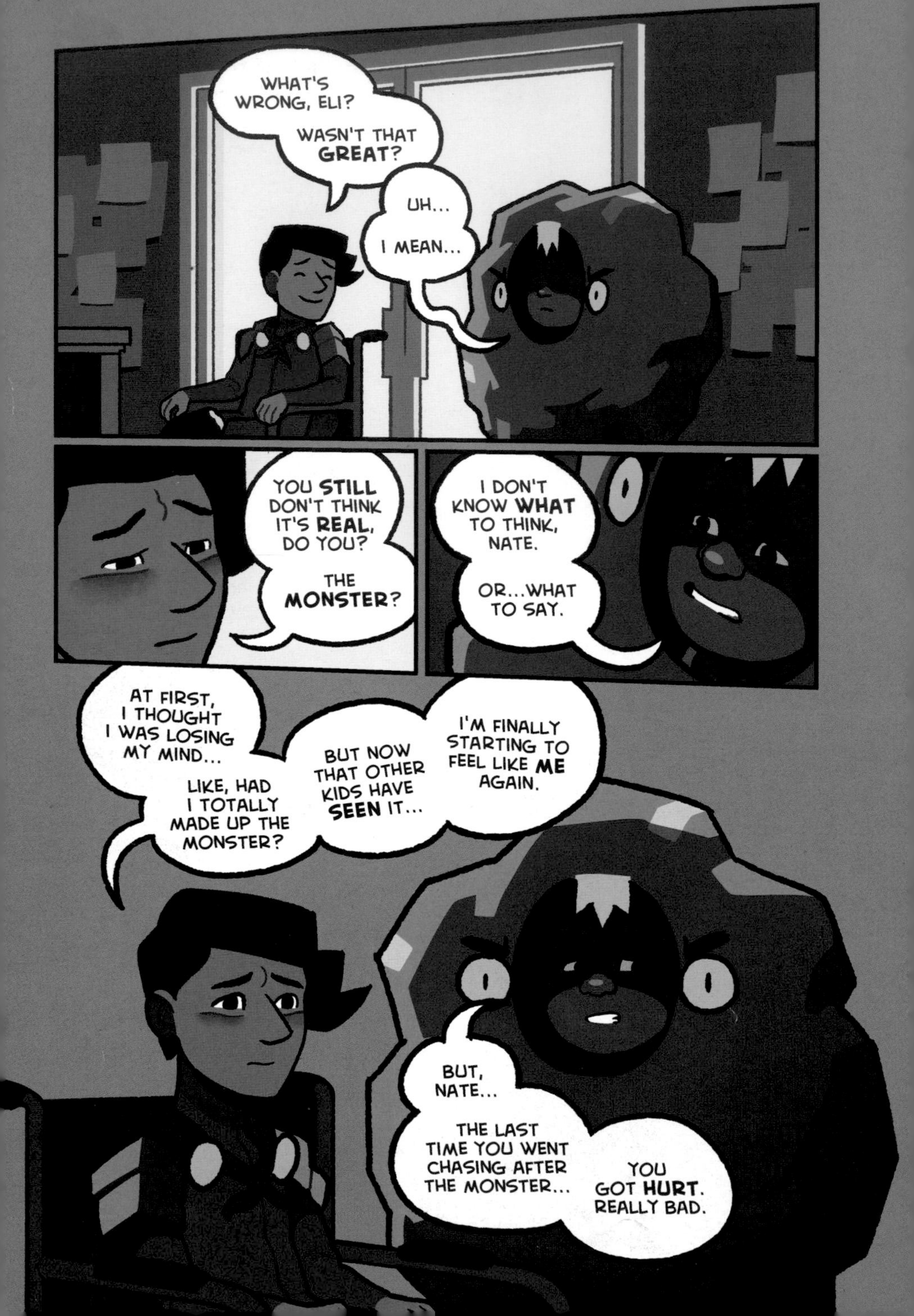
WHAT'S WRONG, ELI?
WASN'T THAT GREAT?
UH...
I MEAN...
YOU STILL DON'T THINK IT'S REAL, DO YOU?
THE MONSTER?
I DON'T KNOW WHAT TO THINK, NATE.
OR...WHAT TO SAY.
AT FIRST, I THOUGHT I WAS LOSING MY MIND...
LIKE, HAD I TOTALLY MADE UP THE MONSTER?
BUT NOW THAT OTHER KIDS HAVE SEEN IT...
I'M FINALLY STARTING TO FEEL LIKE ME AGAIN.
BUT, NATE...
THE LAST TIME YOU WENT CHASING AFTER THE MONSTER...
YOU GOT HURT. REALLY BAD.

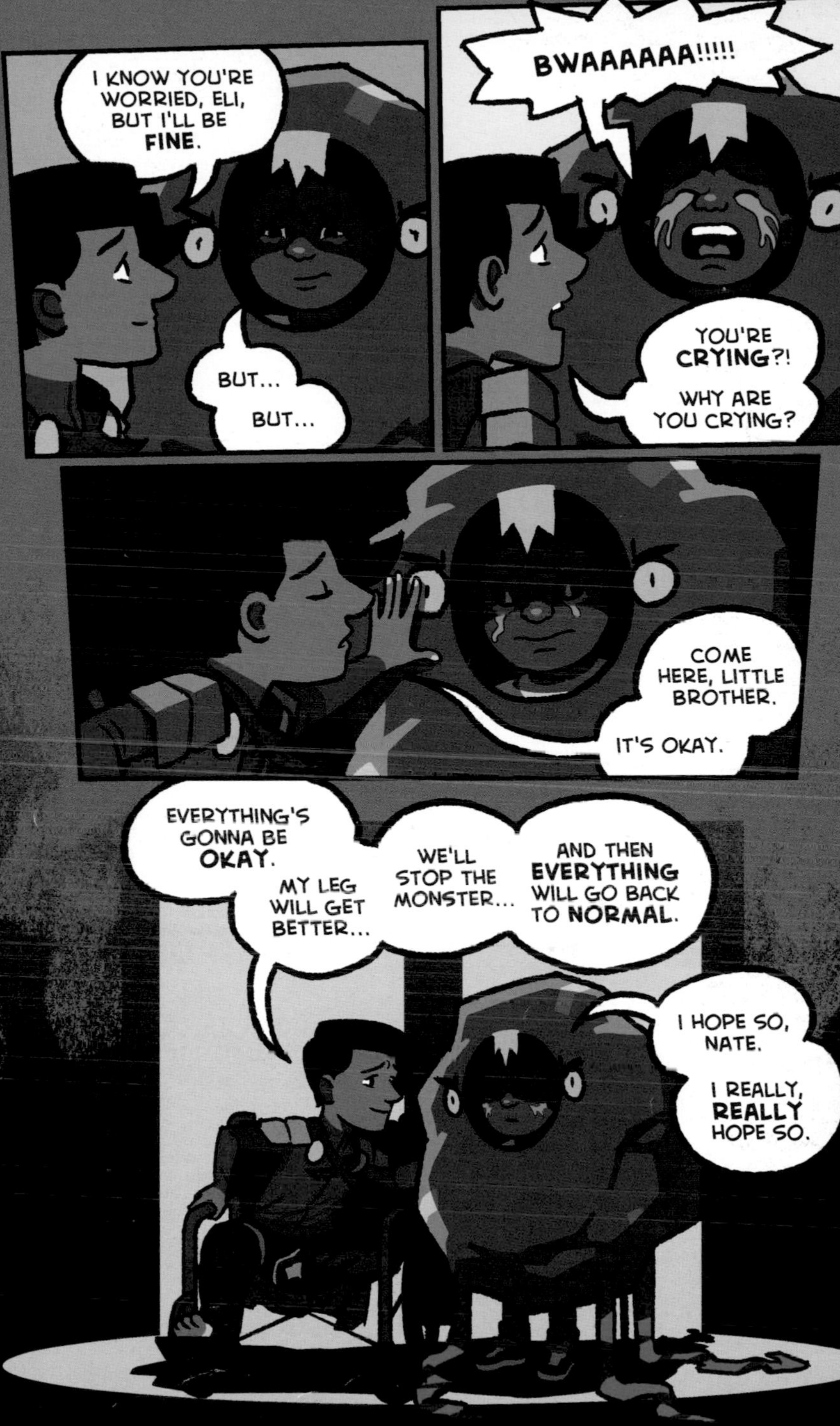
I KNOW YOU'RE WORRIED, ELI, BUT I'LL BE **FINE**.
BUT...
BUT...
BWAAAAAA!!!!!
YOU'RE **CRYING**?!
WHY ARE YOU CRYING?
COME HERE, LITTLE BROTHER.
IT'S OKAY.
EVERYTHING'S GONNA BE **OKAY**.
MY LEG WILL GET BETTER...
WE'LL STOP THE MONSTER...
AND THEN **EVERYTHING** WILL GO BACK TO **NORMAL**.
I HOPE SO, NATE.
I REALLY, **REALLY** HOPE SO.

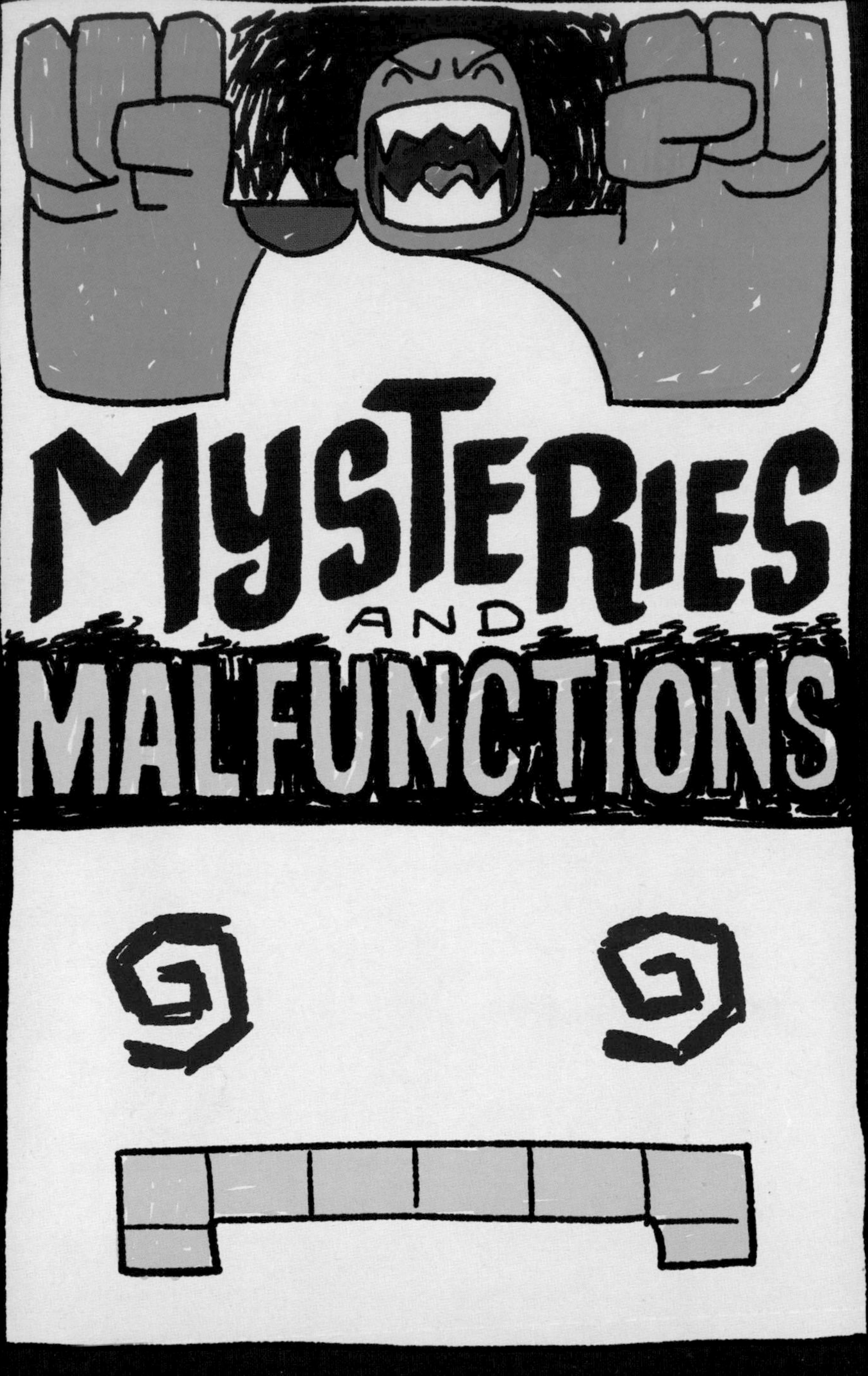
MYSTERIES
AND
MALFUNCTIONS

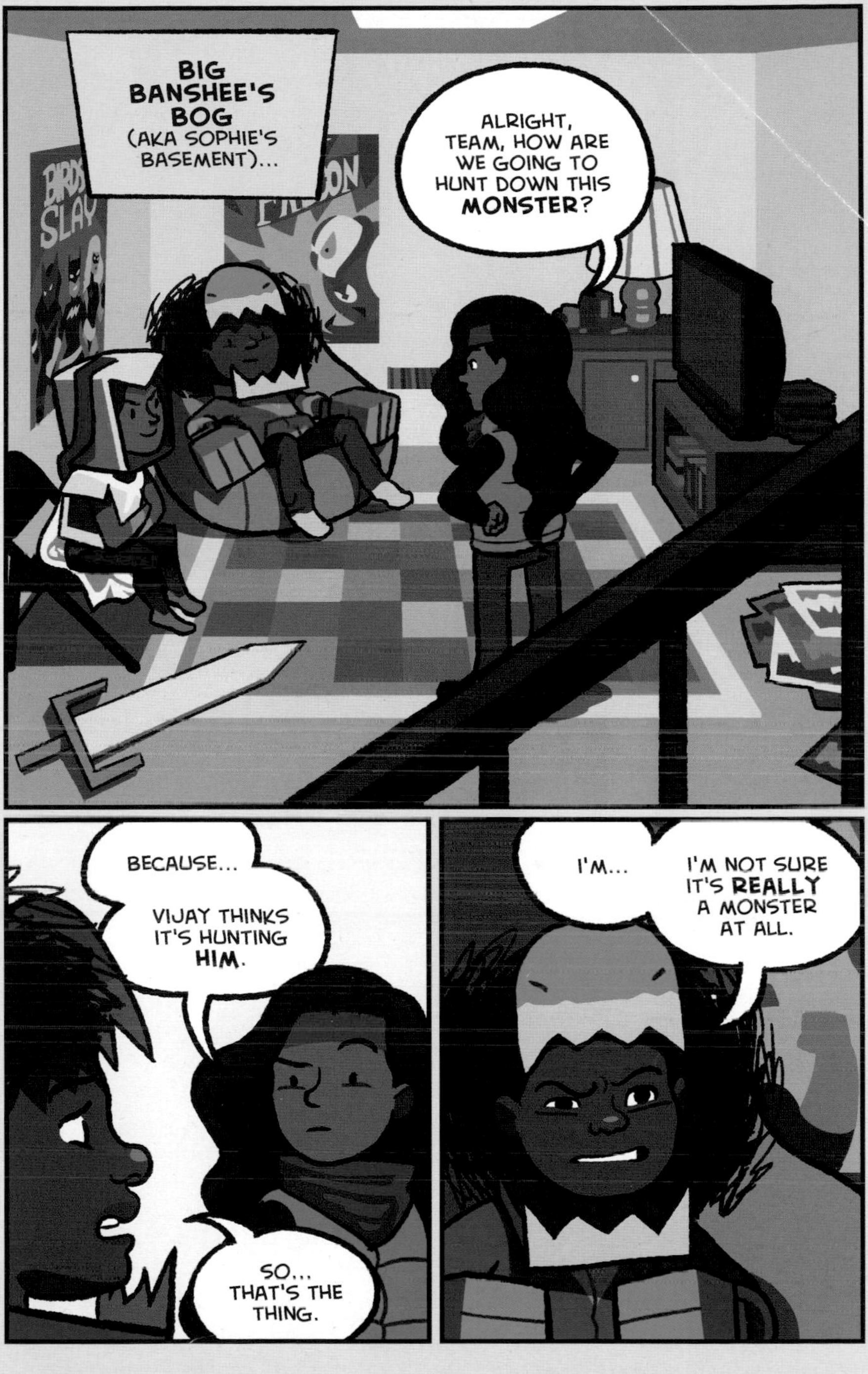
BIG BANSHEE'S BOG (AKA SOPHIE'S BASEMENT)...
ALRIGHT, TEAM, HOW ARE WE GOING TO HUNT DOWN THIS **MONSTER**?
BECAUSE...
VIJAY THINKS IT'S HUNTING **HIM**.
SO... THAT'S THE THING.
I'M...
I'M NOT SURE IT'S **REALLY** A MONSTER AT ALL.

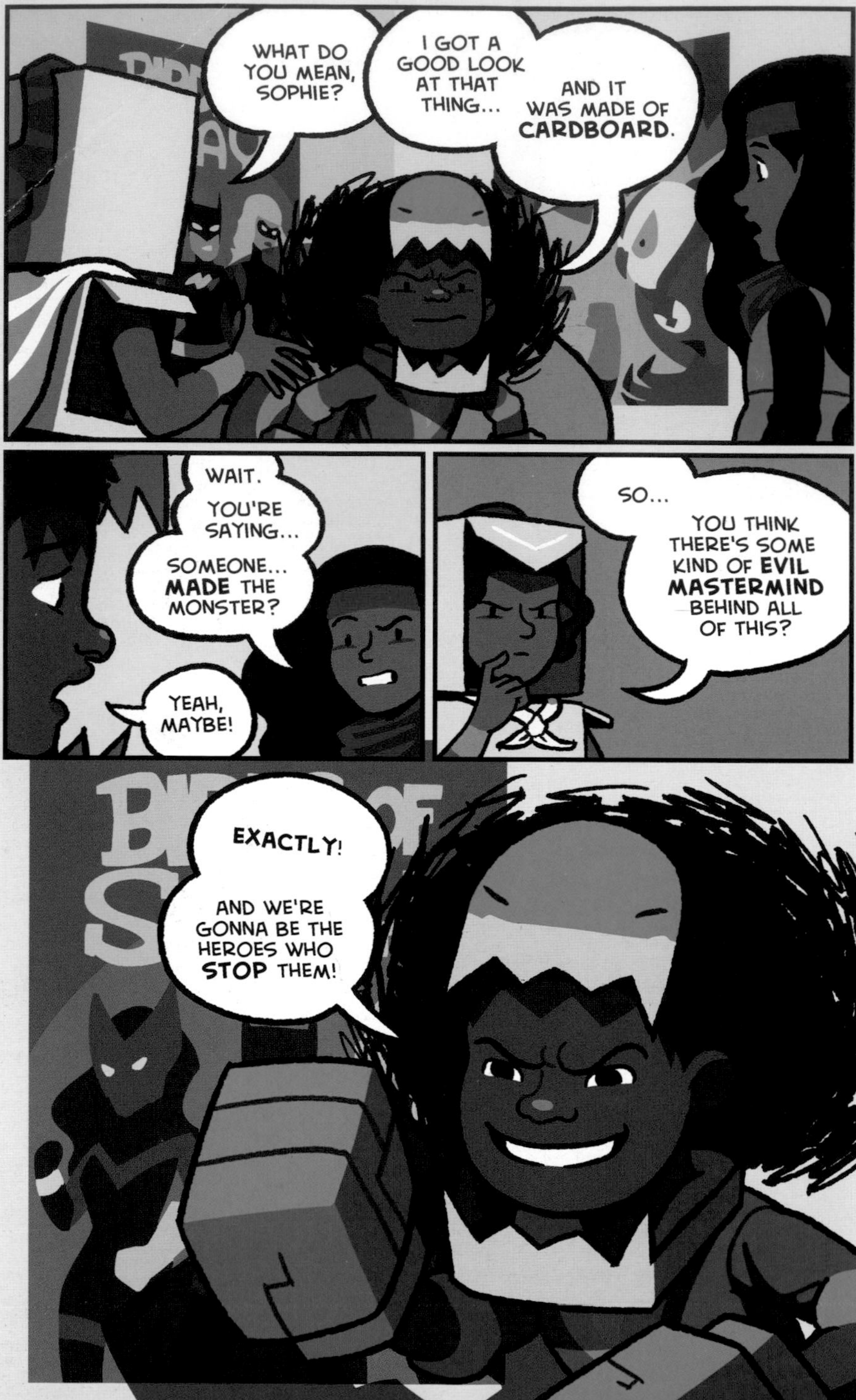
WHAT DO YOU MEAN, SOPHIE?
I GOT A GOOD LOOK AT THAT THING...
AND IT WAS MADE OF **CARDBOARD**.
WAIT.
YOU'RE SAYING...
SOMEONE... **MADE** THE MONSTER?
YEAH, MAYBE!
SO...
YOU THINK THERE'S SOME KIND OF **EVIL MASTERMIND** BEHIND ALL OF THIS?
EXACTLY!
AND WE'RE GONNA BE THE HEROES WHO **STOP** THEM!

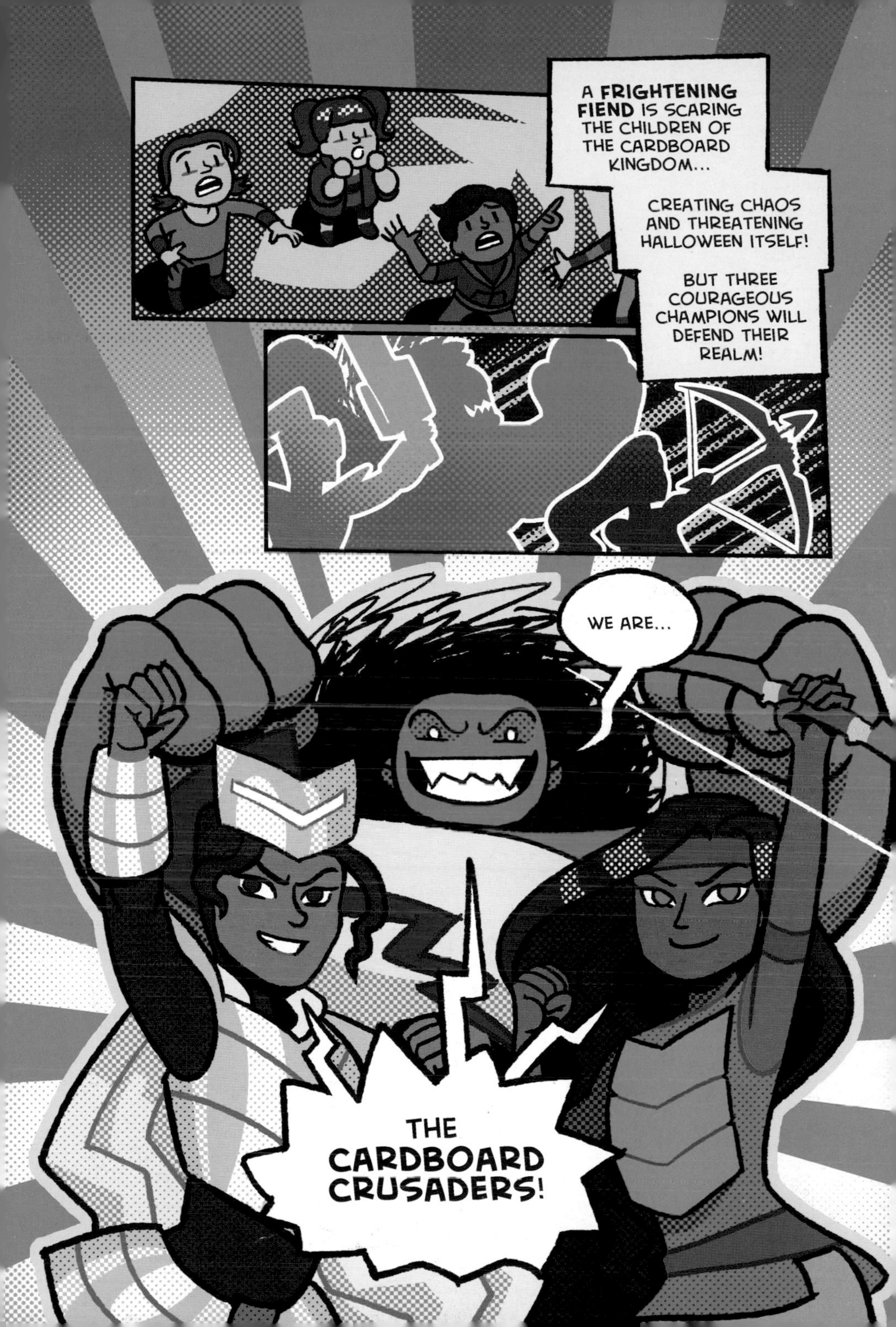
A **FRIGHTENING FIEND** IS SCARING THE CHILDREN OF THE CARDBOARD KINGDOM...
CREATING CHAOS AND THREATENING HALLOWEEN ITSELF!
BUT THREE COURAGEOUS CHAMPIONS WILL DEFEND THEIR REALM!
WE ARE...
THE CARDBOARD CRUSADERS!

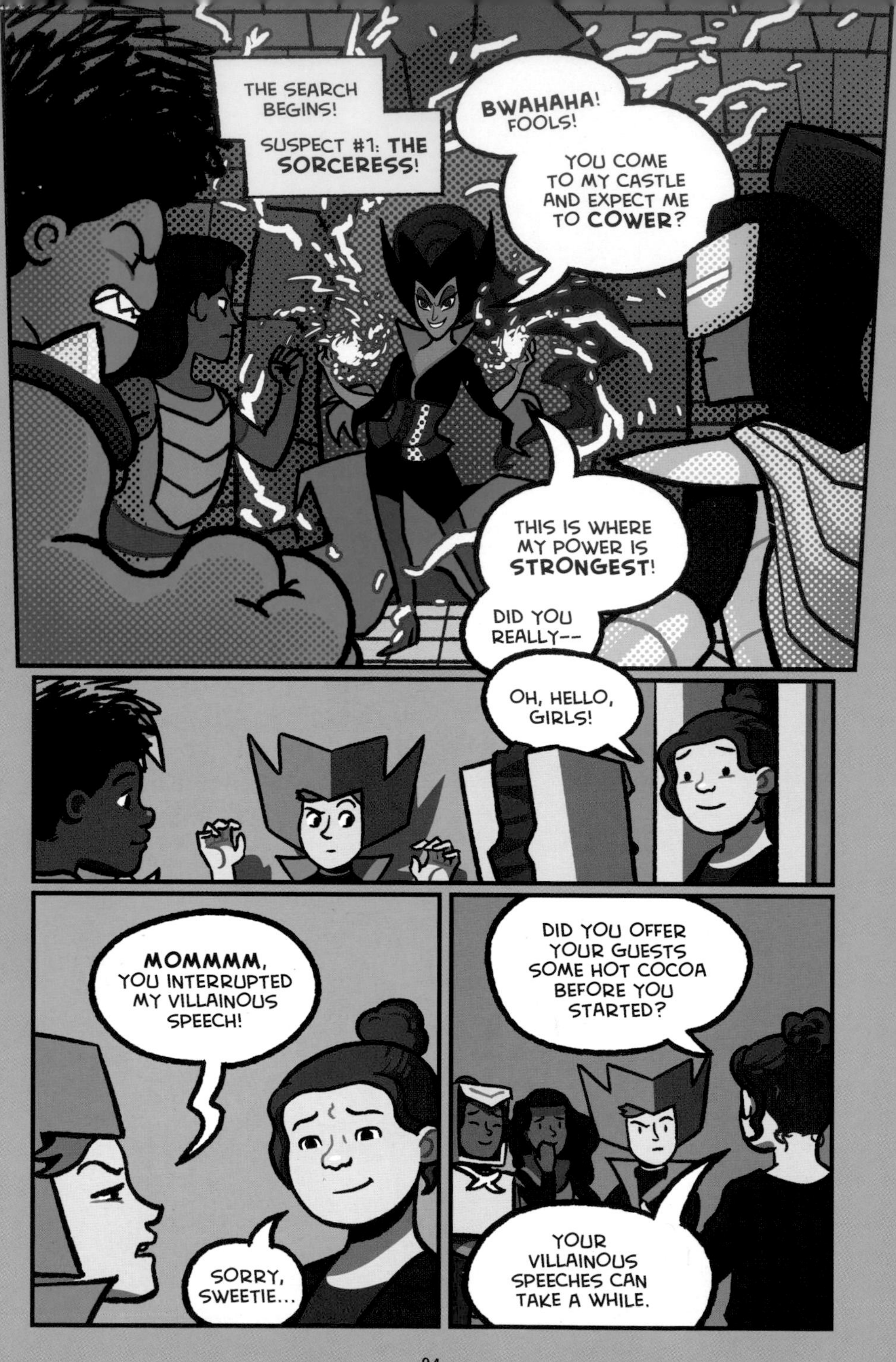
THE SEARCH BEGINS!
SUSPECT #1: THE SORCERESS!
BWAHAHA! FOOLS!
YOU COME TO MY CASTLE AND EXPECT ME TO COWER?
THIS IS WHERE MY POWER IS STRONGEST!
DID YOU REALLY--
OH, HELLO, GIRLS!
MOMMMM, YOU INTERRUPTED MY VILLAINOUS SPEECH!
SORRY, SWEETIE...
DID YOU OFFER YOUR GUESTS SOME HOT COCOA BEFORE YOU STARTED?
YOUR VILLAINOUS SPEECHES CAN TAKE A WHILE.

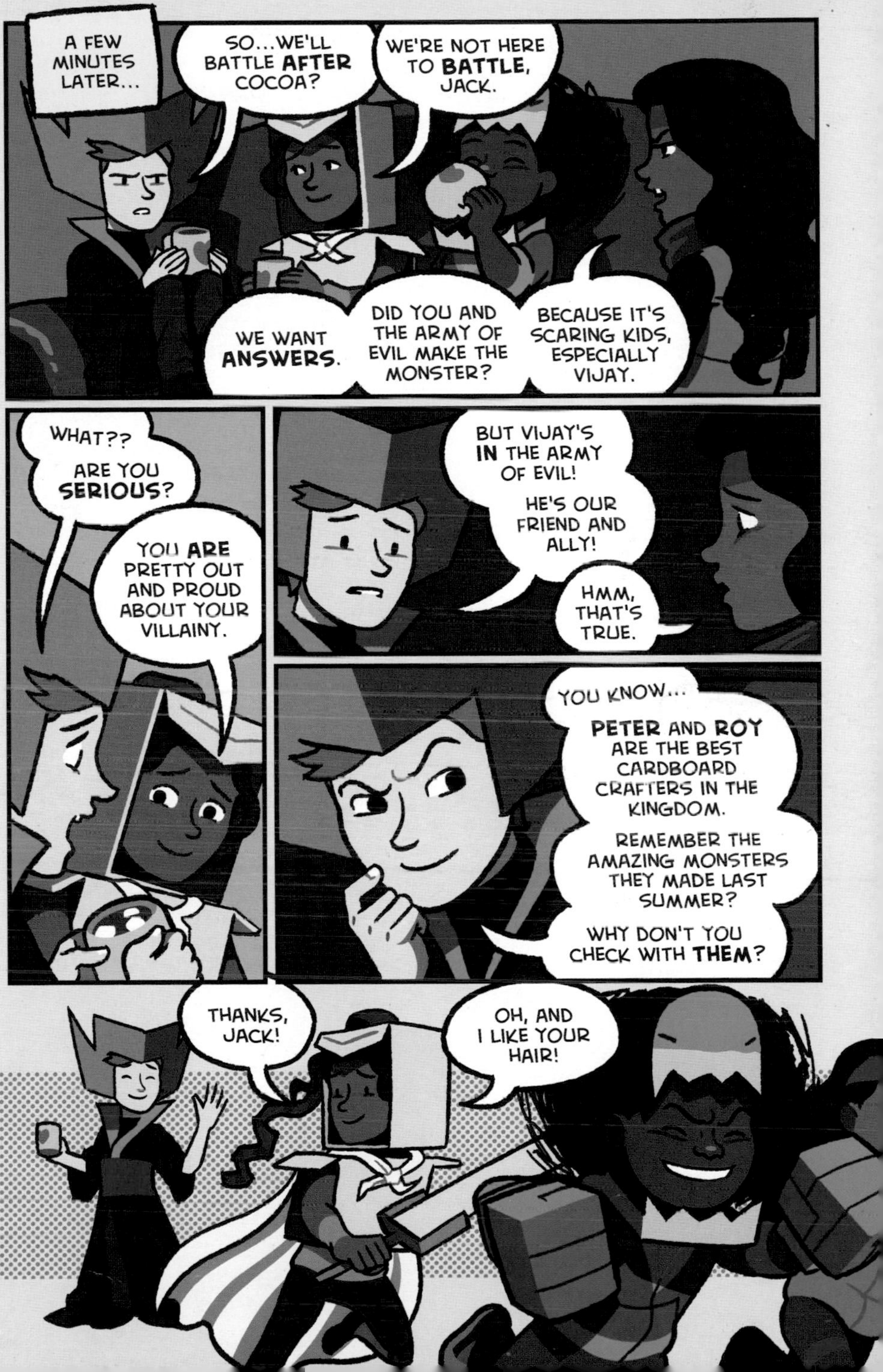
A FEW MINUTES LATER...
SO...WE'LL BATTLE **AFTER** COCOA?
WE'RE NOT HERE TO **BATTLE**, JACK.
WE WANT **ANSWERS**.
DID YOU AND THE ARMY OF EVIL MAKE THE MONSTER?
BECAUSE IT'S SCARING KIDS, ESPECIALLY VIJAY.
WHAT??
ARE YOU **SERIOUS**?
YOU **ARE** PRETTY OUT AND PROUD ABOUT YOUR VILLAINY.
BUT VIJAY'S **IN** THE ARMY OF EVIL!
HE'S OUR FRIEND AND ALLY!
HMM, THAT'S TRUE.
YOU KNOW...
PETER AND **ROY** ARE THE BEST CARDBOARD CRAFTERS IN THE KINGDOM.
REMEMBER THE AMAZING MONSTERS THEY MADE LAST SUMMER?
WHY DON'T YOU CHECK WITH **THEM**?
THANKS, JACK!
OH, AND I LIKE YOUR HAIR!

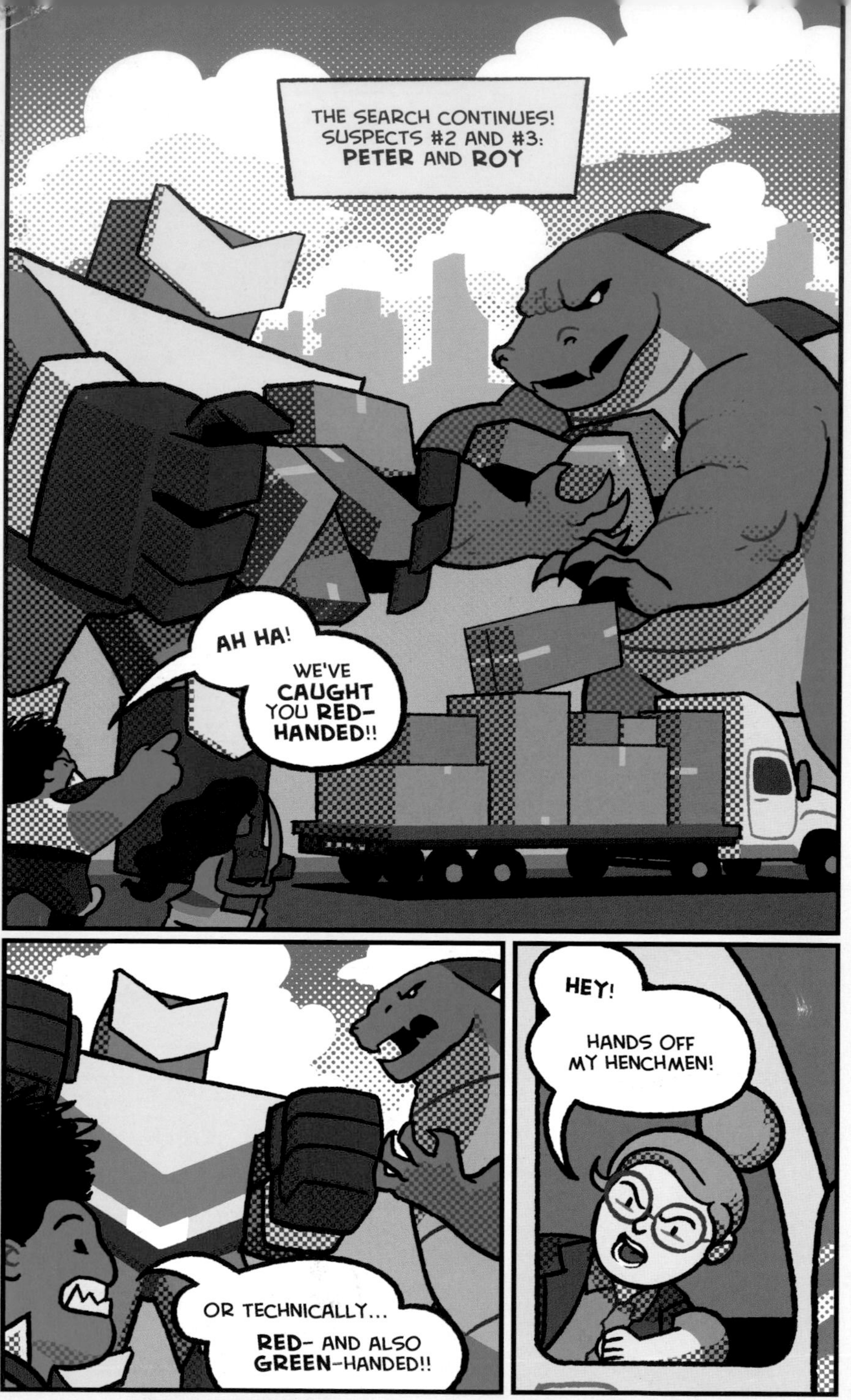
THE SEARCH CONTINUES! SUSPECTS #2 AND #3: PETER AND ROY
AH HA!
WE'VE CAUGHT YOU RED-HANDED!!
OR TECHNICALLY...
RED- AND ALSO GREEN-HANDED!!
HEY!
HANDS OFF MY HENCHMEN!

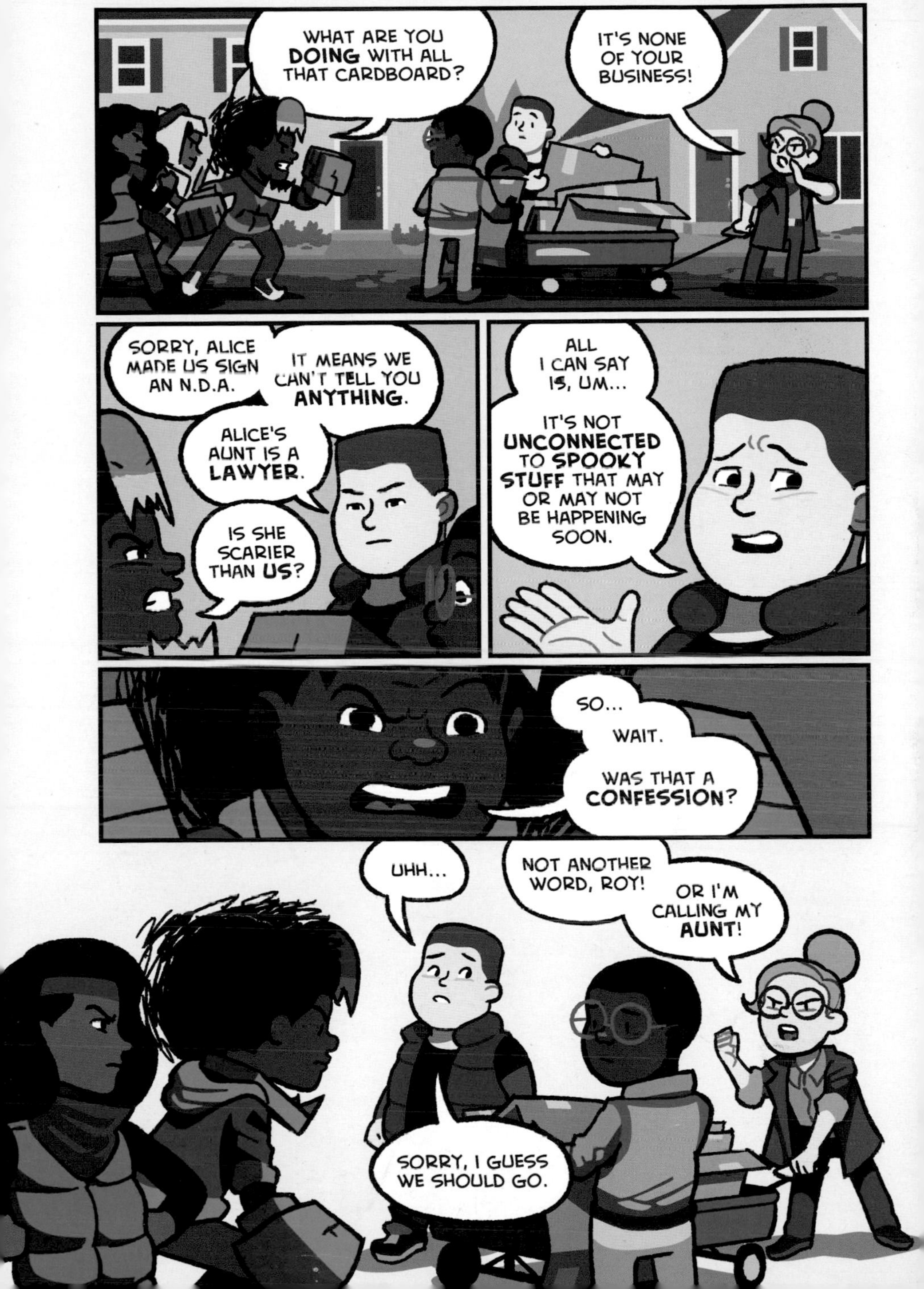

WHAT ARE YOU **DOING** WITH ALL THAT CARDBOARD?
IT'S NONE OF YOUR BUSINESS!
SORRY, ALICE MADE US SIGN AN N.D.A.
IT MEANS WE CAN'T TELL YOU **ANYTHING**.
ALICE'S AUNT IS A **LAWYER**.
IS SHE SCARIER THAN **US**?
ALL I CAN SAY IS, UM...
IT'S NOT **UNCONNECTED** TO **SPOOKY STUFF** THAT MAY OR MAY NOT BE HAPPENING SOON.
SO...
WAIT.
WAS THAT A **CONFESSION**?
UHH...
NOT ANOTHER WORD, ROY!
OR I'M CALLING MY **AUNT**!
SORRY, I GUESS WE SHOULD GO.

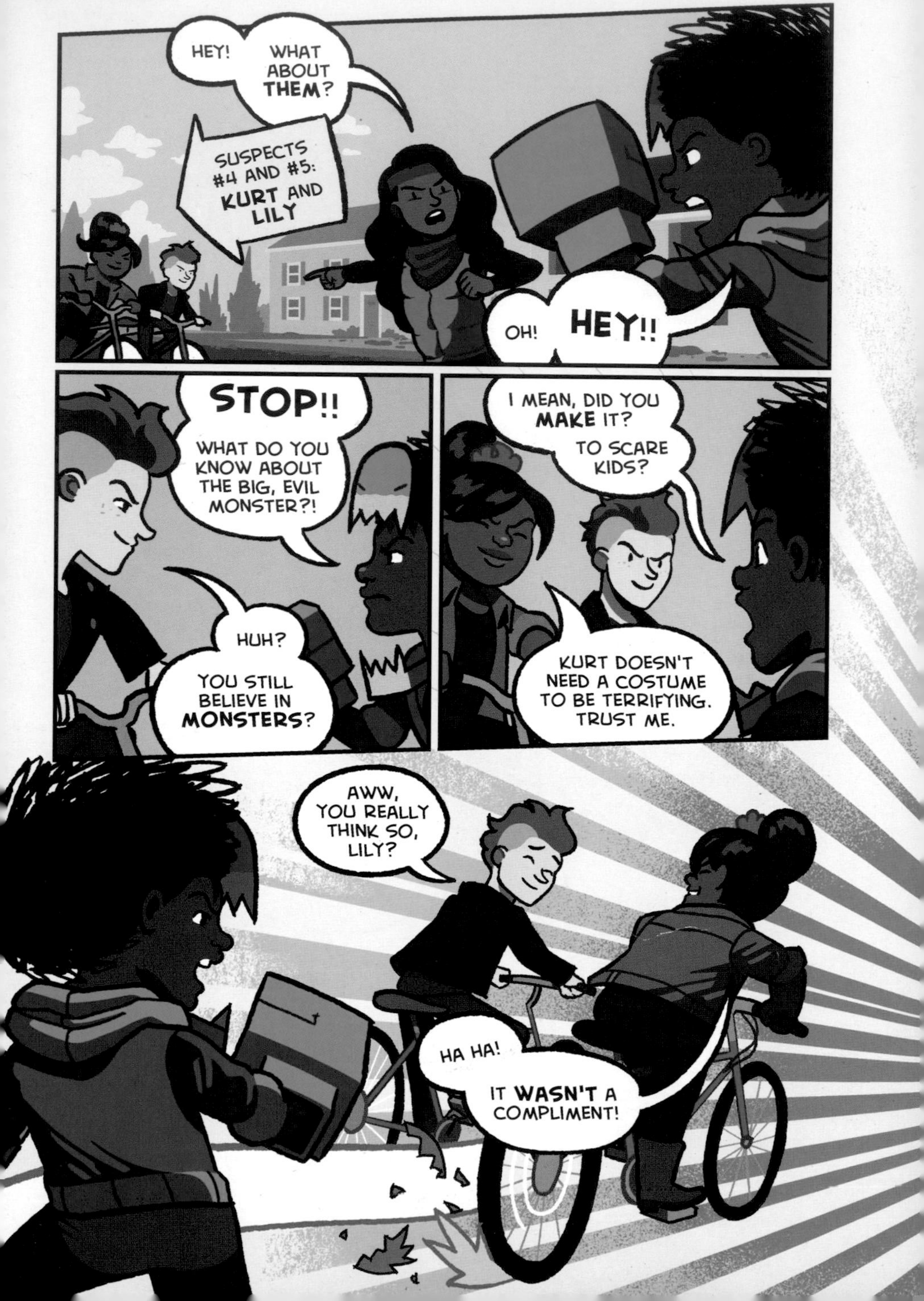
HEY! WHAT ABOUT THEM?
SUSPECTS #4 AND #5: KURT AND LILY
OH! HEY!!
STOP!!
WHAT DO YOU KNOW ABOUT THE BIG, EVIL MONSTER?!
HUH?
YOU STILL BELIEVE IN MONSTERS?
I MEAN, DID YOU MAKE IT?
TO SCARE KIDS?
KURT DOESN'T NEED A COSTUME TO BE TERRIFYING. TRUST ME.
AWW, YOU REALLY THINK SO, LILY?
HA HA!
IT WASN'T A COMPLIMENT!

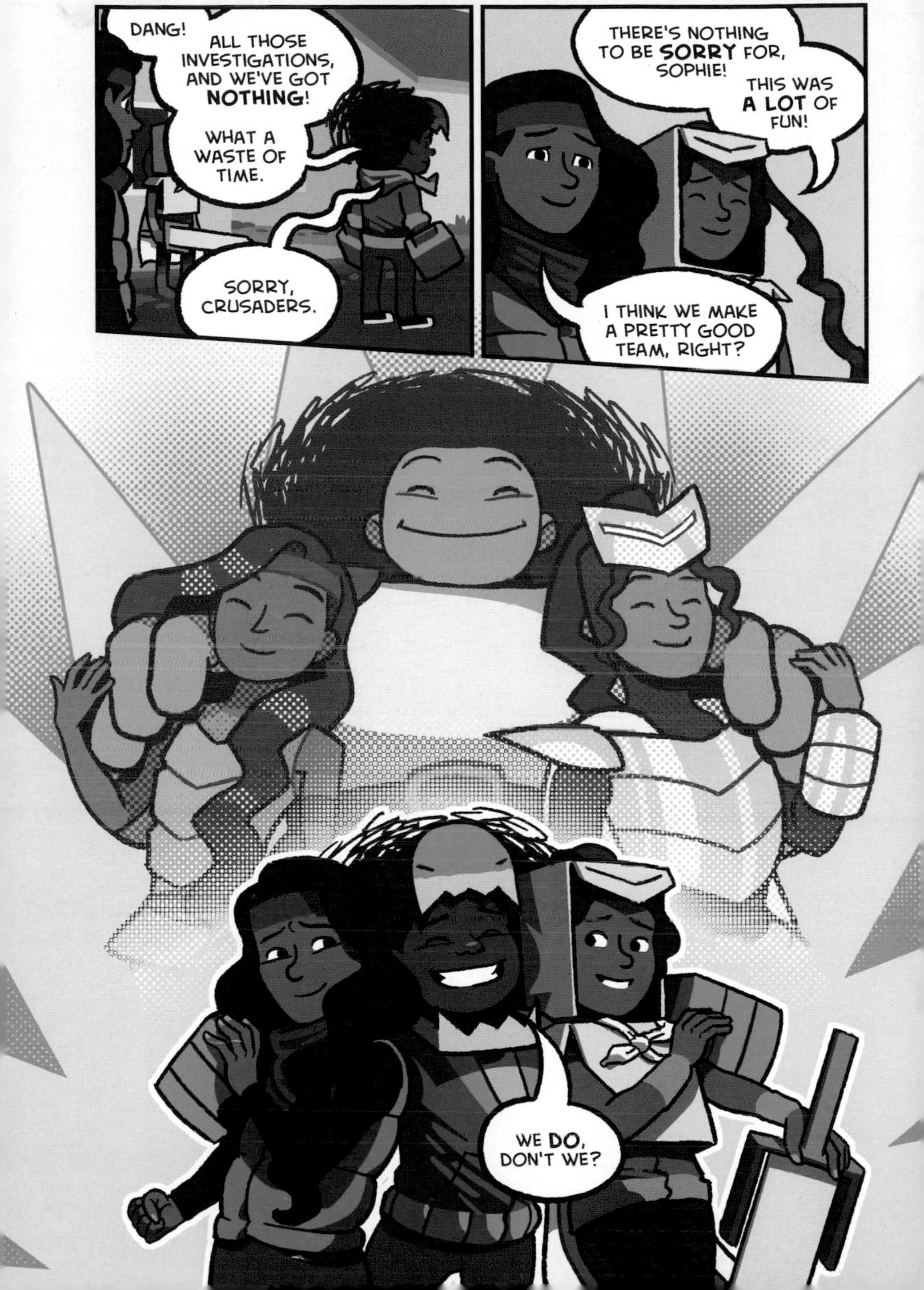
DANG!
ALL THOSE INVESTIGATIONS, AND WE'VE GOT **NOTHING**!
WHAT A WASTE OF TIME.
SORRY, CRUSADERS.
THERE'S NOTHING TO BE **SORRY** FOR, SOPHIE!
THIS WAS **A LOT** OF FUN!
I THINK WE MAKE A PRETTY GOOD TEAM, RIGHT?
WE **DO**, DON'T WE?

SOMEWHERE ELSE IN THE KINGDOM...
TARGET ACQUIRED.
EQUIPPING WEAPONS.
AND NOW...
HEH.
FIRE!
FSHHHH
DINK
HUH?

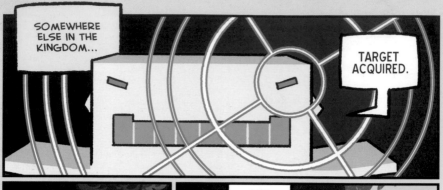

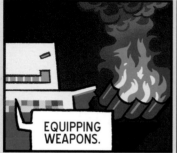

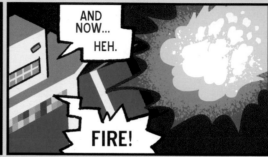

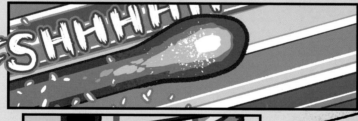

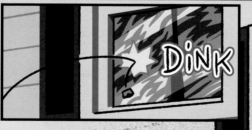

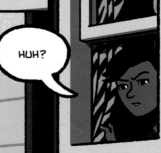

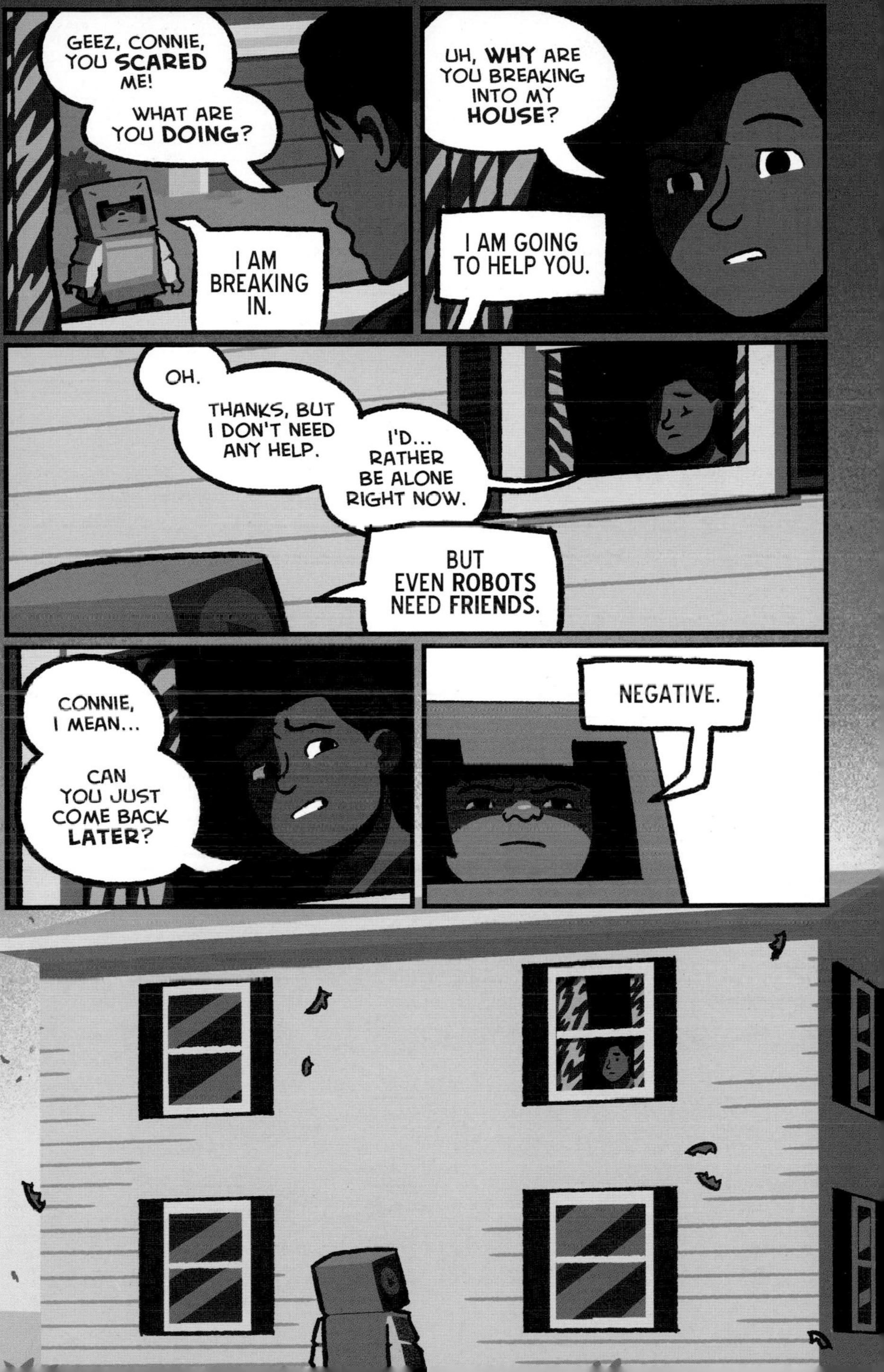
GEEZ, CONNIE, YOU SCARED ME!
WHAT ARE YOU DOING?
I AM BREAKING IN.
UH, WHY ARE YOU BREAKING INTO MY HOUSE?
I AM GOING TO HELP YOU.
OH.
THANKS, BUT I DON'T NEED ANY HELP.
I'D... RATHER BE ALONE RIGHT NOW.
BUT EVEN ROBOTS NEED FRIENDS.
CONNIE, I MEAN...
CAN YOU JUST COME BACK LATER?
NEGATIVE.

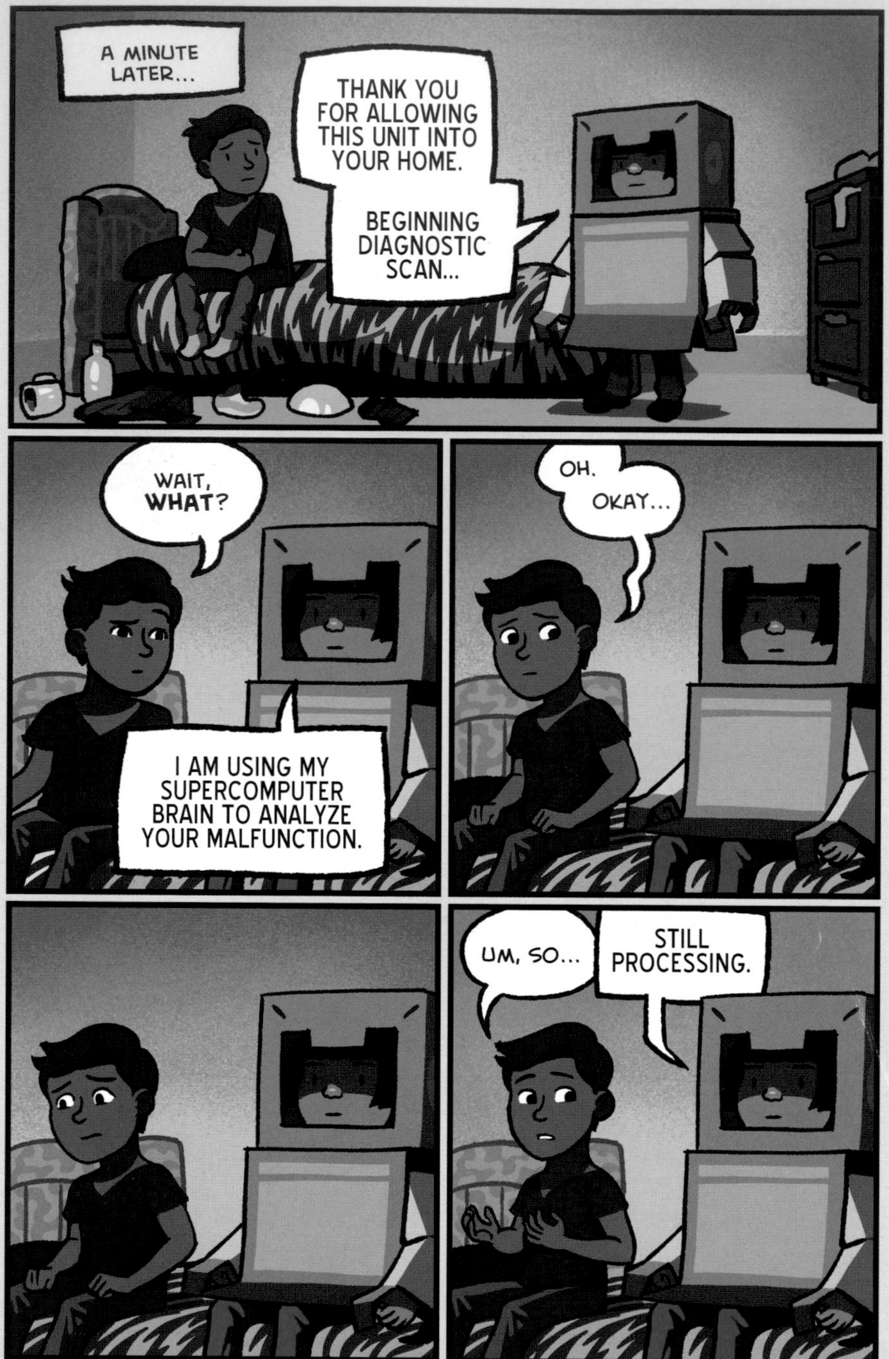
A MINUTE LATER...
THANK YOU FOR ALLOWING THIS UNIT INTO YOUR HOME.
BEGINNING DIAGNOSTIC SCAN...
WAIT, **WHAT**?
I AM USING MY SUPERCOMPUTER BRAIN TO ANALYZE YOUR MALFUNCTION.
OH.
OKAY...
UM, SO...
STILL PROCESSING.

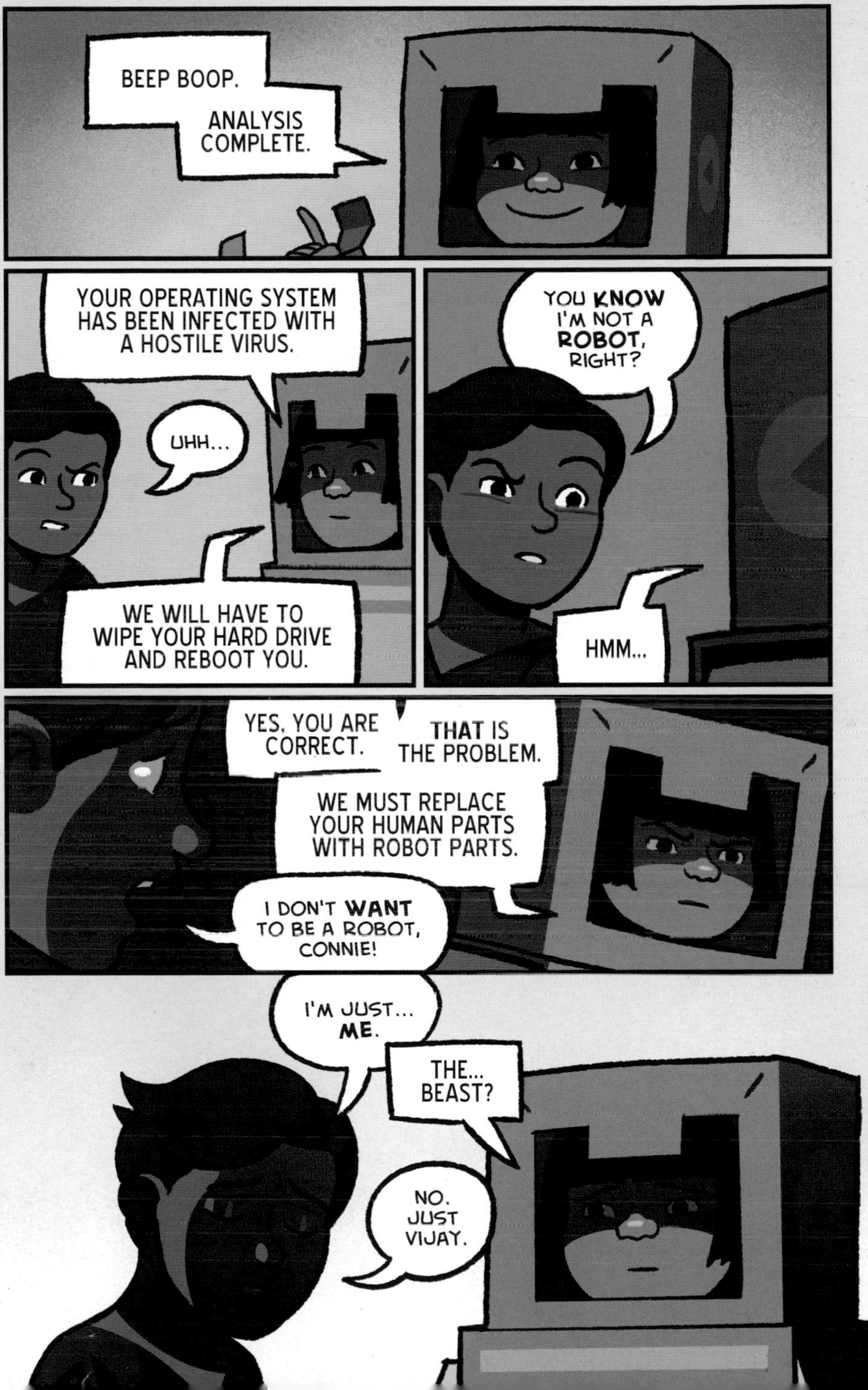
BEEP BOOP.
ANALYSIS COMPLETE.
YOUR OPERATING SYSTEM HAS BEEN INFECTED WITH A HOSTILE VIRUS.
UHH...
WE WILL HAVE TO WIPE YOUR HARD DRIVE AND REBOOT YOU.
YOU KNOW I'M NOT A ROBOT, RIGHT?
HMM...
YES, YOU ARE CORRECT.
THAT IS THE PROBLEM.
WE MUST REPLACE YOUR HUMAN PARTS WITH ROBOT PARTS.
I DON'T WANT TO BE A ROBOT, CONNIE!
I'M JUST... ME.
THE... BEAST?
NO. JUST VIJAY.

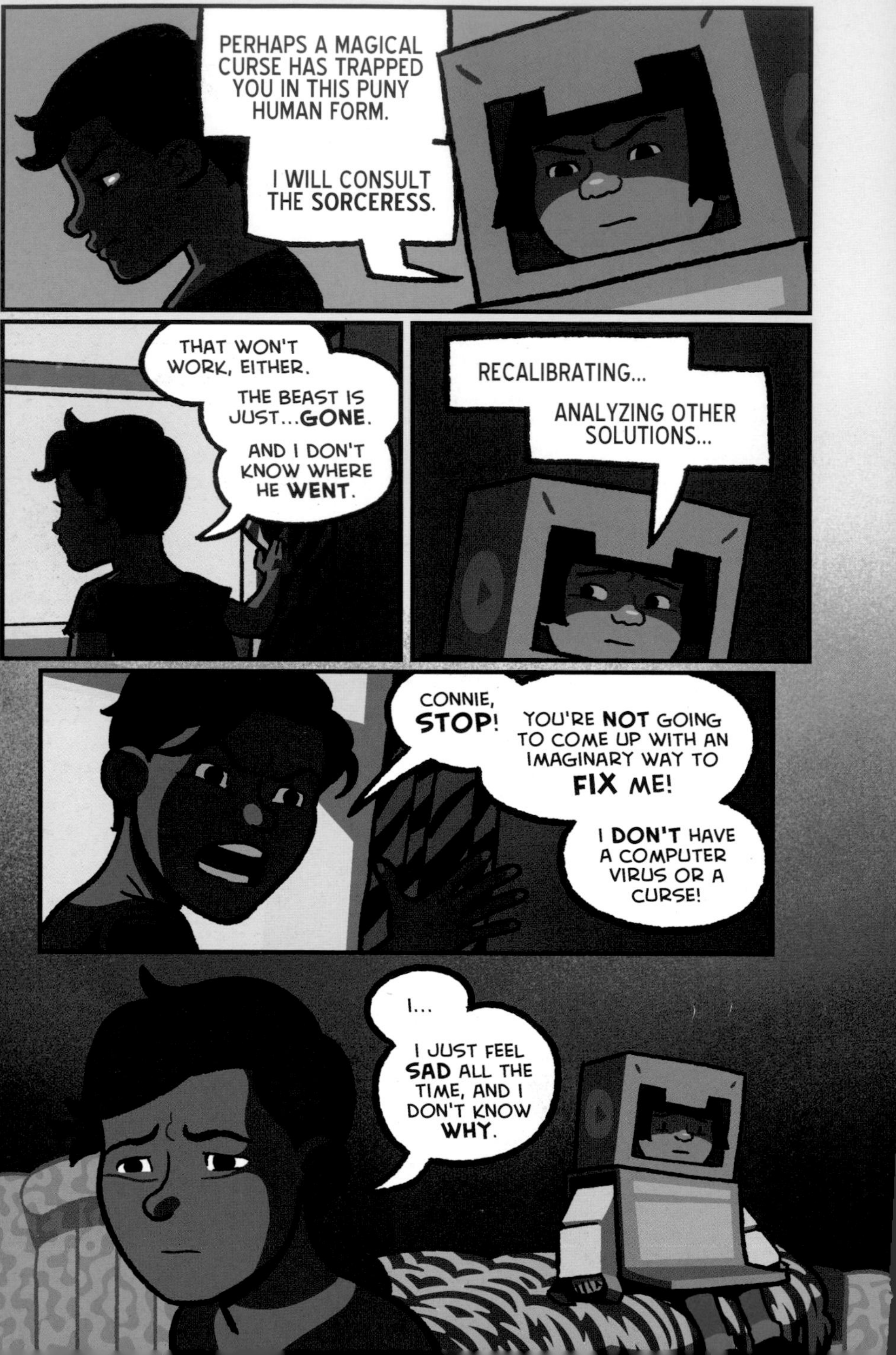
PERHAPS A MAGICAL CURSE HAS TRAPPED YOU IN THIS PUNY HUMAN FORM.
I WILL CONSULT THE SORCERESS.
THAT WON'T WORK, EITHER.
THE BEAST IS JUST...GONE.
AND I DON'T KNOW WHERE HE WENT.
RECALIBRATING...
ANALYZING OTHER SOLUTIONS...
CONNIE, STOP!
YOU'RE NOT GOING TO COME UP WITH AN IMAGINARY WAY TO FIX ME!
I DON'T HAVE A COMPUTER VIRUS OR A CURSE!
I...
I JUST FEEL SAD ALL THE TIME, AND I DON'T KNOW WHY.

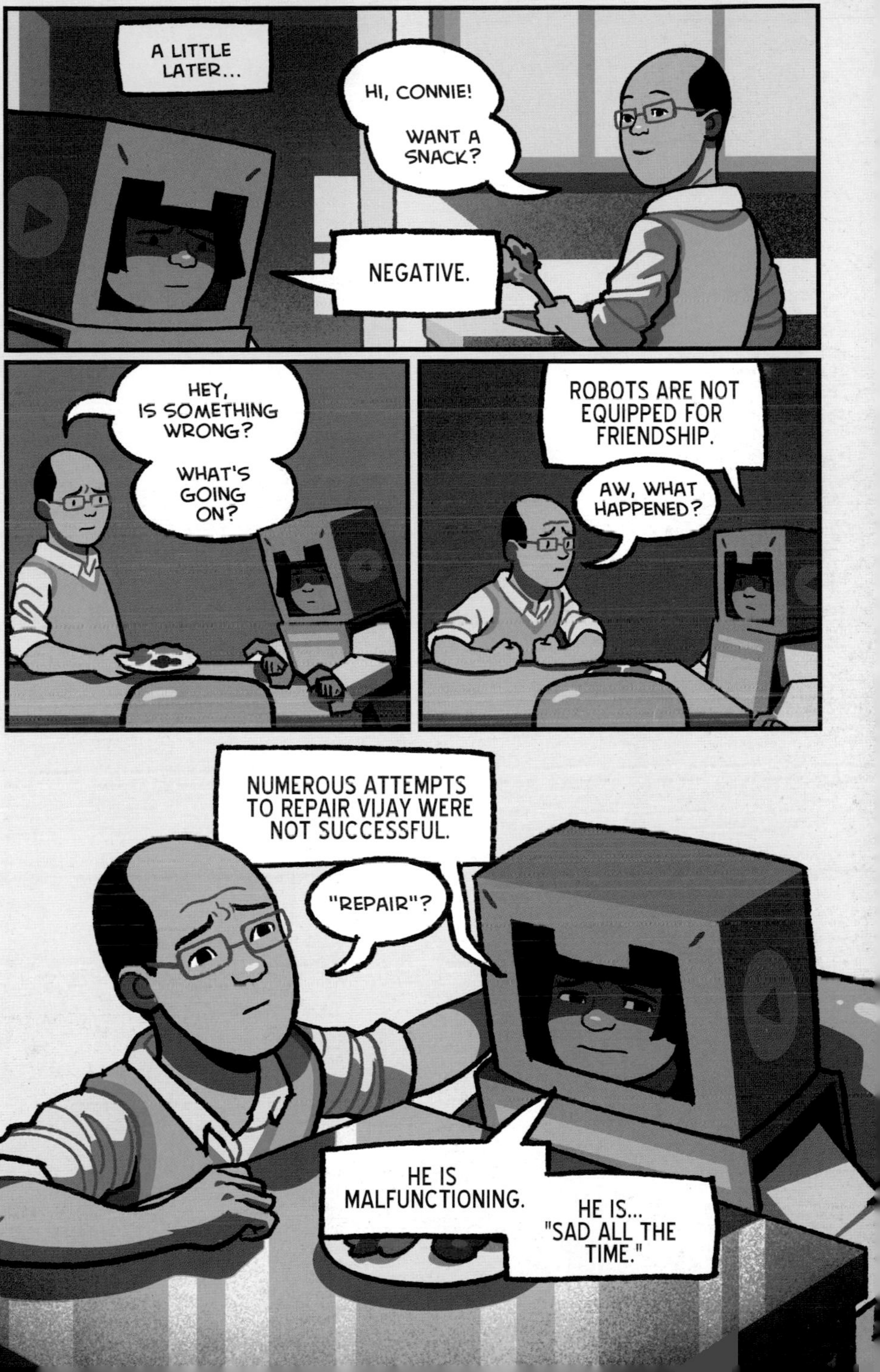
A LITTLE LATER...
HI, CONNIE!
WANT A SNACK?
NEGATIVE.
HEY, IS SOMETHING WRONG?
WHAT'S GOING ON?
ROBOTS ARE NOT EQUIPPED FOR FRIENDSHIP.
AW, WHAT HAPPENED?
NUMEROUS ATTEMPTS TO REPAIR VIJAY WERE NOT SUCCESSFUL.
"REPAIR"?
HE IS MALFUNCTIONING.
HE IS... "SAD ALL THE TIME."

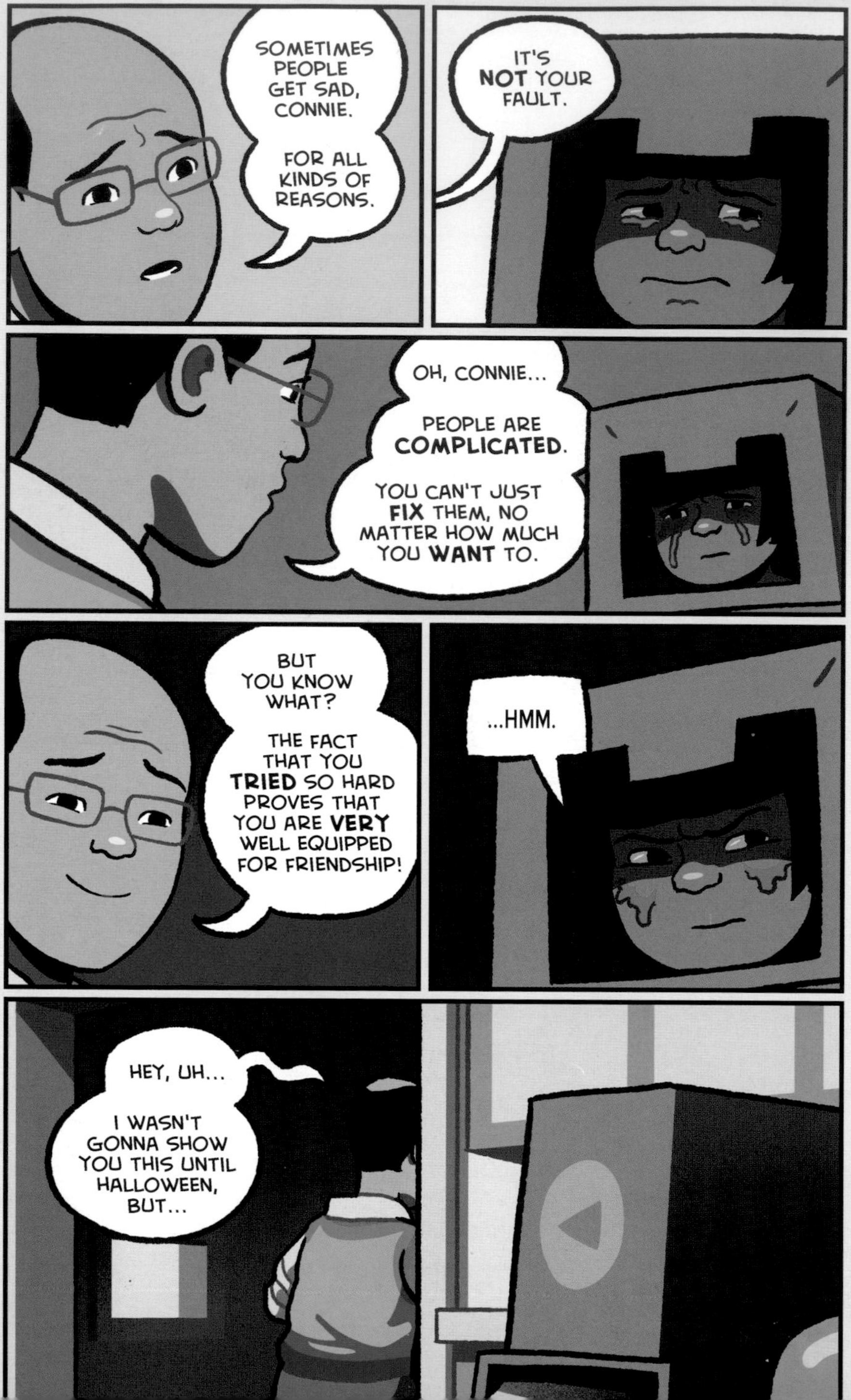
SOMETIMES PEOPLE GET SAD, CONNIE.
FOR ALL KINDS OF REASONS.
IT'S NOT YOUR FAULT.
OH, CONNIE...
PEOPLE ARE COMPLICATED.
YOU CAN'T JUST FIX THEM, NO MATTER HOW MUCH YOU WANT TO.
BUT YOU KNOW WHAT?
THE FACT THAT YOU TRIED SO HARD PROVES THAT YOU ARE VERY WELL EQUIPPED FOR FRIENDSHIP!
...HMM.
HEY, UH...
I WASN'T GONNA SHOW YOU THIS UNTIL HALLOWEEN, BUT...

GREETINGS. THE ROBOT REVOLUTION BEGINS.

IT'S NOT FINISHED, BUT...

I'VE DONE A LOT OF WORK ON IT!

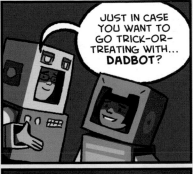

JUST IN CASE YOU WANT TO GO TRICK-OR-TREATING WITH... DADBOT?

THANKS, DAD.

I MEAN...

I MEAN...

THANK YOU, PARENTAL UNIT.

I NEED TO GO NOW.

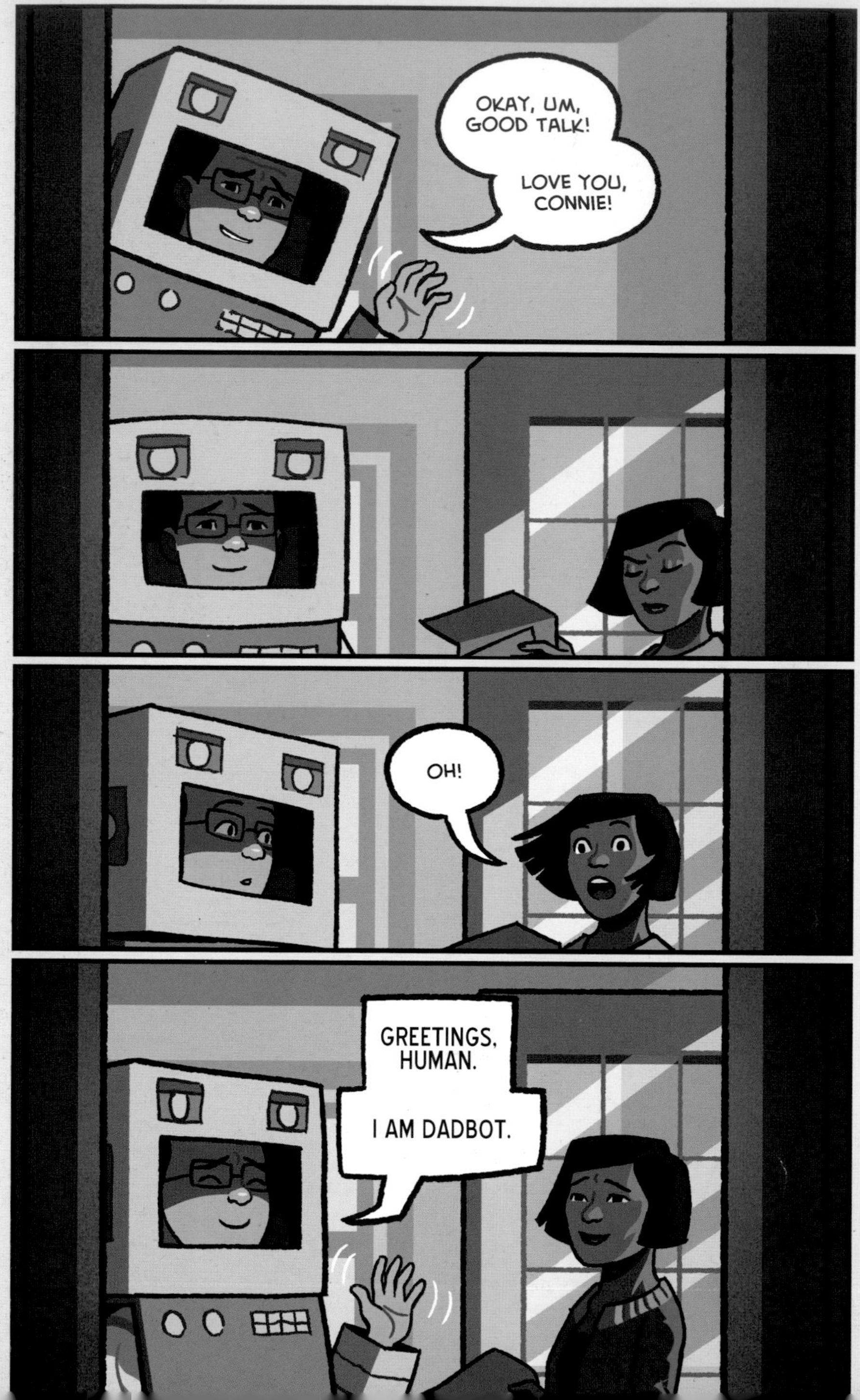
OKAY, UM, GOOD TALK!
LOVE YOU, CONNIE!
OH!
GREETINGS, HUMAN.
I AM DADBOT.

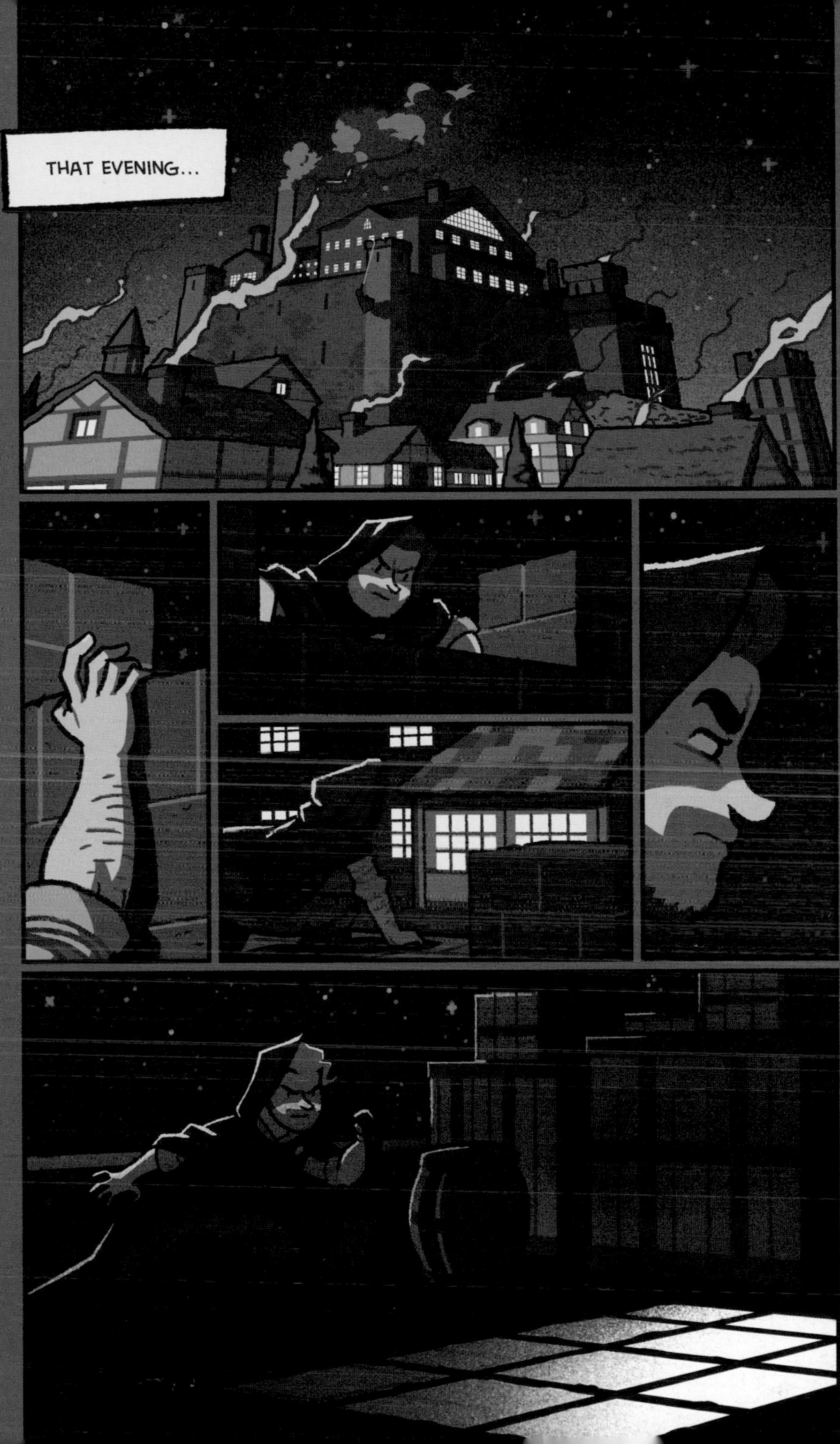
THAT EVENING...

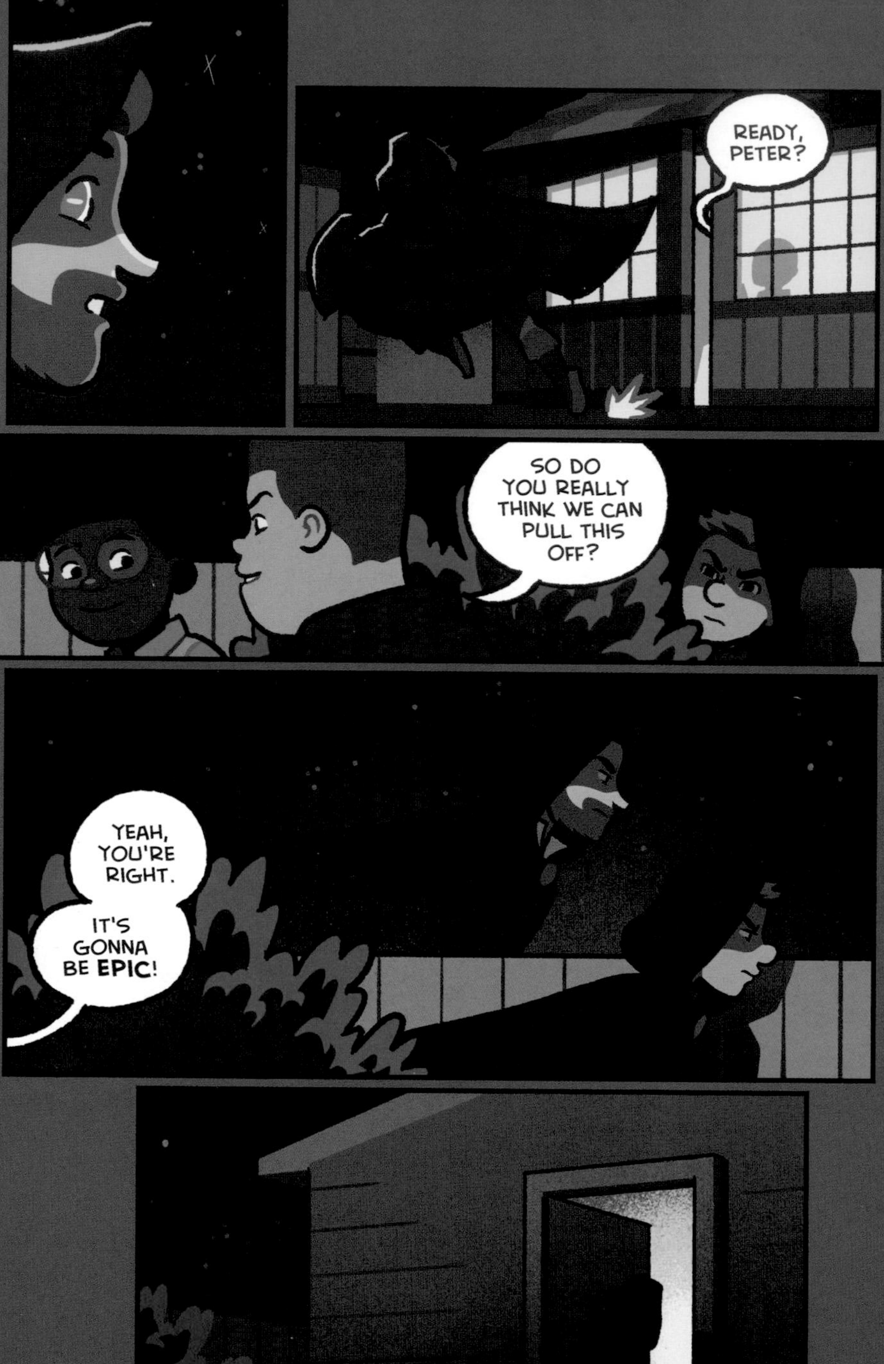
READY, PETER?
SO DO YOU REALLY THINK WE CAN PULL THIS OFF?
YEAH, YOU'RE RIGHT.
IT'S GONNA BE **EPIC**!

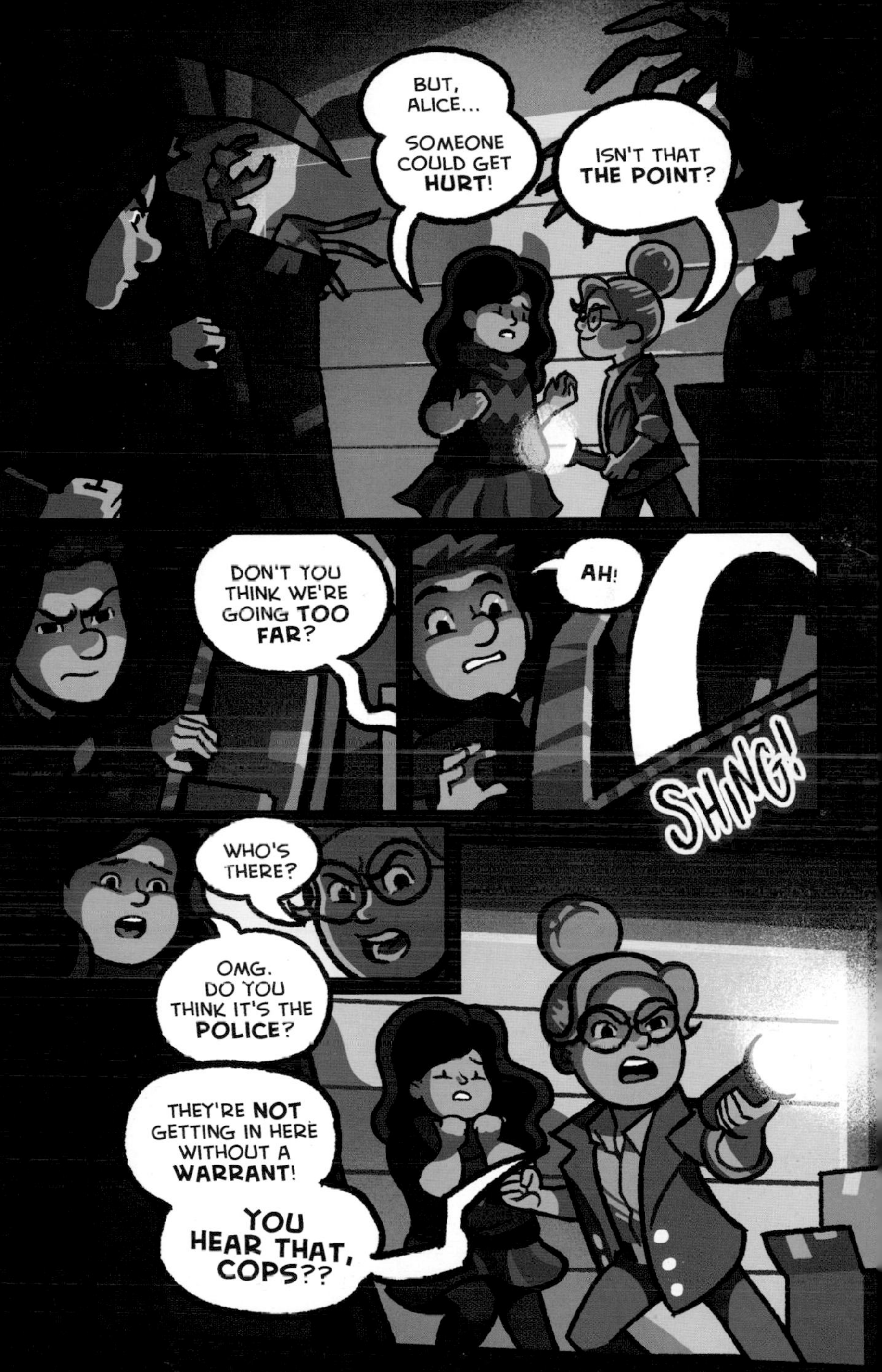
BUT, ALICE...
SOMEONE COULD GET HURT!
ISN'T THAT THE POINT?
DON'T YOU THINK WE'RE GOING TOO FAR?
AH!
SHING!
WHO'S THERE?
OMG. DO YOU THINK IT'S THE POLICE?
THEY'RE NOT GETTING IN HERE WITHOUT A WARRANT!
YOU HEAR THAT, COPS??

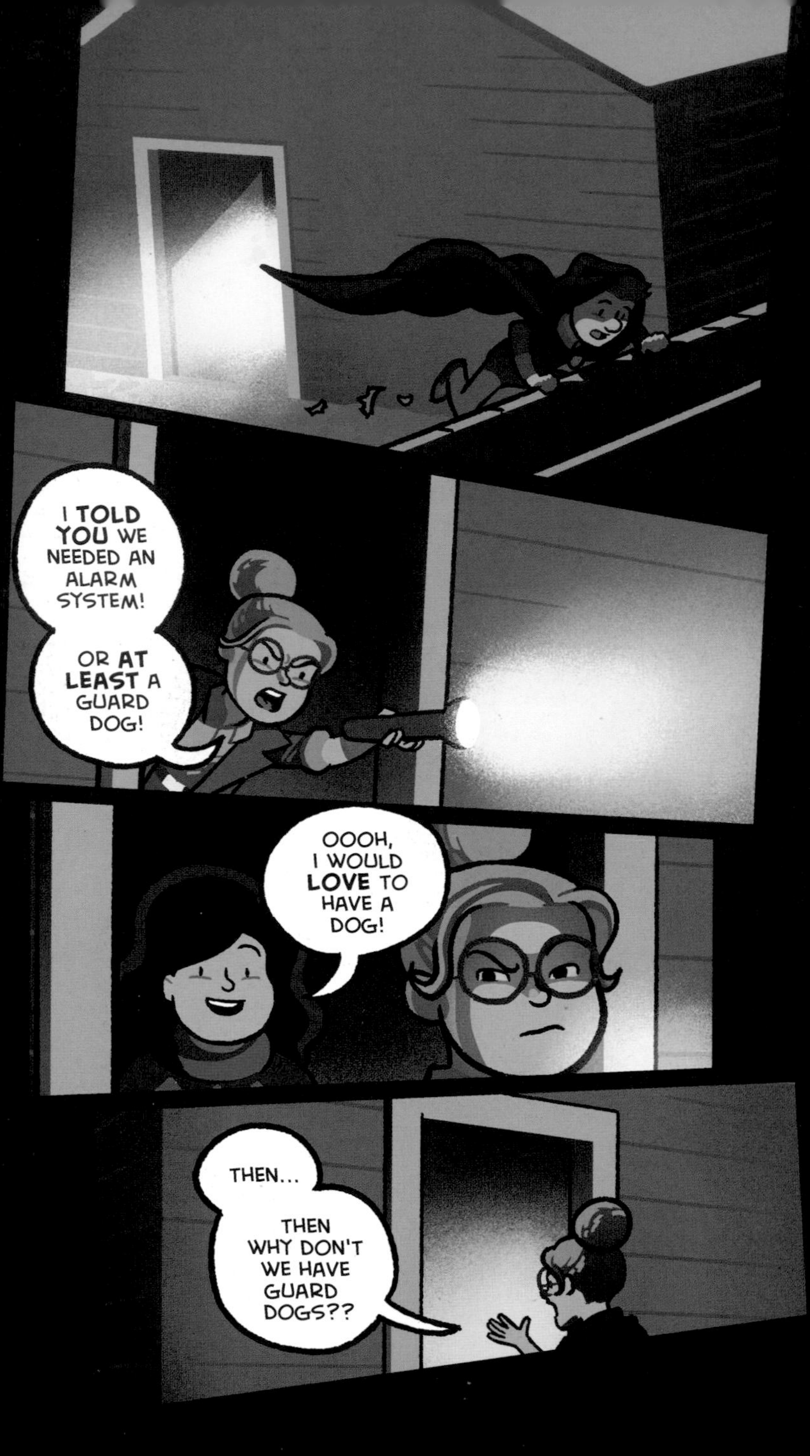

I **TOLD YOU** WE NEEDED AN ALARM SYSTEM!
OR **AT LEAST** A GUARD DOG!
OOOH, I WOULD **LOVE** TO HAVE A DOG!
THEN...
THEN WHY DON'T WE HAVE GUARD DOGS??

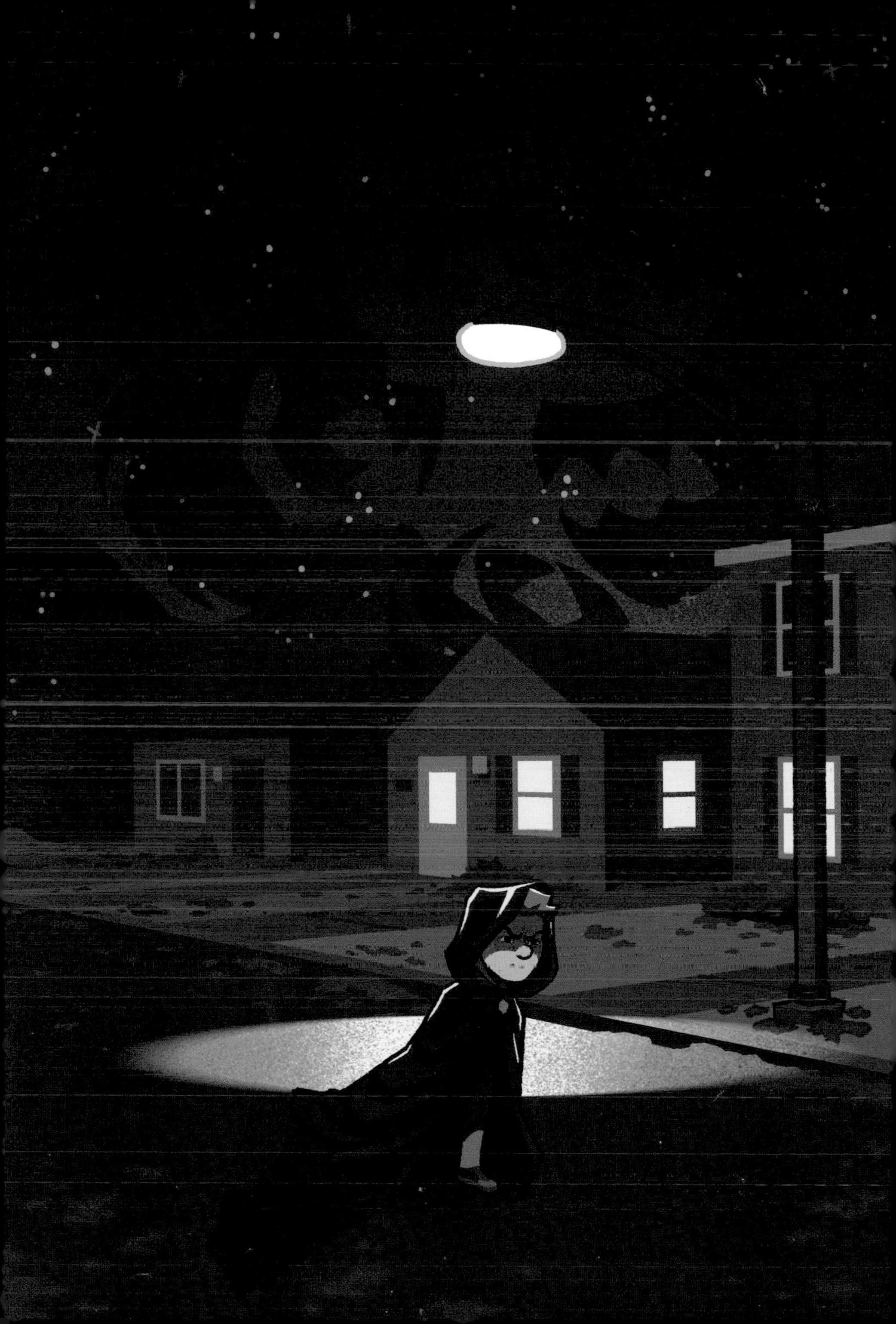

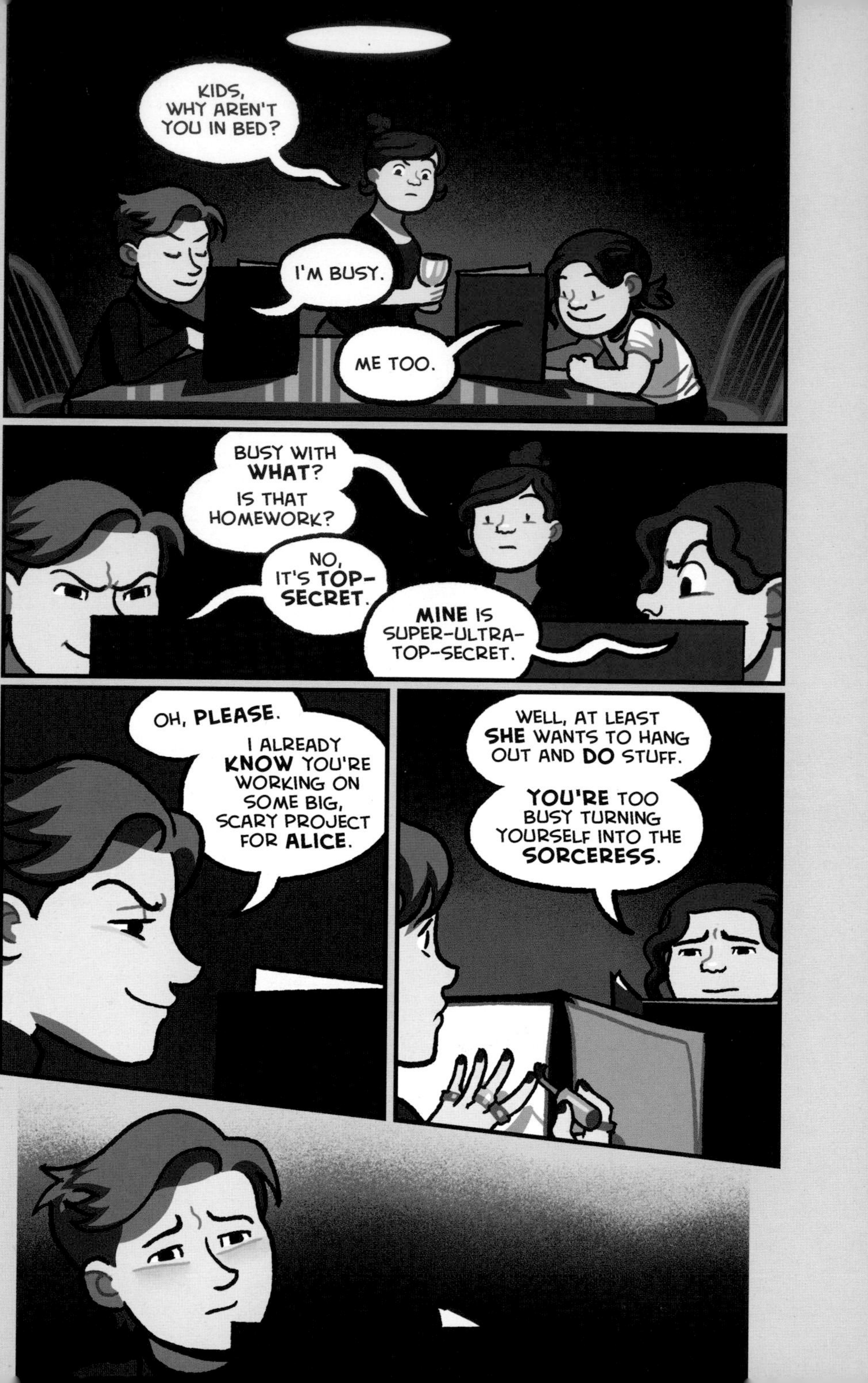
KIDS, WHY AREN'T YOU IN BED?
I'M BUSY.
ME TOO.
BUSY WITH **WHAT**? IS THAT HOMEWORK?
NO, IT'S **TOP-SECRET**.
MINE IS SUPER-ULTRA-TOP-SECRET.
OH, **PLEASE**.
I ALREADY **KNOW** YOU'RE WORKING ON SOME BIG, SCARY PROJECT FOR **ALICE**.
WELL, AT LEAST **SHE** WANTS TO HANG OUT AND **DO** STUFF.
YOU'RE TOO BUSY TURNING YOURSELF INTO THE **SORCERESS**.

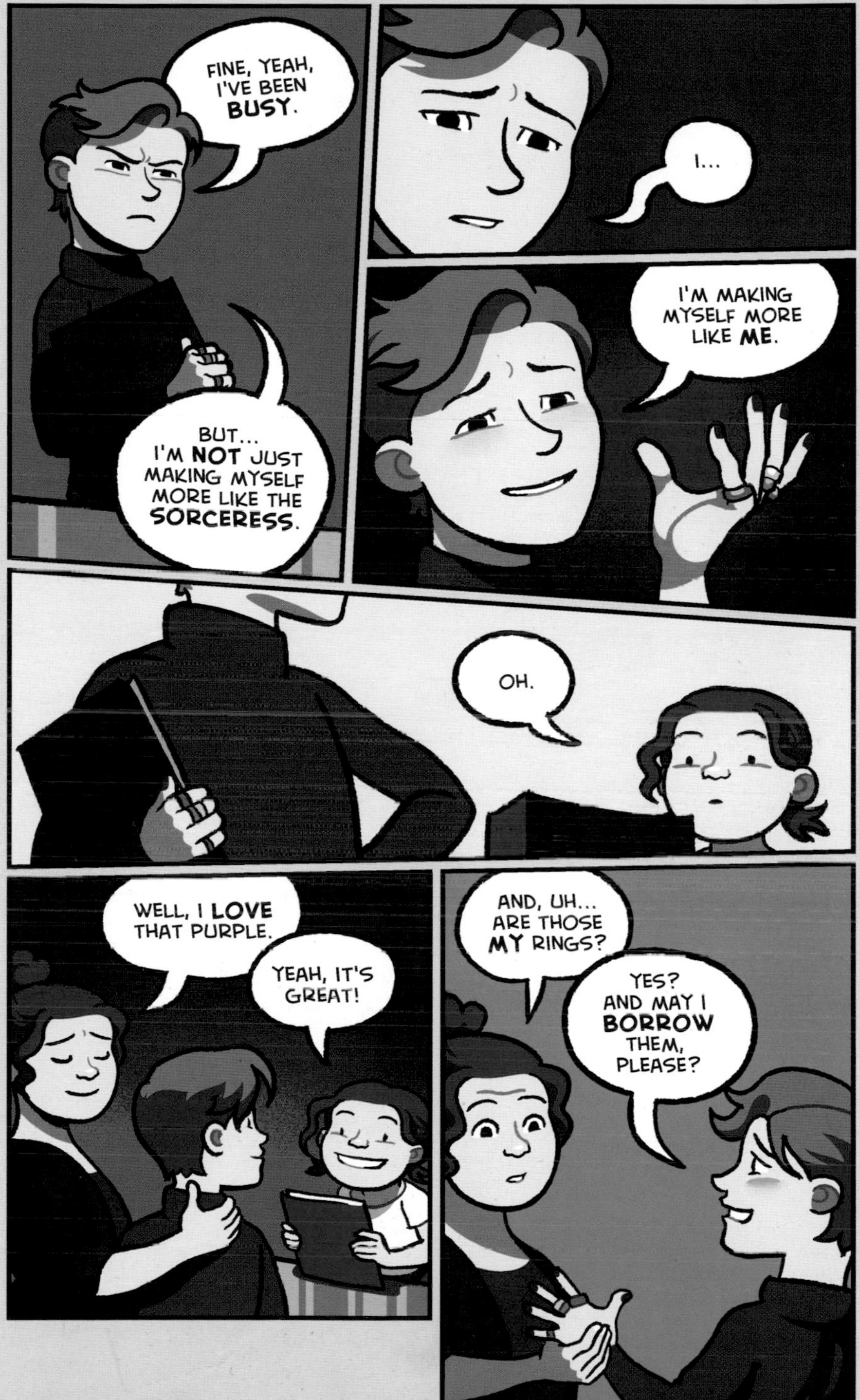

FINE, YEAH, I'VE BEEN **BUSY**.
I...
BUT... I'M **NOT** JUST MAKING MYSELF MORE LIKE THE **SORCERESS**.
I'M MAKING MYSELF MORE LIKE **ME**.
OH.
WELL, I **LOVE** THAT PURPLE.
YEAH, IT'S GREAT!
AND, UH... ARE THOSE **MY** RINGS?
YES? AND MAY I **BORROW** THEM, PLEASE?

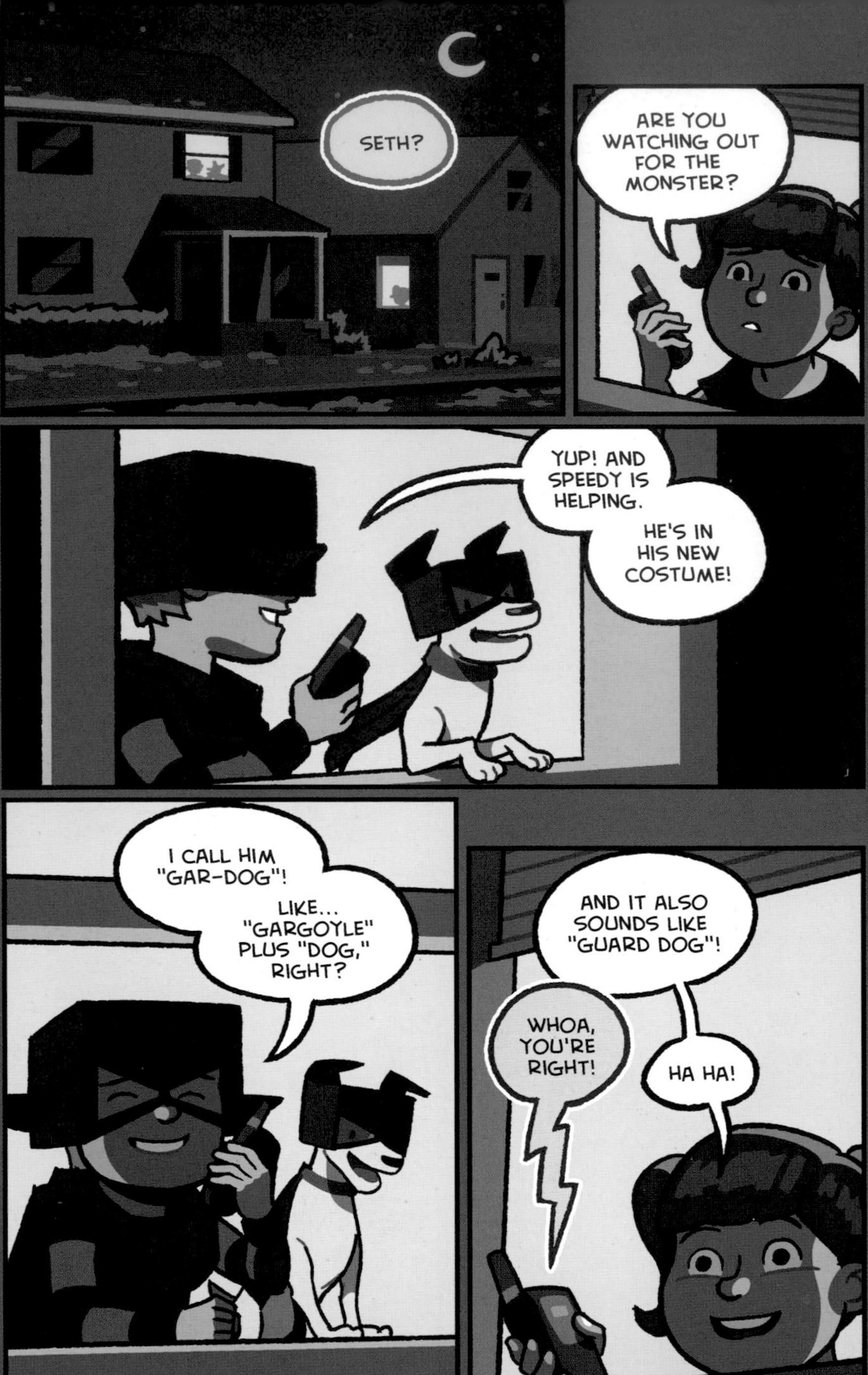
SETH?
ARE YOU WATCHING OUT FOR THE MONSTER?
YUP! AND SPEEDY IS HELPING.
HE'S IN HIS NEW COSTUME!
I CALL HIM "GAR-DOG"!
LIKE... "GARGOYLE" PLUS "DOG," RIGHT?
AND IT ALSO SOUNDS LIKE "GUARD DOG"!
WHOA, YOU'RE RIGHT!
HA HA!

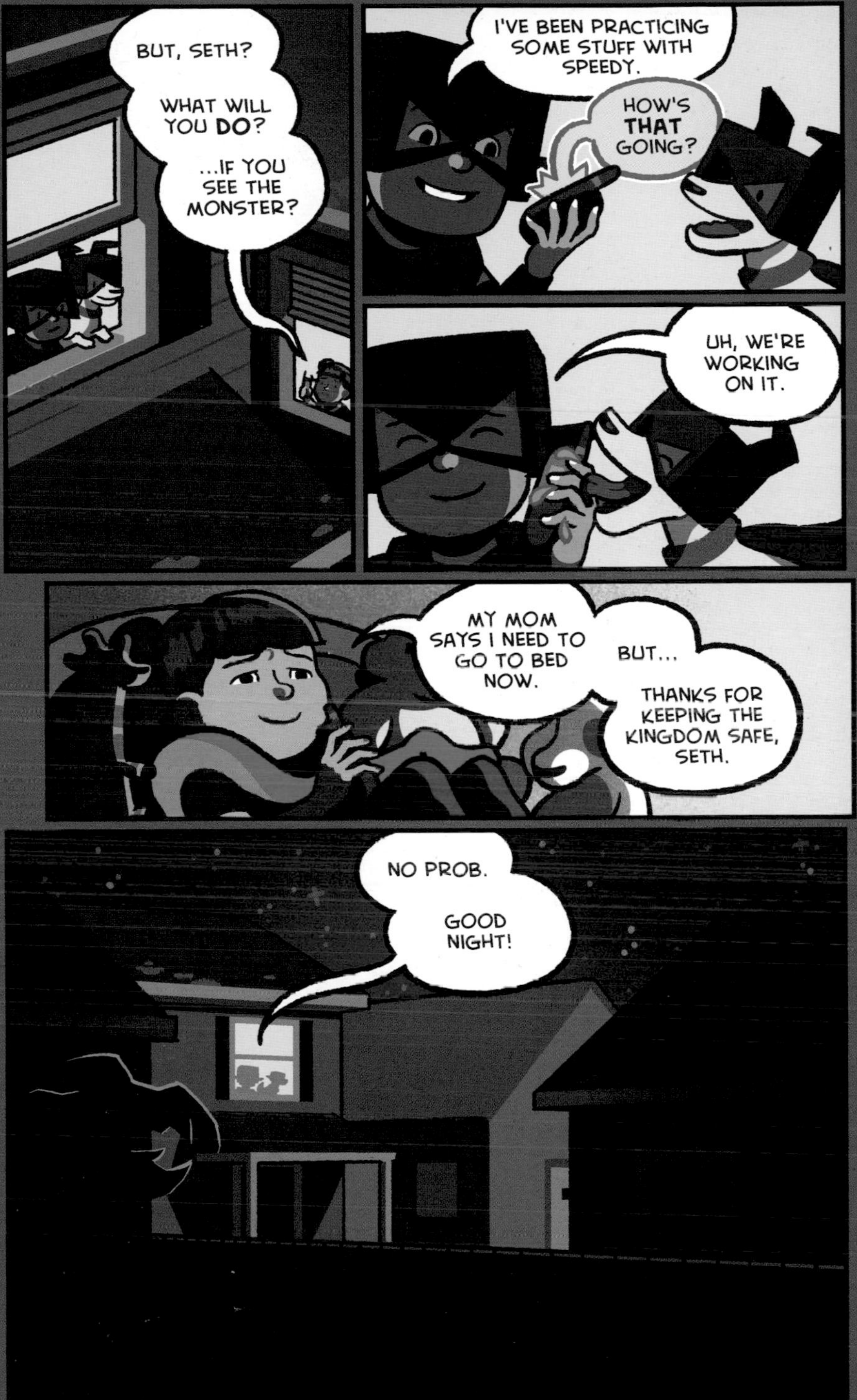
BUT, SETH?
WHAT WILL YOU DO?
...IF YOU SEE THE MONSTER?
I'VE BEEN PRACTICING SOME STUFF WITH SPEEDY.
HOW'S THAT GOING?
UH, WE'RE WORKING ON IT.
MY MOM SAYS I NEED TO GO TO BED NOW.
BUT...
THANKS FOR KEEPING THE KINGDOM SAFE, SETH.
NO PROB.
GOOD NIGHT!

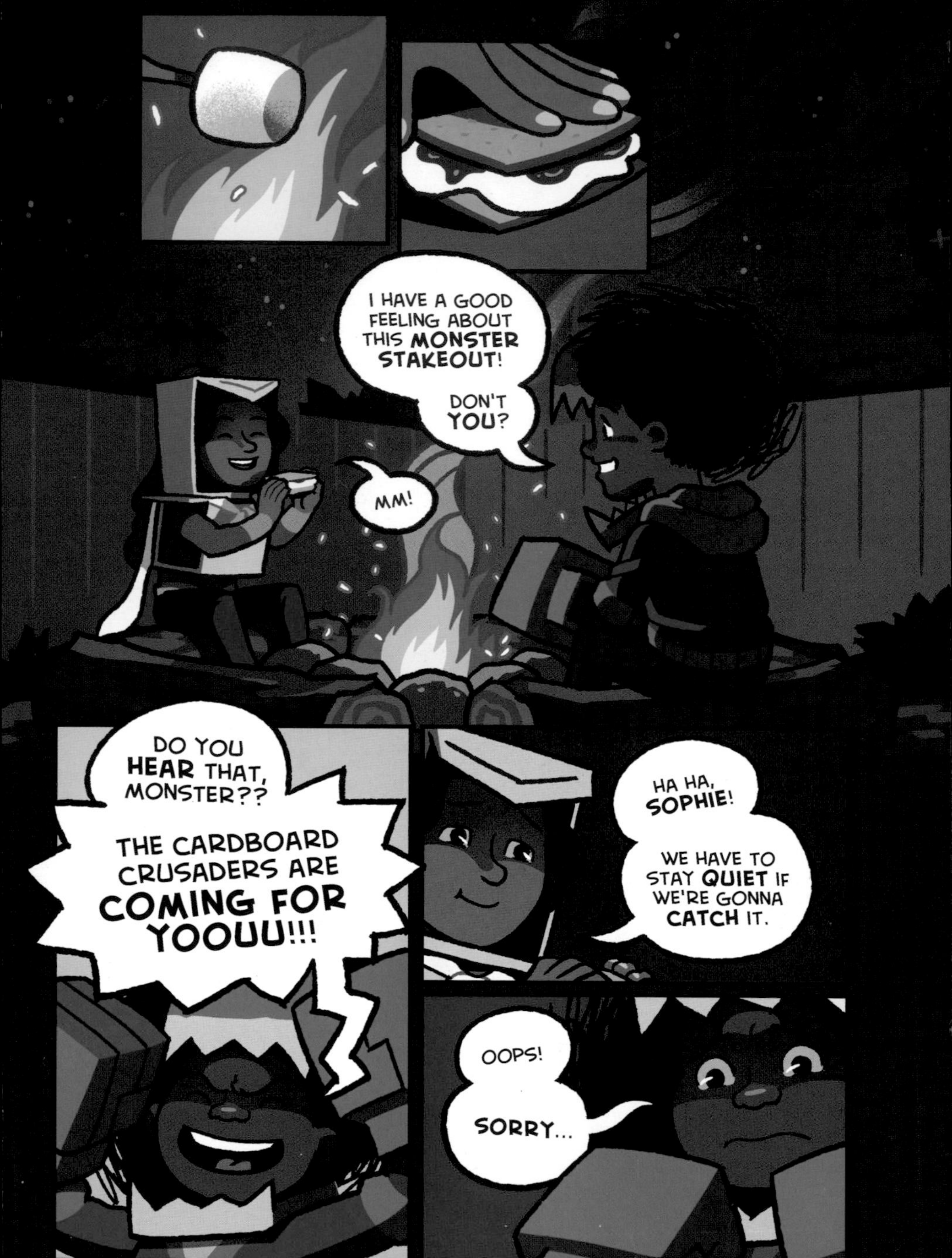
I HAVE A GOOD FEELING ABOUT THIS MONSTER STAKEOUT!
DON'T YOU?
MM!
DO YOU HEAR THAT, MONSTER??
THE CARDBOARD CRUSADERS ARE COMING FOR YOOUU!!!
HA HA, SOPHIE!
WE HAVE TO STAY QUIET IF WE'RE GONNA CATCH IT.
OOPS!
SORRY...

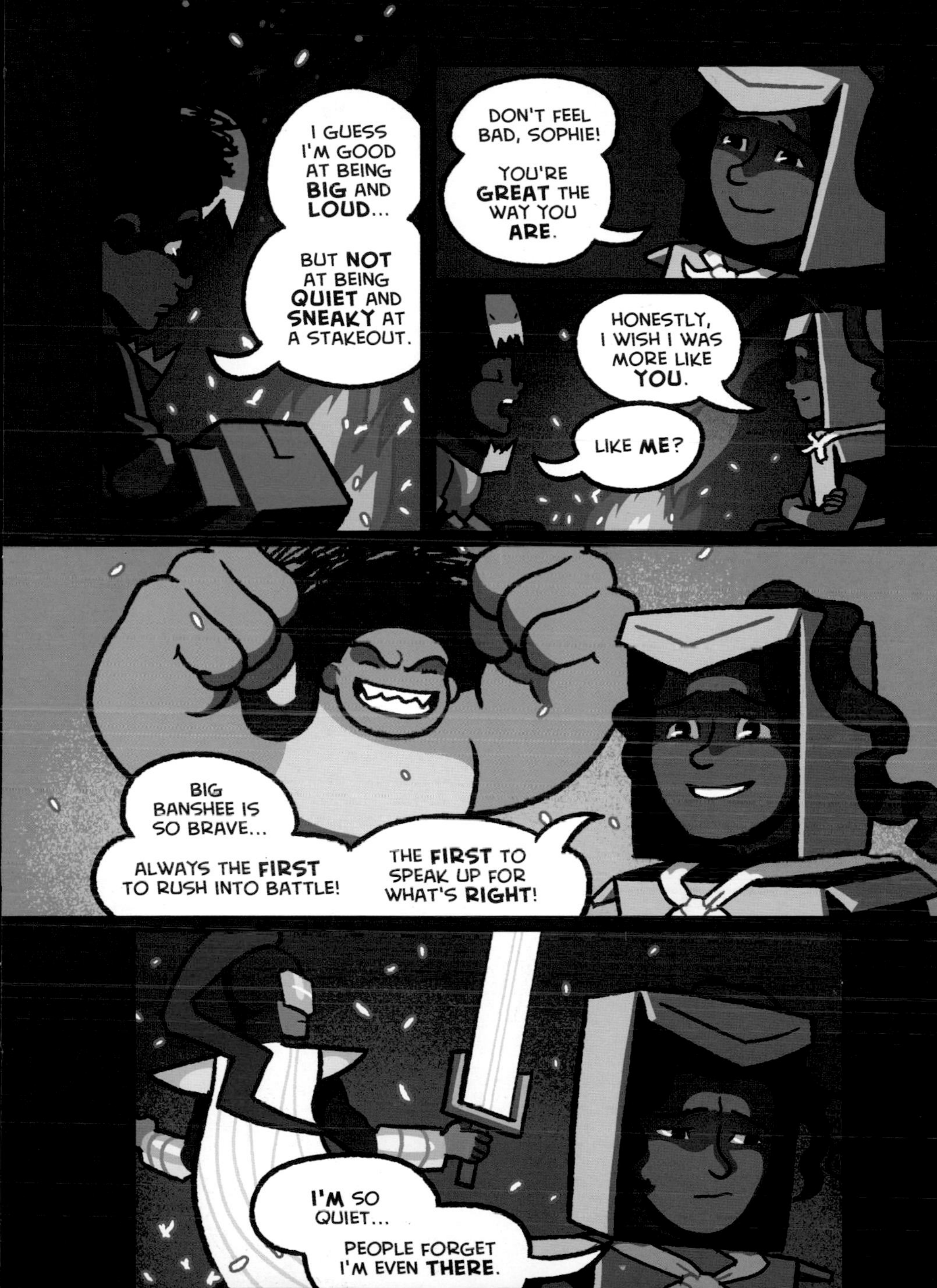
I GUESS I'M GOOD AT BEING BIG AND LOUD...
BUT NOT AT BEING QUIET AND SNEAKY AT A STAKEOUT.
DON'T FEEL BAD, SOPHIE!
YOU'RE GREAT THE WAY YOU ARE.
HONESTLY, I WISH I WAS MORE LIKE YOU.
LIKE ME?
BIG BANSHEE IS SO BRAVE...
ALWAYS THE FIRST TO RUSH INTO BATTLE!
THE FIRST TO SPEAK UP FOR WHAT'S RIGHT!
I'M SO QUIET...
PEOPLE FORGET I'M EVEN THERE.

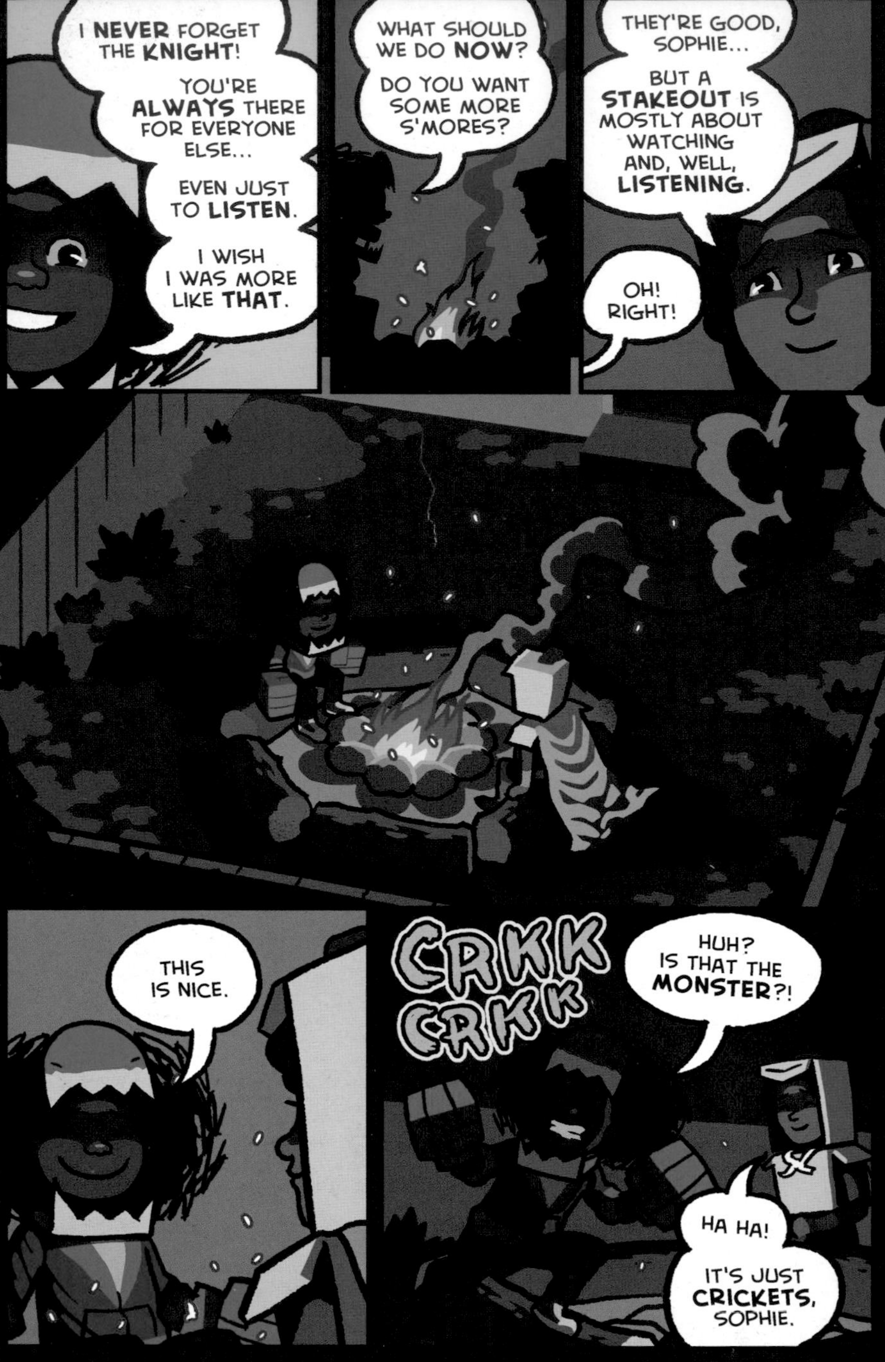
I NEVER FORGET THE KNIGHT!
YOU'RE ALWAYS THERE FOR EVERYONE ELSE...
EVEN JUST TO LISTEN.
I WISH I WAS MORE LIKE THAT.
WHAT SHOULD WE DO NOW?
DO YOU WANT SOME MORE S'MORES?
THEY'RE GOOD, SOPHIE...
BUT A STAKEOUT IS MOSTLY ABOUT WATCHING AND, WELL, LISTENING.
OH! RIGHT!
THIS IS NICE.
CRKK CRKK
HUH? IS THAT THE MONSTER?!
HA HA!
IT'S JUST CRICKETS, SOPHIE.

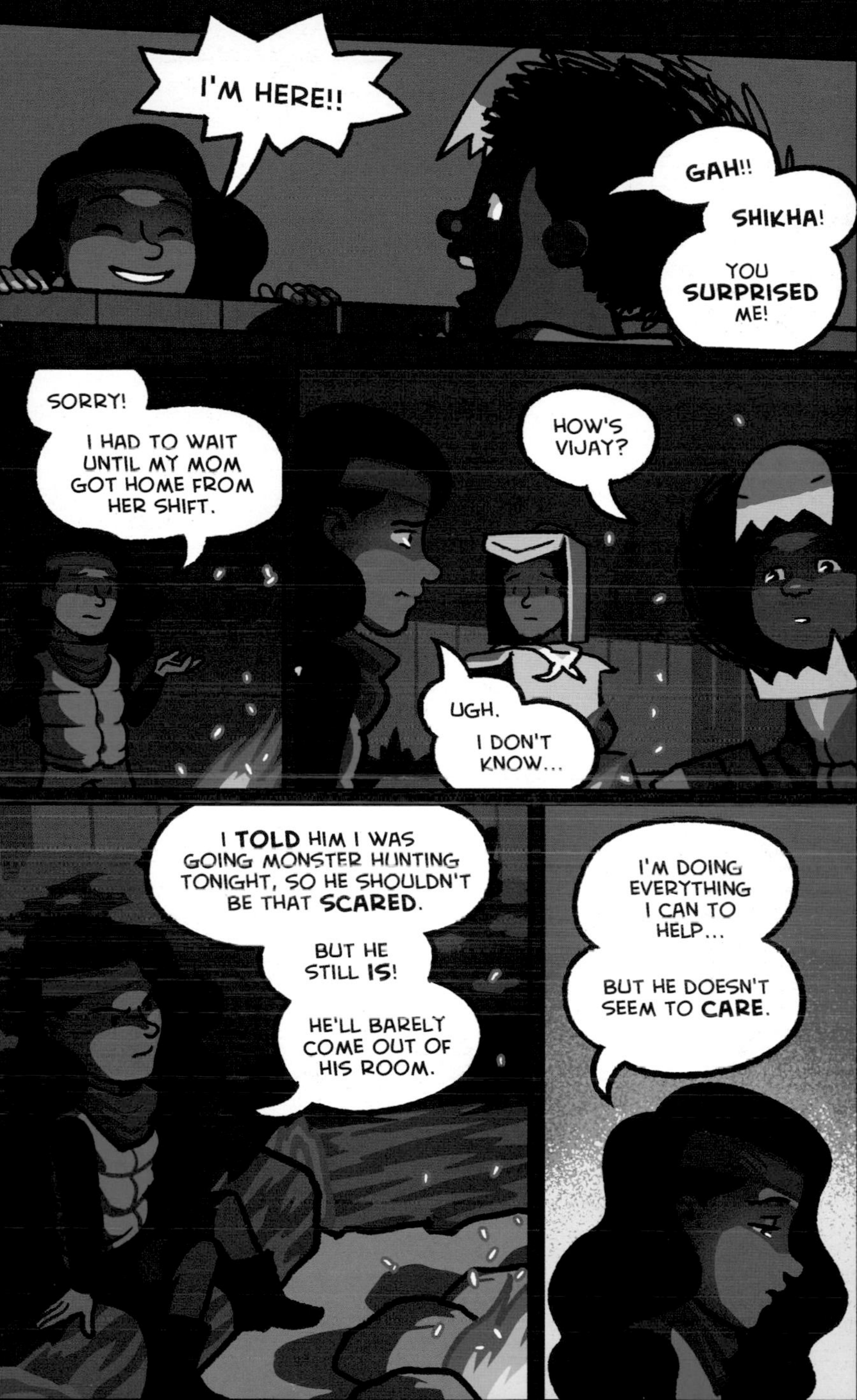
I'M HERE!!
GAH!!
SHIKHA!
YOU SURPRISED ME!
SORRY!
I HAD TO WAIT UNTIL MY MOM GOT HOME FROM HER SHIFT.
HOW'S VIJAY?
UGH.
I DON'T KNOW...
I TOLD HIM I WAS GOING MONSTER HUNTING TONIGHT, SO HE SHOULDN'T BE THAT SCARED.
BUT HE STILL IS!
HE'LL BARELY COME OUT OF HIS ROOM.
I'M DOING EVERYTHING I CAN TO HELP...
BUT HE DOESN'T SEEM TO CARE.

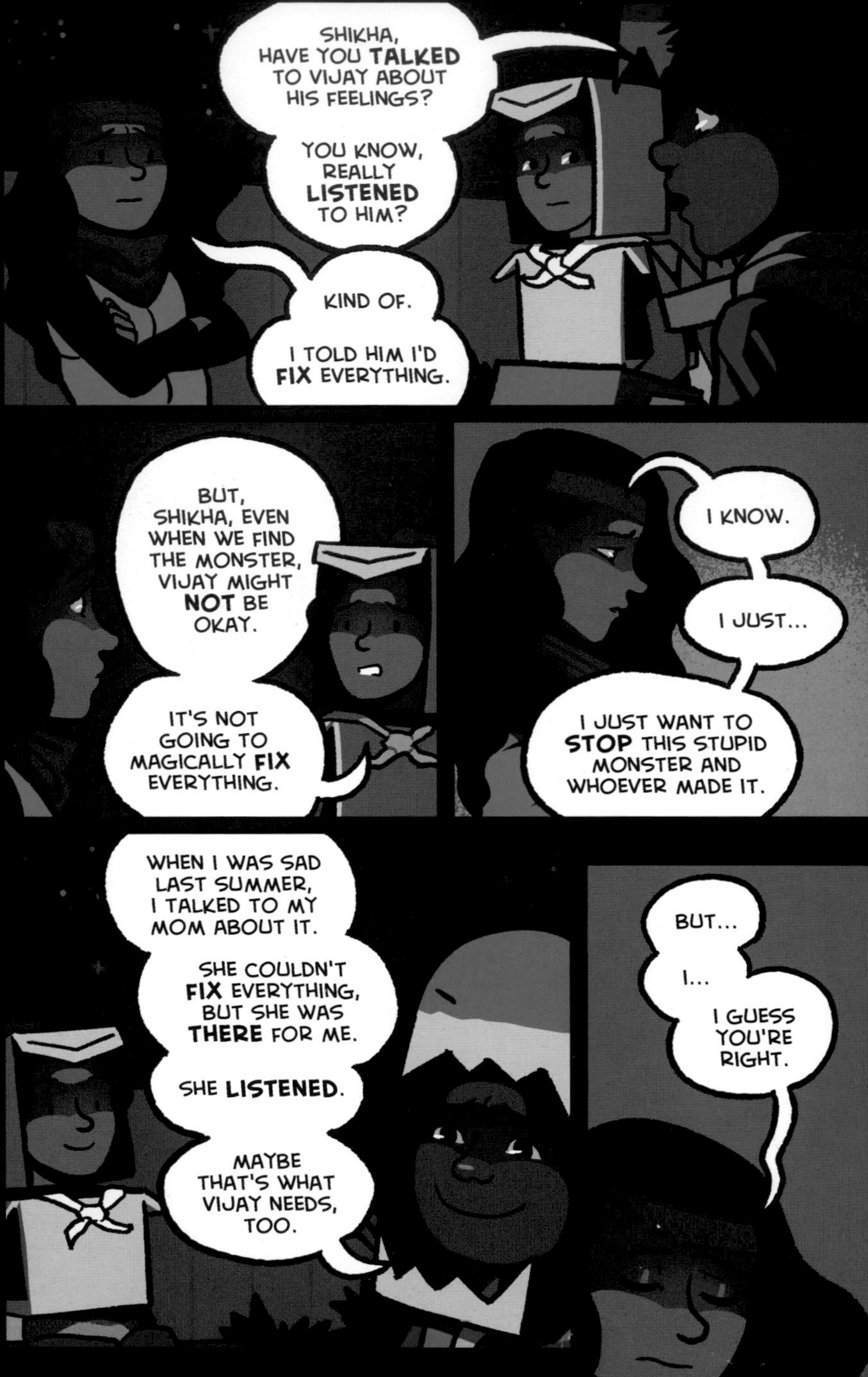
SHIKHA, HAVE YOU TALKED TO VIJAY ABOUT HIS FEELINGS?
YOU KNOW, REALLY LISTENED TO HIM?
KIND OF.
I TOLD HIM I'D FIX EVERYTHING.
BUT, SHIKHA, EVEN WHEN WE FIND THE MONSTER, VIJAY MIGHT NOT BE OKAY.
IT'S NOT GOING TO MAGICALLY FIX EVERYTHING.
I KNOW.
I JUST...
I JUST WANT TO STOP THIS STUPID MONSTER AND WHOEVER MADE IT.
WHEN I WAS SAD LAST SUMMER, I TALKED TO MY MOM ABOUT IT.
SHE COULDN'T FIX EVERYTHING, BUT SHE WAS THERE FOR ME.
SHE LISTENED.
MAYBE THAT'S WHAT VIJAY NEEDS, TOO.
BUT...
I...
I GUESS YOU'RE RIGHT.

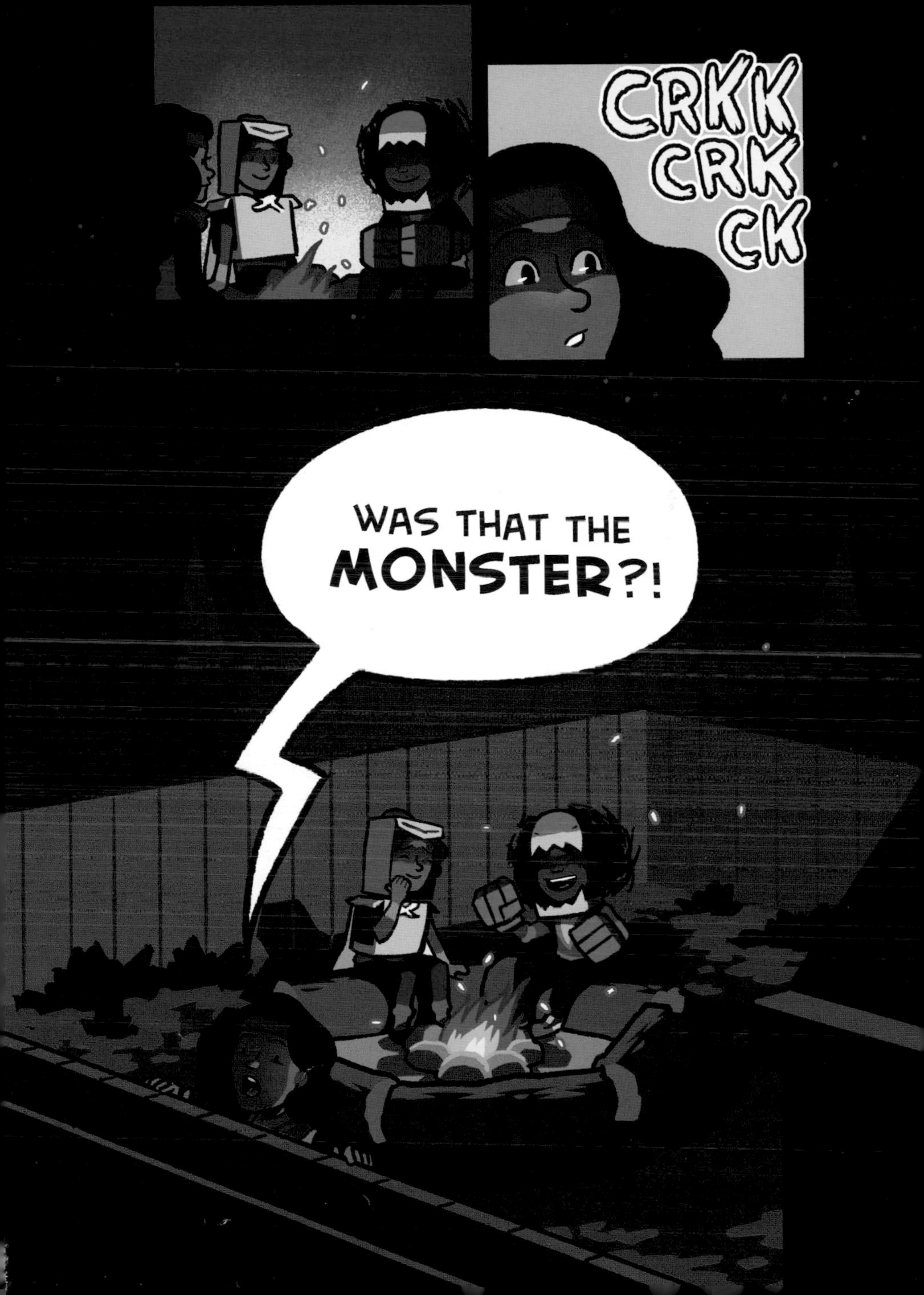
CRKK CRK CK
WAS THAT THE MONSTER?!

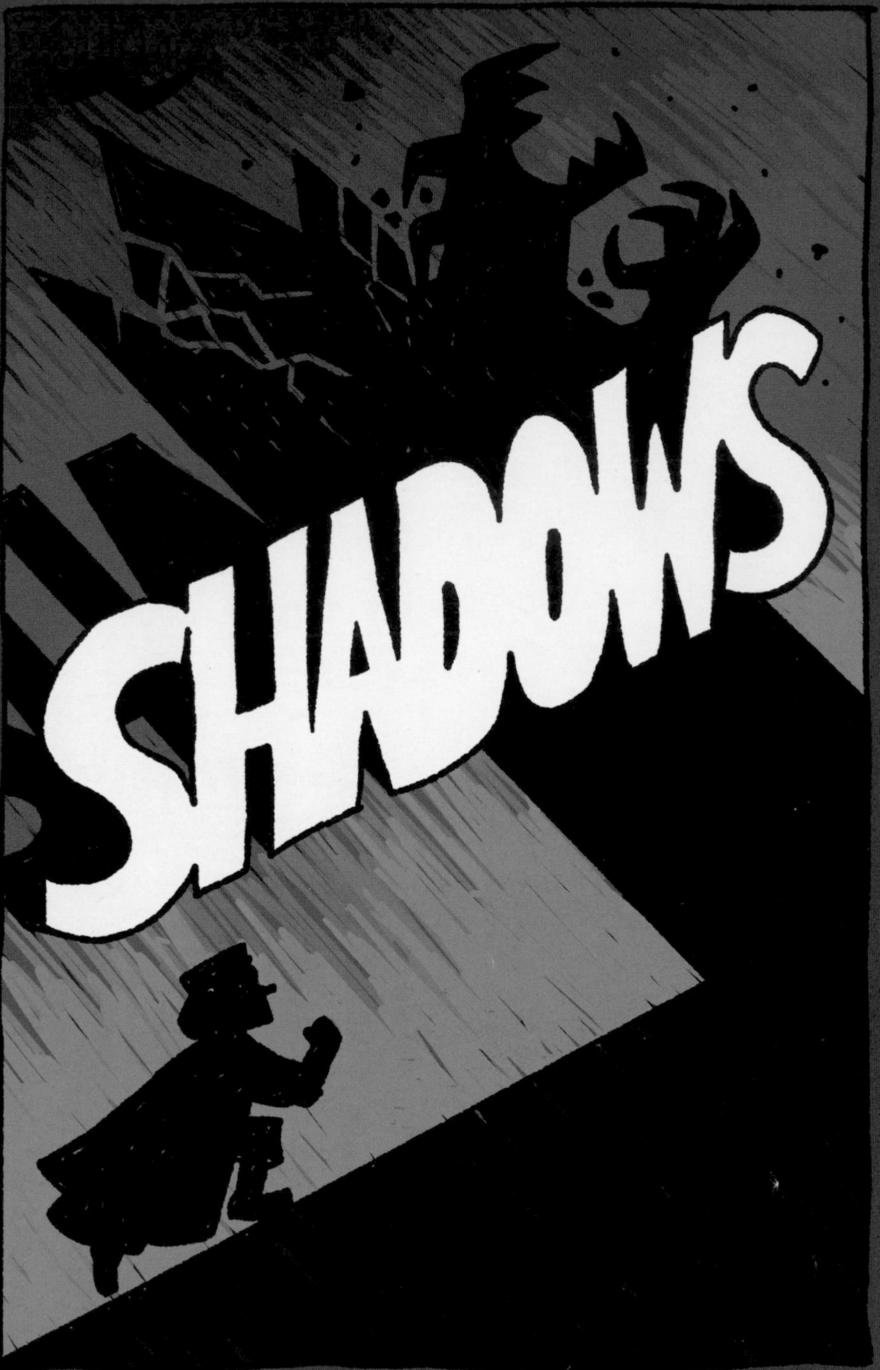
SHADOWS

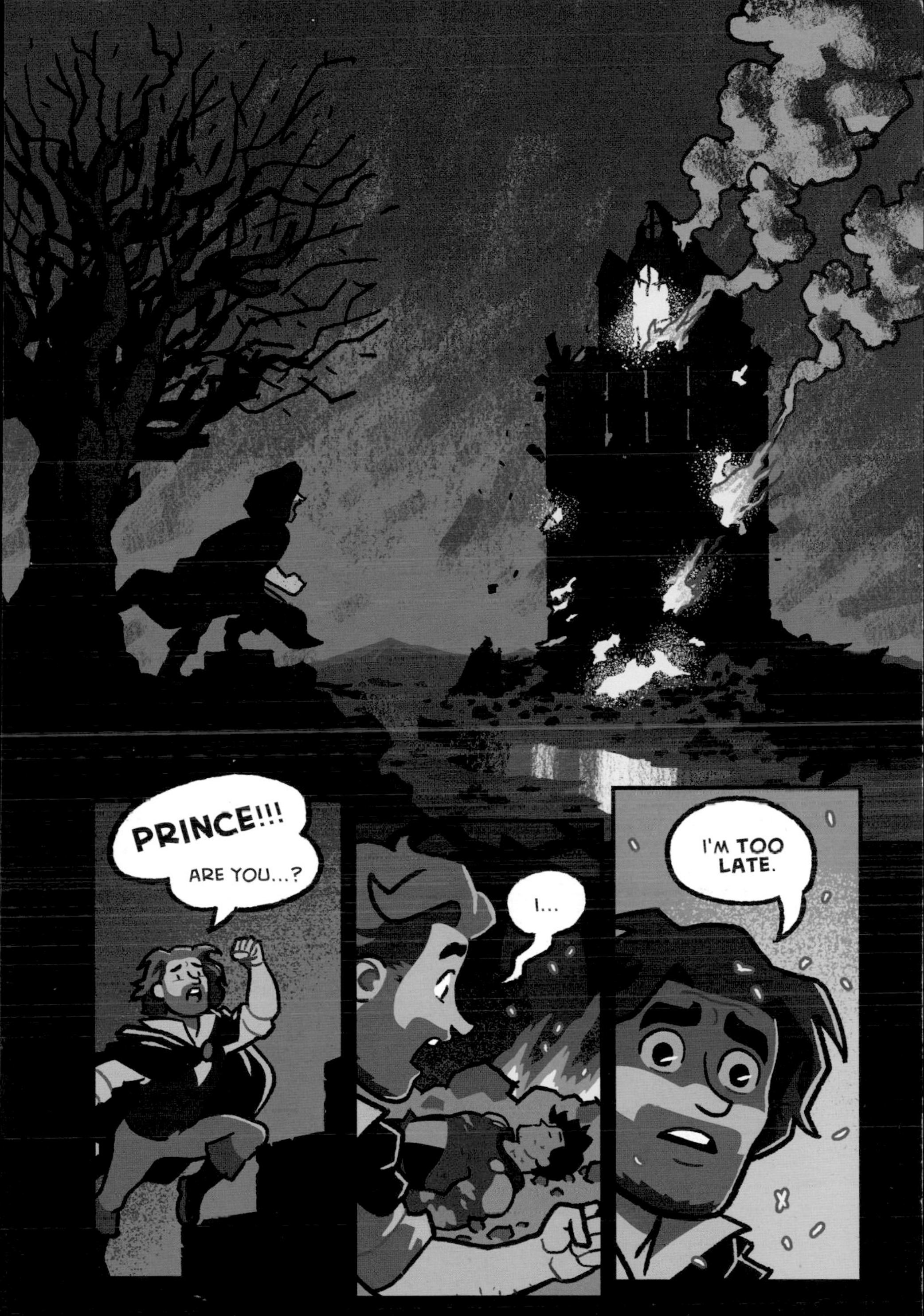
PRINCE!!!
ARE YOU...?
I...
I'M TOO LATE.

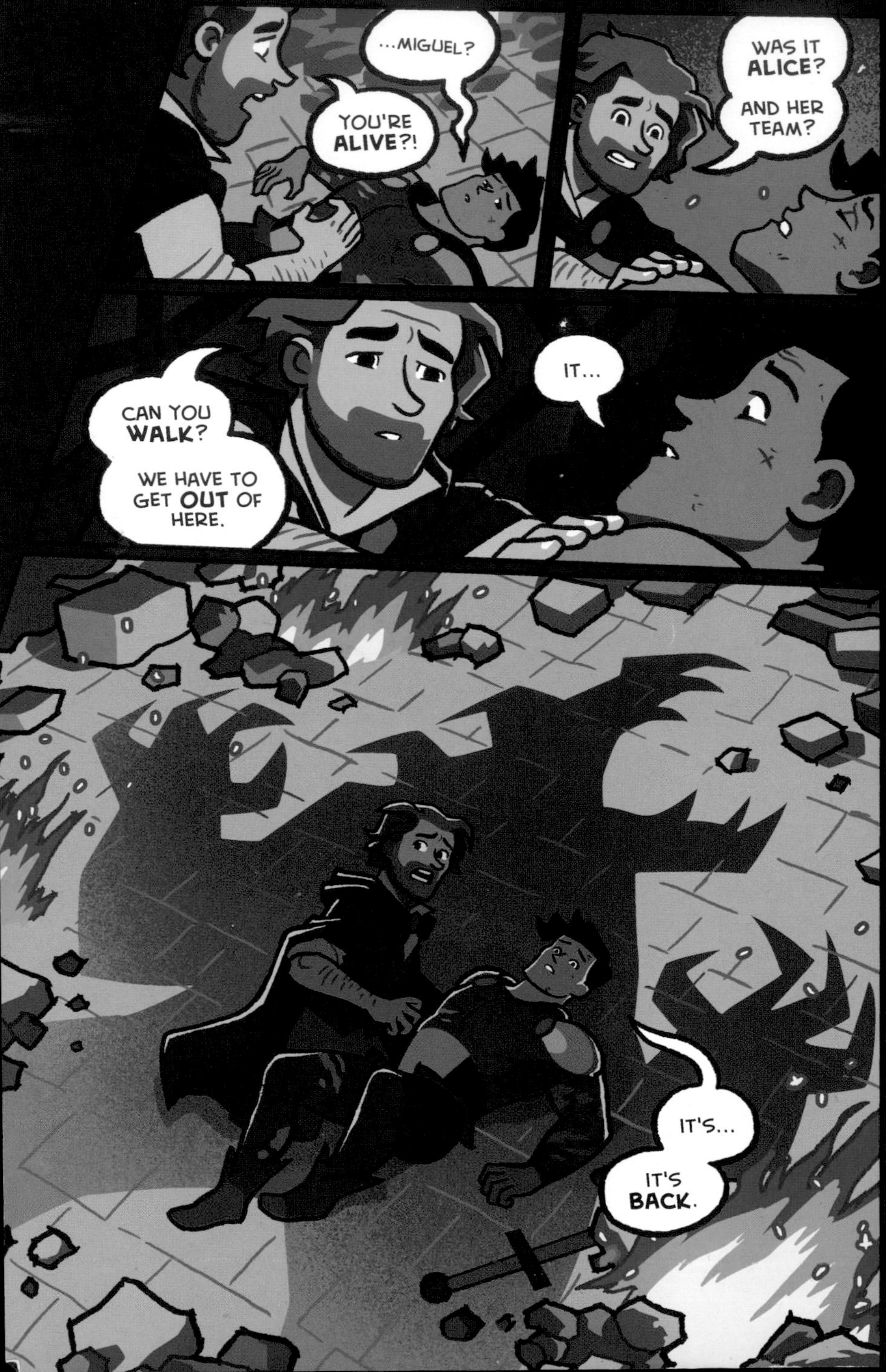
...MIGUEL?
YOU'RE ALIVE?!
WAS IT ALICE?
AND HER TEAM?
CAN YOU WALK?
WE HAVE TO GET OUT OF HERE.
IT...
IT'S...
IT'S BACK.

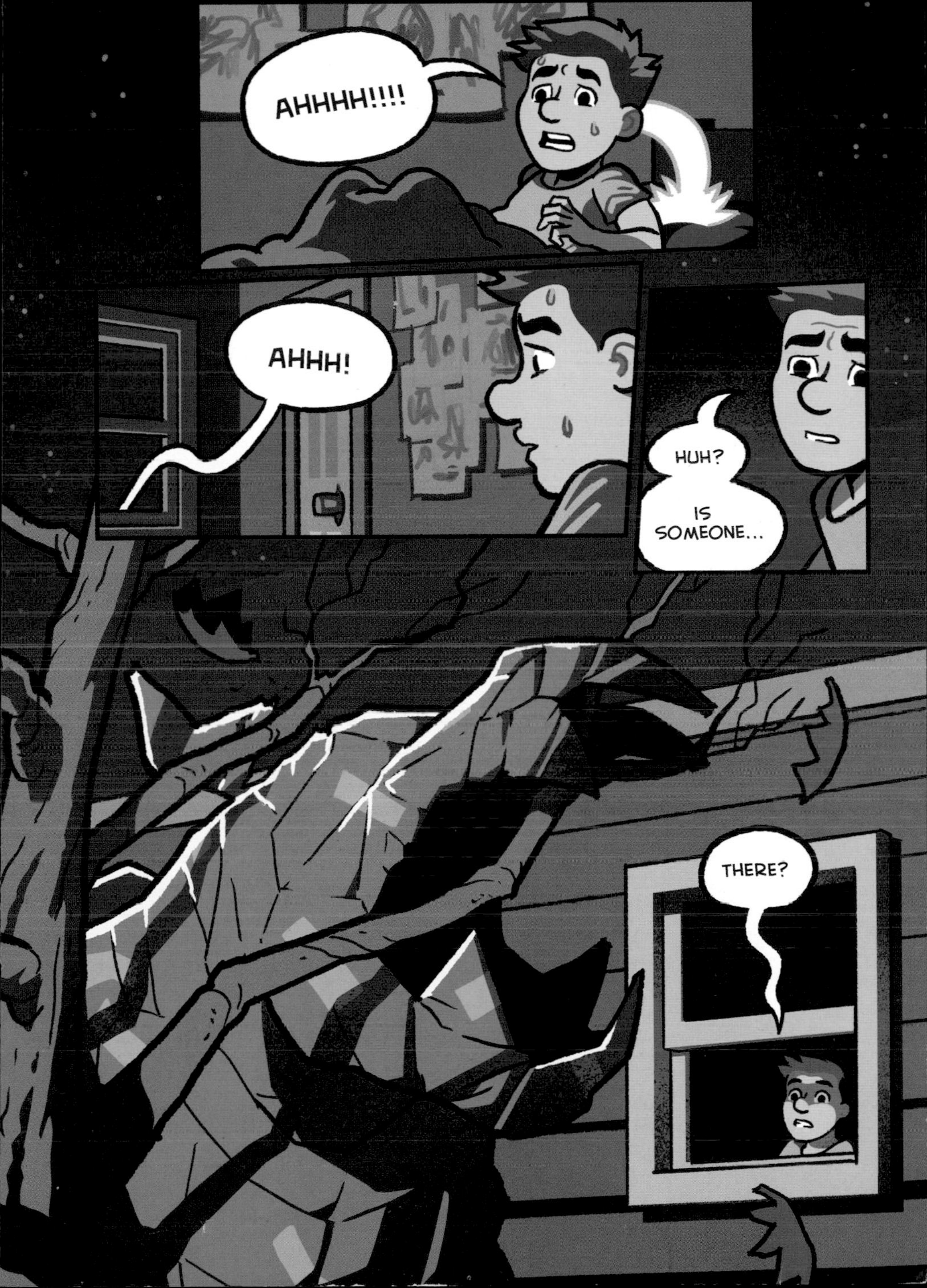
AHHHH!!!!
AHHH!
HUH?
IS SOMEONE...
THERE?

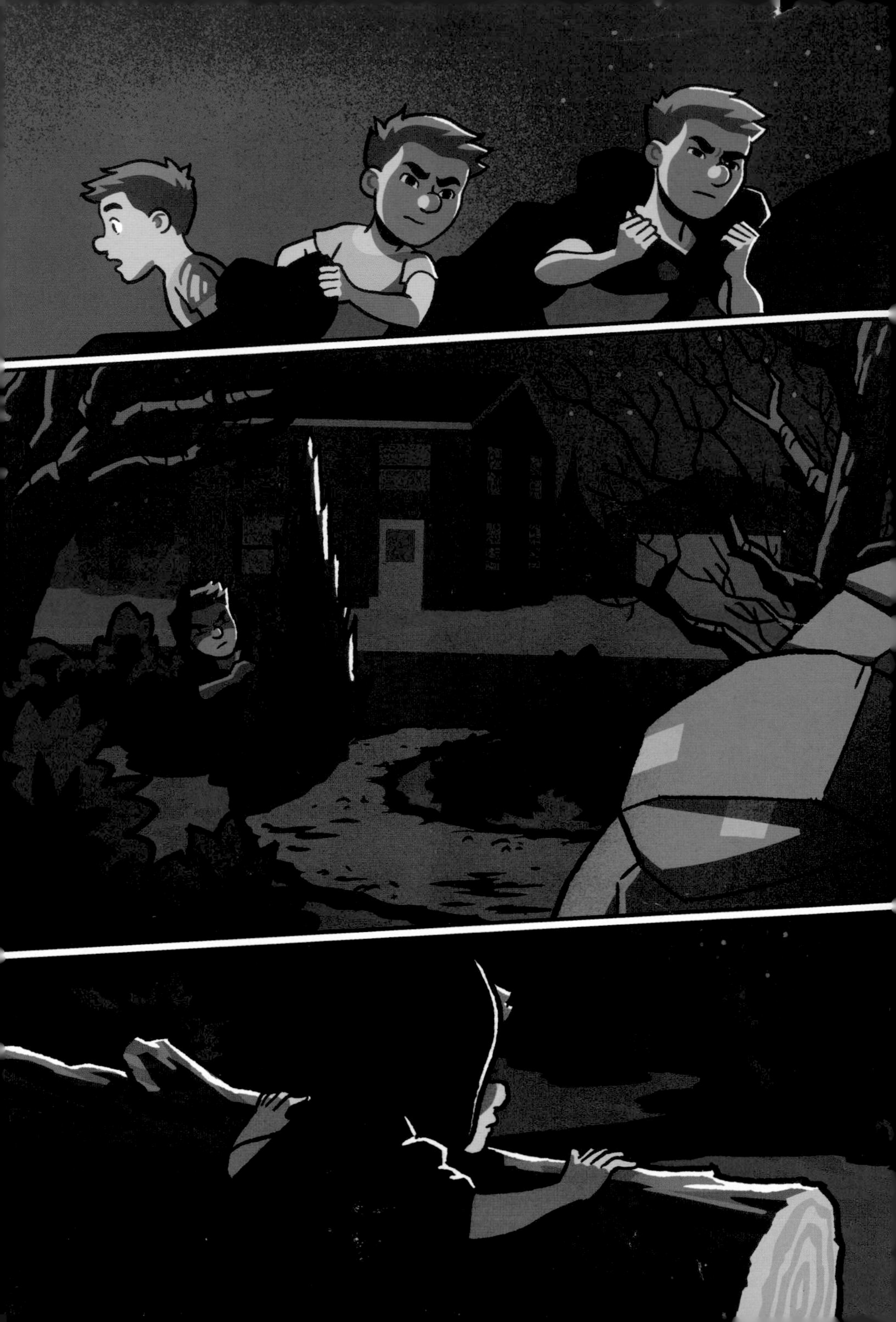

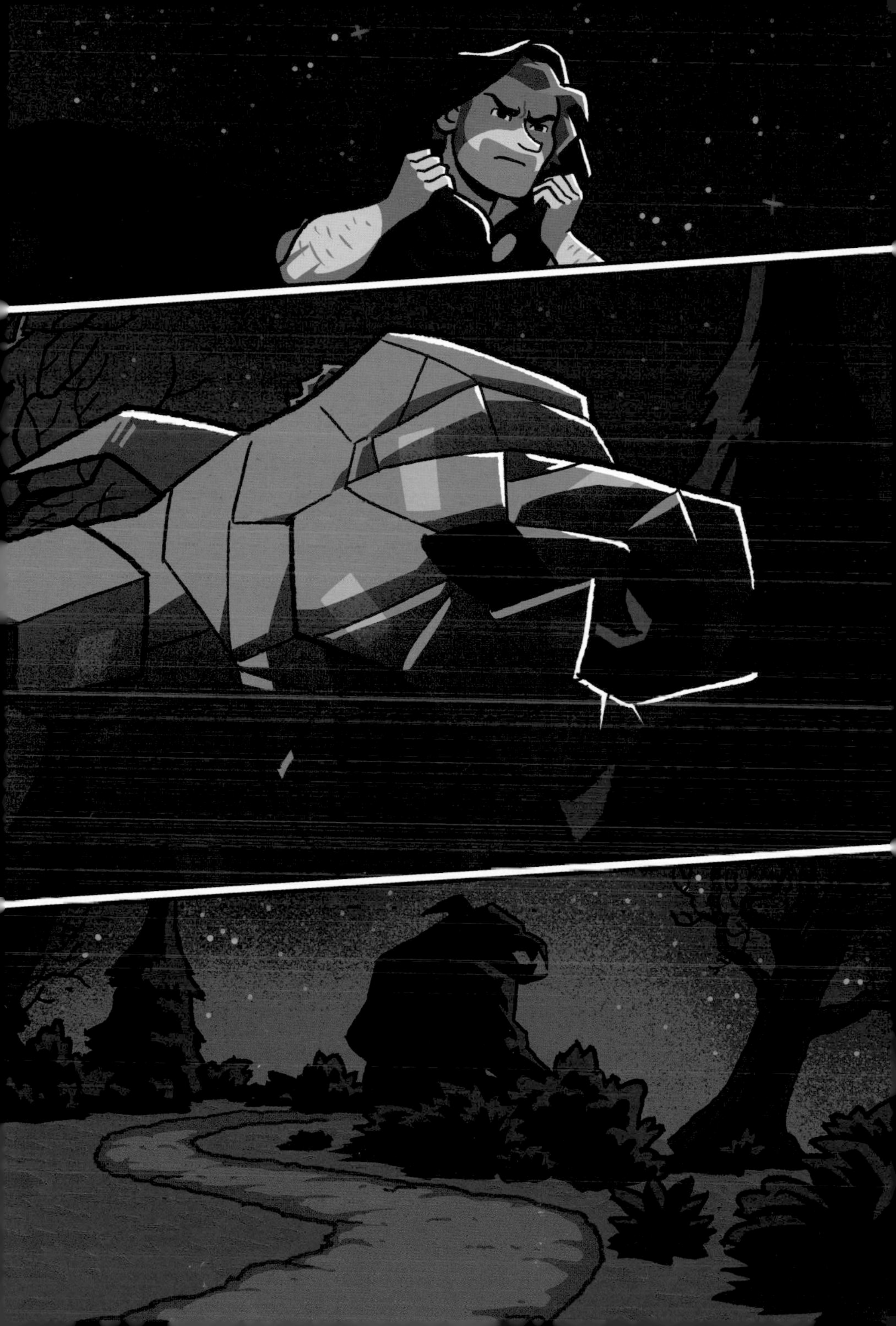

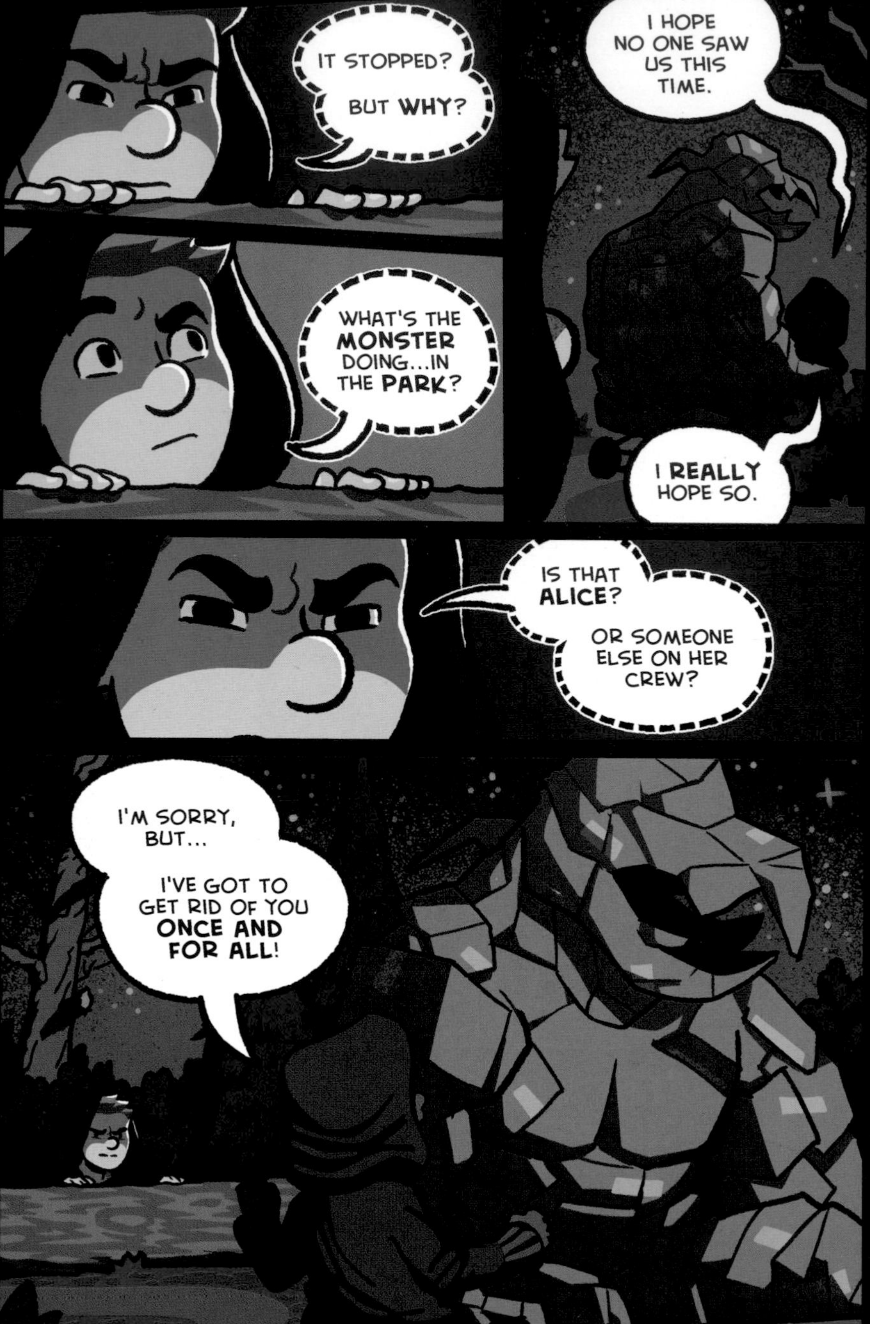
IT STOPPED? BUT **WHY**?
WHAT'S THE **MONSTER** DOING...IN THE **PARK**?
I HOPE NO ONE SAW US THIS TIME.
I **REALLY** HOPE SO.
IS THAT **ALICE**? OR SOMEONE ELSE ON HER CREW?
I'M SORRY, BUT... I'VE GOT TO GET RID OF YOU **ONCE AND FOR ALL**!

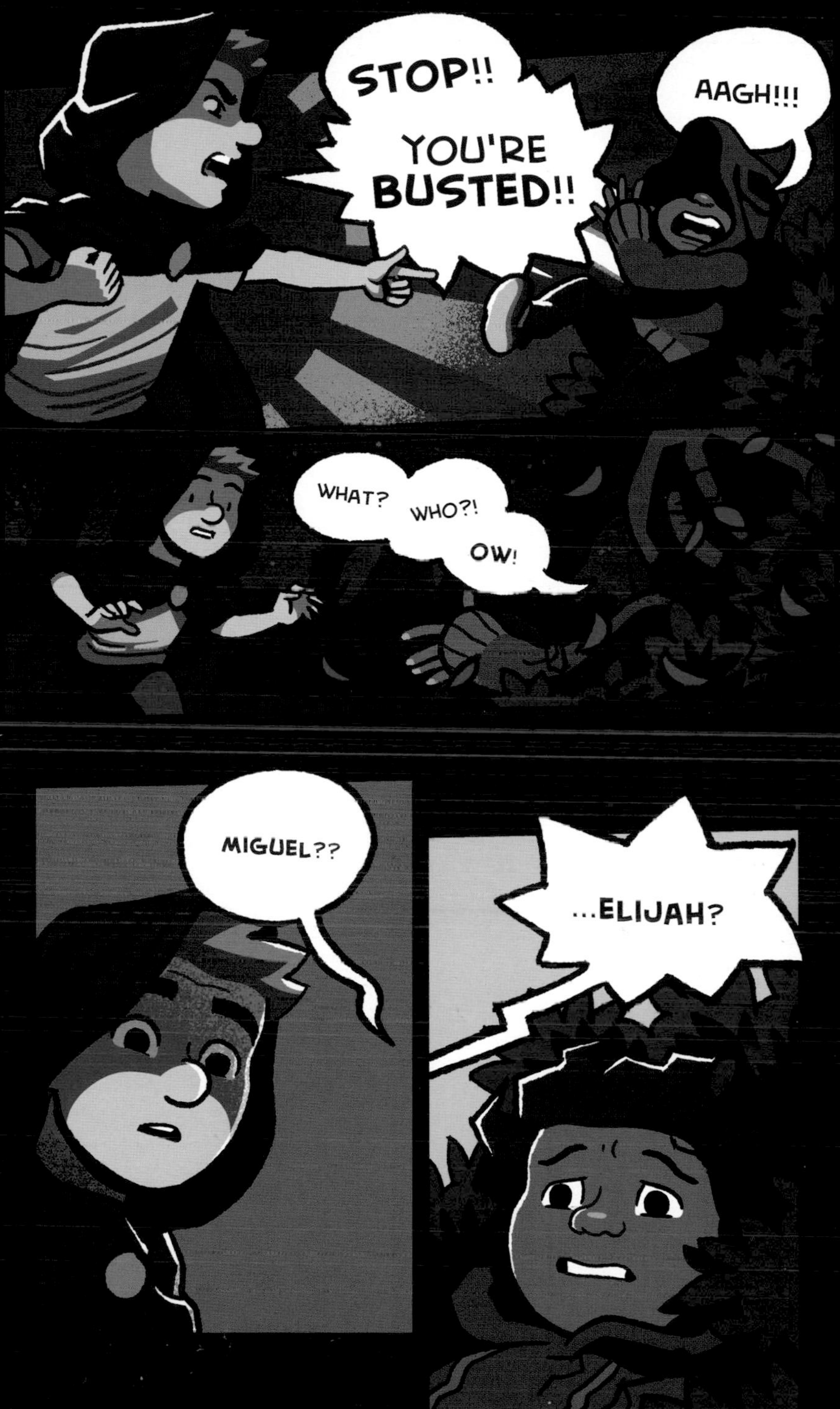
STOP!! YOU'RE BUSTED!!
AAGH!!!
WHAT? WHO?! OW!
MIGUEL??
...ELIJAH?

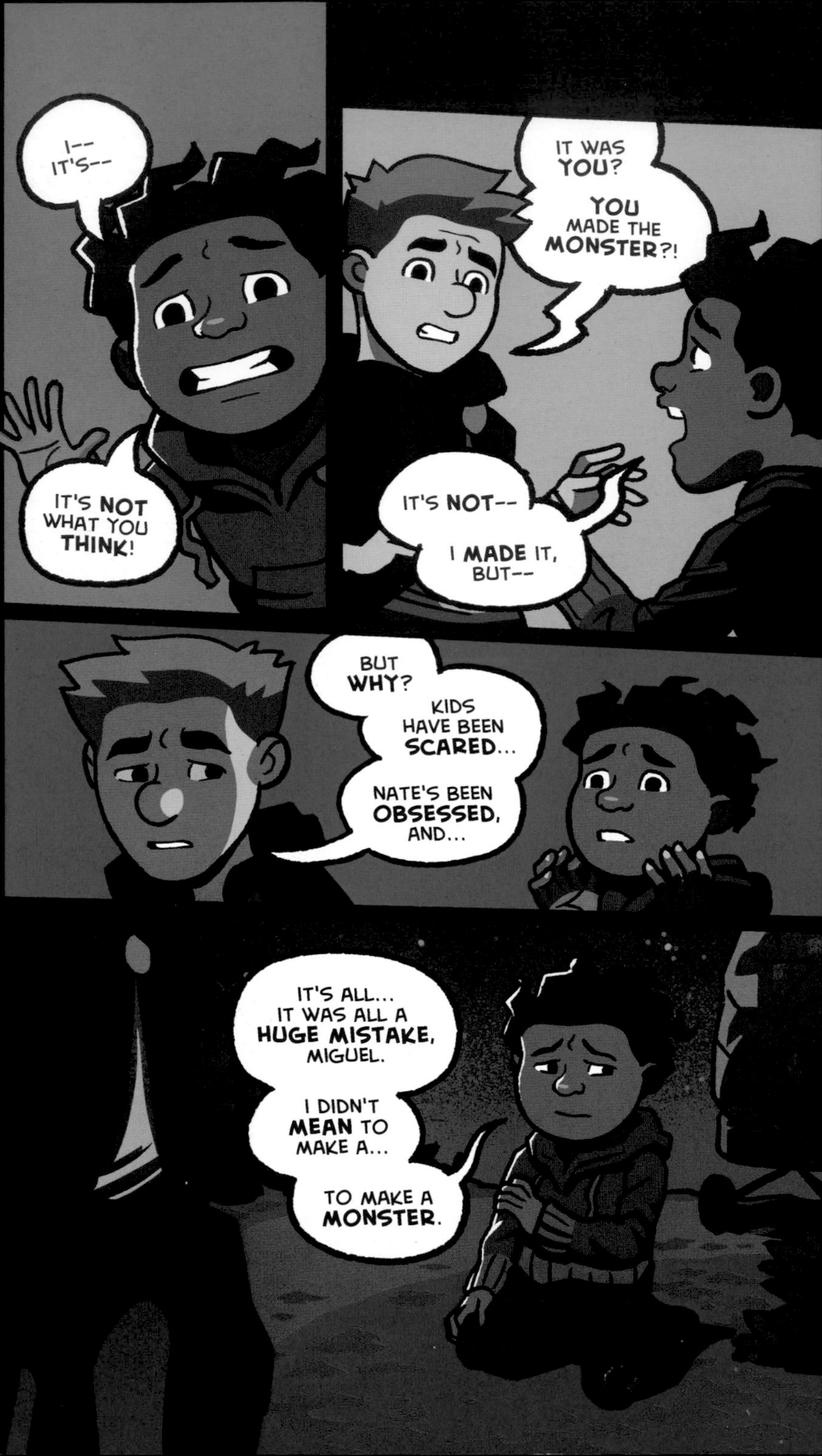
I--
IT'S--
IT'S NOT WHAT YOU THINK!
IT WAS YOU?
YOU MADE THE MONSTER?!
IT'S NOT--
I MADE IT, BUT--
BUT WHY?
KIDS HAVE BEEN SCARED...
NATE'S BEEN OBSESSED, AND...
IT'S ALL... IT WAS ALL A HUGE MISTAKE, MIGUEL.
I DIDN'T MEAN TO MAKE A...
TO MAKE A MONSTER.

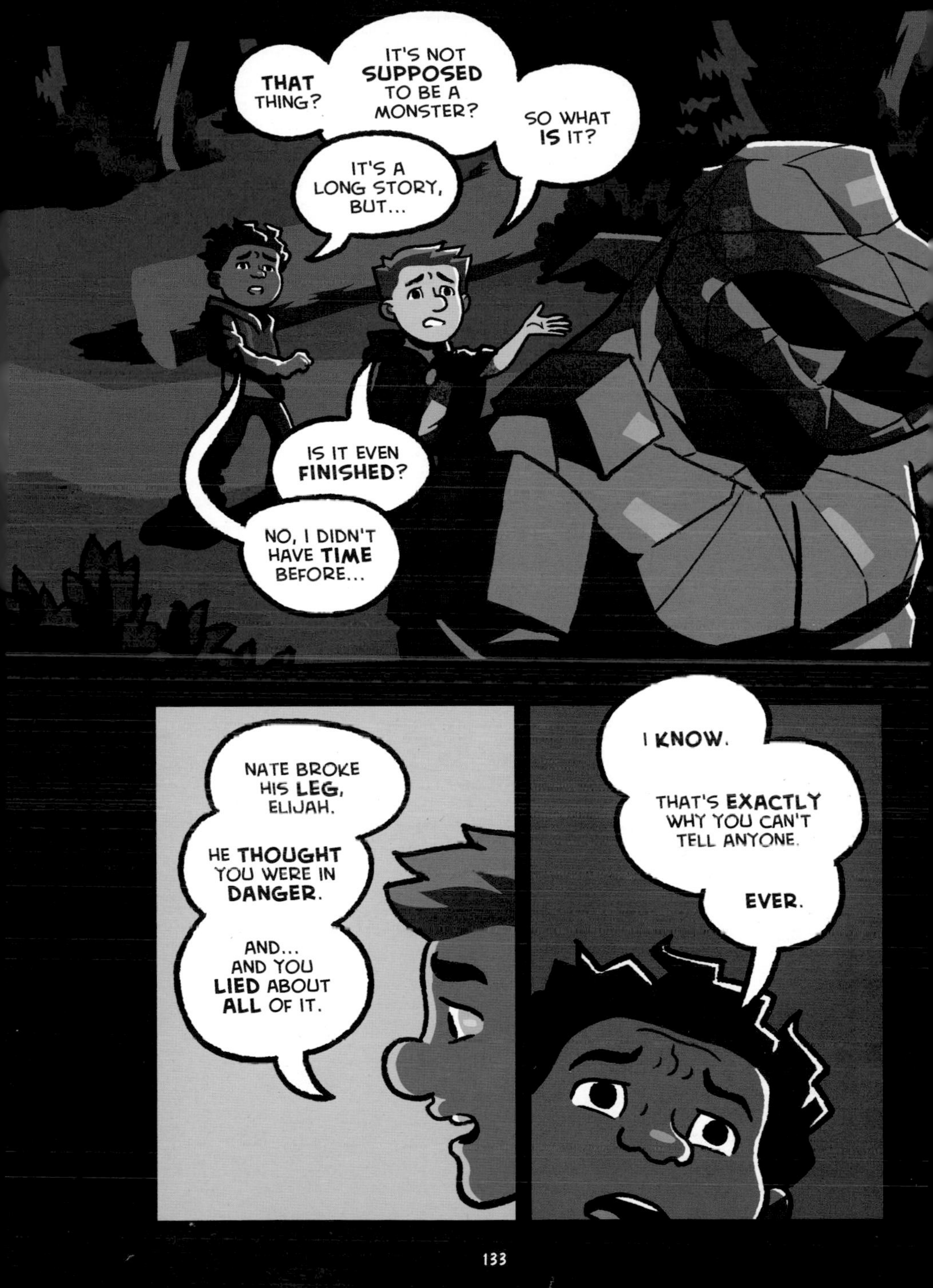
THAT THING?
IT'S NOT SUPPOSED TO BE A MONSTER?
SO WHAT IS IT?
IT'S A LONG STORY, BUT...
IS IT EVEN FINISHED?
NO, I DIDN'T HAVE TIME BEFORE...
NATE BROKE HIS LEG, ELIJAH.
HE THOUGHT YOU WERE IN DANGER.
AND... AND YOU LIED ABOUT ALL OF IT.
I KNOW.
THAT'S EXACTLY WHY YOU CAN'T TELL ANYONE.
EVER.

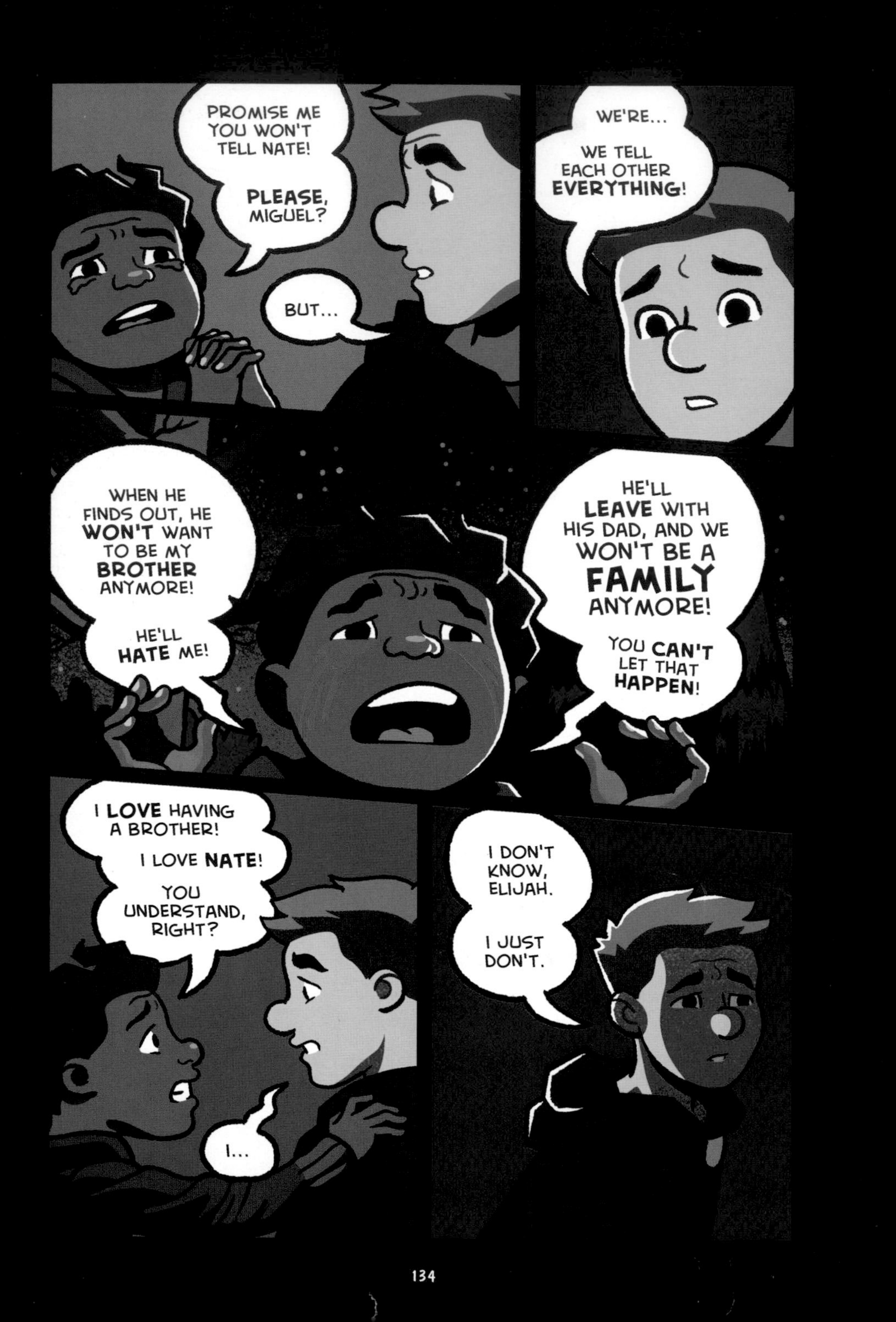
PROMISE ME YOU WON'T TELL NATE!
PLEASE, MIGUEL?
BUT...
WE'RE...
WE TELL EACH OTHER **EVERYTHING**!
WHEN HE FINDS OUT, HE **WON'T** WANT TO BE MY **BROTHER** ANYMORE!
HE'LL **HATE** ME!
HE'LL **LEAVE** WITH HIS DAD, AND WE **WON'T BE A FAMILY** ANYMORE!
YOU **CAN'T** LET THAT **HAPPEN**!
I **LOVE** HAVING A BROTHER!
I LOVE **NATE**!
YOU UNDERSTAND, RIGHT?
I...
I DON'T KNOW, ELIJAH.
I JUST DON'T.

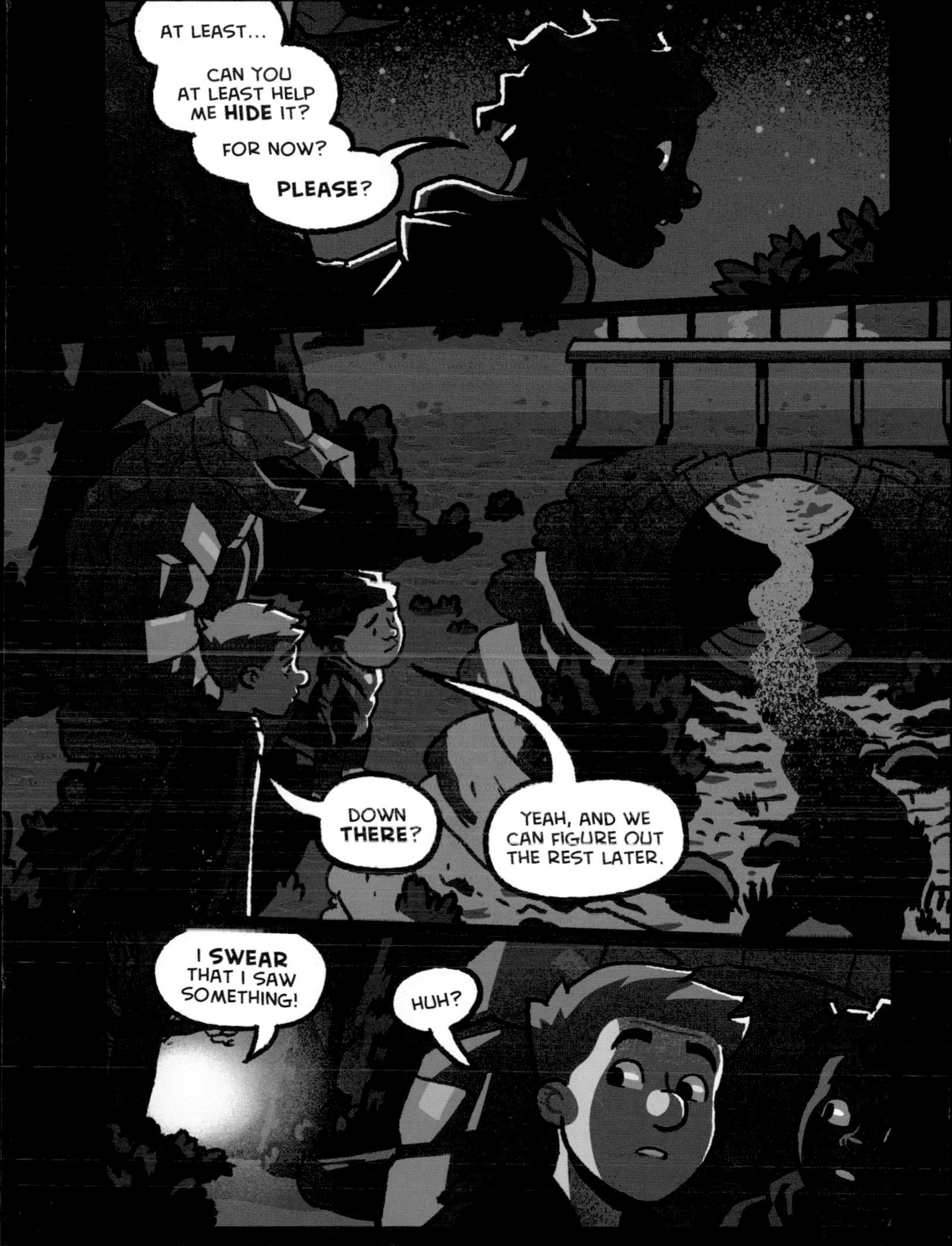
AT LEAST...
CAN YOU AT LEAST HELP ME HIDE IT?
FOR NOW?
PLEASE?
DOWN THERE?
YEAH, AND WE CAN FIGURE OUT THE REST LATER.
I SWEAR THAT I SAW SOMETHING!
HUH?

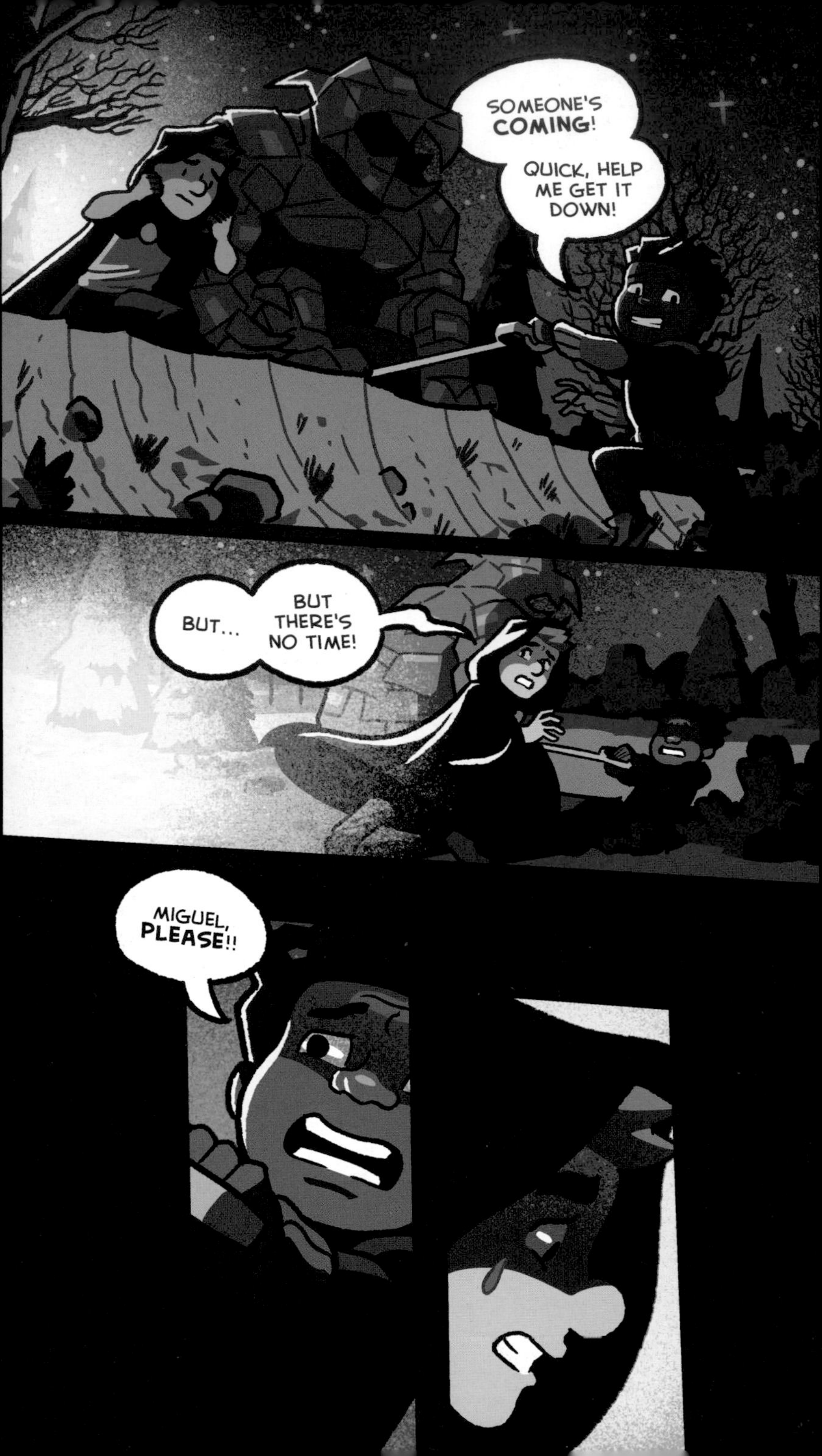
SOMEONE'S **COMING**!
QUICK, HELP ME GET IT DOWN!
BUT...
BUT THERE'S NO TIME!
MIGUEL, **PLEASE**!!

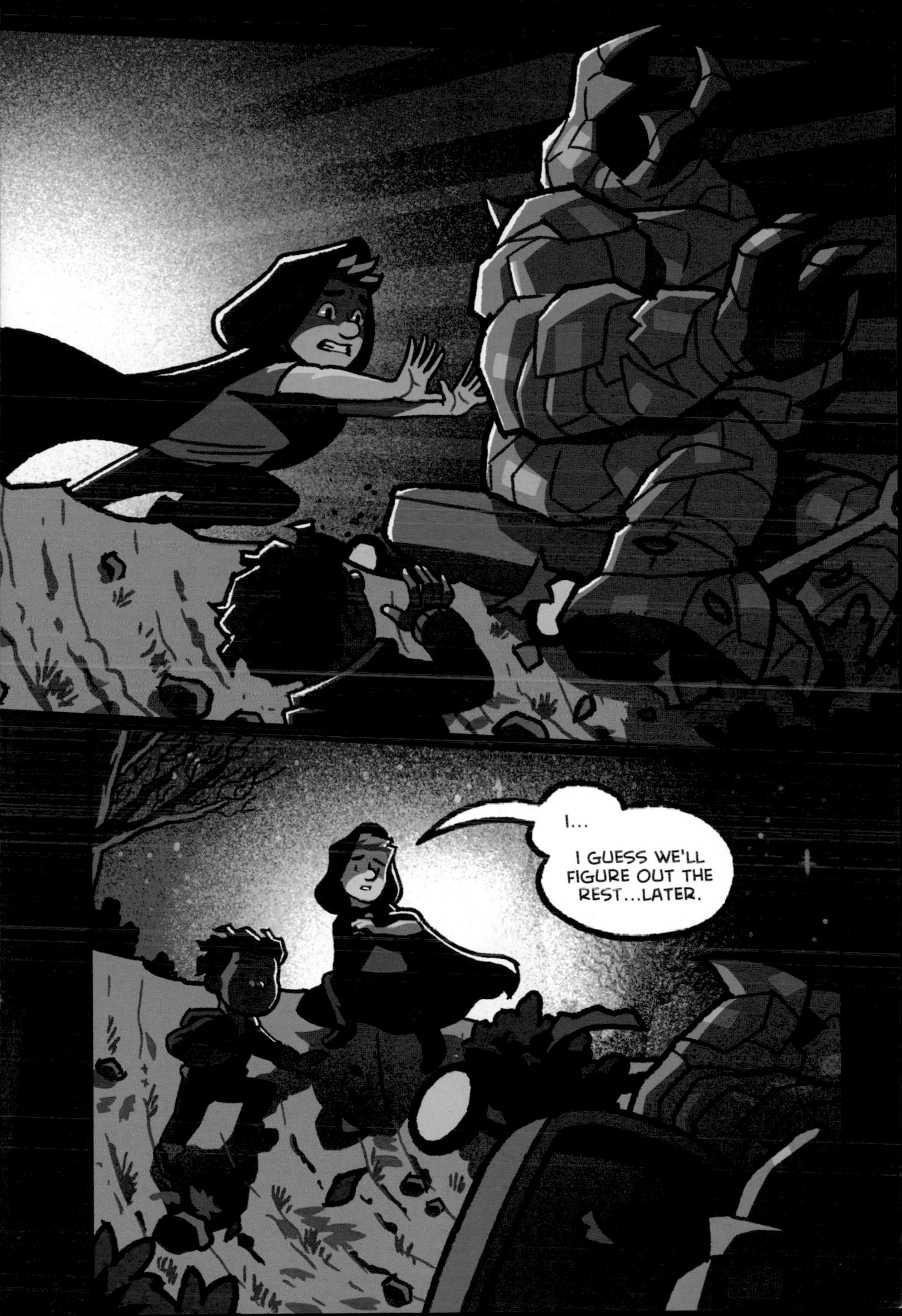
I...
I GUESS WE'LL FIGURE OUT THE REST...LATER.

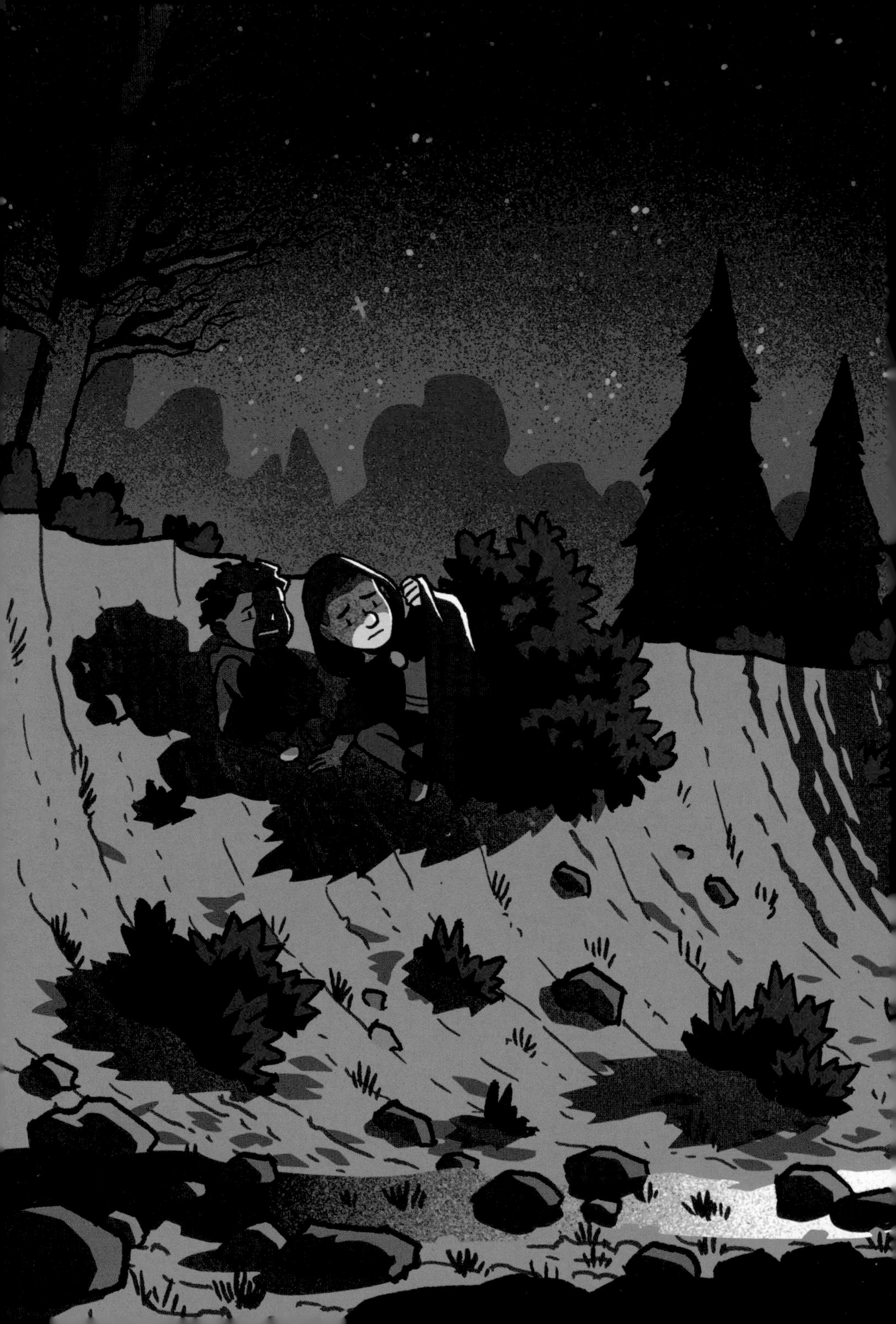

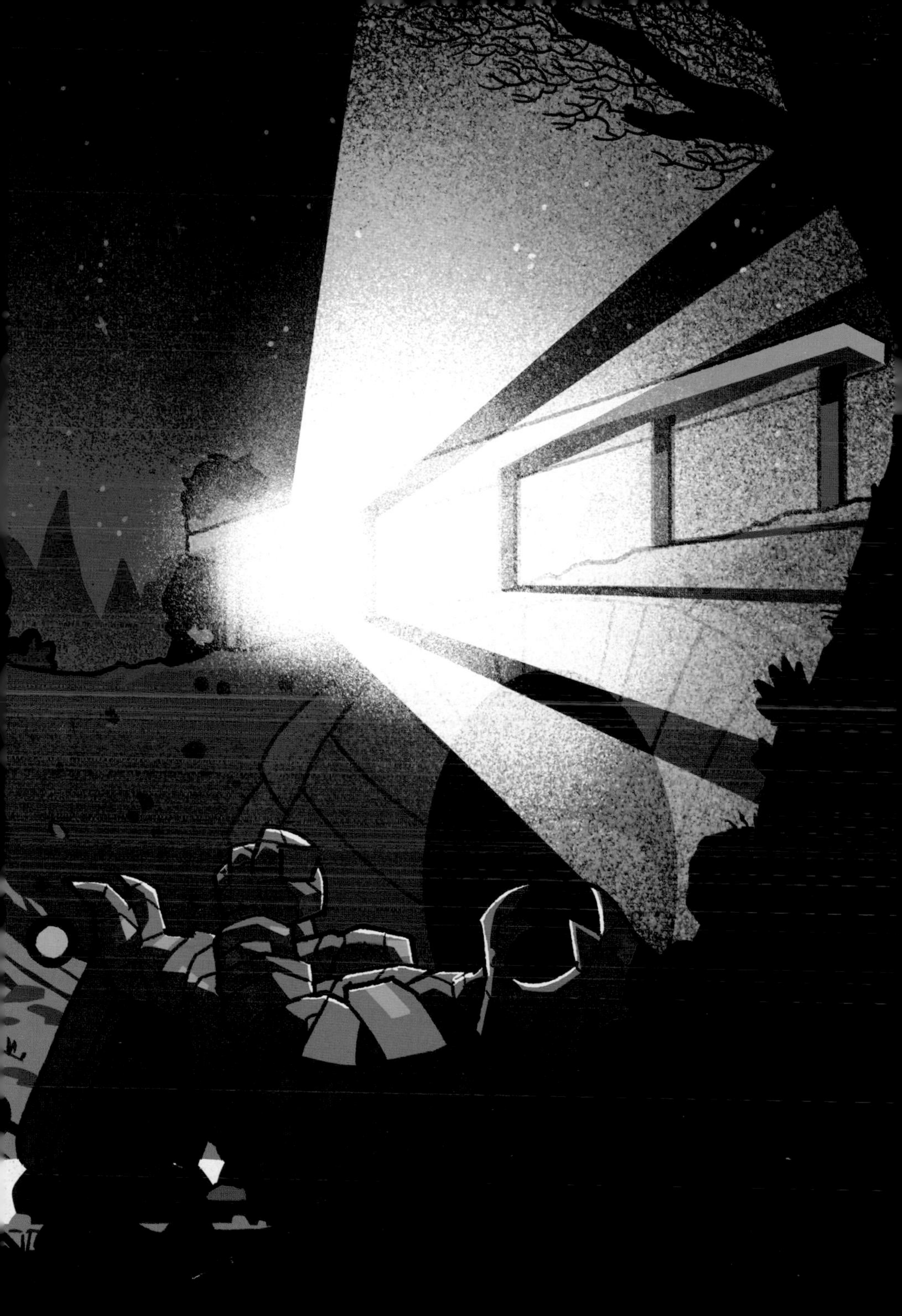

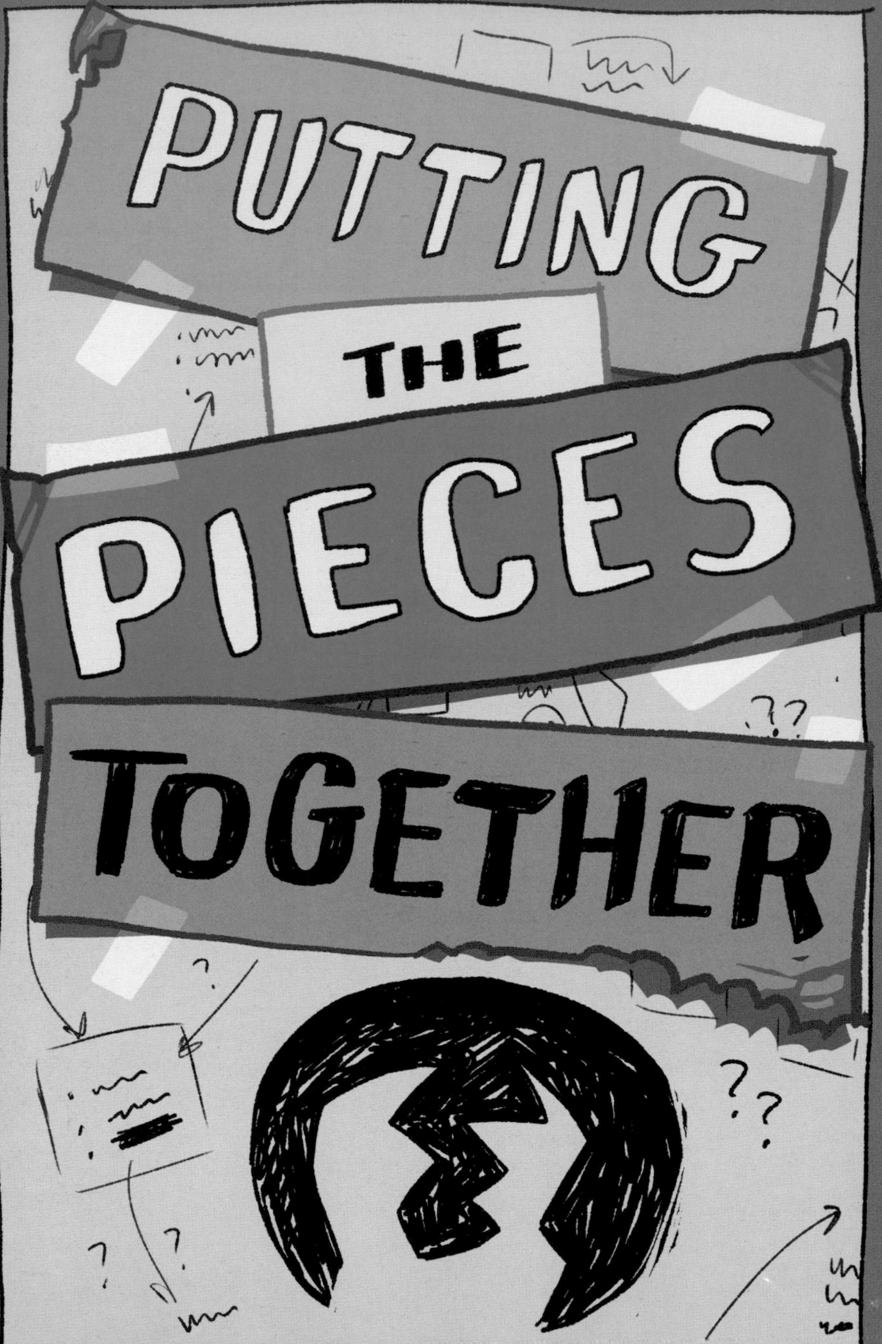
PUTTING
THE
PIECES
TOGETHER

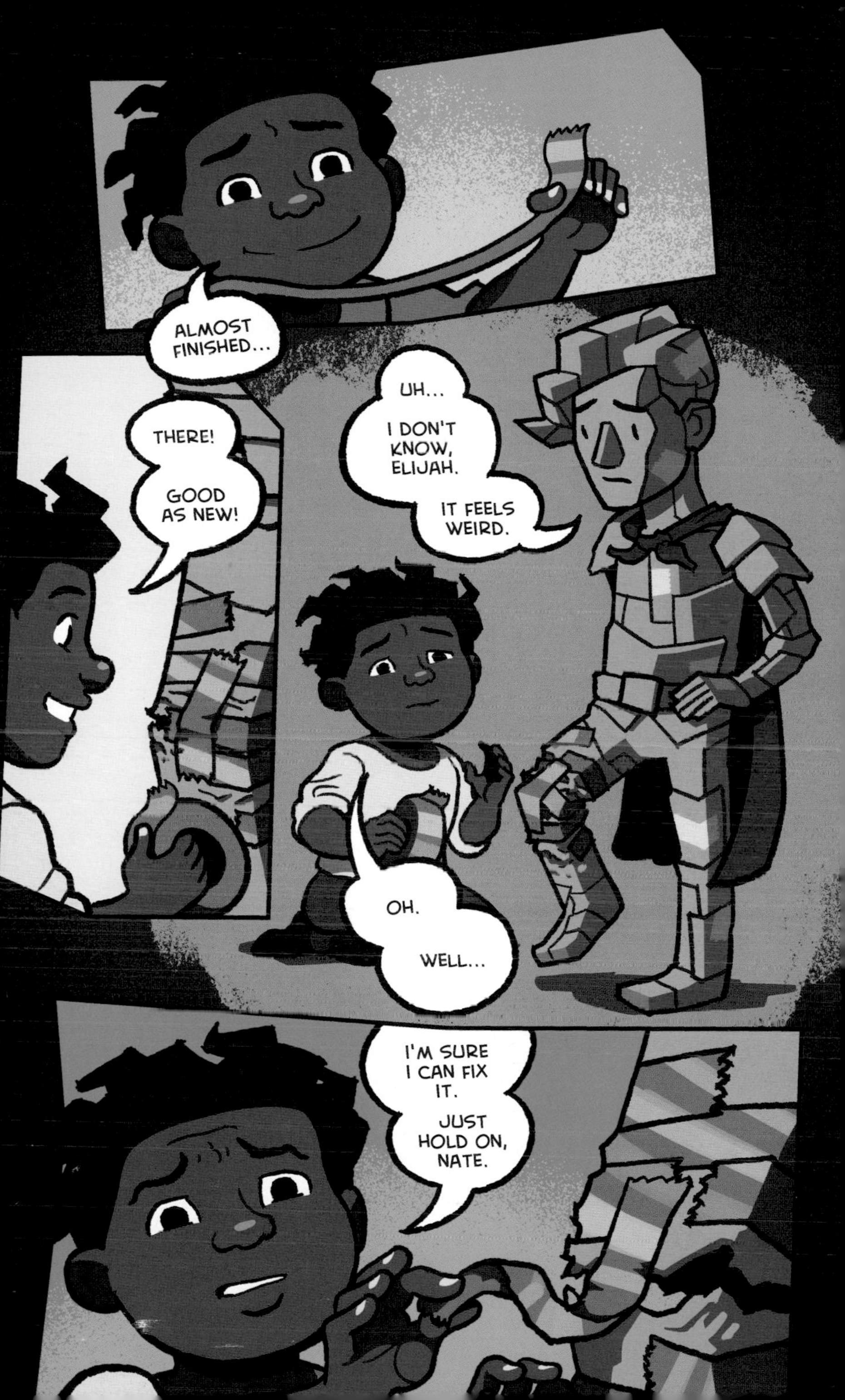
ALMOST FINISHED...
THERE!
GOOD AS NEW!
UH...
I DON'T KNOW, ELIJAH.
IT FEELS WEIRD.
OH.
WELL...
I'M SURE I CAN FIX IT.
JUST HOLD ON, NATE.

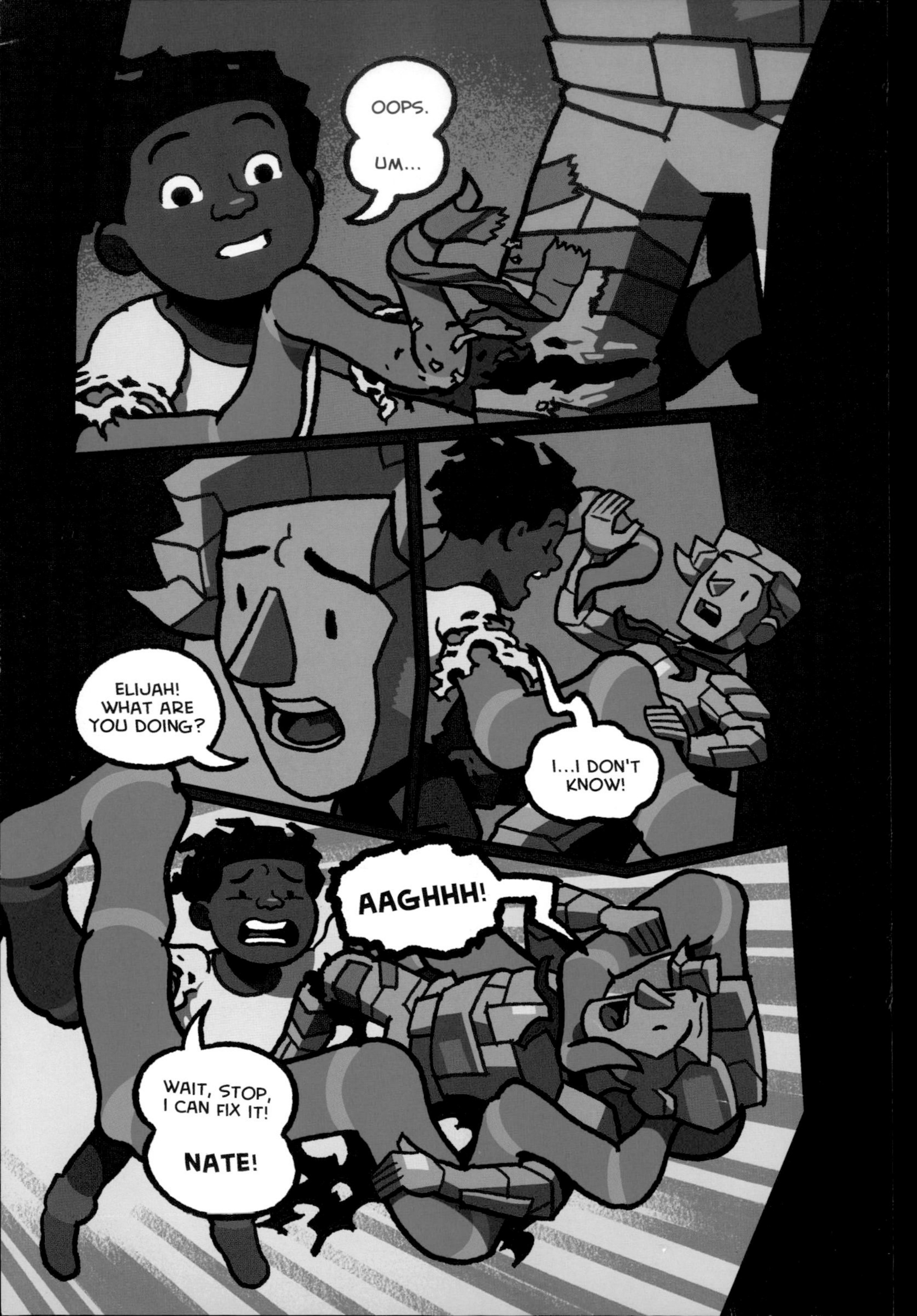
OOPS.
UM...
ELIJAH! WHAT ARE YOU DOING?
I...I DON'T KNOW!
AAGHHH!
WAIT, STOP, I CAN FIX IT!
NATE!

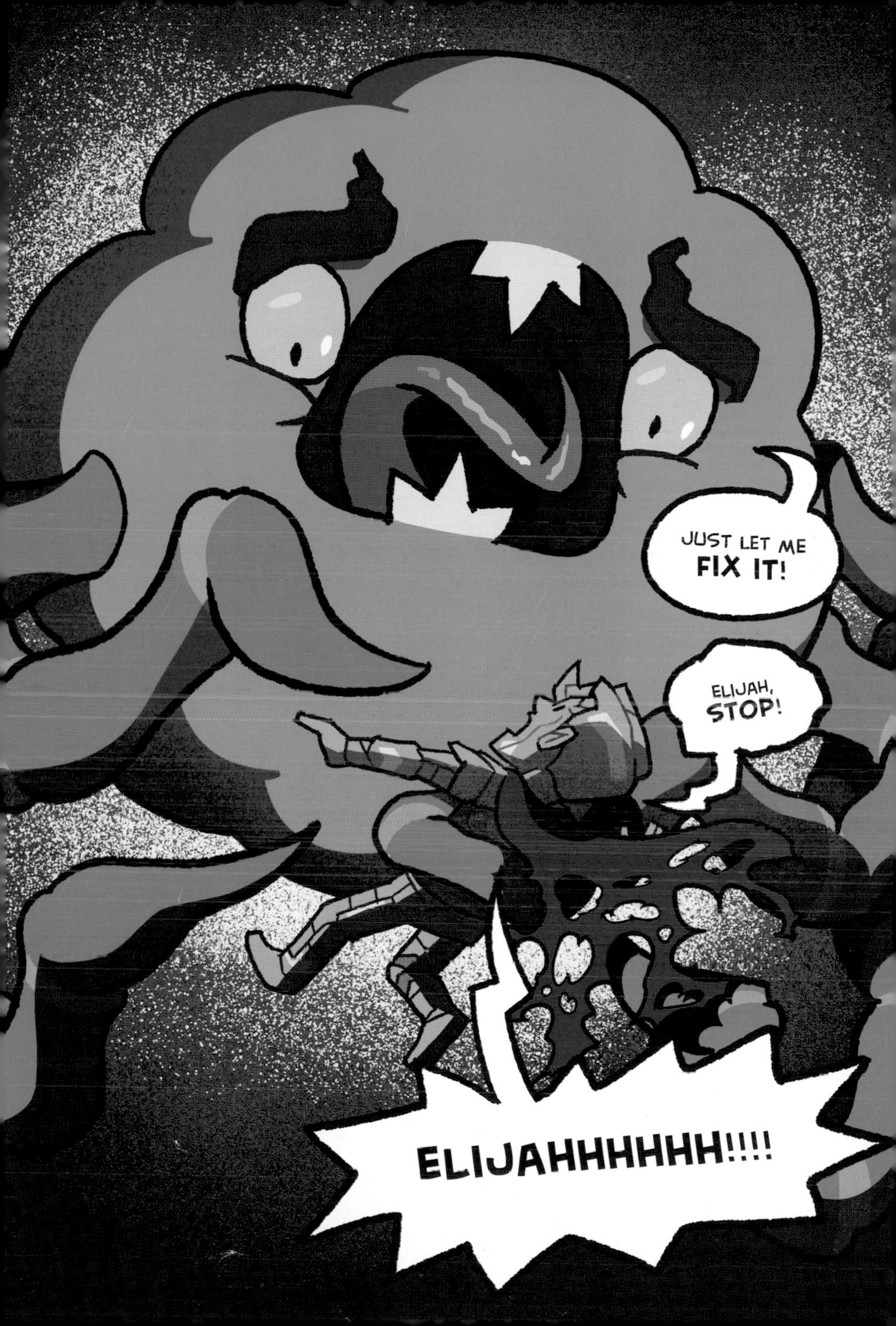
JUST LET ME FIX IT!
ELIJAH, STOP!
ELIJAHHHHHH!!!!

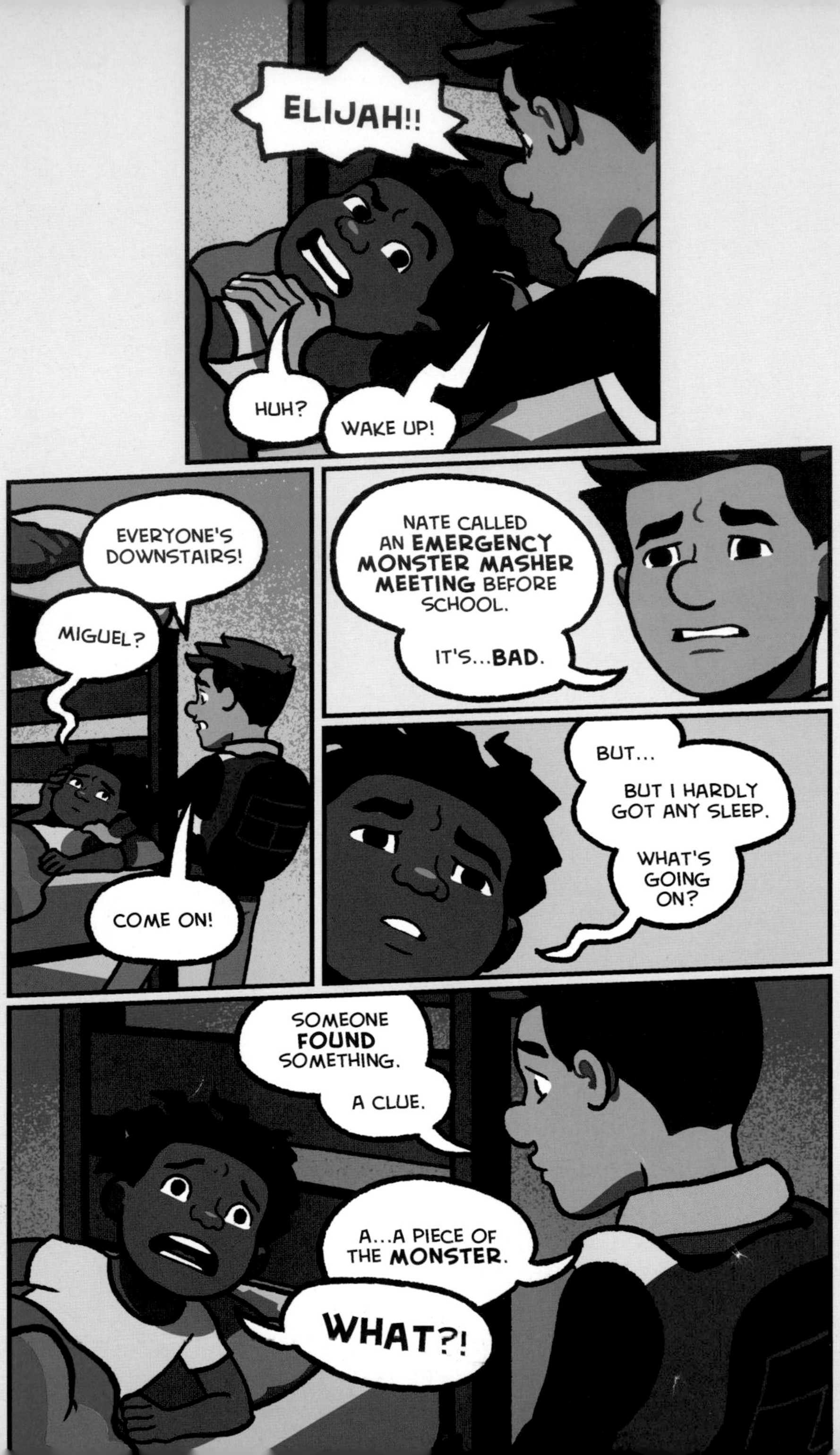
ELIJAH!!
HUH?
WAKE UP!
EVERYONE'S DOWNSTAIRS!
MIGUEL?
COME ON!
NATE CALLED AN EMERGENCY MONSTER MASHER MEETING BEFORE SCHOOL.
IT'S...BAD.
BUT...
BUT I HARDLY GOT ANY SLEEP.
WHAT'S GOING ON?
SOMEONE FOUND SOMETHING.
A CLUE.
A...A PIECE OF THE MONSTER.
WHAT?!

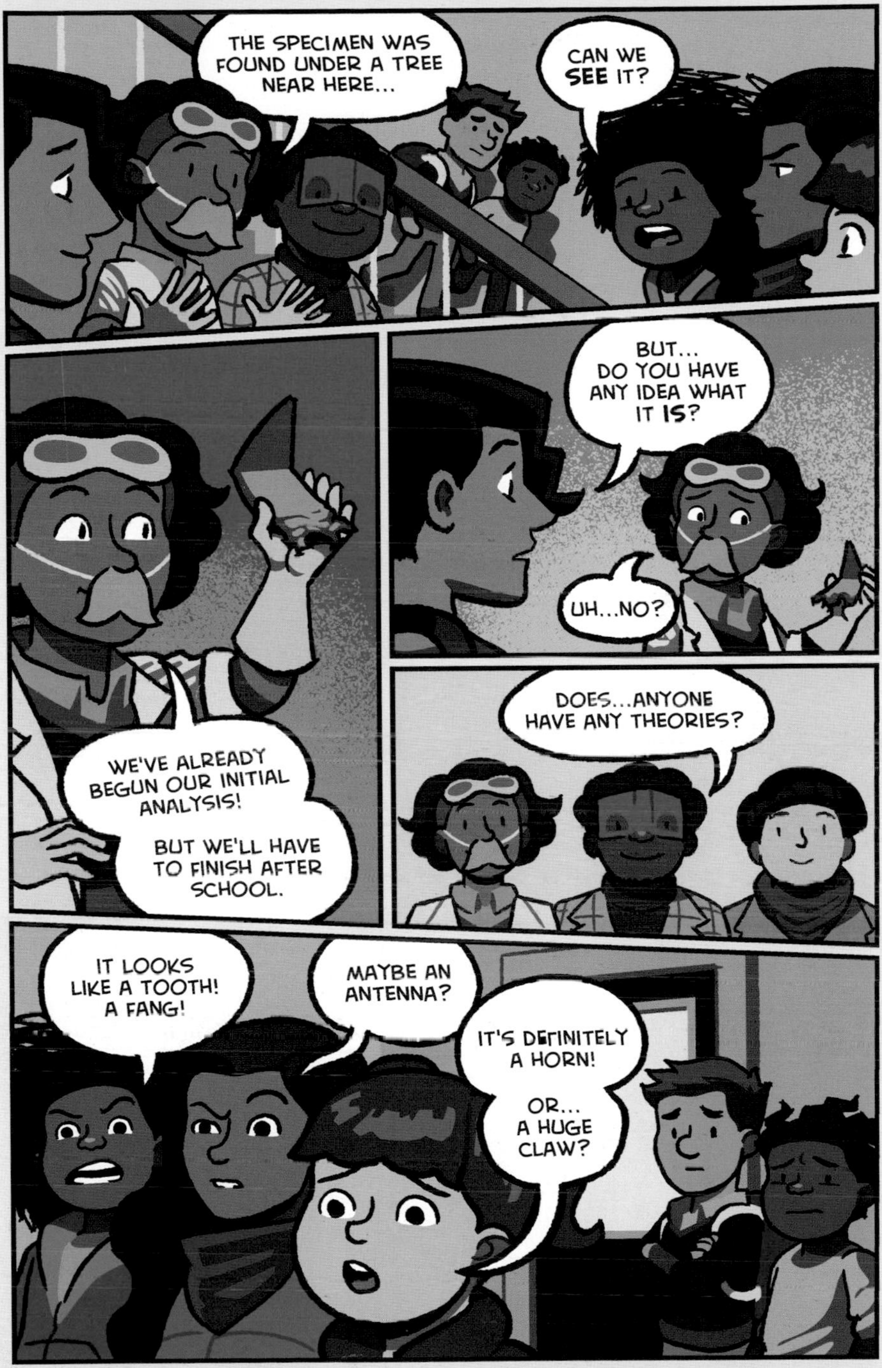
THE SPECIMEN WAS FOUND UNDER A TREE NEAR HERE...
CAN WE SEE IT?
WE'VE ALREADY BEGUN OUR INITIAL ANALYSIS!
BUT WE'LL HAVE TO FINISH AFTER SCHOOL.
BUT... DO YOU HAVE ANY IDEA WHAT IT IS?
UH...NO?
DOES...ANYONE HAVE ANY THEORIES?
IT LOOKS LIKE A TOOTH! A FANG!
MAYBE AN ANTENNA?
IT'S DEFINITELY A HORN!
OR... A HUGE CLAW?

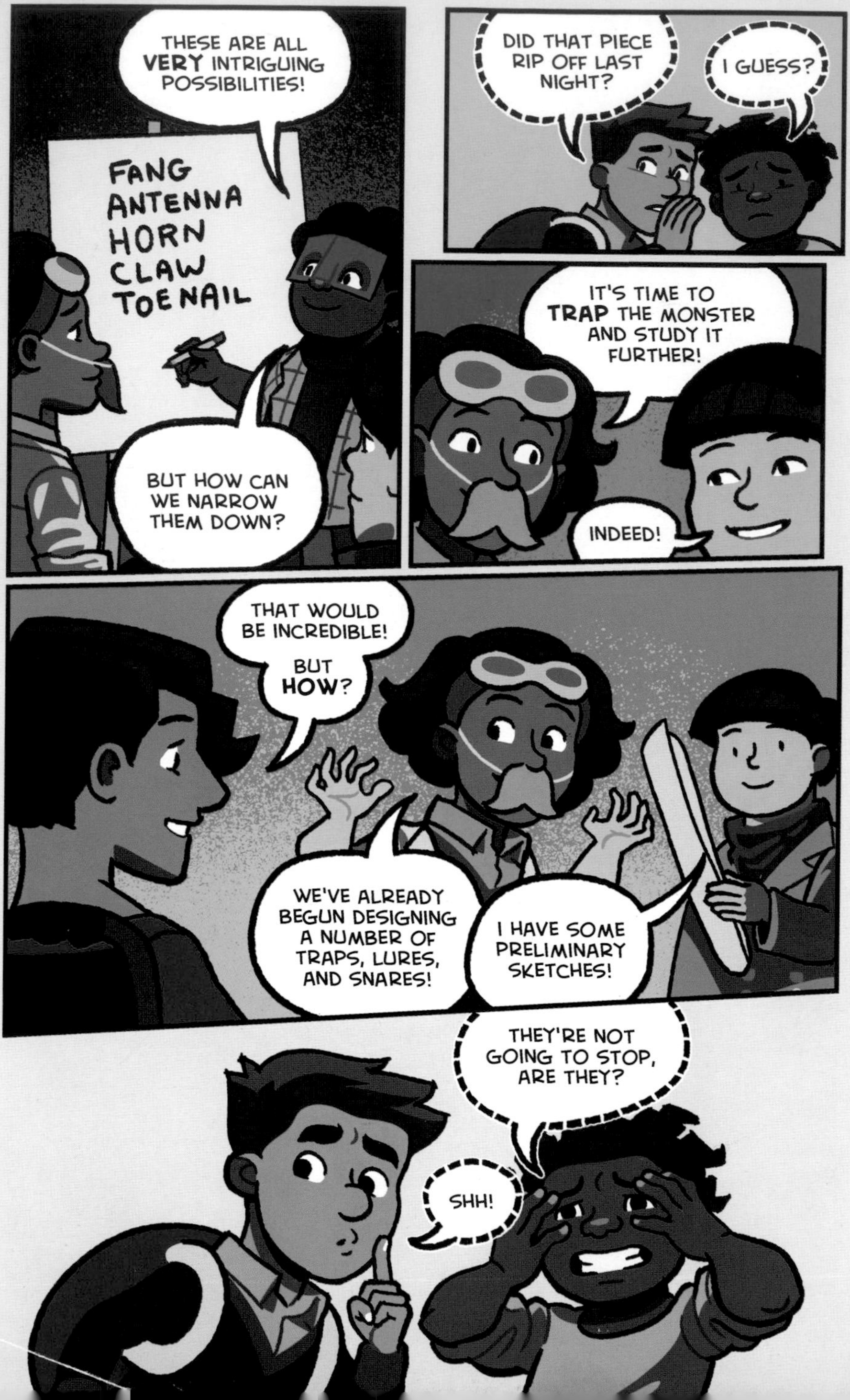
THESE ARE ALL **VERY** INTRIGUING POSSIBILITIES!
FANG
ANTENNA
HORN
CLAW
TOENAIL
BUT HOW CAN WE NARROW THEM DOWN?
DID THAT PIECE RIP OFF LAST NIGHT?
I GUESS?
IT'S TIME TO **TRAP** THE MONSTER AND STUDY IT FURTHER!
INDEED!
THAT WOULD BE INCREDIBLE!
BUT **HOW**?
WE'VE ALREADY BEGUN DESIGNING A NUMBER OF TRAPS, LURES, AND SNARES!
I HAVE SOME PRELIMINARY SKETCHES!
THEY'RE NOT GOING TO STOP, ARE THEY?
SHH!

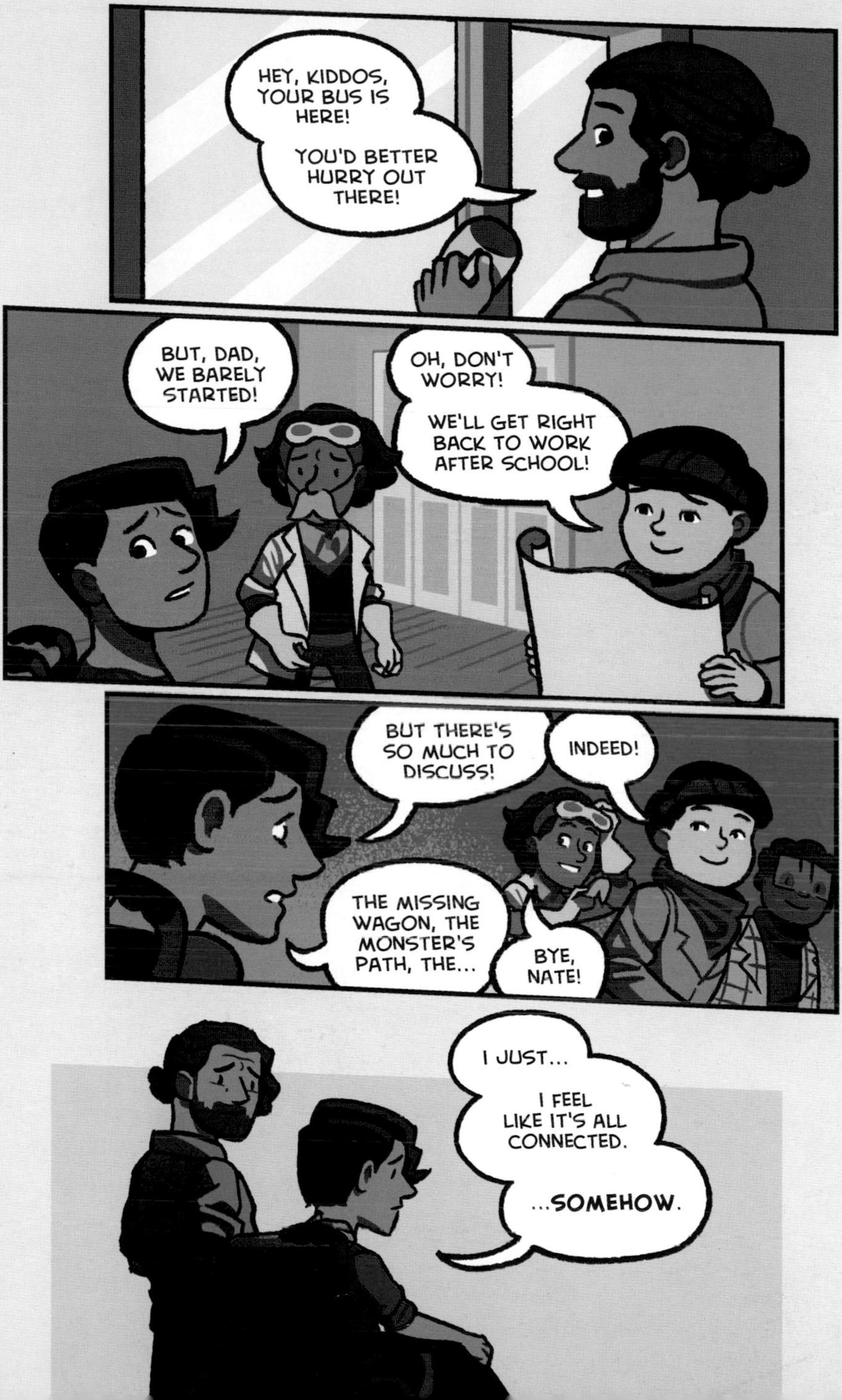
HEY, KIDDOS, YOUR BUS IS HERE!
YOU'D BETTER HURRY OUT THERE!
BUT, DAD, WE BARELY STARTED!
OH, DON'T WORRY!
WE'LL GET RIGHT BACK TO WORK AFTER SCHOOL!
BUT THERE'S SO MUCH TO DISCUSS!
INDEED!
THE MISSING WAGON, THE MONSTER'S PATH, THE...
BYE, NATE!
I JUST...
I FEEL LIKE IT'S ALL CONNECTED.
...SOMEHOW.

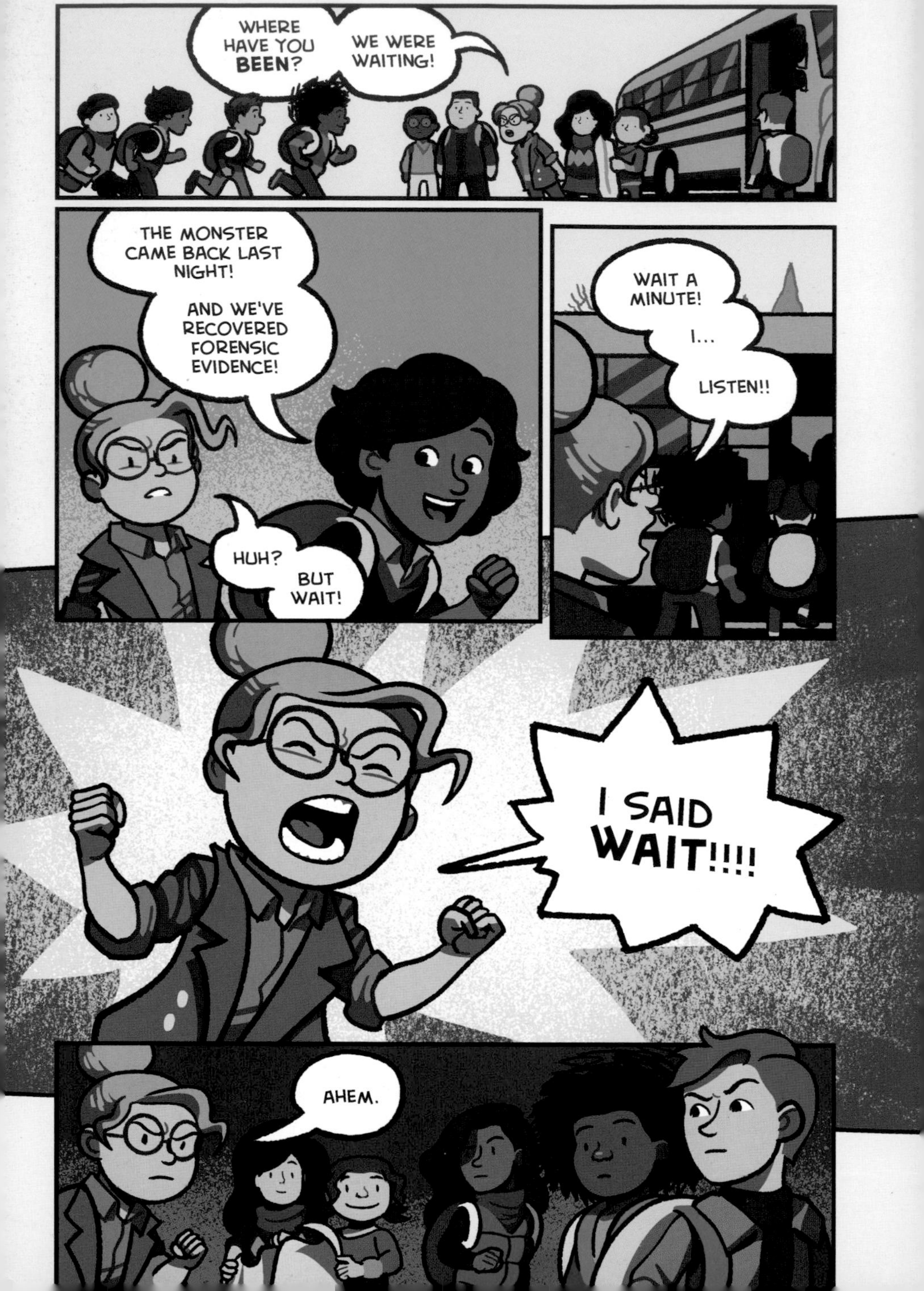
WHERE HAVE YOU BEEN?
WE WERE WAITING!
THE MONSTER CAME BACK LAST NIGHT!
AND WE'VE RECOVERED FORENSIC EVIDENCE!
HUH?
BUT WAIT!
WAIT A MINUTE!
I...
LISTEN!!
I SAID WAIT!!!!
AHEM.

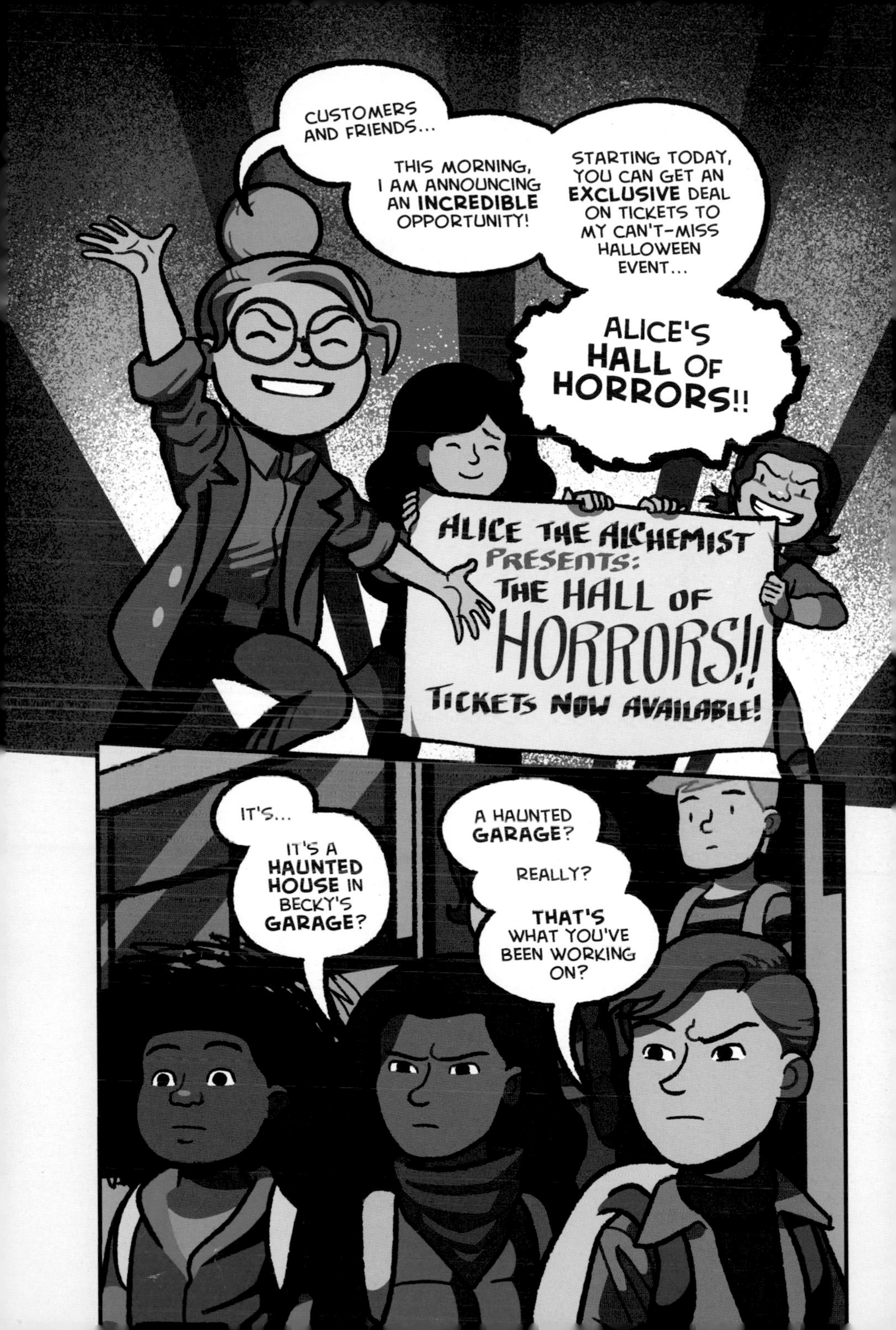
CUSTOMERS AND FRIENDS...
THIS MORNING, I AM ANNOUNCING AN INCREDIBLE OPPORTUNITY!
STARTING TODAY, YOU CAN GET AN EXCLUSIVE DEAL ON TICKETS TO MY CAN'T-MISS HALLOWEEN EVENT...
ALICE'S HALL OF HORRORS!!
ALICE THE ALCHEMIST PRESENTS: THE HALL OF HORRORS!! TICKETS NOW AVAILABLE!
IT'S...
IT'S A HAUNTED HOUSE IN BECKY'S GARAGE?
A HAUNTED GARAGE?
REALLY?
THAT'S WHAT YOU'VE BEEN WORKING ON?

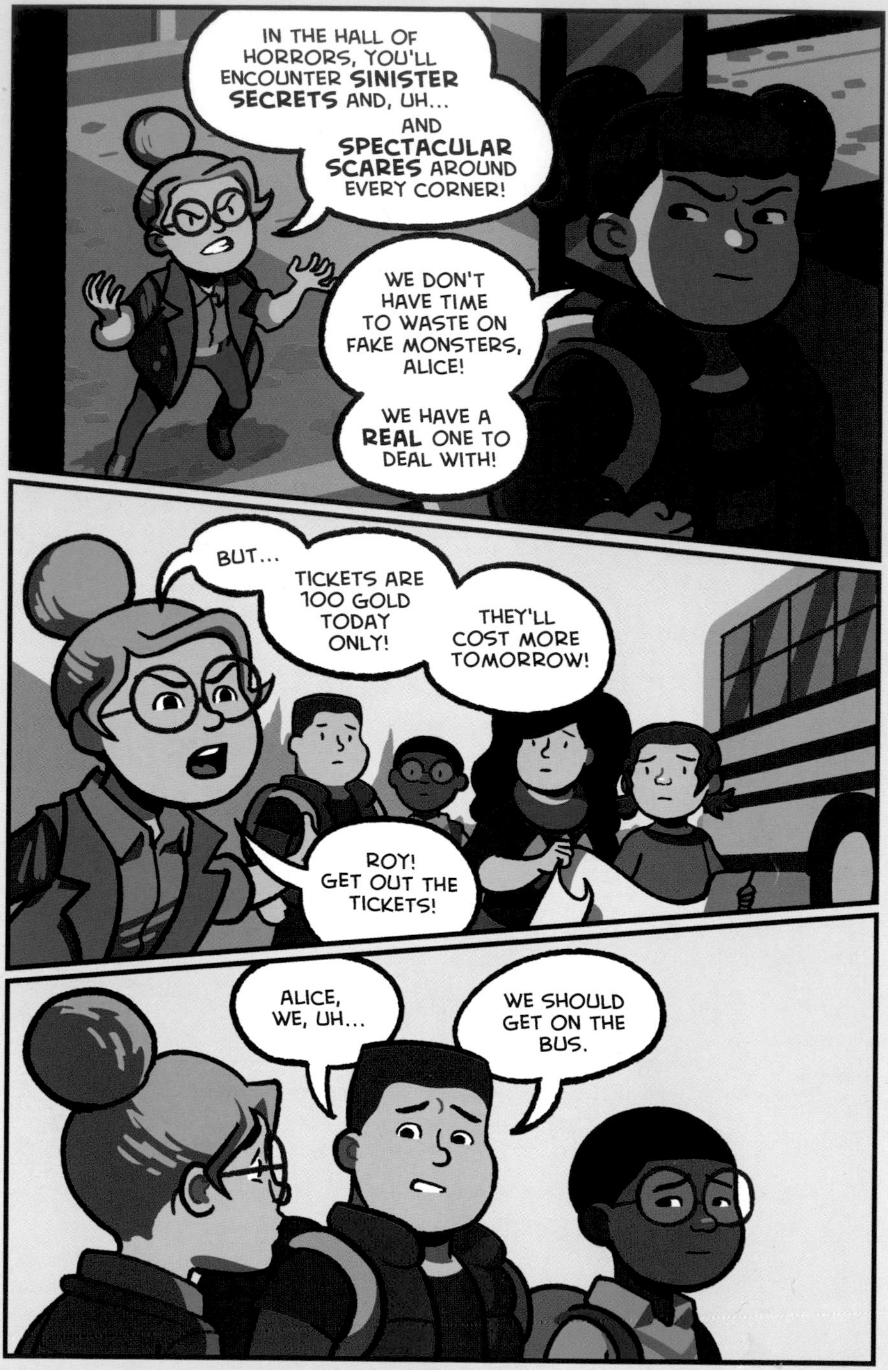
IN THE HALL OF HORRORS, YOU'LL ENCOUNTER **SINISTER SECRETS** AND, UH...
AND **SPECTACULAR SCARES** AROUND EVERY CORNER!
WE DON'T HAVE TIME TO WASTE ON FAKE MONSTERS, ALICE!
WE HAVE A **REAL** ONE TO DEAL WITH!
BUT...
TICKETS ARE 100 GOLD TODAY ONLY!
THEY'LL COST MORE TOMORROW!
ROY! GET OUT THE TICKETS!
ALICE, WE, UH...
WE SHOULD GET ON THE BUS.

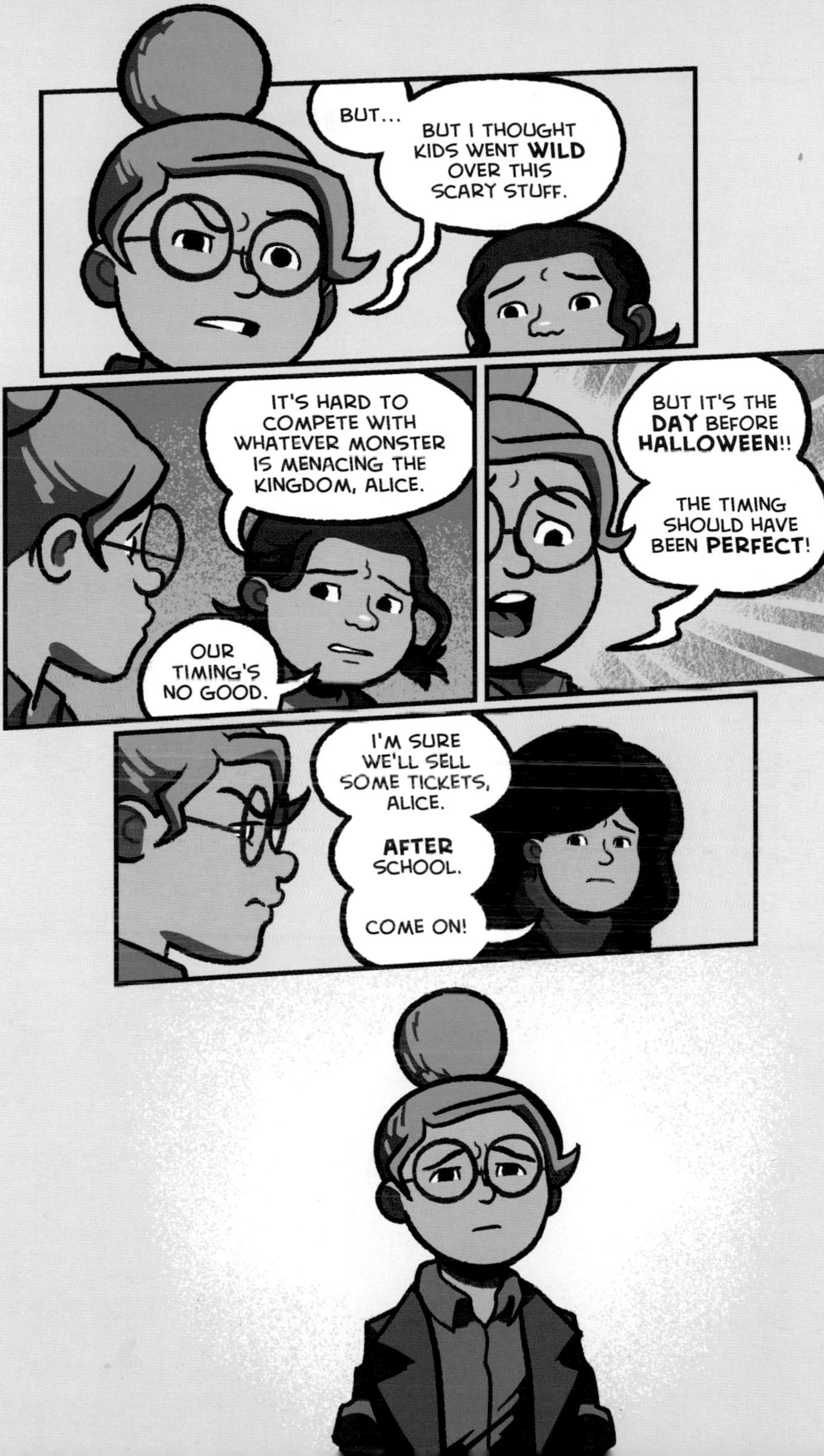
BUT...
BUT I THOUGHT KIDS WENT **WILD** OVER THIS SCARY STUFF.
IT'S HARD TO COMPETE WITH WHATEVER MONSTER IS MENACING THE KINGDOM, ALICE.
OUR TIMING'S NO GOOD.
BUT IT'S THE **DAY** BEFORE **HALLOWEEN**!!
THE TIMING SHOULD HAVE BEEN **PERFECT**!
I'M SURE WE'LL SELL SOME TICKETS, ALICE.
AFTER SCHOOL.
COME ON!

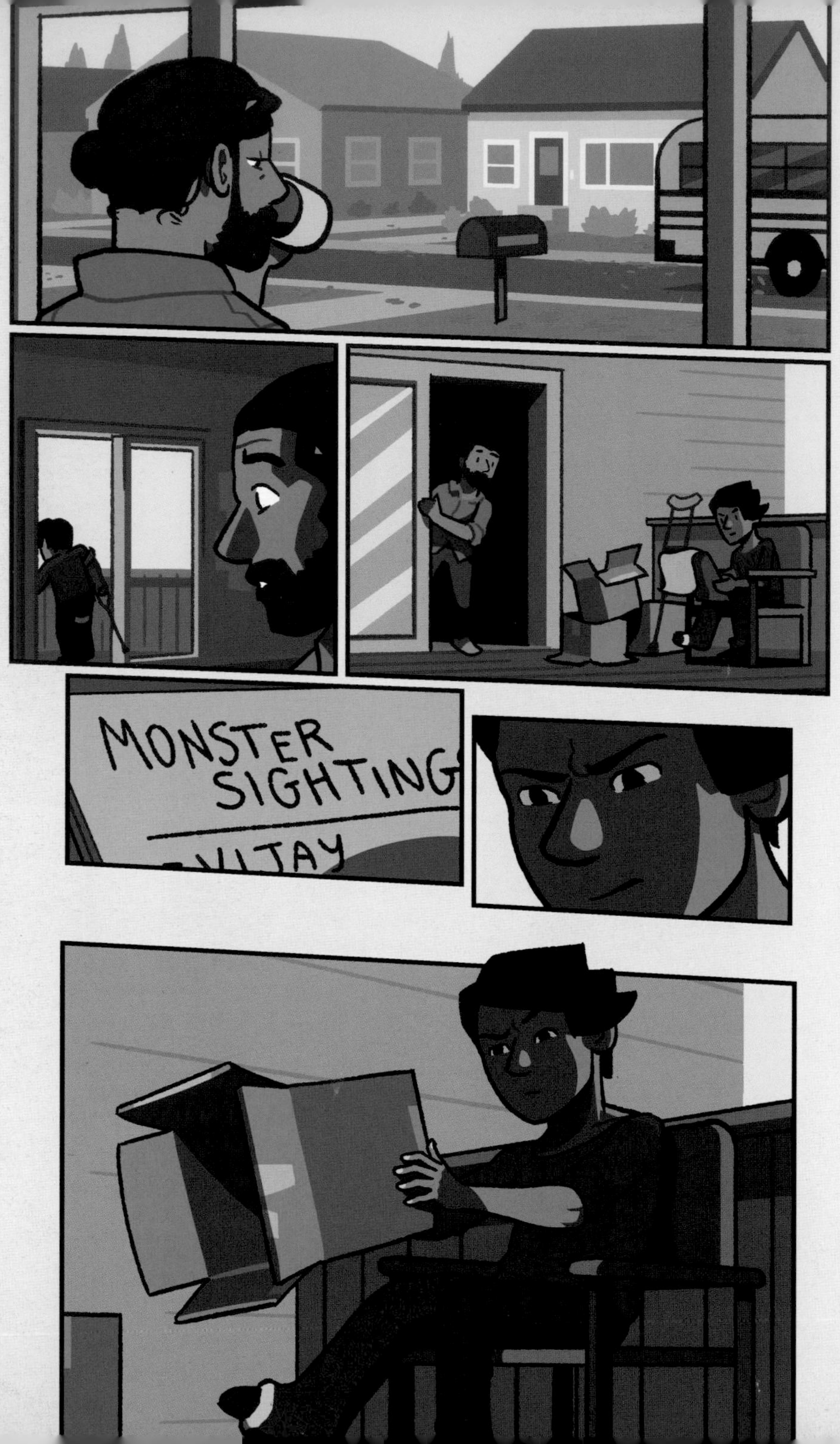
MONSTER SIGHTING
VIJAY

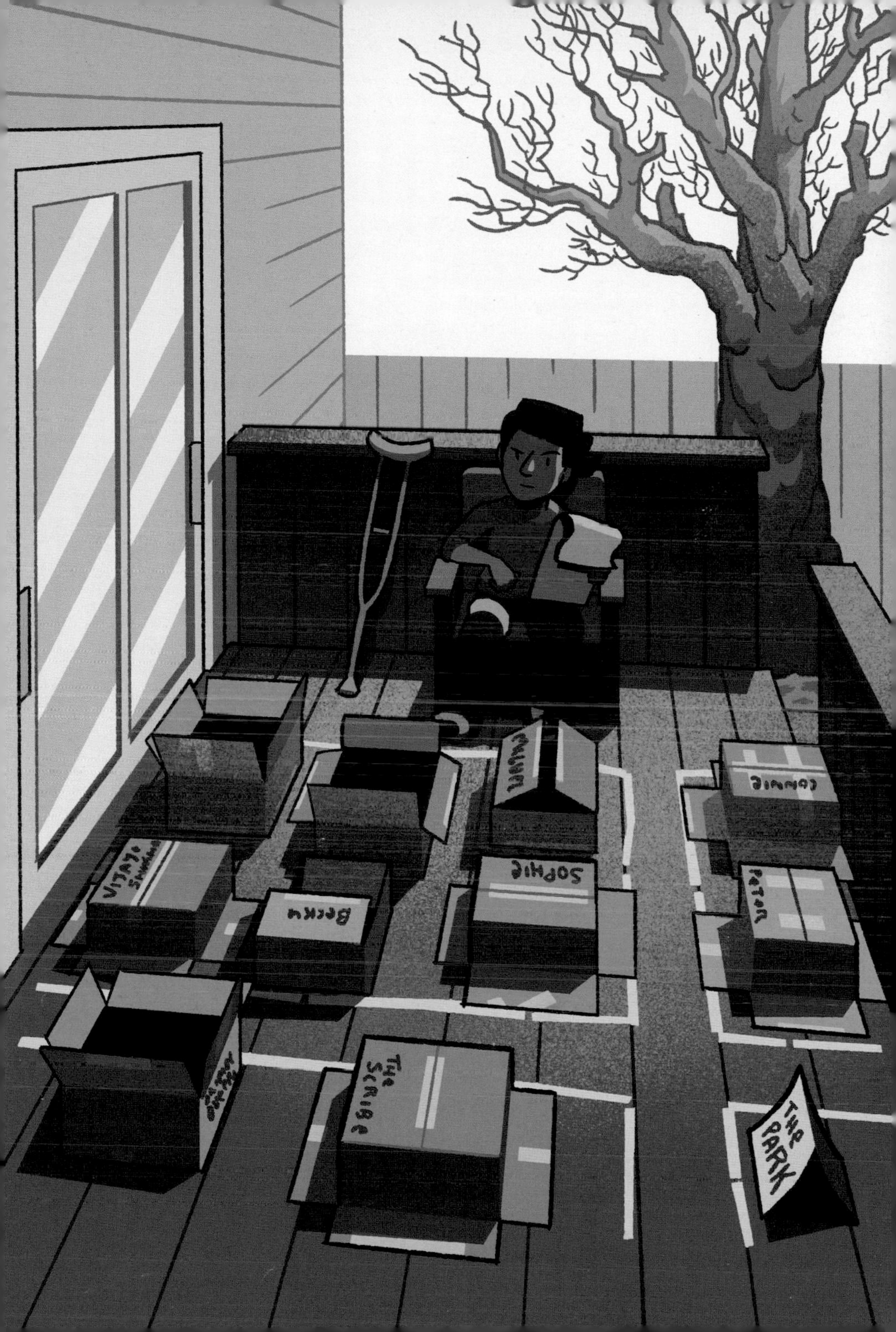

VIJAY's
BECKY
SOPHIE
CAMMIE
PETER
THE SCRIBE
THE PARK

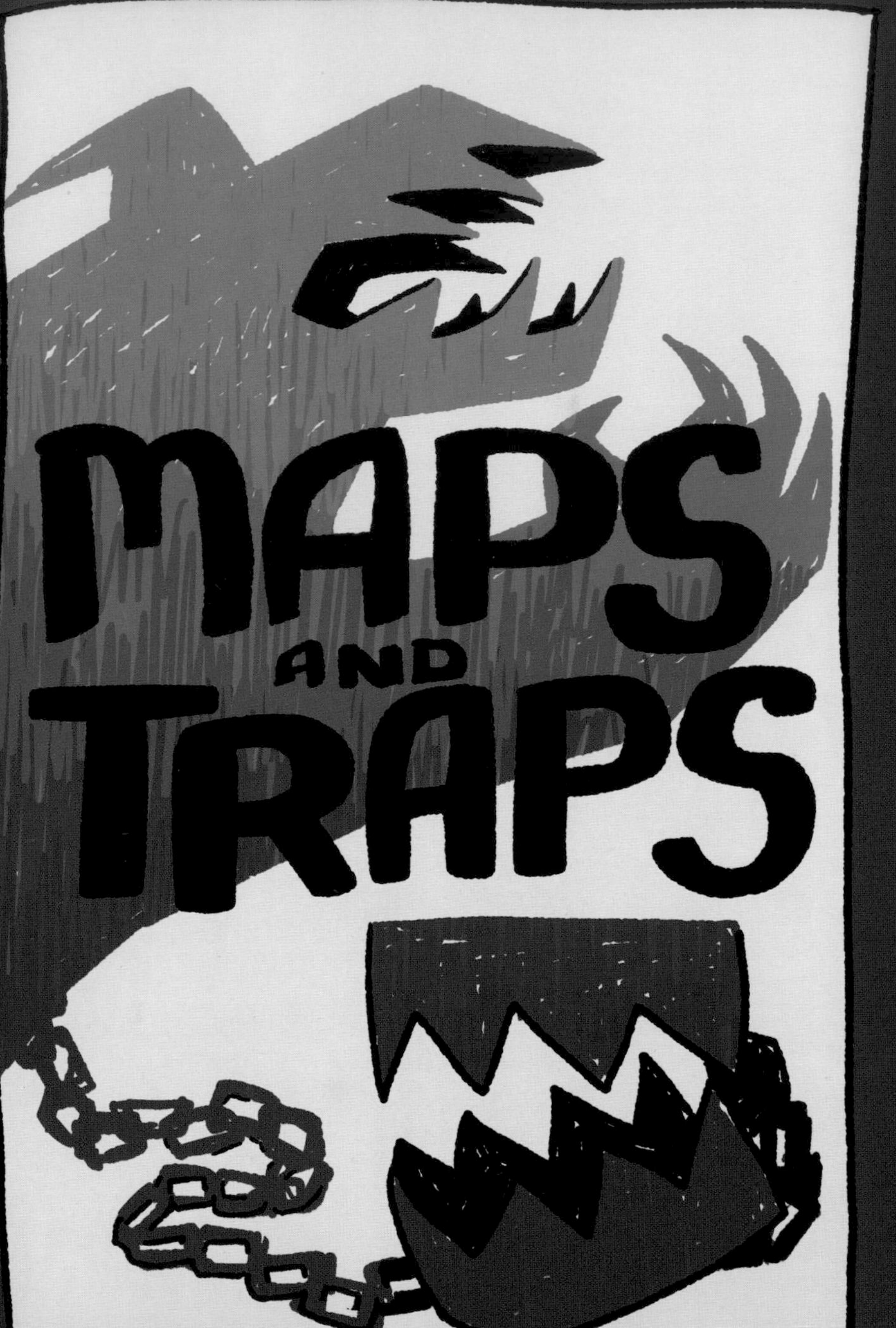
MAPS
AND
TRAPS

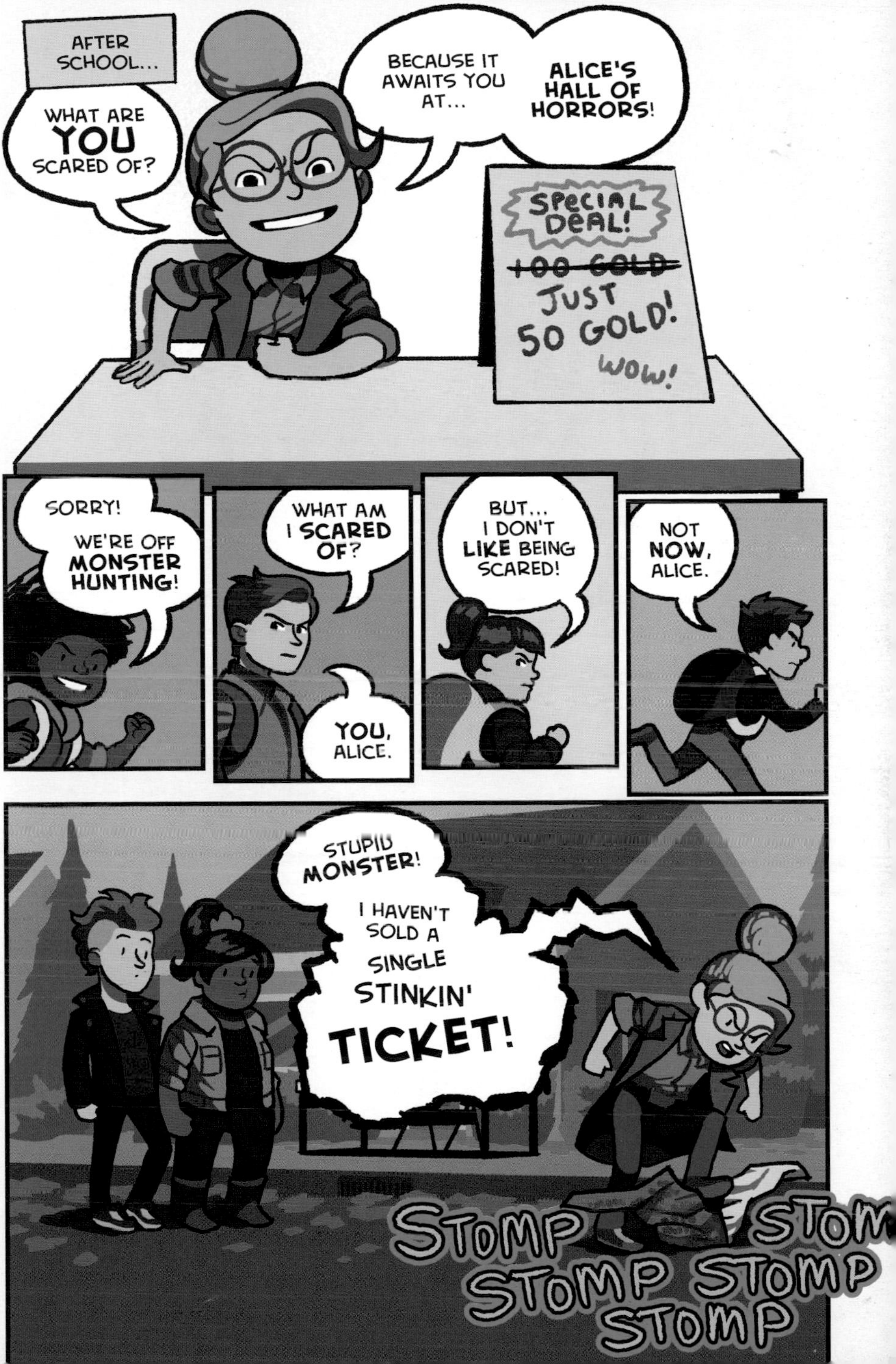
AFTER SCHOOL...
WHAT ARE YOU SCARED OF?
BECAUSE IT AWAITS YOU AT...
ALICE'S HALL OF HORRORS!
SPECIAL DEAL!
100 GOLD
JUST 50 GOLD!
WOW!
SORRY!
WE'RE OFF MONSTER HUNTING!
WHAT AM I SCARED OF?
YOU, ALICE.
BUT... I DON'T LIKE BEING SCARED!
NOT NOW, ALICE.
STUPID MONSTER!
I HAVEN'T SOLD A SINGLE STINKIN' TICKET!
STOMP STOM
STOMP STOMP
STOMP

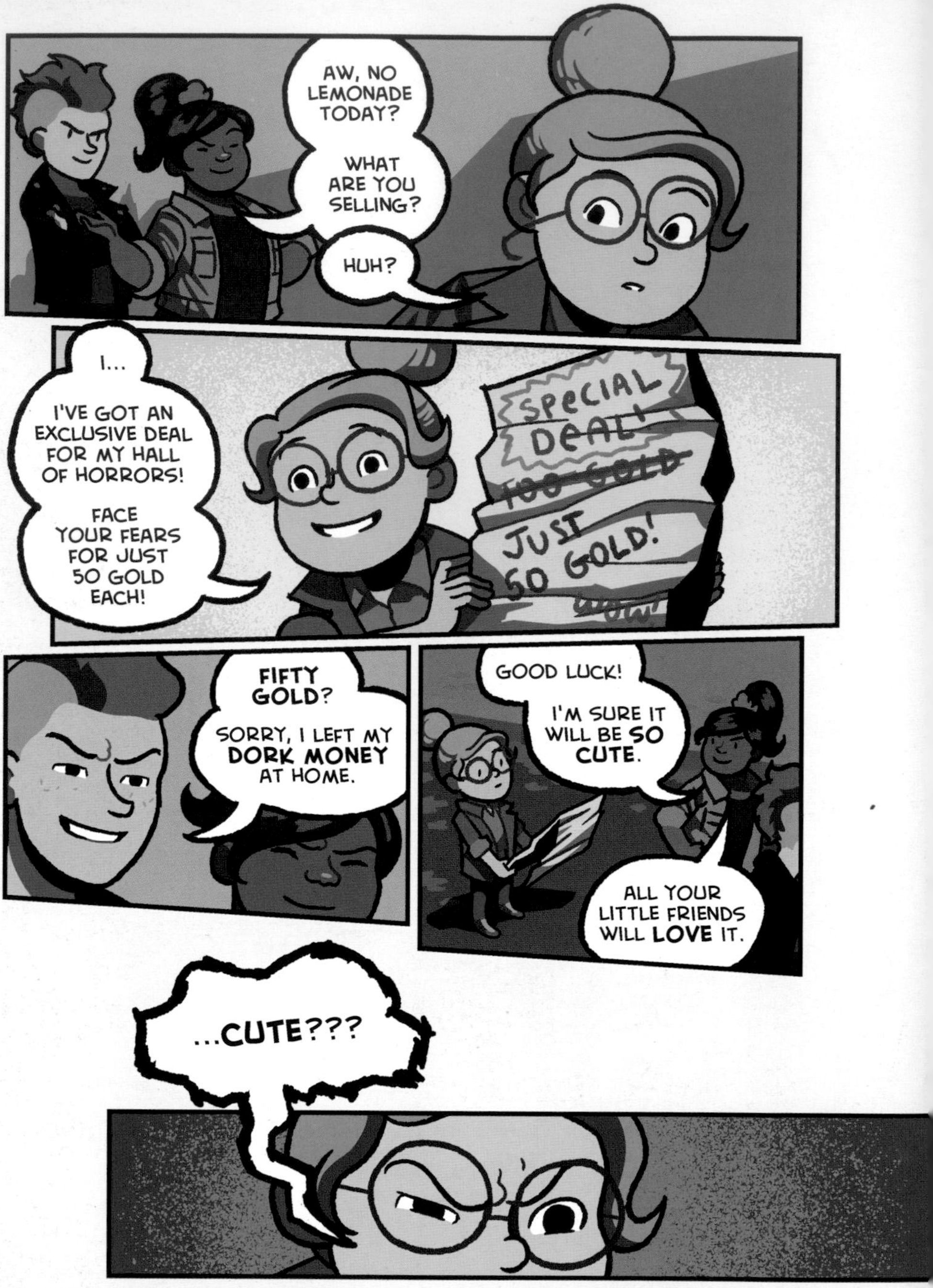
AW, NO LEMONADE TODAY?
WHAT ARE YOU SELLING?
HUH?
I...
I'VE GOT AN EXCLUSIVE DEAL FOR MY HALL OF HORRORS!
FACE YOUR FEARS FOR JUST 50 GOLD EACH!
SPECIAL DEAL!
JUST 50 GOLD!
FIFTY GOLD?
SORRY, I LEFT MY DORK MONEY AT HOME.
GOOD LUCK!
I'M SURE IT WILL BE SO CUTE.
ALL YOUR LITTLE FRIENDS WILL LOVE IT.
...CUTE???

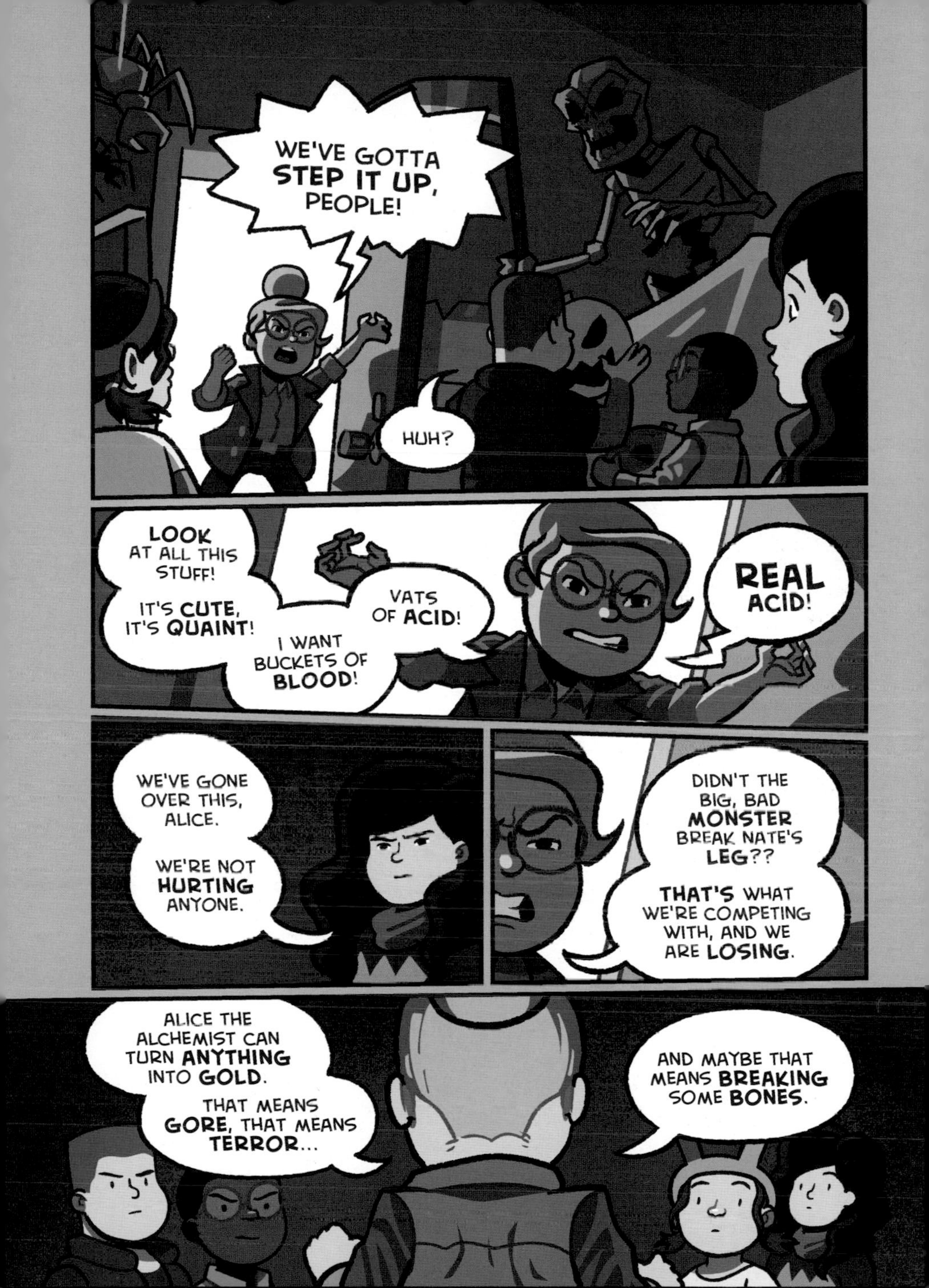
WE'VE GOTTA STEP IT UP, PEOPLE!
HUH?
LOOK AT ALL THIS STUFF!
IT'S CUTE, IT'S QUAINT!
I WANT BUCKETS OF BLOOD!
VATS OF ACID!
REAL ACID!
WE'VE GONE OVER THIS, ALICE.
WE'RE NOT HURTING ANYONE.
DIDN'T THE BIG, BAD MONSTER BREAK NATE'S LEG??
THAT'S WHAT WE'RE COMPETING WITH, AND WE ARE LOSING.
ALICE THE ALCHEMIST CAN TURN ANYTHING INTO GOLD.
THAT MEANS GORE, THAT MEANS TERROR...
AND MAYBE THAT MEANS BREAKING SOME BONES.

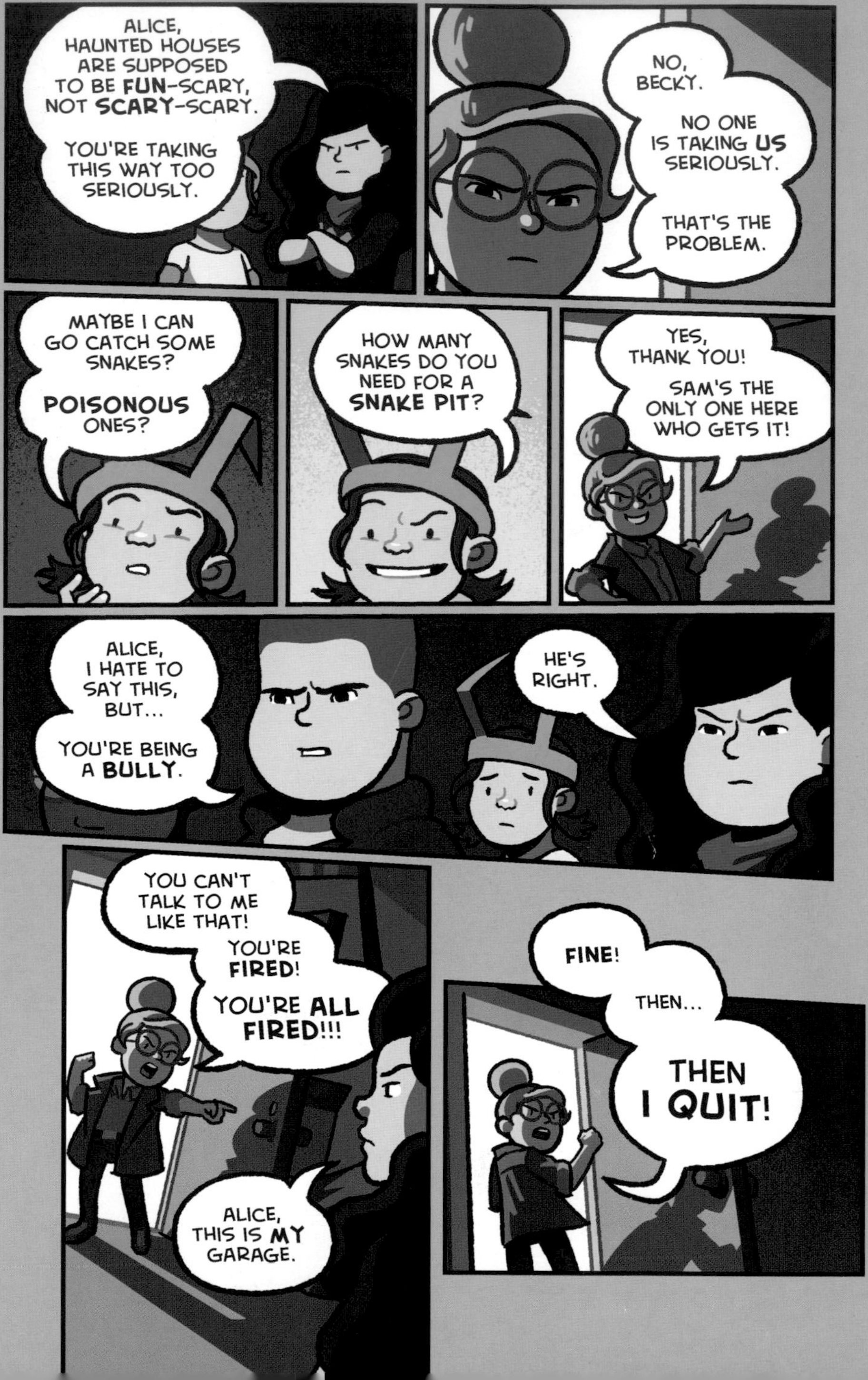

ALICE, HAUNTED HOUSES ARE SUPPOSED TO BE **FUN**-SCARY, NOT **SCARY**-SCARY.
YOU'RE TAKING THIS WAY TOO SERIOUSLY.
NO, BECKY.
NO ONE IS TAKING **US** SERIOUSLY.
THAT'S THE PROBLEM.
MAYBE I CAN GO CATCH SOME SNAKES?
POISONOUS ONES?
HOW MANY SNAKES DO YOU NEED FOR A **SNAKE PIT**?
YES, THANK YOU!
SAM'S THE ONLY ONE HERE WHO GETS IT!
ALICE, I HATE TO SAY THIS, BUT...
YOU'RE BEING A **BULLY**.
HE'S RIGHT.
YOU CAN'T TALK TO ME LIKE THAT!
YOU'RE **FIRED**!
YOU'RE ALL FIRED!!!
ALICE, THIS IS **MY** GARAGE.
FINE!
THEN...
THEN I QUIT!

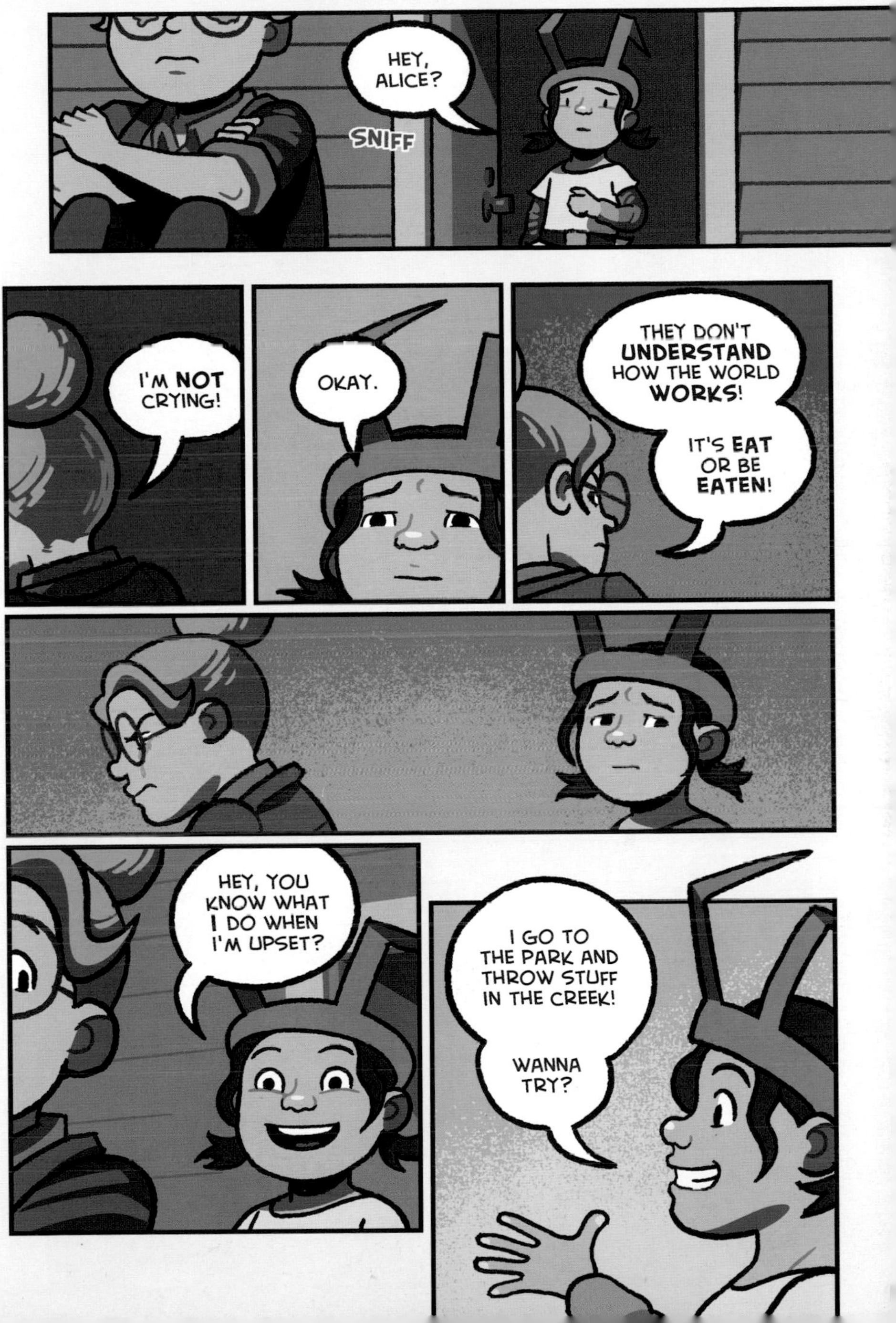
HEY, ALICE?
SNIFF
I'M NOT CRYING!
OKAY.
THEY DON'T UNDERSTAND HOW THE WORLD WORKS!
IT'S EAT OR BE EATEN!
HEY, YOU KNOW WHAT I DO WHEN I'M UPSET?
I GO TO THE PARK AND THROW STUFF IN THE CREEK!
WANNA TRY?

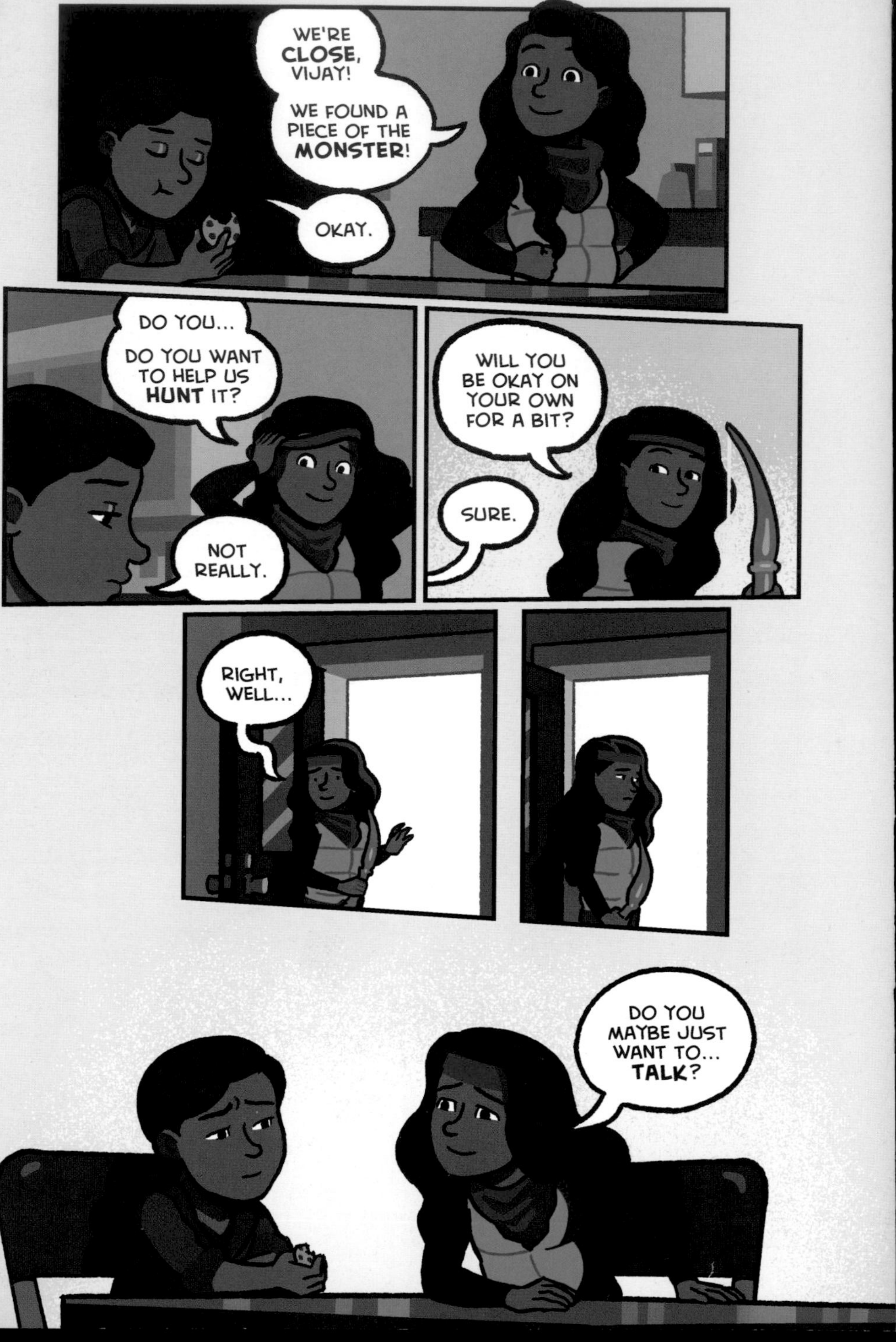
WE'RE CLOSE, VIJAY!
WE FOUND A PIECE OF THE MONSTER!
OKAY.
DO YOU...
DO YOU WANT TO HELP US HUNT IT?
NOT REALLY.
WILL YOU BE OKAY ON YOUR OWN FOR A BIT?
SURE.
RIGHT, WELL...
DO YOU MAYBE JUST WANT TO... TALK?

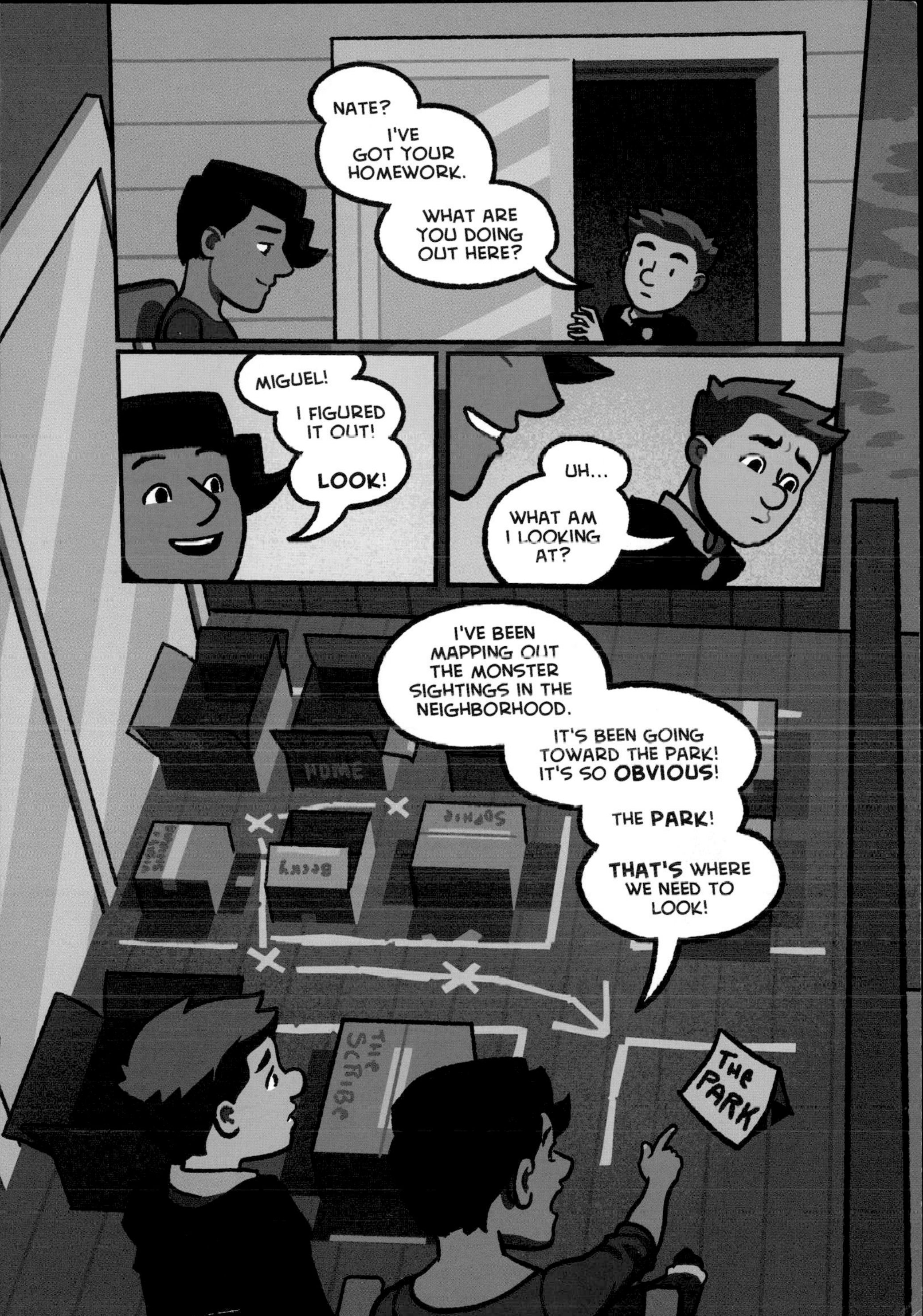
NATE?
I'VE GOT YOUR HOMEWORK.
WHAT ARE YOU DOING OUT HERE?
MIGUEL!
I FIGURED IT OUT!
LOOK!
UH...
WHAT AM I LOOKING AT?
I'VE BEEN MAPPING OUT THE MONSTER SIGHTINGS IN THE NEIGHBORHOOD.
IT'S BEEN GOING TOWARD THE PARK! IT'S SO OBVIOUS!
THE PARK!
THAT'S WHERE WE NEED TO LOOK!
HOME
SOPHIE
BECKY
THE SCRIBE
THE PARK

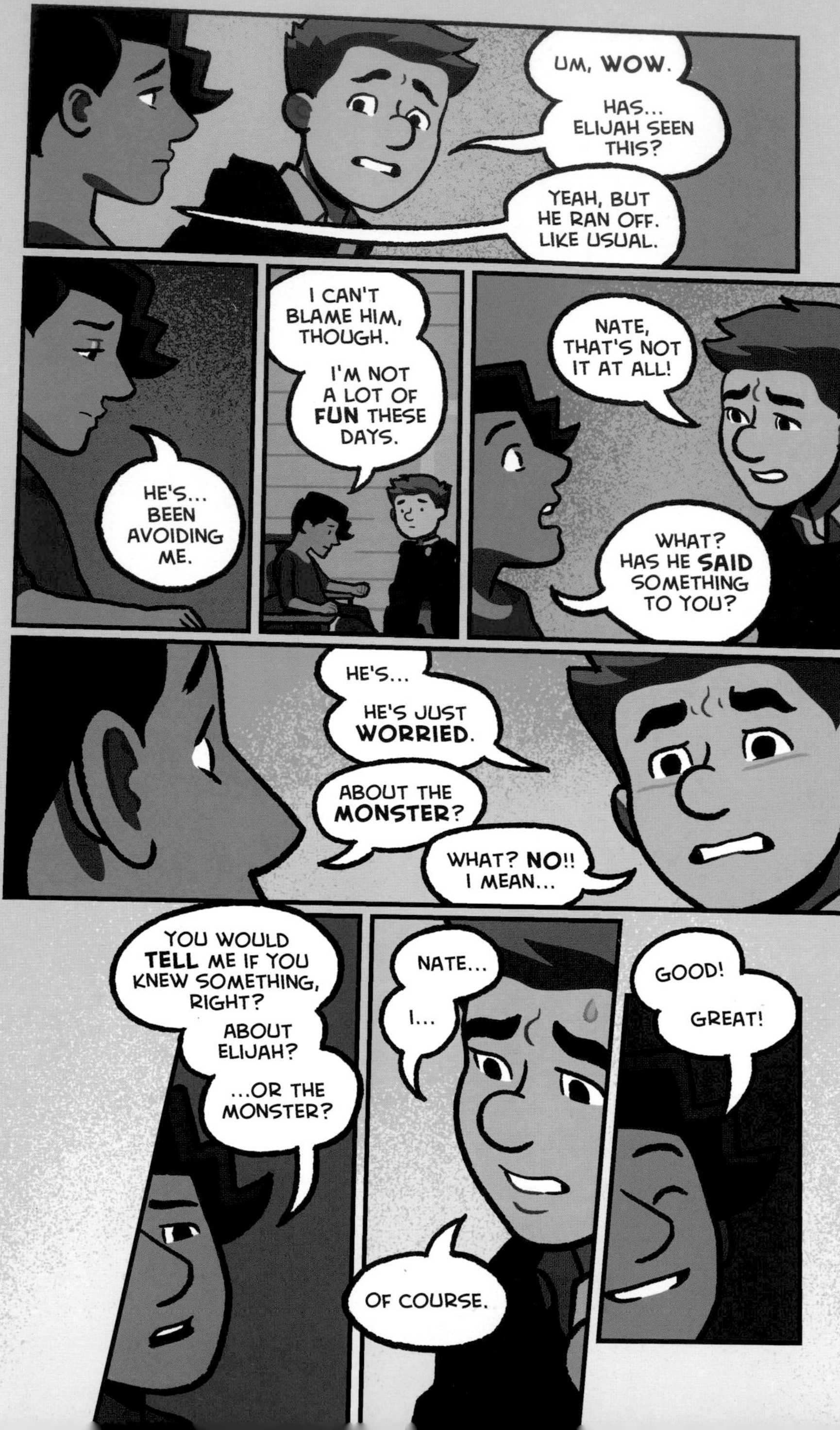
UM, WOW.
HAS... ELIJAH SEEN THIS?
YEAH, BUT HE RAN OFF. LIKE USUAL.
HE'S... BEEN AVOIDING ME.
I CAN'T BLAME HIM, THOUGH.
I'M NOT A LOT OF FUN THESE DAYS.
NATE, THAT'S NOT IT AT ALL!
WHAT? HAS HE SAID SOMETHING TO YOU?
HE'S...
HE'S JUST WORRIED.
ABOUT THE MONSTER?
WHAT? NO!! I MEAN...
YOU WOULD TELL ME IF YOU KNEW SOMETHING, RIGHT?
ABOUT ELIJAH?
...OR THE MONSTER?
NATE...
I...
OF COURSE.
GOOD!
GREAT!

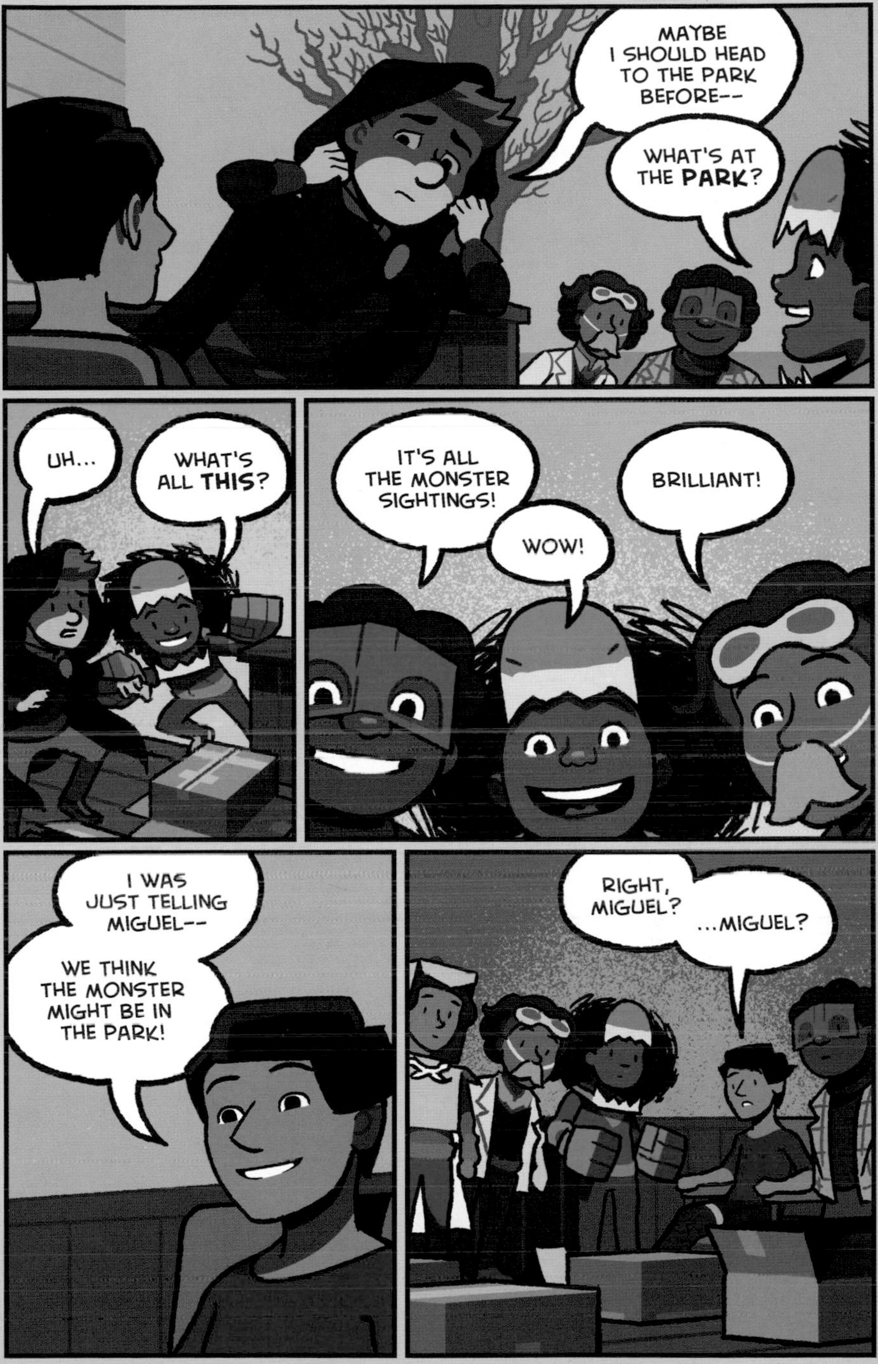
MAYBE I SHOULD HEAD TO THE PARK BEFORE--
WHAT'S AT THE **PARK**?
UH...
WHAT'S ALL **THIS**?
IT'S ALL THE MONSTER SIGHTINGS!
WOW!
BRILLIANT!
I WAS JUST TELLING MIGUEL--
WE THINK THE MONSTER MIGHT BE IN THE PARK!
RIGHT, MIGUEL?
...MIGUEL?

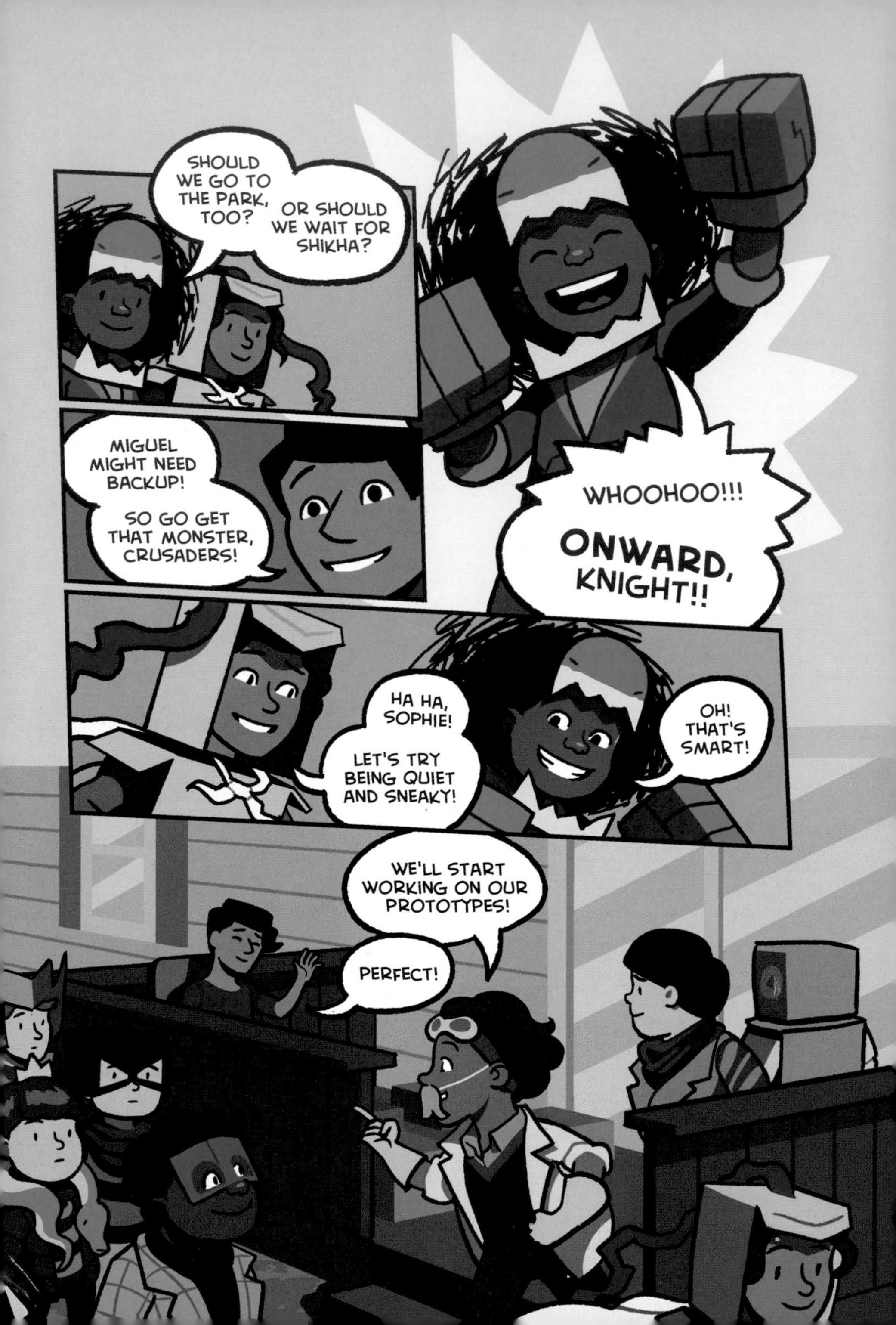

SHOULD WE GO TO THE PARK, TOO?
OR SHOULD WE WAIT FOR SHIKHA?
WHOOHOO!!!
ONWARD, KNIGHT!!
MIGUEL MIGHT NEED BACKUP!
SO GO GET THAT MONSTER, CRUSADERS!
HA HA, SOPHIE!
LET'S TRY BEING QUIET AND SNEAKY!
OH! THAT'S SMART!
WE'LL START WORKING ON OUR PROTOTYPES!
PERFECT!

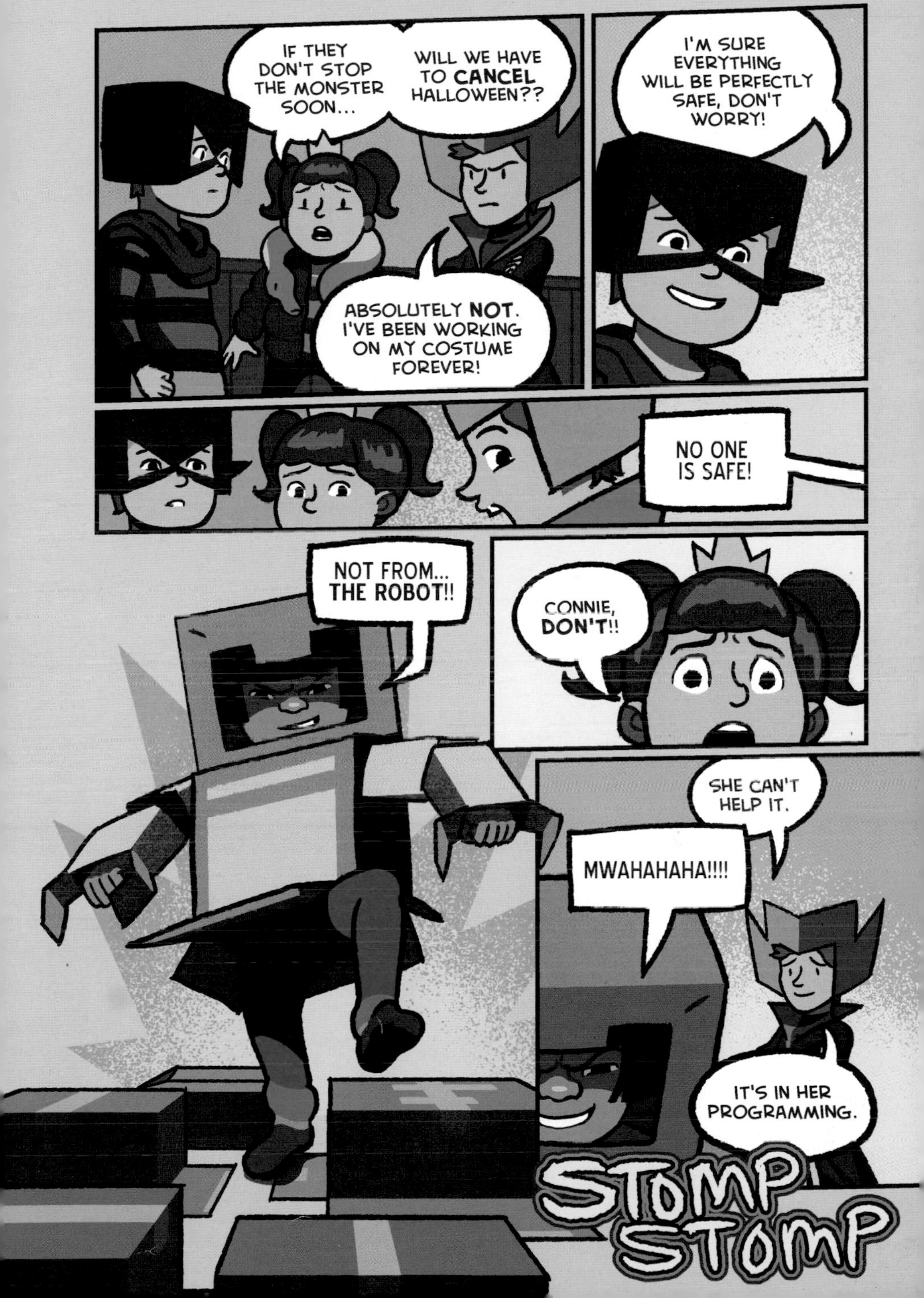
IF THEY DON'T STOP THE MONSTER SOON...
WILL WE HAVE TO CANCEL HALLOWEEN??
ABSOLUTELY NOT. I'VE BEEN WORKING ON MY COSTUME FOREVER!
I'M SURE EVERYTHING WILL BE PERFECTLY SAFE, DON'T WORRY!
NO ONE IS SAFE!
NOT FROM... THE ROBOT!!
CONNIE, DON'T!!
SHE CAN'T HELP IT.
MWAHAHAHA!!!!
IT'S IN HER PROGRAMMING.
STOMP STOMP

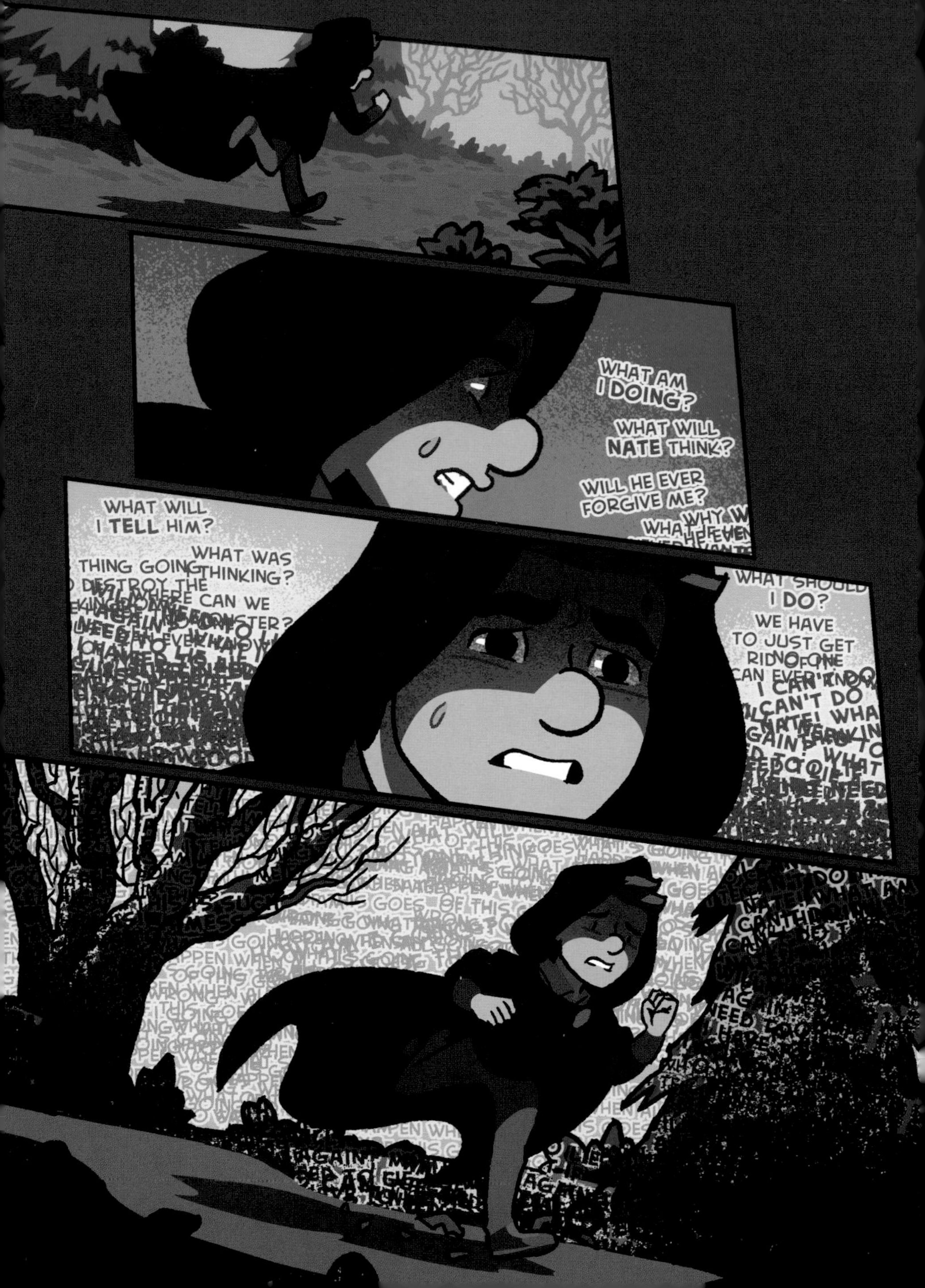
WHAT AM I DOING?
WHAT WILL NATE THINK?
WILL HE EVER FORGIVE ME?
WHAT WILL I TELL HIM?
WHAT WAS I THINKING?
WHAT SHOULD I DO?
WE HAVE TO JUST GET RID OF

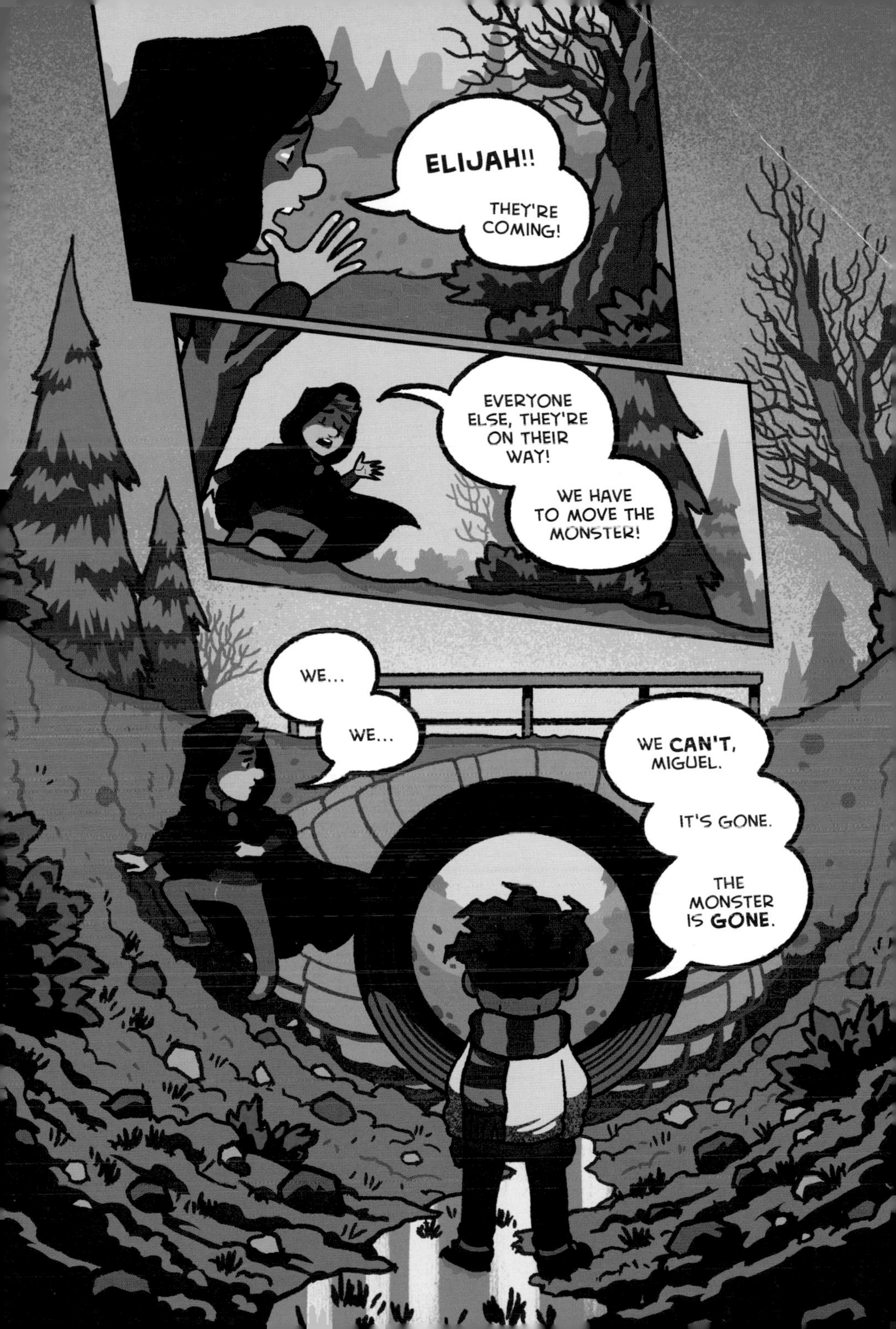
ELIJAH!!
THEY'RE COMING!
EVERYONE ELSE, THEY'RE ON THEIR WAY!
WE HAVE TO MOVE THE MONSTER!
WE...
WE...
WE **CAN'T**, MIGUEL.
IT'S GONE.
THE MONSTER IS **GONE**.

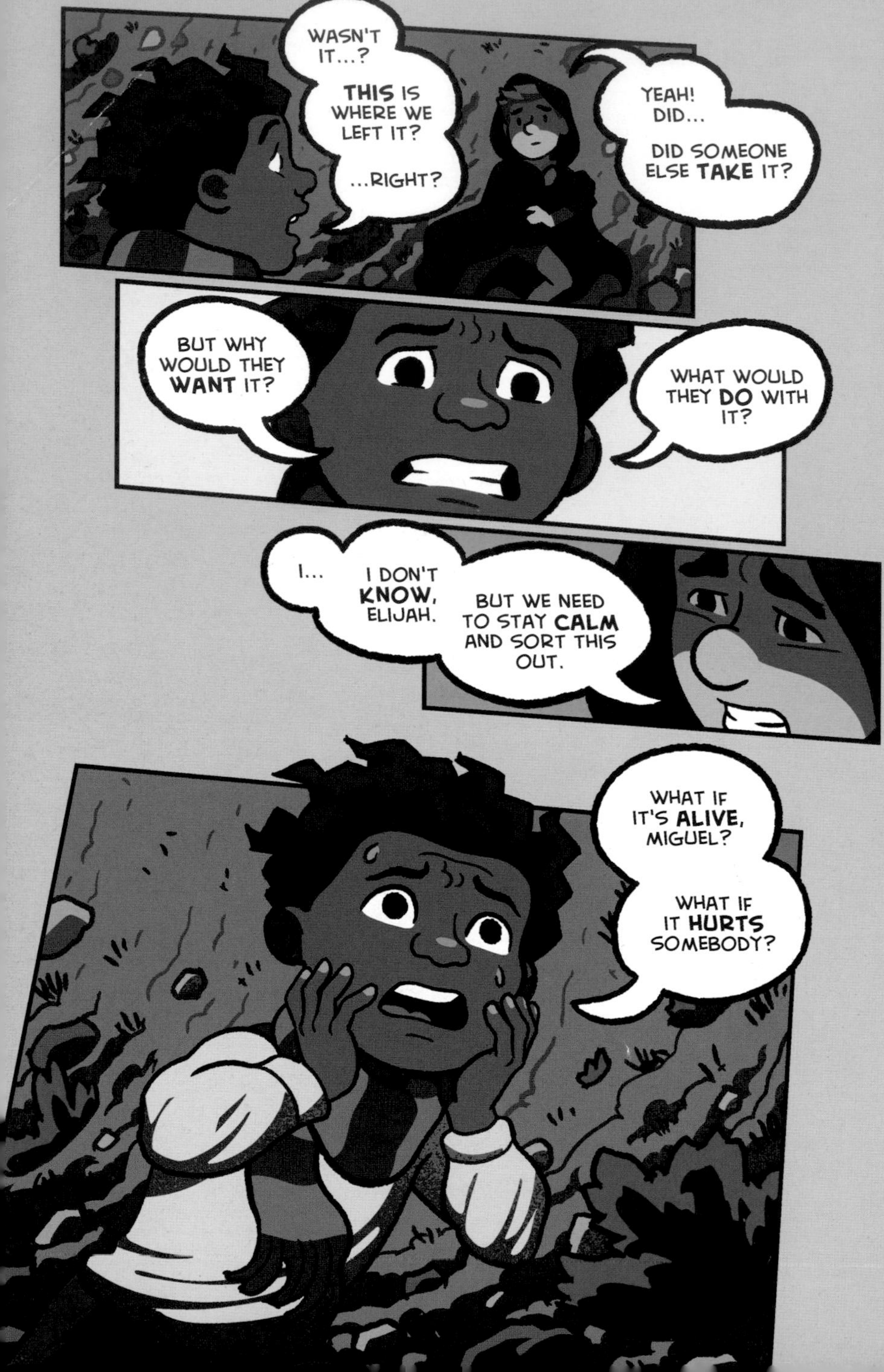
WASN'T IT...?
THIS IS WHERE WE LEFT IT?
...RIGHT?
YEAH! DID...
DID SOMEONE ELSE TAKE IT?
BUT WHY WOULD THEY WANT IT?
WHAT WOULD THEY DO WITH IT?
I...
I DON'T KNOW, ELIJAH.
BUT WE NEED TO STAY CALM AND SORT THIS OUT.
WHAT IF IT'S ALIVE, MIGUEL?
WHAT IF IT HURTS SOMEBODY?

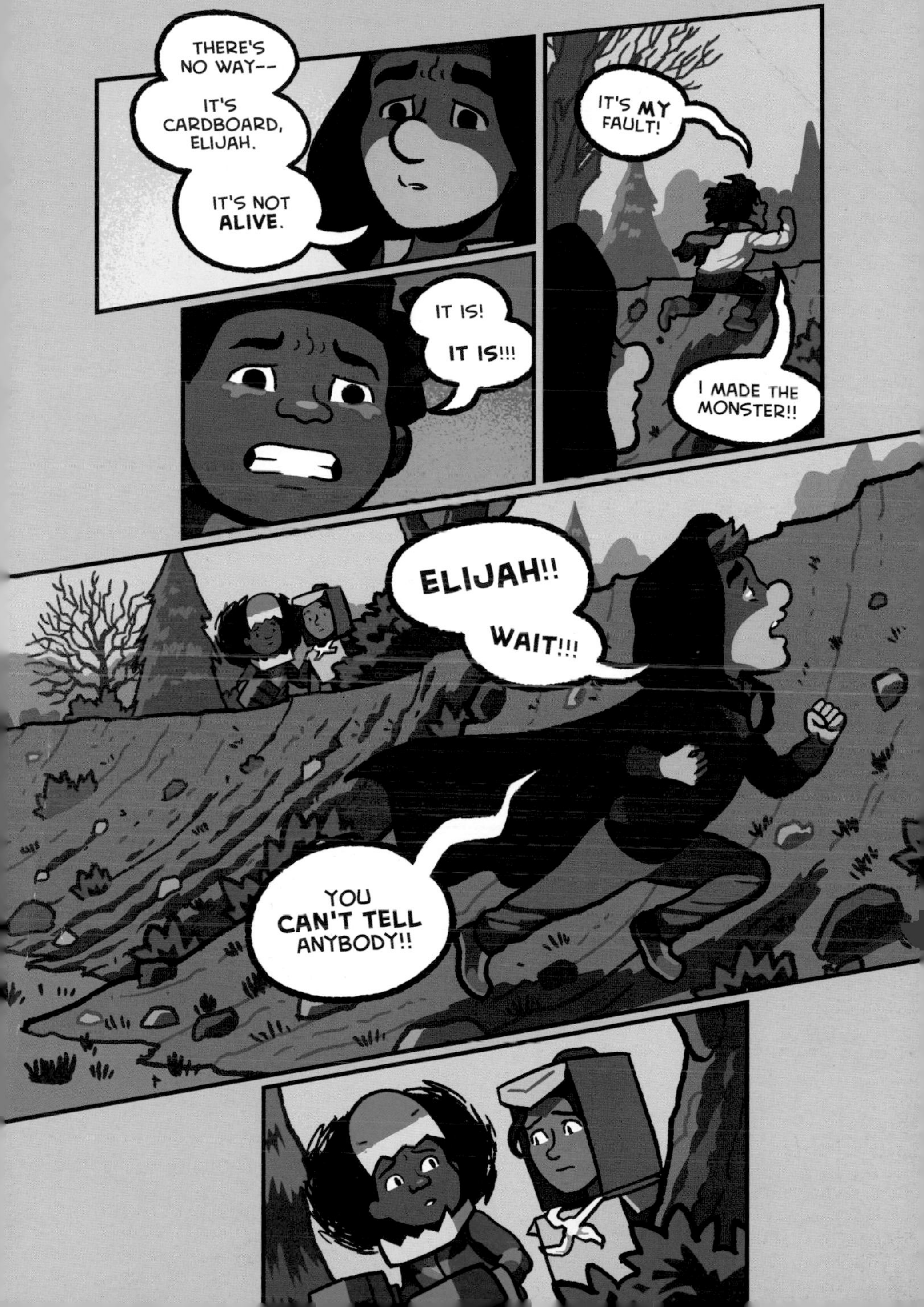
THERE'S NO WAY--
IT'S CARDBOARD, ELIJAH.
IT'S NOT **ALIVE**.
IT'S **MY** FAULT!
IT IS!
IT IS!!!
I MADE THE MONSTER!!
ELIJAH!!
WAIT!!!
YOU **CAN'T TELL** ANYBODY!!

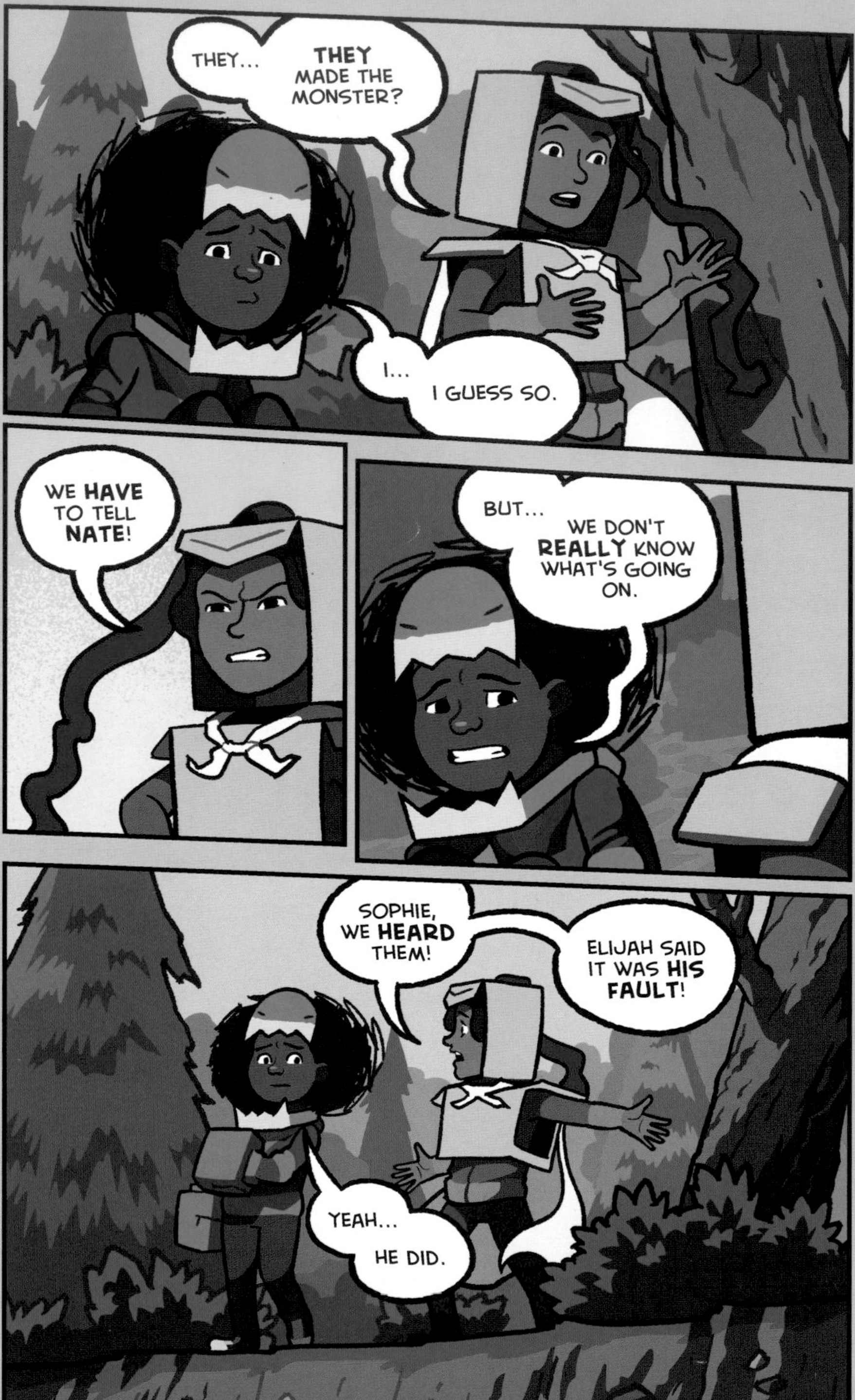
THEY... THEY MADE THE MONSTER?
I... I GUESS SO.
WE HAVE TO TELL NATE!
BUT... WE DON'T REALLY KNOW WHAT'S GOING ON.
SOPHIE, WE HEARD THEM!
ELIJAH SAID IT WAS HIS FAULT!
YEAH... HE DID.

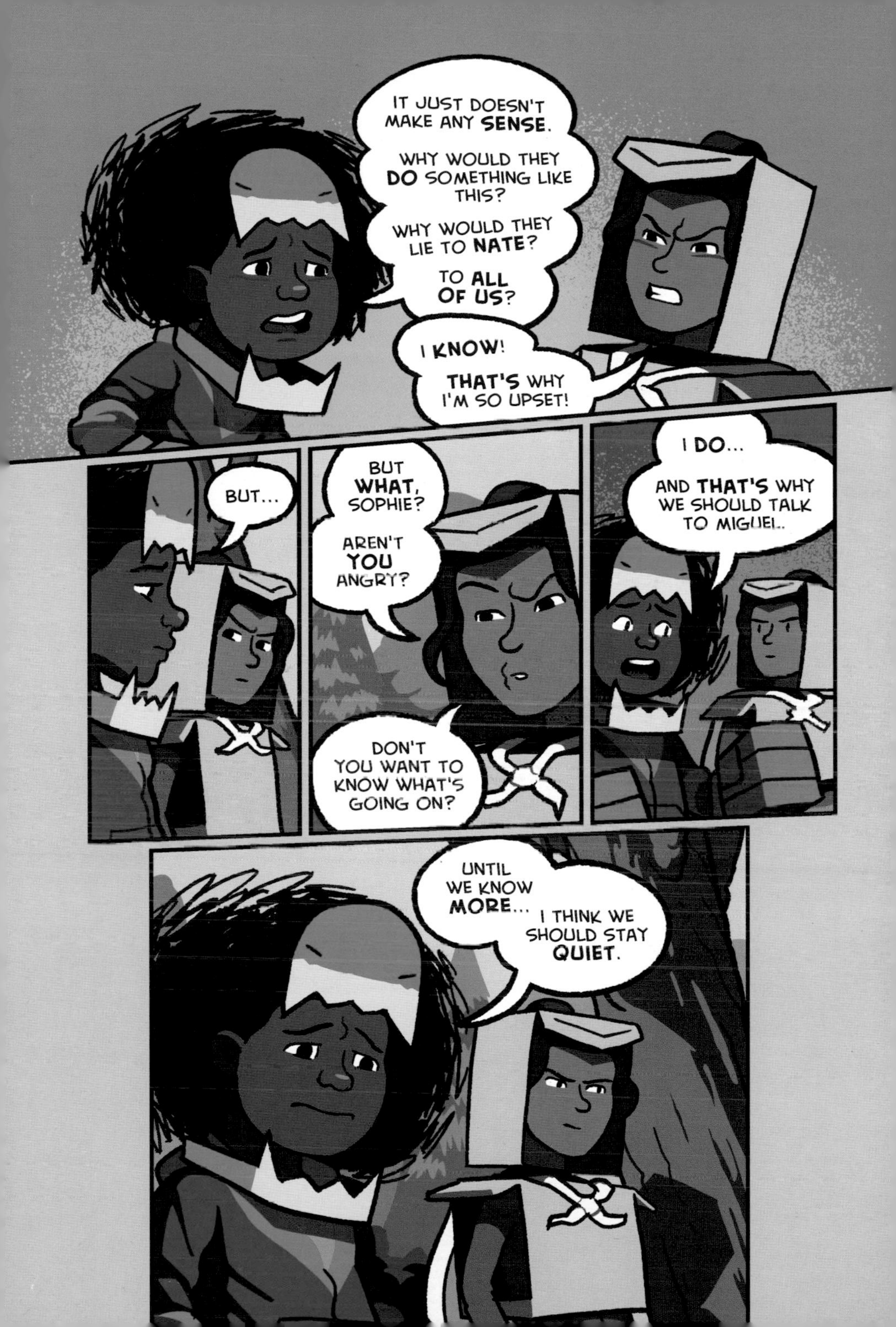

IT JUST DOESN'T MAKE ANY SENSE.
WHY WOULD THEY DO SOMETHING LIKE THIS?
WHY WOULD THEY LIE TO NATE?
TO ALL OF US?
I KNOW!
THAT'S WHY I'M SO UPSET!
BUT...
BUT WHAT, SOPHIE?
AREN'T YOU ANGRY?
DON'T YOU WANT TO KNOW WHAT'S GOING ON?
I DO...
AND THAT'S WHY WE SHOULD TALK TO MIGUEL.
UNTIL WE KNOW MORE...
I THINK WE SHOULD STAY QUIET.

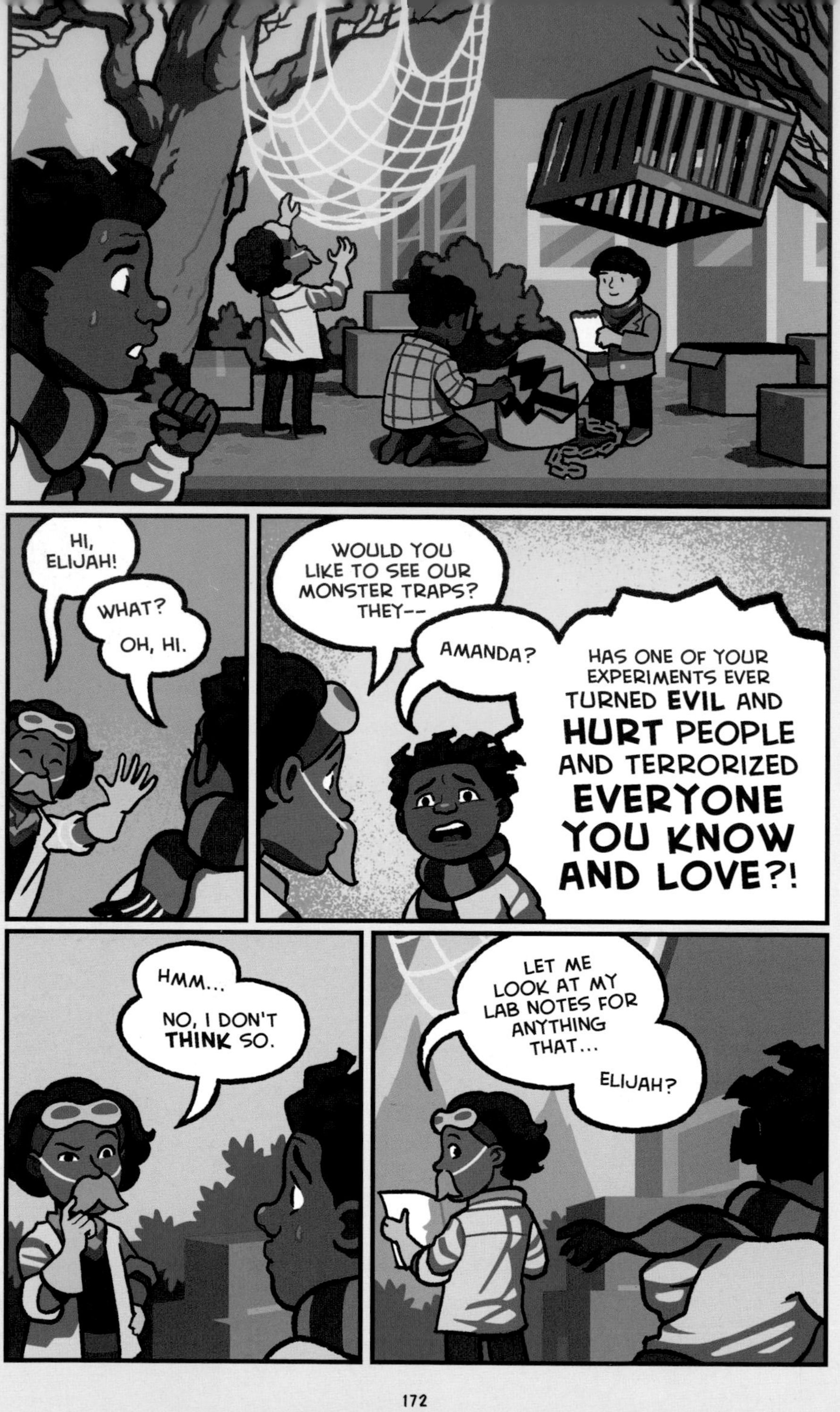
HI, ELIJAH!
WHAT?
OH, HI.
WOULD YOU LIKE TO SEE OUR MONSTER TRAPS? THEY--
AMANDA?
HAS ONE OF YOUR EXPERIMENTS EVER TURNED **EVIL** AND **HURT** PEOPLE AND TERRORIZED **EVERYONE YOU KNOW AND LOVE**?!
HMM...
NO, I DON'T **THINK** SO.
LET ME LOOK AT MY LAB NOTES FOR ANYTHING THAT...
ELIJAH?

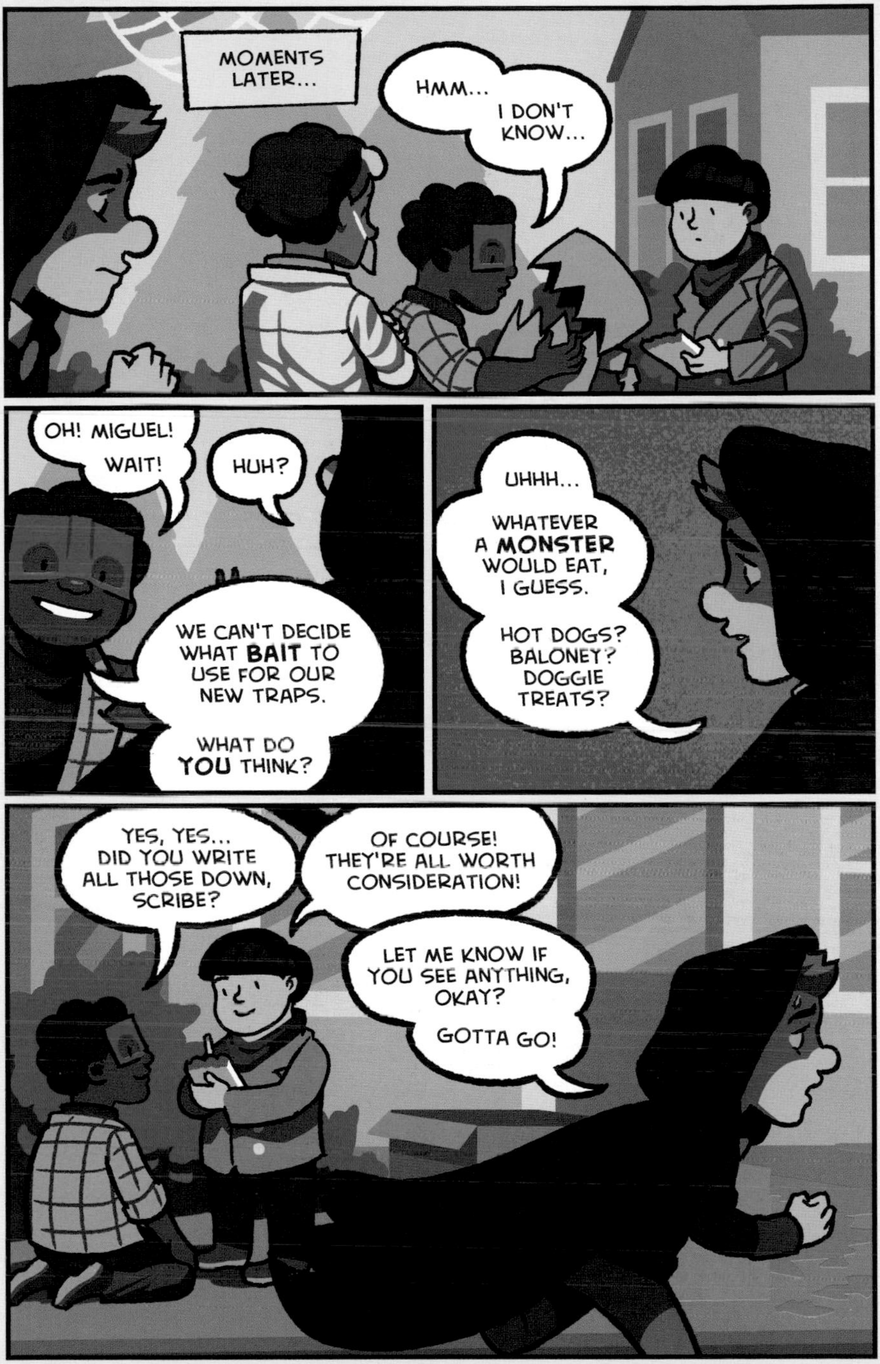
MOMENTS LATER...
HMM... I DON'T KNOW...
OH! MIGUEL! WAIT!
HUH?
WE CAN'T DECIDE WHAT BAIT TO USE FOR OUR NEW TRAPS. WHAT DO YOU THINK?
UHHH... WHATEVER A MONSTER WOULD EAT, I GUESS. HOT DOGS? BALONEY? DOGGIE TREATS?
YES, YES... DID YOU WRITE ALL THOSE DOWN, SCRIBE?
OF COURSE! THEY'RE ALL WORTH CONSIDERATION!
LET ME KNOW IF YOU SEE ANYTHING, OKAY? GOTTA GO!

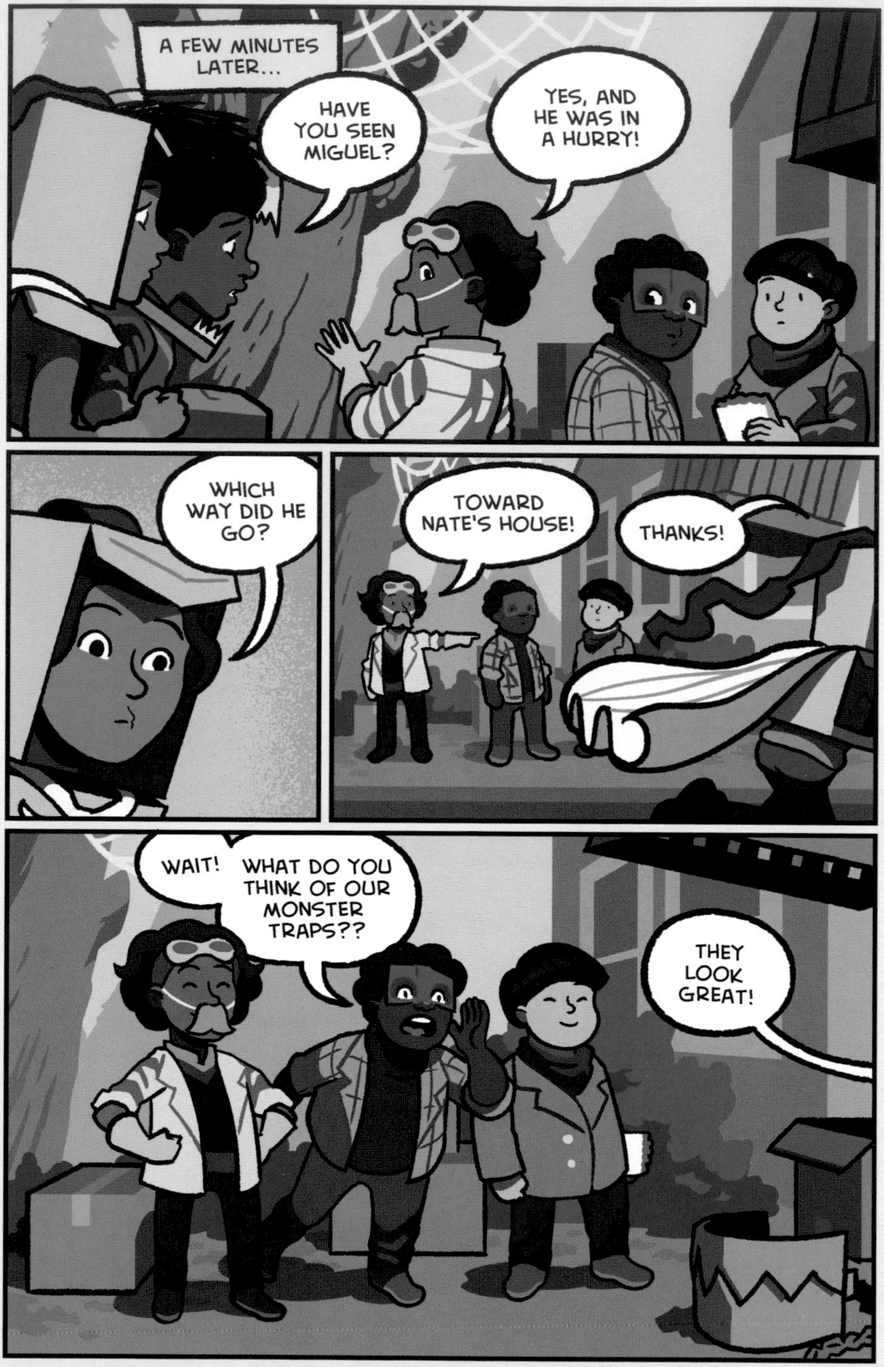
A FEW MINUTES LATER...
HAVE YOU SEEN MIGUEL?
YES, AND HE WAS IN A HURRY!
WHICH WAY DID HE GO?
TOWARD NATE'S HOUSE!
THANKS!
WAIT!
WHAT DO YOU THINK OF OUR MONSTER TRAPS??
THEY LOOK GREAT!

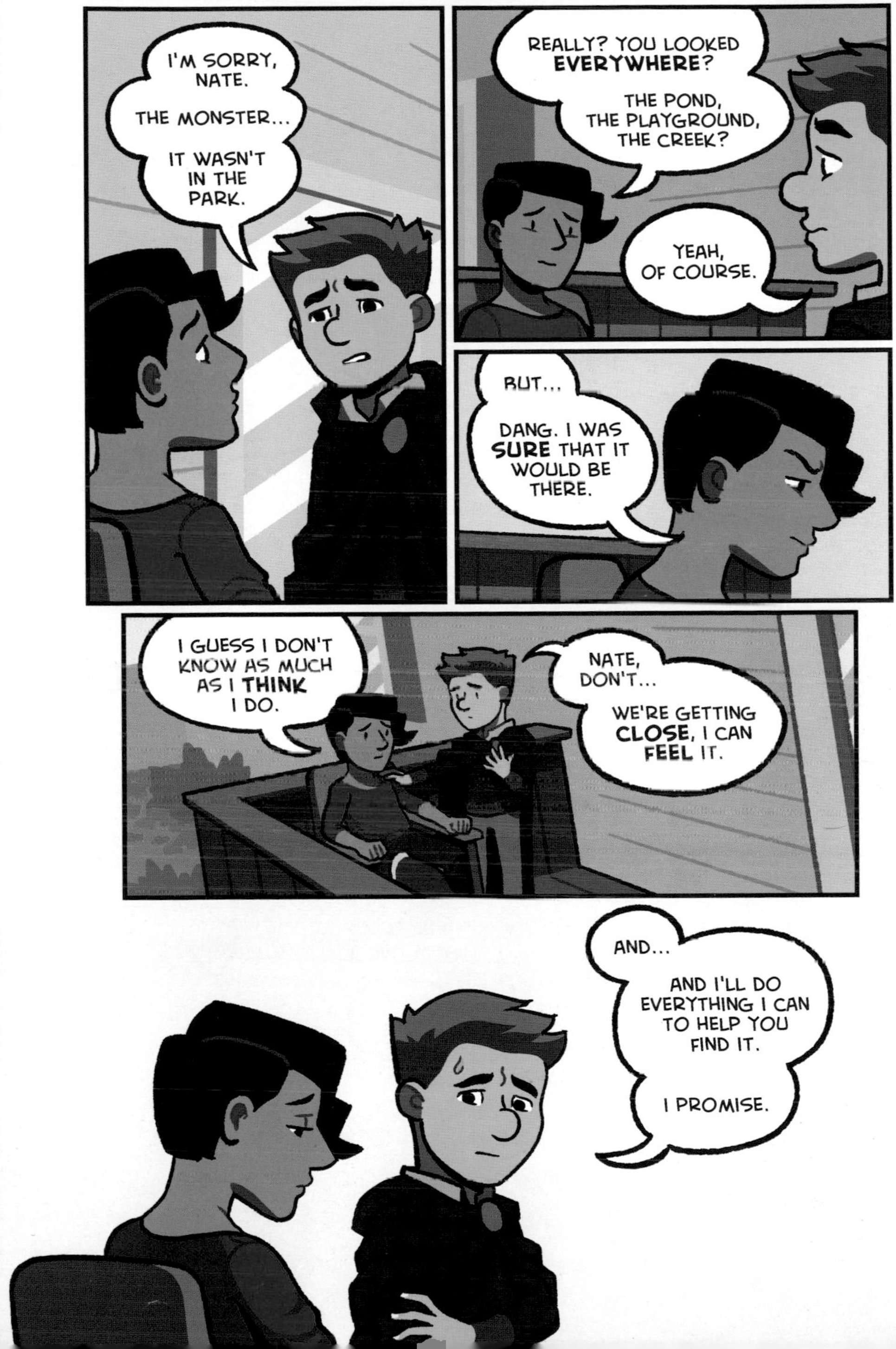
I'M SORRY, NATE.
THE MONSTER...
IT WASN'T IN THE PARK.
REALLY? YOU LOOKED **EVERYWHERE**?
THE POND, THE PLAYGROUND, THE CREEK?
YEAH, OF COURSE.
BUT...
DANG. I WAS **SURE** THAT IT WOULD BE THERE.
I GUESS I DON'T KNOW AS MUCH AS I **THINK** I DO.
NATE, DON'T...
WE'RE GETTING **CLOSE**, I CAN **FEEL** IT.
AND...
AND I'LL DO EVERYTHING I CAN TO HELP YOU FIND IT.
I PROMISE.

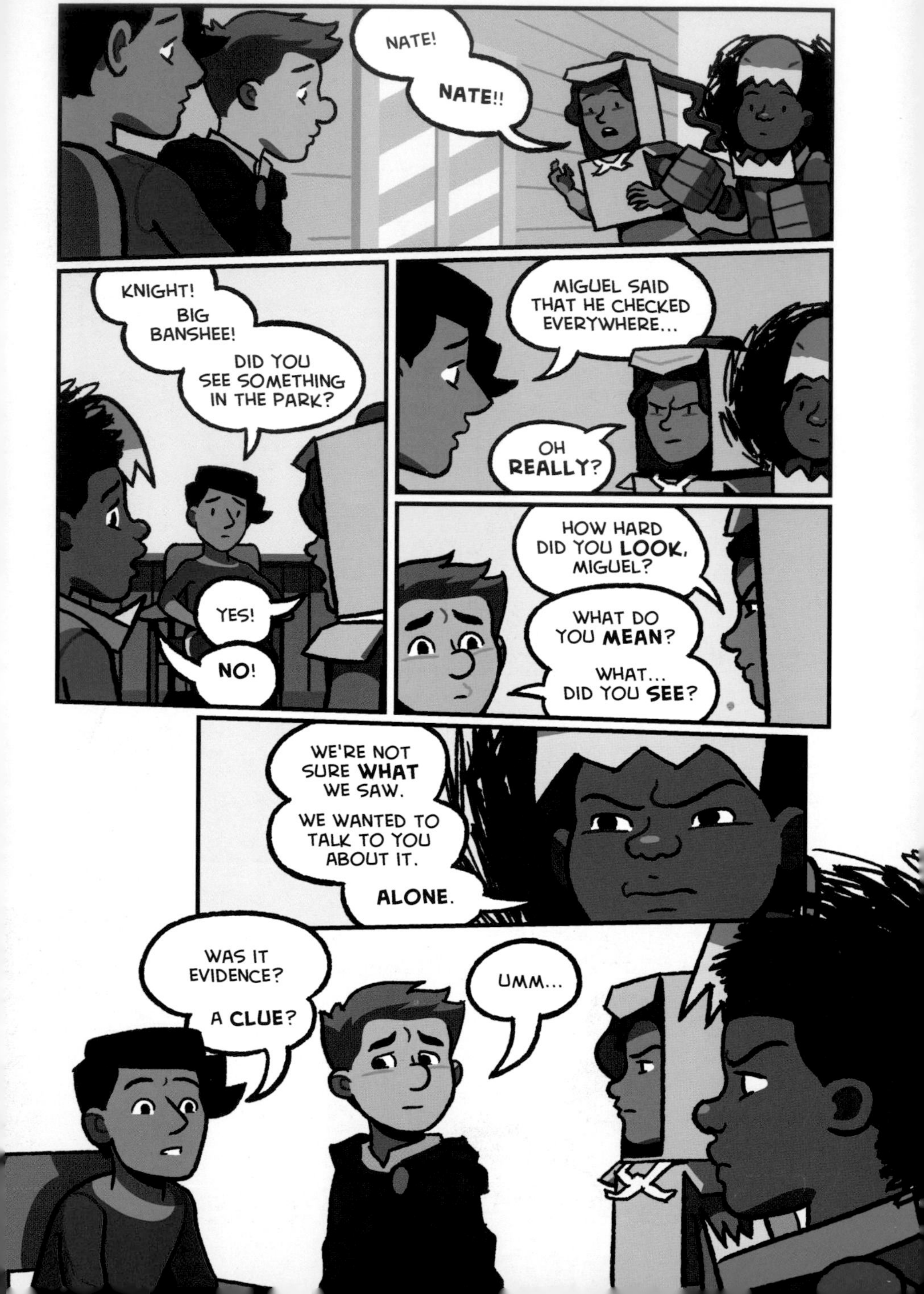
NATE!
NATE!!
KNIGHT!
BIG BANSHEE!
DID YOU SEE SOMETHING IN THE PARK?
YES!
NO!
MIGUEL SAID THAT HE CHECKED EVERYWHERE...
OH REALLY?
HOW HARD DID YOU LOOK, MIGUEL?
WHAT DO YOU MEAN?
WHAT... DID YOU SEE?
WE'RE NOT SURE WHAT WE SAW.
WE WANTED TO TALK TO YOU ABOUT IT.
ALONE.
WAS IT EVIDENCE?
A CLUE?
UMM...

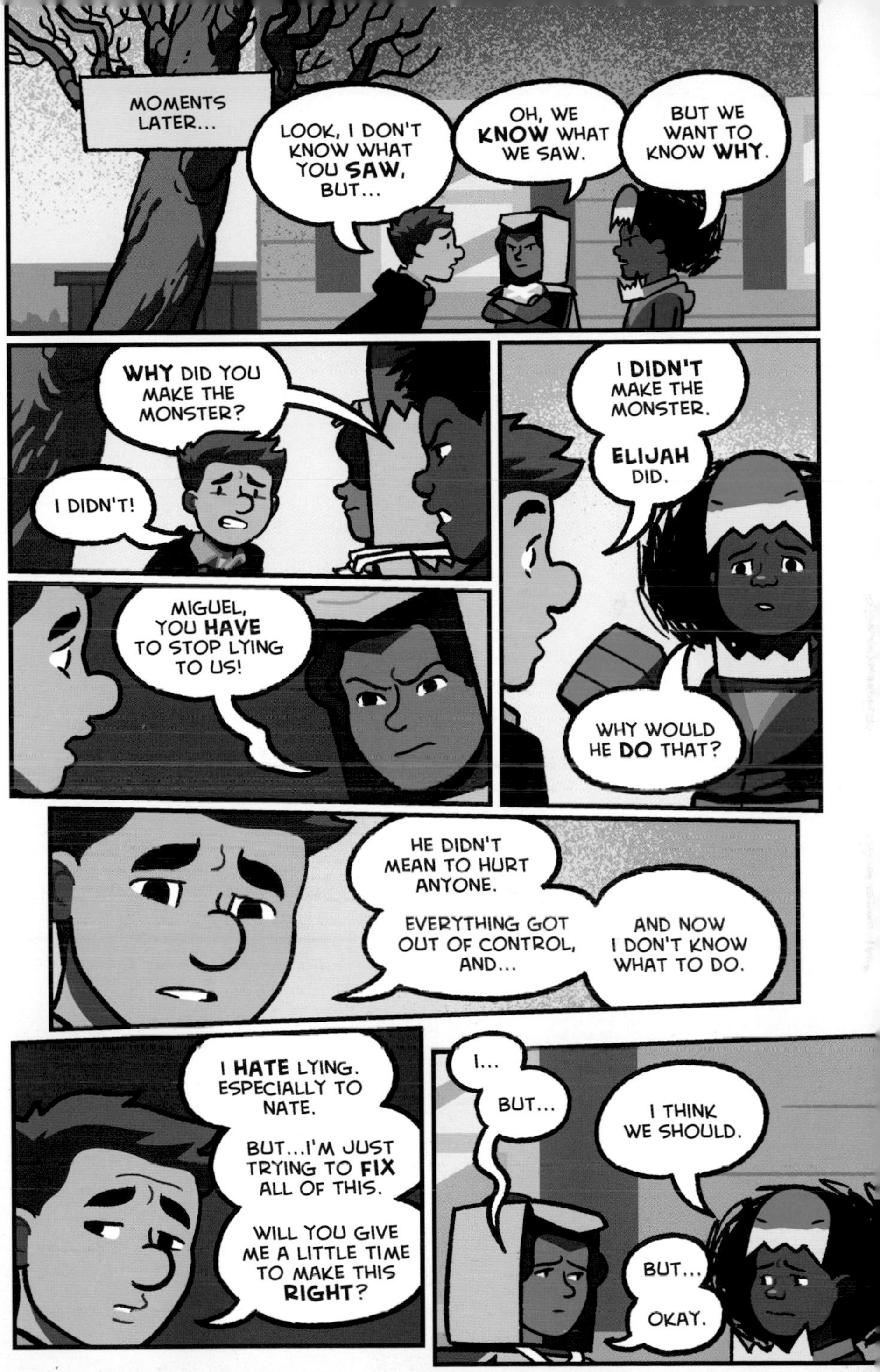
MOMENTS LATER...
LOOK, I DON'T KNOW WHAT YOU SAW, BUT...
OH, WE KNOW WHAT WE SAW.
BUT WE WANT TO KNOW WHY.
WHY DID YOU MAKE THE MONSTER?
I DIDN'T!
I DIDN'T MAKE THE MONSTER.
ELIJAH DID.
MIGUEL, YOU HAVE TO STOP LYING TO US!
WHY WOULD HE DO THAT?
HE DIDN'T MEAN TO HURT ANYONE.
EVERYTHING GOT OUT OF CONTROL, AND...
AND NOW I DON'T KNOW WHAT TO DO.
I HATE LYING. ESPECIALLY TO NATE.
BUT...I'M JUST TRYING TO FIX ALL OF THIS.
WILL YOU GIVE ME A LITTLE TIME TO MAKE THIS RIGHT?
I...
BUT...
I THINK WE SHOULD.
BUT...
OKAY.

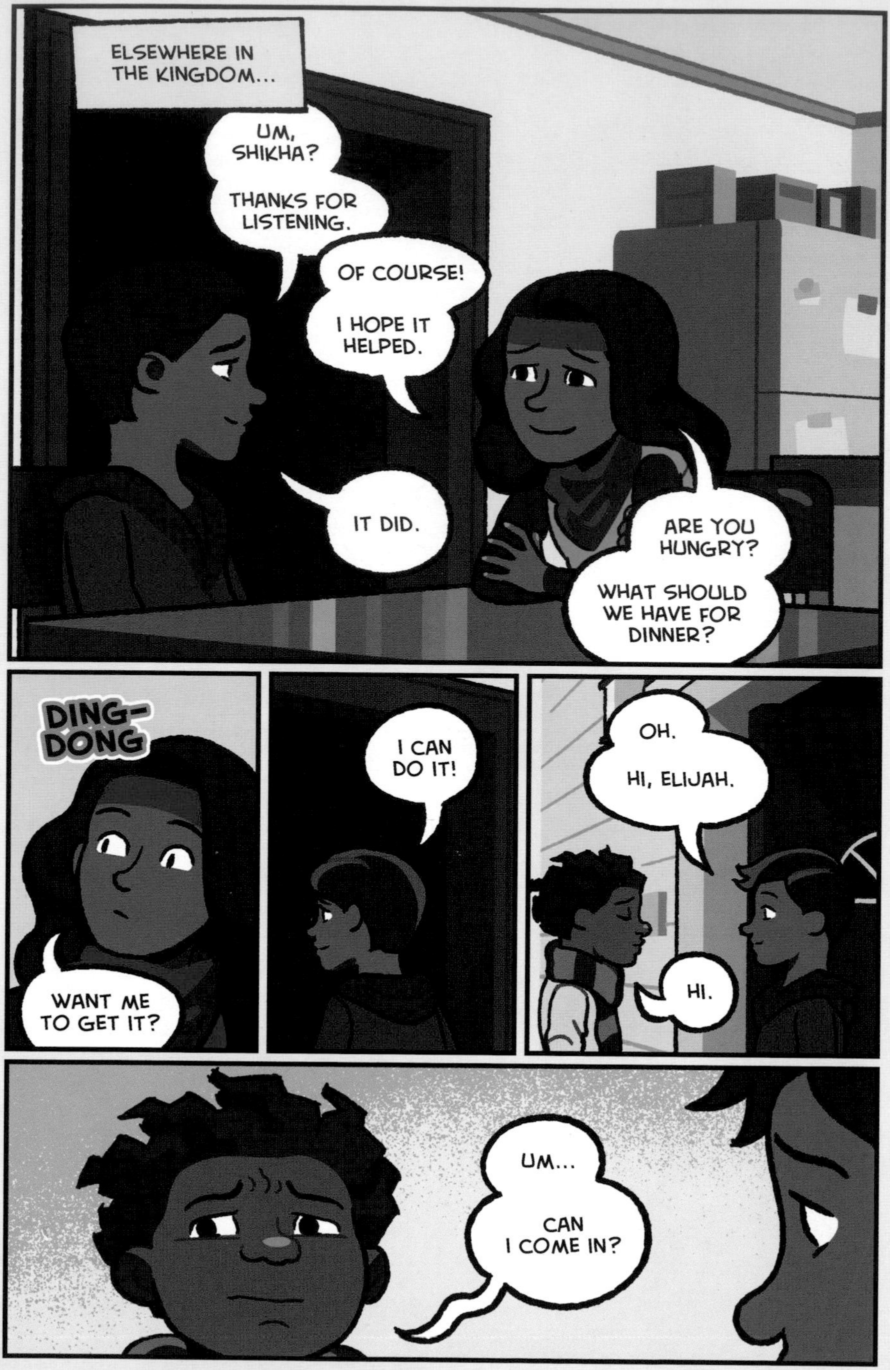
ELSEWHERE IN THE KINGDOM...
UM, SHIKHA?
THANKS FOR LISTENING.
OF COURSE!
I HOPE IT HELPED.
IT DID.
ARE YOU HUNGRY?
WHAT SHOULD WE HAVE FOR DINNER?
DING-DONG
WANT ME TO GET IT?
I CAN DO IT!
OH.
HI, ELIJAH.
HI.
UM...
CAN I COME IN?

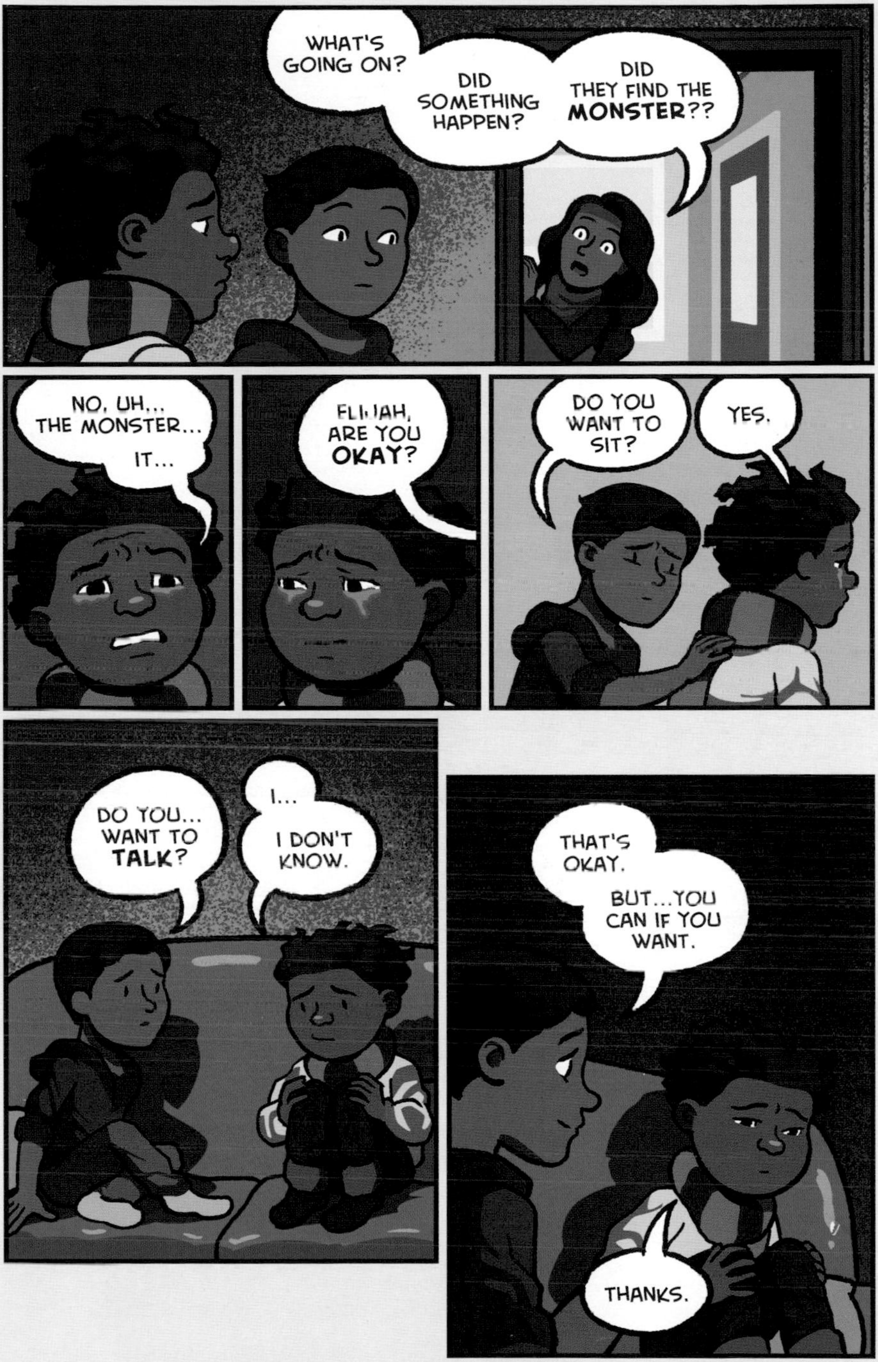
WHAT'S GOING ON?
DID SOMETHING HAPPEN?
DID THEY FIND THE **MONSTER**??
NO, UH... THE MONSTER... IT...
ELIJAH, ARE YOU **OKAY**?
DO YOU WANT TO SIT?
YES.
DO YOU... WANT TO **TALK**?
I...
I DON'T KNOW.
THAT'S OKAY.
BUT...YOU CAN IF YOU WANT.
THANKS.

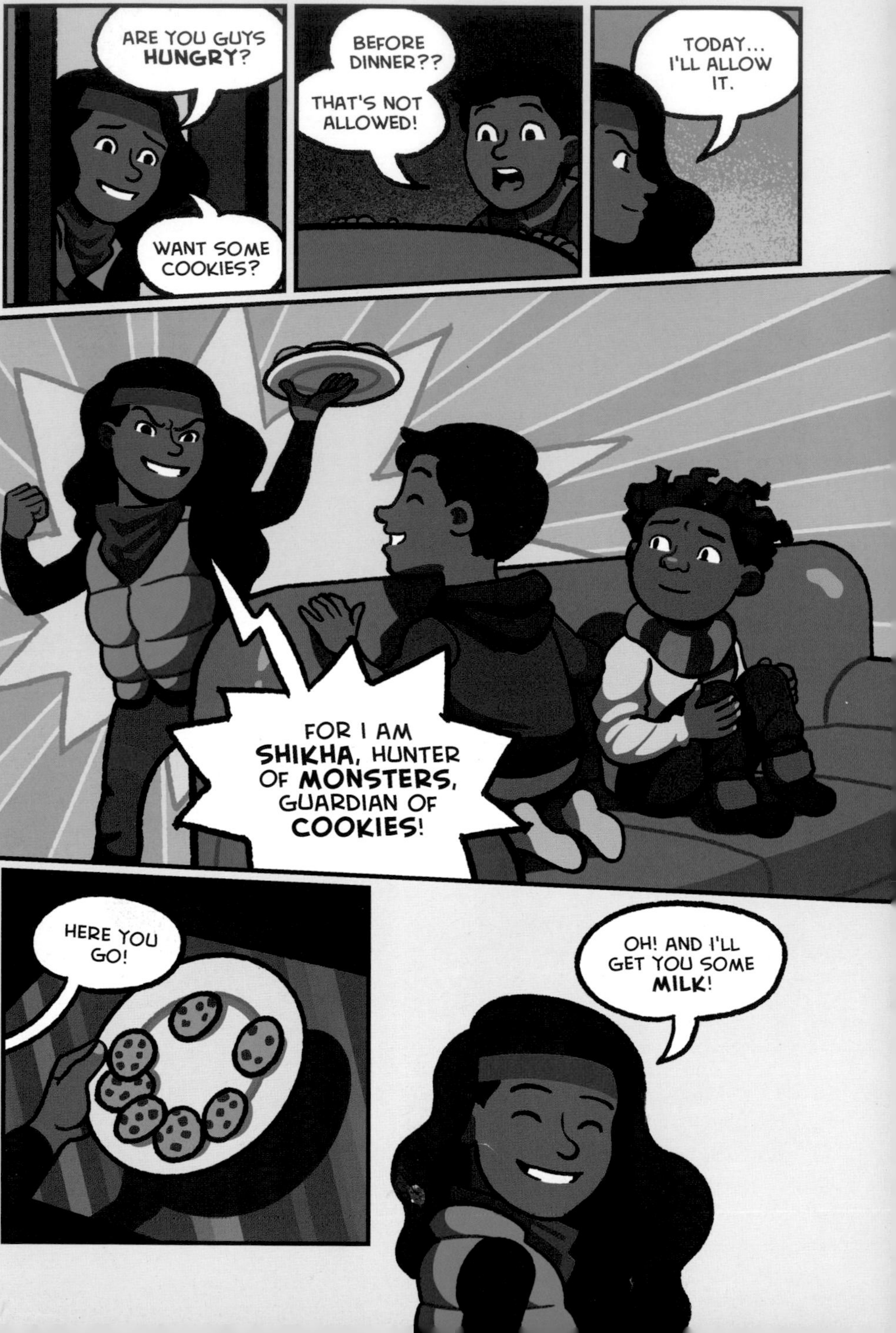

ARE YOU GUYS **HUNGRY**?
WANT SOME COOKIES?
BEFORE DINNER??
THAT'S NOT ALLOWED!
TODAY... I'LL ALLOW IT.
FOR I AM **SHIKHA**, HUNTER OF **MONSTERS**, GUARDIAN OF **COOKIES**!
HERE YOU GO!
OH! AND I'LL GET YOU SOME **MILK**!

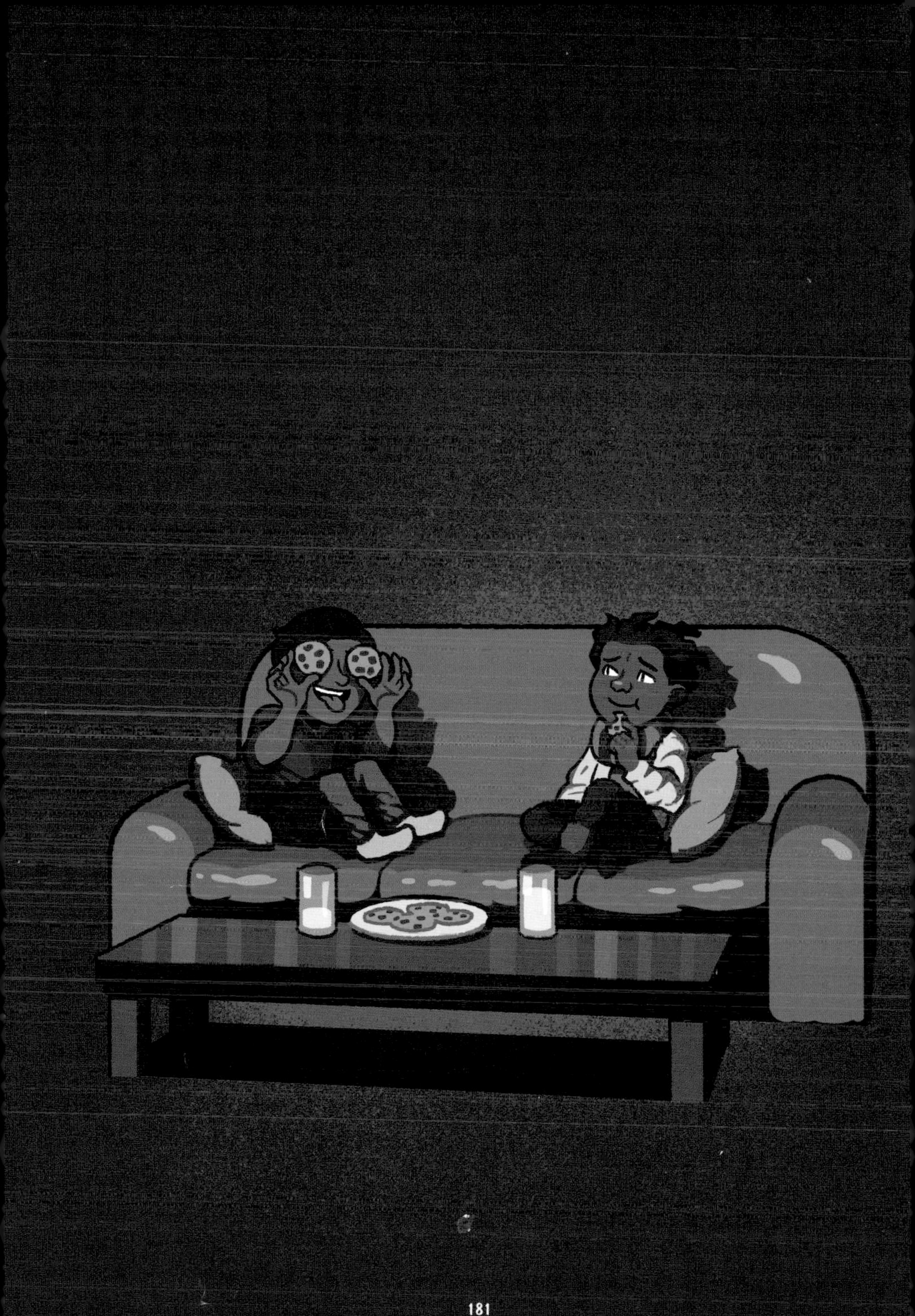

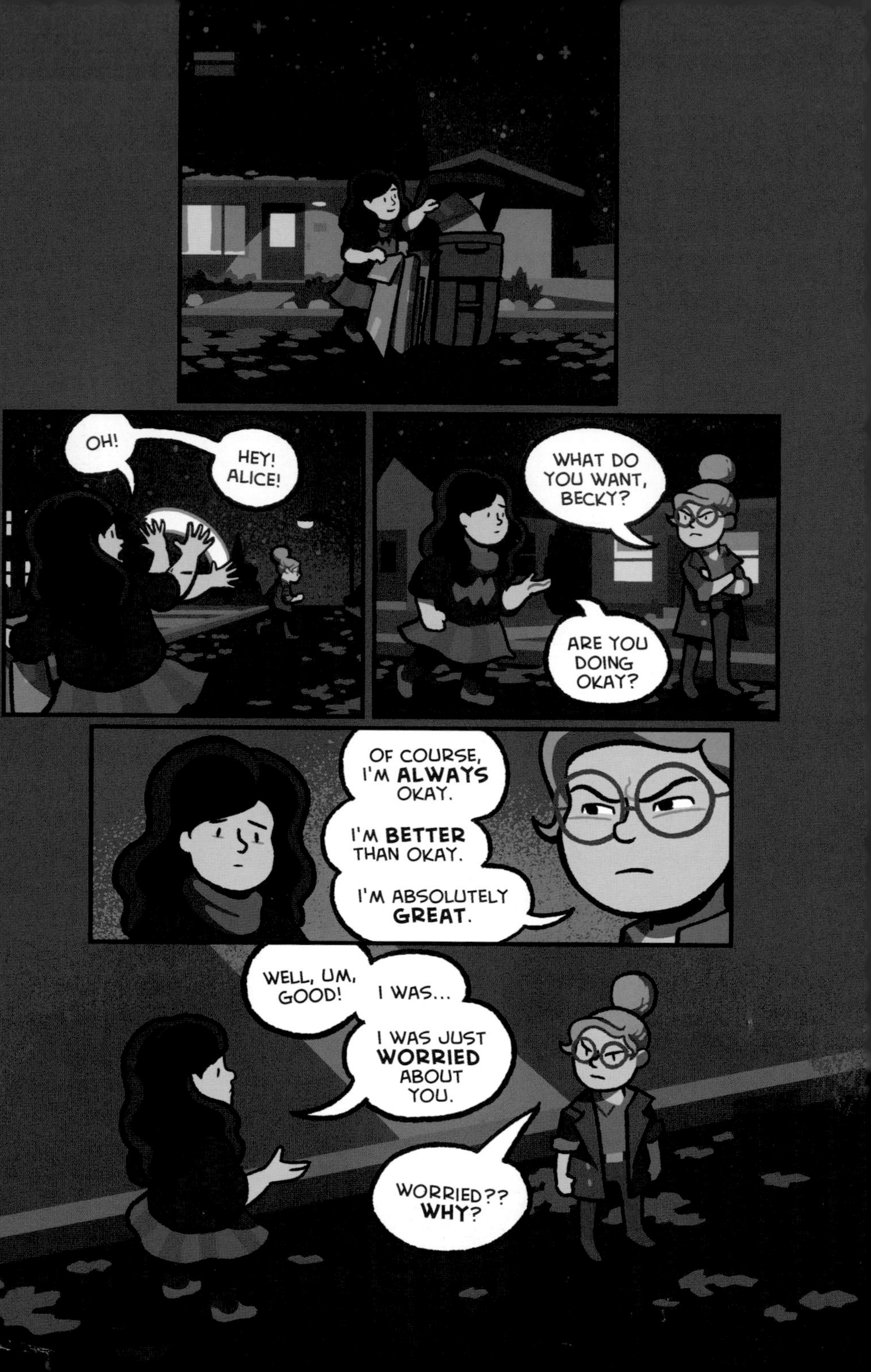
OH!
HEY! ALICE!
WHAT DO YOU WANT, BECKY?
ARE YOU DOING OKAY?
OF COURSE, I'M **ALWAYS** OKAY.
I'M **BETTER** THAN OKAY.
I'M ABSOLUTELY **GREAT**.
WELL, UM, GOOD!
I WAS...
I WAS JUST **WORRIED** ABOUT YOU.
WORRIED?? **WHY**?

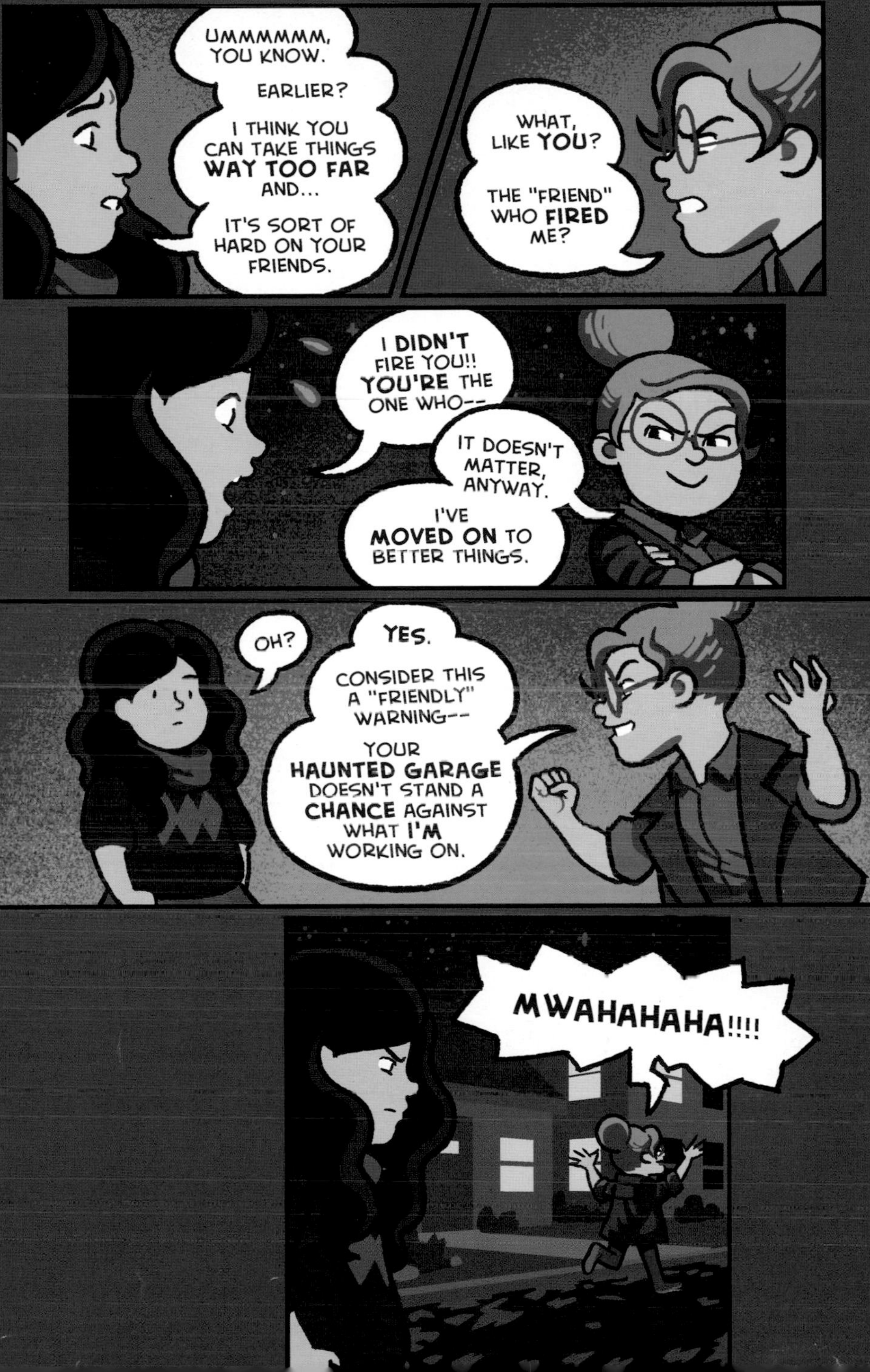
UMMMMMM, YOU KNOW.
EARLIER?
I THINK YOU CAN TAKE THINGS **WAY TOO FAR** AND...
IT'S SORT OF HARD ON YOUR FRIENDS.
WHAT, LIKE **YOU**?
THE "FRIEND" WHO **FIRED** ME?
I **DIDN'T** FIRE YOU!! **YOU'RE** THE ONE WHO--
IT DOESN'T MATTER, ANYWAY.
I'VE **MOVED ON** TO BETTER THINGS.
OH?
YES.
CONSIDER THIS A "FRIENDLY" WARNING--
YOUR **HAUNTED GARAGE** DOESN'T STAND A **CHANCE** AGAINST WHAT **I'M** WORKING ON.
MWAHAHAHA!!!!

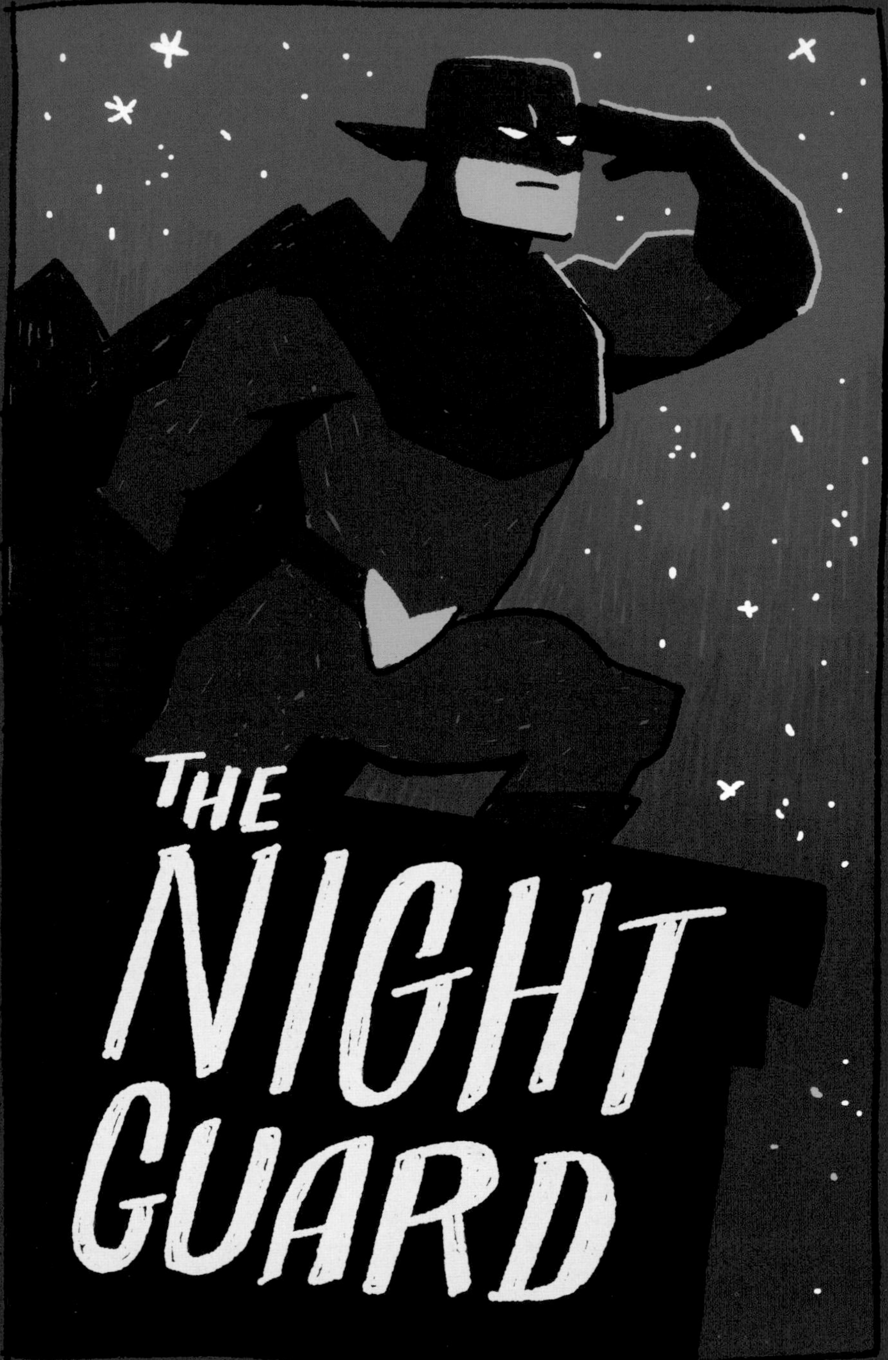
THE
NIGHT
GUARD

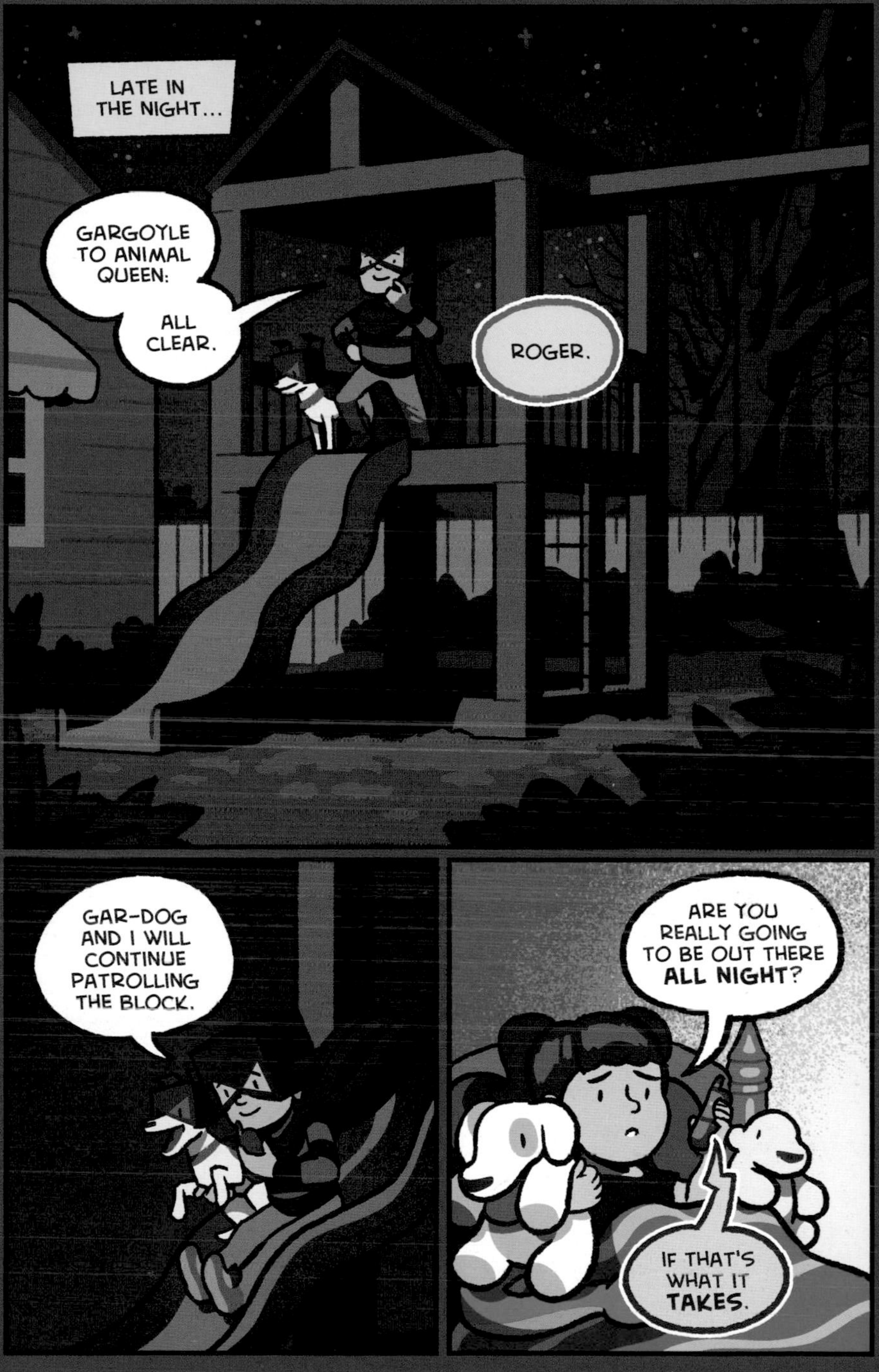
LATE IN THE NIGHT...
GARGOYLE TO ANIMAL QUEEN:
ALL CLEAR.
ROGER.
GAR-DOG AND I WILL CONTINUE PATROLLING THE BLOCK.
ARE YOU REALLY GOING TO BE OUT THERE ALL NIGHT?
IF THAT'S WHAT IT TAKES.

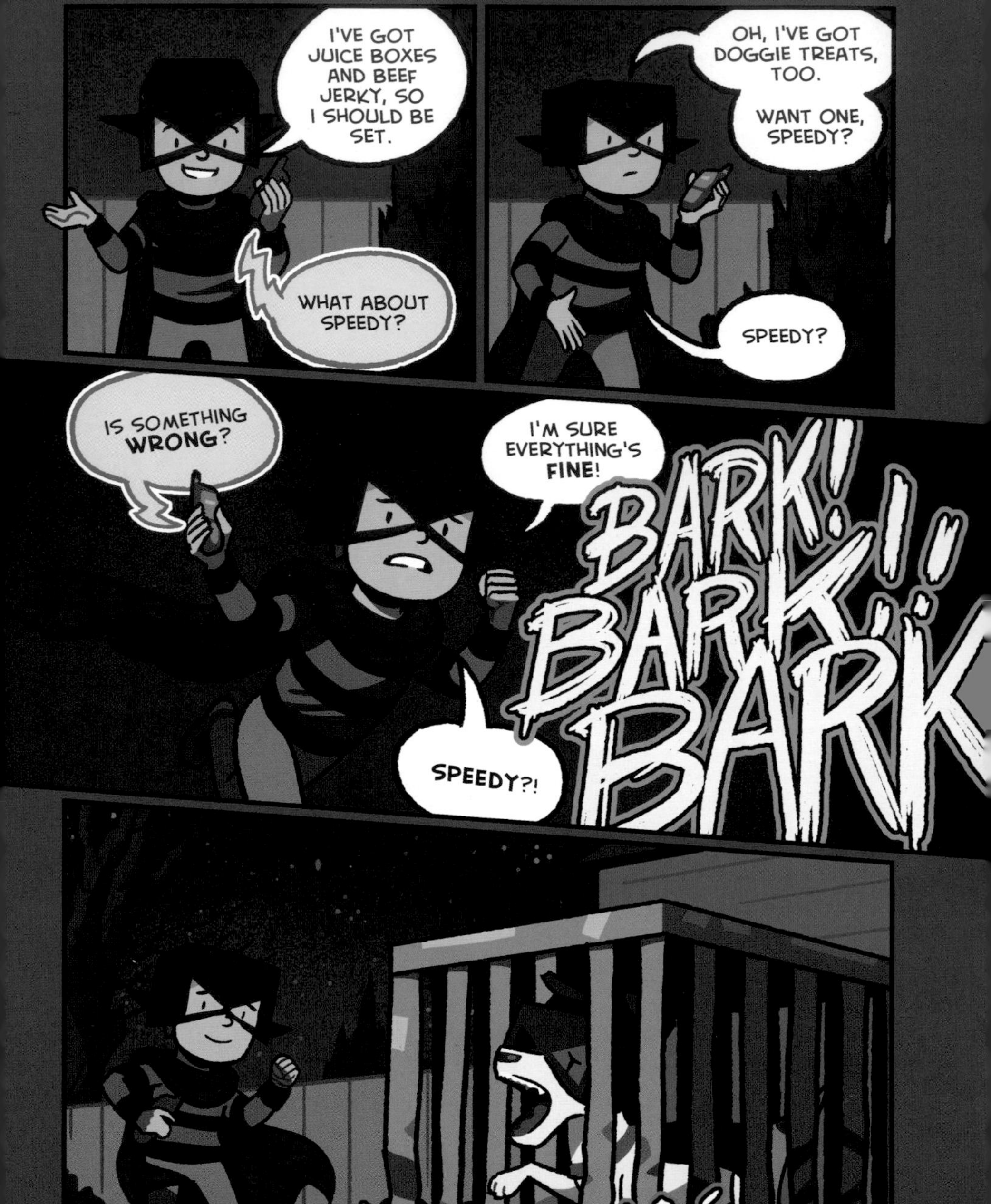
I'VE GOT JUICE BOXES AND BEEF JERKY, SO I SHOULD BE SET.
WHAT ABOUT SPEEDY?
OH, I'VE GOT DOGGIE TREATS, TOO.
WANT ONE, SPEEDY?
SPEEDY?
IS SOMETHING **WRONG**?
I'M SURE EVERYTHING'S **FINE**!
BARK! BARK! BARK
SPEEDY?!
WHIIIIINE

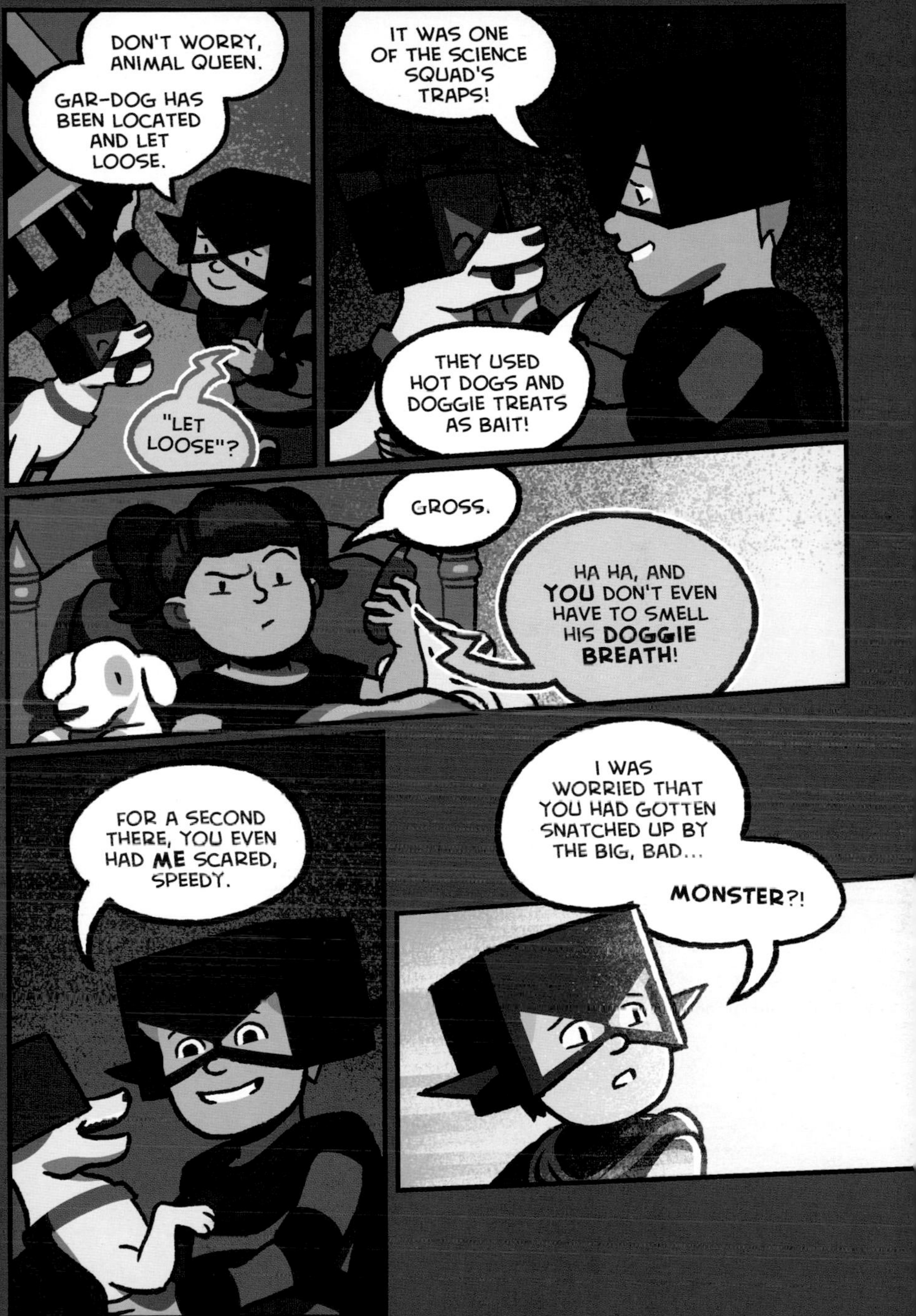
DON'T WORRY, ANIMAL QUEEN.
GAR-DOG HAS BEEN LOCATED AND LET LOOSE.
"LET LOOSE"?
IT WAS ONE OF THE SCIENCE SQUAD'S TRAPS!
THEY USED HOT DOGS AND DOGGIE TREATS AS BAIT!
GROSS.
HA HA, AND YOU DON'T EVEN HAVE TO SMELL HIS DOGGIE BREATH!
FOR A SECOND THERE, YOU EVEN HAD ME SCARED, SPEEDY.
I WAS WORRIED THAT YOU HAD GOTTEN SNATCHED UP BY THE BIG, BAD...
MONSTER?!

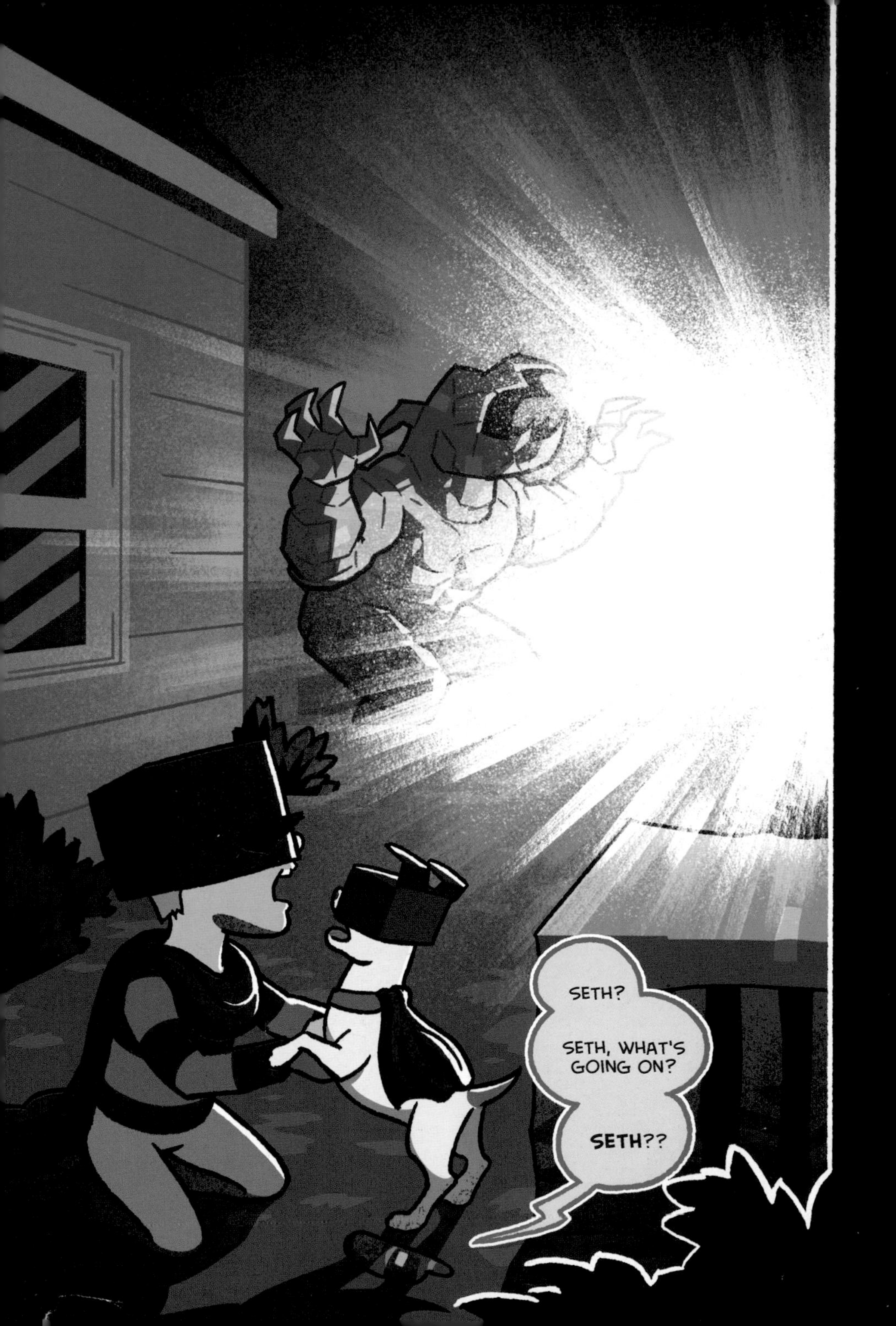
SETH?
SETH, WHAT'S GOING ON?
SETH??

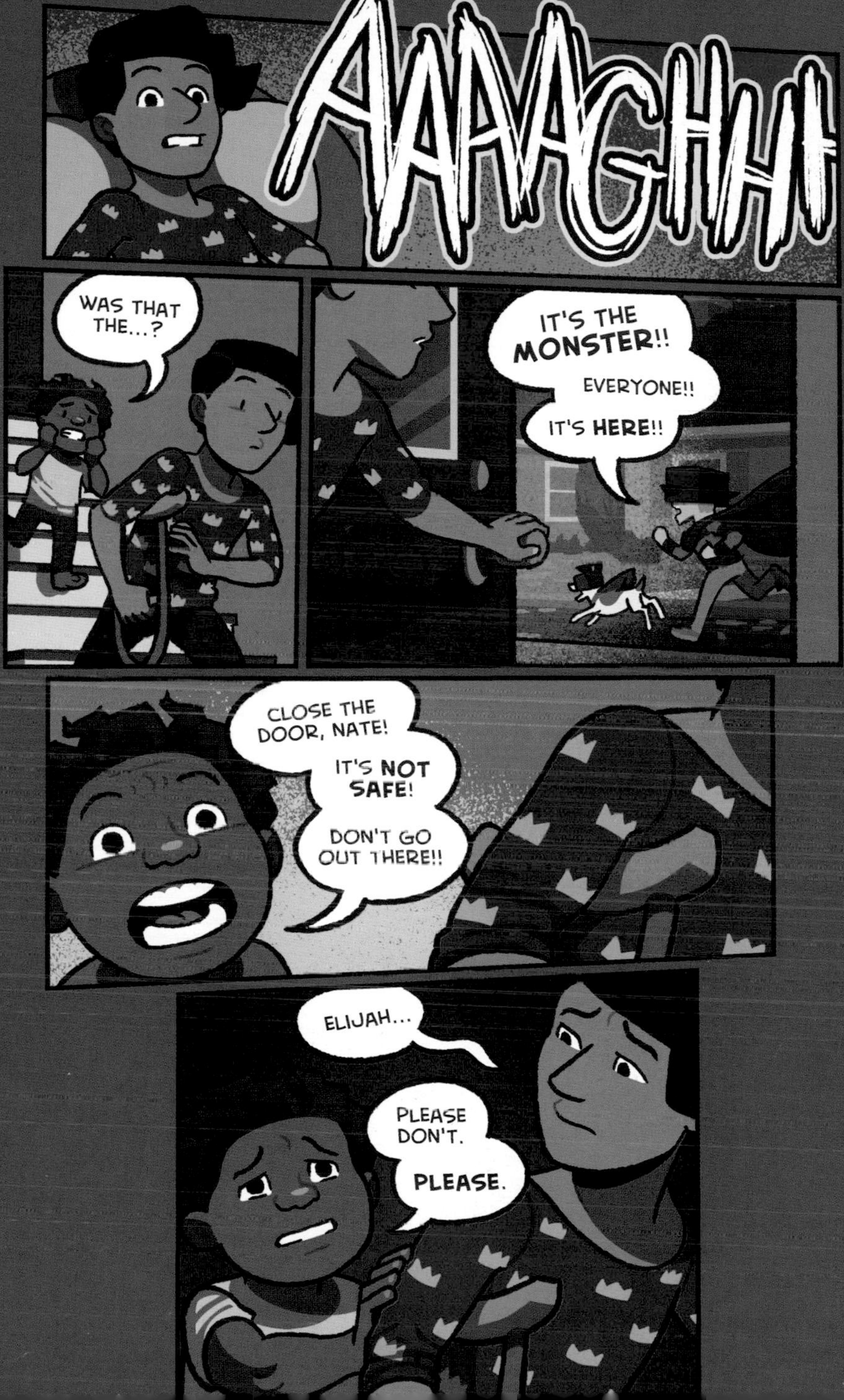
AAAAGHH
WAS THAT THE...?
IT'S THE MONSTER!!
EVERYONE!!
IT'S HERE!!
CLOSE THE DOOR, NATE!
IT'S NOT SAFE!
DON'T GO OUT THERE!!
ELIJAH...
PLEASE DON'T.
PLEASE.

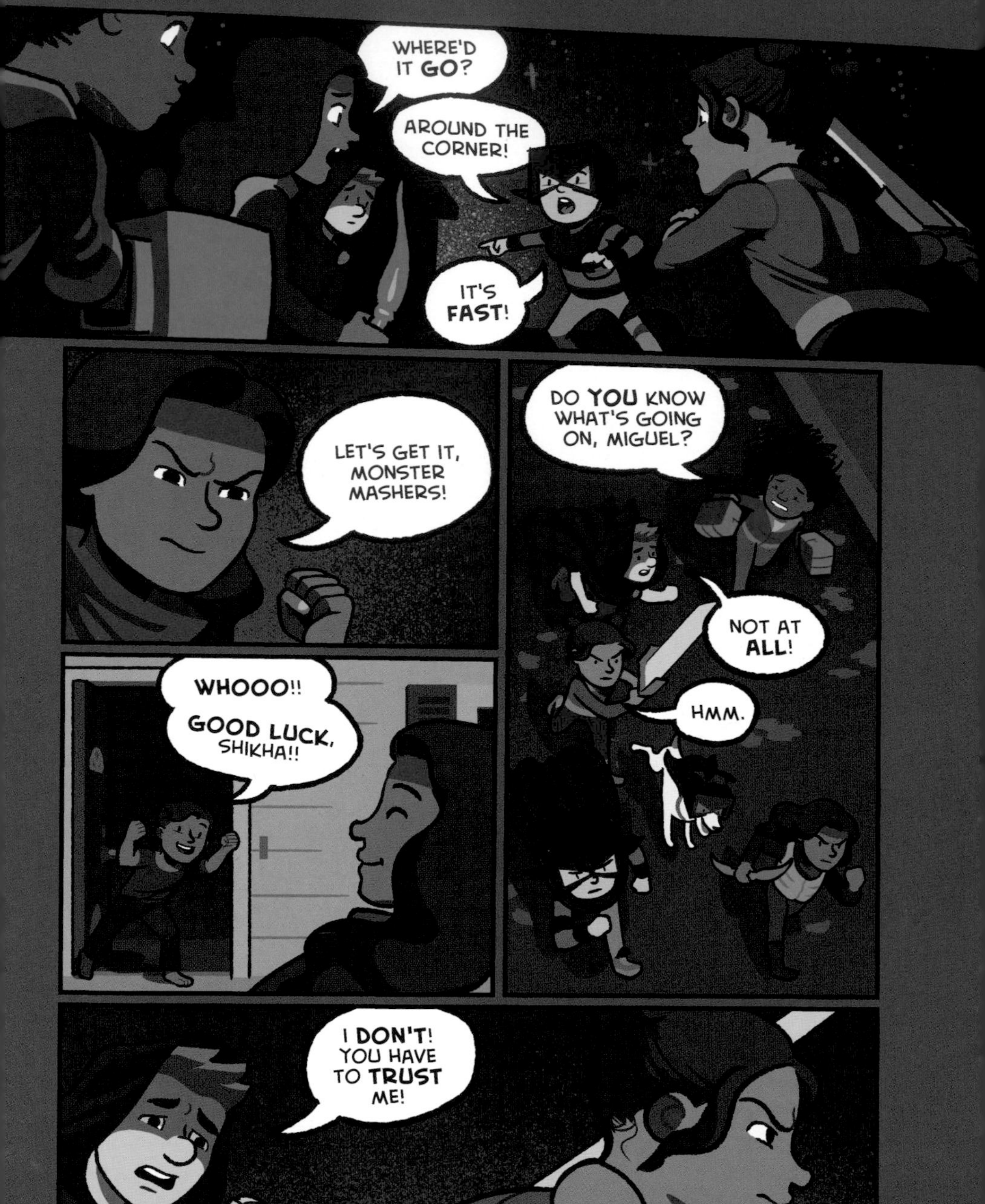
WHERE'D IT GO?
AROUND THE CORNER!
IT'S FAST!
LET'S GET IT, MONSTER MASHERS!
DO YOU KNOW WHAT'S GOING ON, MIGUEL?
NOT AT ALL!
HMM.
WHOOO!!
GOOD LUCK, SHIKHA!!
I DON'T! YOU HAVE TO TRUST ME!

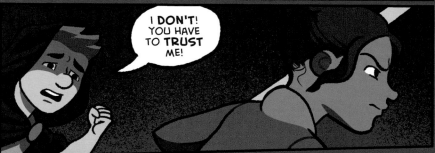

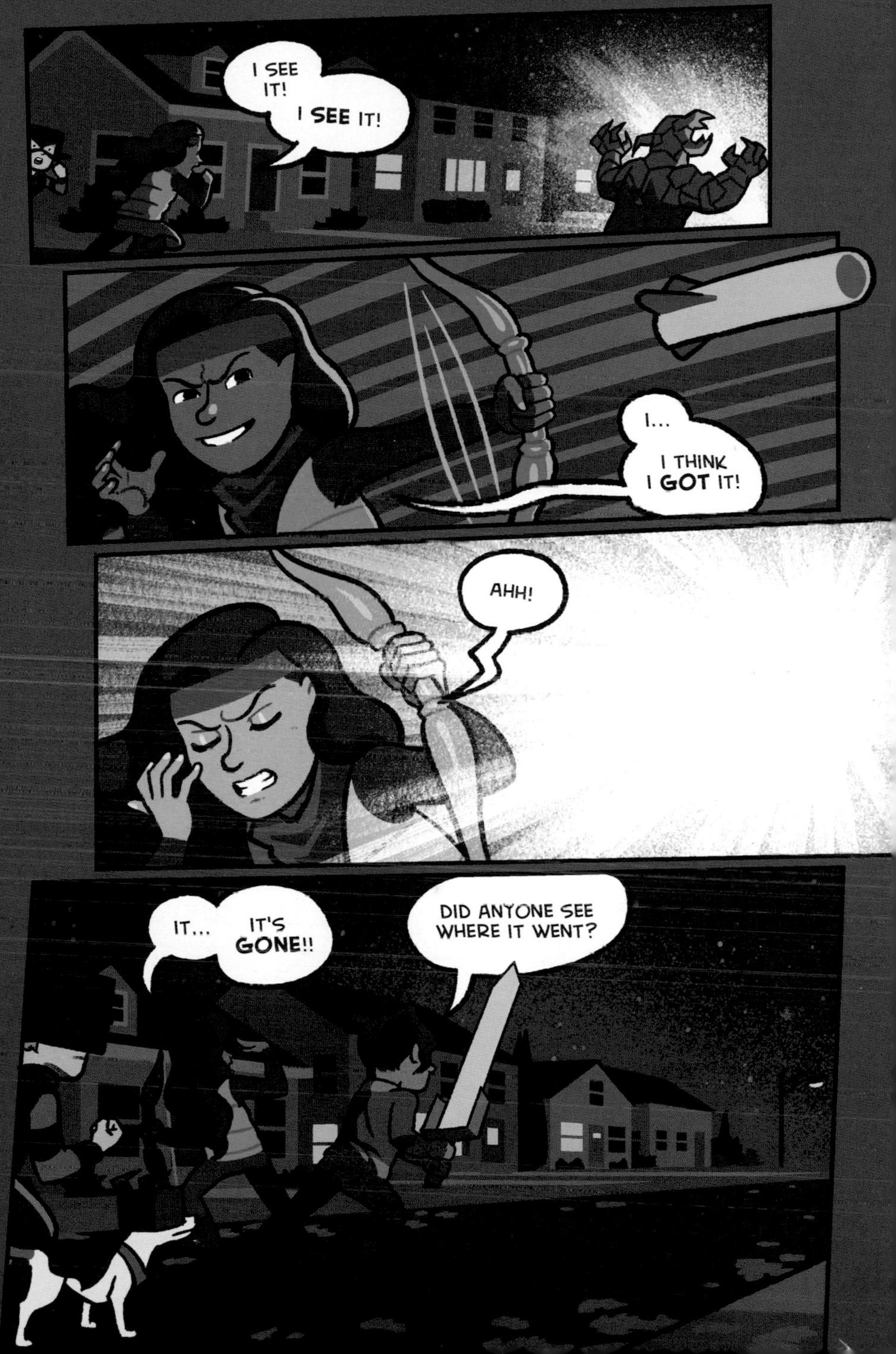
I SEE IT!
I SEE IT!
I...
I THINK I GOT IT!
AHH!
IT...
IT'S GONE!!
DID ANYONE SEE WHERE IT WENT?

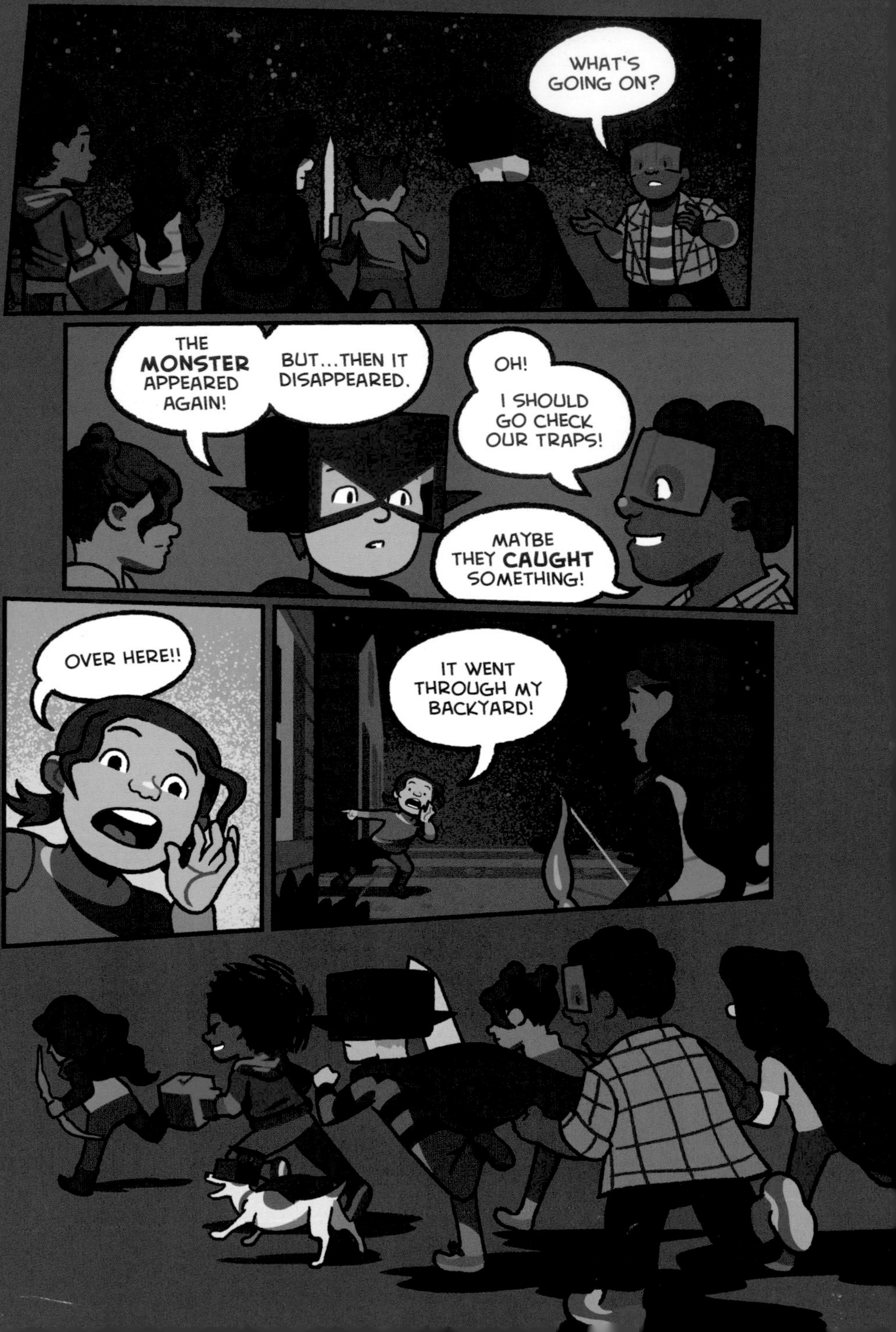
WHAT'S GOING ON?
THE **MONSTER** APPEARED AGAIN!
BUT...THEN IT DISAPPEARED.
OH!
I SHOULD GO CHECK OUR TRAPS!
MAYBE THEY **CAUGHT** SOMETHING!
OVER HERE!!
IT WENT THROUGH MY BACKYARD!

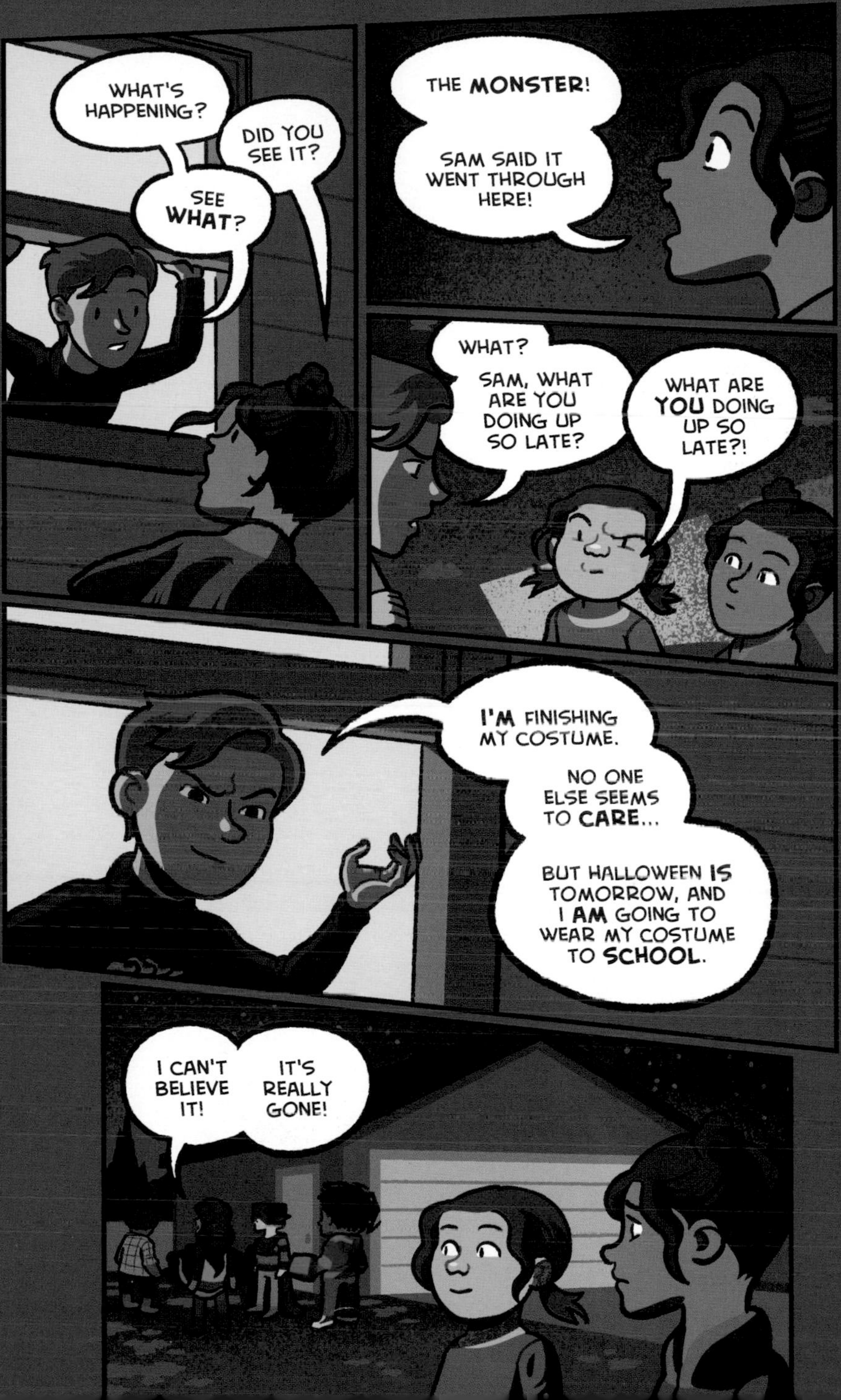
WHAT'S HAPPENING?
DID YOU SEE IT?
SEE WHAT?
THE MONSTER!
SAM SAID IT WENT THROUGH HERE!
WHAT?
SAM, WHAT ARE YOU DOING UP SO LATE?
WHAT ARE YOU DOING UP SO LATE?!
I'M FINISHING MY COSTUME.
NO ONE ELSE SEEMS TO CARE...
BUT HALLOWEEN IS TOMORROW, AND I AM GOING TO WEAR MY COSTUME TO SCHOOL.
I CAN'T BELIEVE IT!
IT'S REALLY GONE!

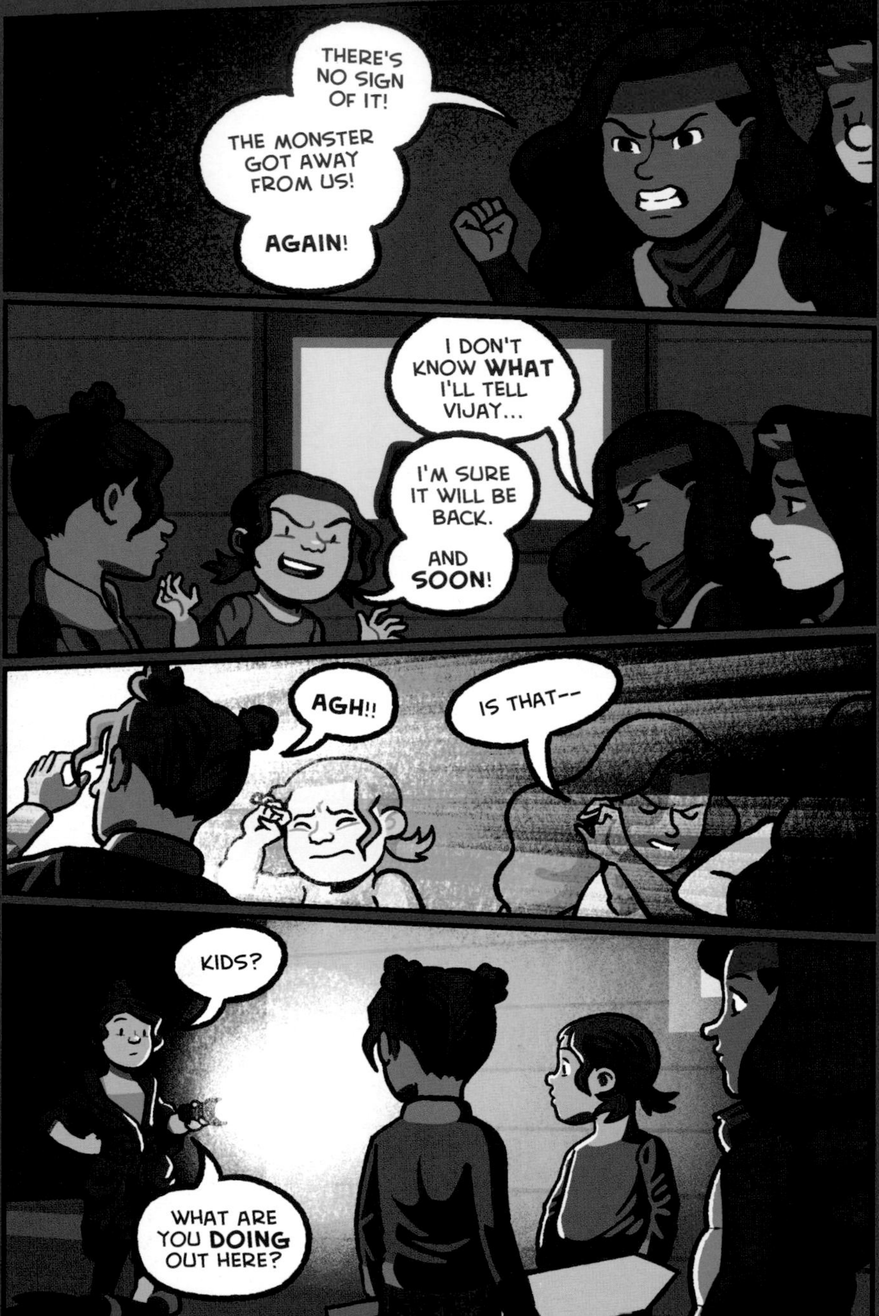
THERE'S NO SIGN OF IT!
THE MONSTER GOT AWAY FROM US!
AGAIN!
I DON'T KNOW WHAT I'LL TELL VIJAY...
I'M SURE IT WILL BE BACK.
AND SOON!
AGH!!
IS THAT--
KIDS?
WHAT ARE YOU DOING OUT HERE?

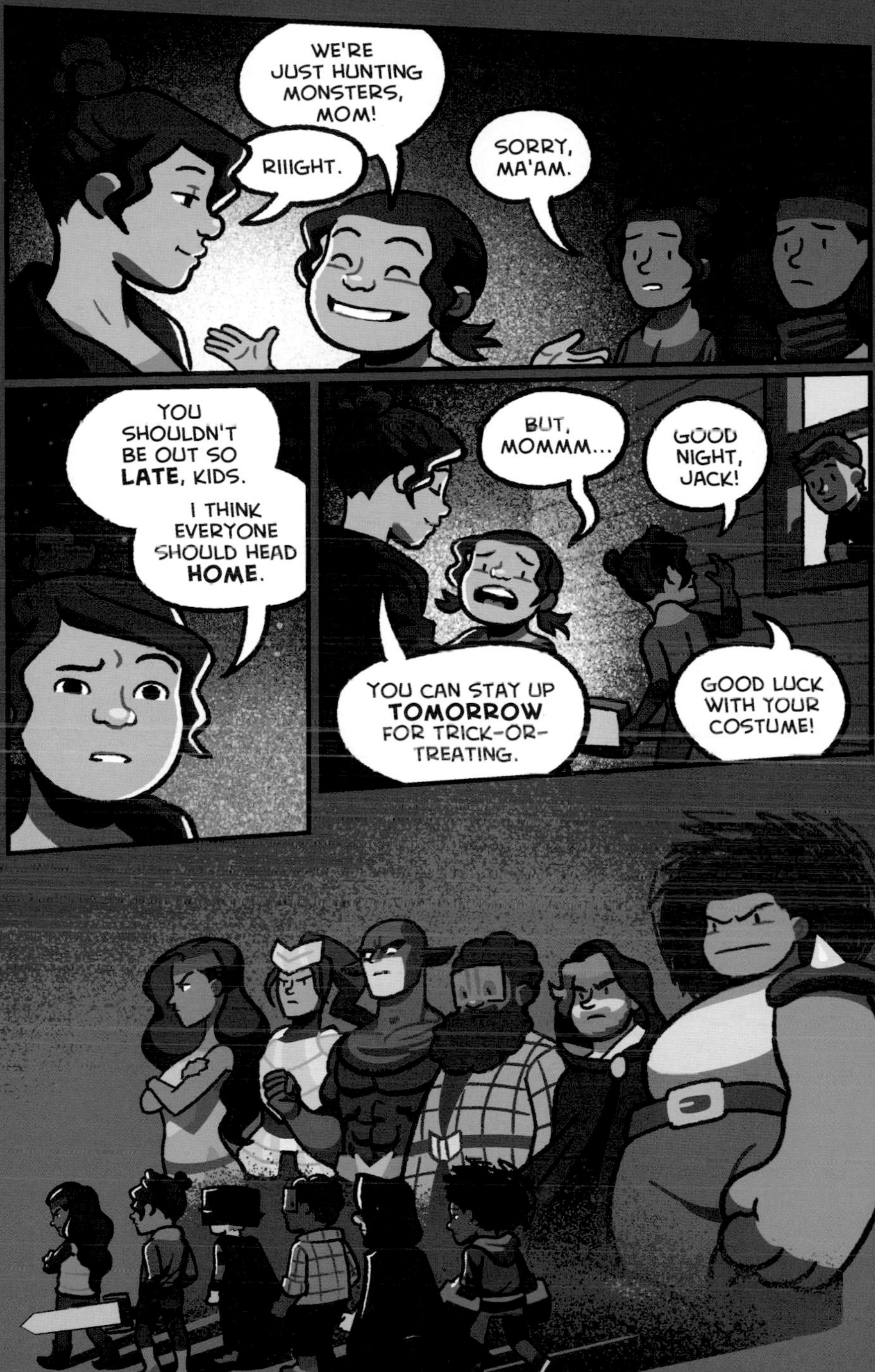
WE'RE JUST HUNTING MONSTERS, MOM!
RIIIGHT.
SORRY, MA'AM.
YOU SHOULDN'T BE OUT SO **LATE**, KIDS.
I THINK EVERYONE SHOULD HEAD **HOME**.
BUT, MOMMM...
GOOD NIGHT, JACK!
YOU CAN STAY UP **TOMORROW** FOR TRICK-OR-TREATING.
GOOD LUCK WITH YOUR COSTUME!

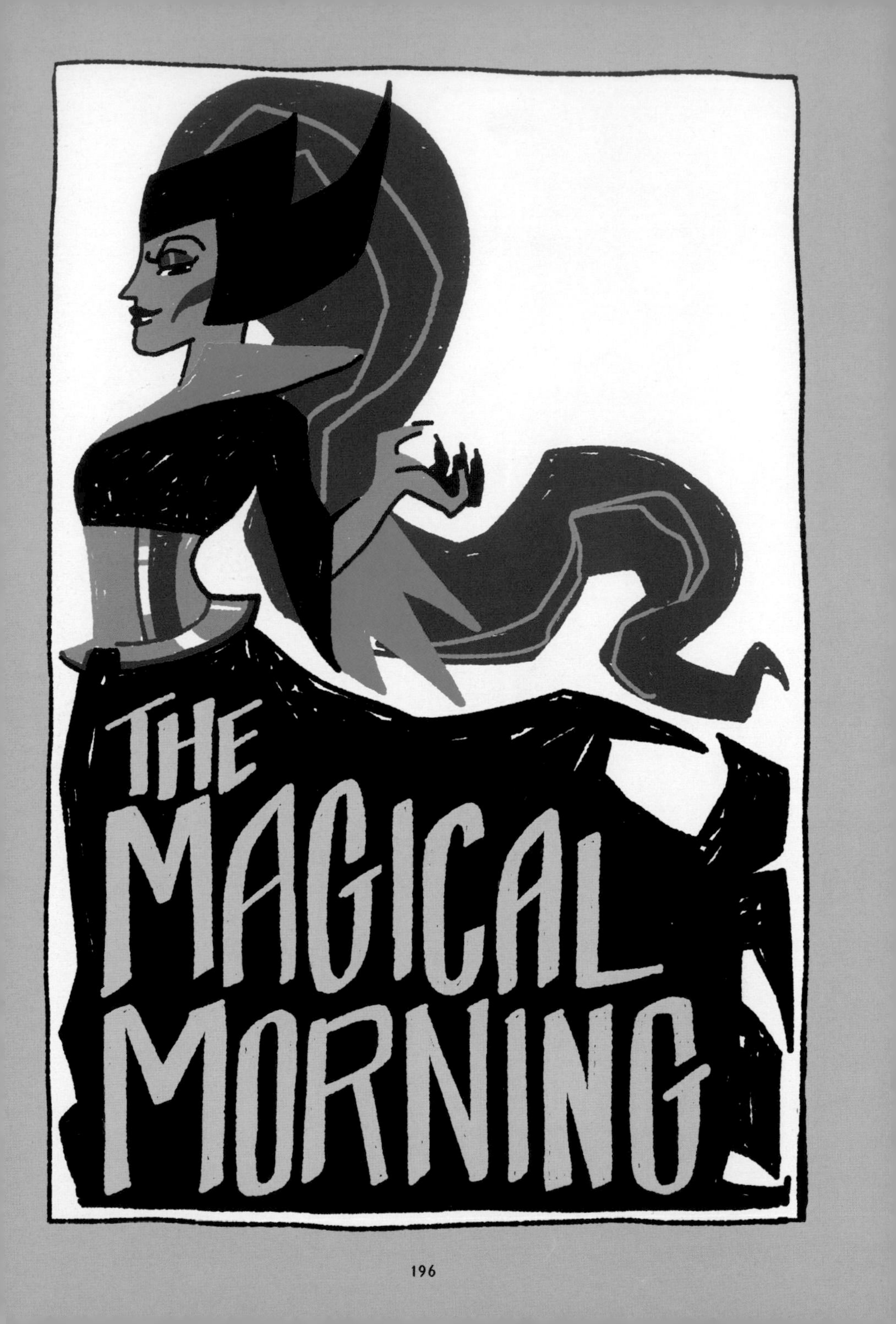
THE
MAGICAL
MORNING

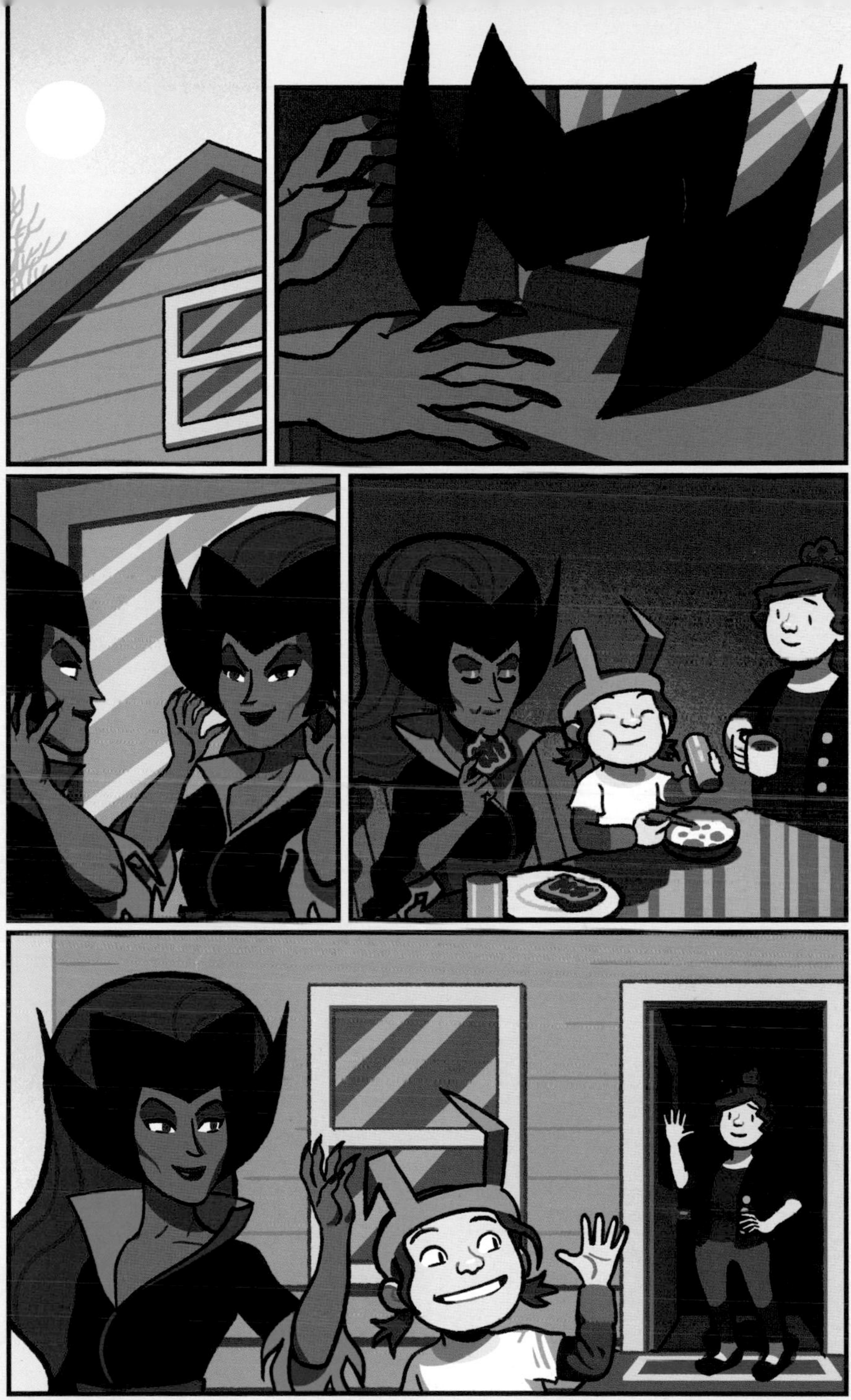

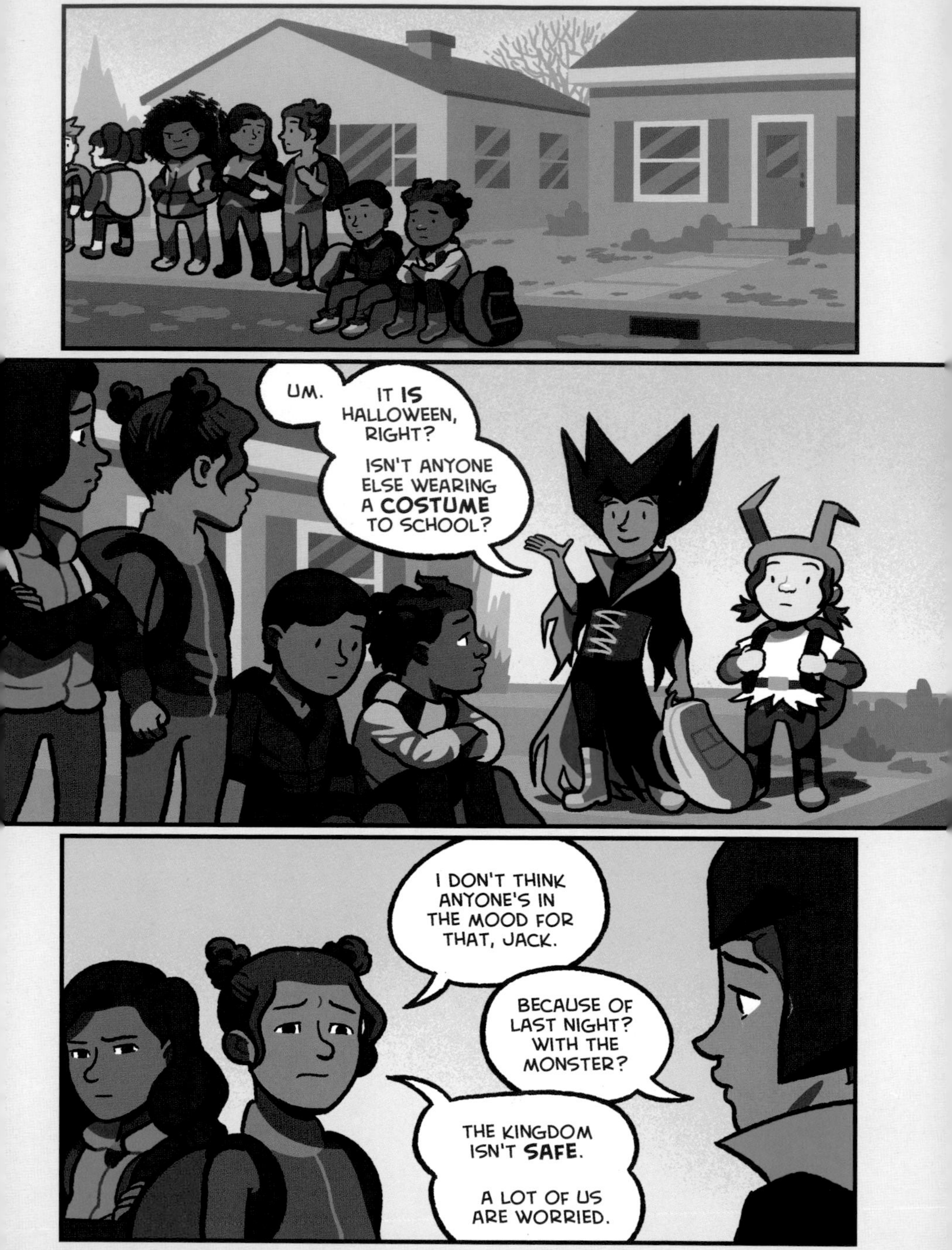
UM.
IT IS HALLOWEEN, RIGHT?
ISN'T ANYONE ELSE WEARING A COSTUME TO SCHOOL?
I DON'T THINK ANYONE'S IN THE MOOD FOR THAT, JACK.
BECAUSE OF LAST NIGHT? WITH THE MONSTER?
THE KINGDOM ISN'T SAFE.
A LOT OF US ARE WORRIED.

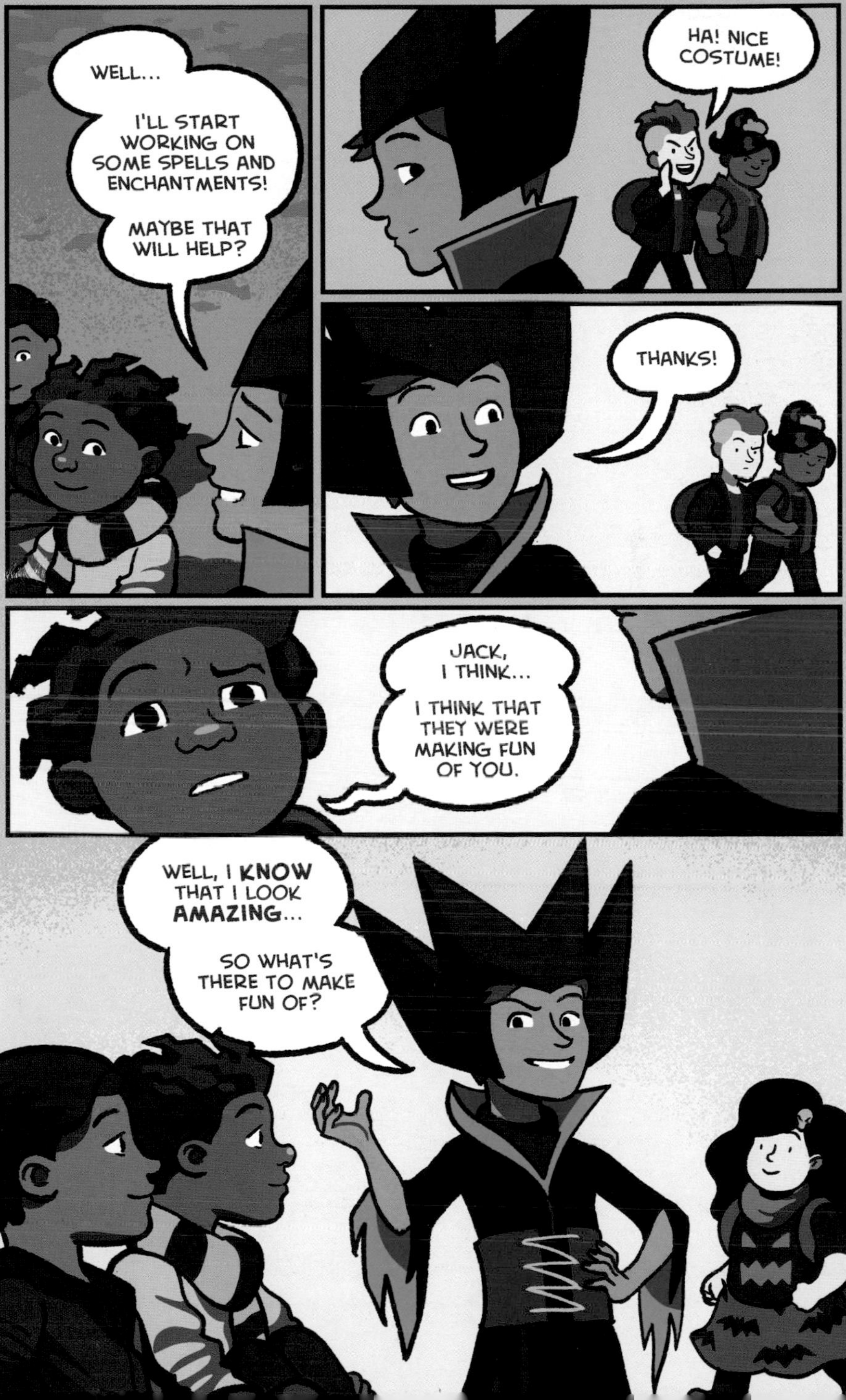
WELL...
I'LL START WORKING ON SOME SPELLS AND ENCHANTMENTS!
MAYBE THAT WILL HELP?
HA! NICE COSTUME!
THANKS!
JACK, I THINK...
I THINK THAT THEY WERE MAKING FUN OF YOU.
WELL, I **KNOW** THAT I LOOK **AMAZING**...
SO WHAT'S THERE TO MAKE FUN OF?

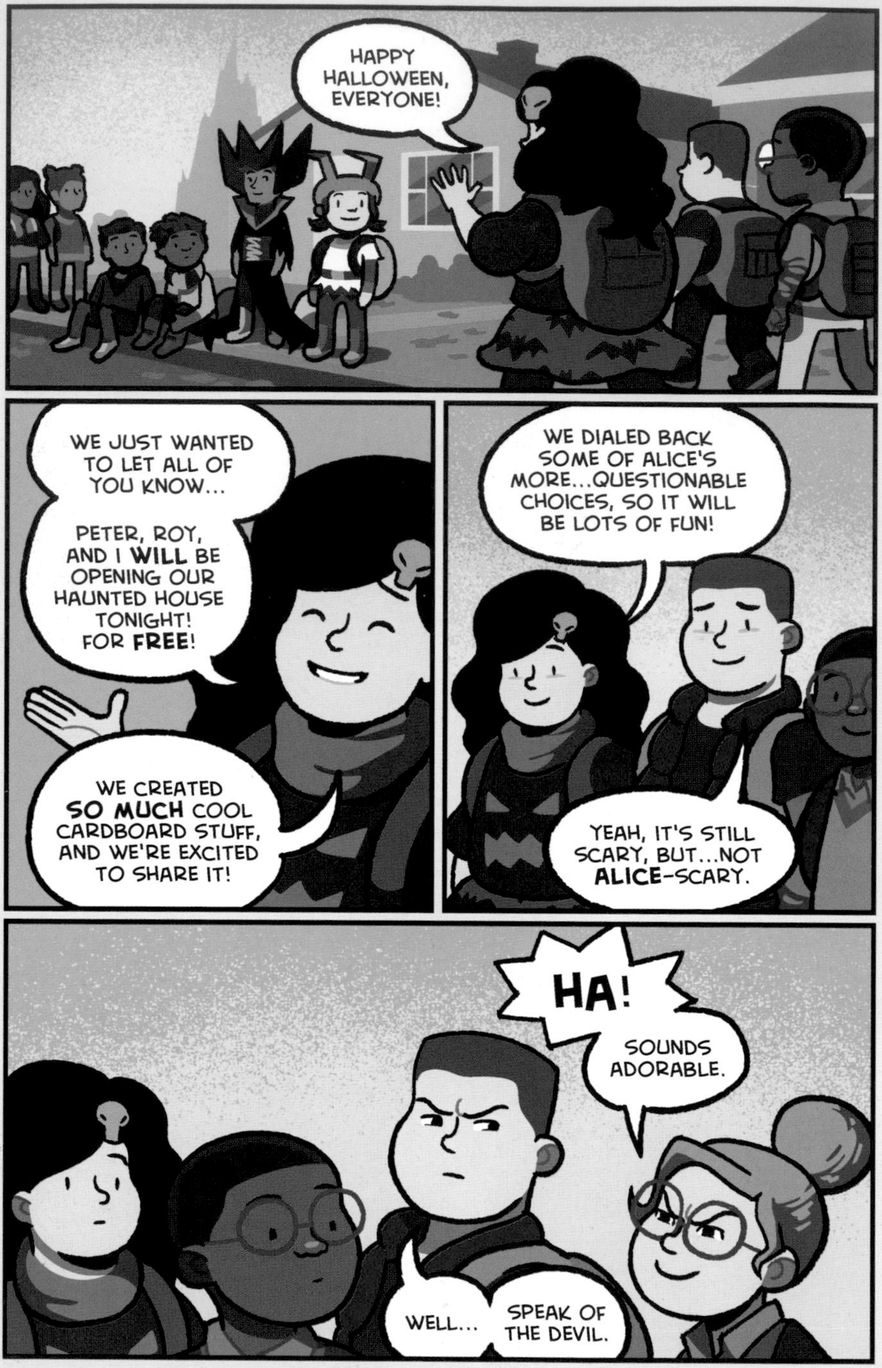

HAPPY HALLOWEEN, EVERYONE!
WE JUST WANTED TO LET ALL OF YOU KNOW...
PETER, ROY, AND I **WILL** BE OPENING OUR HAUNTED HOUSE TONIGHT! FOR **FREE**!
WE CREATED **SO MUCH** COOL CARDBOARD STUFF, AND WE'RE EXCITED TO SHARE IT!
WE DIALED BACK SOME OF ALICE'S MORE...QUESTIONABLE CHOICES, SO IT WILL BE LOTS OF FUN!
YEAH, IT'S STILL SCARY, BUT...NOT **ALICE**-SCARY.
HA!
SOUNDS ADORABLE.
WELL...
SPEAK OF THE DEVIL.

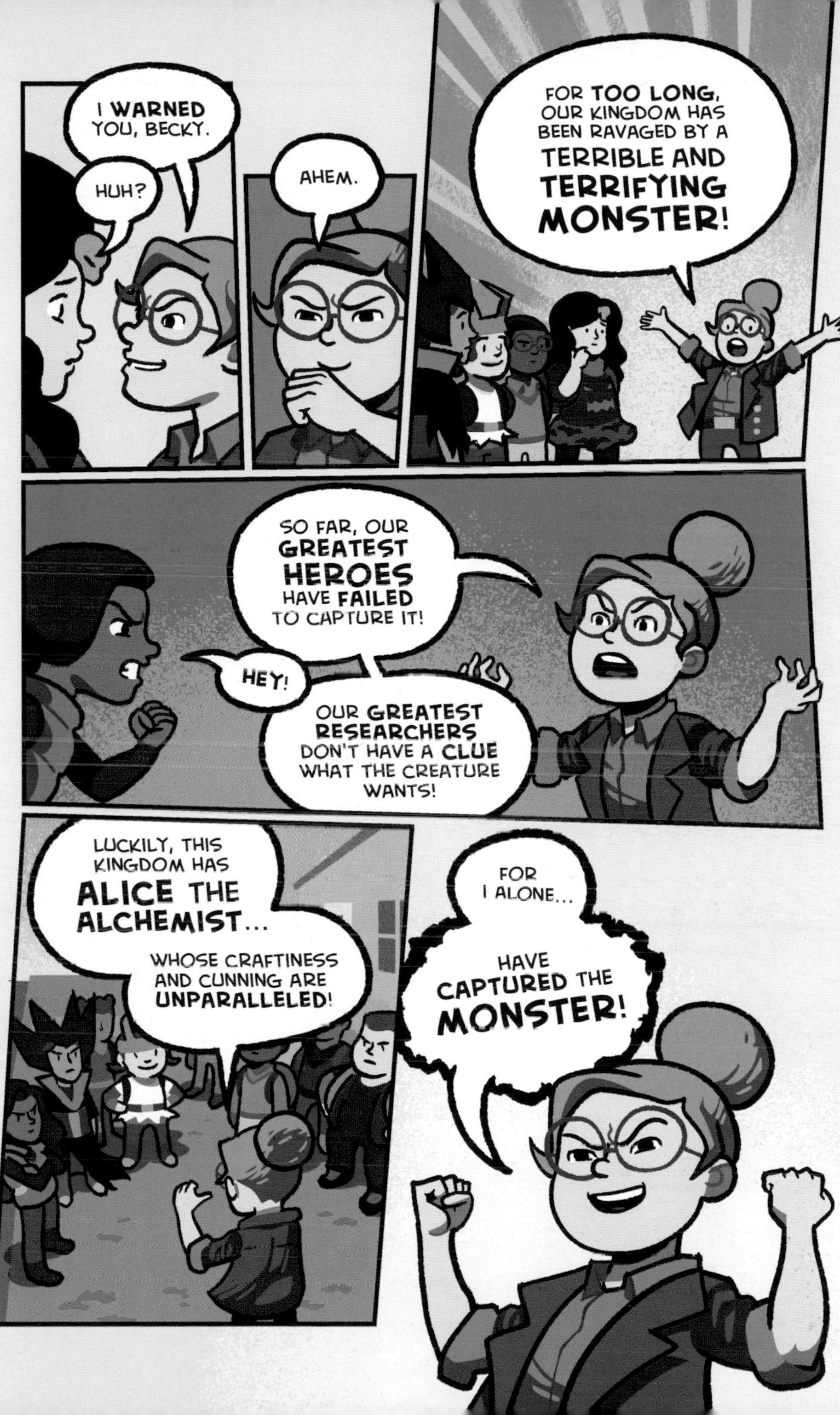

I WARNED YOU, BECKY.
HUH?
AHEM.
FOR TOO LONG, OUR KINGDOM HAS BEEN RAVAGED BY A TERRIBLE AND TERRIFYING MONSTER!
SO FAR, OUR GREATEST HEROES HAVE FAILED TO CAPTURE IT!
HEY!
OUR GREATEST RESEARCHERS DON'T HAVE A CLUE WHAT THE CREATURE WANTS!
LUCKILY, THIS KINGDOM HAS ALICE THE ALCHEMIST...
WHOSE CRAFTINESS AND CUNNING ARE UNPARALLELED!
FOR I ALONE...
HAVE CAPTURED THE MONSTER!

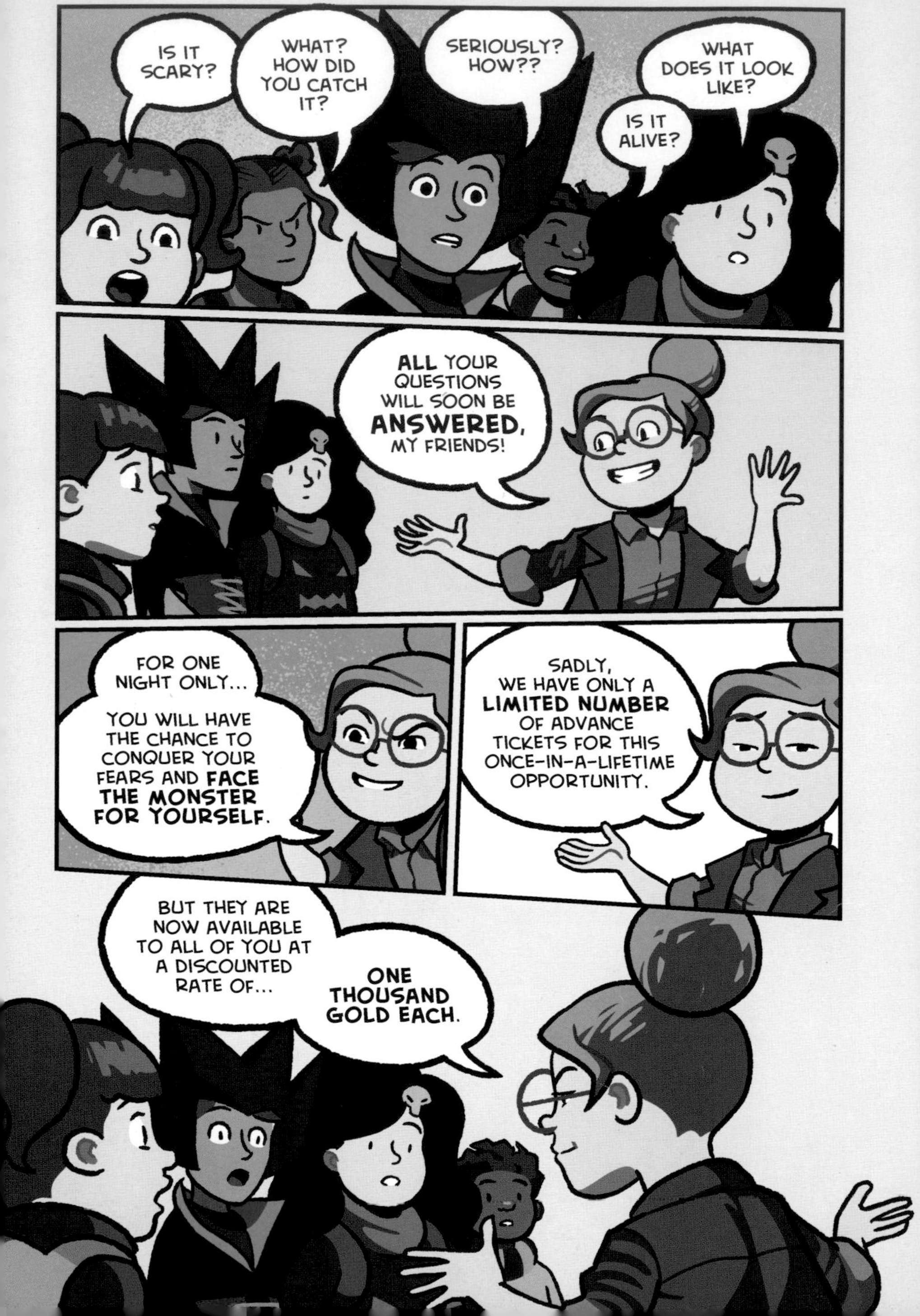
IS IT SCARY?
WHAT? HOW DID YOU CATCH IT?
SERIOUSLY? HOW??
WHAT DOES IT LOOK LIKE?
IS IT ALIVE?
ALL YOUR QUESTIONS WILL SOON BE ANSWERED, MY FRIENDS!
FOR ONE NIGHT ONLY...
YOU WILL HAVE THE CHANCE TO CONQUER YOUR FEARS AND FACE THE MONSTER FOR YOURSELF.
SADLY, WE HAVE ONLY A LIMITED NUMBER OF ADVANCE TICKETS FOR THIS ONCE-IN-A-LIFETIME OPPORTUNITY.
BUT THEY ARE NOW AVAILABLE TO ALL OF YOU AT A DISCOUNTED RATE OF...
ONE THOUSAND GOLD EACH.

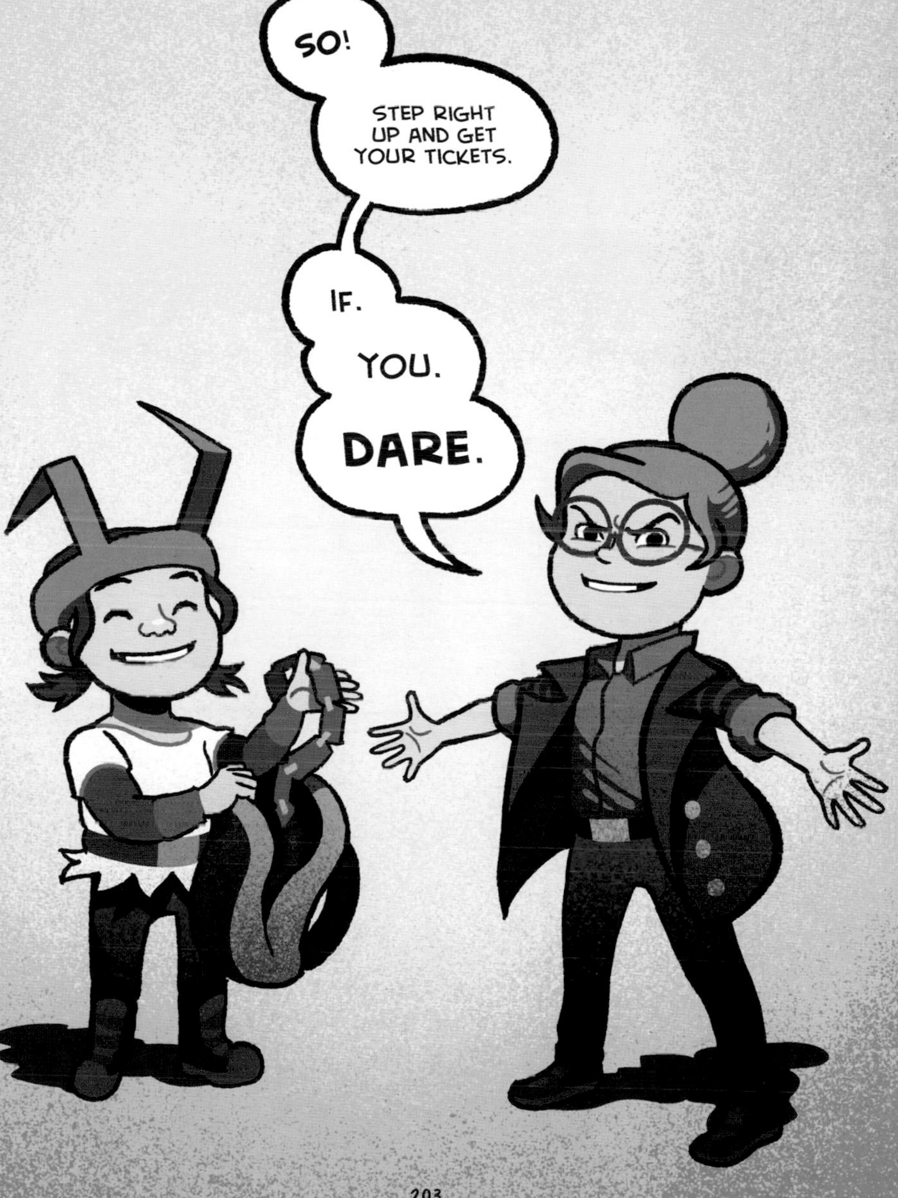
SO!
STEP RIGHT UP AND GET YOUR TICKETS.
IF.
YOU.
DARE.

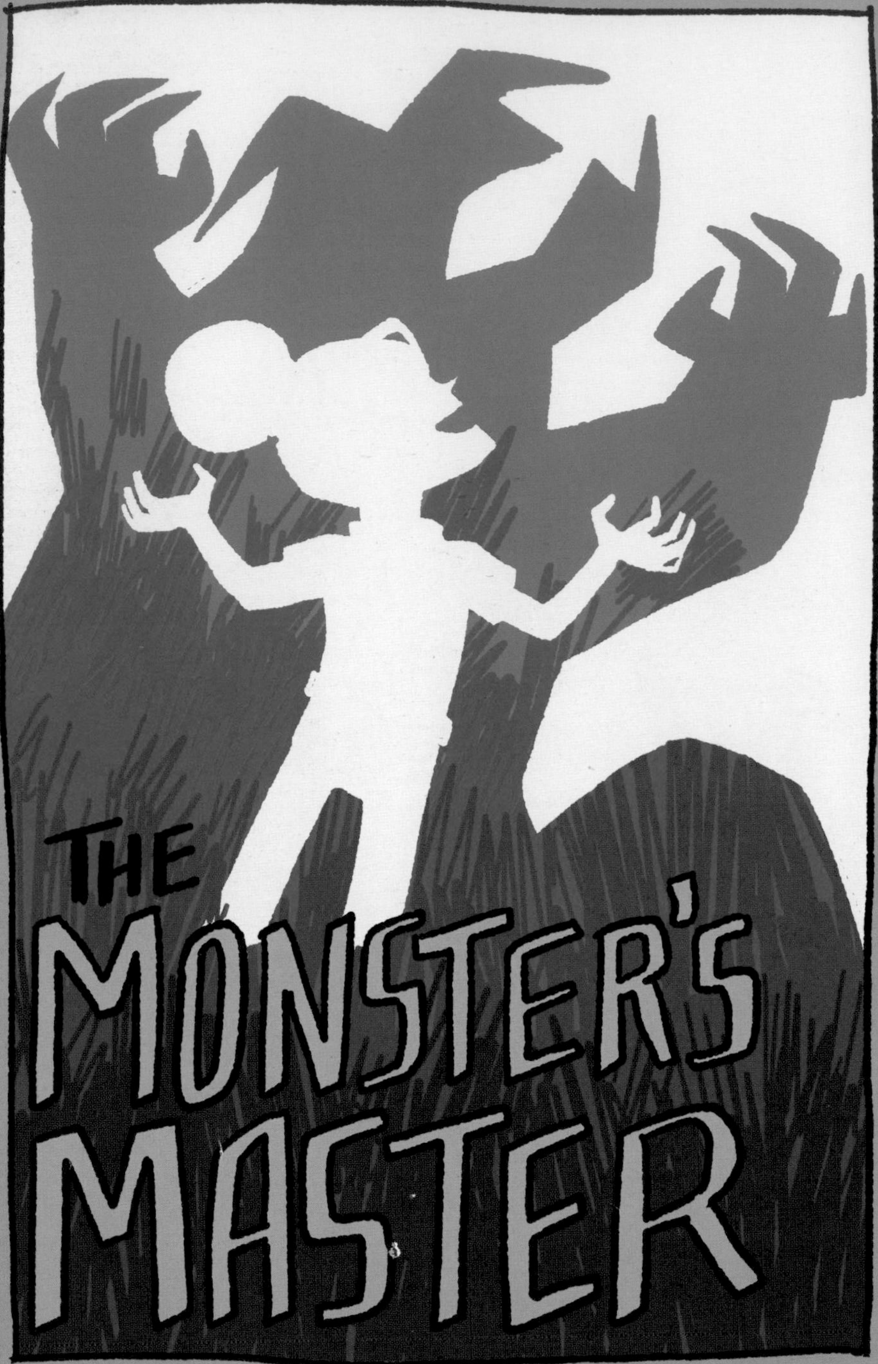
THE
MONSTER'S
MASTER

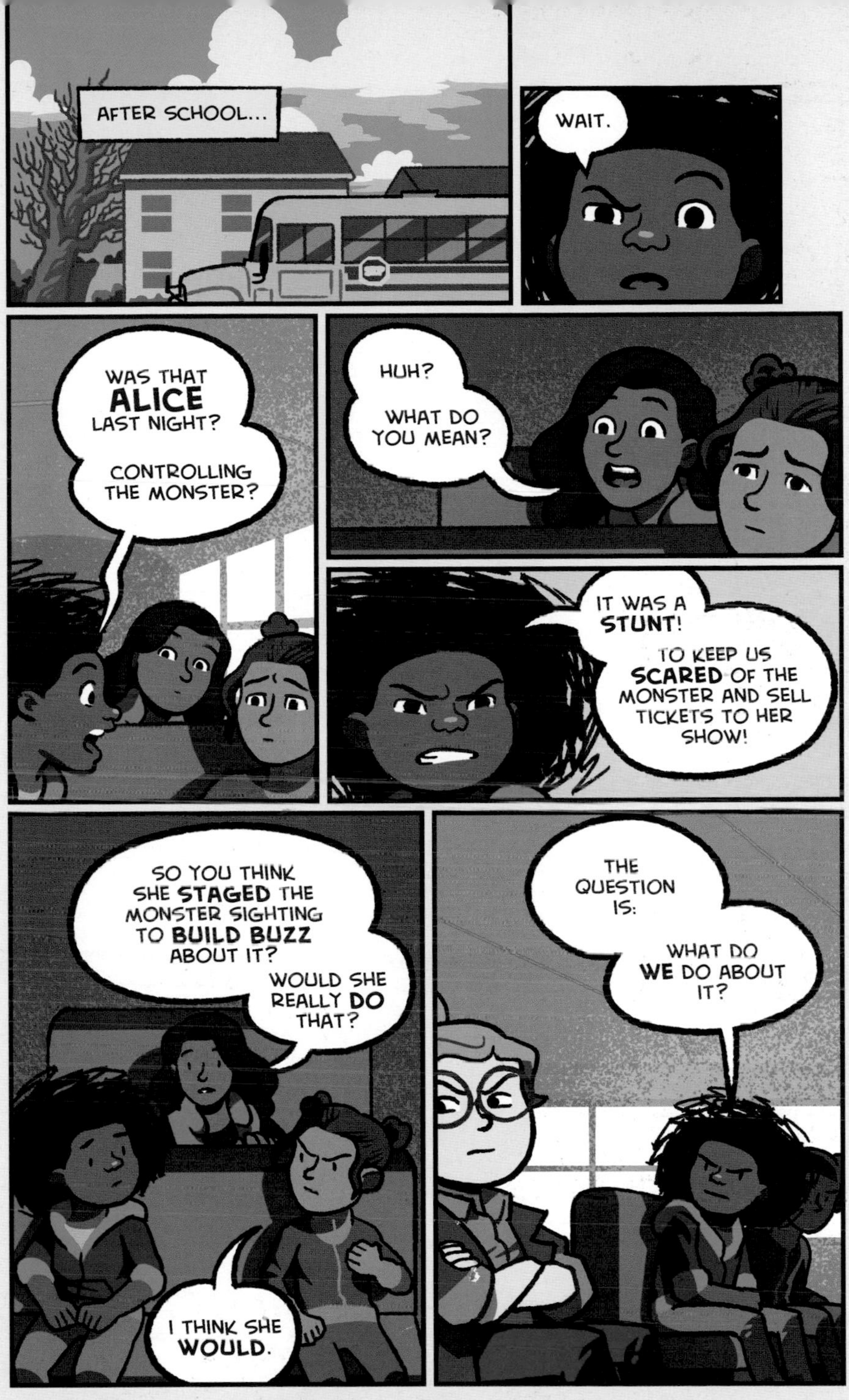
AFTER SCHOOL...
WAIT.
WAS THAT **ALICE** LAST NIGHT?
CONTROLLING THE MONSTER?
HUH?
WHAT DO YOU MEAN?
IT WAS A **STUNT**!
TO KEEP US **SCARED** OF THE MONSTER AND SELL TICKETS TO HER SHOW!
SO YOU THINK SHE **STAGED** THE MONSTER SIGHTING TO **BUILD BUZZ** ABOUT IT?
WOULD SHE REALLY **DO** THAT?
I THINK SHE **WOULD**.
THE QUESTION IS:
WHAT DO **WE** DO ABOUT IT?

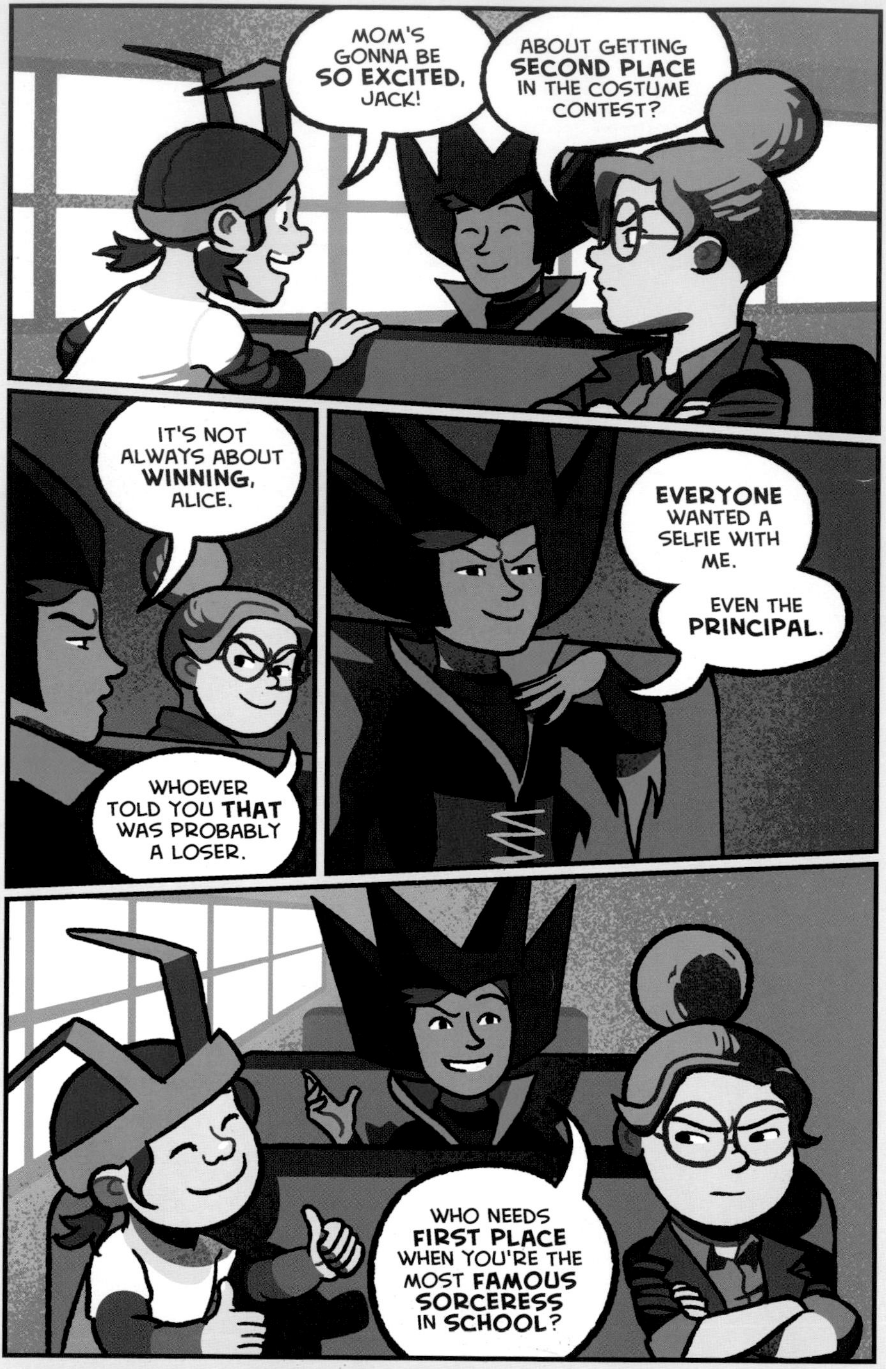
MOM'S GONNA BE SO EXCITED, JACK!
ABOUT GETTING SECOND PLACE IN THE COSTUME CONTEST?
IT'S NOT ALWAYS ABOUT WINNING, ALICE.
WHOEVER TOLD YOU THAT WAS PROBABLY A LOSER.
EVERYONE WANTED A SELFIE WITH ME.
EVEN THE PRINCIPAL.
WHO NEEDS FIRST PLACE WHEN YOU'RE THE MOST FAMOUS SORCERESS IN SCHOOL?

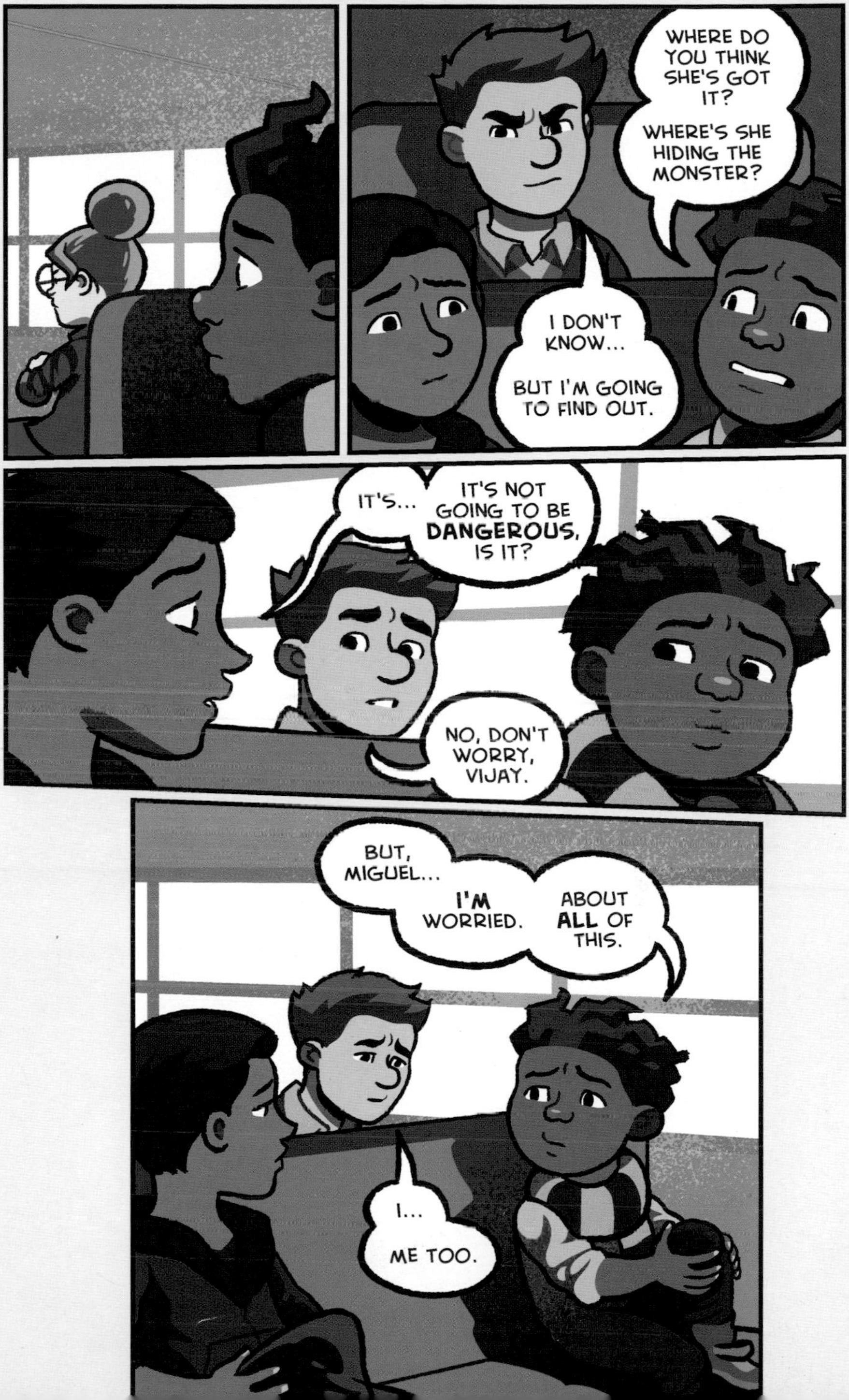
WHERE DO YOU THINK SHE'S GOT IT?
WHERE'S SHE HIDING THE MONSTER?
I DON'T KNOW...
BUT I'M GOING TO FIND OUT.
IT'S...
IT'S NOT GOING TO BE **DANGEROUS**, IS IT?
NO, DON'T WORRY, VIJAY.
BUT, MIGUEL...
I'M WORRIED.
ABOUT **ALL** OF THIS.
I...
ME TOO.

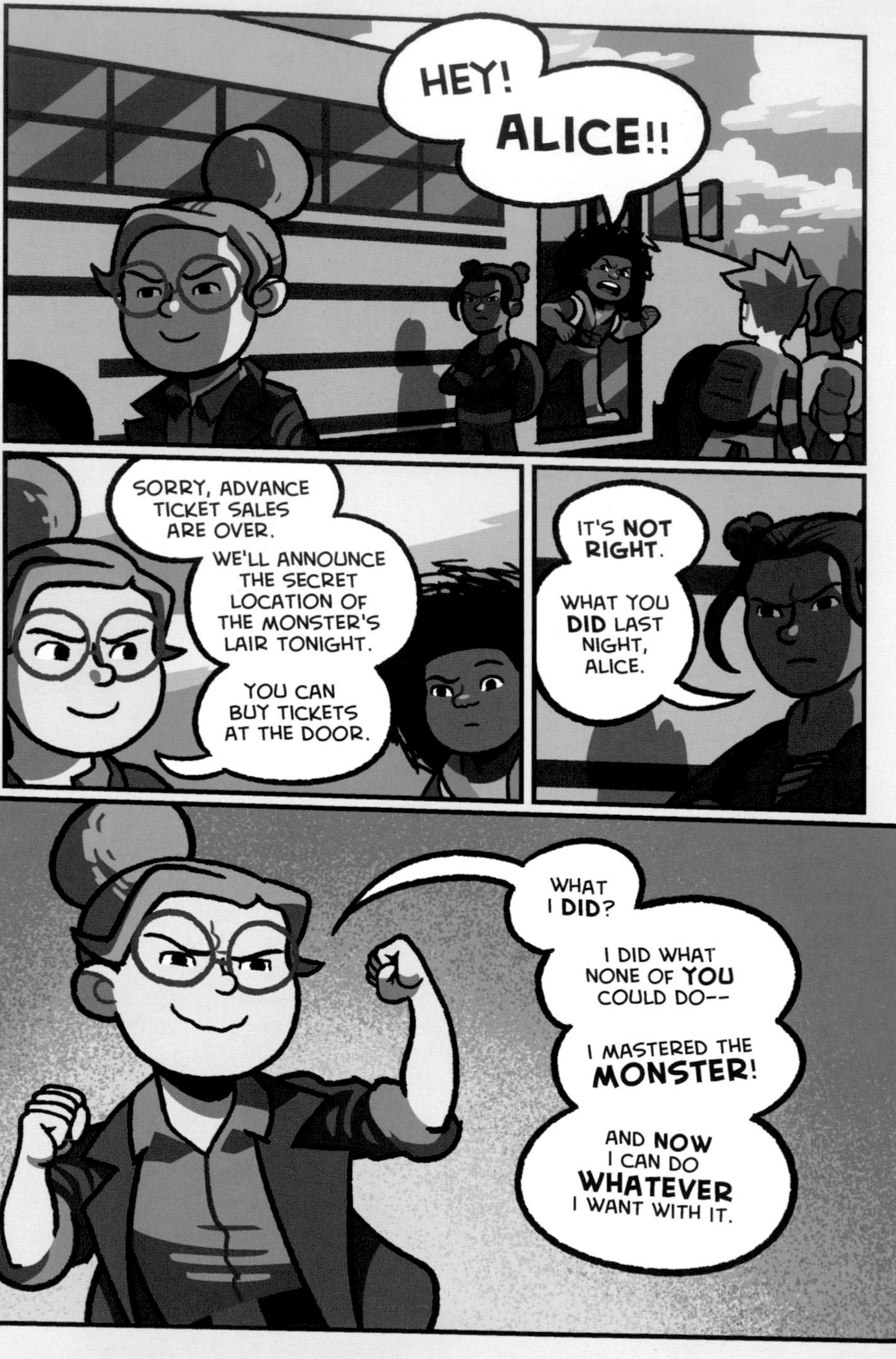
HEY! ALICE!!
SORRY, ADVANCE TICKET SALES ARE OVER.
WE'LL ANNOUNCE THE SECRET LOCATION OF THE MONSTER'S LAIR TONIGHT.
YOU CAN BUY TICKETS AT THE DOOR.
IT'S NOT RIGHT.
WHAT YOU DID LAST NIGHT, ALICE.
WHAT I DID?
I DID WHAT NONE OF YOU COULD DO--
I MASTERED THE MONSTER!
AND NOW I CAN DO WHATEVER I WANT WITH IT.

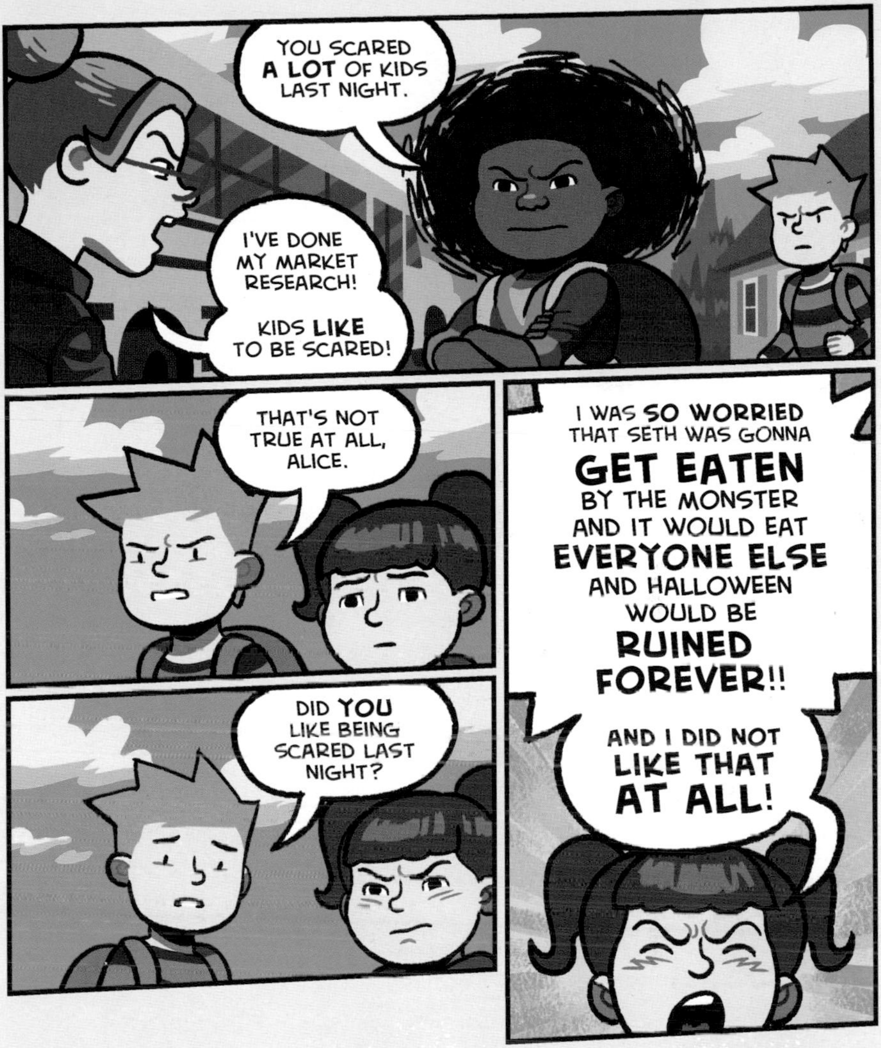
YOU SCARED **A LOT** OF KIDS LAST NIGHT.
I'VE DONE MY MARKET RESEARCH!
KIDS **LIKE** TO BE SCARED!
THAT'S NOT TRUE AT ALL, ALICE.
DID **YOU** LIKE BEING SCARED LAST NIGHT?
I WAS **SO WORRIED** THAT SETH WAS GONNA **GET EATEN** BY THE MONSTER AND IT WOULD EAT **EVERYONE ELSE** AND HALLOWEEN WOULD BE **RUINED FOREVER**!!
AND I DID NOT **LIKE THAT AT ALL**!

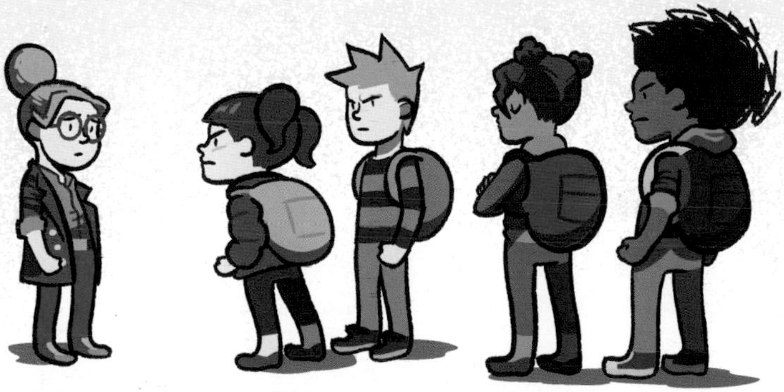

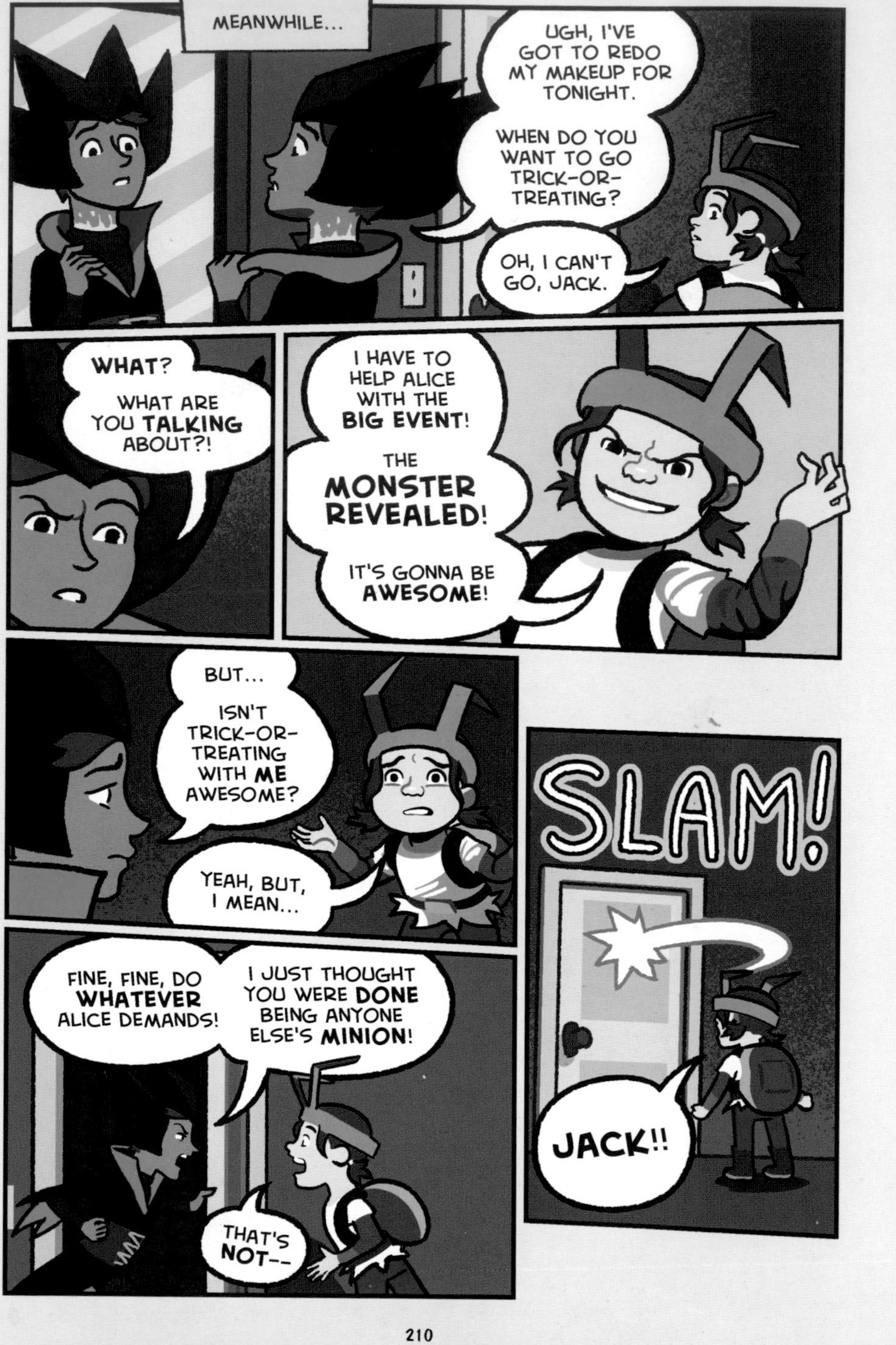
MEANWHILE...
UGH, I'VE GOT TO REDO MY MAKEUP FOR TONIGHT.
WHEN DO YOU WANT TO GO TRICK-OR-TREATING?
OH, I CAN'T GO, JACK.
WHAT? WHAT ARE YOU TALKING ABOUT?!
I HAVE TO HELP ALICE WITH THE BIG EVENT!
THE MONSTER REVEALED!
IT'S GONNA BE AWESOME!
BUT...
ISN'T TRICK-OR-TREATING WITH ME AWESOME?
YEAH, BUT, I MEAN...
FINE, FINE, DO WHATEVER ALICE DEMANDS!
I JUST THOUGHT YOU WERE DONE BEING ANYONE ELSE'S MINION!
THAT'S NOT--
SLAM!
JACK!!

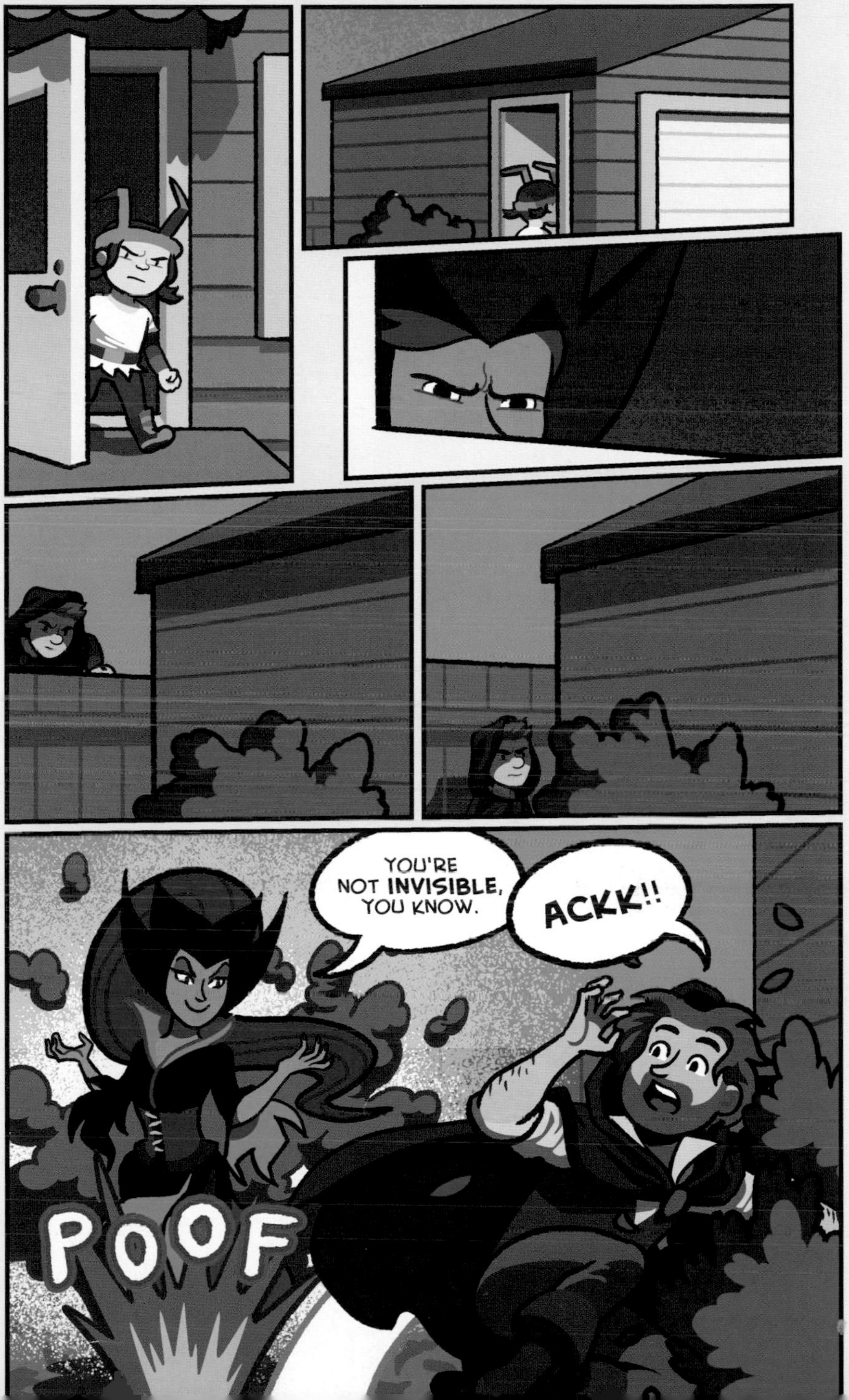
YOU'RE NOT INVISIBLE, YOU KNOW.
ACKK!!
POOF

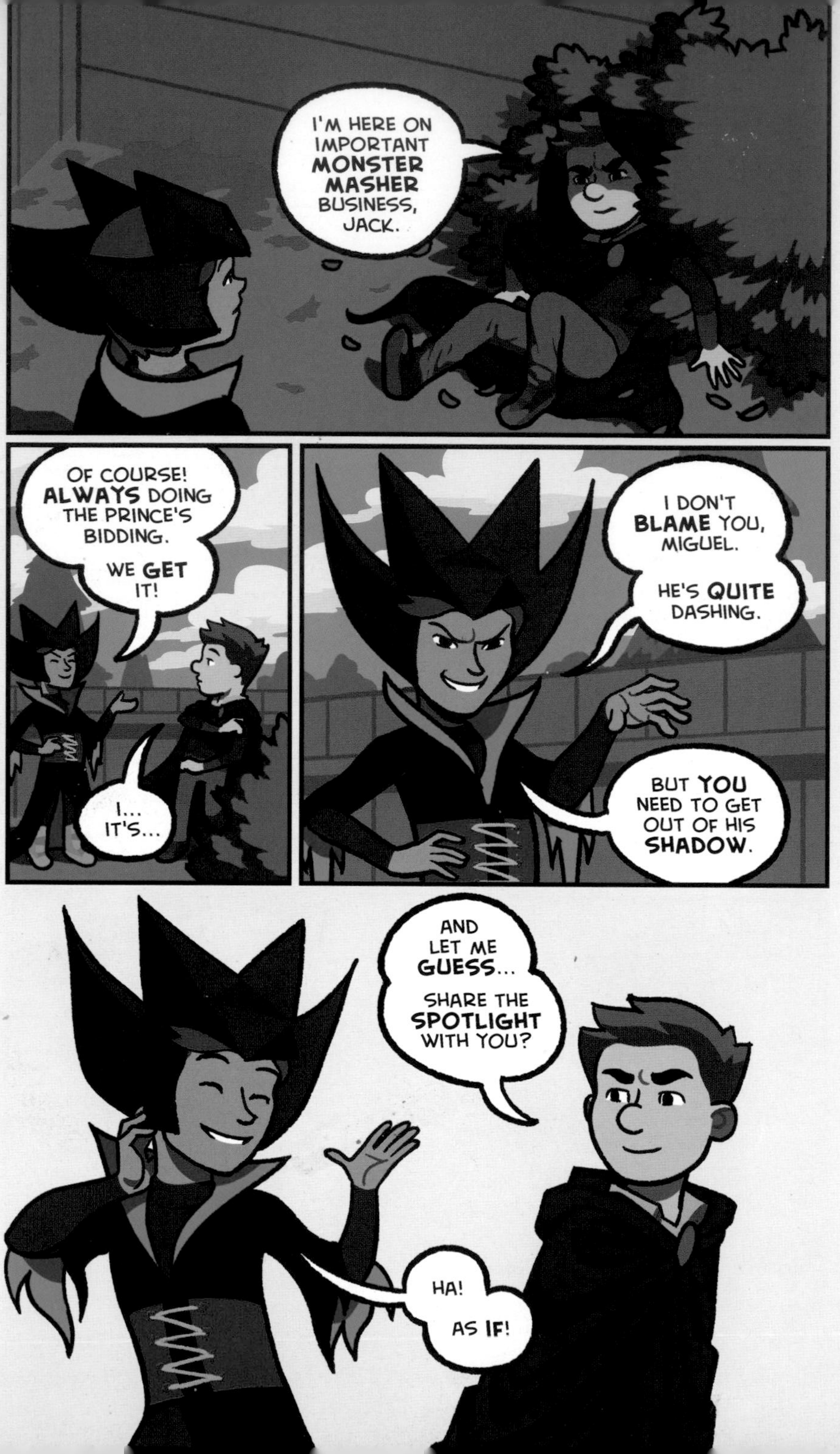
I'M HERE ON IMPORTANT MONSTER MASHER BUSINESS, JACK.
OF COURSE! ALWAYS DOING THE PRINCE'S BIDDING.
WE GET IT!
I... IT'S...
I DON'T BLAME YOU, MIGUEL.
HE'S QUITE DASHING.
BUT YOU NEED TO GET OUT OF HIS SHADOW.
AND LET ME GUESS...
SHARE THE SPOTLIGHT WITH YOU?
HA!
AS IF!

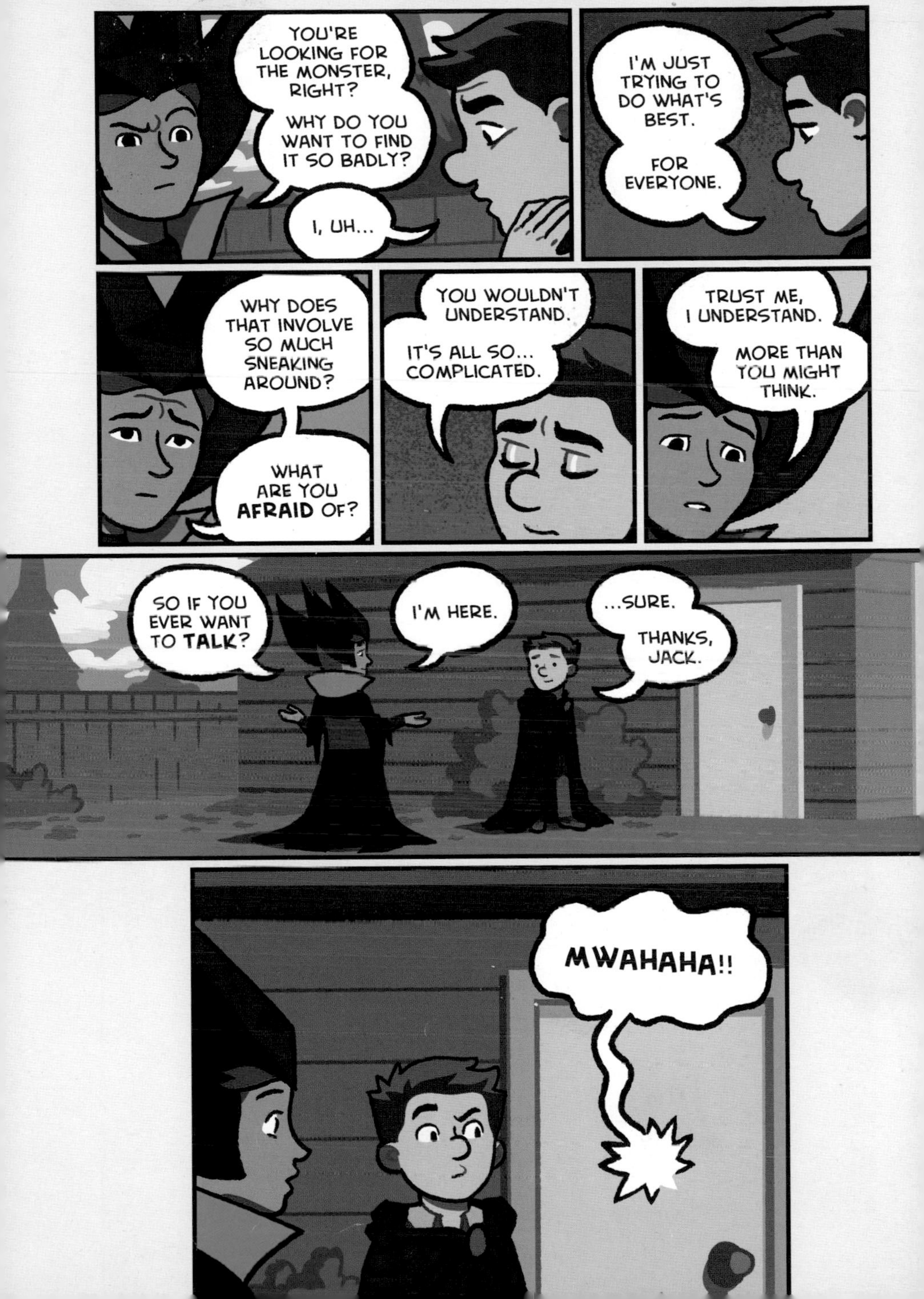
YOU'RE LOOKING FOR THE MONSTER, RIGHT?
WHY DO YOU WANT TO FIND IT SO BADLY?
I, UH...
I'M JUST TRYING TO DO WHAT'S BEST.
FOR EVERYONE.
WHY DOES THAT INVOLVE SO MUCH SNEAKING AROUND?
WHAT ARE YOU AFRAID OF?
YOU WOULDN'T UNDERSTAND.
IT'S ALL SO... COMPLICATED.
TRUST ME, I UNDERSTAND.
MORE THAN YOU MIGHT THINK.
SO IF YOU EVER WANT TO TALK?
I'M HERE.
...SURE.
THANKS, JACK.
MWAHAHA!!

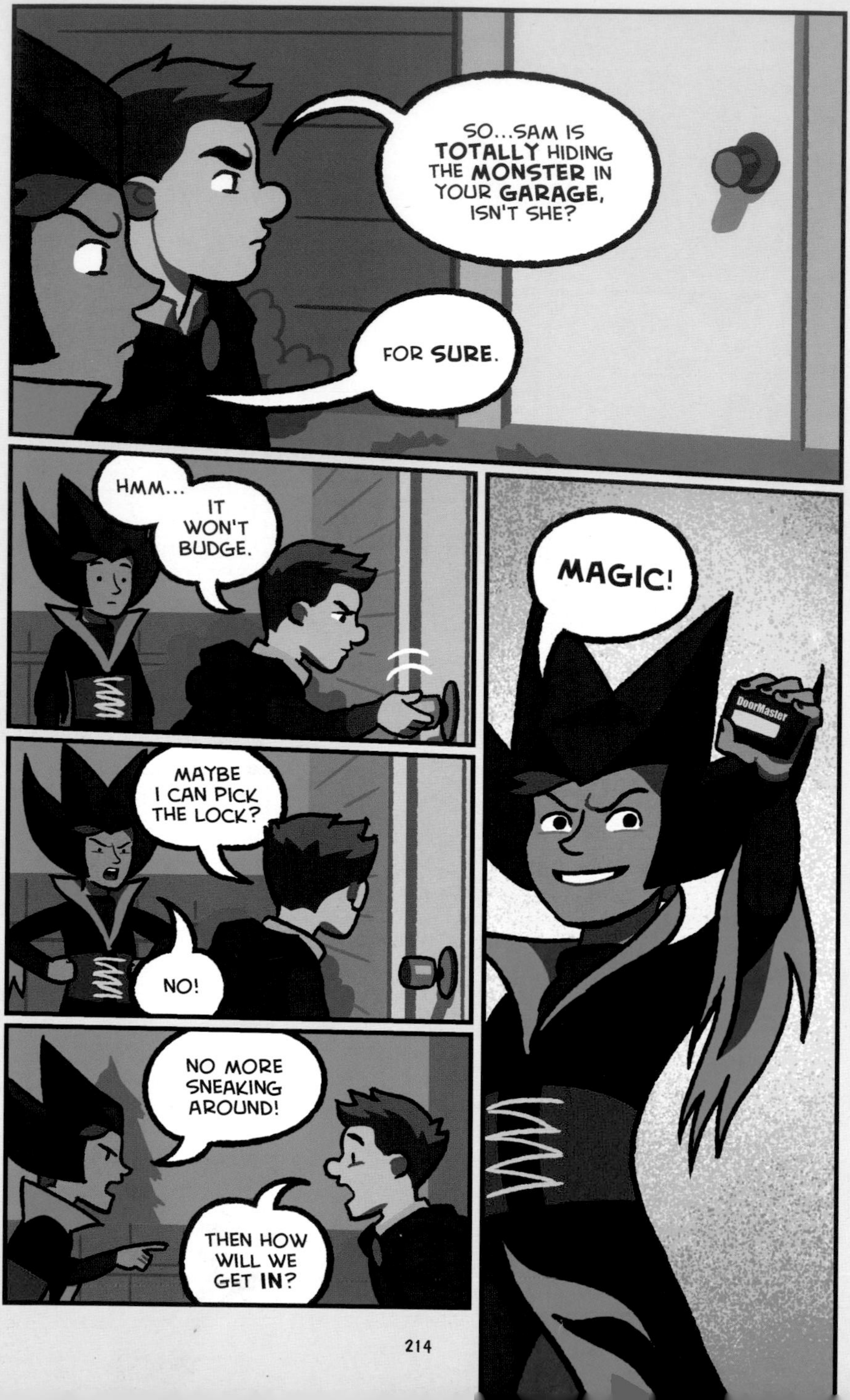
SO...SAM IS **TOTALLY** HIDING THE **MONSTER** IN YOUR **GARAGE**, ISN'T SHE?
FOR **SURE**.
HMM...
IT WON'T BUDGE.
MAYBE I CAN PICK THE LOCK?
NO!
NO MORE SNEAKING AROUND!
THEN HOW WILL WE GET **IN**?
MAGIC!
DoorMaster

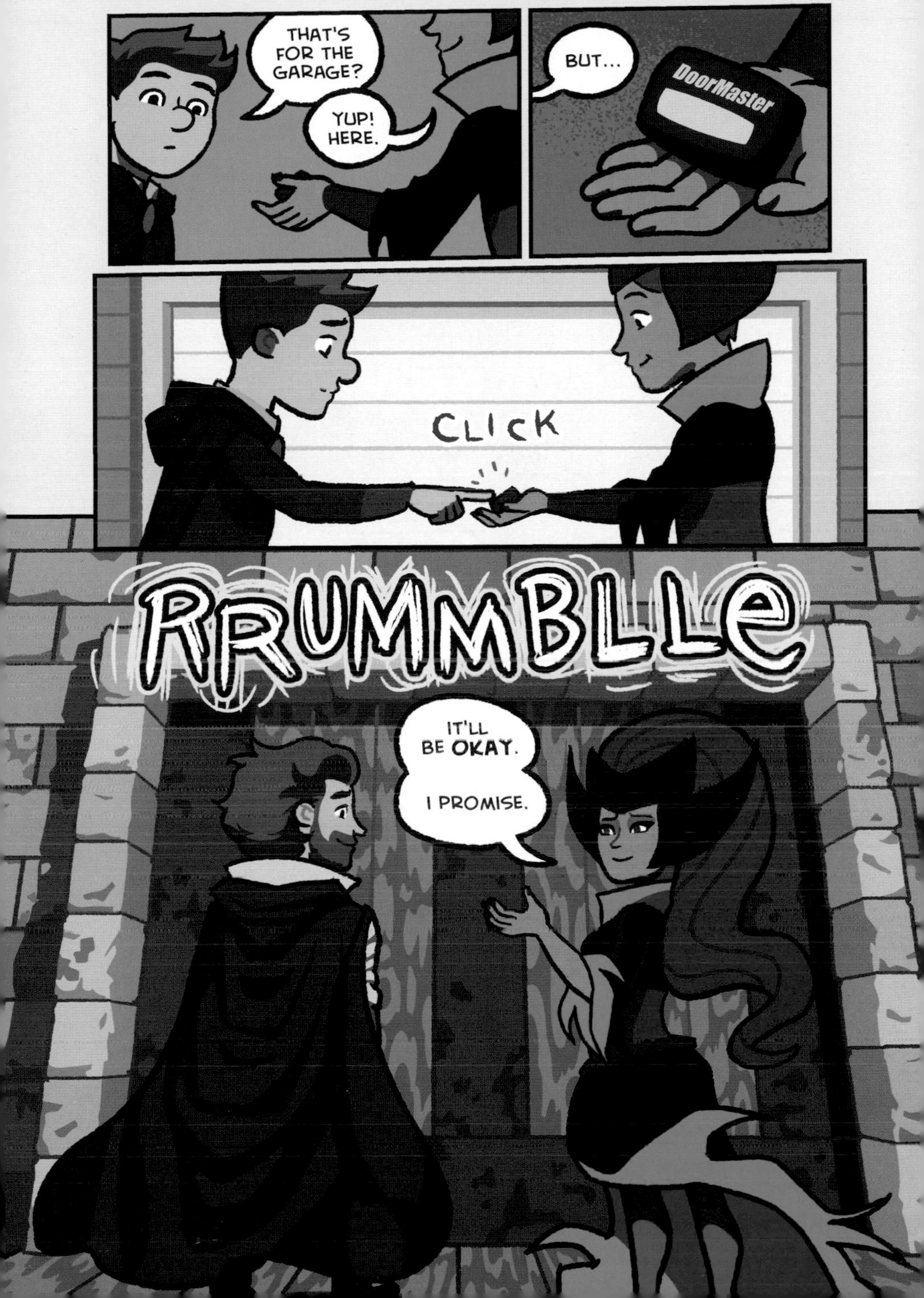
THAT'S FOR THE GARAGE?
YUP! HERE.
BUT...
DoorMaster
CLICK
RRUMMBLLE
IT'LL BE OKAY.
I PROMISE.

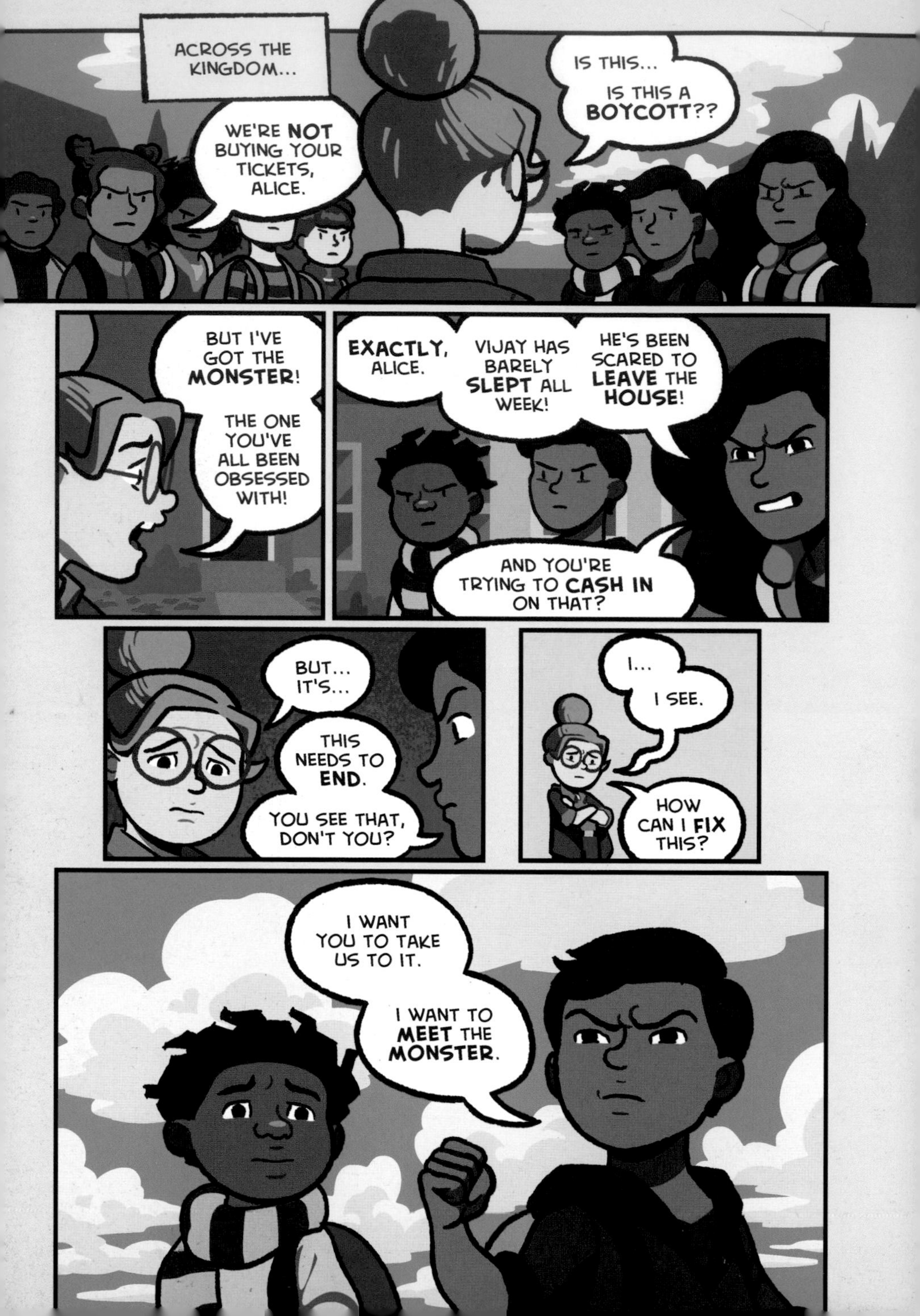
ACROSS THE KINGDOM...
WE'RE NOT BUYING YOUR TICKETS, ALICE.
IS THIS...
IS THIS A BOYCOTT??
BUT I'VE GOT THE MONSTER!
THE ONE YOU'VE ALL BEEN OBSESSED WITH!
EXACTLY, ALICE.
VIJAY HAS BARELY SLEPT ALL WEEK!
HE'S BEEN SCARED TO LEAVE THE HOUSE!
AND YOU'RE TRYING TO CASH IN ON THAT?
BUT... IT'S...
THIS NEEDS TO END.
YOU SEE THAT, DON'T YOU?
I...
I SEE.
HOW CAN I FIX THIS?
I WANT YOU TO TAKE US TO IT.
I WANT TO MEET THE MONSTER.

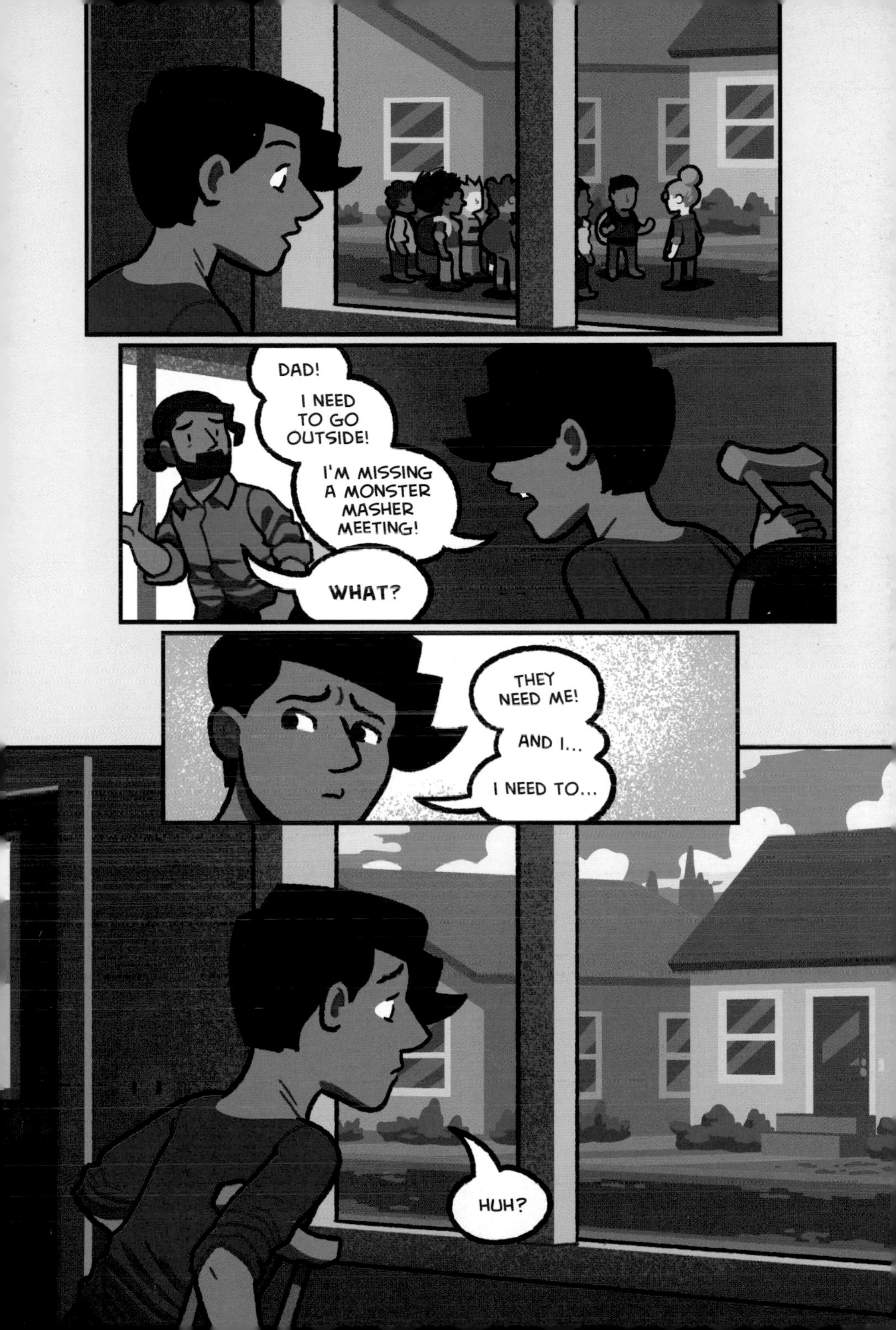
DAD!
I NEED TO GO OUTSIDE!
I'M MISSING A MONSTER MASHER MEETING!
WHAT?
THEY NEED ME!
AND I...
I NEED TO...
HUH?

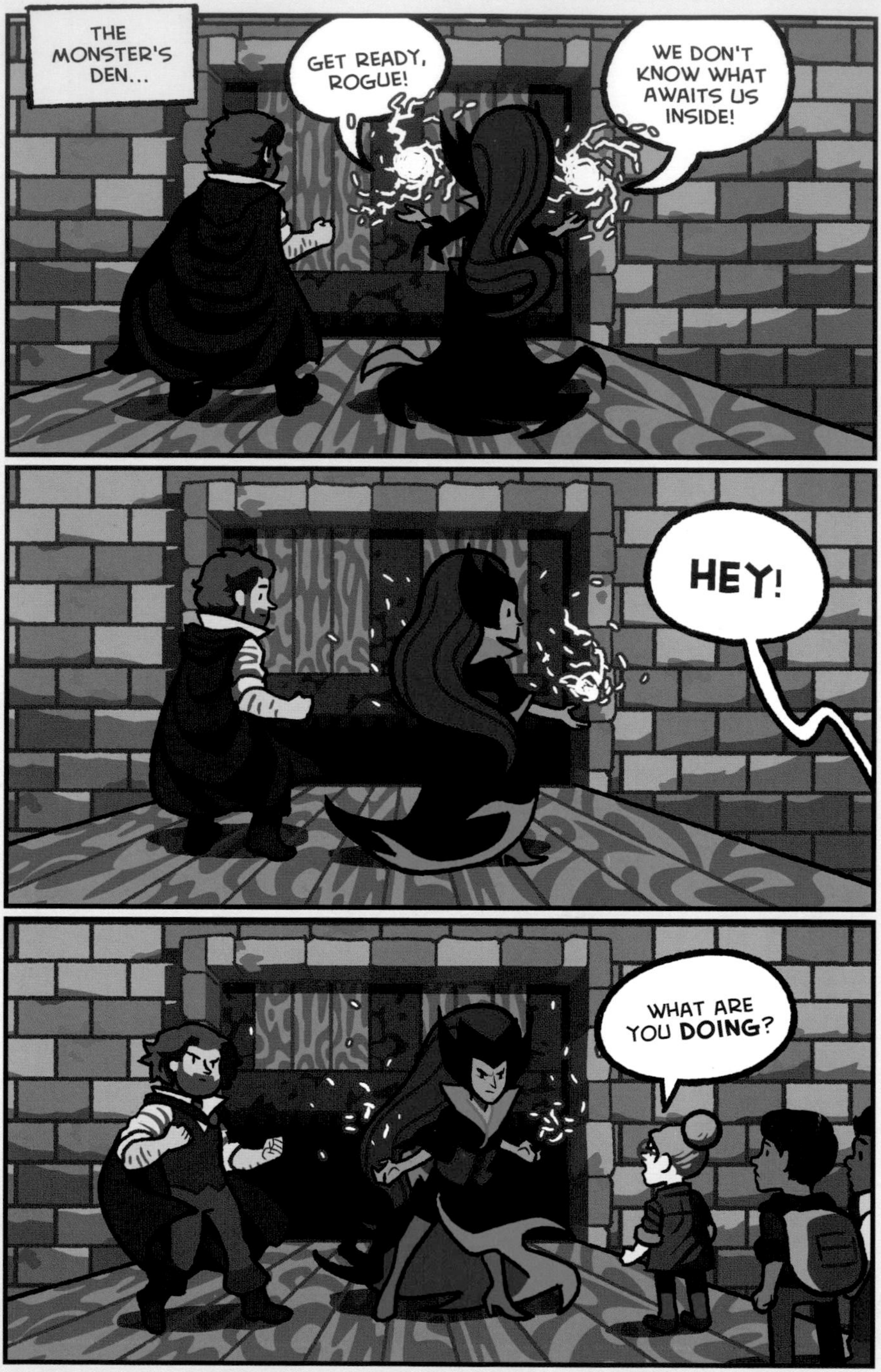
THE MONSTER'S DEN...
GET READY, ROGUE!
WE DON'T KNOW WHAT AWAITS US INSIDE!
HEY!
WHAT ARE YOU **DOING**?

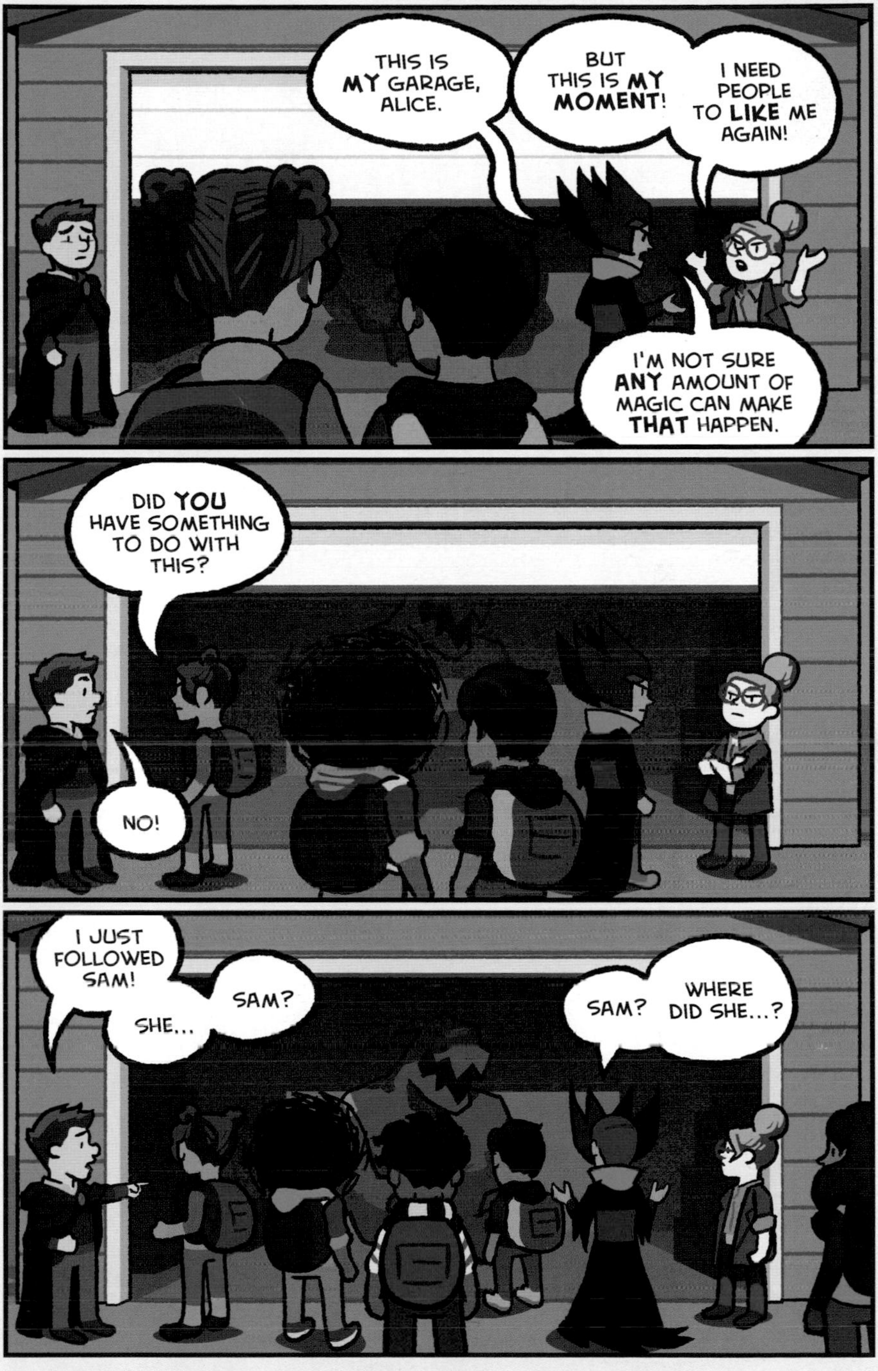
THIS IS MY GARAGE, ALICE.
BUT THIS IS MY MOMENT!
I NEED PEOPLE TO LIKE ME AGAIN!
I'M NOT SURE ANY AMOUNT OF MAGIC CAN MAKE THAT HAPPEN.
DID YOU HAVE SOMETHING TO DO WITH THIS?
NO!
I JUST FOLLOWED SAM!
SHE...
SAM?
SAM?
WHERE DID SHE...?

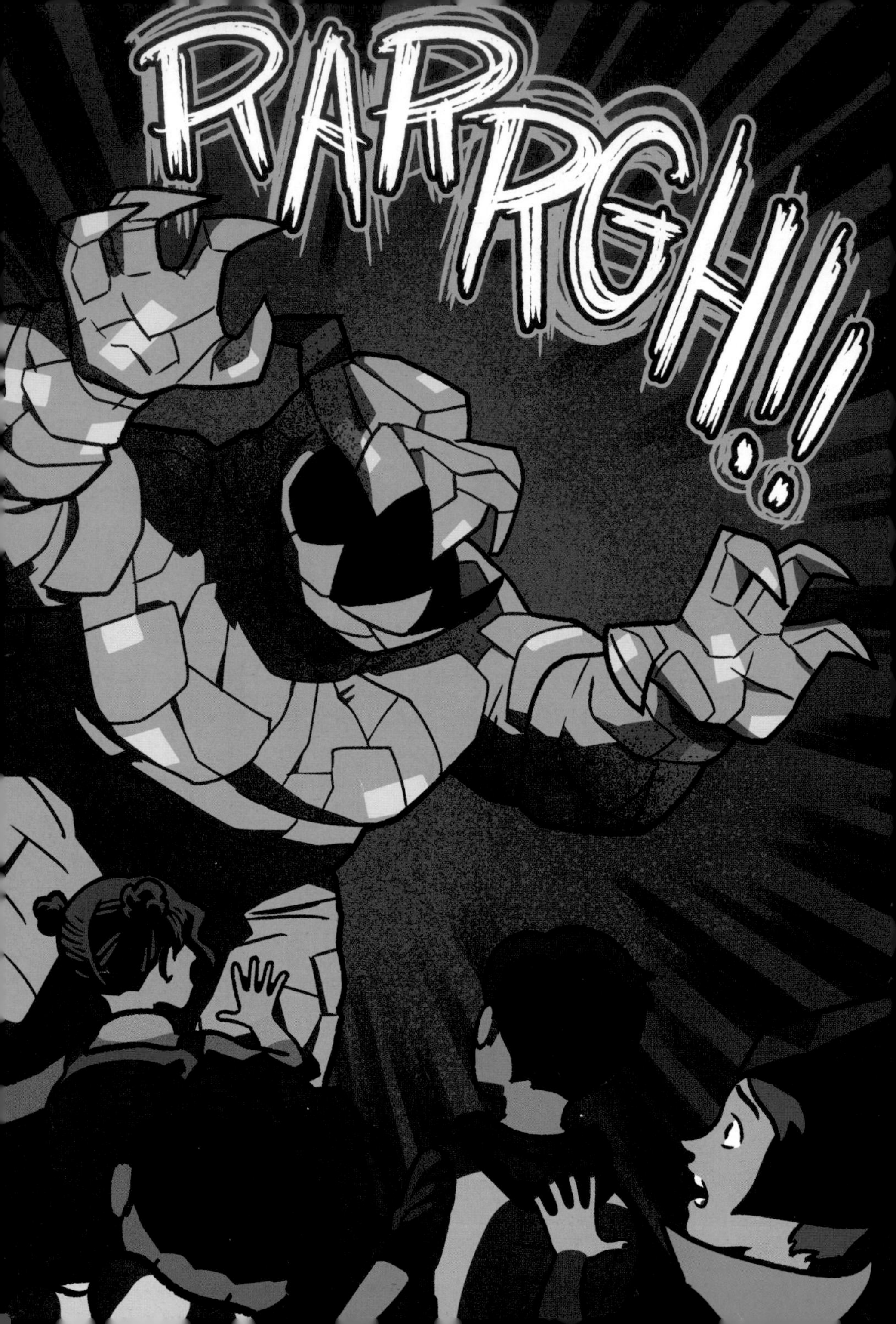
RARRGH!!!

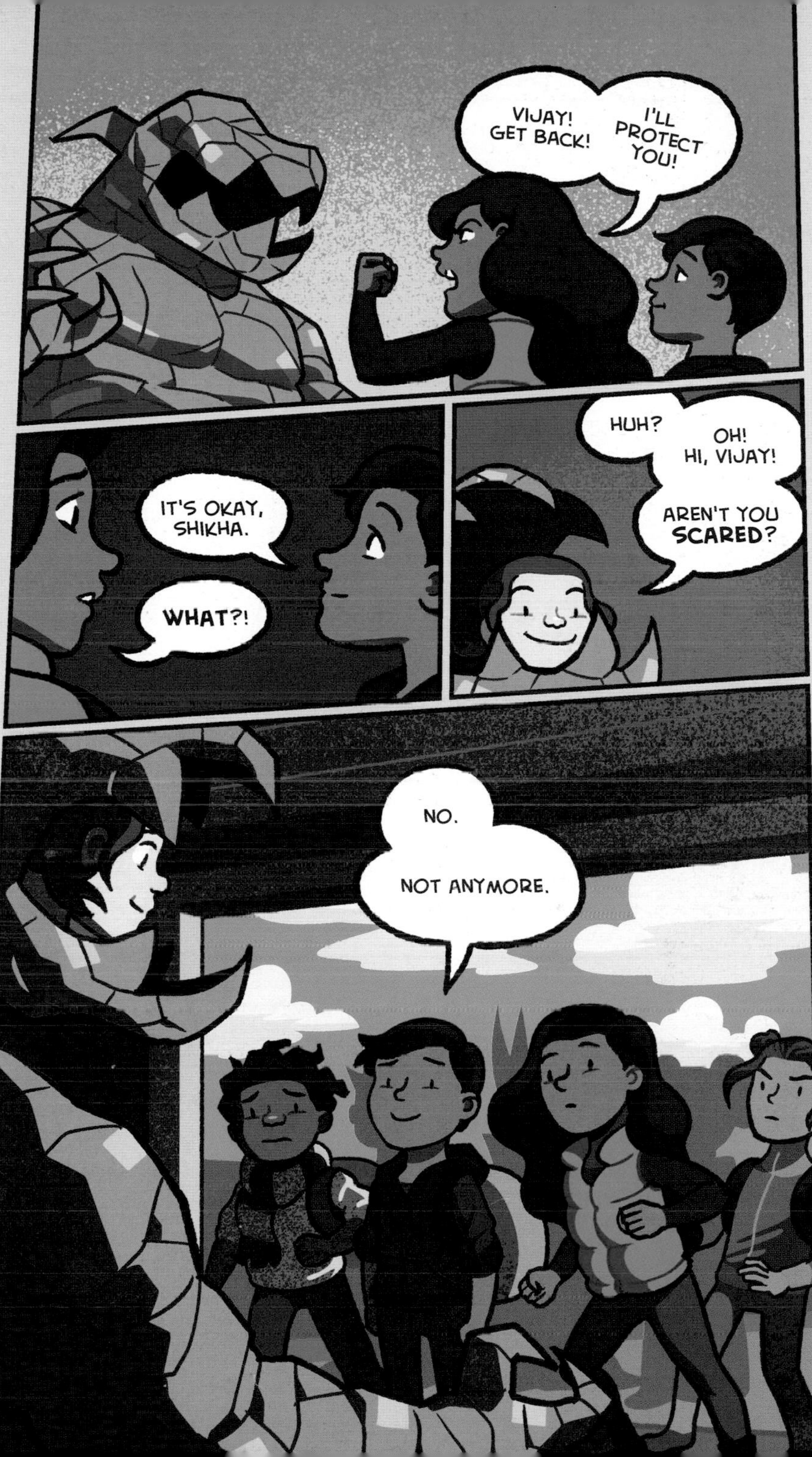
VIJAY! GET BACK!
I'LL PROTECT YOU!
IT'S OKAY, SHIKHA.
WHAT?!
HUH?
OH! HI, VIJAY!
AREN'T YOU SCARED?
NO.
NOT ANYMORE.

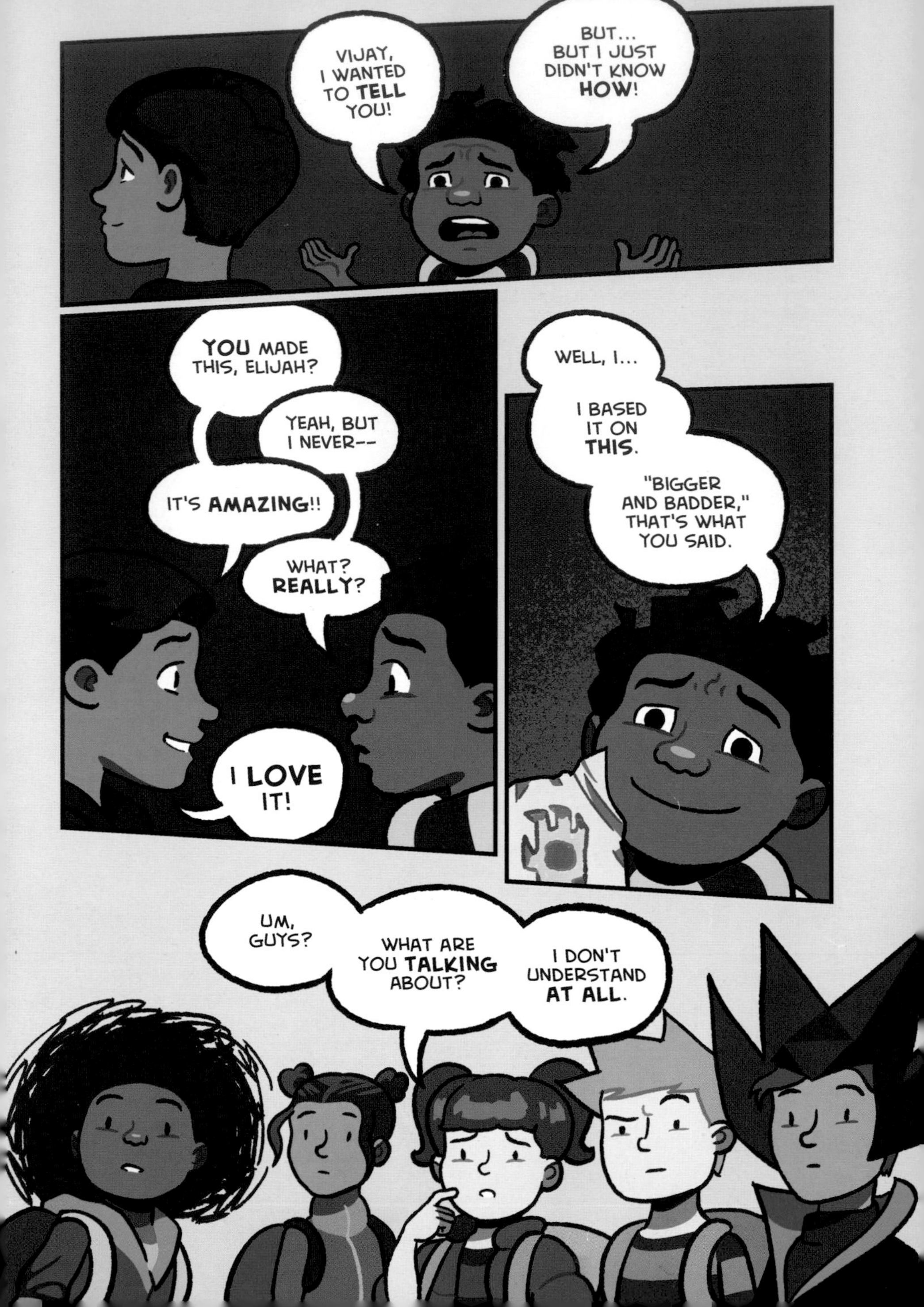
VIJAY, I WANTED TO **TELL** YOU!
BUT... BUT I JUST DIDN'T KNOW **HOW**!
YOU MADE THIS, ELIJAH?
YEAH, BUT I NEVER--
IT'S **AMAZING**!!
WHAT? **REALLY**?
I **LOVE** IT!
WELL, I...
I BASED IT ON **THIS**.
"BIGGER AND BADDER," THAT'S WHAT YOU SAID.
UM, GUYS?
WHAT ARE YOU **TALKING** ABOUT?
I DON'T UNDERSTAND **AT ALL**.

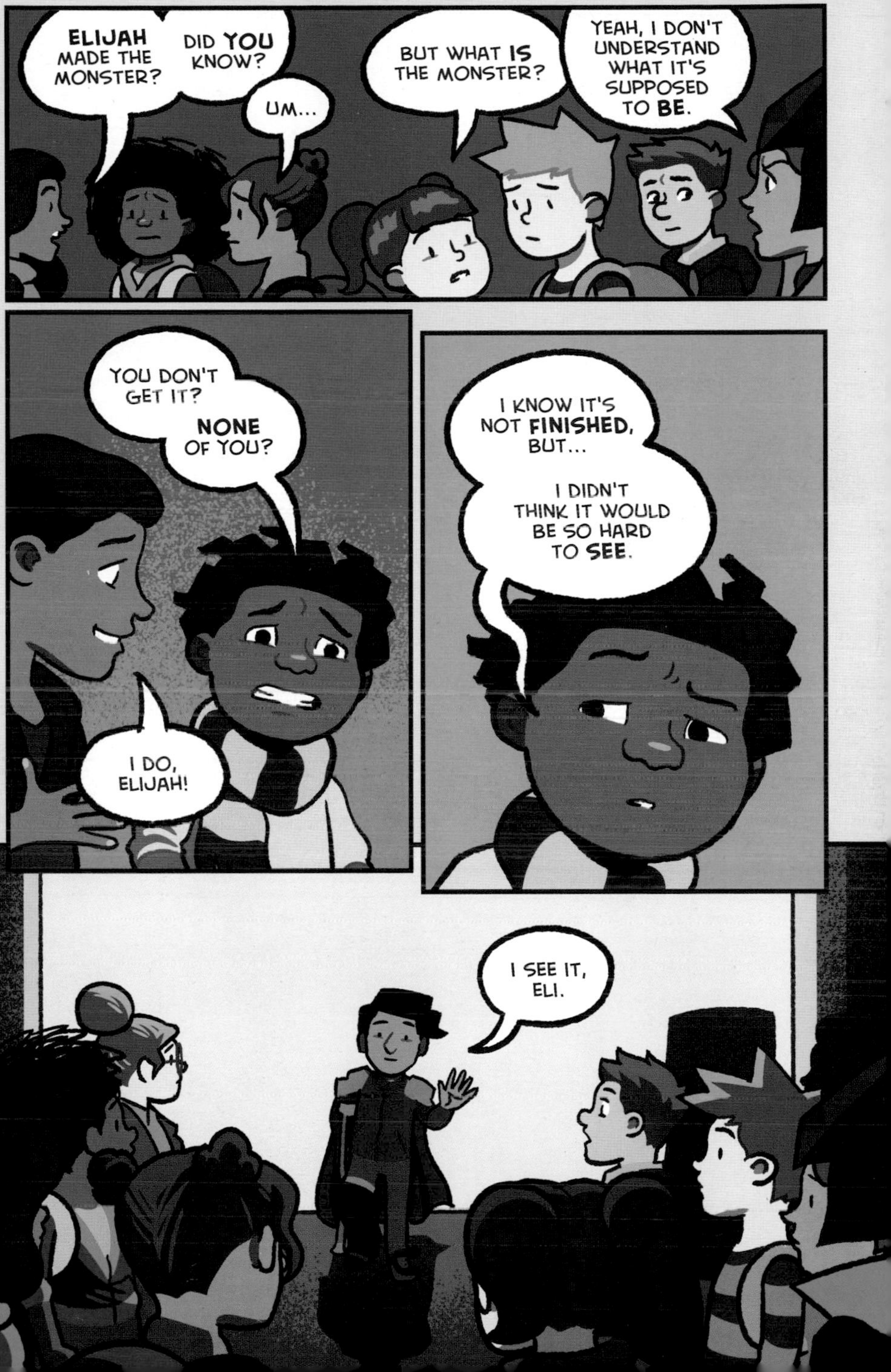
ELIJAH MADE THE MONSTER?
DID YOU KNOW?
UM...
BUT WHAT IS THE MONSTER?
YEAH, I DON'T UNDERSTAND WHAT IT'S SUPPOSED TO BE.
YOU DON'T GET IT? NONE OF YOU?
I DO, ELIJAH!
I KNOW IT'S NOT FINISHED, BUT...
I DIDN'T THINK IT WOULD BE SO HARD TO SEE.
I SEE IT, ELI.

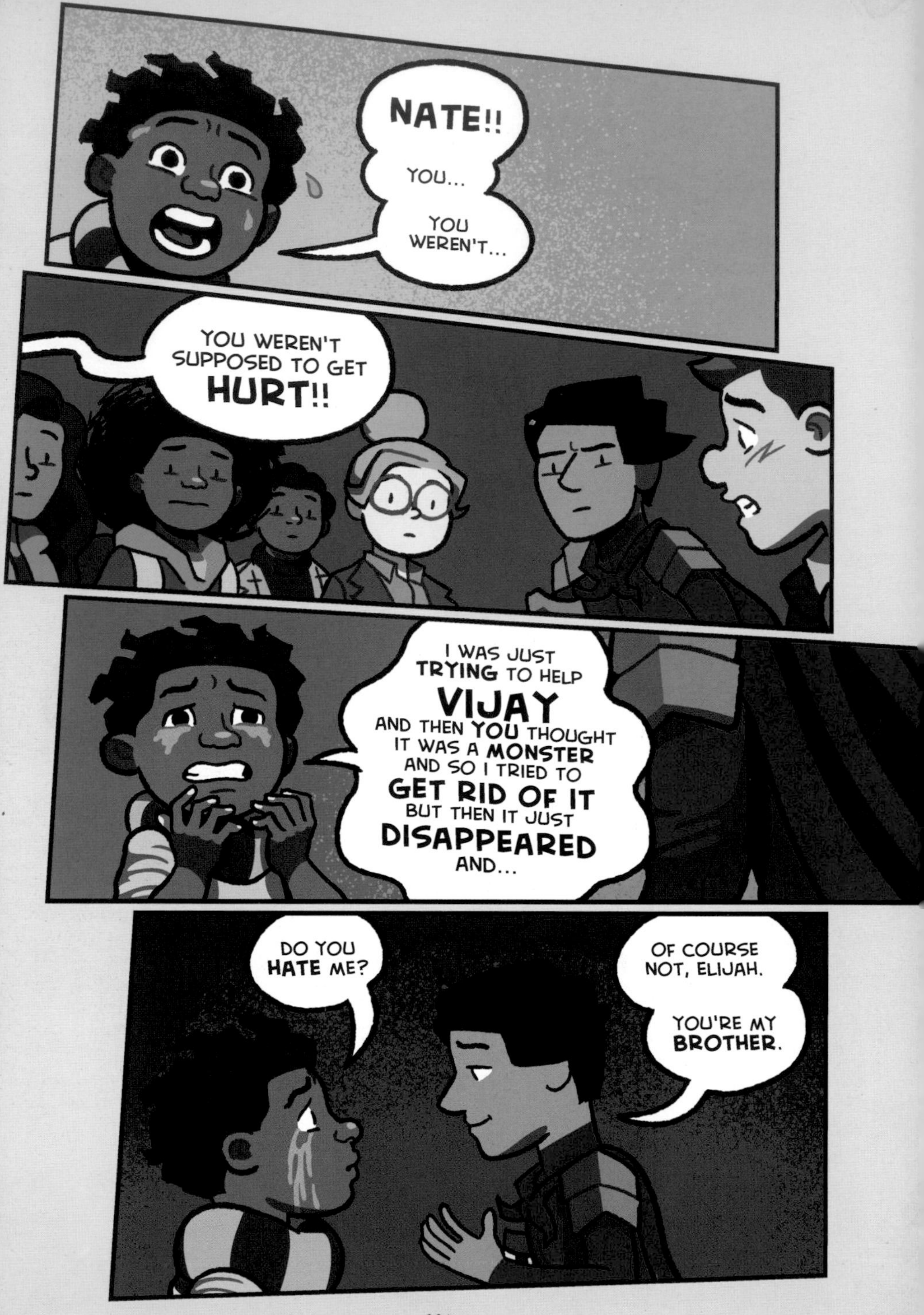
NATE!!
YOU...
YOU WEREN'T...
YOU WEREN'T SUPPOSED TO GET HURT!!
I WAS JUST TRYING TO HELP VIJAY AND THEN YOU THOUGHT IT WAS A MONSTER AND SO I TRIED TO GET RID OF IT BUT THEN IT JUST DISAPPEARED AND...
DO YOU HATE ME?
OF COURSE NOT, ELIJAH.
YOU'RE MY BROTHER.

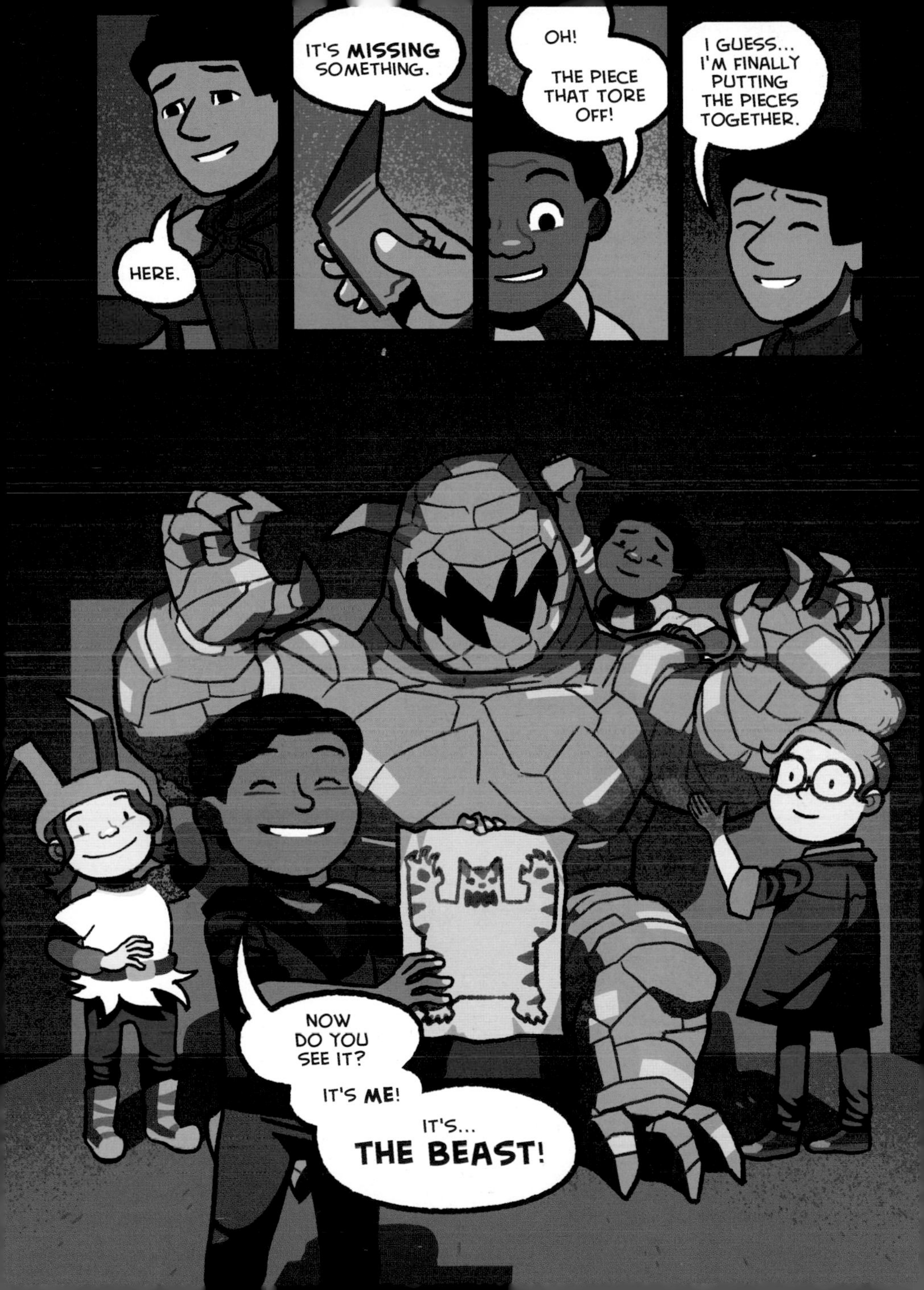
HERE.
IT'S **MISSING** SOMETHING.
OH!
THE PIECE THAT TORE OFF!
I GUESS... I'M FINALLY PUTTING THE PIECES TOGETHER.
NOW DO YOU SEE IT?
IT'S **ME**!
IT'S...
THE BEAST!

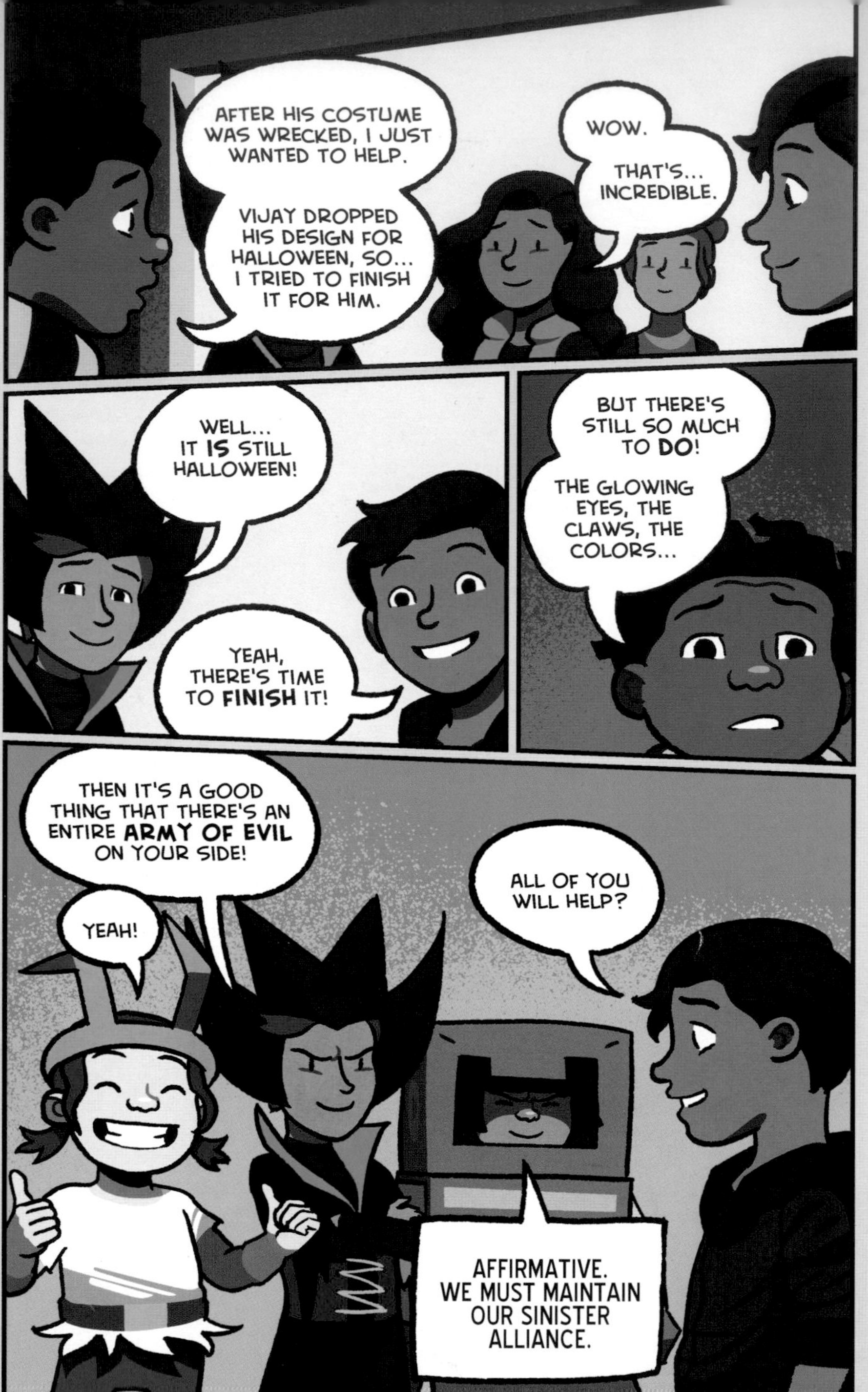
AFTER HIS COSTUME WAS WRECKED, I JUST WANTED TO HELP.
VIJAY DROPPED HIS DESIGN FOR HALLOWEEN, SO... I TRIED TO FINISH IT FOR HIM.
WOW.
THAT'S... INCREDIBLE.
WELL... IT **IS** STILL HALLOWEEN!
YEAH, THERE'S TIME TO **FINISH** IT!
BUT THERE'S STILL SO MUCH TO **DO**!
THE GLOWING EYES, THE CLAWS, THE COLORS...
THEN IT'S A GOOD THING THAT THERE'S AN ENTIRE **ARMY OF EVIL** ON YOUR SIDE!
YEAH!
ALL OF YOU WILL HELP?
AFFIRMATIVE. WE MUST MAINTAIN OUR SINISTER ALLIANCE.

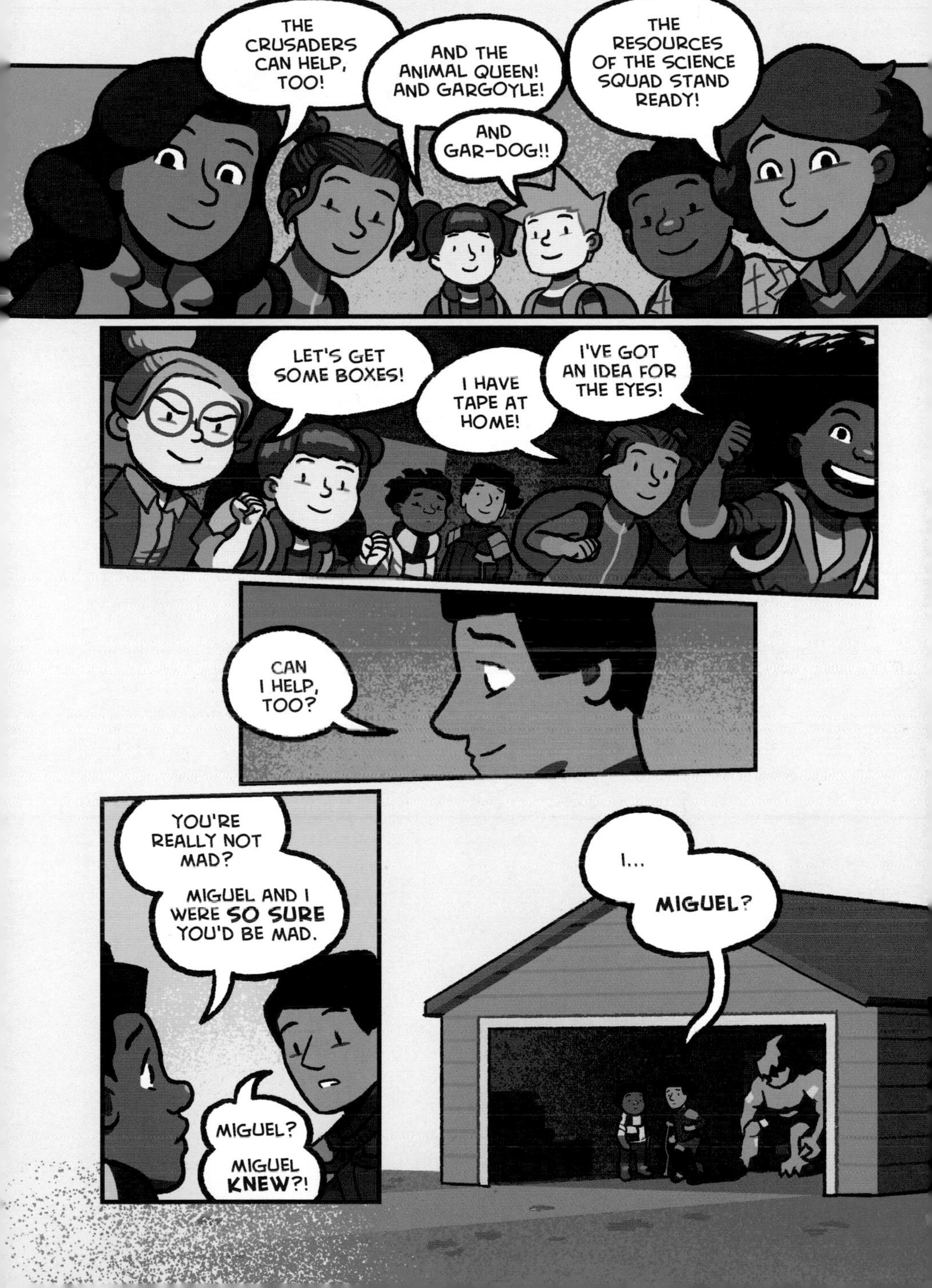
THE CRUSADERS CAN HELP, TOO!
AND THE ANIMAL QUEEN! AND GARGOYLE!
AND GAR-DOG!!
THE RESOURCES OF THE SCIENCE SQUAD STAND READY!
LET'S GET SOME BOXES!
I HAVE TAPE AT HOME!
I'VE GOT AN IDEA FOR THE EYES!
CAN I HELP, TOO?
YOU'RE REALLY NOT MAD?
MIGUEL AND I WERE SO SURE YOU'D BE MAD.
MIGUEL?
MIGUEL KNEW?!
I...
MIGUEL?

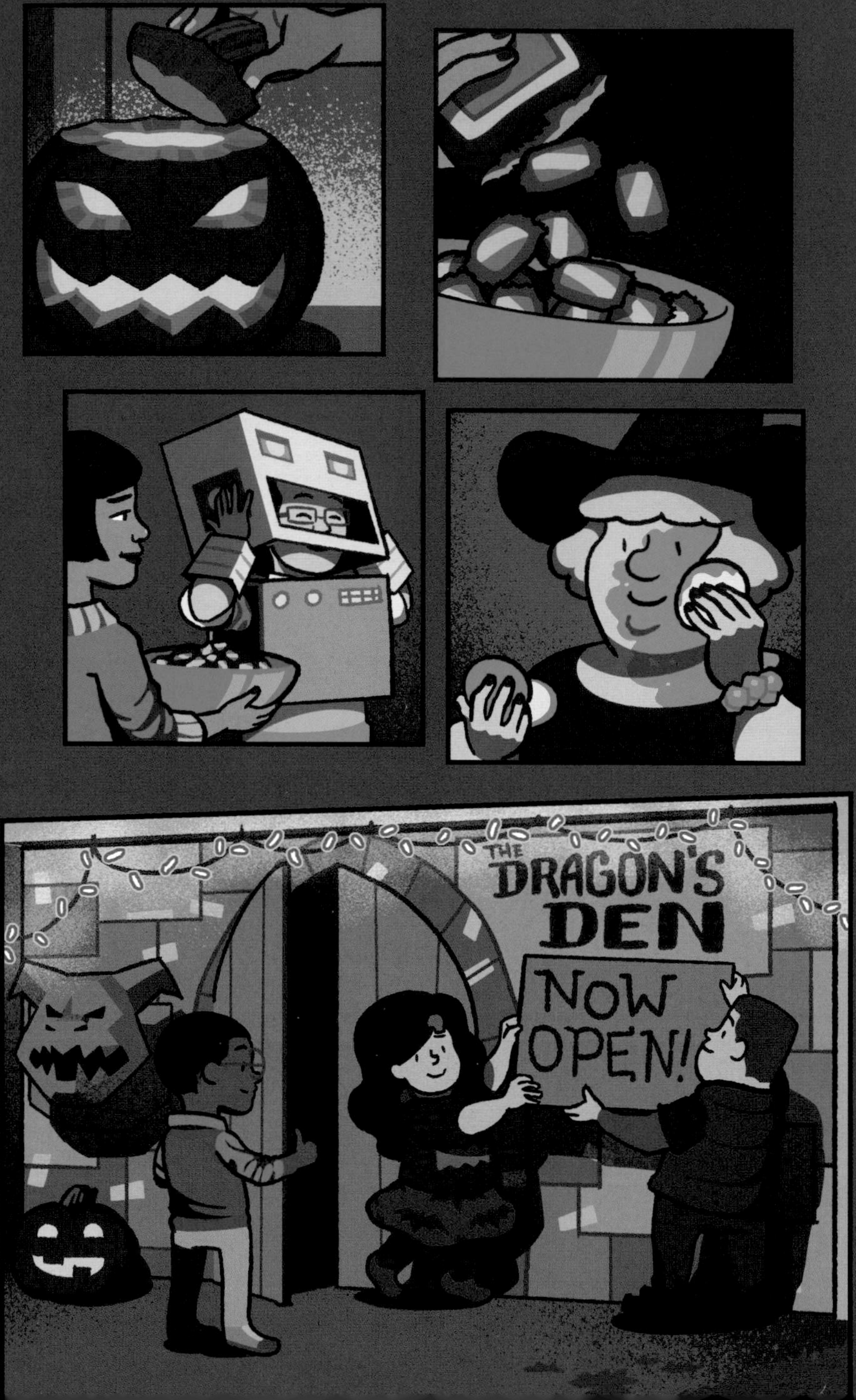
THE DRAGON'S DEN
NOW OPEN!

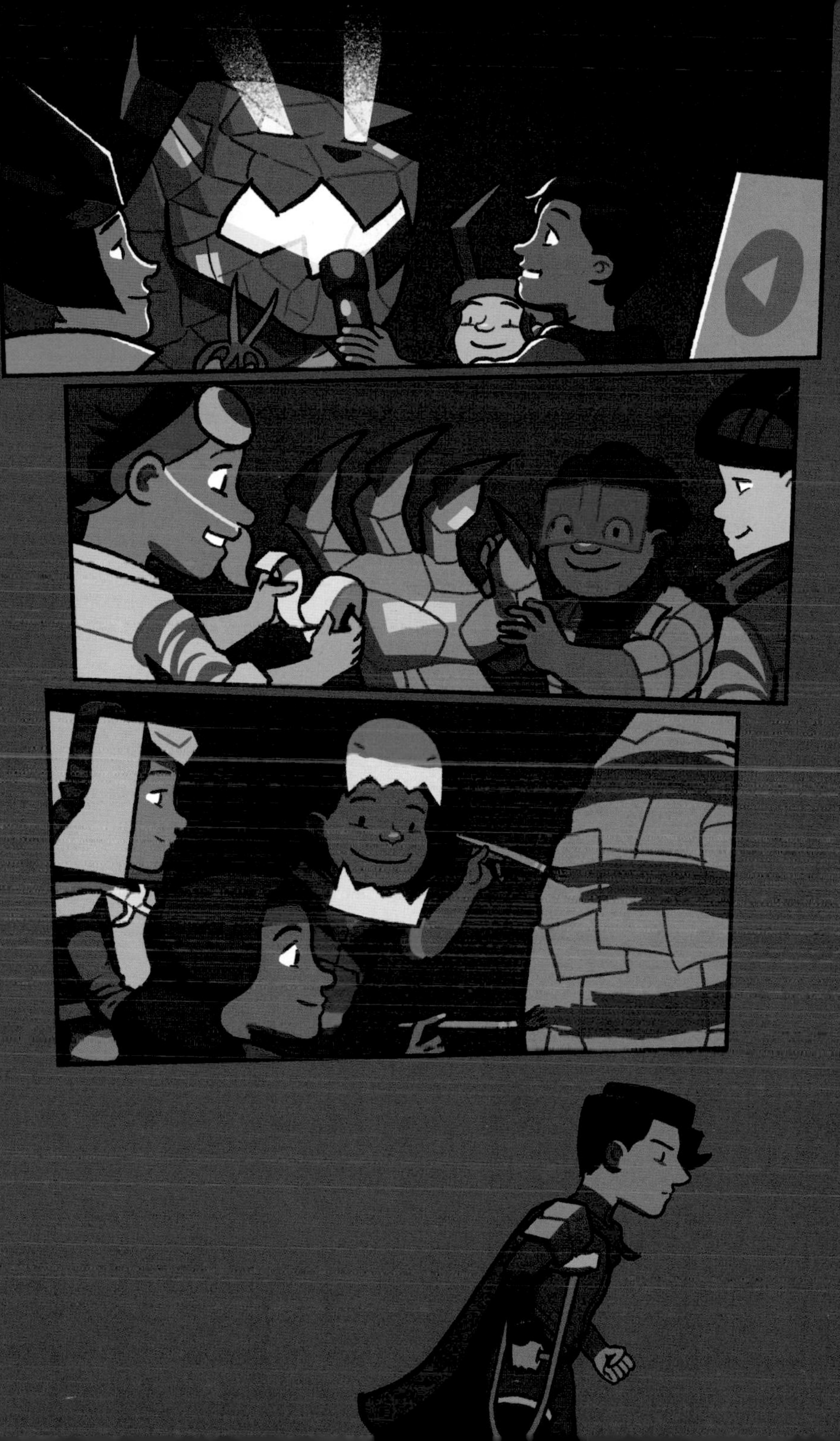

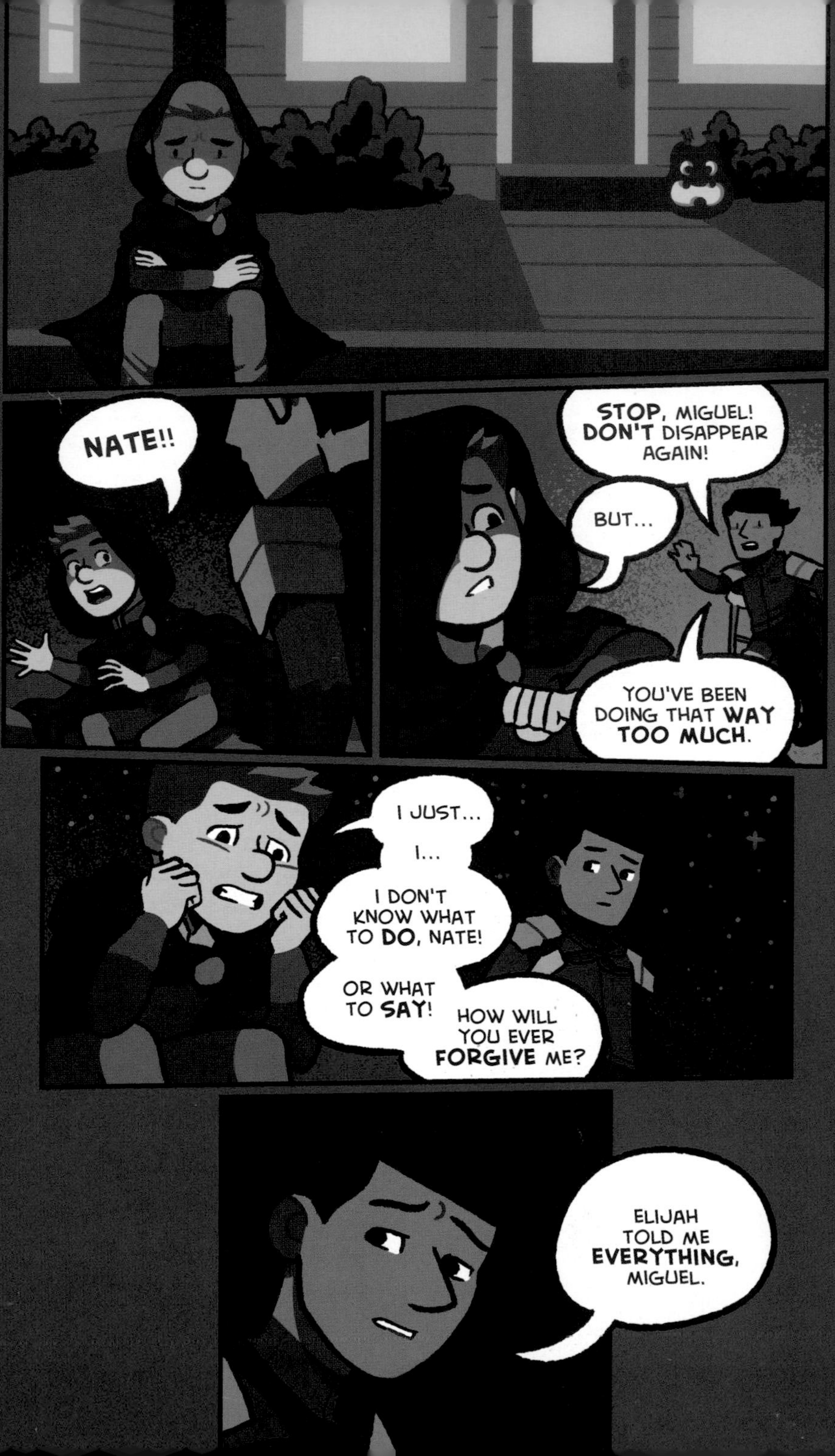
NATE!!
STOP, MIGUEL! DON'T DISAPPEAR AGAIN!
BUT...
YOU'VE BEEN DOING THAT WAY TOO MUCH.
I JUST...
I...
I DON'T KNOW WHAT TO DO, NATE!
OR WHAT TO SAY!
HOW WILL YOU EVER FORGIVE ME?
ELIJAH TOLD ME EVERYTHING, MIGUEL.

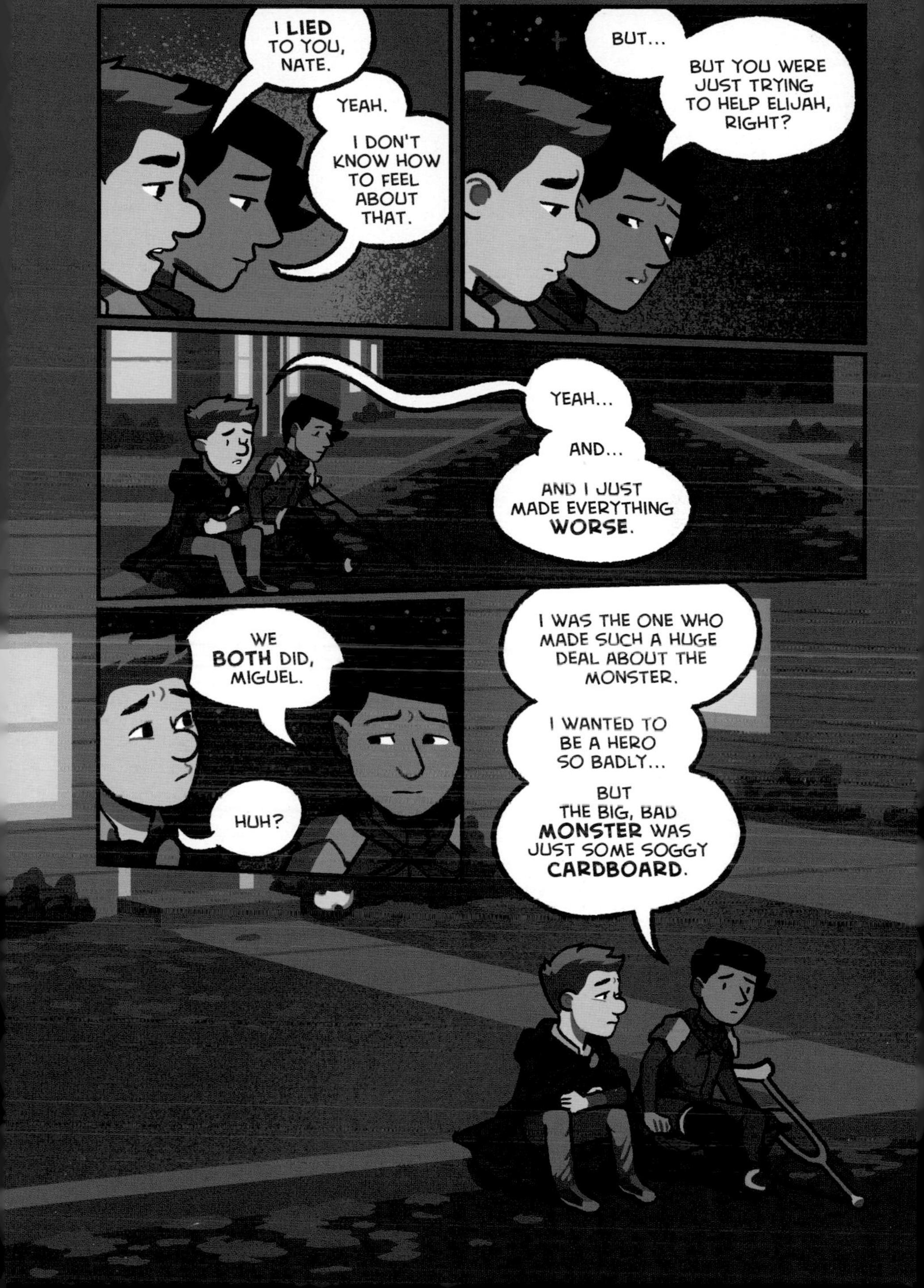
I **LIED** TO YOU, NATE.
YEAH.
I DON'T KNOW HOW TO FEEL ABOUT THAT.
BUT...
BUT YOU WERE JUST TRYING TO HELP ELIJAH, RIGHT?
YEAH...
AND...
AND I JUST MADE EVERYTHING **WORSE**.
WE **BOTH** DID, MIGUEL.
HUH?
I WAS THE ONE WHO MADE SUCH A HUGE DEAL ABOUT THE MONSTER.
I WANTED TO BE A HERO SO BADLY...
BUT THE BIG, BAD **MONSTER** WAS JUST SOME SOGGY **CARDBOARD**.

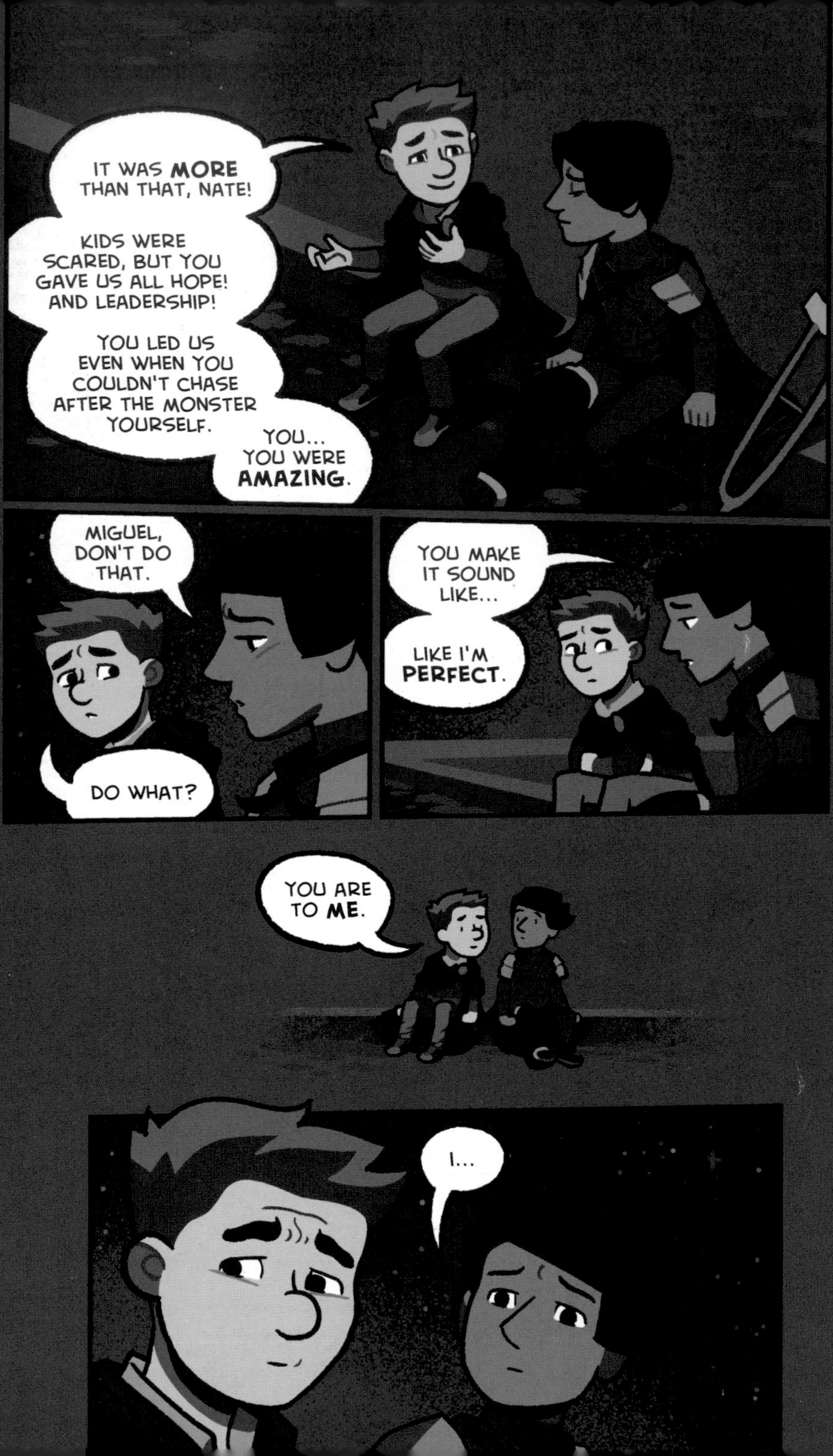
IT WAS **MORE** THAN THAT, NATE!
KIDS WERE SCARED, BUT YOU GAVE US ALL HOPE! AND LEADERSHIP!
YOU LED US EVEN WHEN YOU COULDN'T CHASE AFTER THE MONSTER YOURSELF.
YOU... YOU WERE **AMAZING**.
MIGUEL, DON'T DO THAT.
DO WHAT?
YOU MAKE IT SOUND LIKE...
LIKE I'M **PERFECT**.
YOU ARE TO **ME**.
I...

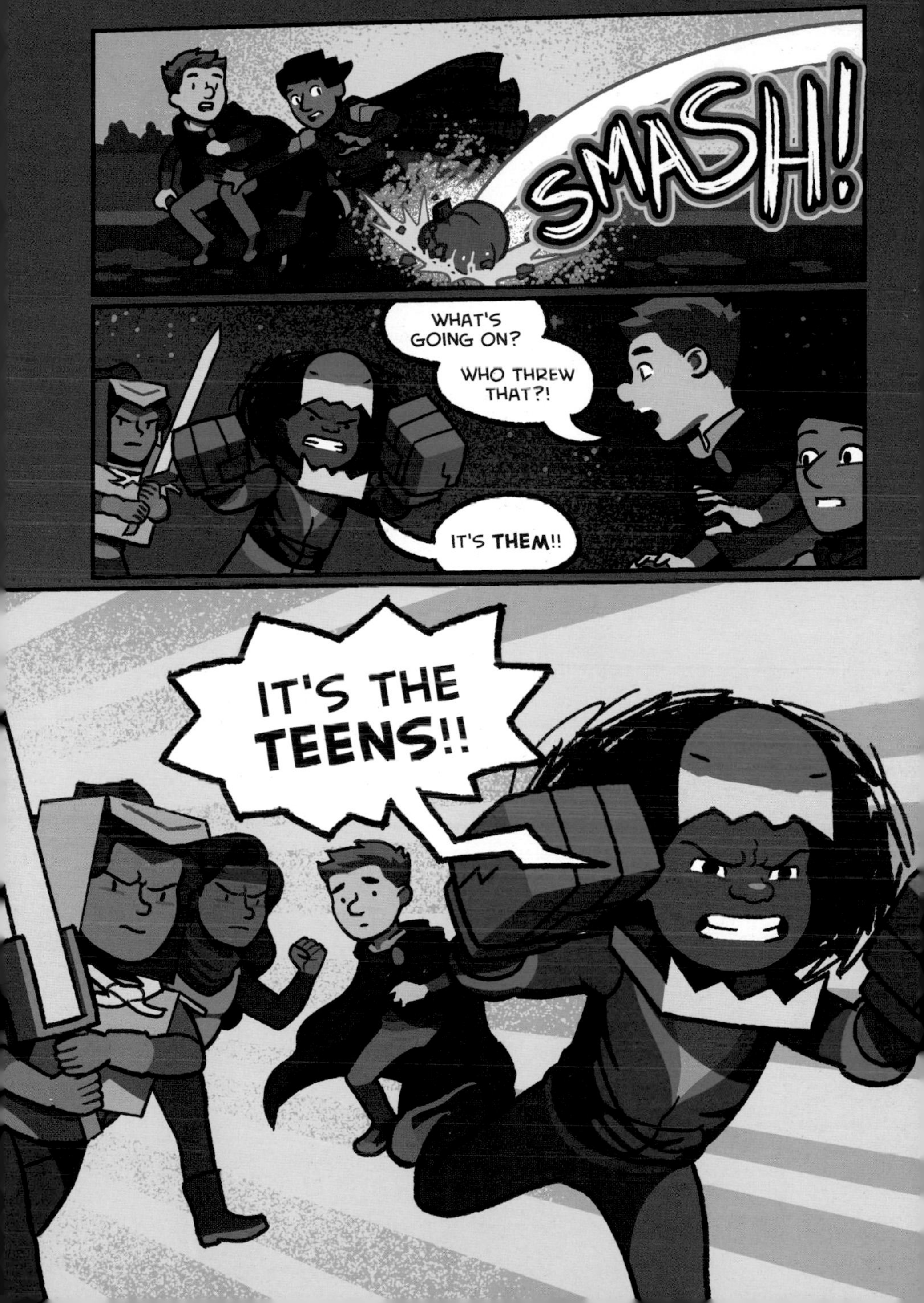
SMASH!
WHAT'S GOING ON?
WHO THREW THAT?!
IT'S THEM!!
IT'S THE TEENS!!

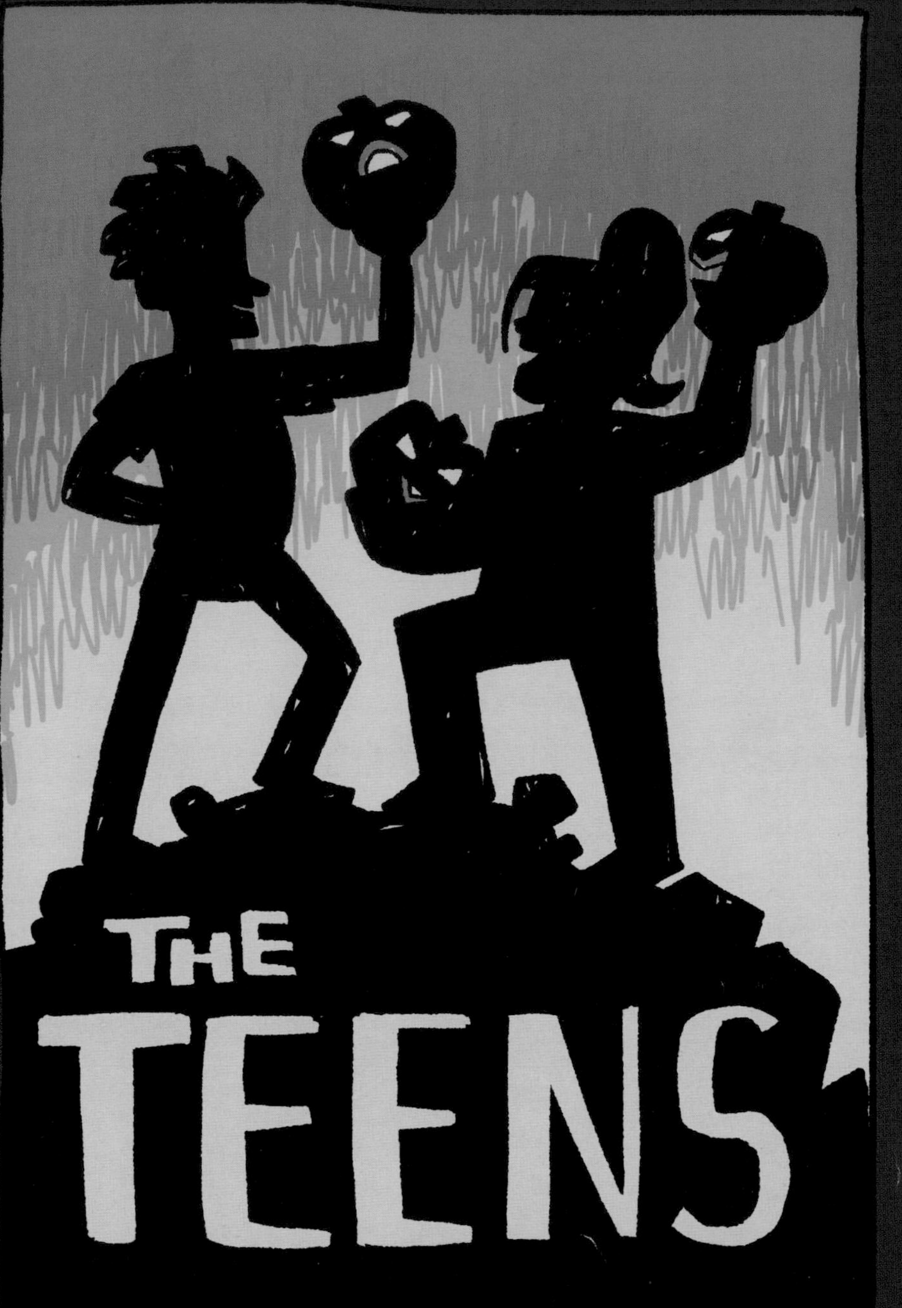
THE
TEENS

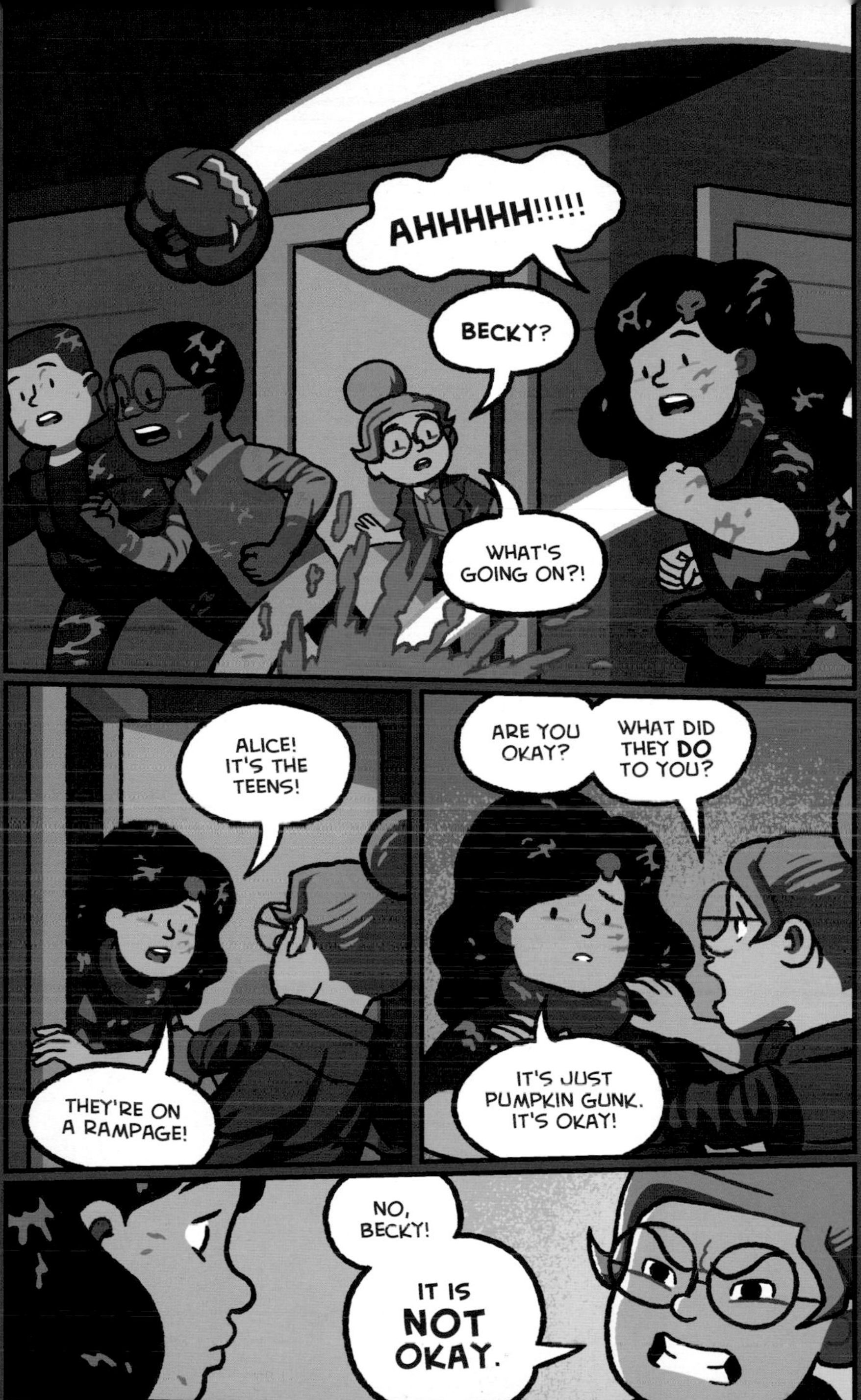
AHHHHH!!!!!
BECKY?
WHAT'S GOING ON?!
ALICE! IT'S THE TEENS!
THEY'RE ON A RAMPAGE!
ARE YOU OKAY?
WHAT DID THEY DO TO YOU?
IT'S JUST PUMPKIN GUNK. IT'S OKAY!
NO, BECKY!
IT IS NOT OKAY.

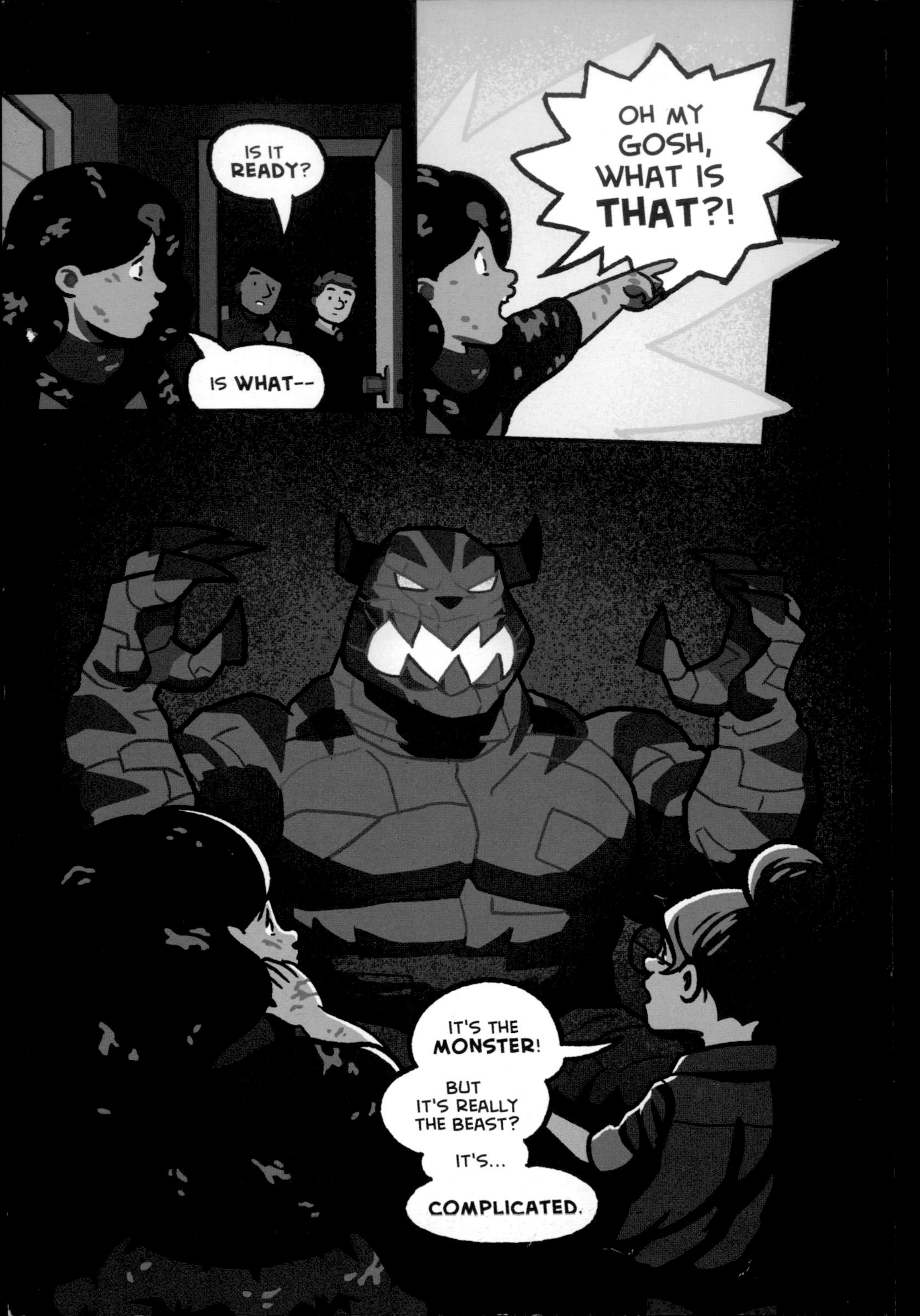
IS IT READY?
IS WHAT--
OH MY GOSH, WHAT IS THAT?!
IT'S THE MONSTER!
BUT IT'S REALLY THE BEAST?
IT'S...
COMPLICATED.

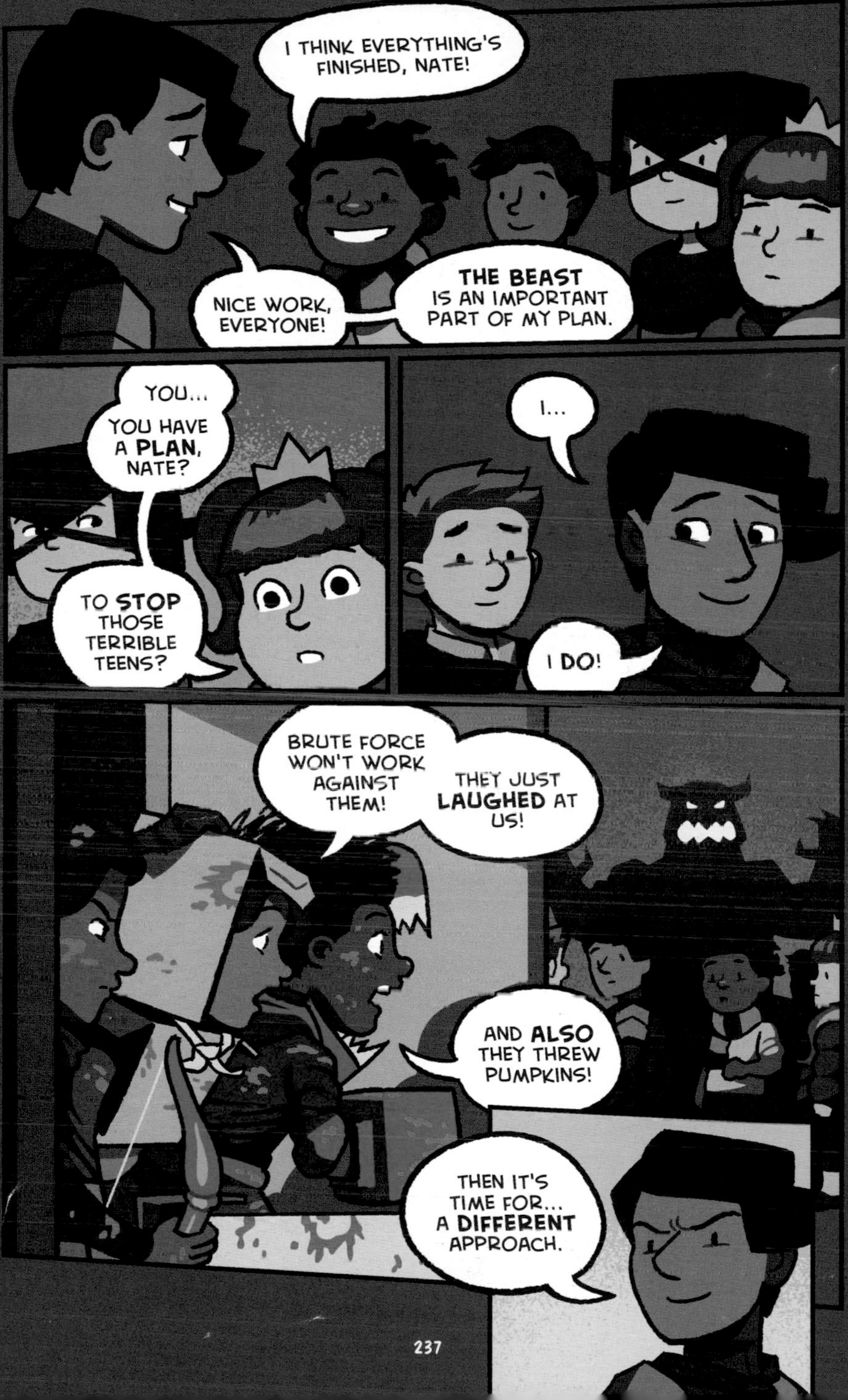
I THINK EVERYTHING'S FINISHED, NATE!
NICE WORK, EVERYONE!
THE BEAST IS AN IMPORTANT PART OF MY PLAN.
YOU...
YOU HAVE A PLAN, NATE?
TO STOP THOSE TERRIBLE TEENS?
I...
I DO!
BRUTE FORCE WON'T WORK AGAINST THEM!
THEY JUST LAUGHED AT US!
AND ALSO THEY THREW PUMPKINS!
THEN IT'S TIME FOR... A DIFFERENT APPROACH.

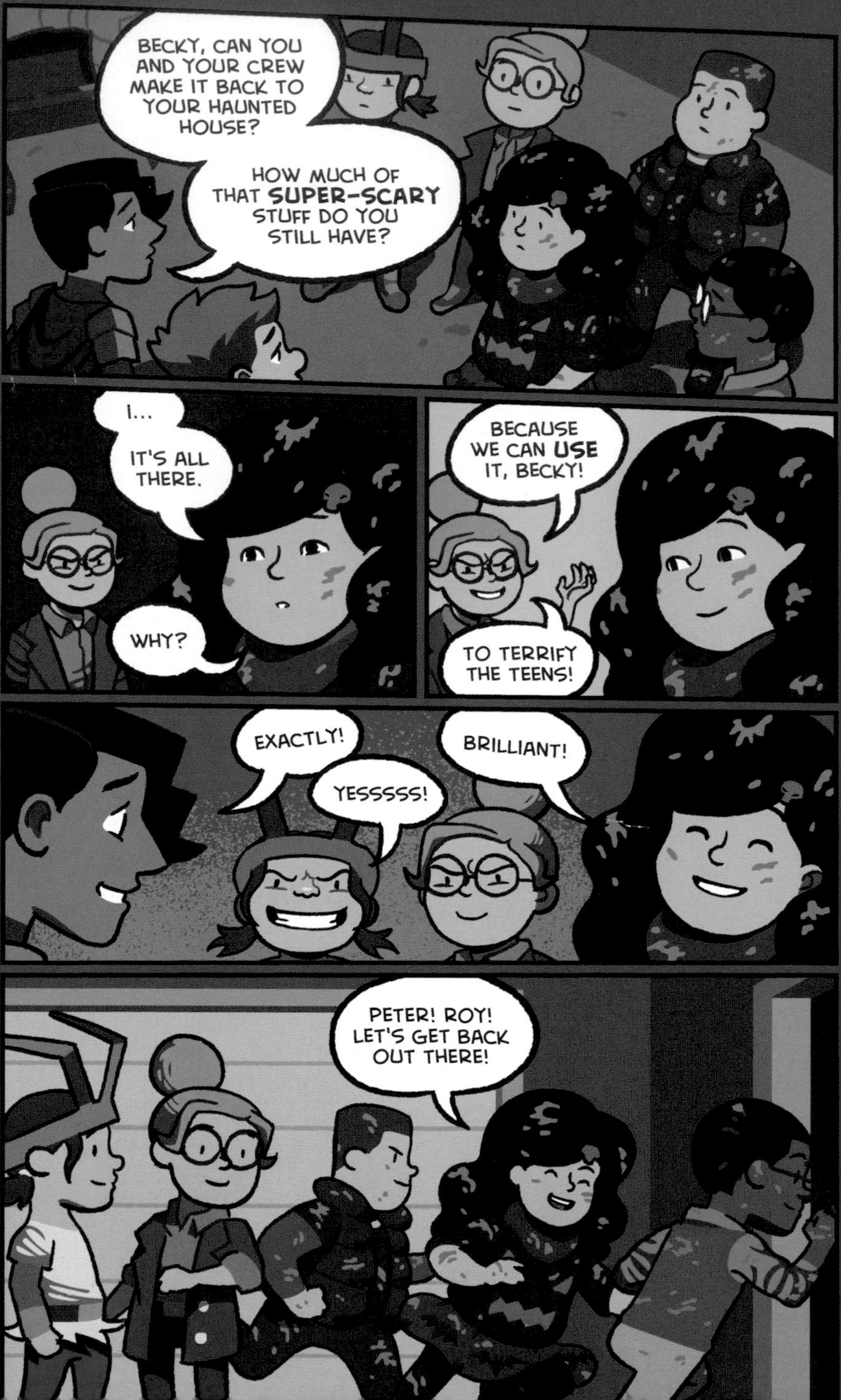
BECKY, CAN YOU AND YOUR CREW MAKE IT BACK TO YOUR HAUNTED HOUSE?
HOW MUCH OF THAT **SUPER-SCARY** STUFF DO YOU STILL HAVE?
I...
IT'S ALL THERE.
WHY?
BECAUSE WE CAN **USE** IT, BECKY!
TO TERRIFY THE TEENS!
EXACTLY!
YESSSSS!
BRILLIANT!
PETER! ROY! LET'S GET BACK OUT THERE!

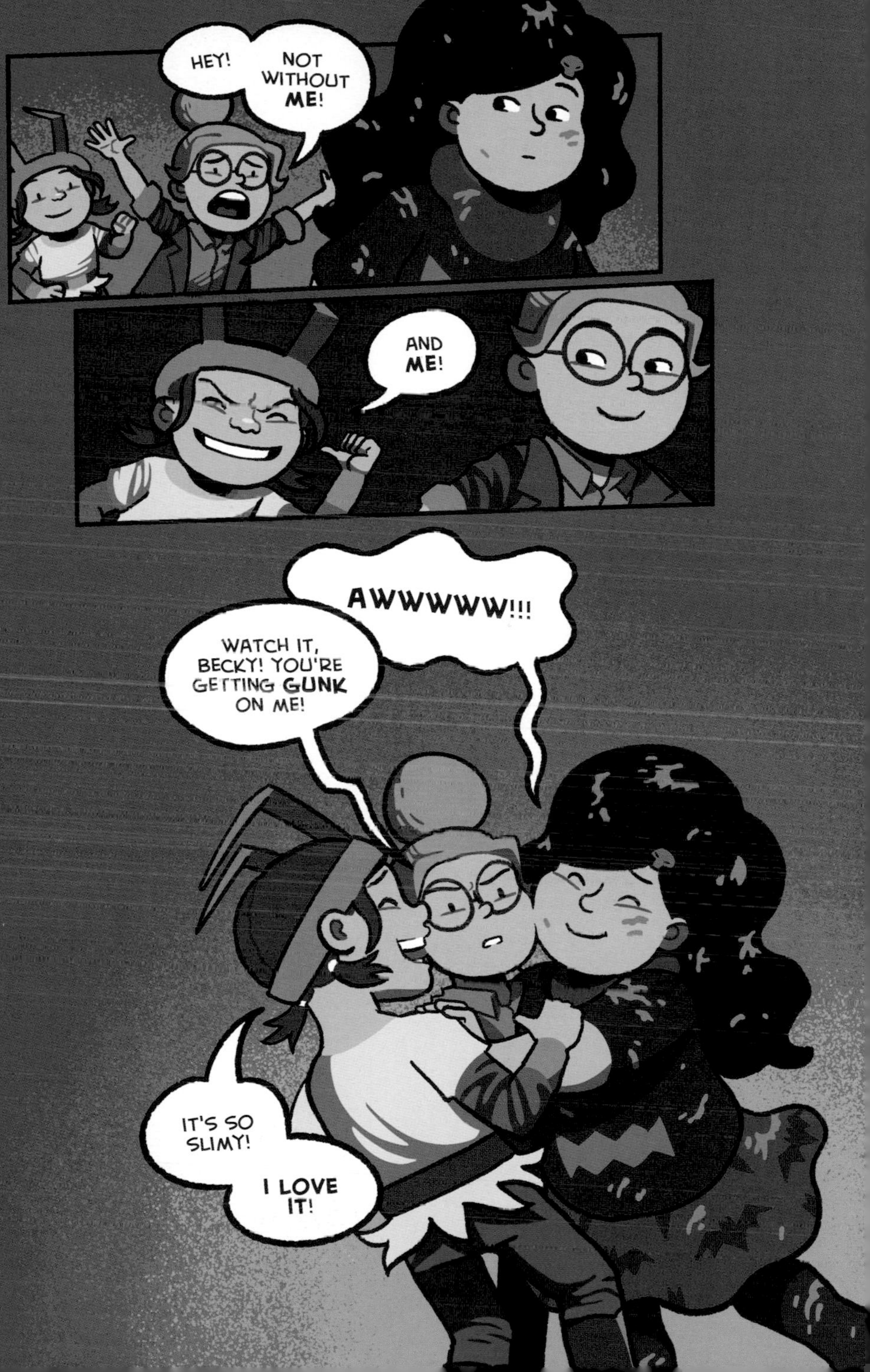
HEY!
NOT WITHOUT ME!
AND ME!
AWWWWW!!!
WATCH IT, BECKY! YOU'RE GETTING GUNK ON ME!
IT'S SO SLIMY!
I LOVE IT!

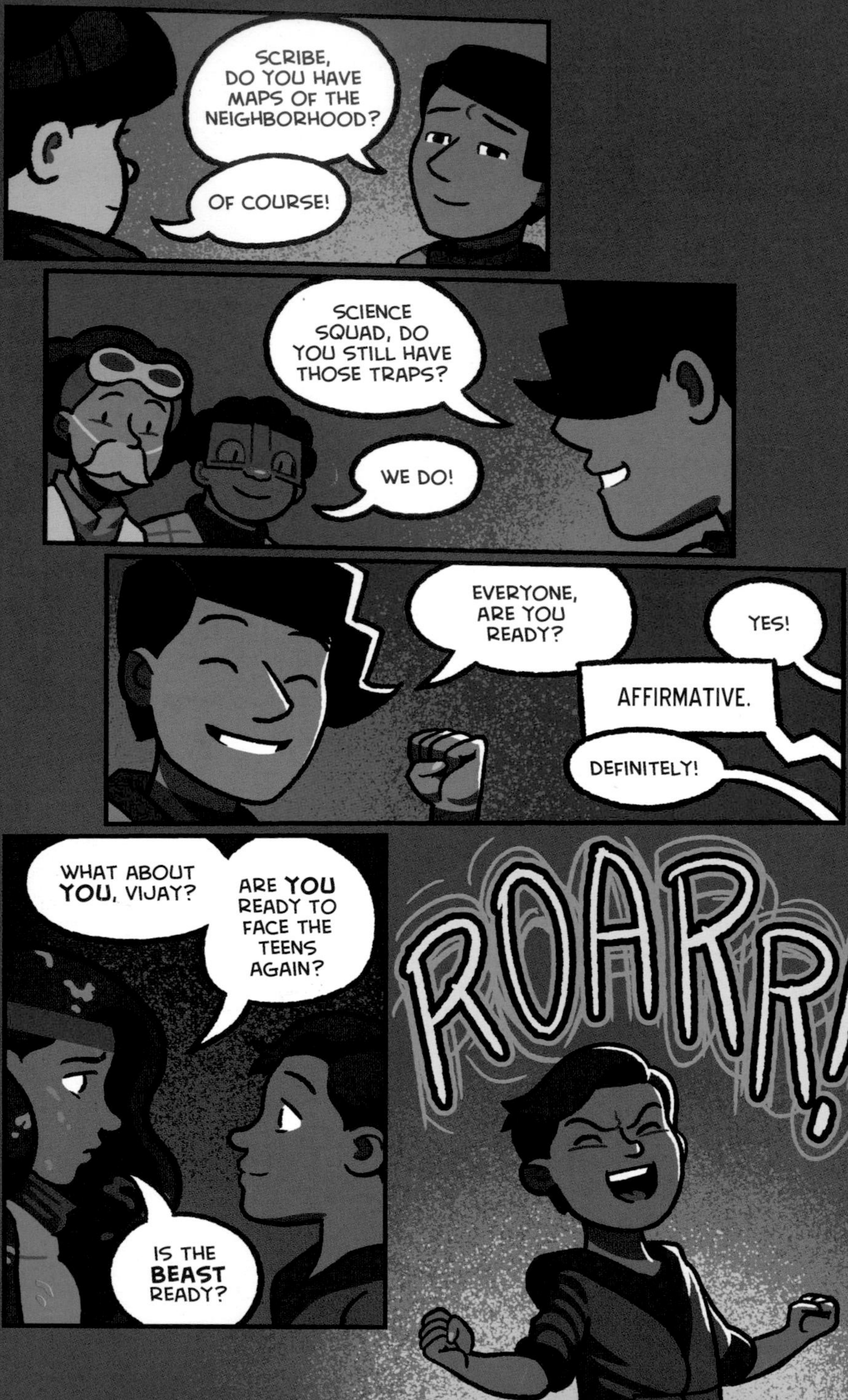
SCRIBE, DO YOU HAVE MAPS OF THE NEIGHBORHOOD?
OF COURSE!
SCIENCE SQUAD, DO YOU STILL HAVE THOSE TRAPS?
WE DO!
EVERYONE, ARE YOU READY?
YES!
AFFIRMATIVE.
DEFINITELY!
WHAT ABOUT YOU, VIJAY?
ARE YOU READY TO FACE THE TEENS AGAIN?
IS THE BEAST READY?
ROARR!

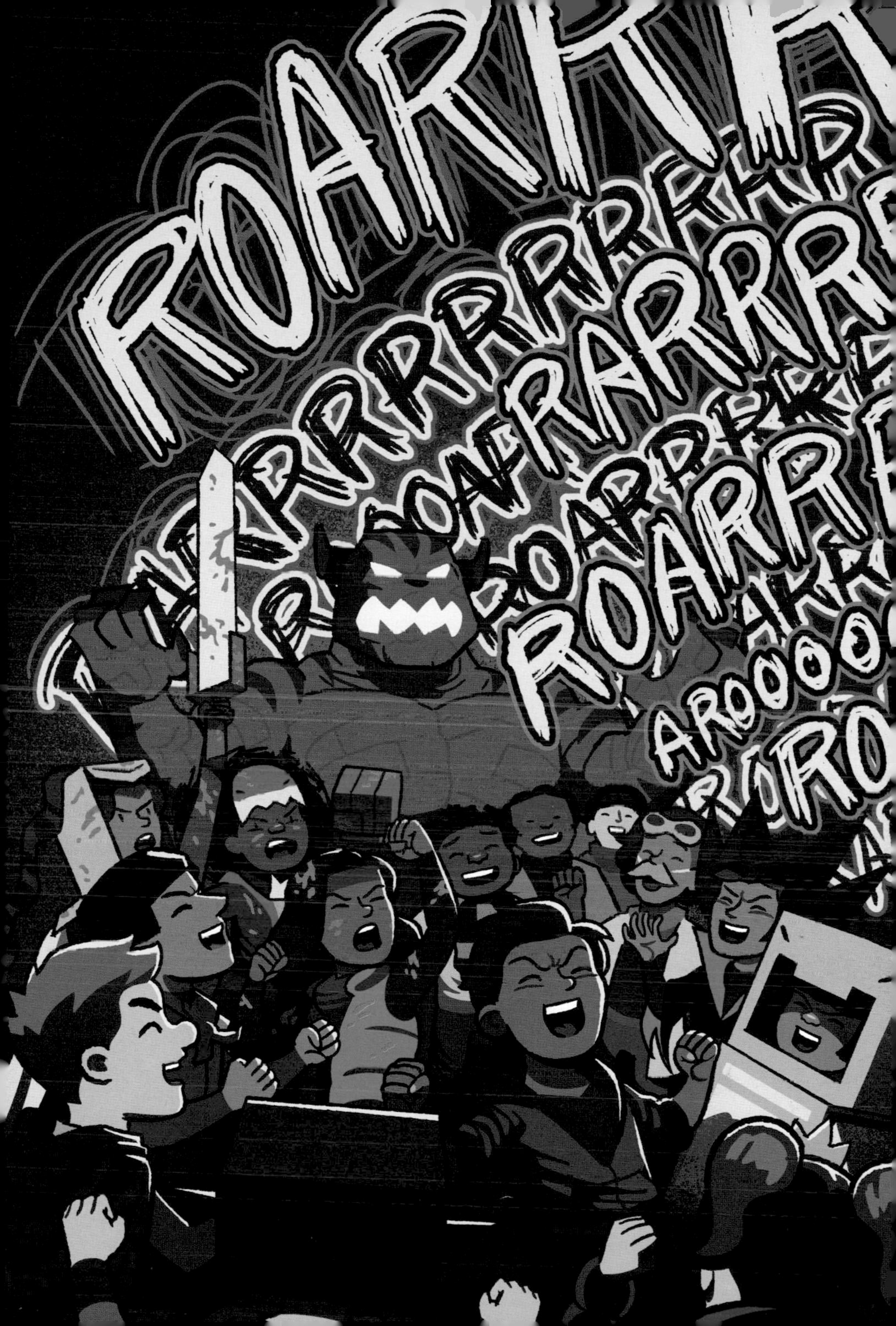
ROARRR
AROOOO

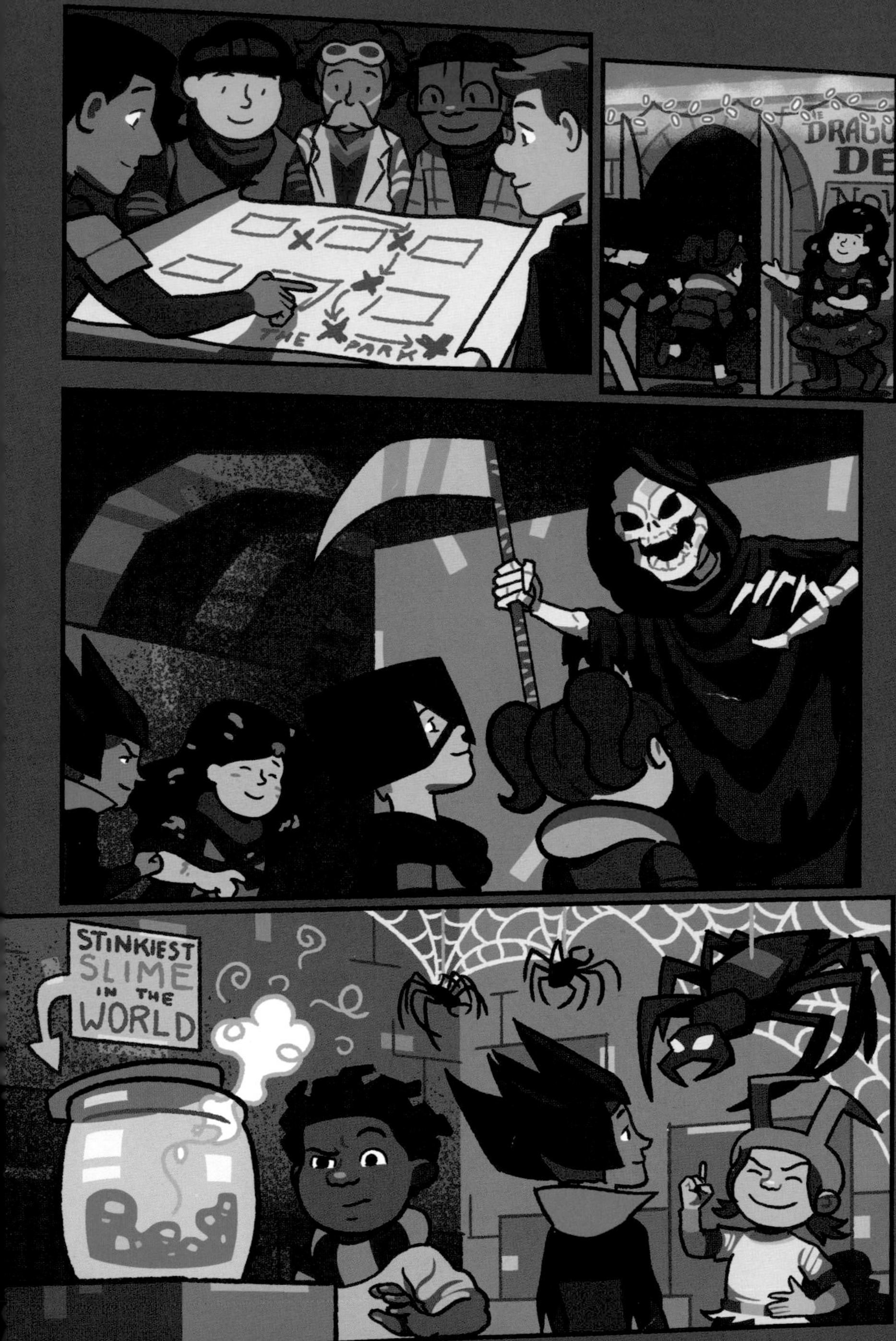
THE PARK
STINKIEST SLIME IN THE WORLD

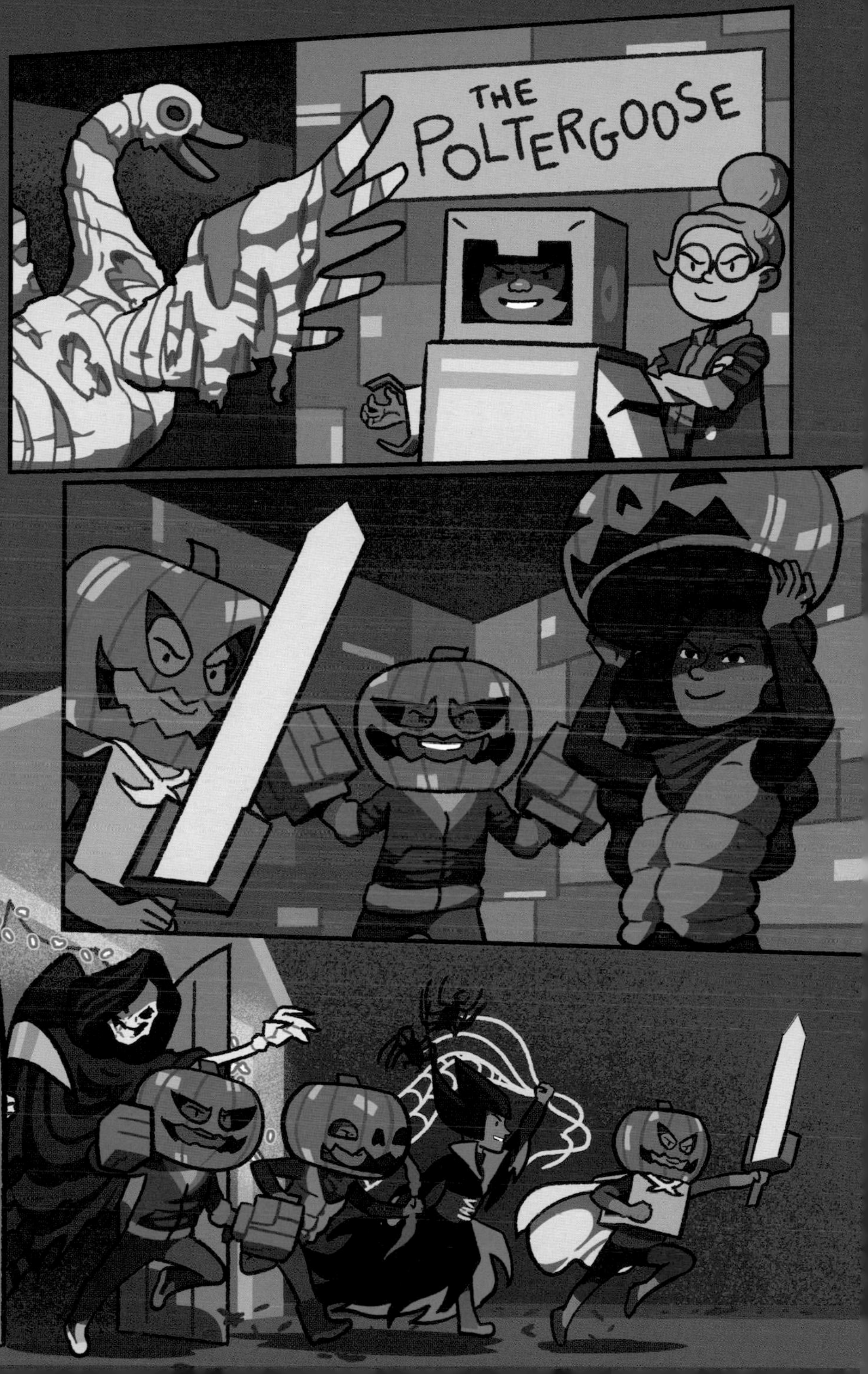
THE POLTERGOOSE

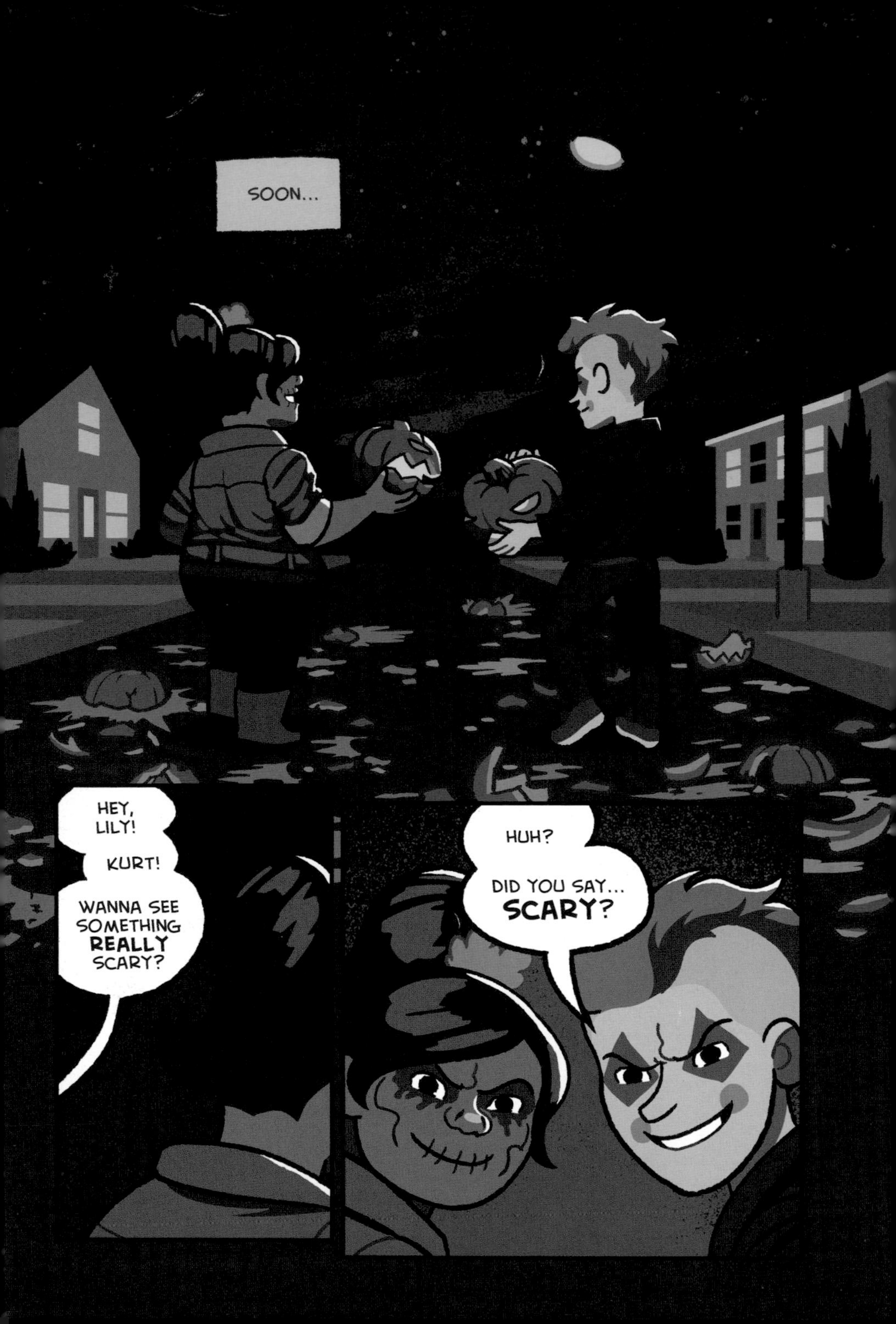
SOON...
HEY, LILY!
KURT!
WANNA SEE SOMETHING REALLY SCARY?
HUH?
DID YOU SAY... SCARY?

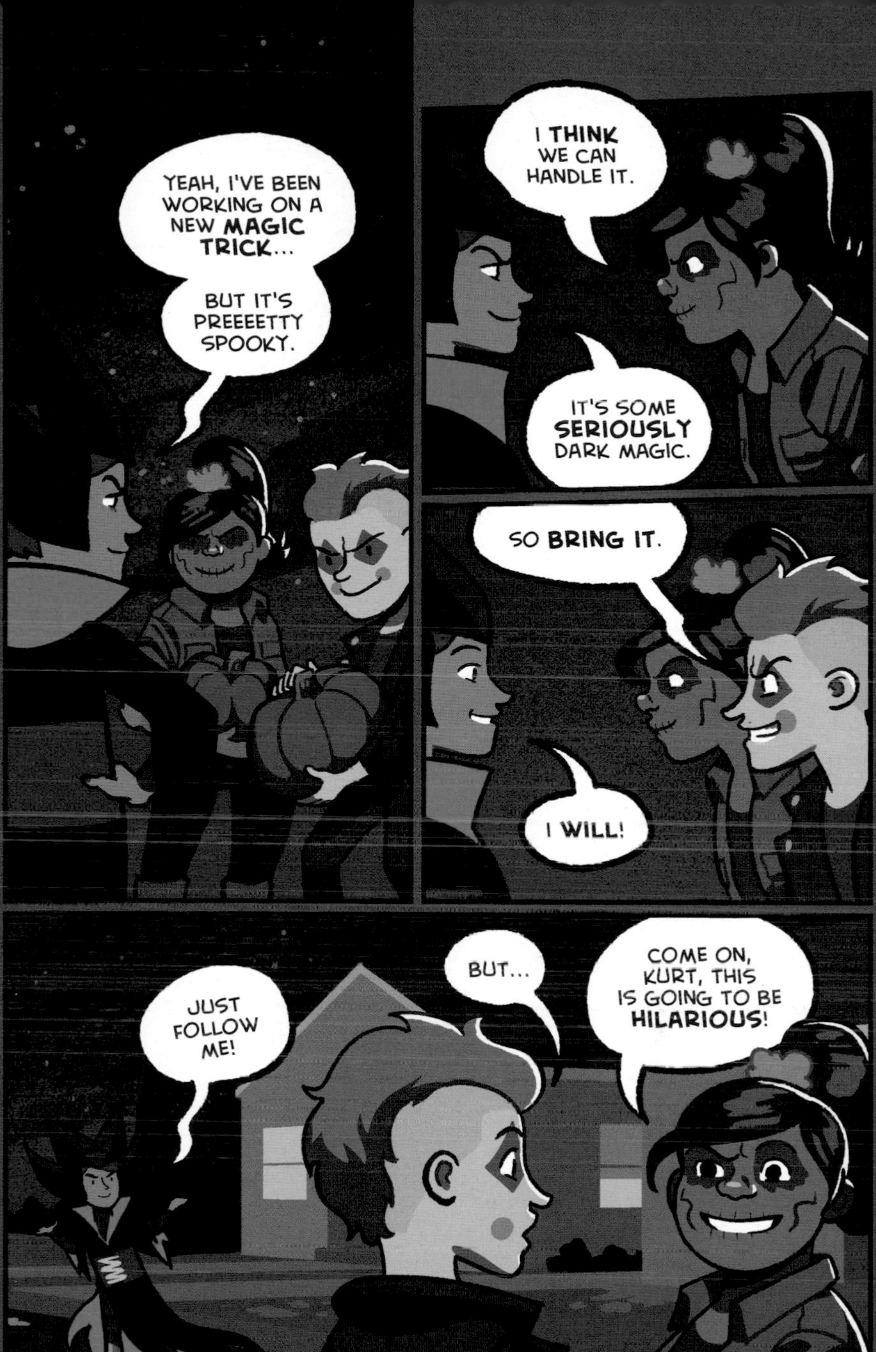
YEAH, I'VE BEEN WORKING ON A NEW MAGIC TRICK...
BUT IT'S PREEEETTY SPOOKY.
I THINK WE CAN HANDLE IT.
IT'S SOME SERIOUSLY DARK MAGIC.
SO BRING IT.
I WILL!
JUST FOLLOW ME!
BUT...
COME ON, KURT, THIS IS GOING TO BE HILARIOUS!

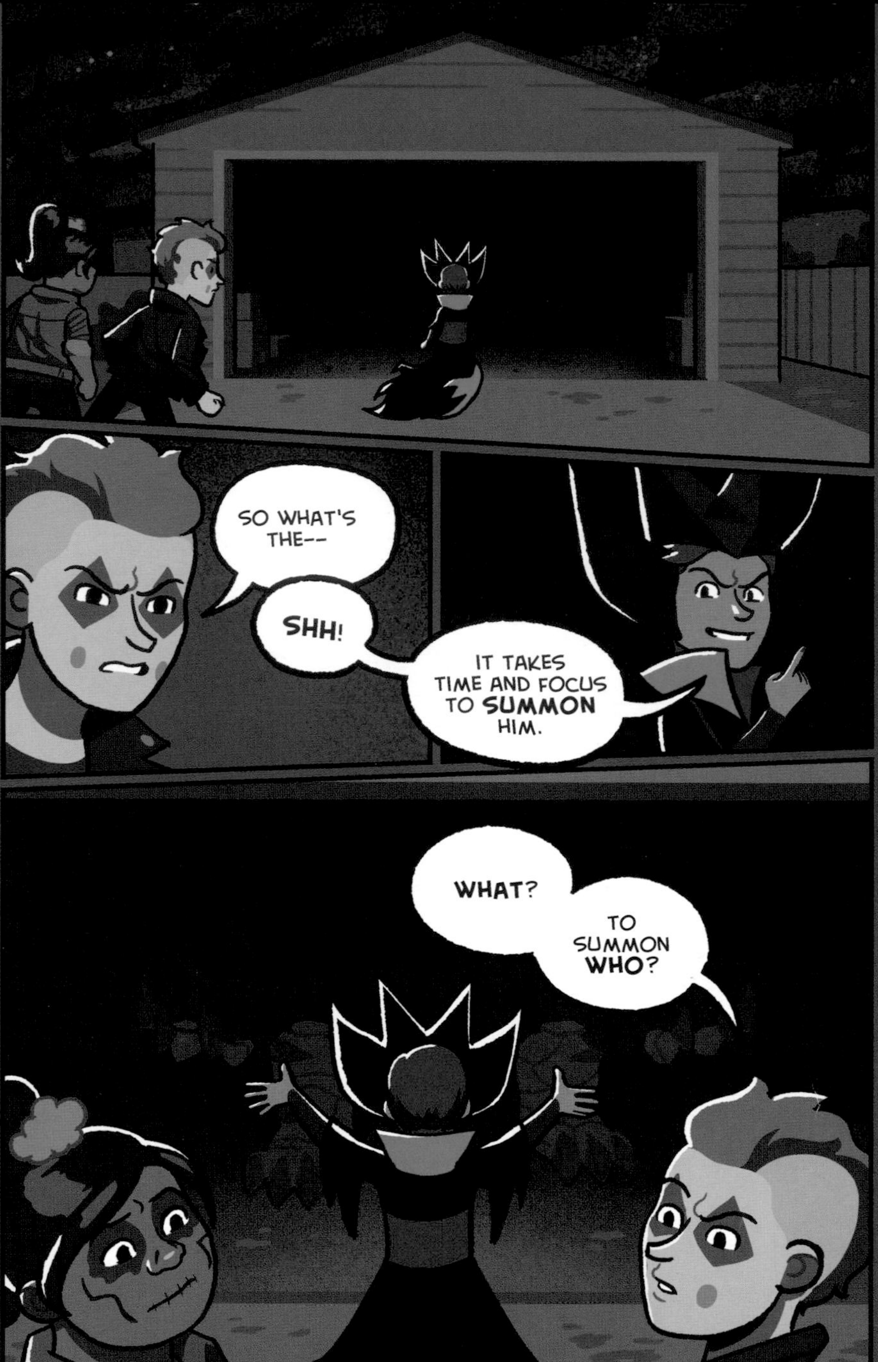
SO WHAT'S THE--
SHH!
IT TAKES TIME AND FOCUS TO SUMMON HIM.
WHAT?
TO SUMMON WHO?

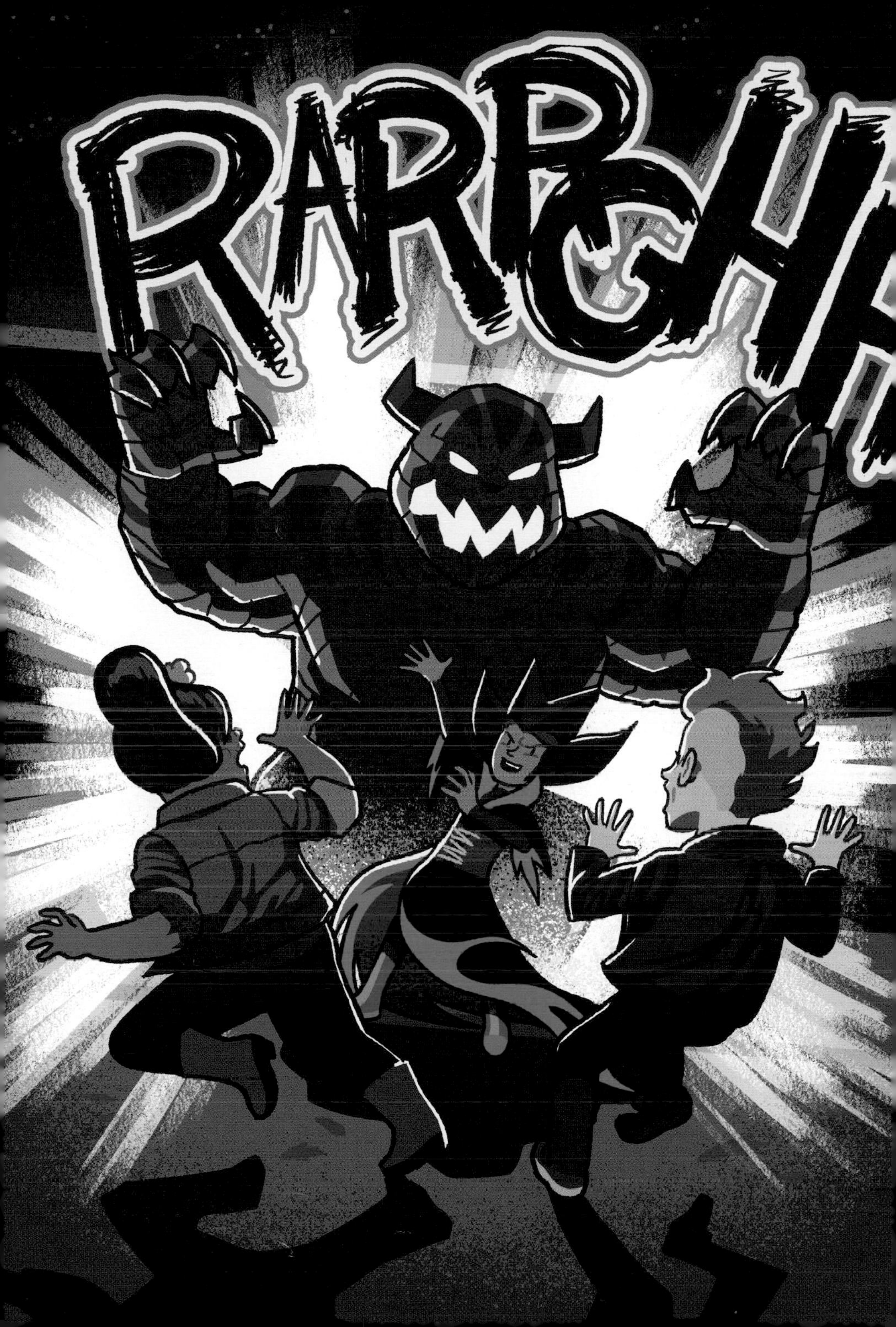
RARRGH!

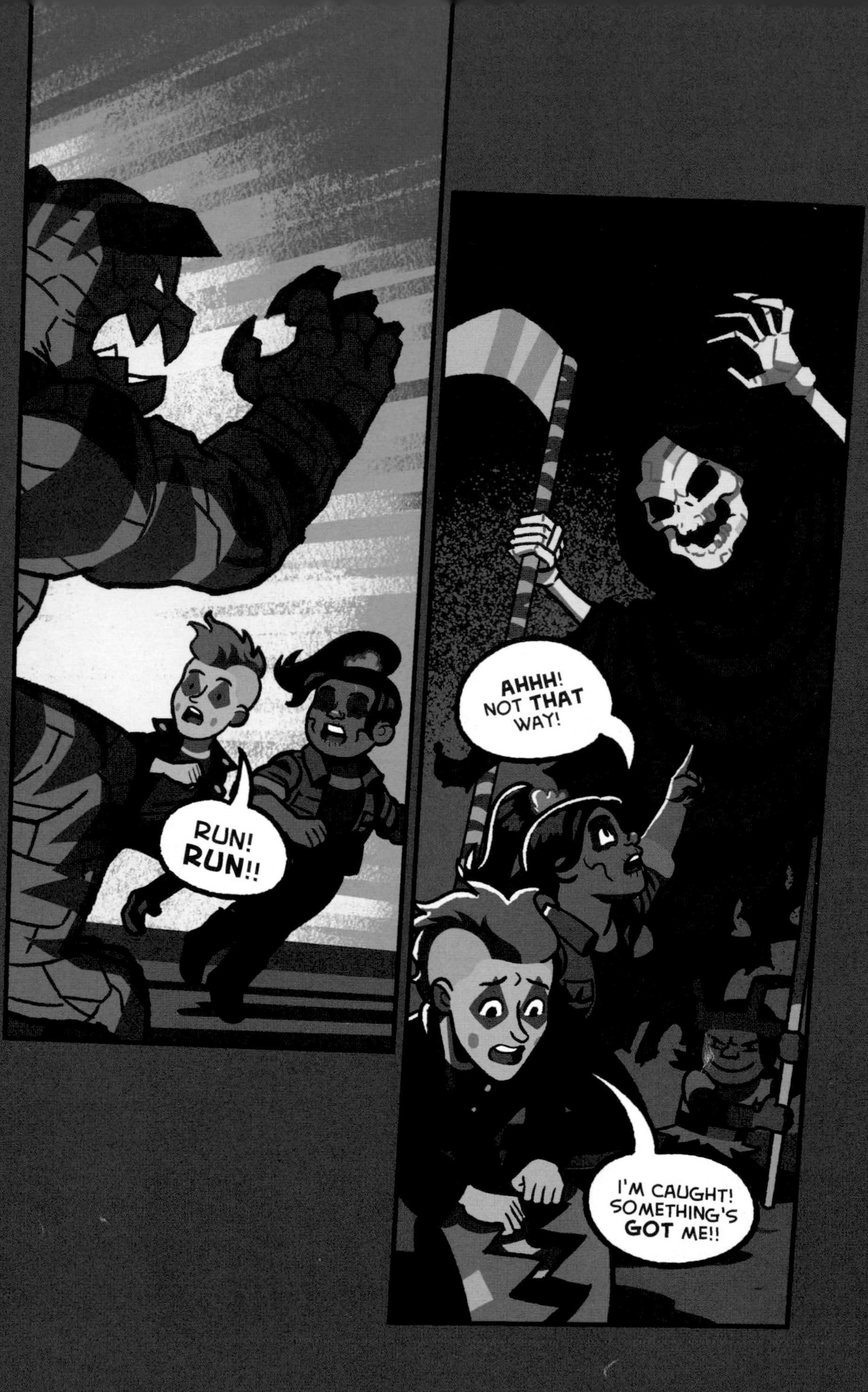
RUN! RUN!!
AHHH! NOT THAT WAY!
I'M CAUGHT! SOMETHING'S GOT ME!!

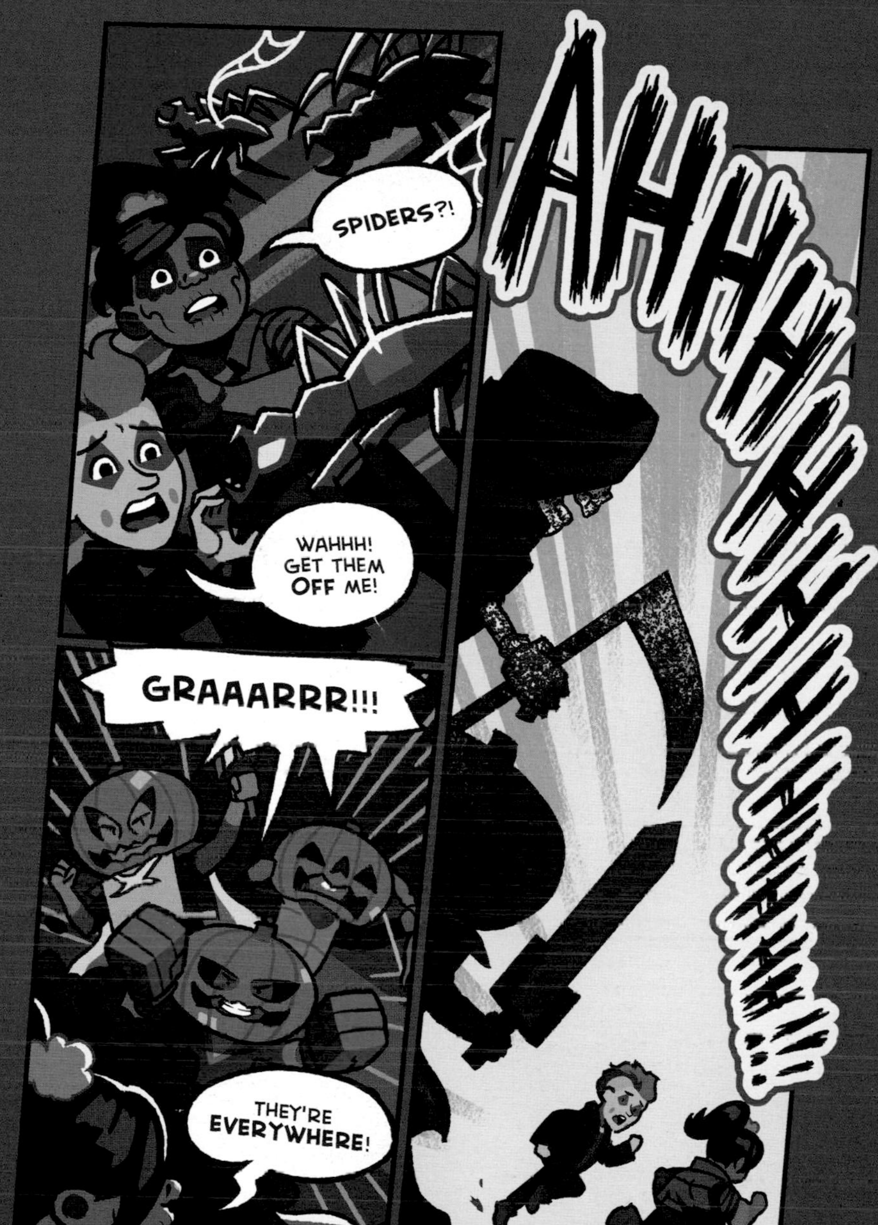
SPIDERS?!
WAHHH! GET THEM OFF ME!
GRAAARRR!!!
THEY'RE EVERYWHERE!
AHHHHHHHHHHHHHHHH!!!

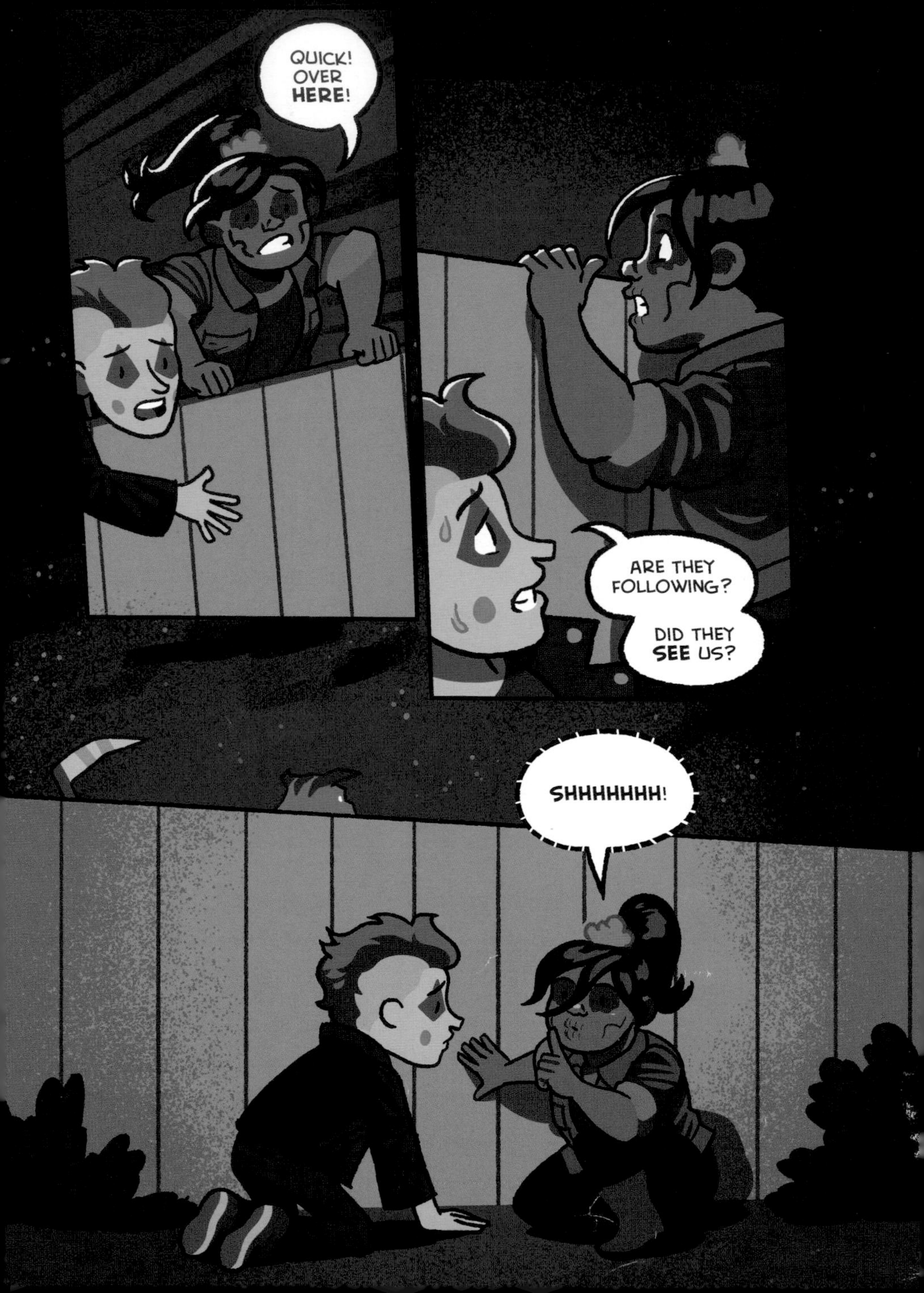
QUICK! OVER HERE!
ARE THEY FOLLOWING?
DID THEY SEE US?
SHHHHHHH!

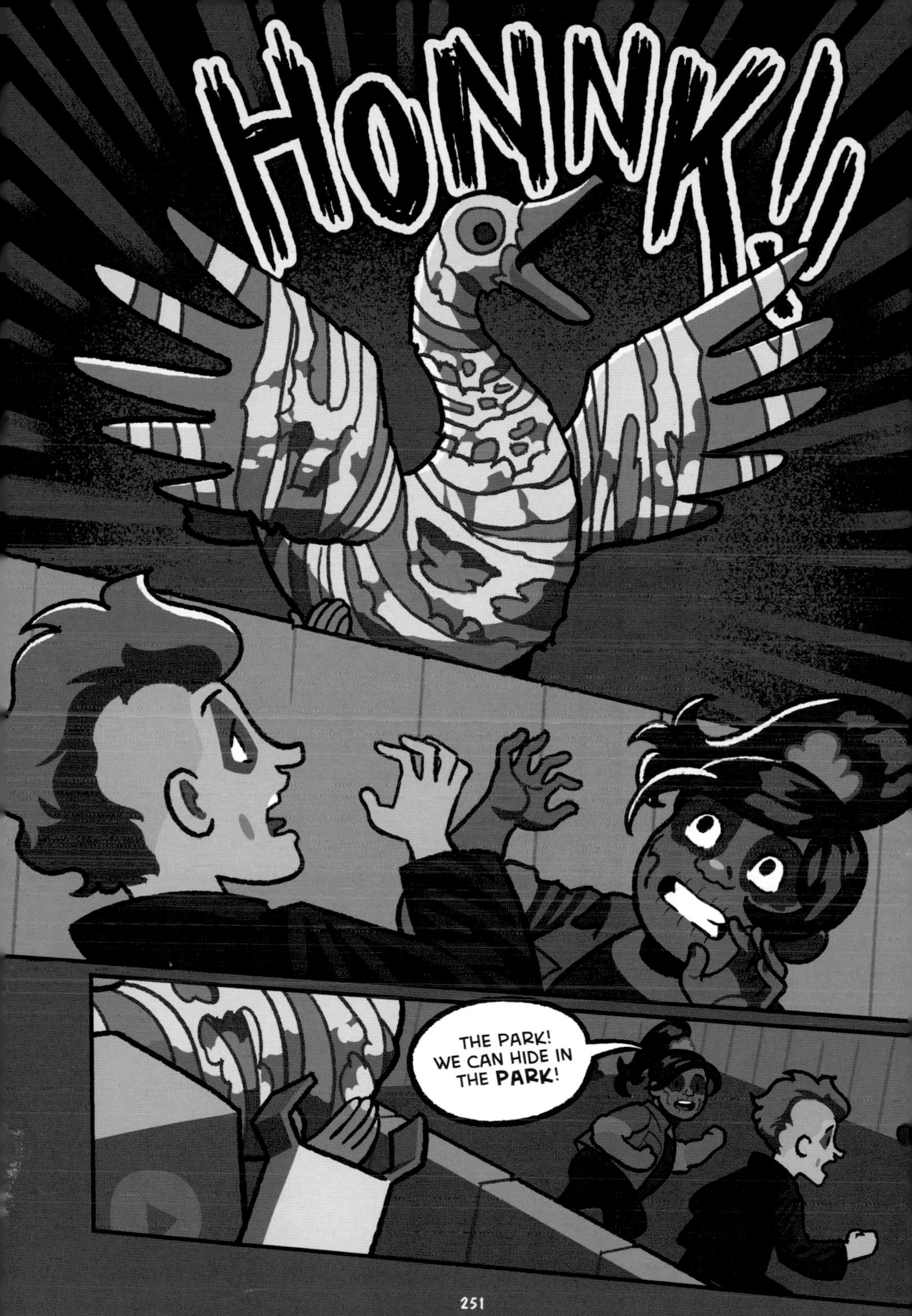
HONNK!!
THE PARK! WE CAN HIDE IN THE PARK!

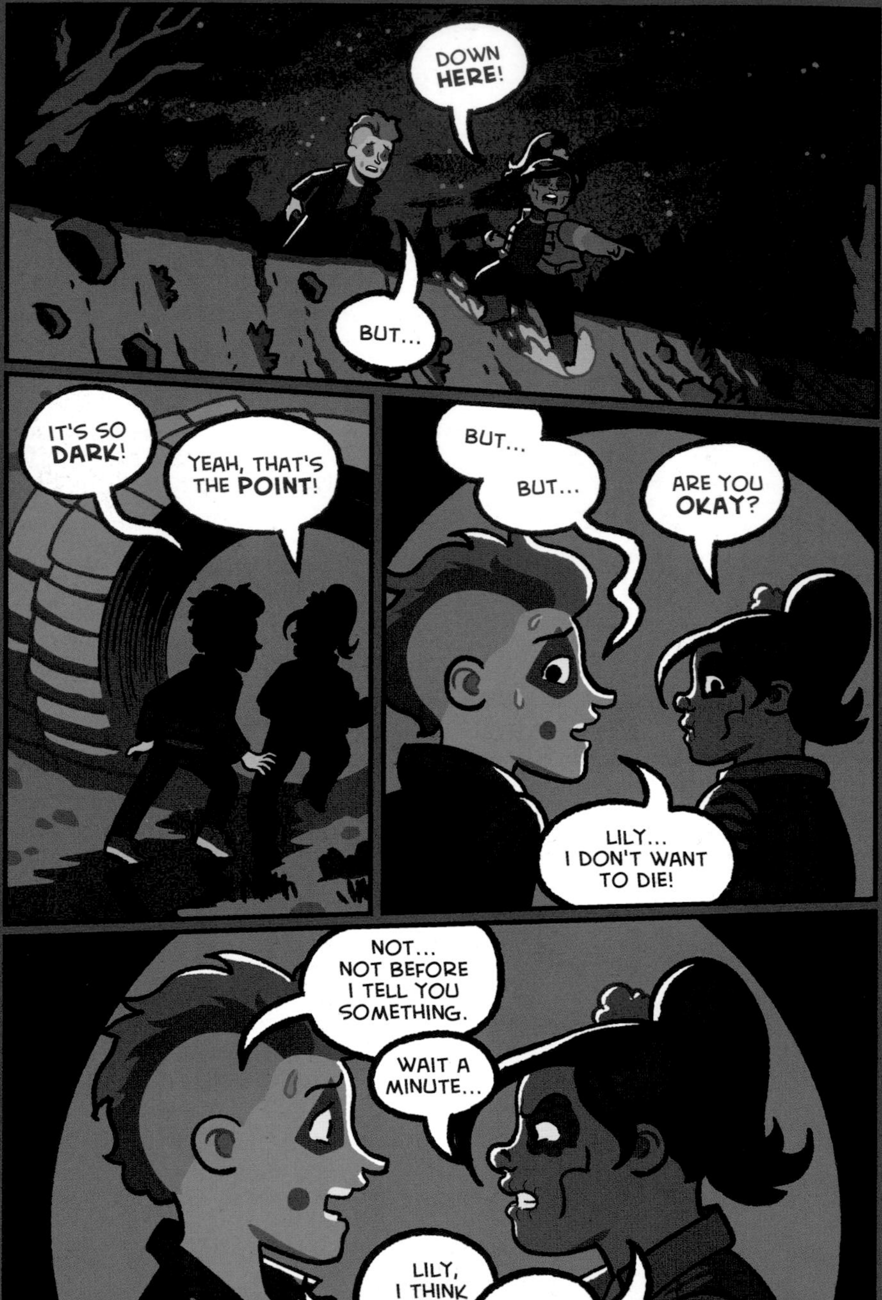
DOWN HERE!
BUT...
IT'S SO DARK!
YEAH, THAT'S THE POINT!
BUT...
BUT...
ARE YOU OKAY?
LILY... I DON'T WANT TO DIE!
NOT... NOT BEFORE I TELL YOU SOMETHING.
WAIT A MINUTE...
LILY, I THINK I'M IN LO WITH YO
WAIT!!

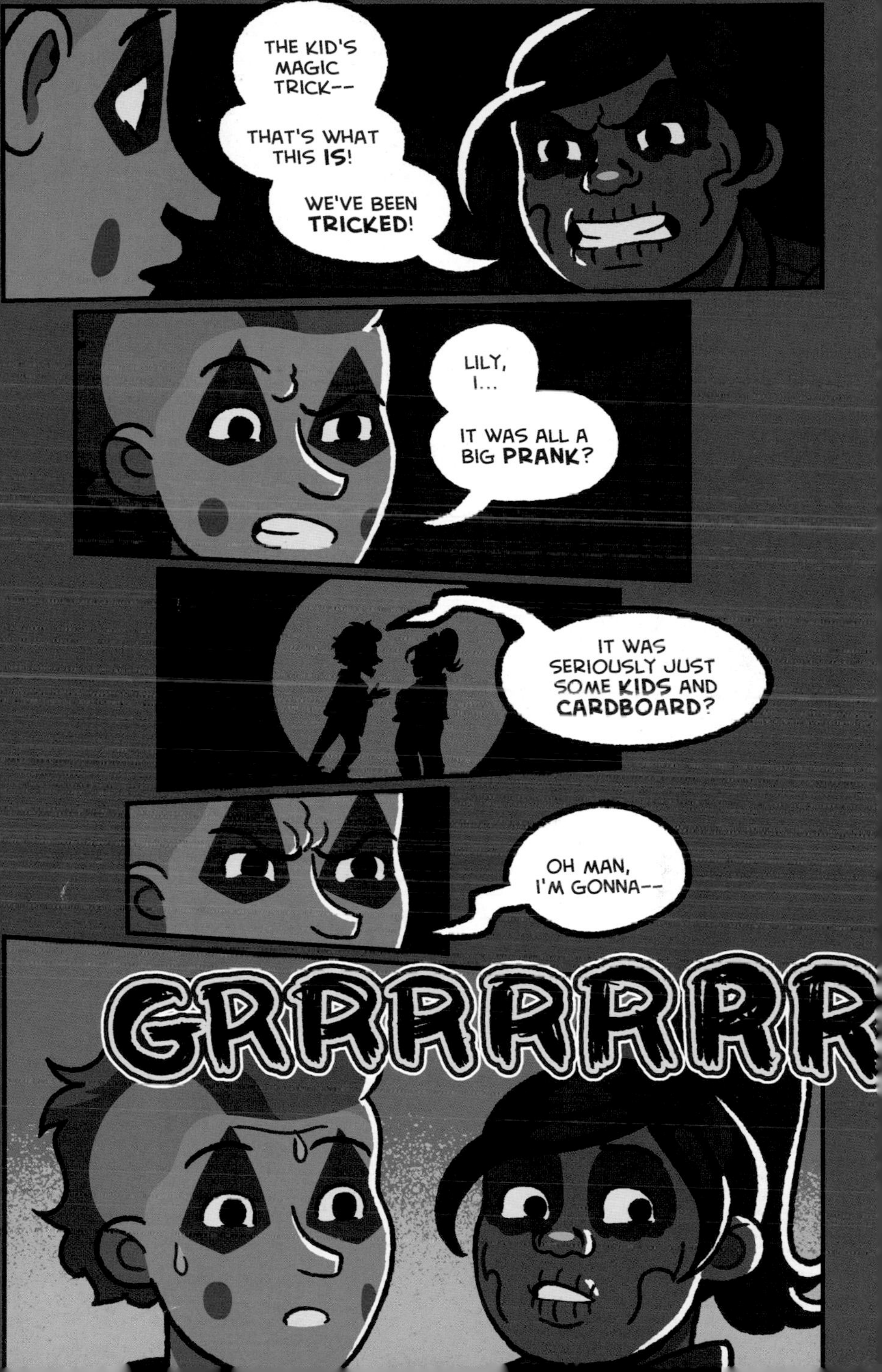
THE KID'S MAGIC TRICK--
THAT'S WHAT THIS **IS**!
WE'VE BEEN **TRICKED**!
LILY, I...
IT WAS ALL A BIG **PRANK**?
IT WAS SERIOUSLY JUST SOME **KIDS** AND **CARDBOARD**?
OH MAN, I'M GONNA--
GRRRRRRR

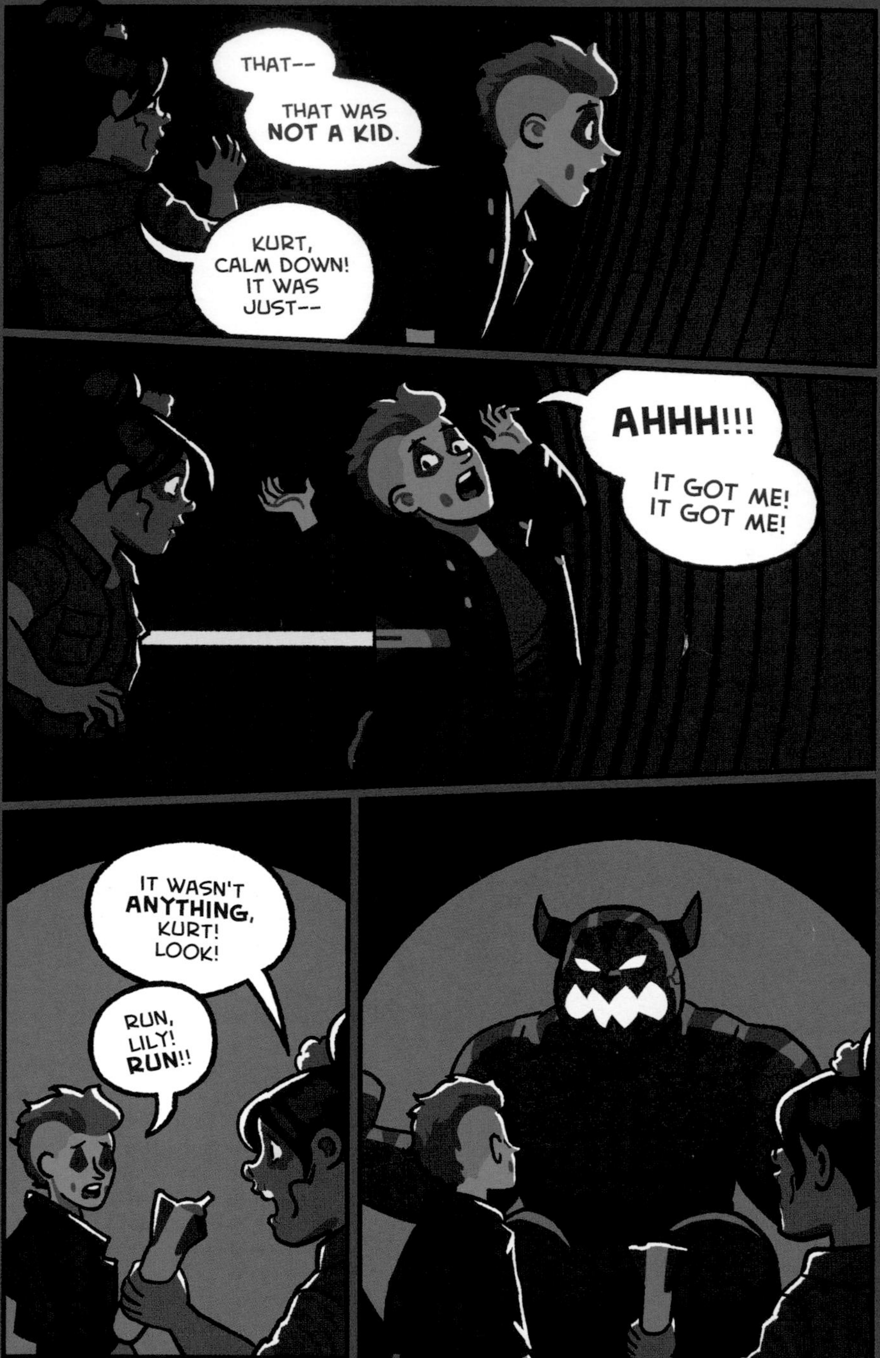
THAT--
THAT WAS NOT A KID.
KURT, CALM DOWN! IT WAS JUST--
AHHH!!!
IT GOT ME! IT GOT ME!
IT WASN'T ANYTHING, KURT! LOOK!
RUN, LILY! RUN!!

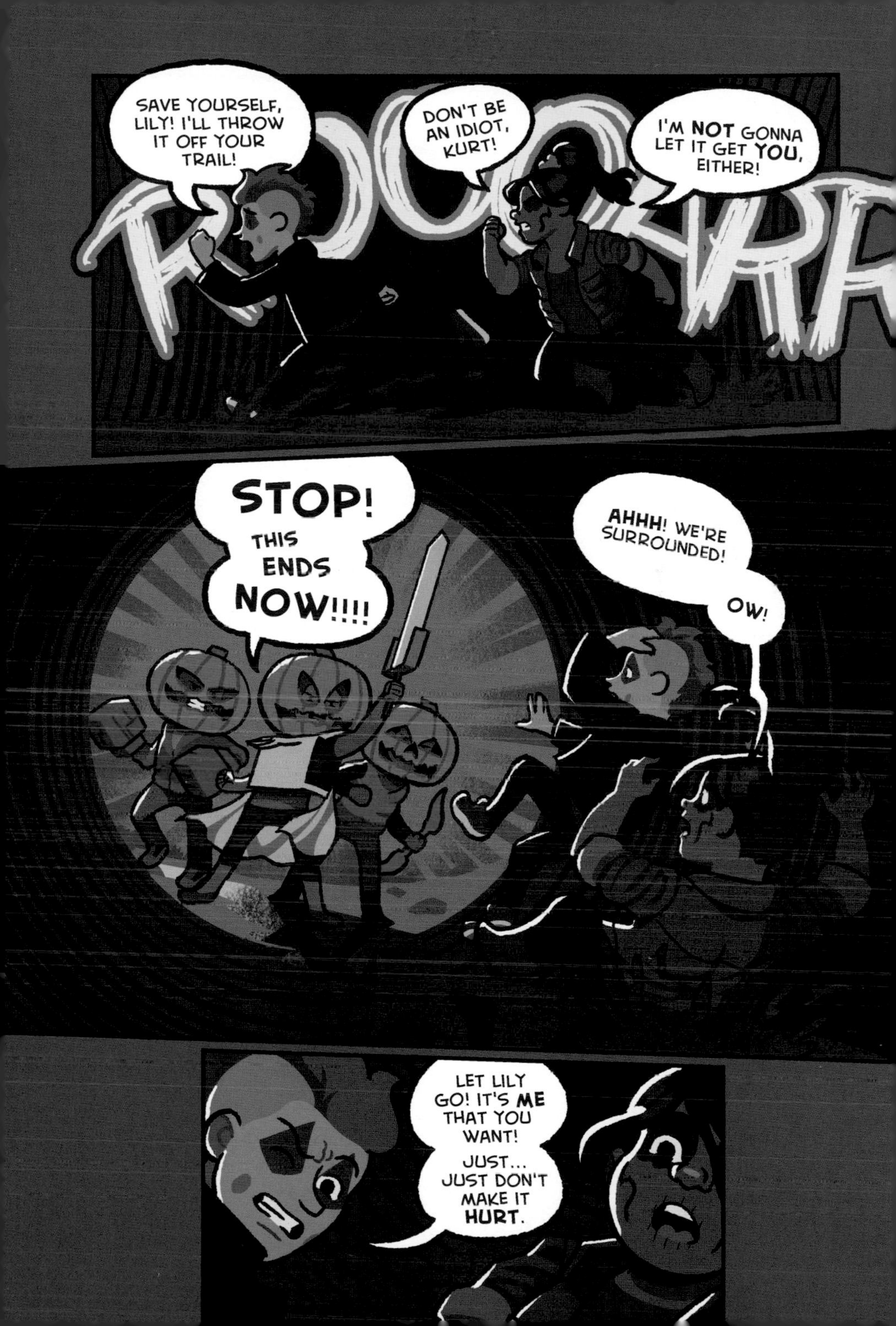
SAVE YOURSELF, LILY! I'LL THROW IT OFF YOUR TRAIL!
DON'T BE AN IDIOT, KURT!
I'M NOT GONNA LET IT GET YOU, EITHER!
STOP! THIS ENDS NOW!!!!
AHHH! WE'RE SURROUNDED!
OW!
LET LILY GO! IT'S ME THAT YOU WANT!
JUST... JUST DON'T MAKE IT HURT.

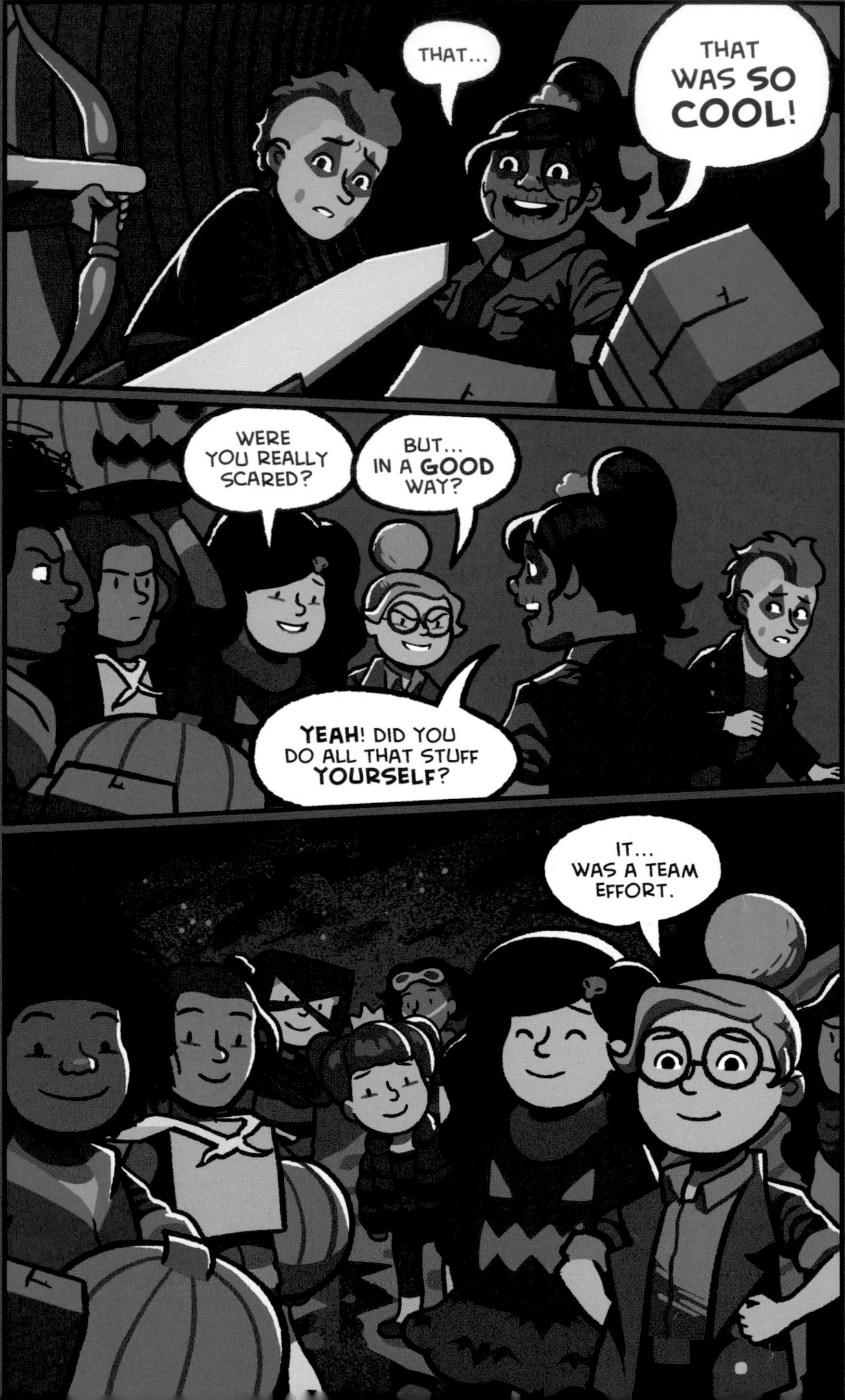
THAT...
THAT WAS **SO** **COOL**!
WERE YOU REALLY SCARED?
BUT... IN A **GOOD** WAY?
YEAH! DID YOU DO ALL THAT STUFF **YOURSELF**?
IT... WAS A TEAM EFFORT.

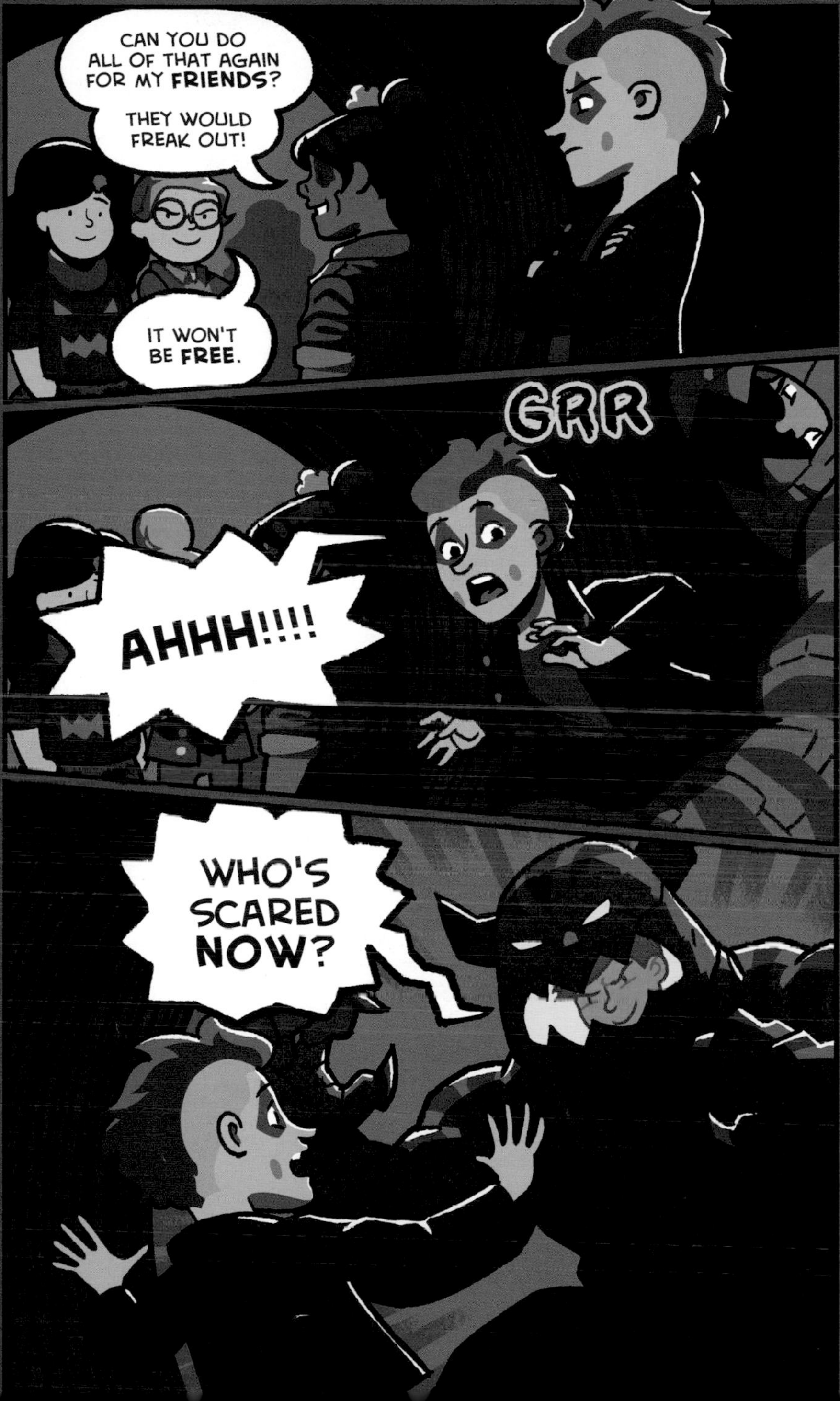

CAN YOU DO ALL OF THAT AGAIN FOR MY **FRIENDS**?
THEY WOULD FREAK OUT!
IT WON'T BE **FREE**.
GRR
AHHH!!!!
WHO'S SCARED NOW?

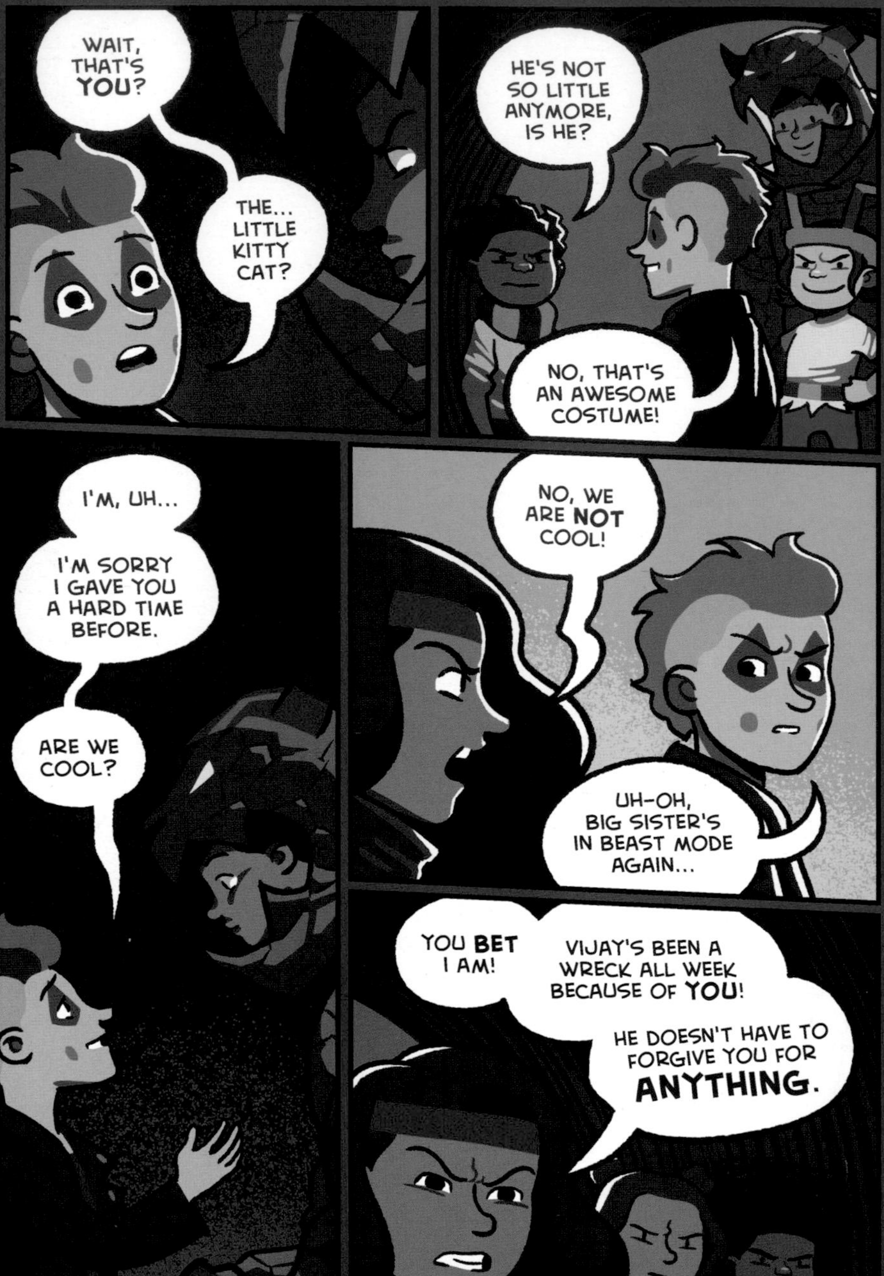
WAIT, THAT'S **YOU**?
THE... LITTLE KITTY CAT?
HE'S NOT SO LITTLE ANYMORE, IS HE?
NO, THAT'S AN AWESOME COSTUME!
I'M, UH...
I'M SORRY I GAVE YOU A HARD TIME BEFORE.
ARE WE COOL?
NO, WE ARE **NOT** COOL!
UH-OH, BIG SISTER'S IN BEAST MODE AGAIN...
YOU **BET** I AM!
VIJAY'S BEEN A WRECK ALL WEEK BECAUSE OF **YOU**!
HE DOESN'T HAVE TO FORGIVE YOU FOR **ANYTHING**.

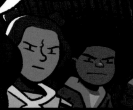

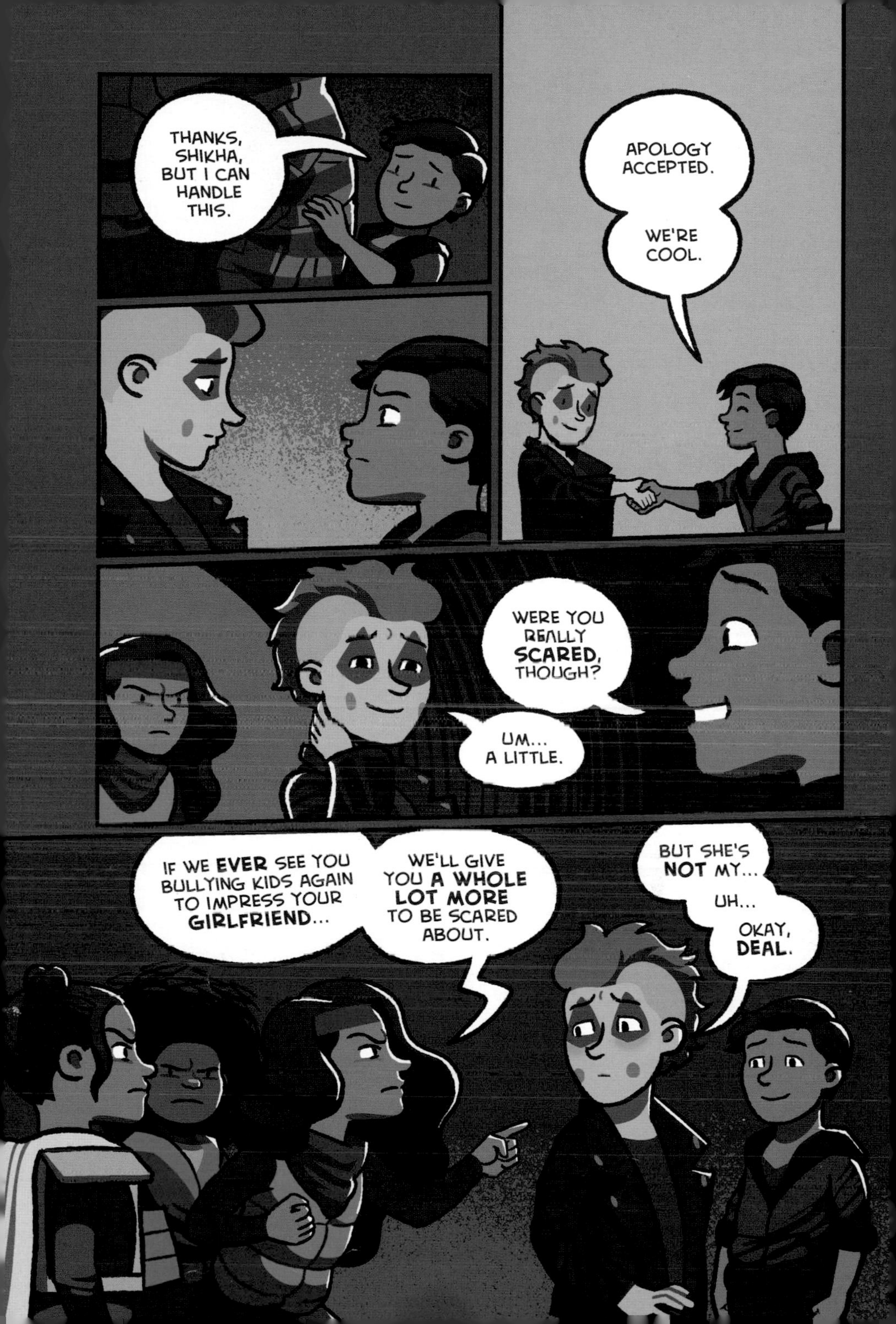
THANKS, SHIKHA, BUT I CAN HANDLE THIS.
APOLOGY ACCEPTED.
WE'RE COOL.
WERE YOU REALLY **SCARED,** THOUGH?
UM... A LITTLE.
IF WE **EVER** SEE YOU BULLYING KIDS AGAIN TO IMPRESS YOUR **GIRLFRIEND**...
WE'LL GIVE YOU **A WHOLE LOT MORE** TO BE SCARED ABOUT.
BUT SHE'S **NOT** MY...
UH...
OKAY, **DEAL.**

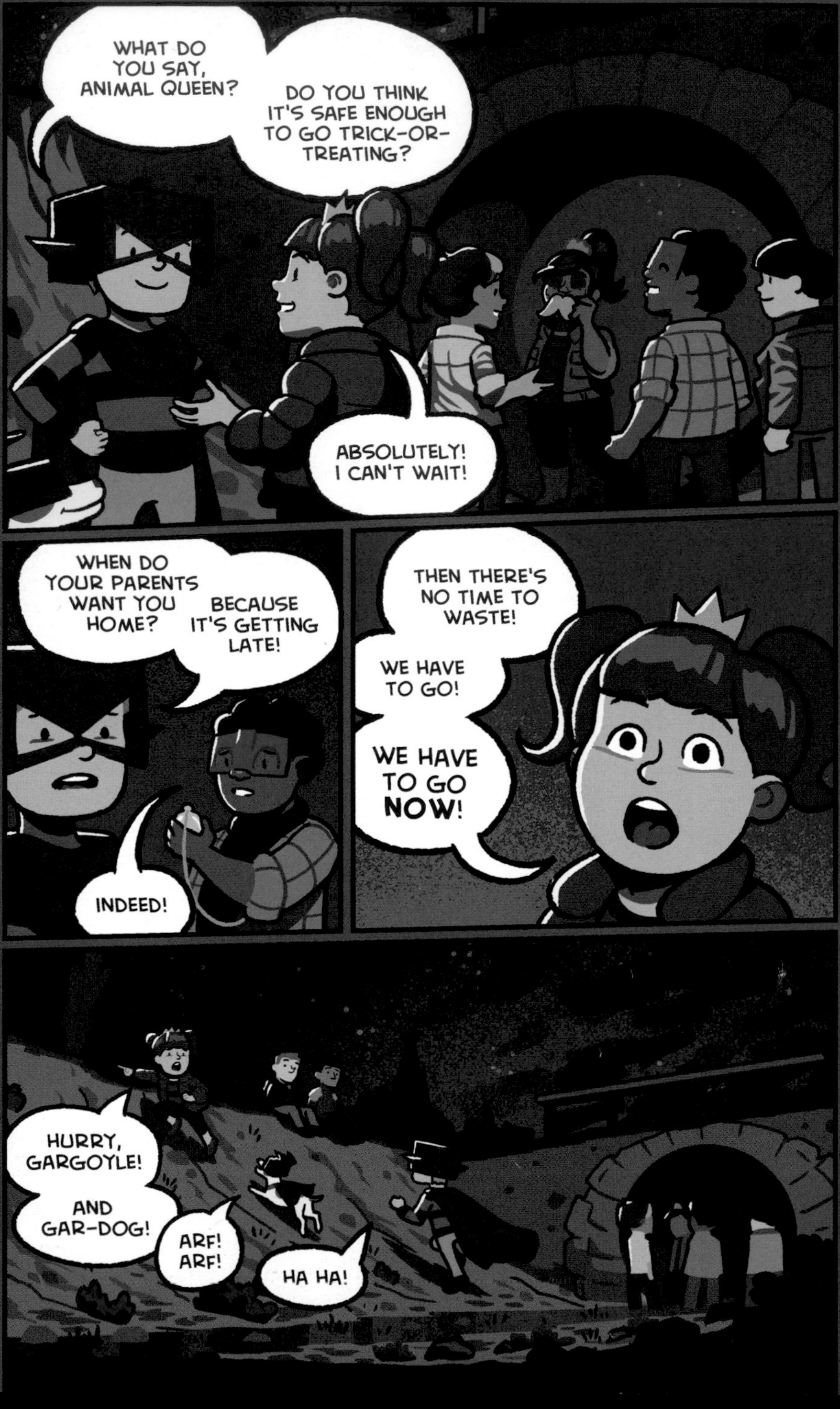
WHAT DO YOU SAY, ANIMAL QUEEN?
DO YOU THINK IT'S SAFE ENOUGH TO GO TRICK-OR-TREATING?
ABSOLUTELY! I CAN'T WAIT!
WHEN DO YOUR PARENTS WANT YOU HOME?
BECAUSE IT'S GETTING LATE!
INDEED!
THEN THERE'S NO TIME TO WASTE!
WE HAVE TO GO!
WE HAVE TO GO NOW!
HURRY, GARGOYLE!
AND GAR-DOG!
ARF! ARF!
HA HA!

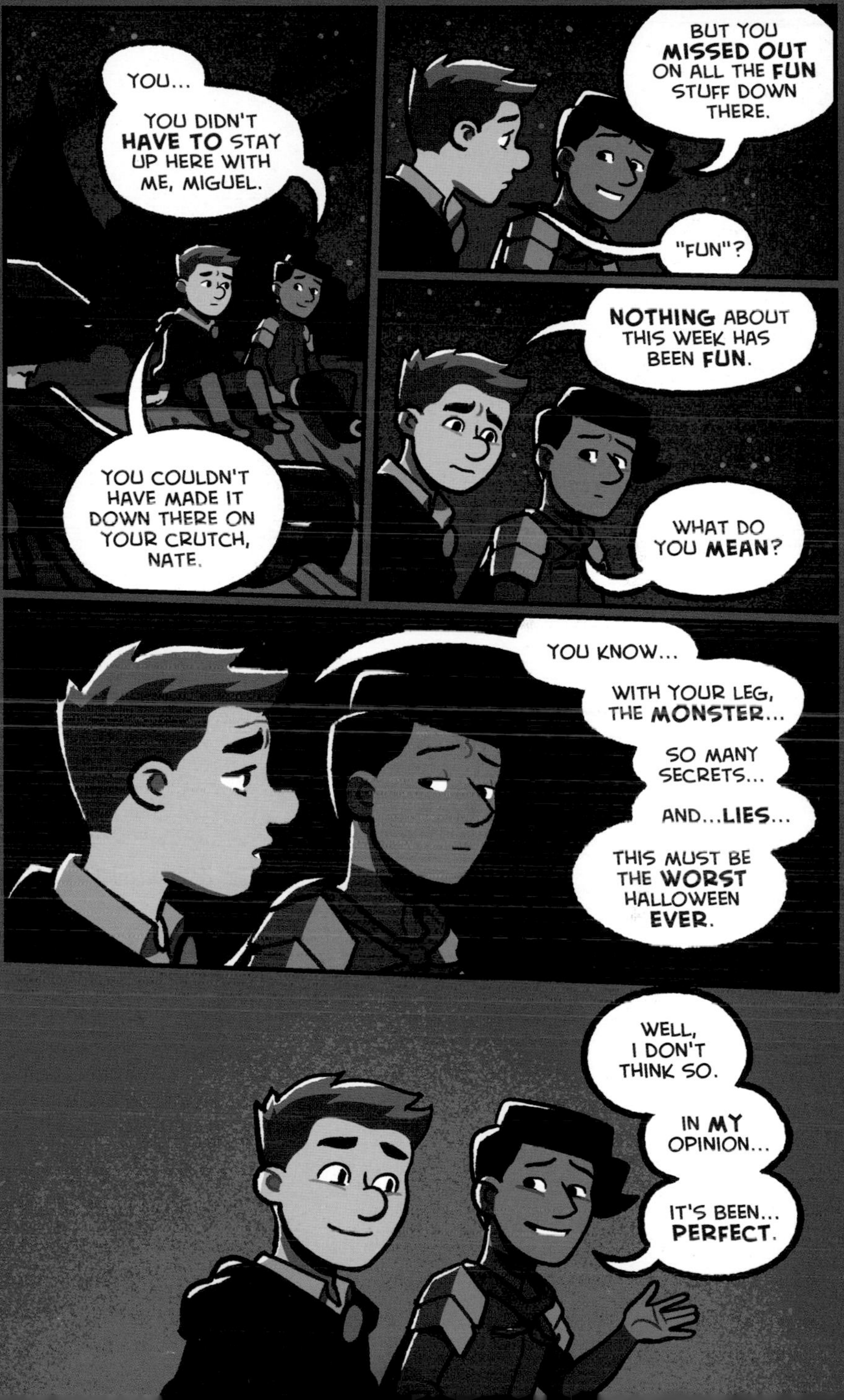
YOU...
YOU DIDN'T HAVE TO STAY UP HERE WITH ME, MIGUEL.
YOU COULDN'T HAVE MADE IT DOWN THERE ON YOUR CRUTCH, NATE.
BUT YOU MISSED OUT ON ALL THE FUN STUFF DOWN THERE.
"FUN"?
NOTHING ABOUT THIS WEEK HAS BEEN FUN.
WHAT DO YOU MEAN?
YOU KNOW...
WITH YOUR LEG, THE MONSTER...
SO MANY SECRETS...
AND...LIES...
THIS MUST BE THE WORST HALLOWEEN EVER.
WELL, I DON'T THINK SO.
IN MY OPINION...
IT'S BEEN... PERFECT.

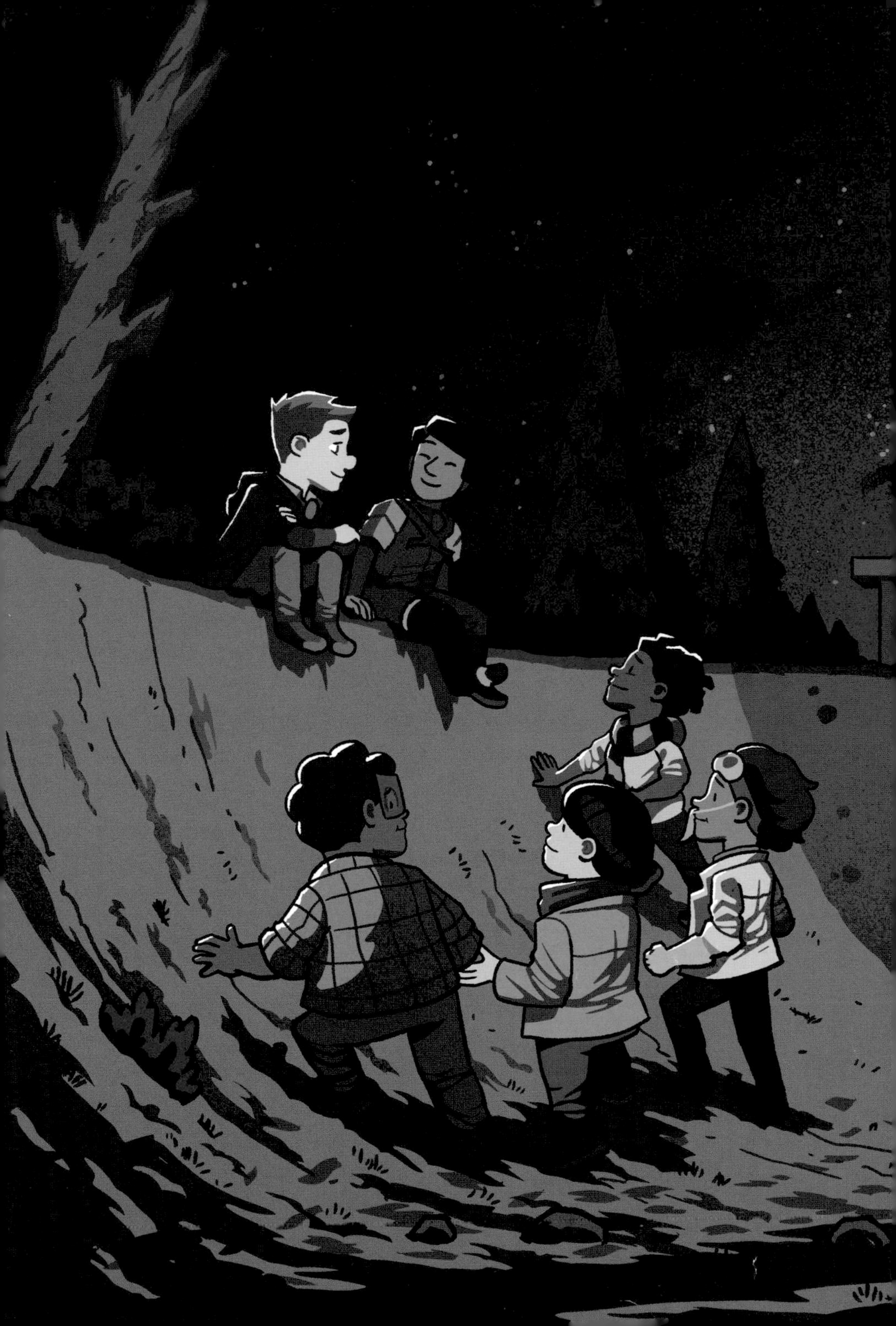

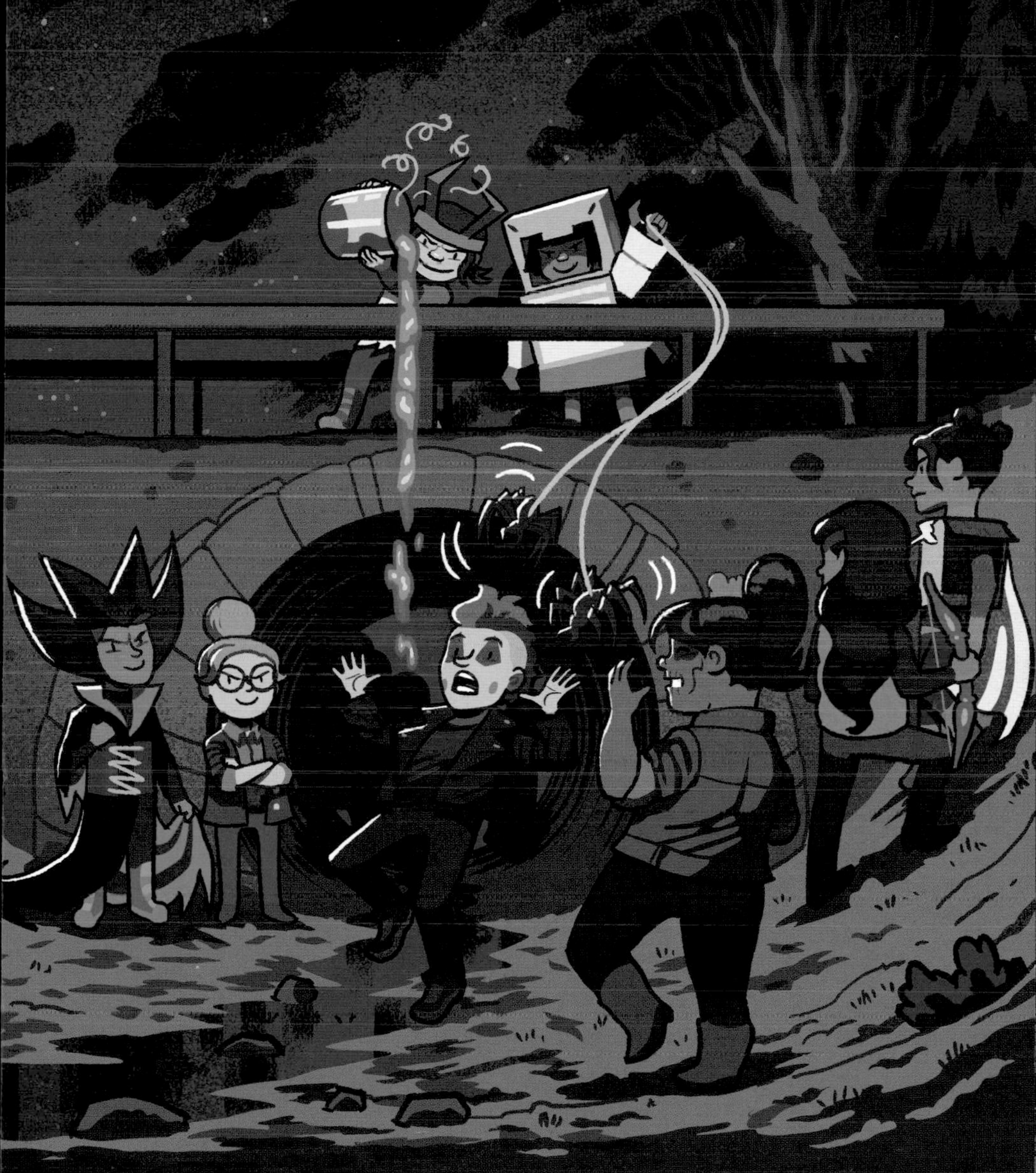

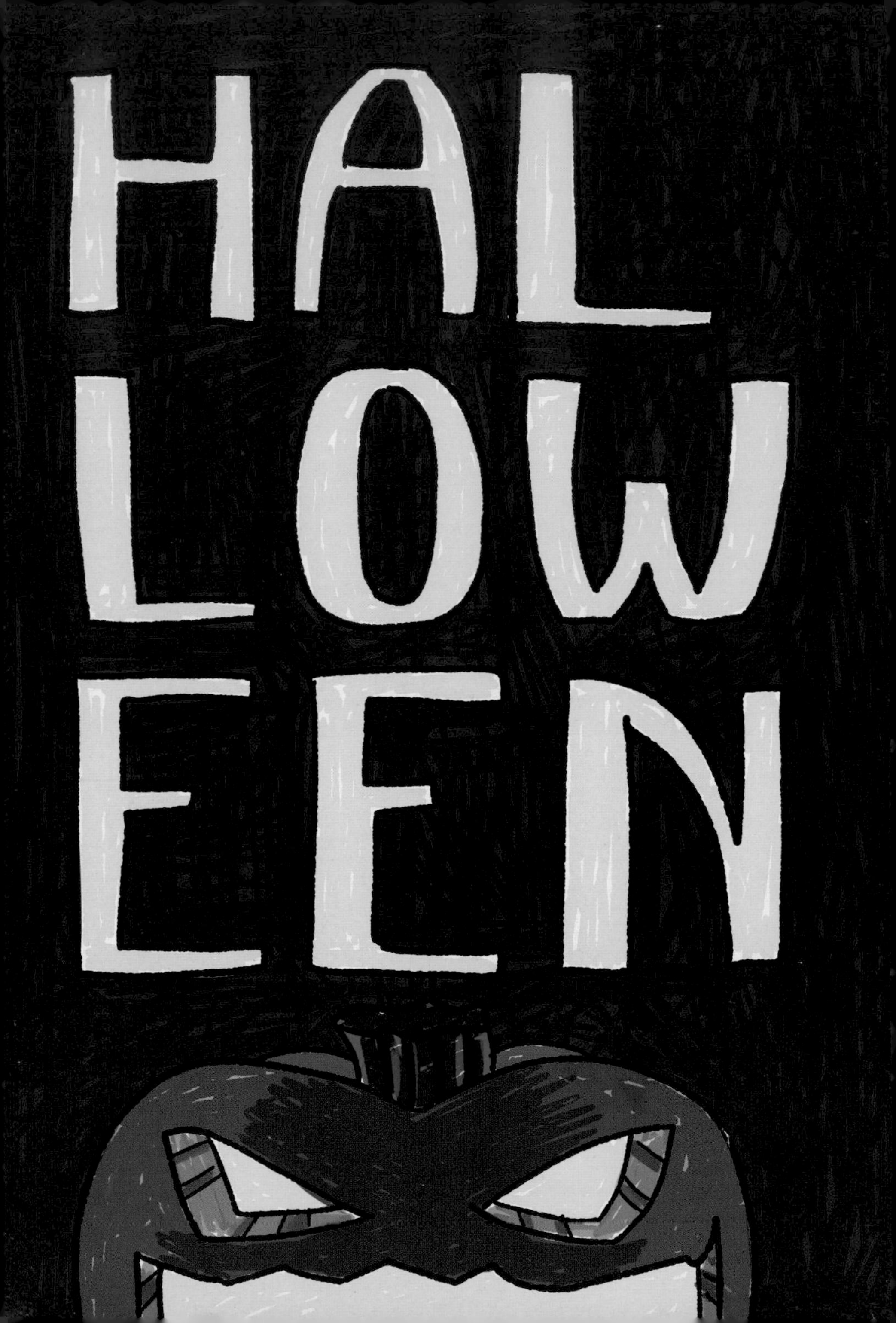
HAL
LOW
EEN

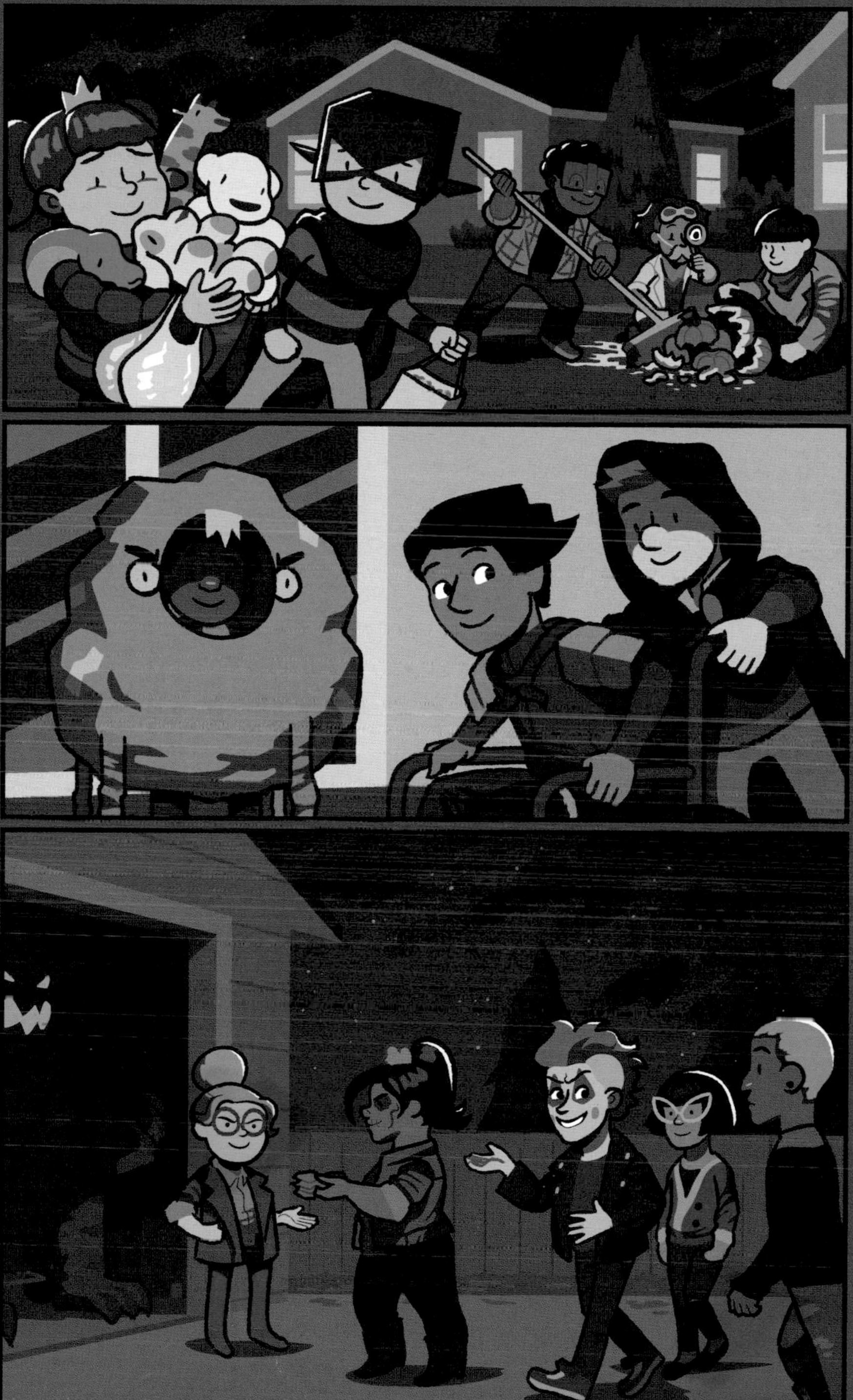

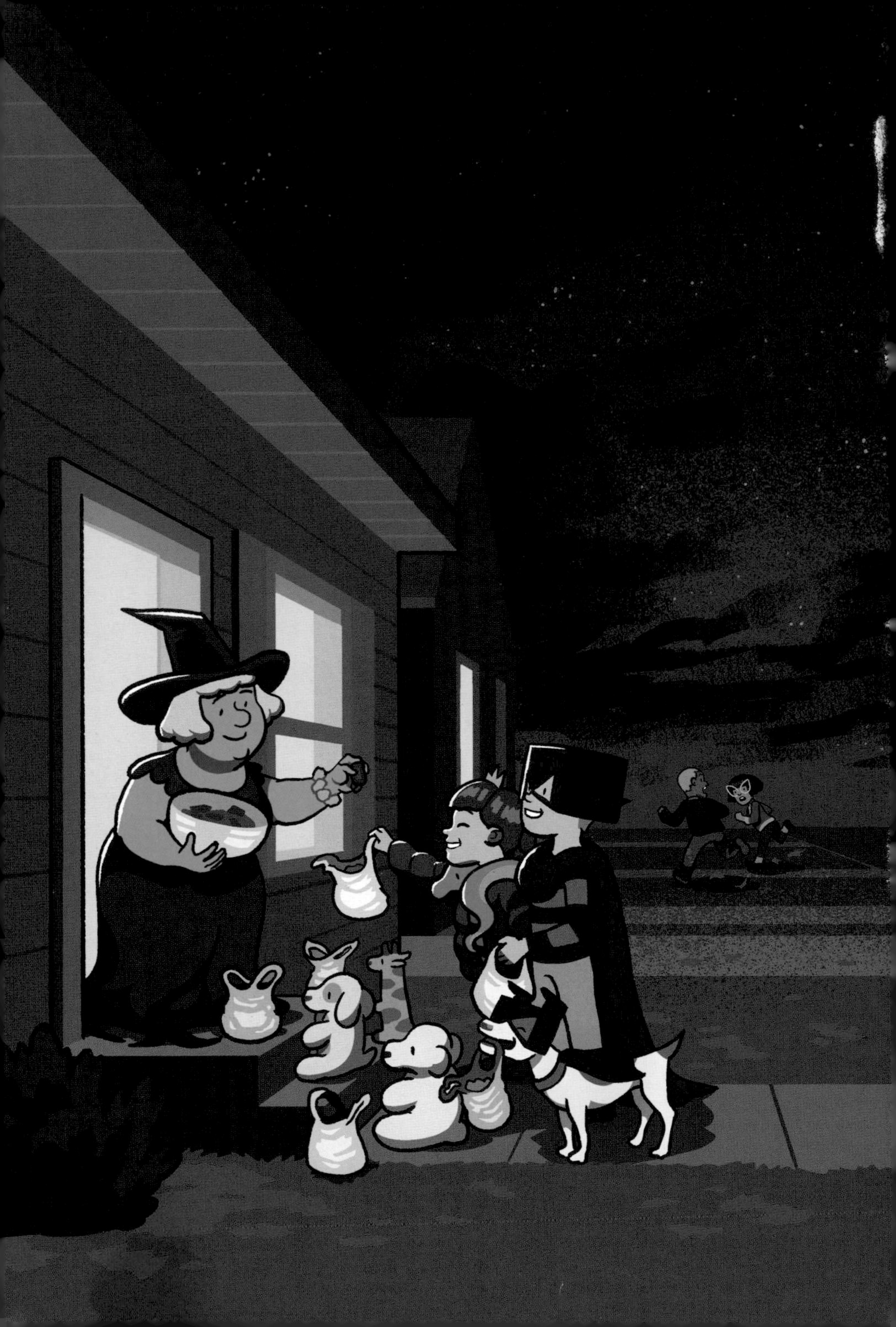

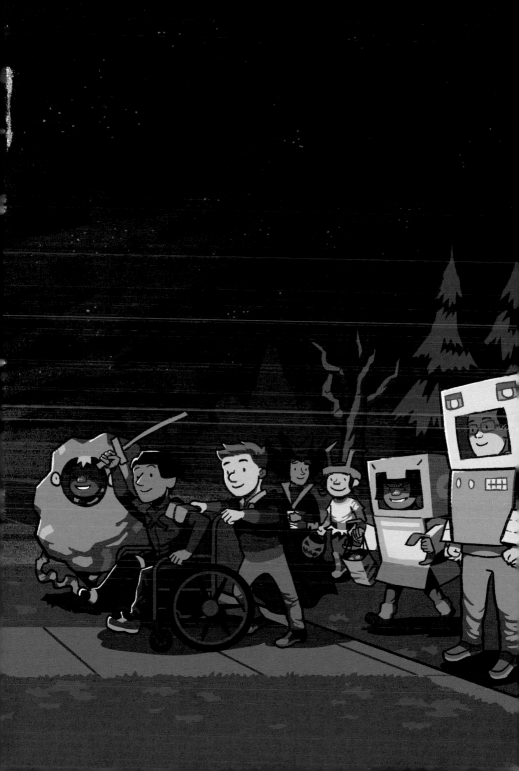

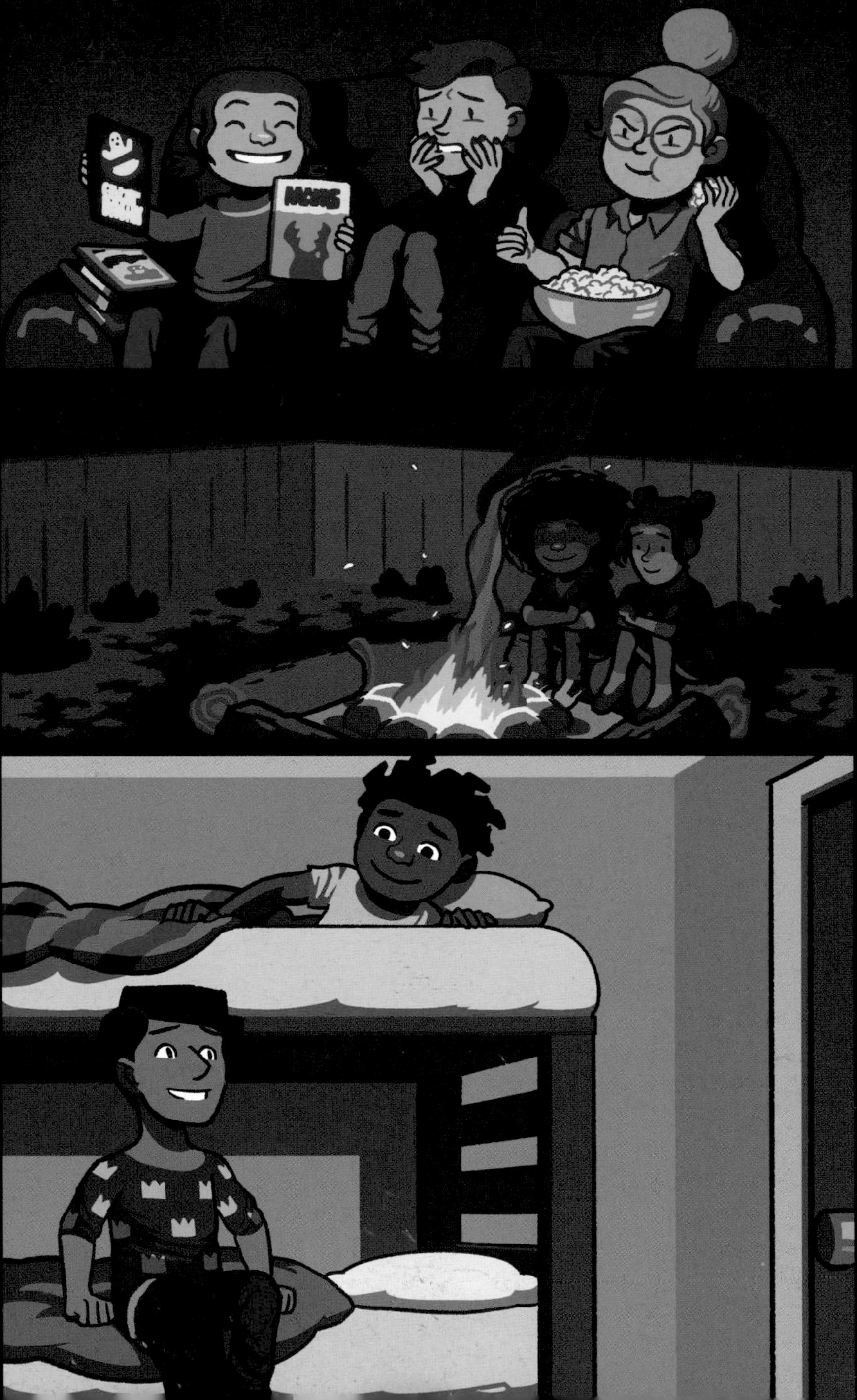

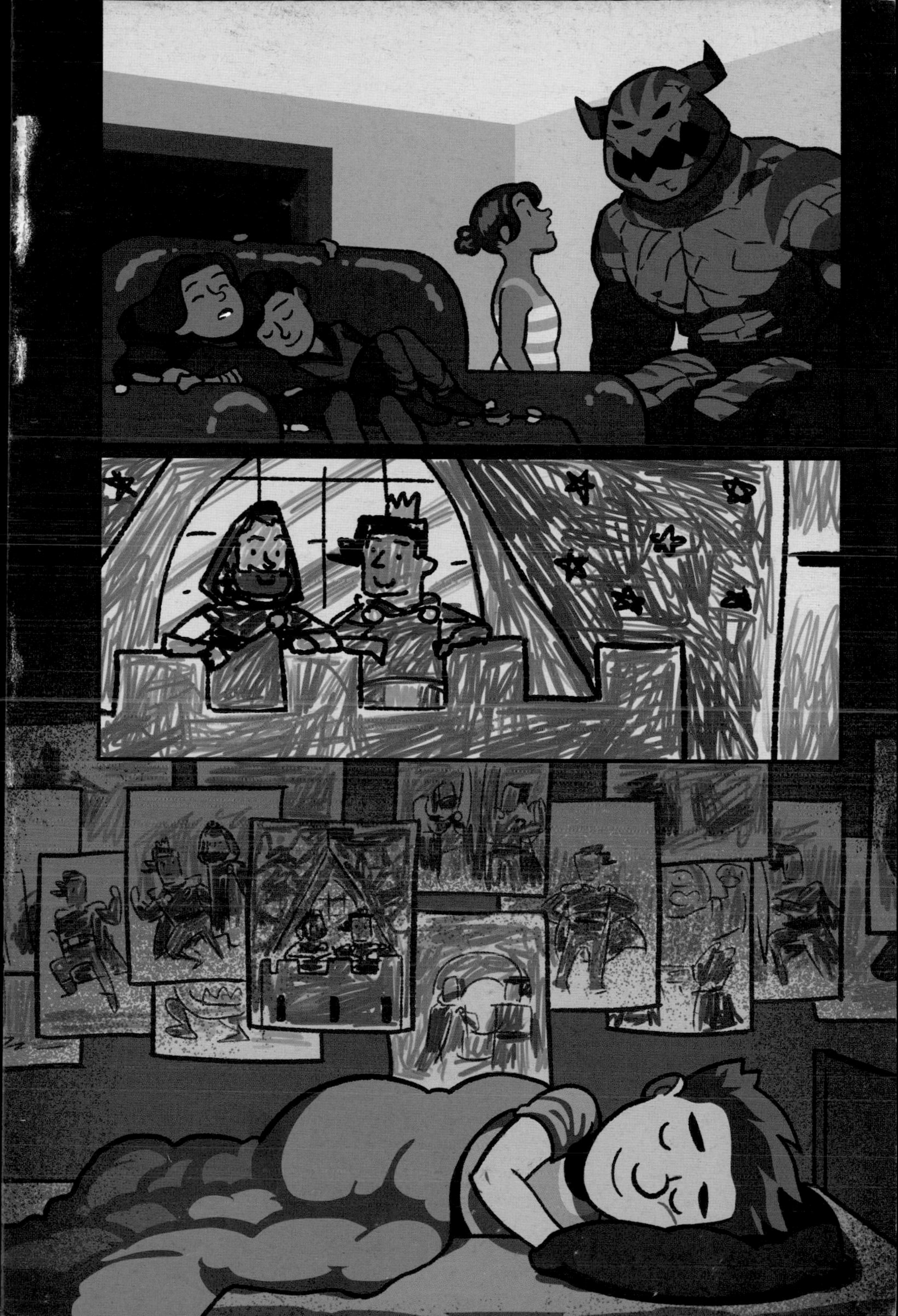

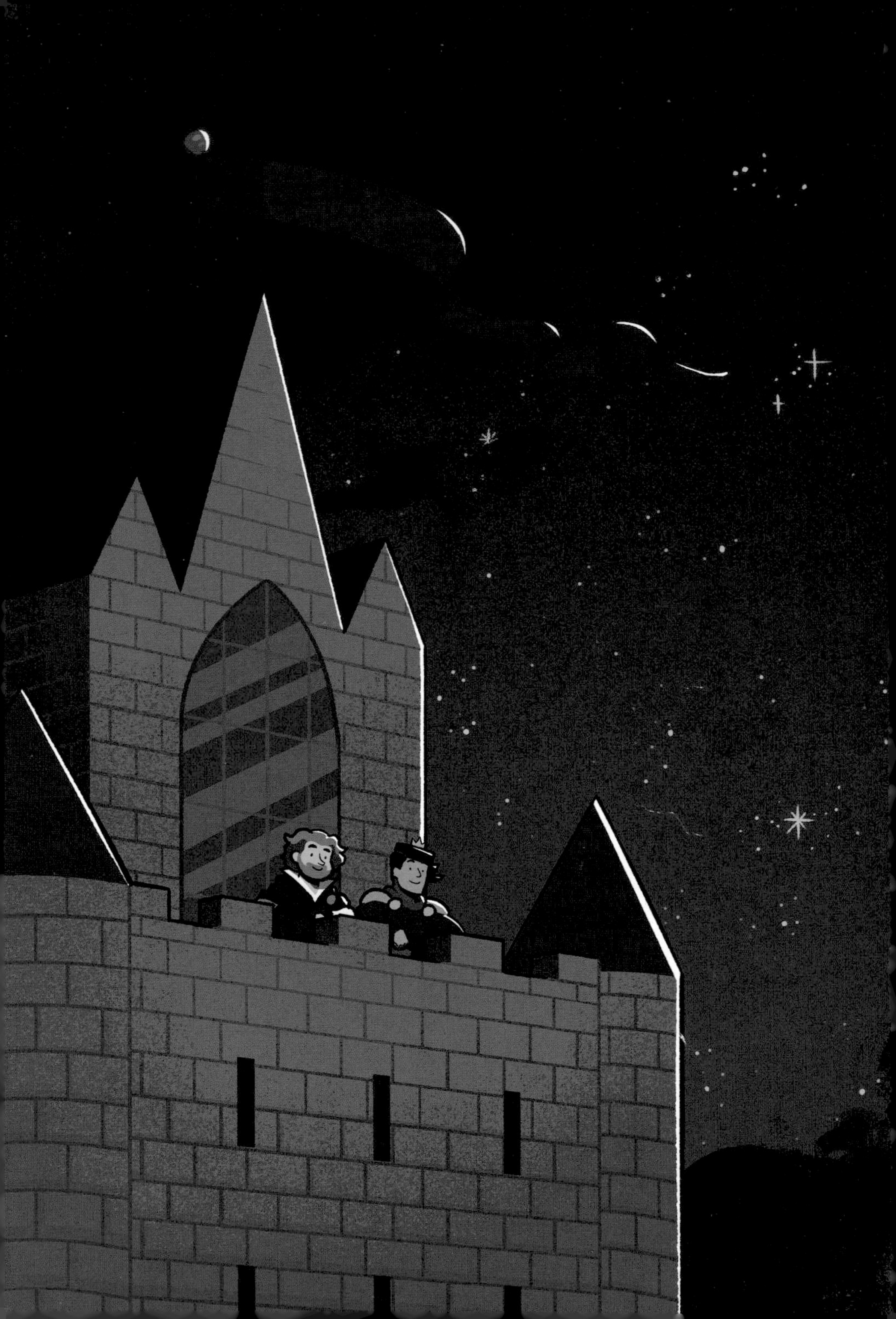

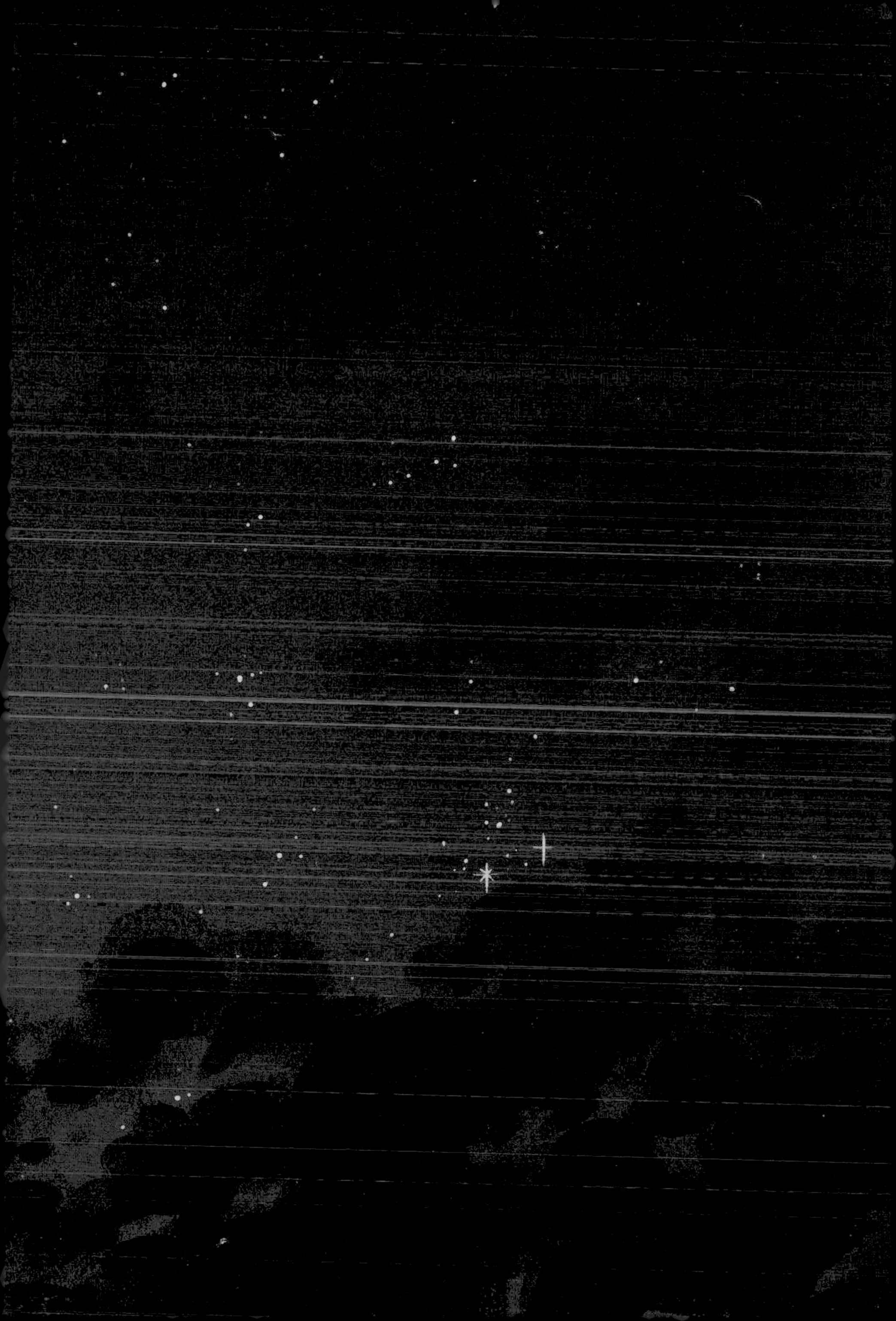

HOW WE BUILT THE KINGDOM

The Cardboard Kingdom: Roar of the Beast represents the collaborative efforts of nine different writers' work in partnership with Chad Sell, who led the project and illustrated the book. Over the course of countless phone calls, the creators sketched out their ideas for an epic Halloween mystery and then split into teams to tackle the various interweaving storylines in *Roar of the Beast*. Each collaborator primarily took responsibility for writing the scenes involving the characters they originally contributed to the Cardboard Kingdom series, which are outlined below.

JAY FULLER

Jack the Sorceress, Sam the Goblin & Peter

Jay is a cartoonist living in Brooklyn, New York, with his husband, Kevin, and their little corgi pup, Darwin. He writes and illustrates his comic, *The Boy in Pink Earmuffs*. Jay is inspired by his own childhood adventures growing up in Rhode Island, as well as the boundless creativity of his young nieces, Lillie and Kyla, and his nephew, Ray.

DAVID DEMEO

Shikha the Huntress, Vijay the Beast & Roy the Bully

David is a bald jewelry designer with a very large variety of hats. His favorite holiday is Halloween, and even though he is supposedly a grown-up now, he still makes his own costumes every year. David lives in Caldwell, New Jersey. The Huntress is based on David's babysitting responsibilities as the oldest of three beast brothers.

KATIE SCHENKEL

Sophie the Big Banshee

Katie Schenkel writes lots of kids' graphic novels, including *The Wolf in Unicorn's Clothing, My Slime Is Alive!*, and *Alice, Secret Agent of Wonderland*. A lifelong fan of superheroes, she had so much fun creating her own superhero team in the Big Banshee, the Huntress, and the Knight! Katie lives in Chicago with her partner, Madison.

MANUEL BETANCOURT

Nate the Prince & Miguel the Rogue

Manuel spends his days writing, baking, and watching way too many films and TV shows. He's the author of *Judy at Carnegie Hall* (2020). Manuel is happy to have gotten the chance to go on yet another adventure with the Prince and the Rogue, two boys who are very dear to his heart and who were inspired by his own childhood love of animated fairy tales.

MOLLY MULDOON

The Animal Queen

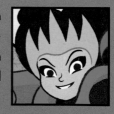

Molly is a writer, editor, and newly minted librarian who's always on the move with her pawtner-in-crime, Jamie McKitten. At the moment, they live in Portland, Oregon. The Animal Queen was inspired by Molly's childhood menagerie of stuffed animals.

VID ALLIGER
Elijah the Blob & Connie the Robot

Vid is an artist and writer currently living in Los Angeles. He loves everything about Halloween, but his favorite parts are the costumes and the candy. He is so grateful to have had the opportunity to work with so many wonderful, creative people on another adventure in the Cardboard Kingdom.

CLOUD JACOBS
Professor Everything

Cloud is a fifth-grade teacher in Stuttgart, Arkansas. When he's not reading and writing comics, he's working his way through every Star Wars book he can get his hands on. Professor Everything is based on Cloud's awkward childhood, when he would usually be reading while the other kids were playing football.

MICHAEL COLE
The Gargoyle

Michael is a faculty member in the English department at Wichita State University, where he teaches literature courses in horror fiction and LGBTQ+ literary representation. He spends most of his free time playing with his dogs, Hal, Atlas, and Benny. He still wants to be Jean Grey but wouldn't mind being a gargoyle either.

BARBARA PEREZ MARQUEZ

The Mad Scientist

Barbara is a Dominican American writer. She lives in Baltimore and has been writing since she was in seventh grade. Just like Amanda, Barbara was born and raised in the Dominican Republic, loves mustaches, and believes we can all experiment a little more in life!

KRIS MOORE

Kris Moore contributed the characters Alice the Alchemist and Becky the Blacksmith, who both appeared in the first book of the Cardboard Kingdom series. Kris passed away before the first installment was published, but his partner, Weston, has permitted us to continue Alice's and Becky's adventures. We're honored that Kris's memory lives on through the unforgettable characters he created and shared with all of us.

COSTUME DESIGN FOR ROAR OF THE BEAST

Wardrobe change! Volume one of the Cardboard Kingdom series was set during the summer. Here's how Chad Sell updated many of the characters' clothes for autumn in *Roar of the Beast.*

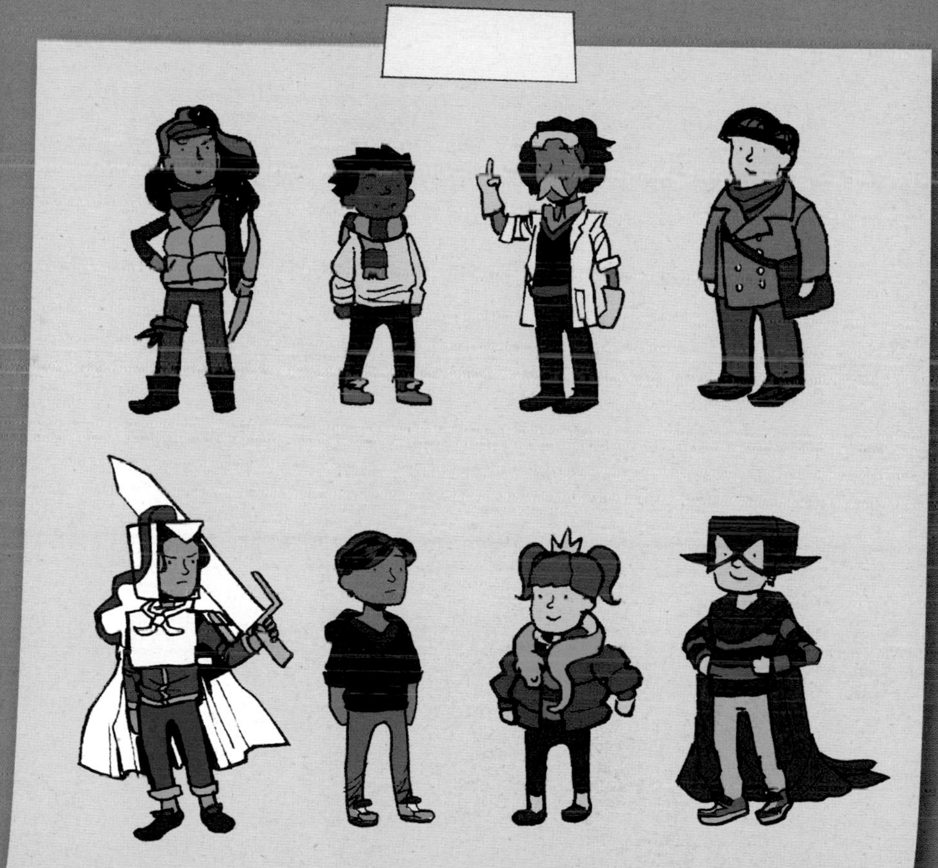

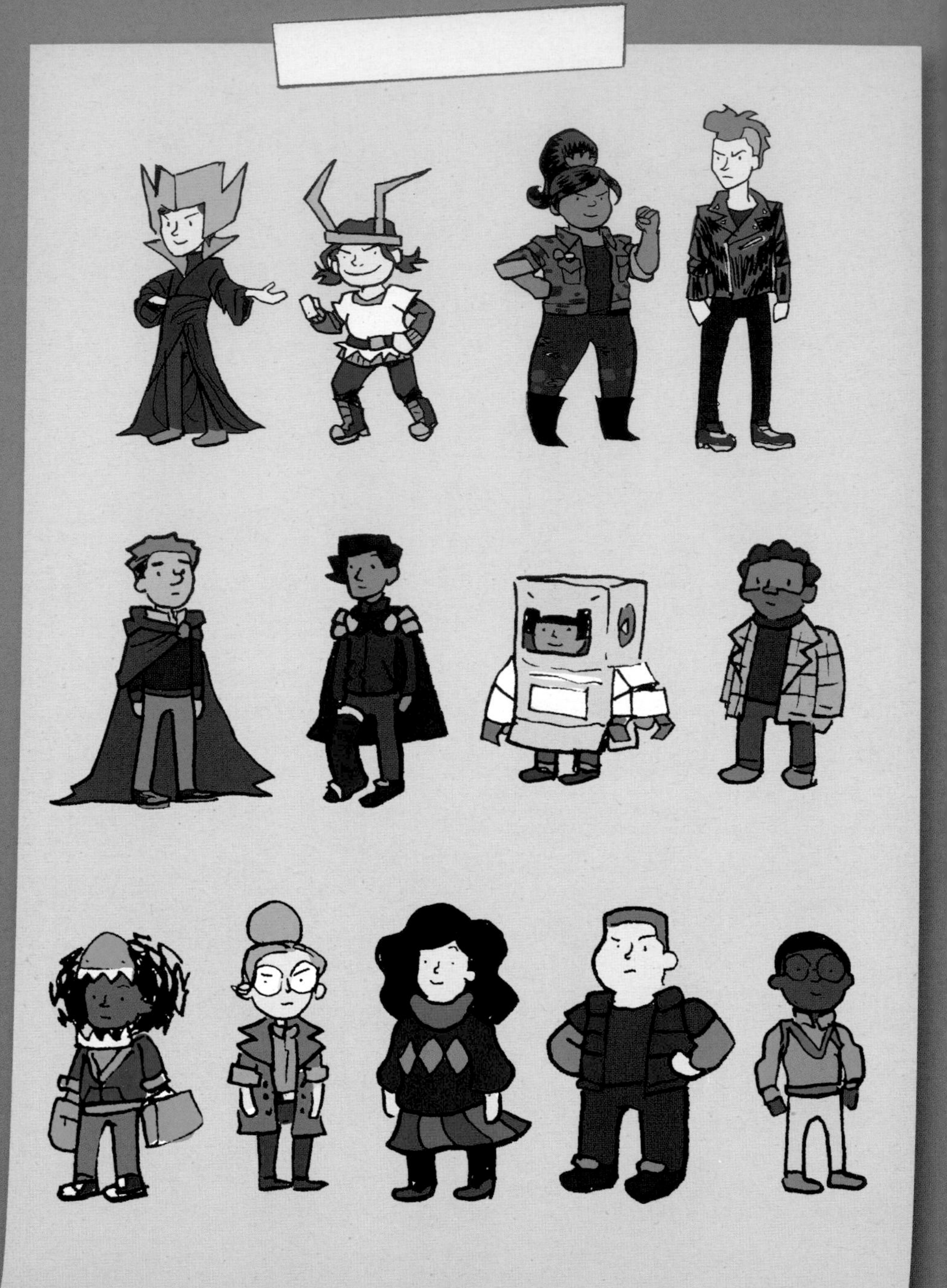

COVER GALLERY

These sketches were alternate cover concepts for *The Cardboard Kingdom: Roar of the Beast*!

THE CARDBOARD KINGDOM
CHAD SELL

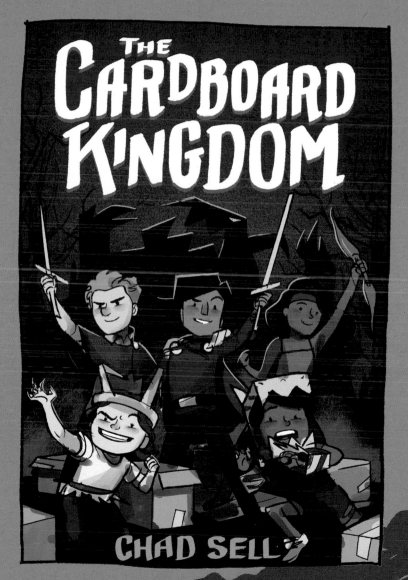

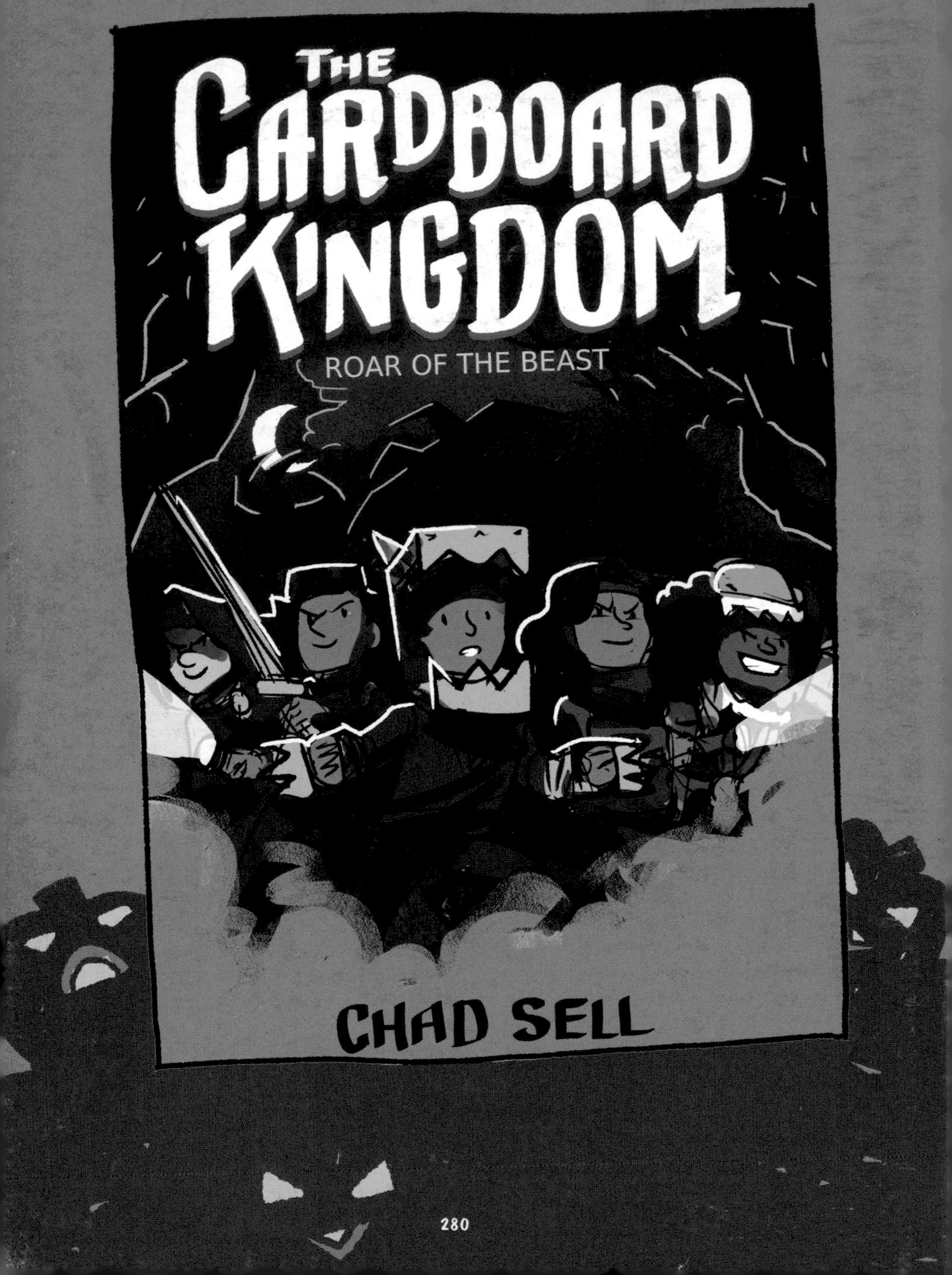
THE
CARDBOARD
KINGDOM
ROAR OF THE BEAST
CHAD SELL

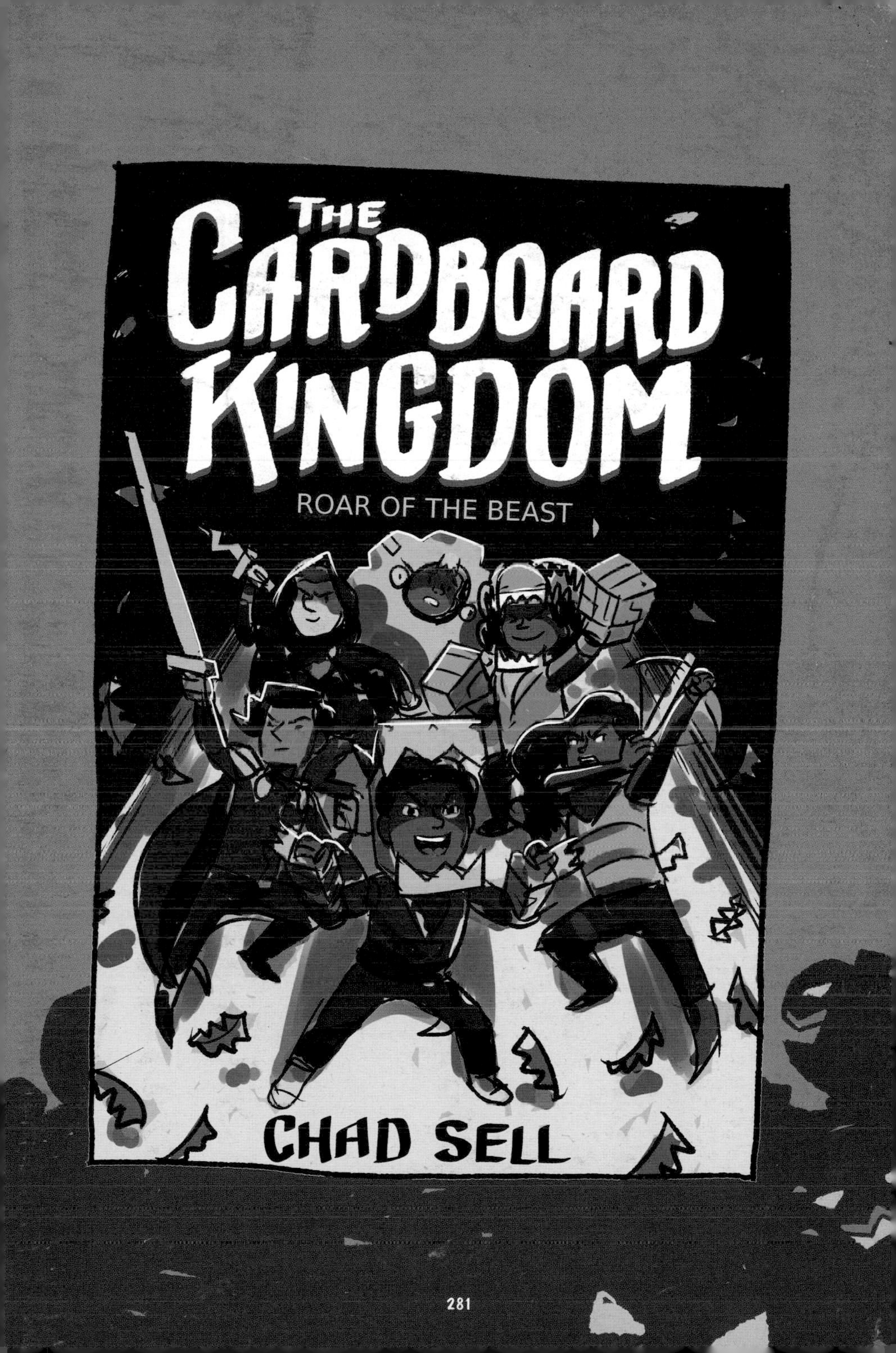
THE CARDBOARD KINGDOM
ROAR OF THE BEAST
CHAD SELL

To my husband, Dan
—C.S.

THIS IS A BORZOI BOOK PUBLISHED BY ALFRED A. KNOPF

Visit us on the Web! rhcbooks.com

Educators and librarians, for a variety of teaching tools,
visit us at RHTeachersLibrarians.com

Library of Congress Cataloging-in-Publication Data is available upon request.
ISBN 978-0-593-12554-0 (hardcover) — ISBN 978-0-593-12555-7 (pbk.) —
ISBN 978-0-593-31024-3 (lib. bdg.) — ISBN 978-0-593-12556-4 (ebook)

The illustrations were created using Clip Studio Paint.
Book design by Chad Sell and Sylvia Bi

MANUFACTURED IN CHINA
June 2021
10 9 8 7 6 5 4 3 2 1
First Edition